Miss Ravenel's Conversion
from Secession to Loyalty

Check patriotic gore:
Edmund Wilson

W. J. Cash
The mind of the South

A CHARLES E. MERRILL STANDARD EDITION

CHARLES E. MERRILL STANDARD EDITIONS

Under the General Editorship of
Matthew J. Bruccoli and Joseph Katz

Exact reprints, whenever possible facsimiles, of authoritative texts of significant literary works. Each volume is introduced in an appropriate manner by a major scholar, critic, or author.

John William DeForest

Miss Ravenel's Conversion from Secession to Loyalty

Introduced by

Arlin Turner

Duke University

CHARLES E. MERRILL PUBLISHING COMPANY
A Bell & Howell Company
Columbus, Ohio

This text of *Miss Ravenel's Conversion from Secession to Loyalty* is a facsimile of the first impression, first edition published by Harper & Brothers, 1867—from a copy in the Kent State University Library.

Standard Book Number: 675-09391-0 Clothbound
edition
675-09390-2 Paperbound
edition

Library of Congress Catalog Number: 75-100633

1 2 3 4 5 6 7 8 9 10 — 78 77 76 75 74 73 72
71 70 69

Printed in the United States of America

Introduction

Arlin Turner

William Dean Howells included *Miss Ravenel's Conversion from Secession to Loyalty* among his literary passions. He thought it "the best novel suggested by the Civil War" and in fact one of the best American novels he had read. When it first appeared in 1867, he added, it "was of an advanced realism, before realism was known by name." Howells failed, as he noted, to persuade many critics or readers of his time to his opinion that De Forest belongs among "the masters of American fiction" or to his enthusiasm for De Forest's "keen and accurate touch in character, his wide scope, and his unerring rendition of whatever he has attempted to

report of American life."[1] But since a new edition of the novel was
published in 1939, Howells's judgment has been generally supported. Van Wyck Brooks remarked that De Forest wrote "with a
breadth of understanding and a truth to actuality that were certainly unique at the moment."[2] Arthur Hobson Quinn found him
to be the most realistic among the novelists who began writing in
the 1850's, and remarked that he "could paint relentlessly the portraits of real men and women" and in *Miss Ravenel's Conversion*
portrayed "war in its sordid reality."[3] Gordon S. Haight declared
in the same vein that "war had never been depicted so truthfully"
before this novel, and he called De Forest "the first American
writer to deserve the name of realist."[4] Albert E. Stone, Jr., has
argued that *Miss Ravenel's Conversion* is the best of the Civil War
novels.[5]

Miss Ravenel's Conversion embodies the unflinching veracity
praised by Howells and others after him because it relies heavily
on experiences and observations which were still fresh with the
author and were of great moment to him. That is not to say that
De Forest was a beginning writer who responded to the experience
of Civil War by writing a fictional masterpiece. He was a professional author with five books to his credit before he entered the
Union Army, and he began at once recording events and observations and preserving them for later use in his novel.

John William De Forest (1826-1906) was a native of Connecticut and in particular knew life at New Haven and at Yale College,
such as he later introduced into *Miss Ravenel's Conversion*. As a
young man he traveled several years in the Near East and in
Europe, and he became a student of foreign languages and litera-
tures, especially French and Italian. He knew the works of
Shakespeare, Sterne, Milton, Bunyan, Thackeray, Dickens, Dante,
Balzac, Cervantes, Irving, Hawthorne, Emerson, and Harriet
Beecher Stowe; and he referred to enough additional authors to
suggest a considerable literary acquaintance. His first book, published in 1851, was a scholarly *History of the Indians of Connecticut from the Earliest Known Period to 1850*. Two travel books,

---

[1]*My Literary Passions* (New York, 1895), p. 223.

[2]*New England: Indian Summer* (New York, 1940), p. 240.

[3]*American Fiction* (New York, 1936), pp. 166, 168.

[4]"Realism Defined," in *Literary History of the United States,* ed. Robert
E. Spiller and others (New York, 1948), II, 881.

[5]"Best Novel of the Civil War," *American Heritage,* XIII (June, 1962),
84-88.

Oriental Acquaintance; or Letters from Syria (1856) and *European Acquaintance; Being Sketches of People in Europe* (1858), were apprentice efforts which showed De Forest determined to write but uncertain as to both the material and the literary form he would employ. *Witching Times,* a novel serialized in *Putnam's Monthly Magazine* beginning in December, 1856, but not issued in book form during the author's lifetime, reflects his scholarly excursions into Increase Mather, Cotton Mather, Robert Calef, and other historians of the Salem witch delusion of 1692. It reflects also his fondness for circumstantial detail and a degree of realism in character and action. In his second novel, *Seacliff; or The Mystery of the Westervelts* (1859), De Forest turned to America in his own time for his setting and showed some concern for actuality, but he was more interested in a slight mystery story and a display of erudition and cleverness. The aspects of *Seacliff* most significant to the author's development as a novelist are the variety among the characters he introduces and his attempts to make them psychologically believable.

On June 5, 1856, De Forest was married to Harriet Silliman Shepard, whose father held college professorships in both Amherst College and the Medical College of Charleston, South Carolina, and divided each year between the two colleges. As a consequence, De Forest visited Charleston in the years preceding the Civil War. Early in 1862 he was commissioned a captain in the United States Army and took command of a unit he had recruited, Company I of the Twelfth Connecticut Volunteers. With the Twelfth Connecticut under General Benjamin Butler he went first to Ship Island, then to New Orleans at the time the city fell to the Union fleet under Farragut; he served under General Nathaniel P. Banks in the campaigns west of New Orleans and at Fort Hudson; later he served in Virginia under General Philip H. Sheridan. At the end of his term of service, he was discharged on December 2, 1864. He entered the Army again on February 10 as captain and was stationed in Washington; comissioned as brevet major on May 15 of the next year, he served in the Freedman's Bureau at Greenville, South Carolina, until he was mustered out on January 1, 1868.

De Forest took up his literary pen as soon as he was free from the military campaigns. In September, 1864, in fact, he published the first in a series of articles on the war: "The First Time Under Fire," in *Harper's New Monthly Magazine.* As soon as he sailed for Ship Island in 1862 he began writing careful, detailed letters to his wife and asked her to save them for him. Even while recovering

his health after the Virginia campaign in 1864, he began writing
Miss Ravenel's Conversion. By October, 1865, publication arrangements were under discussion with the Harper firm. The book was
published in May, 1867, while De Forest was still assigned to the
Freedman's Bureau in South Carolina.

Miss Ravenel's Conversion differs conspicuously from De Forest's
earlier work. A statement he made years afterward shows how
clearly he realized that increased reliance on his own experiences
accounted for one of the major differences: "I came to know the
value of personal knowledge of one's subject and the art of drawing upon life for one's characters. In my younger days everything
was romance. . . . From *Miss Ravenel* on I have written from life
and have been a realist."[6] Extensive parallels exist between
De Forest's experiences and those he gives Colburne in the novel.
Each marries the daughter of a professor in New England who
holds a second appointment in Charleston and who is an authority
in mineralogy. Each is commissioned a captain in the Union Army
and recruits a company which he commands under General Butler
at Ship Island and in New Orleans and later under General Banks
in several engagements in Louisiana, and still later in the battle
of Cedar Creek in the Shenandoah Valley of Virginia. Each is
mustered out without being promoted because of political favorit-
ism to other officers. The state of Barataria and New Boston in
the book are readily identified as Connecticut and New Haven.
The novel keeps without change the geographical names and the
names of military and civilian leaders in Louisiana.

Because De Forest began writing *Miss Ravenel's Conversion*
while he was recovering from exhaustion in recent battles (such
as Colburne also experiences), he could draw on fresh memories
for the factual details he wanted to include. It is evident, moreover, that he wrote with manuscripts open before him, letters or
other accounts, in which at times he had described the fighting
literally while the shells were exploding around him. De Forest
published five magazine narratives of his war experiences, one of
them, "The First Time Under Fire,"[7] before, but the others after
he wrote *Miss Ravenel's Conversion*. Some years later he revised
these narratives, mainly by reducing the technical military details
and touching up the style, and combined them with other matter,
chiefly from letters written to his wife during the war, to make a

---

[6]Quoted in James F. Light, *John William De Forest* (New York, 1965),
p. 89. I am indebted to this work for the main facts of De Forest's life.

[7]In *Harper's New Monthly Magazine,* XXIX (September, 1864), 475-482.

book-length manuscript entitled *A Volunteer's Adventures: A Union Captain's Record of the Civil War*. He did not publish the work, and it was not in print until 1946.[8] This autobiographical account reveals the quality and the slant of the author's mind and suggests how much the novel draws on his experiences, and also how fully it reflects his interests and attitudes. Both accounts use the phrase "*pum-pum-pum* of cannon" in reporting the battle of Port Hudson. The *Adventures* contains the following passage:

> The enemy's artillery at this time made a tremendous uproar; the shells howled and burst over our heads incessantly and deafeningly. Every minute or two some lordly tree, eighteen inches or two feet in diameter, flew asunder with a roar and toppled crashing to earth. For some minutes I admired without enjoying this sublime massacre of the monarchs of the forest. (pp. 108-109)

The author of this passage is conscious of details and of the effects he wants to achieve. The corresponding passage from the novel indicates De Forest's habits in converting a factual account into fiction. The incident and the tone are not greatly altered, but the effectiveness has been augmented by the addition of concrete detail and dramatic statement:

> At this moment, and for two hours afterward, the uproar of heavy guns, bursting shells, falling trees and flying splinters was astonishing, stunning, horrible, doubled as it was by the sonorous echoes of the forest. Magnolias, oaks and beeches eighteen inches or two feet in diameter were cut asunder with a deafening scream of shot and of splitting fibres, the tops falling after a pause of majestic deliberation, not sidewise, but stem downwards, like a descending parachute, and striking the earth with a dull shuddering thunder. They seemed to give up their life with a roar of animate anguish, as if they were savage beasts, or as if they were inhabited by Afreets and Demons. (p. 281)

Two other passages, the first from the *Adventures* and the second from the novel, may be quoted to illustrate further the author's fictional use of observed incident:

---

[8]Edited by James H. Croushore, with an introduction by Stanley T. Williams (New Haven). This and subsequent passages from the *Adventures* are quoted with the permission of the Yale University Press. *A Union Officer in the Reconstruction* was edited by James H. Croushore and David Morris Potter (New Haven, 1948) from a similar manuscript which De Forest prepared, but did not publish, dealing with his experiences in the Freedman's Bureau.

... a color corporal near me dropped his musket and spun around
with a broad stream of blood dribbling down his face. I supposed
for a moment that he was a dead man; but the ball had merely
run along the upper edge of his leathern forepiece, driving it
through the skin; there was nothing worse than a shallow gash
from temple to temple. (p. 109)

I saw a broad flow of blood stream down the face of a color-corporal who stood within arm's-length of me. I thought he was surely
a dead man; but it was only one of the wonderful escapes of battle.
The bullet had skirted his cap where the fore-piece joins the cloth,
forcing the edge of the leather through the skin, and making a
clean cut to the bone from temple to temple. (p. 283)

De Forest had come to believe that a novelist has obligations to
truth and actuality. In an essay of 1868 entitled "The Great American Novel" he called for a novel which will give a "picture of
ordinary emotions and manners of American existence." *Uncle
Tom's Cabin* has shortcomings, he noted, but he could commend it
because there is "a national breadth to the picture, truthful out-
lining of character, natural speaking, and plenty of strong feeling."[9]
It was his purpose in *Miss Ravenel's Conversion*, just as it had
been in his letters from the battlefields, to describe or to suggest the
thoughts and feelings of the ordinary soldier experiencing not only
exaltation or resignation or terror in the presence of danger, but
also the misery of dust, heat, and blistered feet, and the boredom
of military routine, "the Sahara-like flatness of ordinary camp life"
(p. 367). Colburne wrote Dr. Ravenel that the soldiers suffered
from "wearisome *ennui*" even though they could hear from their
waiting transports Farragut's fleet shelling the forts on the lower
Mississippi in order to clear the approach to New Orleans (p. 123).
The letters De Forest sent his wife, as they appear in *A Volunteer's
Adventures*, present his intimately personal responses to experiences in camp, on long marches, or in battle; but they present also
a contrasting formal, almost clinical analysis of the responses an
ordinary soldier, any soldier, would have to such experiences. The
occurrences of the novel are shown from the same antithetical or
complementary perspectives, and the resulting composite portrayal
accounts for the particular quality of the realism.

---

[9]In the *Nation*, VI (January 9, 1868), 27-29. The title of this essay gave
prominence to an idea which was already being discussed and which, together with the phrase of De Forest's title, has appeared often since, as in
William Carlos Williams's *The Great American Novel* (1923).

To satisfy a natural curiosity or to record observations for fictional uses — probably to serve both purposes — De Forest gave close attention to what might be called the psychology of courage and fear. A passage in *A Volunteer's Adventures* indicates this interest of his and summarizes the conclusions he had reached. It reflects also the ironic touch he often employed in handling the conventional views of war, social institutions, and human nature. The passage follows a narrative of severe fighting at Port Hudson.

> The thoughtful among my readers, those who care less for objective incidents than for their effect upon the human soul, will ask me if I liked the business. With a courage which entitles me to honorable mention at the headquarters of the veracities, I reply that I did not like it, except in some expansive moments when this or that stirring success filled me with excitement. Certain military authors who never heard a bullet whistle have written copiously for the marines, to the general effect that fighting is delightful. It is not; it is just tolerable; you can put up with it; but you can't honestly praise it. Bating a few flashes of elation which come in moments of triumph or in the height of a breathless charge, when "the air is all a yell and the earth is all a flame," it is much like being in a rich cholera district in the height of the season.
>
> Profoundly, infinitely true, true of every species and of every individual, is the copybook maxim, "Self-preservation is the first law of nature." The man who does not dread to die or to be mutilated is a lunatic. The man who, dreading these things, still faces them for the sake of duty and honor is a hero. (pp. 123-124)

Such a sentence as the last above, in its approach to the conventional view which De Forest normally disparaged, is not compatible with the tone of either the work in which it occurs or *Miss Ravenel's Conversion*. In both books, incidents of fear and cowardice are recorded. In *A Volunteer's Adventures*, there is a calm account of a sergeant who, upon hearing enemy bullets in his first encounter, "faced about and started rearward." The narrative continues:

> I never saw anything done more naturally and promptly. He did not look wild with fright; he simply looked alarmed and resolved to get out of danger; it was the simplest and most persuaded expression of countenance imaginable. He was not a thorough coward, and never afterward turned tail that I know of; but he was confounded by the peril of the moment and thought of nothing but getting away from it.

It would have been lawful and right to pistol him, for he ran a risk of guiding the regiment rearward and bringing about defeat. In a great rage and with sabre uplifted, I pounced upon him as he was struggling through the color corporals, all of whom were pushing forward eagerly and gallantly. "Forward, or I'll split your head open," I shouted, catching him by the shoulder and facing him about. He obeyed in silence, with a curious dazed expresssion, and I pushed him into his place in the front rank of the color guard. (p. 63)

A parallel incident is reported in the novel, but rather than fear it is an instance of cowardice:

Every regiment has its two or three cowards, or perhaps its half-dozen, weakly-nerved creatures, whom nothing can make fight, and who never do fight. One abject hound, a corporal with his disgraced stripes upon his arm, came by with a ghastly backward glare of horror, his face colorless, his eyes projecting, and his chin shaking. Colburne cursed him for a poltroon, struck him with the flat of his sabre, and dragged him into the ranks of his own regiment; but the miserable creature was too thoroughly unmanned by the great horror of death to be moved to any show of resentment or even of courage by the indignity; he only gave an idiotic stare with outstretched neck toward the front, then turned with a nervous jerk, like that of a scared beast, and rushed rearward. (p. 282)

This incident is embedded in an account of Colburne's company under extremely heavy artillery shelling, when the soldiers, "hardened as they were to scenes of ordinary battle," turned grim faces in every direction, "in an instinctive search for cover." Colburne "smiled grimly to see the paralyzed terror" of the men. He too was overwhelmed, he wrote, by the "mere physical power" of the cannonading, and he continued: "When one of our men was borne by me with half his foot torn off by a round of shot, the splintered bones projecting clean and white from the ragged raw flesh, I grew so sick that perhaps I might have fainted if a brother officer had not given me a sip of whiskey from his canteen" (p. 283).

Thus, twenty-five years before *The Red Badge of Courage*, De Forest described war with little heroics and little glamor, but instead with a full measure of dirt, stench, blood, exhaustion, pain, boredom, and despair; and with such courage, fear, cowardice, and venality as would be the average among ordinary men. He realized that he was allowing far more unpleasantness and indelicacy to enter his novel than editors and publishers of the time would readily accept; but he achieved a thorough naturalness in describing corpses "black with putrifaction" (p. 294), or an artilleryman "with his brains bulging from a bullet-hole in his forehead, while a dark claret-colored streak crossed his face" (p. 289), or the field hospital with its "great pools of clotted blood, amidst which lay amputated fingers, hands, arms, feet and legs, only a little more ghastly in color than the faces of those who waited their turn on the table," or a soldier, shot through the body, who "lay speechless and dying, but quivering from head to foot with a prolonged though probably unconscious agony," and who "continued to shudder thus for half an hour, when he gave one superhuman throe, and then lay quiet for ever" (p. 292).

In marshaling such details as these and in analyzing the soldiers' responses to the experiences of war, De Forest was not far different from Stephen Crane. There is a great difference, however, which lies mainly in DeForest's frequent obtrusion as author to discuss the characters and the action with the reader, in contrast to Crane's detachment as a dispassionate observer and reporter whose comment is not stated but is borne by the spare language he employs and by the irony of his view.

In scenes away from the battlefield De Forest kept no less firmly his resolve to present "ordinary emotions and manners." In the fourth chapter he remarks, at the conclusion of a conversation between Colburne and Lillie Ravenel: "Next in flatness to the ordinary talk of two lovers comes, I think, the ordinary talk of two young persons of the opposite sexes. . . . When therefore I report the conversation of these two uncorrupted young persons as being of a moderately dull quality, I flatter myself that I am publishing the very truth of nature" (pp. 53-54). Trivial conversations abound in the novel, with the author indicating often that he knows they are trivial. When Colburne and Lillie first met in New Orleans, "they behaved in a disappointingly well-bred manner," the author notes, and he adds, "Melodramatically considered real life is frequently a failure." But such tongue-in-cheek remarks as this notwithstanding, De Forest consciously used the scenes of low-key conversation — in the manner William Dean Howells was to develop fully later — to establish the tempo and the quality of life among his characters and to advance the plot almost unawares to the reader.

Again, as with the battle scenes, the author takes liberties with the rules of decency and propriety which prevailed in the novel of his time, though serious rebellion did not tempt him, apparently, and his editors were ready to blue-pencil any grossly offending passages. His first contract with the Harper firm, late in 1865, pro-

vided for serial publication, deferring the decision as to book publication. But a new contract was signed a year later and his novel
appeared directly in book form, to avoid compromising the status
of *Harper's* as a family magazine. While serialization was still being
considered, De Forest wrote the publisher that he would not object
to "reform of the story" to make it "proper for families" but that
he thought "it ought to be understood, for the sake of *vraisem-
blance*, that the Colonel did frequently swear and that the Louisiana lady was not quite as good as she should be."[10] As the book
was published, Colonel Carter does more swearing — and much of
the time without the disguise of dashes or asterisks — than was
normal among his contemporaries on the pages of fiction, but by no
means more, on the author's testimony, than would have been normal to a contemporary army officer of his character. Mrs. Larue
remains largely in the background, but her guilt in seducing Colonel Carter, not to mention other activities only hinted, is of a
degree to condemn her — in a Howells novel or in most others published during the next several decades — to punishment rather
than the prosperous care-free future which lies before her at the
close of the book.

In his attempt to portray actuality, De Forest undertakes to
analyze Lillie's feelings when Colonel Carter proposes to her, when
she is pregnant with his child, when she learns that he has been
unfaithful and later that he is dead, and when she responds to
Colburne's love. In the frank, though restrained, explanation that
Lillie did not realize the full meaning of connubial love when her
husband left her to join his troops two days after their marriage
(p. 245), De Forest suggests that he had the interest and perhaps
the understanding for subtler exposition of her thoughts and emotions, along with those of other characters, including Mrs. Larue
and Colonel Carter, if he could have ignored the current proprieties.

De Forest's habits of turning phrases or ideas, with homely or
even earthy overtones at times, suggest a clear leaning toward
realism. Some people are "as easy to wear as old slippers," but
"others pinch your moral corns in a most grievous manner" (pp.
103-4). Colonel Carter says Mrs. Larue "was sweeter on him than a
pailful of syrup" (p. 182). Occasionally there is a detail which the
author likely knew many of his contemporaries would think indelicate, but included nevertheless. Colonel Carter sat one evening "in
vexatious thought, slapping his mosquito bites," and after deciding

---

[10]Quoted in Light, *John William De Forest*, p. 87.

to go to bed, "kicked off his trousers (long since unbuttoned)"
(p. 194).

It is significant that even though the war episodes dominate the
narrative, the book takes its title from Lillie Ravenel. The author's
greatest interest is in the characters. Three of them are conspicuously Thackerayan and in fact can be paired with characters in
Vanity Fair: Lillie and Amelia, Colburne and Dobbin, Colonel
Carter and Rawdon. Others of the characters show a Dickensian
extravagance and are closer to caricature than to believable char-
acterization: John Whitewood, Jr., the product of a typical Puritan
university; his sister, an inevitable spinster of twenty-five; the
New England woman of a type the author said he had known since
childhood ("thin-lipped, hollow-cheeked, narrow-chested, with only
one lung and an intermittent digestion, without a single rounded
outline or graceful movement, . . . a sad example of what the New
England east winds can do in enfeebling and distorting the human
form divine") (p. 24); the cowardly, corrupt Major Gazaway; and
the hard-fighting, hard-drinking Lieutenant Van Zandt. Mrs. Larue
is a plausible character only in broad outline. She is a Creole, but
except for her French phrases and pronunciation, she has no traits
identifying her with the New Orleans Creoles, whose distinctive
qualities had to wait until George W. Cable began presenting them,
from close knowledge, in the 1870's.

Dr. Ravenel is a composite character who has a major role as
spokesman for the author. He is so generally the voice of understanding and good sense that he is forced drastically out of character when he is made into the ignorant, inept tenderfoot who
takes a gun and joins the soldiers in defending Fort Winthrop. A
Southerner who has fled the South to escape what he considers the
stigma of slavery and the error of secession, he voices much of
De Forest's attack on slavery and the Southern institutions which
had supported it; or better, he shares this role with the author,
for the abundant authorial comment, in the manner of Thackeray,
ranges over this and many other topics. De Forest shows himself
not a profound social critic but a citizen distressed at abuses
around him and ready to attack them in his fictional works, aware
that his attacks provide substance for his plots and issues for
delineating his characters. He recognized the possibilities, moreover, of introducing irony, satire, caricature, and other types of
humor into his social criticism.

Colonel Carter's Southern origin gives De Forest occasion to
pass judgment on various aspects of Southern society. Carter was

"a Virginian born, and of a family which sat in the upper seats of the southern oligarchy. Furthermore, he had married a wife and certain appertaining human property in Louisiana; and although he had buried the first, and dissolved the second (as Cleopatra did pearls) in the wine cup, it was reasonable to suppose that they had exercised an establishing influence on his character; for what Yankee even was ever known to remain an abolitionist after having once tasted the pleasure of living by the labor of others?" (p. 119). De Forest's visits in Charleston before the Civil War and his service in Greenville during Reconstruction, when he was finishing his novel, gave him a knowledge and probably a tolerance of the South that otherwise would have been unlikely for him — a soldier only a few months distant from the Southern battlefields. Colonel Carter has the faults which, to the minds of both the author and Dr. Ravenel, come with the heritage as a "high-born southern gentleman" (p. 99), but for a while his better nature prevails and he seems to have no worse faults than his fondness for liquor — which De Forest makes clear, however, he considers a major fault. Lillie's love comes close, it seems, to redeeming Carter, before he falls to the triple temptations of drink, the wiles of Mrs. Larue, and financial dishonesty. To the end, he remains an excellent soldier, holds the admiration of his troops, including Colburne, and he meets death in the best military tradition.

Dr. Ravenel states and restates his indictment of slavery, and with it the Southern planter aristocracy. The slaveholding society, he believes, was "a compendium of injustice and wickedness" (p. 206). Mrs. Stowe's Uncle Tom is to his mind "a pure fiction," for no man, whatever his innate possibilities, could experience the degradation of slavery without retaining irremovable marks (p. 269). Colburne can admire Dr. Ravenel and Lillie in their program of labor and education for the freed slaves, but he and the author ("as a truthful historian," in his words) share the belief that "there were some rotten specks in the social fruit which the Doctor was trying to raise from this barbarous stock" (p. 267). In the last quarter of the book the characters view the war from its final stages, when the outcome is certain, and approach the perspective which was possible to De Forest in Greenville a year and more after the final surrender. Colburne says the cause of the plain people is being fought out "against an aristocracy" (p. 369); Dr. Ravenel sees the war as "a struggle of the plain people against an oligarchy" (p. 92) and sees in the outcome "the triumph of laboring men," for, he says, "Slavery meant in reality to create an idle nobility" (p. 500); "The pro-slavery South meant oligarchy, and imitated the manners of the European nobility" (p. 506).

De Forest cast a wide net for social abuses to bring under castigation. Military red-tape and promotion by political or family preferment he could condemn with the force generated in his own experience. Similarly he could castigate the Puritan heritage from personal acquaintance. Puritanism, he says in the second chapter, "is absolutely noxious to social gayeties, amenities and graces. I say this in sorrow and not in anger, for New England is the land of my birth and Puritanism is the creed of my ancestors" (p. 22). The same chapter describes New England caricatures present at the Whitefords' dinner party.

The breadth of social issues discussed in *Miss Ravenel's Conversion* has a parallel in the geographical span, from Connecticut to Louisiana. The natural scene receives little attention, but through unobtrusive strokes here and there, the camps and the battlefields are portrayed with convincing reality, especially the terrain of Ship Island, along the bayous of southwestern Louisiana, and at Port Hudson on the Mississippi River. But the author's greatest achievement lies in his characters. Dr. Ravenel is a satisfying composite of common sense, firm conviction, and uncompromising hatred of sham and wrong. Lillie suffers early in the story from De Forest's tendency toward caricature, but the changes she experiences later are plausible in themselves and give her strength and interest enough for the central position she occupies in the novel. Colonel Carter and Mrs. Larue stay in the reader's awareness for their believable humanity, for the admixture of strength and weakness in each, the warring of admirable against despicable traits for dominance. The complex humanity of these characters was in part responsible, it seems, for the slight reception the book had when it was published. William Dean Howells offered the following suggestion: "A certain scornful bluntness in dealing with the disguises in which women natures reveal themselves is perhaps at the root of that dislike which most women have felt for his fiction, and which in a nation of women readers has prevented it from ever winning a merited popularity." Howells himself recalled Mrs. Larue as "very lurid" and said he could not think of her without shuddering.[11] Readers in 1867 were not prepared

---

[11]*Heroines of Fiction* (New York, 1901), II, 153, 157.

for such characters as Mrs. Larue, or for the frankness and unpleasantness and indelicacy they encountered on De Forest's
pages, or for the unexcited portrayal of the commonplace which
Howells and others soon would teach them to read.

If *Miss Ravenel's Conversion* had won critical acclaim and had
shown promise that such works would provide the income
De Forest needed from his pen, he might have continued to
develop the robust strain of realism to which he was undoubtedly
inclined. But the reception of the novel offered so little encouragement that when he revised it in 1887 looking forward to a new
edition which did not materialize, he made extensive deletions,
including a number of the indelicate passages, as if attempting to
placate his readers. The following deleted passage will suggest the
nature of many others cut out in the revision. It appears in a conversation between Colonel Carter and Colburne in which Carter,
at the happiest period of his life, soon after his marriage to Lillie,
is explaining in what he calls an Emersonianism how humanity is
perfected in the unity of man and woman: "You remember Baron
Munchausen's horse; how he was cut in two, and the halves got on
very poorly without each other; and how they were reunited with
mutual benefit. Now this is the history of every bachelor and single
woman, who having miserably tried for a while to go it alone,
finally coalesce happily in one flesh" (p. 358). Later, on the deck
of the *Creole*, when Mrs. Larue has all but gained her conquest of
Colonel Carter and says she is afraid he does not love her, the passage reads in the original: "He was not hypocrite enough to say,
'I *do* love you'; he could only kiss her repeatedly, penitently and in
silence" (p. 381). In the revised version published in 1939
this passage reads: "He was not hypocrite enough to say, 'I *do*
love you'; he could only press her hand repeatedly and in silence."[12]

De Forest removed also much of the authorial comment, such
as the first paragraph of Chapter XXVI (p. 360), showing that he
had joined Howells, Cable, and others in adopting the dramatic
method which they identified with the Russian novelist Turgenev.
He cut out passages of strictly military discussion (such as the
final paragraph of Chapter XXIV, pp. 345-46), and passages of
wide-swinging social criticism (such as the last six sentences of the
long paragraph on pp. 350-51). These revisions were made, probably, because the author was twenty years farther from the expe-

[12]This edition has an introduction by Gordon S. Haight (New York,
1939), p. 337.

~~riences~~ of the war and from ~~the social issues he had criticized~~ and as a consequence could see his book more as a literary work than when he wrote it.

De Forest continued to be "distinctly a man's novelist," as Howells called him, and he wrote important novels and stories which are properly called realistic, but he did not have the steady, consistent development which William Dean Howells and Henry James were to have.[13] But if he had not published *Miss Ravenel's Conversion* to furnish others an example and to prepare the way among publishers, critics, and readers, the development of realistic fiction by Howells and James — with Stephen Crane added, and others who followed him — might have taken a different course from the one it followed.

allusion to Whitman

not a very large leisure class

---

[13]The best of De Forest's later works include *Kate Beaumont* (1872), a novel of South Carolina as he knew it from 1855 to the opening of the war and during his service in the Freedman's Bureau; two novels exposing political corruption: *Honest John Vane* (1875) and *Playing the Mischief* (1875); and *The Bloody Chasm* (1881), a story treating Southern problems of the Reconstruction era, including poverty especially. Others of his works are *Overland* (1871), *The Wetherel Affair* (1873), *Justine's Lovers* (1878), *Irene the Missionary* (1879), *A Lover's Revolt* (1898), *The Downing Legends: Stories in Rhyme* (1901), and *Poems: Medley and Palestina* (1902).

MISS RAVENEL'S CONVERSION

FROM

SECESSION TO LOYALTY.

By J. W. DE FOREST,

AUTHOR OF "EUROPEAN ACQUAINTANCE," "SEACLIFF,"
ETC., ETC.

NEW YORK:

HARPER & BROTHERS, PUBLISHERS,

FRANKLIN SQUARE.

1867.

CONTENTS.

MISS RAVENEL'S CONVERSION.

CHAPTER I.

MR. EDWARD COLBURNE BECOMES ACQUAINTED WITH MISS LILLIE RAVENEL.

It was shortly after the capitulation of loyal Fort Sumter to rebellious South Carolina that Mr. Edward Colburne of New Boston made the acquaintance of Miss Lillie Ravenel of New Orleans.

An obscure American author remarks in one of his rejected articles, (which he had the kindness to read to me from the manuscript) that every great historical event reverberates in a very remarkable manner through the fortunes of a multitude of private and even secluded individuals. No volcanic eruption rends a mountain without stirring the existence of the mountain's mice. It was unquestionably the southern rebellion which brought Miss Ravenel and Mr. Colburne into interesting juxtaposition. But for this gigantic political upturning it is probable that the young lady would never gave visited New Boston where the young gentleman then lived, or, visiting it and meeting him there, would have been a person of no necessary importance in his eyes. But how could a most loyal, warm-hearted youth fail to be interested in a pretty and intelligent girl who was exiled from her home because her father would not be a rebel?

New Boston, by the way, is the capital city of the little Yankee State of Barataria. I ask pardon for this geographical impertinence of introducing a seventh State into New England, and solemnly affirm that I do not mean to disturb thereby the congressional balance of the republic. I make the arrangement with no political object, but solely for my private convenience, so that I may tell my story freely without being accused of misrepresenting this private individual, or insulting that public functionary, or burlesquing any self-satisfied community. Like Sancho Panza's famous island of the same name, Barataria was surrounded by land, at least to a much greater extent than most islands.

It was through Ravenel the father that Colburne made the acquaintance of Miss Ravenel. In those days, not yet a soldier, but only a martially disposed young lawyer and wrathful patriot, he used to visit the New Boston House nearly every evening, running over all the journals in the reading-room, devouring the telegraphic reports that were brought up hot from the newspaper offices, and discussing the great political events of the time with the heroes and sages of the city. One evening he found nobody in the reading-room but a stranger, a tall gentleman of about fifty, with a baldish head and a slight stoop in the shoulders, attired in an English morning-suit of modest snuff-color. He was reading the New York Evening Post through a rather dandified eyeglass. Presently he put the eyeglass in his vest pocket, produced a pair of steel-bowed spectacles, slipped them on his nose and resumed his reading with an air of increased facility and satisfaction. He was thus engaged, and Colburne was waiting for the Post, raging meanwhile over that copperhead sheet, The New Boston Index, when there was a pleasant rustle of female attire in the hall which led by the reading-room.

"Papa, put on your eyeglass," said a silver voice which Colburne liked. "Do take off those horrid spectacles. They make you look as old as Ararat."

"My dear, the eyeglass makes me feel as old as you say," responded papa.

· "Well, stop reading then and come up stairs," was the young person's next command. "I've had such an awful afternoon with those pokey people. I want to tell you———"

Here she caught sight of Colburne regarding her fixedly in the mirror, and with another rustle of vesture she suddenly slid beyond reach of the angle of incidence and refraction.

The stranger laid down the Post in his lap, pocketed his spectacles, and, looking about him, caught sight of Colburne.

"I beg your pardon, sir," said he with a frank, friendly, man of the world sort of smile. "I have kept the evening paper a long time. Will you have it?"

To our young gentleman the civility of this well-bred, middle-aged personage was somewhat imposing, and consequently he made his best bow and would not accept of the Post until positively assured that the other had entirely done with it. Moreover he would not commence reading immediately because that might seem like a tacit reproach; so he uttered a few patriotic common-places on the news of the day, and thereby gave occasion for this history.

"Yes, a sad struggle, a sad struggle—especially for the South," assented the unnamed gentleman. "You can't imagine how unprepared they are for it. The South is just like the town's poor rebelling against the authorities; the more successful they are, the more sure to be ruined."

While he spoke he looked in the young and strange face of his hearer with as much seeming earnestness as if the latter had been an old acquaintance whose opinions were of value to him. There was an amiable fascination in the sympathetic grey eyes and the persuasive smile. He caught Colburne's expression of interest and proceeded.

"Nobody can tell me anything about those unlucky, misguided people. I am one of them by birth—I have lived among them nearly all my life—I know them. They

A 2

are as ill-informed as Hottentots. They have no more idea of their relative strength as compared to that of the United States than the Root-diggers of the Rocky Mountains. They are doomed to perish by their own ignorance and madness."

"It will probably be a short struggle," said Colburne, speaking the common belief of the North.

"I don't know—I don't know about that; we mustn't be too sure of that. You must understand that they are barbarians, and that all barbarians are obstinate and reckless. They will hold out like the Florida Seminoles. They will resist like jackasses and heroes. They won't know any better. They will be an honor to the fortitude and a sarcasm on the intelligence of human nature. They will become an example in history of much that is great, and all that is foolish."

interesting prophecy

"May I ask what part of the South you have resided in?" inquired Colburne.

"I am a South Carolinian born. But I have lived in New Orleans for the last twenty years, summers excepted. A man can't well live there the year round. He must be away occasionally, to clear his system of its malaria physical and moral. It is a Sodom. I consider it a proof of depravity in any one to want to go there. But there was my work, and there I staid—as little as possible. I staid till this stupid, barbarous Ashantee rebellion drove me out."

"I am afraid you will be an exile for some time, sir," observed Colburne, after a short silence during which he regarded the exiled stranger with patriotic sympathy.

"I am afraid so," was the answer, uttered in a tone which implied serious reflection if not sadness.

He remembers the lost home, the sacrificed wealth, the undeserved hostility, the sentence of outlawry which should have been a meed of honor, thought the enthusiastic young patriot. The voice of welcome ought to greet him, the hand of friendship ought to aid him, here among loyal men.

"I hope you stay some time in New Boston, sir," he observed aloud. "If I can be of the slightest benefit to you, I shall be most happy. Allow me to offer you my card, sir."

"Oh! Thank you. You are extremely kind," said the stranger. He bowed very politely and smiled very cordially as he took the bit of pasteboard; but at the same time there was a slight fixity of surprise in his eye which made the sensitive Colburne color. He read the name on the card; then, with a start as of reminiscence, glanced at it again; then leaned forward and peered into the young man's face with an air of eager curiosity.

"Are you—is it possible!—are you related to Doctor Edward Colburne of this place who died fourteen or fifteen years ago?"

"I am his son, sir."

"Is it possible! I am delighted to meet you. I am most sincerely and earnestly gratified. I knew your father well. I had particular occasion to know him as a fellow beginner in mineralogy at a time when the science was little studied in this country. We corresponded and exchanged specimens. My name is Ravenel. I have been for twenty years professor of theory and practice in the Medical College of New Orleans. An excellent place for a dissecting class, by the way. So many negroes are whipped to death, so many white gentlemen die in their boots, as the saying is, that we rarely lack for subjects.— But you must have been quite young when you had the misfortune—and science had the misfortune—to lose your father. Really, you have quite his look about the eyes and forehead. What profession may I ask?"

"Law," said Colburne, who was flushed with pleasure over the acquisition of this charming acquaintance, so evidently to him a man of the world, a savant, a philosopher, and a patriotic martyr.

"Law—that is a smattering of it—just enough to have an office and do notary work."

"A good profession! A grand profession! But I should have expected your father's son to be a physician or a mineralogist."

He took off his spectacles and surveyed Colburne's frank, handsome face with evidently sincere interest. He seemed as much occupied with this young stranger's history and prospects as he had been a moment before with his own beliefs and exile.

At this stage of the conversation one of the hotel servants entered the room and said, "Sir, the young lady wishes you would come up stairs, if you please, sir."

"Oh, certainly," answered the stranger, or, as I may now call him, the Doctor. "Mr. Colburne, come up to my room, if you are at leisure. I shall be most happy to have a longer conversation with you."

Colburne was in the usual quandary of young and modest men on such occasions. He wished to accept the invitation; he feared that he ought not to take advantage of it; he did not know how to decline it. After a lightning-like consideration of the *pros* and *cons*, after a stealthy glance at his toilet in the mirror, he showed the good sense and had the good luck to follow Doctor Ravenel to his private parlor. As they entered, the same silver voice which Colburne had heard below, exclaimed, "Why papa! What has kept you so long? I have been as lonely as a mouse in a trap."

"Lillie, let me introduce Mr. Colburne to you," answered papa. "My dear sir, take this arm chair. It is much more comfortable than those awkward mahogany uprights. Don't suppose that I want it. I prefer the sofa, I really do."

Miss Ravenel, I suppose I ought to state in this exact place, was very fair, with lively blue eyes and exceedingly handsome hair, very luxuriant, very wavy and of a flossy blonde color lighted up by flashes of amber. She was tall and rather slender, with a fine form and an uncommon grace of manner and movement. Colburne was flattered by the quick blush and pretty momentary flutter of embarrassment with which she received him. This same irrepressible blush and flutter often interested those male individuals who were fortunate enough to make Miss Ravenel's acquaintance. Each young fellow thought that she was specially interested in himself; that the depths of her womanly nature were stirred into pleasurable excitement by his advent. And it was frequently not altogether a mistake. Miss Ravenel was interested in people, in a considerable number of people, and often at first sight. She had her father's sympathetic character, as well as his graceful cordiality and consequent charm of manner, the whole made more fascinating by being veiled in a delicate gauze of womanly dignity. As to her being as lovely as a houri, I confess that there were different opinions on that question, and I do not care to settle it, as I of course might, by a tyrannical affirmation.

It is curious how resolutely most persons demand that the heroine of a story shall be extraordinarily handsome. And yet the heroine of many a love affair in our own lives is not handsome; and most of us fall in love, quite earnestly and permanently in love too, with rather plain women. Why then should I strain my conscience by asserting broadly and positively that Miss Ravenel was a first class beauty? But I do affirm without hesitation that, like her father, she was socially charming. I go farther: she was also very loveable and (I beg her pardon) very capable of loving; although up to this time she did not feel sure that she possessed either of these two qualities.

She had simply bowed with a welcoming smile and that flattering blush, but without speaking or offering her hand, when Colburne was presented. I suspect that she waited for her father to give her a key to the nature of the interview and an intimation as to whether she should join in the conversation. She was quite capable of such small forethought, and Doctor Ravenel was worthy of the trust.

" Mr. Colburne is the son of Doctor Colburne, my dear,"

he observed as soon as his guest was seated. "You have heard me speak of the Doctor's premature and lamented death. I think myself very fortunate in meeting his son."

"You are very kind to call on us, Mr. Colburne," said the silver voice with a musical accent which almost amounted to a singsong. "I hope you don't hate Southerners," she added with a smile which made Colburne feel for a moment as if he could not heartily hate Beauregard, then the representative man of the rebellion. "We are from Louisiana, you know."

"I regret to hear it," answered Colburne.

"Oh, don't pity us," she laughed. "It is not such a bad place."

"Please don't misunderstand me. I meant that I regret your exile from your home."

"Thank you for that. I don't know whether papa will thank you or not. He doesn't appreciate Louisiana. I don't believe he is conscious that he has suffered a misfortune in being obliged to quit it. I am. New Boston is very pretty, and the people are very nice. But you know how it is; it is bad to lose one's home."

"My dear, I can't help laughing at your grand misfortune," said the Doctor. "We are something like the Hebrews when they lost Pharaoh king of Egypt, or like people who lose a sinking wreck by getting on a sound vessel. Besides, our happy home turned us out of doors."

The Doctor felt that he had a right to abuse his own, especially after it had ill-treated him.

"Were you absolutely exiled, sir?" asked Colburne.

"I had to take sides. Those unhappy Chinese allow no neutrals—nothing but themselves, the central flowery people, and outside barbarians. They have fed on the poor blacks until they can't abide a man who isn't a cannibal. He is a reproach to them, and they must make away with him. They remind me of a cracker whom I met at a cross road tavern in one of my journeys through the north of Georgia. This man, a red-nosed, tobacco-drizzling, whiskey-perfumed·giant, invited me to drink with him, and, when I declined, got furious and wanted to fight me. I told him that I never drank whiskey and that it made me sick, and finally suceeeded in pacifying him without touching his poison. In fact he made me a kind of apology for having offered to cut my throat. 'Wa'al, fact is, stranger,' said he, '*I*,' (laying an accent as strong as his liquor on the personal pronoun) '*I* use whiskey.'—You understand the inference, I suppose : a man who refused whiskey was a contradiction, a reproach to his personality : such a man he could not suffer to live. It was the Brooks and Sumner affair over again. Brooks says, 'Fact is *I* believe in slavery,' and immediately hits Sumner over the head for not believing in it."

"Something like my grandfather, who, when he had to diet, used to want the whole family to live on dry toast," observed Colburne. "For the time being he believed in the universal propriety and necessity of toast."

"Were you in danger of violence before you left New Orleans ?" he presently asked. "I beg pardon if I am too curious."

"Violence ? Why, not precisely ; not immediate violence. The breaking-off point was this. I must explain that I dabble in chemistry as well as mineralogy. Now in all that city of raw materialism, of cotton-bale and sugar-hogshead instinct—I can't call it intelligence—there was not a man of southern principles who knew enough of chemistry to make a fuse. They wanted to possess themselves of the United States forts in their State. They supposed that they would be obliged to shell them. The shells they had plundered from the United States arsenal ; but the fuses were wanting. A military committee requested me to fabricate them. Of course I was driven to make an immediate choice between rebellion and loyalty. I took the first steamboat to New York, getting off just in time to escape the system of surveillance which the vigilance committees established."

It may seem odd to some sensible people that this learned gentleman of over fifty should expose his own history
so freely to a young fellow whom he had not seen until
half an hour before.   But it was a part of the Doctor's
character to suppose that humanity took an interest in him
just as he took an interest in all humanity; and his natural frankness had been increased by contact with the prevailing communicativeness of his open-hearted fellow-citizens of the South. I dare say that he would have unfolded
the tale of his exile to an intelligent stage-driver by whom
he might have chanced to sit, with as little hesitation as
he poured it into the ears of this graduate of a distinguished university and representative of a staid puritanical
aristocracy. He had no thought of claiming admiration
for his self-sacrificing loyalty.   His story was worth telling, not because it was connected with his interests, but
because it had to do with his sentiments and convictions.
Why should he not relate it to a stranger who was evidently capable of sympathising with those sentiments and
appreciating those convictions ?

But there was another reason for the Doctor's frankness.
At that time every circumstance of the opening civil war,
every item of life that came from hostile South to indignant North, was regarded by all as a species of public
property. If you put down your name on a hotel register
as arrived from Charleston, Savannah, Mobile, New Orleans, or any other point south of Mason & Dixon's line,
you were immediately addressed and catechised.   People
wanted to know how you escaped, and why you tried to
escape; and were ready to accord you any credit you demanded for perilous adventures and patriotic motives;
and did not perceive it nor think a bit ill of you if you
showed yourself somewhat of a romancer and braggart.
And you, on the other hand, did not object to telling your
story, but let it out as naturally as a man just rescued
from drowning opens his heart to the sympathising crowd
which greets him on the river bank.

Now Miss Ravenel was a rebel. Like all young people and almost all women she was strictly local, narrowly geographical in her feelings and opinions. She was colored by the soil in which she had germinated and been nurtured; and during that year no flower could be red, white and blue in Louisiana. Accordingly the young lady listened to the Doctor's story of his self-imposed exile and to his sarcasms upon the people of her native city with certain pretty little starts and sniffs of disapprobation which reminded Colburne of the counterfeit spittings of a kitten playing anger. She could not under any provocation quarrel with her father, but she could perseveringly and energetically disagree with his opinions. When he had closed his tirade and history she broke forth in a defence of her darling Dixie.

"Now, papa, you are too bad. Mr. Colburne, don't you think he is too bad? Just see here. Louisiana is my native State, and papa has lived there half his life. He could not have been treated more kindly, nor have been thought more of, than he was by those Ashantees, as he calls them, until he took sides against them. If you never lived with the Southerners you don't know how pleasant they are. I don't mean those rough creatures from Arkansas and Texas, nor the stupid Acadians, nor the poor white trash. There are low people everywhere. But I do say that the better classes of Louisiana and Mississippi and Georgia and South Carolina and Virginia, yes, and of Tennessee and Kentucky, are right nice. If they don't know all about chemistry and mineralogy, they can talk delightfully to ladies. They are perfectly charming at receptions and dinner parties. They are so hospitable, too, and generous and courteous! Now I call that civilization. I say that such people are civilized."

"They have taught you Ashantee English, though," smiled the Doctor, who has not yet fully realized the fact that his daughter has become a young lady, and ought no longer to be criticised like a school girl. "I am afraid

Mr. Colburne won't understand what 'right nice' means."

"Oh, yes he will. Do try to understand it, Mr. Colburne," answers Miss Ravenel, coloring to her temples and fluttering like a canary whose cage has been shaken, but still smiling good-naturedly. Her father's satire, delivered before a stranger, touched her, but could not irritate a good temper softened by affection.

"I must be allowed to use those Ashantee phrases once in a while," she went on. "We learn them from our old mammas; that is, you know, our nice old black nurses. Well, I admit that the mammas are not grammarians. I admit that Louisiana is not perfect. But it is my Louisiana. And, papa, it ought to be your Louisiana. I think we owe fealty to our State, and should go with it wherever it goes. Don't you believe in State rights, Mr. Colburne? Wouldn't you stand by Barataria in any and every case?"

"Not against the Union, Miss Ravenel," responded the young man, unshaken in his loyalty even by that earnest look and winning smile.

"Oh dear! how can you say so!" exclaims the lovely advocate of secession. "I thought New Englanders—all but Massachusetts people—would agree with us. Wasn't the Hartford Convention held in New England?"

"I can't help admiring your knowledge of political history. But the Hartford Convention is a byeword of reproach among us now. We should as soon think of being governed by the Blue Laws."

At this declaration Miss Ravenel lost hope of converting her auditor. She dropped back in her corner of the sofa, clasping her hands and pouting her lips with a charming earnestness of mild desperation.

Well, the evening passed away delightfully to the young patriot, although it grieved his soul to find Miss Ravenel such a traitor to the republic. It was nearly twelve when he bade the strangers good night and apologized for staying so late, and accepted an invitation to call next day, and hoped they would continue to live in New Boston. He actually trembled with pleasure when Lillie at parting gave him her hand in the frank southern fashion. And after he had reached his cosy bedroom on the opposite side of the public square he had to smoke a segar to compose himself to sleep, and succeeded so ill in his attempt to secure speedy slumber that he heard the town clock ring out one and then two of the morning before he lost his consciousness.

" Oh dear! papa, how he did hang on!" said Miss Ravenel as soon as the door had shut behind him.

Certainly it was late, and she had a right to be impatient with the visitor, especially as he was a Yankee and an abolitionist. But Miss Ravenel, like most young ladies, was a bit of a hypocrite in talking of young men, and was not so very ill pleased at the bottom of her heart with the hanging on of Mr. Colburne.

CHAPTER II.

MISS RAVENEL BECOMES ACQUAINTED WITH LIEUTENANT-
COLONEL CARTER.

MR. COLBURNE was not tardy in calling on the Ravenels nor careless in improving chances of encountering them by seeming accident. His modesty made him afraid of being tiresome, and his sensitiveness of being ridiculous; but neither the one terror nor the other prevented him from inflicting a good deal of his society upon the interesting exiles. Three weeks after his introduction it was his good fortune to be invited to meet them at a dinner party given them by Professor Whitewood of his own Alma Mater, the celebrated Winslow University.

The Whitewood house was of an architecture so com-

mon in New Boston that in describing it I run no risk of
identifying it to the curious.　Exteriorly it was a square
box of brick, stuccoed to represent granite; interiorly it
consisted of four rooms on each floor, divided by a hall up
and down the centre.　This was the original construction,
to which had been added a greenhouse, into which you
passed through the parlor, carefully balanced by a study
into which you passed through the library.　Trim, regular, geometrical, one half of the structure weighing to an
ounce just as much as the other half, and the whole perhaps forming some exact fraction of the entire avoirdupois
of the globe, the very furniture distributed at measured
distances, it was precisely such a building as the New Boston soul would naturally create for itself.　Miss Ravenel
noticed this with a quickness of perception as to the relations of mind and matter which astonished and amused
Mr. Colburne.

"If I should be transported on Aladdin's carpet," she
said, "fast asleep, to some unknown country, and should
wake up and find myself in such a house as this, I should
know that I was in New Boston.　How the Professor must
enjoy himself here !　This room is exactly twenty feet one
way by twenty feet the other.　Then the hall is just ten
feet across by just forty in length.　The Professor can look
at it and say, Four times ten is forty.　Then the greenhouse and the study balance each other like the paddle-
boxes of a steamer.　Why will you all be so square ?"

"But how shall we become triangular, or circular, or
star-shaped, or cruciform ?" asked Colburne.　"And what
would be the good of it if we should get into those forms ?"

"You would be so much more picturesque.　I should
enjoy myself so much more in looking at you."

"I am so sorry you don't like us."

"How it grieves you !" laughed the young lady.　A
flush of rose mounted her cheek as she said this; but I
must beg the reader to recollect that Miss Ravenel blushed
at anything and nothing.

"Now here are buildings of all shapes and colors," she proceeded, turning over the leaves of a photographic album which contained views of Venetian architecture. "Don't you see that these were not built by New Bostonians?"

They were in the library, whither Miss Whitewood had conducted them to exhibit her father's fine collection of photographs and engravings. A shy but hospitable and thoughtful maiden, incapable of striking up a flirtation of her own, and with not a selfish matrimonial in her head, but still quite able to sympathise with the loves of others, Miss Whitewood had seated her two guests at their art banquet, and then had gently withdrawn herself from the study so that they might talk of what they chose without restraint. It was already reported, with or without reason, that Mr. Colburne was interested in the fascinating young exile from Louisiana, and that she was not so indifferent to him as she evidently was to most of the New Boston beaux. This was the reason why that awkward but good Miss Whitewood, twenty-five years old and without a suitor, be it remembered, had brought them into the quiet of the study. Meantime the door was wide open into the hall, and exactly opposite to it was another door wide open into the parlor, where, in full view of the young people, sat all the old people, meaning thereby Doctor Ravenel, Professor Whitewood, Mrs. Whitewood, and her prematurely middle-aged daughter. The three New Bostonians were listening with evident delight to the fluent and zealous Louisianian. But, instead of entering upon his conversation, which consisted chiefly of lively satire and declamation directed against slavery and its rebellious partizans, let us revert for a tiresome moment or two, while dinner is preparing and other guests are arriving, to the subject on which Miss Ravenel has been teasing Mr. Colburne.

New Boston is not a lively nor a sociable place. The principal reason for this is that it is inhabited chiefly by New Englanders. Puritanism, the prevailing faith of that

land and race, is not only not favorable but is absolutely
noxious to social gayeties, amenities and graces. I say
this in sorrow and not in anger, for New England is the
land of my birth and Puritanism is the creed of my progenitors. And I add as a mere matter of justice, that, deficient as the New Bostonians are in timely smiles and appropriate compliments, bare as they are of jollities and an-
gular in manners and opinions, they have strong sympathies for what is clearly right, and can become enthusiastic in a matter of conscience and benevolence. If they
have not learned how to love the beautiful, they know how
to love the good and true. But Puritanism is not the only
reason why the New Bostonians are socially stiff and unsympathetic. The city is divided into more than the ordinary number of cliques and coteries, and they are hedged
from each other by an unusually thorny spirit of repulsion.
From times now far beyond the memory of the oldest inhabitant, the capsheaf in the social pyramid has been allotted by common consent, without much opposition on the
part of the other inhabitants, to the president and professors of Winslow University, their families, and the few
whom they choose to honor with their intimacy. In early
days this learned institution was chiefly theological and its
magnates all clerical ; and it was inevitable that men bearing the priestly dignity should hold high rank in a puritan
community. Eighty or a hundred years ago, moreover,
the professor, with his salary of a thousand dollars yearly was a nabob of wealth in a city where there were not
ten merchants and not one retired capitalist who could
boast an equal income. Finally, learning is a title to consideration which always has been and still is recognized
by the majority of respectable Americans. An objectionable feature of this sacred inner circle of society is that it
contains none of those seraphim called young gentlemen.
The sons of the professors, excepting the few who become
tutors and eventually succeed their fathers, leave New
Boston for larger fields of enterprise ; the daughters of the

professors, enamored of learning and its votaries alone, will not dance, nor pic-nic, much less intermarry, with the children of shop-keepers, shippers and manufacturers ; and thus it happens that almost the only beaux whom you will discover at the parties given in this Upper Five Hundred are slender and beardless undergraduates.

From the time of Colburne's introduction to the Ravenels it was the desire of his heart to make New Boston a pleasant place to them ; and by dint of spreading abroad the fame of their patriotism and its ennobling meed of martyrdom, he was able, in those excitable days, to infect with the same fancy all his relatives and most of his acquaintances ; so that in a short time the exiles received quite a number of hospitable calls and invitations. The Doctor, travelled man of the world as he was, made no sort of difficulty in enjoying or seeming to enjoy these attentions. If he did not sincerely and heartily relish the New Bostonians, so different in flavor of manner and education from the society in which he had been educated, he at least made them one and all believe that they were luxuries to his palate. He became shortly the most popular man for a dinner party or an evening conversazione that was ever known in that city of geometry and puritanism. Except when they had wandered outside of New Boston, or rather, I should say, outside of New England, and got across the ocean, or south of Mason and Dixon's line, these good and grave burghers had never beheld such a radiant, smiling, universally sympathetic and perennially sociable gentleman of fifty as Ravenel. A most interesting spectacle was it to see him meet and greet one of the elder magnates of the university, usually a solid and sincere but shy and somewhat unintelligible person, who always meant three or four times as much as he said or looked, and whose ice melted away from him leaving him free to smile, as our southern friend fervently grasped his frigid hand and beamed with tropical warmth into his arctic spirit. Such a greeting was as exhilarating as a pint of sherry to the sad, sedentary scholar, who had just come from a weary day's grubbing among Hebrew roots, and whose afternoon recreation had been a walk in the city cemetery.

There were not wanting good people who feared the Doctor; who were suspicious of this inexhaustible courtesy and alarmed at these conversational powers of fascination; who doubted whether poison might not infect the pleasant talk, as malaria fills the orange-scented air of Louisiana.

"I consider him a very dangerous man; he might do a great deal of harm if he chose," remarked one of those conscientious but uncharitable ladies whom I have regarded since my childhood with a mixture of veneration and dislike. Thin-lipped, hollow-cheeked, narrow-chested, with only one lung and an intermittent digestion, without a single rounded outline or graceful movement, she was a sad example of what the New England east winds can do in enfeebling and distorting the human form divine. Such are too many of the New Boston women when they reach that middle age which should be physically an era of adipose, and morally of charity. Even her smile was a woful phenomenon; it seemed to be rather a symptom of pain than an expression of pleasure; it was a kind of griping smile, like that of an infant with the colic.

"If he chose! What harm would he choose to do?" expostulated Colburne, for whose ears this warning was intended.

"I can't precisely make out whether he is orthodox or not," replied the inexorable lady. "And if he *is* heterodox, what an awful power he has for deceiving and leading away the minds of the young! He is altogether too agreeable to win my confidence until I know that he is guided and restrained by grace."

"That is the most unjust thing that I ever heard of," broke out Colburne indignantly. "To condemn a man because he is charming! If the converse of the rule is true, Mrs. Ruggles—if unpleasant people are to be admired because they are such—then some of us New Bostonians ought to be objects of adoration."

"I have my opinions, Mr. Colburne," retorted the lady, who was somewhat stung, although not clever enough to comprehend how badly.

"It makes a great difference with an object who looks at it," continued the young man. "I sometimes wonder what the ants think of us human beings. Do they understand our capacities, duties and destinies? Or do they look upon us from what might be called a pismire point of view?"

Colburne could say such things because he was a popular favorite. To people who, like the New Bostonians, did not demand a high finish of manner, this young man was charming. He was sympathetic, earnest in his feelings, as frank as such a modest fellow could be, and among friends had any quantity of expansion and animation. He would get into a gale of jesting and laughter over a game of whist, provided his fellow players were in anywise disposed to be merry. On such occasions his eyes became so bright and his cheeks so flushed that he seemed luminous with good humor. His laugh was sonorous, hearty, and contagious; and he was not at all fastidious as to what he laughed at: it was sufficient for him if he saw that you meant to be witty. In conversation he was very pleasant, and had only one questionable trick, which was a truly American habit of hyperbole. When he was excited he had a droll, absent-minded way of running his fingers through his wavy brown hair, until it stood up in picturesque masses which were very becoming. His forehead was broad and clear; his complexion moderately light, with a strong color in the cheeks; his nose straight and handsome, and other features sufficiently regular; his eyes of a light hazel, and remarkable for their gentleness. There was nothing hidden, nothing stern, in his expression —you saw at a glance that he was the embodiment of frankness and good nature. In person he was strongly

B

built, and he had increased his vigor by systematic exercise. He had been one of the best gymnasts and oarsmen in college, and still kept up his familiarity with swinging-bars and racing shells. His firm white arms were well set on broad shoulders and a full chest; and a pair of long, vigorous legs completed an uncommonly fine figure. Pardonably proud of the strength which he had in part created, he loved to exhibit gymnastic feats, and to talk of the matches in which he had been stroke-oar. It was the only subject on which he exhibited personal vanity. To sum up, he was considered in his set the finest and most agreeable young man in New Boston.

Let us now return to the dinner of Professor Whitewood. The party consisted of eight persons; the male places being filled by Professor Whitewood, Doctor Ravenel, Colburne, and a Lieutenant-Colonel Carter; the female by Mrs. and Miss Whitewood, Miss Ravenel, and John Whitewood, Jr. This last named individual, the son and heir of the host, a youth of twenty years of age, was a very proper person to fill the position of fourth lady. Thin, pale and almost sallow, with pinched features surmounted by a high and roomy forehead, tall, slender, narrow-chested and fragile in form, shy, silent, and pure as the timidest of girls, he was an example of what can be done with youthful blood, muscle, mind and feeling by the studious severities of a puritan university. Miss Ravenel, accustomed to far more masculine men, felt a contempt for him at the first glance, saying to herself, How dreadfully ladylike! She was far better satisfied with the appearance of the stranger, Lieutenant-Colonel Carter. A little above the middle height he was, with a full chest, broad shoulders and muscular arms, brown curling hair, and a monstrous brown mustache, forehead not very high, nose straight and chin dimpled, brown eyes at once audacious and mirthful, and a dark rich complexion which made one think of pipes of sherry wine as well as of years of sunburnt adventure. When he was presented to her he looked her full in the eyes with a bold flash of interest which caused her to color from her forehead to her shoulders. In age he might have been anywhere from thirty-three to thirty-seven. In manner he was a thorough man of the world without the insinuating suavity of her father, but with all his self-possession and readiness.

Colburne had not expected this alarming phenomenon. He was clever enough to recognize the stranger's gigantic social stature at a glance, and like the Israelitish spies in the presence of the Amakim, he felt himself shrink to a grasshopper mediocrity.

At table the company was arranged as follows. At the head sat Mrs. Whitewood, with Dr. Ravenel on her right, and Miss Whitewood on her left. At the foot was the host, flanked on the right by Miss Ravenel and on the left by Lieutenant-Colonel Carter. The two central side places were occupied by young Whitewood and Colburne, the latter being between Miss Whitewood and Miss Ravenel. With a quickness of perception which I suspect he would not have shown had not his heart been interested in the question he immediately decided that Doctor Ravenel was intended to go *tete-a-tete* with Mrs. Whitewood, and this strange officer with Miss Ravenel, while he was to devote himself to Miss Whitewood. The worrying thought drove every brilliant idea from his head. He could no more talk and be merry than could that hermaphrodite soul whose lean body and cadaverous countenance fronted him on the opposite side of the table. Miss Whitewood, who was nearly as great a student as her brother, was almost as deficient in the powers of speech ; she made an effort, first in the direction of the coming Presentation Day, then towards somebody's notes on Cicero, finally upon the weather ; at last, with a woman's sympathetic divination, she guessed the cause of Colburne's gloom, and sank into a pitying silence. As for Mrs. Whitewood, amiable woman and excellent housewife, though an invalid, her conversational faculty consisted in listening. Thus nobody talked except the Ravenels, Lieutenant-Colonel Carter, and Professor Whitewood.

Colburne endeavored to conceal his troubled condition by a smile of counterfeit interest in the conversation. Then he grew ashamed of himself, and tearing off his fictitious smirk, substituted a look of stern thought, thereby exhibiting an honest countenance, but not one suitable to the occasion. There was sherry on the table; not because wine-bibbing was a habit of the Whitewoods, inasmuch as the hostess had brought it out of the family medical stores with a painful twinge of conscience; but there it was, in deference to the supposed tastes of the army gentleman and the strangers from the south. Colburne was tempted to rouse himself with a glass of it, but did not, being a pledged member of a temperance society. Instead of this he made a gallant moral effort, and succeeded in talking copiously to the junior Whitewood. But as what he said is of little consequence to our story, let us go back a few moments and learn what it was that had depressed his spirits.

" I am delighted to meet some one from Louisiana, Miss Ravenel," said the Lieutenant-Colonel, after the master of the house had said grace.

" Why? Are you a Louisianian?" asked the young lady with a blush of interest which was the first thing that troubled Colburne.

" Not precisely. I came very near calling myself such at one time, I liked the State and the people so much. I was stationed there for several years."

" Indeed! At New Orleans?"

" Not so fortunate," replied the Lieutenant Colonel with a smile and a slight bow, which was as much as to say that, if he had been stationed there, he might have hoped for the happiness of knowing Miss Ravenel earlier. " I was stationed in the arsenal at Baton Rouge."

" I never was at Baton Rouge; I mean I never visited there. I have passed there repeatedly in going up and down the river, just while the boat made its landings, you know. What a beautiful place it is! I don't mean the buildings, but the situation, the bluffs."

"Precisely. Great relief to get to Baton Rouge and see a hill or two after staying in the lowlands."

"Oh! don't say anything against the lowlands," begged Miss Ravenel.

"I won't," promised the Lieutenant Colonel. "Give you my word of honor I won't do it, not even in the strictest privacy."

There was a cavalier dash in the gentleman's tone and manner; he looked and spoke as if he felt himself quite good enough for his company. And so he was, at least in respect to descent and social position; for no family in Virginia boasted a purer strain of old colonial blue blood than the Carters. In addition the Lieutenant Colonel was a gentleman by right of a graduation from West Point, and of a commission in the regular service which dated back to the times when there were no volunteers and few civilian appointments, and when by consequence army officers formed a caste of aristocratic military brahmins. From the regular service, however, in which he had been only a lieutenant, his name had vanished several years previous. His lieutenant-colonelcy was a volunteer commission issued by the governor of the State. It was in the Second Barataria, a three-months' regiment, which was shortly to distinguish itself by a masterly retreat from Bull Run. Carter had injured his ancle by a fall from his horse, and was away from the army on a sick leave of twenty days, avoiding the hospitals of Washington, and giving up his customary enjoyments in New York for the sake of attending to business which will transpire during this narrative. His leave had nearly expired, but he had applied to the War Department for an extension of ten days, and was awaiting an answer from that awful headquarters with the utmost tranquillity. If he found himself in the condition of being absent without leave, he knew how to explain things to a military commission or a board of inquiry.

The Lieutenant-Colonel liked the appearance of the young person whom he had been invited to meet. In the first place, he said to himself, she had a charming mixture of girlish freshness and of the thorough-bred society air which he considered indispensable to a lady. In the second place she looked somewhat like his late wife; and although he had been a wasteful and neglectful husband, he still kept a moderately soft spot in his heart for the memory of the departed one; not being in this respect different, I understand, from the majority of widowers. He saw that Miss Ravenel was willing to talk any kind of nothing so long as she could talk of her native State, and that therefore he could please her without much intellectual strain or chance of rivalry. Consequently he prattled and made prattle for some minutes about Louisiana.

"Were you acquainted with the McAllisters?" he wanted to know. "Very natural that you shouldn't be. They lived up the river, and seldom went to the city. They had such a noble plantation, though! You could enjoy the true, old-style, princely Louisiana hospitality there. Splendid life, that of a southern planter. If I hadn't been in the army—or rather, if I could have done everything that I fancied, I should have become a sugar planter. Of course I should have run myself out, for it takes a frightful capital and some business faculty, or else the best of luck. By the way, I am afraid those fine fellows will all of them come to grief if this war continues five or six years."

"Five or six years!" exclaimed Professor Whitewood in astonishment, but not in dismay, so utter was his incredulity. "Do you suppose, Colonel, that the rebels can resist for five or six years?"

"Why not? Ten or twelve millions of people on their own ground, and difficult ground too, will make a terrific resistance. They are as well prepared as we are, and better. Frederic of Prussia wasn't conquered in seven years. I don't see anything unreasonable in allowing these fellows five or six. By the way," he laughed, " I am giving you an honest professional opinion. Talking outside—to the rabble—talking as a patriot," (here he laughed again) " and not as an officer, I say three months. Do it in three months, gentlemen !" he added, setting his head back and swelling his chest in imitation of the conventional popular orator.

Miss Ravenel laughed outright to hear the enemies of her section satirized.

" But how will the South stand a contest of five or six years ?" queried the Professor.

" Oh, badly, of course ; get whipped, of course ; that is, if we develope energy and military talent. We have the resources to thrash them. War in the long run is pretty much a matter of arithmetical calculation. Oh, Miss Ravenel, I was about to ask you, did you know the Slidells ?"

" Very slightly."

" Why slightly ? Didn't you like them ? I thought they were very agreeable people ; though, to be sure, they were *parvenus.*"

" They were very ultra, you know ; and papa was of the other party."

" Oh, indeed !" said the Lieutenant-Colonel, turning his head and surveying Ravenel with curiosity, not because he was loyal, but because he was the young lady's papa. " How I regret that I had no chance to make your father's acquaintance in Louisiana. Give you my honor that I wasn't so simple as to prefer Baton Rouge to New Orleans. I tried to get ordered to the crescent city, but the War Department was obdurate. I am confident," he added, with his audacious smile, half flattering and half quizzical, " that if the Washington people had known *all* that I lost by not getting to New Orleans, they would have relented."

It was perfectly clear to Miss Ravenel that he meant to

pay her a compliment. It occurred to her that she was
probably in short dresses when the gallant Lieutenant-
Colonel was on duty at Baton Rouge, and thus missed a
chance of seeing her in New Orleans.   But she did not
allude to this ludicrous possibility ; she only colored at his
audacity, and said, " Oh, it's such a lovely city ! I think
it is far preferable to New York."

" But is it not a very wicked city ?" asked the host,
quite seriously.

" Mr. Whitewood ! How can you say that to me, a native of it ?" she laughed.

" Jerusalem," pursued the Professor, getting out of his
scrape with a kind of ponderous dexterity, like an elephant
backing off a shaky bridge, and taking his time about it,
like Noah spending a hundred and twenty years in building his ark—" Jerusalem proved her wickedness by casting
out the prophets.   It seems to me that your presence here,
and that of your father, as exiles, is sufficient proof of the
iniquity of New Orleans."

" Upon my honor, Professor !" burst out the Lieutenant-
Colonel, " you beat the best man I ever saw at a compliment."

It was now Professor Whitewood's pale and wrinkled
cheek which flushed, partly with gratification, partly with
embarrassment.   His wife surveyed him in mild astonishment, almost fearing that he had indulged in much sherry.

The Lieutenant-Colonel, by the way, had taken to the
wine in a style which showed that he was used to the
taste of it, and liked the effects. His conversation grew
more animated ; his bass voice rang from end to end of
the table, startling Mrs. Whitewood ; his fine brown eyes
flashed, and a few drops of perspiration beaded his brow.
It must not be supposed that the sherry alone could do as
much as this for so old a campaigner. That afternoon, as
he lounged and yawned in the reading-room of the New
Boston House, he had thought of Professor Whitewood's
invitation, and, feeling low-spirited and stupid, had con-

cluded not to go to the dinner, although in the morning he
had sent a note of acceptance.   Then, feeling low-spirited
and stupid, as I said, he took a glass of ale, and subsequently a stiffish whiskey-punch, following up the treatment with a segar, which by producing a dryness of the
throat, induced him to try another whiskey-punch.   Forti-
fied by twenty-five cents' worth of liquor (at the then
prices) he felt his ambition and industry revive. By Jove,
Carter, he said to himself, you must go to that dinner-
party.   Whitewood is just one of those pious heavy-
weights who can bring this puritanical governor to
terms.   Put on your best toggery, Carter, and make your
bow, and say how-de-do.

Thus it was that when the Professor's sherry entered into the Lieutenant-Colonel, it found an ally there which aided it to produce the afore-mentioned signs of excitement.
Colburne, I grieve to say, almost rejoiced in detecting
these symptoms, thinking that surely Miss Ravenel would
not fancy a man who was, to say the least, inordinately
convivial.   Alas! Miss Ravenel had been too much accustomed to just such gentlemen in New Orleans society to
see anything disgusting or even surprising in the manner
of the Lieutenant-Colonel.   She continued to prattle with
him in her pleasantest manner about Louisiana, not in the
least restrained by Colburne's presence, and only now and
then casting an anxious glance at her father; for Ravenel
the father, man of the world as he was, did not fancy the
bacchanalian New Orleans type of gentility, having observed that it frequently brought itself and its wife and
children to grief.

The dinner lasted an hour and a half, by which time it
was nearly twilight.   The ordinary prandial hour of the
Whitewoods, as well as of most fashionable New Boston
people, was not later than two o'clock in the afternoon,
but this had been considered a special occasion on account
of the far-off origin of some of the guests, and the meal had
therefore commenced at five.   On leaving the table the

party went into the parlor and had coffee. Then Miss Ravenel thought it wise to propitiate her father's searching eye by quitting the Lieutenant-Colonel with his pleasant wordly ways and his fascinating masculine maturity, and going to visit the greenhouse in company with that pale bit of human celery, John Whitewood. Carter politely stood up to the rack for a while with Miss Whitewood, but, finding it dry fodder to his taste, soon made his adieux. Colburne shortly followed, in a state of mind to question the goodness of Providence in permitting lieutenant-colonels.

CHAPTER III.

MR. COLBURNE TAKES A SEGAR WITH LIEUTENANT-COLONEL CARTER.

As Colburne neared his house he saw the Lieutenant-Colonel standing in the flare of a street lamp and looking up at the luminary with an air of puzzled consideration. With a temperance man's usual lack of charity to people given to wine, the civilian judged that the soldier was disgracefully intoxicated, and, instead of thinking how to conduct him quietly home, was about to pass him by on the other side. The Lieutenant-Colonel turned and recognized the young man. In other states of feeling he would have cut him there and then, on the ground that it was not binding on him to continue a chance acquaintance. But being full at the moment of that comprehensive love of fellow existences which some constitutions extract from inebriating fluids, he said,

"Ah! how are you? Glad to come across you again."

Colburne nodded, smiled and stopped, saying, "Can I do anything for you?"

" Will you smoke ?" asked the Lieutenant-Colonel, offering a segar. " But how to light it ? there's the rub. I've just broken my last match against this cursed wet lamp-post—never thought of the dew, you know—and was studying the machine itself, to see if I could get up to it and into it."

" I have matches," said Colburne. He produced them; they lighted and walked on together.

Being a great fancier of good segars, and of moonlit summer walks under New Boston elms, I should like here to describe how sweetly the fragrance of the Havanas rose through the still, dewy air into the interlacing arches of nature's cathedral aisles. The subject would have its charms, not only for the great multitude of my brother smokers, but for many young ladies who dearly love the smell of a segar because they like the creatures who use them. At a later period of this history, if I see that I am likely to have the necessary space and time, I may bloom into such pleasant episodes.

" Come to my room," said the soldier, taking the arm of the civilian. " Hope you have nothing better to do. We will have a glass of ale."

Colburne would have been glad to refuse. He was modest enough to feel himself at a disadvantage in the company of men of fashion ; and moreover he was just sufficiently jealous of the Lieutenant-Colonel not to desire to fraternize with him. Finally, a strong suspicion troubled his mind that this military personage, indifferent to New Boston opinions, and evidently a wine-bibber, might proceed to get publicly drunk, thus making a disagreeable scene, with a chance of future scandal. Why then did not Colburne decline the invitation? Because he was young, good-natured, modest, and wanting in that social tact and courage which most men only acquire by much intercourse with a great variety of their fellow creatures. The Lieutenant-Colonel's walk was the merest trifle unsteady, or at least careless, and his herculean arm, solid and knotted as an apple-tree limb, swayed repeatedly against Colburne, eliciting from him a stroke-oarsman's approbation. Proud of his own biceps, the young man had to acknowledge its comparative inferiority in volume and texture.

"Are you a gymnast, Colonel?" he asked. "Your arm feels like it."

"Sword exercise," answered the other. "Very good thing to work off a heavy dinner. What do you do here? Boat it, eh? That's better yet, I fancy."

"But the sword exercise is just the thing for your profession."

"Pshaw!—beg pardon. But do you suppose that we in these times ever fight hand to hand? No sir. Gunpowder has killed all that."

"Perhaps there never was much real hand to hand fighting," suggested Colburne. "Look at the battle of Pharsalia. Two armies of Romans, the best soldiers of antiquity, meet each other, and the defeated party loses fifteen thousand men killed and wounded, while the victors lose only about two hundred. Is that fighting? Isn't it clear that Pompey's men began to run away when they got within about ten feet of Cæsar's?"

"By Jove! you're right. Bully for you! You would make a soldier. Yes. And if Cæsar's men had had long-range rifles, Pompey's men would have run away at a hundred yards. All victories are won by moral force—by the terror of death rather than by death itself."

"Then it is not the big battalions that carry the day," inferred Colburne. "The weakest battalions will win, if they will stand."

"But they won't stand, by Jove! As soon as they see they are the weakest, they run away. Modern war is founded on the principle that one man is afraid of two. Of course you must make allowance for circumstances, strength of position, fortifications, superior discipline, and superior leadership. Circumstances are sometimes strong enough to neutralize numbers.—Look here. Are you in-terested in these matters? Why don't you go into the army? What the devil are you staying at home for when the whole nation is arming, or will soon have to arm?"

"I"—stammered Colburne—"I *have* thought of apply-ing for a quartermaster's position."

"A quartermaster's!" exclaimed the Lieutenant-Colonel, without seeking to disguise his contempt. "What for? To keep out of the fighting?"

"No," said Colburne, meekly. "But I do know a little of the ways of business, and I know nothing of tactics and discipline. I could no more drill a company than I could sail a ship. I should be like the man who mounted such a tall horse that he not only couldn't manage him, but couldn't get off till he was thrown off. I should be dis-missed for incompetency."

"But you can learn all that. You can learn in a month. You are a college man, aint you?—you can learn more in a month than these boors from the militia can in ten years. I tell you that the fellows who are in command of compa-nies in my regiment, and in all the volunteer regiments that I know, are not fit on an average to be corporals. The best of them are from fair to middling. You are a college man, aint you? Well, when I get a regiment you shall have a company in it. Come up to my quarters, and let's talk this over."

Arrived at his room, Carter rang for Scotch ale and se-gars. In the course of half an hour he became exceedingly open-hearted, though not drunk in the ordinary and disa-greeable acceptation of the word.

"I'll tell you why I am on here," said he. "It's my mother's native State—old Baratarian family—Standishes, you know—historically Puritan and colonial. The White-woods are somehow related to me. By the way, I'm a Virginian. I suppose you think it queer to find me on this side. No you don't, though; you don't believe in the State Right of secession. Neither do I. I was edu-

cated a United States soldier. I follow General Scott.
No Virginian need be ashamed to follow old Fuss and
Feathers. We used to swear by him in the army. Great
Scott! the fellows said. Well, as I had to give up my father's State, I have come to my mother's. I want old Barataria to distinguish herself. Now's the chance. We are
going to have a long war. I want the State to be prepared and come out strong; it's the grandest chance she'll
ever have to make herself famous. I've been to see the
Governor. I said to him, ' Governor, now's your chance ;
now's the chance for Barataria ; now's my chance. It's
going to be a long war. Don't depend on volunteering—
it won't last. Get a militia system ready which will
classify the whole population, and bring it into the fight
as fast as it's needed. Make the State a Prussia. If you'll
allow me, I'll draw up a plan which shall make Barataria
a military community, and put her at the head of the
Union for moral and physical power. Appoint me your
chief of staff, and I'll not only draw up the plan, but put
it in force. Then give me a division, or only a brigade,
and I'll show you what well-disciplined Baratarians can
do on the battle-field. Now what do you think the Governor answered ?—Governor's a dam fool!'"

" Oh, no !" protested Colburne, astonished ; for the chief
magistrate of Barataria was highly respected.

"I don't mean individually—not a natural-born fool,"
explained the Lieutenant-Colonel—" but a fool from the
necessity of the case ; mouthpiece, you see, of a stupid day
and generation. What can he do ? he asks. I admit it.
He can't do anything but what Democracy permits. Lose
the next election, he says. Well, I suppose he would; and
that won't answer. Governor's wise in his day and generation, although a fool by the eternal laws of military
reason.—I don't know as I talk very clearly. But you get
at my meaning, don't you ?—Well, I had a long argument, and gave it up. We must go on volunteering, and
commissioning the rusty militia-men and greasy dema-

gogues who bring in the companies. The rank and file is magnificent—can't be equalled—too good. But such an infernally miserable set as the officers average! Some bright young fellows, who can be licked into shape; the rest old deacons, tinkers, military tailors, Jew pedlars broken down stump orators; wrong-headed cubs who have learned just enough of tactics to know how not to do it. Look at the man that I, a Virginian gentleman, a West Pointer, have over me for Colonel. He's an old bloat—an old political bloat. He knows no more of tactical evolutions than he does of the art of navigation. He'll order a battalion which is marching division front to break into platoons. You don't understand that? It's about the same as—well, never mind—it can't be done. Well, this cursed old bloat is engineering to be a General. We don't want such fellows for Generals, nor for Colonels, nor for Captains, nor for privates, by Jove! If Barataria had to fit out frigates instead of regiments, I wonder if she would put such men in command of them. Democracy might demand it. The Governor would know better, but he might be driven to it, for fear of losing the next election.

"Now then," continued the Lieutenant-Colonel, "I come to business. We shall have to raise more regiments. I shall apply for the command of one of them, and shall get it. But I want gentlemen for my officers. I am a gentleman myself, and a West Pointer. I don't want tinkers and pedlars and country deacons. You're a college man, aint you? All right. College men will do for me. I want you to take a company in my regiment, and get in as many more of your set as you can. I'm not firing blank cartridge. My tongue may be thick, but my head is clear. Will you do it?"

"I will," decided Colburne, after a moment of earnest consideration.

The problem occurred to him whether this man, clever as he was, professional soldier as he was, but apparently a follower of rash John Barleycorn, would be a wiser leader in the field than a green but temperate civilian. He could not stop to settle the question, and accepted the Lieutenant-Colonel's leadership by impulse. The latter thanked him cordially, and then laughed aloud, evidently because of that moment of hesitation.

"Don't think I'm this way always," he said. "Never when on duty; Great Scott! no man can say that. Indeed I'm not badly off now. If I willed it I could be as logical as friend Whitewood—I could do a problem in Euclid. But it would be a devil of an effort. You won't demand it of me, will you?"

"It's an odd thing in man," he went on gravely, "how he can govern drunkenness and even sickness. Just as though a powder-magazine should have self-control enough not to explode when some one throws a live coal into it. The only time I ever got drunk clear through, I did it deliberately. I was to Cairo, caught there by a railroad breakdown, and had to stay over a night. Ever at Cairo? It is the dolefullest, cursedest place! If a man is excusable anywhere for drinking himself insensible, it is at Cairo, Illinois. The last thing I recollect of that evening is that I was sitting in the bar-room, feet against a pillar, debating whether I would go quite drunk, or make a fight and stay sober. I said to myself, It's Cairo, and let myself go. My next distinct recollection is that of waking up in a railroad car. I had been half conscious two or three times previously, but had gone to sleep again, without taking notice of my surroundings. This time I looked about me. My carpet-bag was between my feet, and my over-coat in the rack above my head. I looked at my watch; it was two in the afternoon. I turned to the gentleman who shared my seat and said, 'Sir, will you have the goodness to tell me where this train is going?' He stared, as you may suppose, but replied that we were going to Cincinnati. The devil we are! thought I; and I wanted to go to St. Louis. I afterwards came across a man who was able to tell me how I got on the train. He said that I came down at five in the morning, carpet-bag and over-coat in hand, settled my bill in the most rational manner possible, and took the omnibus to the railroad station. Now it's my belief that I could have staved off that drunken fit by obstinacy. I can stave this one off. You shall see."

He emptied his glass, lighted a fresh segar big enough to floor some men without other aid, and commenced walking the room, taking it diagonally from corner to corner, so as to gain a longer sweep.

"Don't stir," he said. "Don't mind me. Start another segar and try the ale. You won't? What an inhuman monster of abstinence!"

"That is the way they bring us up in New Boston. We are so temperate that we are disposed to outlaw the raising of rye."

"You mean in your set. There must be somebody in this city who gets jolly! there is everywhere, so far as I have travelled. You will find a great many fellows like me, and worse, in the old army. And good reason for it; just think of our life. All of us couldn't have nice places in charge of arsenals, or at Newport, or on Governor's Island. I was five years on the frontier and in California before I got to Baton Rouge; and that was not so very delightful, by the way, in yellow fever seasons. Now imagine yourself in command of a company garrisoning Fort Wallah-Wallah on the upper Missouri, seven hundred miles from an opera, or a library, or a lady, or a mince pie, or any other civilizing influence. The Captain is on detached service somewhere. You are the First Lieutenant, and your only companion is Brown the Second Lieutenant. You mustn't be on sociable terms with the men, because you are an officer and a gentleman. You have read your few books, and talked Brown dry. There is no shooting within five miles of the fort; and if you go beyond that distance, the Blackfeet will raise your hair. What is there to save you from suicide but old-rye? That's one way we come to drink so. You are lucky.

You have had no temptations, or almost none, in this little Puritan city."

"There are some bad places and people here. I don't speak of it boastingly."

"Are there?" laughed Carter. "I'm delighted to hear it, by Jove! When my father went through college here, there wasn't a chance to learn anything wicked but hypocrisy. Chance enough for that, judging from the stories he told me. So old Whitewood is no longer the exact model of all the New Bostonians?"

"Not even in the University. There used to be such a solemn set of Professors that they couldn't be recognised in the cemetery because they had so much the air of tombstones. But that old dark-blue lot has nearly died out, and been succeeded by younger men of quite a pleasant cerulean tint. They have studied in Europe. They like Paris and Vienna, and other places that used to be so wicked; they don't think such very small lager of the German theologians; they accept geology, and discuss Darwin with patience."

"Don't get out of my range. Who the devil is Darwin? Never mind; I'll take him for granted; go on with your new-school Professors.

"Oh, I havn't much to say about them. They are quite agreeable. They are what I call men of the world—though I suppose I hardly know what a man of the world is. I dare say I am like the mouse who took the first dog that he saw for the elephant that he had heard of."

The Lieutenant-Colonel stopped his walk and surveyed him, hands in pockets, a smile on his lip, and a silent horse-laugh in his eye.

"Men of the world, are they? By Jove! Well; perhaps so; I havn't met them yet. But if it comes to pointing out men of the world, allow me to indicate our Louisiana friend, Ravenel. There's a fellow who can do the universally agreeable. You couldn't tell this evening which he liked best, Whitewood or me; and I'll be

hanged if the same man can like both of us.   When he
was talking with the Professor he seemed to be saying
to himself, 'Whitewood is my blue-book;" and when he
was talking with me his whole countenance glowed with
an expression which stated that 'Carter is the boy.'
What a diplomatist he would make! I like him immensely.   He has a charming daughter too; not beautiful exactly, but very charming."

Colburne felt an oppression which would not allow him
to discuss the question.   At the same time he was not indignant, but only astonished, perhaps also a little pleased,
at the tone of indifference with which the other spoke of
the young lady.   His soul was so occupied with this new
train of thought that I doubt whether he heard understandingly the conversation of his interlocutor for the next
few minutes.   Suddenly it struck him that Carter was entirely sober, in body and brain.

"Colonel, wouldn't you like to go on a pic-nic?" he
asked abruptly.

"Pic-nic?—political thing?   Why, yes; think I ought
to like it; help along our regiment."

"No, no; not political.   I'm sorry I gave you such an
exalted expectation; now you'll be disappointed.   I mean
an affair of young ladies, beaux, baskets, paper parcels,
sandwiches, cold tongue, biscuits and lemonade."

"Lemonade!" said Carter with a grimace.   "Could a
fellow smoke?"

"I take that liberty."

"Is Miss Ravenel going?"

"Yes."

"I accept.   How do you go?"

"In an omnibus.   I will see that you are taken up—say
at nine o'clock to-morrow morning."

CHAPTER IV.

THE DRAMATIC PERSONAGES GO ON A PIC-NIC, AND STUDY
THE WAYS OF NEW BOSTON.

WHEN the Lieutenant-Colonel awoke in the morning he did not feel much like going on a pic-nic. He had a slight ache in the top of his head, a huskiness in the throat, a woolliness on the tongue, a feverishness in the cuticle, and a crawling tremulousness in the muscles, as though the molecules of his flesh were separately alive and intertwining themselves. He drowsily called to mind a red-nosed old gentleman whom he had seen at a bar, trying in vain to gather up his change with shaky fingers, and at last exclaiming, " Curse the change !" and walking off hastily in evident mortification.

" Ah, Carter ! you will come to that yet," thought the Lieutenant-Colonel.—" To be sure," he added after a moment, " this sobering one's self by main strength of will, as I did last night, is an extra trial, and enough to shake any man's system.—But how about breakfast and that confounded pic-nic ?" was his next reflection. " Carter, temperance man as you are, you must take a cocktail, or you won't be able to eat a mouthful this morning."

He rang ; ordered an eye-opener, stiff ; swallowed it, and looked at his watch. Eight ; never mind ; he would wash and shave ; then decide between breakfast and pic-nic. Thanks to his martial education he was a rapid dresser, and it still lacked a quarter of nine when he appeared in the dining saloon. He had time therefore to eat a mutton chop, but he only looked at it with a disgusted eye, his stomach being satisfied with a roll and a cup of coffee. In the outer hall he lighted a segar, but after smoking about an inch of it, threw the rest away. It was decidedly one of his qualmish mornings, and he was glad to get a full breath of out of door air.

"Is my hamper ready?" he said to one of the hall-boys.
"Sir?"

"My hamper, confound you;" repeated the Lieutenant Colonel, who was more irritable than usual this morning. "The basket that I ordered last night. Go and ask the clerk."

"Yes, sir," said the boy when he returned. "It's all right, sir. There it is, sir, behind the door."

The omnibus, a little late of course, appeared about a quarter past nine. Besides Colburne it contained three ladies, two of about twenty-five and one of thirty-five, accompanied by an equal number of beardless, slender, jauntily dressed youths whom the Lieutenant-Colonel took for the ladies' younger brothers, inferring that pic-nics were family affairs in New Boston. Surveying these juvenile gentlemen with some contempt, he was about to say to Colburne, "Very sorry, my dear fellow, but really don't feel well enough to go out to-day," when he caught sight of Miss Ravenel.

"Are you going?" she asked with a blush which was so indescribably flattering that he instantly responded, "Yes, indeed."

Behind Miss Ravenel came the doctor, who immediately inquired after Carter's health with an air of friendly interest that contrasted curiously with the glance of suspicion which he bent on him as soon as his back was turned. Libbie hastened into the omnibus, very much afraid that her father would order her back to her room. It was only by dint of earnest begging that she had obtained his leave to join the pic-nic, and she knew that he had given it without suspecting that this sherry-loving army gentleman would be of the party.

"But where are your matrons, Mr. Colburne?" asked the doctor. "I see only young ladies, who themselves need matronizing."

The beauty of thirty-five looked graciously at him, and judged him a perfect gentleman.

"Mrs. Whitewood goes out in her own carriage," answered Colburne.

The Doctor bowed, professed himself delighted with the arrangements, wished them all a pleasant excursion, and turned away with a smiling face which became exceedingly serious as he walked slowly up stairs.   It was not thus that young ladies were allowed to go a pleasuring at New Orleans.   The severe proprieties of French manners with regard to *demoiselles* were in considerable favor there.   Her mother never would have been caught in this way, he thought, and was anxious and repentant and angry with himself, until his daughter returned.

In the omnibus Colburne did the introductions; and now Carter discovered that the beardless young gentlemen were not the brothers of the ladies, but most evidently their cavaliers; and was therefore left to infer that the beaux of New Boston are blessed with an immortal youth, or rather childhood.   He could hardly help laughing aloud to think how he had been caught in such a nursery sort of pic-nic.   He glanced from one downy face to another with a cool, mocking look which no one understood but Miss Ravenel, who was the only other person in the party to whom the sight of such juvenile gallants was a rarity. She bit her lips to repress a smile, and desperately opened the conversation.

"I am so anxious to see the Eagle's Nest," she said to one of the students.

"Oh! you never saw it?" he replied.

There were two things in this response which surprised Miss Ravenel.   In the first place the young gentleman blushed violently at being addressed; in the second, he spoke in a very hoarse and weak tone, his voice being not yet established.   Unable to think of anything further to say, he turned for aid to the maiden of thirty-five, between whom and himself there was a tender feeling, as appeared openly later in the day. She set him on his intellectual pins by commencing a conversation on the wooden-spoon exhibition.

"What is the wooden-spoon?" asked Lillie.

"It is a burlesque honor in college," answered the youth. "It used to be given to the stupidest fellow in the graduating class. Now it's given to the jolliest fellow—most popular fellow—smartest fellow, that doesn't take a real honor."

"Allow me to ask, sir, are you a candidate?" inquired the Lieutenant-Colonel.

Miss Ravenel cringed at this unprovoked and not very brilliant brutality. The collegian merely stammered "No, sir," and blushed immoderately. He was too much puzzled by the other's impassable stare to comprehend the sneer at once; but he studied it much during the day, and that night writhed over the memory of it till towards morning. Both Carter and the lady of thirty-five ought to have been ashamed of themselves for taking unfair advantage of the simplicity and sensitiveness of this lad; but the feminine sinner had at least this excuse, that it was the angelic spirit of love, and not the demonaic spirit of scorn, which prompted her conduct. Perceiving that her boy was being abused, she inveigled him into a corner of the vehicle, where they could talk together without interruption. The conversation of lovers is not usually interesting to outsiders except as a subject of laughter; it is frequently stale and flat to a degree which seems incomprehensible when you consider the strong feelings of the interlocutors. This is the ordinary sort of thing, at least in New Boston:—

Lady. (smiling) Did you go out yesterday?

Gent. (smiling) Yes.

Lady. Where?

Gent. Only down to the post-office.

Lady. Many people in the streets?

Gent. Not very many.

And all the while the two persons are not thinking of the walk, nor of the post-office, nor of the people in the streets, nor of anything of which they speak. They are thinking of each other; they are prattling merely to be near each other; they are so full of each other that they cannot talk of foreign subjects interestingly; and so the babble has a meaning which the unsympathetic bye-stander does not comprehend.

After circulating through the city to pick up the various invited ones, the omnibus was joined by a second omnibus and two or three family rockaways. The little fleet of vehicles then sailed into the country, and at the end of an hour's voyage came to anchor under the lee of a wooded cliff called the Eagle's Nest, which was the projected site of the pic-nic. Up the long slope which formed the back of the cliff, a number of baskets and demijohns were carried by the youthful beaux of the party with a child-like zeal which older gallants might not have exhibited. Carter's weighty hamper was taken care of by a couple of juniors, who jumped to the task on learning that it belonged to a United States army officer. He offered repeatedly to relieve them, but they would not suffer it. In a roundabout and inarticulate manner they were exhibiting the fervent patriotism of the time, as well as that perpetual worship which young men pay to their superiors in age and knowledge of the world. And oh! how was virtue rewarded when the basket was opened and its contents displayed! It was not for the roast chicken that the two frolicsome juniors cared: the companion baskets around were crammed with edibles of all manner of flesh and fowl; it was the sight of six bottles of champagne which made their eyes rejoice. But with a holy horror equal to their wicked joy did all the matrons of the party, and indeed more than half of the younger people, stare. Carter's champagne was the only spirit of a vinous or ardent nature present. And when he produced two bunches of segars from his pockets and proceeded to distribute them, the moral excitation reached its height. Immediately there were opposing partisans in the pic-nic: those who meant to take a glass of champagne and smoke a segar, if it were only for the wicked fun of the thing; and those who meant, not only that they would not smoke nor drink themselves, but that nobody else should. These last formed little groups and discussed the affair with conscientious bitterness. But what to do? The atrocity puzzled them by its very novelty. The memory of woman did not go back to the time when an aristocratic New Boston pic-nic had been so desecrated. I say the memory of *woman* advisedly and upon arithmetical calculation; for in this party the age of the males averaged at least five years less than that of the females.

"Why don't you stop it, Mrs. Whitewood?" said the maiden of thirty-five, with girlish enthusiasm. "You are the oldest person here." (Mrs. Whitewood did not look particularly flattered by this statement.) "You have a perfect right to order anything." (Mrs. Whitewood looked as if she would like to order the young lady to let her alone.) "If I were you, I would step out there and say, Gentlemen, this must be stopped."

Mrs. Whitewood might have replied, Why don't you say it yourself?—you are old enough. But she did not; such sarcastic observations never occurred to her good-natured soul; nor, had she been endowed with thousands of similar conceits, would she have dared utter one. It was impossible to rub her up to the business of confronting and putting down the adherents of the champagne basket. She did think of speaking to Lieutenant-Colonel Carter privately about it, but before she could decide in what terms to address him, the last bottle had been cracked, and then of course it was useless to say anything. So in much horror of spirit and with many self-reproaches for her weakness, she gazed helplessly upon what she considered a scene of wicked revelry. In fact there was

C

a good deal of jollity and racket.   The six bottles of
champagne made a pretty strong dose for the unaccustomed heads of the dozen lads and three or four young
ladies who finished them.   Carter himself, cloyed with
the surfeit of yesterday, took almost nothing, to the wonder, and even, I suspect, to the disappointment of the
temperance party.   But he made himself dreadfully obnoxious by urging his Sillery upon every one, including
the Whitewoods and the maiden of thirty-five.   The latter
declined the proffered glass with an air of virtuous indignation which struck him as uncivil, more particularly as
it evoked a triumphant smile from the adherents of lemonade.   With a cruelty without parallel, and for which I
shall not attempt to excuse him, he immediately offered
the bumper to the young gentleman on whose arm the
lady leaned, with the observation, "Madam, I hope you
will allow your son to take a little."

The unhappy couple walked away in a speechless condition.   The two juniors heretofore mentioned burst into
hysterical gulphs of laughter, and then pretended that it
was a simultaneous attack of ·coughing.   There were no
more attempts to put down the audacious army gentleman, and he was accorded that elbow-room which we all
grant to a bull in a china-shop.   He was himself somewhat
shocked by the sensation which he had produced.

"What an awful row!" he whispered to Colburne.   "I
have plunged this nursery into a state of civil war.   When
you said pic-nic, how could I suppose that it was a Sabbath-school excursion?   By the way, it isn't Sunday, is
it?   Do you always do it this way in New Boston?   But
you are not immaculate.   You do some things here which
would draw down the frown of society in other places.
Look at those couples—a young fellow and a girl—strolling off by themselves among the thickets.   Some of them
have been out of sight for half an hour.   I should think it
would make talk.   I should think Mrs. Whitewood, who
seems to be matron in chief, would stop it.   I tell you, it

wouldn't do in New York or Philadelphia, or any such place, except among the lower classes. You don't catch our young Louisianienne making a dryad of herself. I heard one of these lads ask her to take a walk in the grove on top of the hill, and I saw her decline with a blush which certainly expressed astonishment, and, I think, indignation. Now how the devil can these old girls, who have lived long enough to be able to put two and two together, be so dem'd inconsistent? After regarding me with horror for offering them a glass of champagne, they will commit imprudences which make them appear as if they had drunk a bottle of it. And yet, just look. I have too much delicacy to ask one of those young ones to stroll off with me in the bushes.—Won't you have a segar? I don't believe Miss Ravenel objects to tobacco. They smoke in Louisiana; yes, and they chew and drink, too. Shocking fast set. I really hope the child never will marry down there. I take an interest in her. You and I will go out there some day, and reconquer her patrimony, and put her in possession of it, and then ask her which she will have."

Colburne had already talked a good deal with Miss Ravenel. She was so discouraging to the student beaux, and Carter had been so general in his attentions with a view to getting the champagne into circulation, that she had fallen chiefly to the young lawyer. As to the women, she did not much enjoy their conversation. At that time everybody at the North was passionately loyal, especially those who would not in any chance be called upon to fight —and this loyalty was expressed towards persons of secessionist proclivities with a frank energy which the latter considered brutal incivility. From the male sex Miss Ravenel obtained some compassion or polite forbearance, but from her own very little; and the result was that she avoided ladies, and might perhaps have been driven to suffer the boy beaux, only that she could make sure of the society of Colburne. Important as this young gentleman was to her, she could not forbear teasing him concerning the local peculiarities of New Boston. This afternoon she was satirical upon the juvenile gallants.

"You seem to be the only man in New Boston," she said. "I suppose all the males are executed when they are found guilty of being twenty-one. How came you to escape? Perhaps you are the executioner. Why don't you do your office on the Lieutenant-Colonel?"

"I should like to," answered Colburne.

Miss Ravenel colored, but gave no other sign of comprehension.

"I don't like old beaux," persisted Colburne.

"Oh! I do. When I left New Orleans I parted from a beau of forty."

"Forty! How could you come away?"

"Why, you know that I hated to leave New Orleans."

"Yes; but I never knew the reason before. Did you say forty?"

"Yes, sir; just forty. Is there anything strange in a man of forty being agreeable? I don't see that you New Bostonians find it difficult to like ladies of forty. But I havn't told you the worst. I have another beau, whom I like better than anybody, who is fifty-five."

"Your father."

"You are very clever. As you are so bright to-day perhaps you can explain a mystery to me. Why is it that these grown women are so fond of the society of these students? They don't seem to care to get a word from Lieutenant-Colonel Carter. I don't think they are crazy after you. They are altogether absorbed in making the time pass pleasantly to these boys."

"It is so in all little university towns. Can't you understand it? When a girl is fifteen a student is naturally a more attractive object to her than a mechanic or a shopkeeper's boy. She thinks that to be a student is the chief end of man; that the world was created in order that there might be students. Frequently he is a southerner; and you know how charming southerners are."

" Oh, I know all about it."

" Well, the girl of fifteen takes a fancy to a freshman.
She flirts with him all through the four years of his under-
graduate course. Then he departs, promising to come
back, but never keeping his promise. Perhaps by this
time she is really attached to him ; and that, or habit, or
her original taste for romance and strangers, gives her a
cant for life ; she never flirts with anything but a student
afterwards ; can't relish a man who has'nt a flavor of Greek
and Latin. Generally she sticks to the senior class. When
she gets into the thirties she sometimes enters the theological seminary in search of prey. But she never likes
anything which hasn't a student smack. It reminds one
of the story that when a shark has once tasted human
flesh he will not eat any other unless driven to it by hunger."

" What a brutal comparison !"

" One consequence of this fascination," continued Colburne, " is that New Boston is full of unmarried females.
There is a story in college that a student threw a stone at
a dog, and, missing him, hit seven old maids. On the
other hand there are some good results. These old girls
are bookish and mature, and their conversation is improving to the under-graduates. They sacrifice themselves, as woman's wont is, for the good of others."

" If you ever come to New Orleans I will show you a
fascinating lady of thirty. She is my aunt—or cousin—I
hardly know which to call her—Mrs. Larue. She has
beautiful black hair and eyes. She is a true type of Louisiana."

" And you are not. What right had you to be a blonde ?"

" Because I am my father's daughter. His eyes are blue.
He came from the up-country of South Carolina. There
are plenty of blondes there."

This conversation, the reader perceives, is not monu-
mentally grand or important. Next in flatness to the
ordinary talk of two lovers comes, I think, the ordinary

talk of two young persons of the opposite sexes. In the
first place they are young, and therefore have few great
ideas to interchange and but limited ranges of experience
to compare; in the second place they are hampered and
embarrassed by the mute but potent consciousness of sex
and the alarming possibility of marriage. I am inclined
to give much credit to the saying that only married people
and vicious people are agreeably fluent in an assembly of
both sexes. When therefore I report the conversation of
these two uncorrupted young persons as being of a moderately dull quality, I flatter myself that I am publishing the
very truth of nature. But it follows that we had best
finish with this pic-nic as soon as possible. We will suppose the chickens and sandwiches eaten, the champagne
drunk, the segars smoked, the party gathered into the omnibusses and rockaways, and the vehicle in which we are
chiefly interested at the door of the New Boston House.
As the Lieutenant-Colonel enters with Miss Ravenel a
waiter hands him a telegraphic message.

"Excuse me," he says, and reads as they ascend the
stairs together. On the parlor floor he halts and takes
her hand with an air of more seriousness than he has yet
exhibited.

"Miss Ravenel, I must bid you good-bye. I am so sorry!
I leave for Washington immediately. My application for
extension of leave has been refused. I do sincerely hope
that I shall meet you again."

"Good bye," she simply said, not unaware that her
hand had been pressed, and for that reason unable or unwilling to add more.

He left her there, hurried to his room, packed his valise,
and was off in twenty minutes; for when it was necessary
to move quick he could put on a rate of speed not easily
equalled.

Miss Ravenel walked to her father's room in deep meditation. Without stating the fact in words she felt that
the presence of this mature, masculine, worldly gentleman

of the army was agreeable to her, and that his farewell had been an unpleasant surprise. If he was inebriate, dissipated, dangerous, it must be remembered that she did not know it. In simply smelling of wine and segars he had an odor of Louisiana, to which she had been accustomed from childhood even in the grave society of her father's choice, and which was naturally grateful to the homesick sensibilities of the exiled girl.

For the last hour or two Doctor Ravenel had paced his room in no little excitement. He was a notably industrious man, and had devoted the day to writing an article on the mineralogy of Arkansas; but even this labor, the utterance of a life-long scientific enthusiasm, could not divert him from what I may call maternal anxieties. Why did I let her go on that silly expedition? he repeated to himself. It is the last time; absolutely the last.

At this moment she entered the room and kissed him with more than ordinary effusion. She meant to forestall his expected reproof for her unexpectedly long absence; moreover she felt a very little lonely and in need of unusual affection in consequence of that farewell.

"My dear! how late you are!" said the unappeased Doctor. "How could you stay out so? How could you do it? The idea of staying out till dusk; I am astonished. Really, girls have no prudence. They are no more fit to take care of themselves amid the dangers and stupidities of society than so many goslings among the wheels and hoofs of a crowded street."

Do not suppose that Miss Ravenel bore these reproofs with the serene countenance of Fra Angelico's seraphs, softly beaming out of a halo of eternal love. She was very much mortified, very much hurt and even a little angry. A hard word from her father was an exceeding great trial to her. The tears came into her eyes and the color into her cheeks and neck, while all her slender form trembled, not visibly, but consciously, as if her veins were filled with quicksilver.

"Late! Why, no papa!" (Running to the window and pointing to the crimson west.) "Why, the sun is only just gone down. Look for yourself, papa."

"Well; *that* is too late. If for nothing else, just think of the dew,—the chill. I am not pleased. I tell you, Lillie, I am not pleased."

"Now, papa, you are right hard. I do say you are right cruel. How could I help myself? I couldn't come home alone. I couldn't order the pic-nic to break up and come home when I pleased. How could I? Just think of it, papa."

The Doctor was walking up and down the room with his hands behind his back and his head bent forward. He had hardly looked at his daughter: he never looked at her when he scolded her. He gave her a side-glance now, and seeing her eyes full of tears, he was unable to answer her either good or evil. The earnestness of his affection for her made him very sensitive and sore and cowardly, in case of a misunderstanding. She was looking at him all the time that she talked, her face full of her troubled eagerness to exculpate herself; and now, though he said not a word, she knew him well enough to see that he had relented from his anger. Encouraged by this discovery she regained in a moment or two her self-possession. She guessed the real cause, or at least the strongest cause of his vexation, and proceeded to dissipate it.

"Papa, I think there must be something important going on in the army. Lieutenant-Colonel Carter has received a telegraph, and is going on by the next train."

He halted in his walk and faced her with a childlike smile of pleasure.

"Has he, indeed!" he said as gaily as if he had heard of some piece of personal good fortune. Then, more gravely and with a censorious countenance, "Quite time he went, I should say. It doesn't look well for an officer to be enjoying himself here in Barataria when his men may be fighting in Virginia."

Miss Ravenel thought of suggesting that the Lieu-tenant-Colonel had been on sick leave, but concluded that it would not be well to attempt his defence at the present moment.

"Well Lillie," resumed the Doctor, after taking a cou-pleof leisurely turns up and down the room, "I don't know but I have been unjust in blaming you for coming home so late. I must confess that I don't see how you could help it. The fault was not yours. It resulted from the very nature of all such expeditions. It is one of the in-conveniences of pic-nics that common sense is never in-vited or never has time to go. I wonder that Mrs. Whitewood should permit such irrational procedures."

The Doctor was somewhat apt to exaggerate, whether in praise or blame, when he became interested in a subject.

" Well, well, I am chiefly in fault myself," he concluded. "It must be the last time. My dear, you had better take off your things and get ready for tea."

While Lillie was engaged on her toilette the Doctor co-gitated, and came to the conclusion that he must say some-thing against this Carter, but that he had better say it in-directly. So, as they sauntered down stairs to the tea-table he broke out upon the bibulous gentry of Louisiana.

"To-day's Herald will amuse you," he said. "It con-tains the proceedings of a meeting of the planters of St. Dominic Parish. They are opposed to freedom. They object to the nineteenth century. They mean to smash the United States of America. And for all this they pledge their lives, their fortunes, and their sacred honor. It sur-passes all the jokes in Joe Miller. To think of those whiskey-soaked, negro-whipping, man-slaughtering ruffi-ans, with a bottle of Louisiana rum in one hand and a cat-o'-nine-tails in the other, a revolver in one pocket and a bowie-knife in the other, drunken, swearing, gambling, depraved as Satan, with their black wives and mulatto children—to think of such ruffians prating about their sacred honor! Why, they absolutely don't understand the meaning of the words. They have heard of respectable communities possessing such a quality as honor, and they feel bound to talk as if they possessed it. The pirates of the Isle of Pines might as well pledge their honesty and humanity. Their lives, their fortunes, and their sacred honor! Their lives are not worth the powder that will blow them out of existence. Their fortunes will be worth less in a couple of years. And as for their sacred honor, it is a pure figment of ignorant imaginations made delirious by bad whiskey. That drinking is a ruinous vice. When I see a man soaking himself with sherry at a friend's table, after having previously soaked with whiskey in some groggery, I think I see the devil behind his chair putting the infernal mark on the back of his coat. And it is such a common vice in Louisiana. There is hardly a young man free from it. In the country districts, when a young fellow is paying attention to a young lady, the parents don't ask whether he is in the habit of getting drunk; they take that for granted, and only concern themselves to know whether he gets cross-drunk or amiable-drunk. If the former, they have some hesitation; if the latter, they consent to the match thankfully."

Miss Ravenel understood perfectly that her father was cutting at Lieutenant-Colonel Carter over the shoulders of the convivial gentlemen of Louisiana. She thought him unjust to both parties, but concluded that she would not argue the question; being conscious that the subject was rather too delicately near to her feelings to be discussed without danger of disclosures.

"Well, they are rushing to their doom," resumed the Doctor, turning aside to general reflections, either because such was the tendency of his mind, or because he thought that he had demolished the Lieutenant-Colonel. "They couldn't wait for whiskey to finish them, as it does other barbarous races. They must call on the political mountains to crush them. Their slaveholding Sodom will perish for the lack of five just men, or a single just idea. It must be razed and got out of the way, like any other obstacle to the progress of humanity. It must make room for something more consonant with the railroad, electric-telegraph, printing-press, inductive philosophy, and practical Christianity."

CHAPTER V

THE DRAMATIC PERSONAGES GET NEWS FROM BULL RUN.

"Papa, are we going to stay in New Boston forever?" asked Miss Ravenel.

"My dear, I am afraid we shall both have to die some day, after which we can't expect to stay here, pleasant as it might be," replied the Doctor.

"Nonsense, papa! You know what I mean. Are you going to make New Boston a permanent place of residence?"

"How can I tell, my dear? We can't go back to New Orleans at present; and where else should we go? You know that I must consult economy in my choice of a residence. My bank deposits are not monstrous, and there is no telling how long I may be cut off from my resources. New Boston presents two advantages; it gives me some employment and it is tolerably cheap. Through the friendliness of these excellent professors I am kept constantly busy, and am not paid so very badly, though I can't say that I am in any danger of growing suddenly rich. Then I have the run of the university library, which is a great thing. Finally, where else in the United States should we find a prettier or pleasanter little city?"

"The people are dreadfully poky."

"My daughter, I wish you would have the goodness to converse with me in English. I never became thoroughly familiar with the Gold Coast dialects, and not even with the court language of Ashantee."

" It isn't Ashantee at all. Everybody says poky; and it is real poky in you to pretend not to understand it; don't you think so yourself now? Besides these New Bostonians are so ferociously federal! I can't say a word for the South but the women glare at me as though they wanted to hang me on a sour apple tree, like Jeff Davis."

" My dear, if one of these loyal ladies should say a word for her own lawful government in New Orleans, she would be worse than glared at. I doubt whether the wild-mannered cut-throats of your native city would let her off with plain hanging. Let us thank Heaven that we are among civilized people who only glare at us, and do not stick us under the fifth rib, when we differ with them in opinion."

" Oh papa! how bitter you are on the southerners! It seems to me you must forget that you were born in South Carolina and have lived twenty-five years in Louisiana."

" Oh! oh! the beautiful reason for defending organized barbarism! Suppose I had had the misfortune of being born in the Isle of Pines; would you have me therefore be the apologist of piracy? I do hope that I am perfectly free from the prejudices and trammels of geographical morality. My body was born amidst slavery, but my conscience soon found the underground railroad. I am not boasting; at least I hope not. I have had no plantations, no patrimony of human flesh; very few temptations, in short, to bow down to the divinity of Ashantee. I sincerely thank Heaven for these three things, that I never owned a slave, that I was educated at the north, and that I have been able to visit the free civilization of Europe."

" But why did you live in Louisiana if it was such a Sodom, papa?"

" Ah! there you have me. Perhaps it was because I had an expensive daughter to support, and could pick up four or five thousand dollars a year there easier than anywhere else. But you see I am suffering for having given my countenance to sin. I have escaped out of the burning city, like Lot, with only my family. It is my daily wonder, Lillie, that you are not turned into a pillar of salt. The only reason probably is that the age of miracles is over."

"Papa, when I am as old as you are, and you are as young as I am, I'll satirize you dreadfully.—Well, if we are going to live in New Boston, why can't we keep house?"

"It costs more for two people to keep house than to board. Our furniture, rent, food, fuel, lights and servants would come to more than the eighteen dollars a week which we pay here, now that we have given up our parlor. In a civilized country elbow-room is expensive."

"But is it exactly nice to stay forever in a hotel? English travellers make such an outcry about American families living in hotels."

"I know. At the bottom it is bad. But it is a sad necessity of American society. So long as we have untrained servants—black barbarians at the South and mutinous foreigners at the North—many American housekeepers will throw down their keys in despair and rush for refuge to the hotels. And numbers produce respectability, at least in a democracy."

"So we must give up the idea of a nice little house all to ourselves."

"I am afraid so, unless I should happen to find diamonds in the basaltic formation of the Eagle's Nest."

The Doctor falls to his writing, and Miss Ravenel to her embroidery. Presently the young lady, without having anything in particular to say, is conscious of a desire for further conversation, and, after searching for a subject, begins as follows.

"Papa, have you been in the parlor this morning?"

"Yes, my dear," answers papa, scratching away desperately with his old-fashioned quill pen.

" Whom did you see there ?"

" See ?—Where ?—Oh, I saw Mr. Andrew Smith," says
the Doctor, at first absent-minded, then looking a little
quizzical.

" What did he have to say ?"

" Why, my dear, he spoke so low that I couldn't hear
what he said."

" He did !" responds Miss Ravenel, all interest. " What
did that mean ? Why didn't you ask him to repeat it ?"

" Because, my dear, he wasn't talking to me ; he was
talking to Mrs. Smith."

Here Miss Ravenel perceives that her habitual curiosity
is being made fun of, and replies, " Papa, you ought to be
ashamed of yourself."

" My child, you *must* give me some chance to write,"
retorts the Doctor ; " or else you must learn to sit a little
in your own room. Of course I prefer to have you here,
but I do demand that you accord me some infinitesimal degree of consideration."

Father and daughter used to have many conversations
not very dissimilar to the above. It was a constant prattle when they were together, unless the Doctor raised the
standard of revolt and refused to talk in order that he
might work. Ever since Lillie's earliest recollection they
had been on these same terms of sociability, companion-
ship, almost equality. The intimacy and democracy of the
relation arose partly from the Doctor's extreme fondness
for children and young people, and partly from the fact
that he had lost his wife early, so that in his household
life he had for years depended for sympathy upon his
daughter.

Twice or thrice every morning the Doctor was obliged
to remonstrate against Lillie's talkativeness, something
after the manner of an affectionate old cat who allows her
pussy to jump on her back and bite her ears for a half
hour together, but finally imposes quiet by a velvety and
harmless cuffing. Occasionally he avenged himself for

her untimely demands on his attention by reading to her what he considered a successful passage of the article which he might then be composing.   In this, however, he had not the least intention of punishment, but supposed that he was conferring a pleasure.   It was an essential element of this genial, social, sympathetic nature to believe that whatever interested him would necessarily interest those whom he loved and even those with whom he simply came in contact.   When Lillie offered corrections on his style, which happened frequently, he rarely hesitated to accept them.   Vanity he had none, or at any rate displayed none, except on two subjects, his daughter and his scientific fame.   As a proof of this last he gloried in an extensive correspondence with European *savants*, and made Lillie read every one of those queer shaped letters, written on semi-transparent paper and with foreign stamps and postmarks on their envelopes, which reached him from across the Atlantic.   Although medicine was his profession and had provided him with bread, he had latterly fallen in love with mineralogy, and in his vacation wanderings though that mountainous belt which runs from the Carolinas westward to Arkansas and Missouri he had discovered some new species which were eagerly sought for by the directors of celebrated European collections. Great was his delight at receiving in New Boston a weighty box of specimens which he had shipped as freight from New Orleans just previous to his own departure, but which for two months he had mourned over as lost.   It dowered him with an embarrassment of riches.   During a week his bed, sofa, table, wash-stand, chairs and floor were littered with the scraps of paper and tufts of cotton and of Spanish moss which had served as wrappers, and with hundreds of crystals, ores and other minerals.   Over this confusion the Doctor domineered with a face wrinkled by happy anxiety, laying down one queer-colored pebble to pick up another, pronouncing this a Smithite and that a Brownite trying his blowpipe on them and then his hammer, and covering all the furniture with a layer of learned smudge and dust and gravel.

"Papa, you have puckered your forehead up till it is like a baked apple," Lillie would remonstrate. "You look more than five thousand years old; you look as though you might be the grandfather of all the mummies. Now do leave off bothering those poor Smithites and Hivites and Amelekites, and come and take a walk."

"My dear, you havn't the least idea how necessary it is to push one's discoveries to a certainty as quickly as possible," would answer the Doctor, meanwhile peering at a specimen through his magnifying glass. "The world won't wait for me to take your time. If I don't work fast enough in my researches, it will set somebody else at the job. It makes no allowance for Louisiana ideas of leisure and,"—here he suddenly breaks off his moralizing and exclaims, "My dear, this is *not* a Brownite; it is a Robinsonite—a most unquestionable and superb Robinsonite."

"Oh papa! I wish I was an unquestionable Robinsonite; then you would take some sort of interest in me," says Miss Lillie.

But the Doctor is lost in the ocean of his new discovery, and for fifteen minutes has not a word to say on any subject comprehensible to the young lady.

Two hours of every afternoon were devoted by father and daughter to a long walk in company, sometimes a mere shopping or calling tour, but generally an excursion into the pure country of fields and forest as yet so easily reached from the centre of New Boston. The Doctor preserved a reminiscence of his college botany, and attempted to impart some of his knowledge of plants to Lillie. But she was a hopeless scholar; she persisted in caring for little except human beings and such literature as related directly to them, meaning thereby history, biography, novels and poetry; she remained delightfully innocent of all the ologies.

" You ought to have been born four thousand years
ago, Lillie," he exclaimed in despair over some new instance of her incapacity to move in his favorite grooves.
" So far as you are concerned, Linnæus, Humboldt, Lyell,
Faraday, Agassiz and Dana might as well not have lived.
I believe you will go through life without more knowledge of science than just enough to distinguish between a
plant and a pebble."

" I do hope so, papa," replied the incorrigible and delightful ignoramus.

When they met one of their acquaintance on these
walks the Doctor would not allow him to pass with a nod
and a smile, after the unobtrusive New Boston fashion.
He would stop him, shake hands cordially, inquire earnestly after his health and family, and before parting con-
trive to say something personally civil, if not complimentary; all of which would evidently flatter the New
Bostonian, but would also as evidently discompose him
and turn his head, as being a man unaccustomed to much
social incense.

" Papa, you trouble these people," Lillie would sometimes expostulate. " They don't know where to put all
your civilities and courtesies. They don't seem to have
pockets for them."

" My child, I am nothing more than ordinarily polite."

" Nothing more than ordinary in Louisiana, but something very extraordinary here. I have just thought why
all the gentlemen one meets at the South are so civil. It
is because the uncivil ones are shot as fast as they are discovered."

" There is something in that," admitted the Doctor.
" I suppose duelling has something to do with the superficial good manners current down there. But just consider what an impolite thing shooting is in itself. To knock
and jam and violently push a man into the other world is
one of the most boorish and barbarous discourtesies that I
can imagine. How should I like to be treated that way!

I think I never should be reconciled to the fact or its author."

"But these New Bostonians are so poky—so awfully serious."

"I have some consideration for anti-jokers. They are not amusing, but they are generally useful. It is well for the race, no doubt, to have many persons always in solemn earnest. I don't know what the world would come to if every body could see a joke. Possibly it might laugh itself to death."

Frequently on these walks they were met and joined by Mr. Colburne. That young gentleman, frank as his clear hazel eyes and hearty laugh made him appear, was awkwardly sly in bringing about these ostensibly accidental meetings. Not that his clumsy male cunning deceived Miss Ravenel: she was not by any means fond enough of him to fail to see through him; she knew that he walked in her paths with malice aforethought. Her father did not know it, nor suspect it, nor ever, by any innate consciousness or outward hint, feel his attention drawn toward the circumstance. And, what was most absurd of all, Mr. Colburne persisted in fearing that the Doctor, that travelled and learned man of the world, guessed the secret of his slyness, but never once attributed that degree of sharp-sightedness to the daughter. I sometimes get quite out of patience with the ugly sex, it is so densely stupid with regard to these little social riddles. For example, it happened once at a party that while Colburne, who never danced, was talking to Miss Ravenel, another gentleman claimed her hand for a quadrille. She took her place in the set, but first handed her fan to Colburne. Now every lady who observed this action understood that Miss Ravenel had said to Colburne as plainly as it was possible to express the thing without speaking or using force, that she wished him to return to her side as soon as the quadrille was over, and that in fact she preferred his conversation to that of her dancing admirer. But this masculine blunderer comprehended nothing; he grumbled to himself that he was to be put off with the honor of holding a fan while the other fellow ran away with the owner; and so, shoving the toy into his pocket, he absented himself for half an hour, to the justifiable disapprobation of Miss Ravenel, who did not again give him any thing to hold for many evenings.

But this was an exceptional piece of stupidity in Colburne, and probably he would not have been guilty of it but for a spasm of jealousy. He was not grossly deficient in social tact, any more than in natural cleverness or in acquired information. Conversation, and very sensible conversation too, flowed like a river when he came into confluence with the Ravenels. The prevailing subject, as a matter of course, was the rebellion. It was every body's subject; it was the nightmare by night and the delirium by day of the American people; it was the one thing that no one ignored and no one for an hour forgot. The twenty loyal millions of the North shuddered with rage at the insolent wickedness of those conspirators who, merely that they might perpetuate human bondage and their own political supremacy, proposed to destroy the grandest social fabric that Liberty ever built, the city of refuge for oppressed races, the hope of the nations. For men who through such a glorious temple as this could rush with destroying torches and the cry of "Rule or ruin," the North felt a horror more passionate than ever, on any occasion, for any cause, thrilled the bosom of any other people. This indignation was earnest and wide-spread in proportion to the civilization of the century and the intelligence of the population. The hundreds of telegraph lines and thousands of printing presses in the United States, sent the knowledge of every new treason, and the reverberation of every throb of patriotic anger, in a day to all Americans outside of nurseries and lunatic asylums. The excitement of Germany at the opening of the Thirty Years' War, of England previous to the Cromwellian struggle, was torpid and partial in comparison with this outburst of a modern, reading and swiftly-informed free democracy. As yet there was little bloodshed; the old respect for law and confidence in the processes of reason could not at once die, and men still endeavored to convince each other by argument while holding the pistol to each other's heads; but from the St. Lawrence to the Gulf there was a spiritual preparedness for slaughter which was to end in such murderous contests as should make ensanguined Europe rise from its thousand battlefields to stare in wonder.

Women and children were as wild with the patriotic excitement as men. Some of the prettiest and gentlest-born ladies of New Boston waited in a mixed crowd half the night at the railroad station to see the first regiments pass towards Washington, and flung their handkerchiefs, rings, pencil-cases, and other trinkets to the astonished country lads, to show them how the heart of woman blessed the nation's defenders. In no society could you be ten minutes without hearing the words war, treason, rebellion. And so, the subject being every body's subject, the Ravenels and Colburne frequently talked of it. It was quite a sad and sore circumstance to the two gentlemen that the lady was a rebel. To a man who prides himself on his superior capacity and commanding nature, (that is to say, to almost every man in existence) there can be few greater grievances than a woman whom he cannot convert; and more particularly and painfully is this true when she bears some near relationship to him, as for instance that of a wife, sister, daughter and sweetheart. Thus Ravenel the father and Colburne the admirer, fretted daily over the obstinate treasonableness of Miss Lillie. Patriotism she called it, declaring that Louisiana was her country, and that to it she owed her allegiance.

It is worthy of passing remark how loyal the young are to the prevailing ideas of the community in which they are nurtured. You will find adult republicans in

England, but no infant ones; adults monarchists in our own country, but not in our schools and nurseries. I have known an American of fifty whose beliefs, prejudices and tastes were all European, but who could not save his five children from being all Yankee. Accordingly this young lady of nineteen, born and nurtured among Louisianians, held firm for Louisiana in spite of the arguments of the adored papa and the rather agreeable admirer.

The Doctor liked Colburne, and respected his intellect. He rarely tired of talking with him on any subject, and concerning the war they could go on interminally. The only point on which they disagreed was the probable length of the contest; the southerner prophecying that it would last five or six years, and the northerner that the rebels would succumb in as many months. Miss Ravenel sometimes said that the North would give up in a year, and sometimes that the war would last forty years, both of which opinions she had heard sustained in New Orleans. But, whatever she said, she always believed in the superior pluck and warlike skill of the people of her own section.

"Miss Ravenel," said Colburne, "I believe you think that all southerners are giants, so tall that they can't see a Yankee without lying down, and so pugnacious that they never go to church without praying for a chance to fight somebody."

She resented this satire by observing, "Mr. Colburne, if I believe it you ought not to dispute it."

I am inclined to think that the young man in these days rather damaged his chances of winning the young lady's kind regards (to use a hackneyed and therefore decorous phrase) by his stubborn and passionate loyalty to the old starry banner. It was impossible that the two should argue so much on a subject which so deeply interested both without occasionally coming to spiritual blows. But why should Mr. Colburne win the kind regards of Miss Ravenel? If she were his wife, how could he support her?

He had little, and she had nothing.

While they were talking over the war it went on.   One balmy summer day our little debating club of three sat in one of the small iron balconies of the hotel, discussing the great battle which had been fought, and rumor said won, on the heights around Manassas Junction. For a week the city had been wild about the 'on to Richmond' movement; and to-day the excitement culminated in a general joy which was impatient for official announcements, flags, bells and cannon.   It was true that there was one suspicious circumstance; that for twenty-four hours no telegrams concerning the fight had come over the wires from Washington; but, excepting a few habitual croakers and secret copperheads, who were immediately frowned into silence, no one predicted evil tidings.   At the last accounts "the grand army of the Potomac" was driving before it the traitorous battalions of the South; McDowell had gained a great victory, and there was an end of rebellion.

"I don't believe it—I don't believe it," Miss Ravenel repeatedly asseverated, until her father scolded her for her absurd and disloyal incredulity.

"The telegraph is in order again," observed Colburne "I heard one of those men who just passed say so."   Here comes somebody that we know.   Whitewood!—I say, Whitewood!   Any thing on the bulletin-board?"

The pale young student looked up with a face of despair and eyes full of tears.

"It's all up, Colburne," said he.   "Our men are running, throwing away their guns and every thing."

His trembling voice hardly sufficed for even this short story of shame and disaster.   Miss Ravenel, the desperate rebel, jumped to her feet with a nervous shriek of joy and then, catching her father's reproving eye, rushed up stairs and danced it out in her own room.

"It's impossible!" remonstrated Colburne in such excitement that his voice was almost a scream.   "Why, by the last accounts—"

"Oh! that's all gone up," groaned Whitewood, who was in such a state of grief that he could hardly talk intelligibly. "We've got more. We've got the end of the battle. Johnson came up on our right, and we are whipped all to pieces."

"Johnson! Why, where was Patterson?"

"Patterson is an old traitor," shouted Whitewood, pushing wildly on his way as if too sick at heart to talk more.

"It is very sad," observed the Doctor gravely. The thought occurred to him that for his own interests he had better have stayed in New Orleans; but he lost sight of it immediately in his sorrow for the seeming calamity which had befallen country and liberty and the human race.

"Oh! it's horrible—horrible. I don't believe it. I can't believe it," groaned Colburne. "It's too much to bear. I must go home. It makes me too sick to talk."

CHAPTER VI.

MR. COLBURNE SEES HIS WAY CLEAR TO BE A SOLDIER.

Stragglers arrived, and then the regiments. People were not angry with the beaten soldiers, but treated them with tenderness, gave them plentiful cold collations, and lavished indignation on their ragged shoddy uniforms. Then the little State, at first pulseless with despair, took a long breath of relief when it found that Beauregard had not occupied Washington, and set bravely about preparing for far bloodier battles than that of Bull Run.

Lieutenant-Colonel Carter did not return with his regiment; and Colburne read with a mixture of emotions that he had been wounded and taken prisoner while gallantly leading a charge. He marked the passage, and left the paper with his compliments for the Ravenels, after debating at the door of the hotel whether he should call on them, and deciding in the negative. Not being able as yet to appreciate that blessing in disguise, Bull Run, his loyal heart was very sad and sore over it, and he felt a thrill of something like horror whenever he thought of the joyful shriek with which Lillie had welcomed the shocking tidings. He was angry with her, or at least he tried to be. He called up his patriotism, that strongest of New England isms, and resolved that with a secessionist, a woman who wished ill to her country, he would not fall in love. But to be sure of this he must keep away from her; for thus much of love, or of perilous inclination at least, he already had to acknowledge; and moreover, while he was somewhat ashamed of the feeling, he still could not heartily desire to eradicate it. Troubled thus concerning the affairs of the country and of his own heart, he kept aloof from the Ravenels for three or four days. Then he said to himself that he had no cause for avoiding the Doctor, and that to do so was disgraceful treatment of a man who had proved his loyalty by taking up the cross of exile.

This story will probably have no readers so destitute of sympathy with the young and loving, as that they can not guess the result of Colburne's internal struggles. After two or three chance conversations with Ravenel he jumped, or to speak more accurately, he gently slid to the conclusion that it was absurd and unmanly to make a distinction in favor of the father and against the daughter. Quarrel with a woman; how ridiculous! how unchivalrous! He colored to the tips of his repentant ears as he thought of it and of what Miss Ravenel must think of it. He hastened to call on her before the breach which he had made between her and himself should become untraversable; for although the embargo on their intercourse had lasted only about a week, it already seemed to him a lapse of time measureable by months; and this very naturally, inasmuch as during that short interval he had lived a life of anguish as a man and a patriot. Accordingly the old intimacy was resumed, and the two young people seldom passed forty-eight hours apart. But of the rebellion they said little, and of Bull Run nothing. These were such sore subjects to him that he did not wish to speak of them except to the ear of sympathy; and she, divining his sensitiveness, would not give him pain notwithstanding that he was an abolitionist and a Yankee. If the Doctor, ignorant of what passed in these young hearts, turned the conversation on the war, Lillie became silent, and Colburne, appreciating her forbearance, tried to say very little. Thus without a compact, without an explanation, they accorded in a strain of mutual charity which predicted the ultimate conversion of one or the other.

Moreover, Colburne asked himself, what right had he to talk if he did not fight? If he wanted to answer this woman's outcry of delight over the rout of Bull Run, the place to do it was not a safe parlor, but a field of victorious battle. Why did he not act in accordance with these truly chivalrous sentiments? Why not fall into one of the new regiments which his gallant little State was organizing to continue the struggle? Why not march on with the soul of old John Brown, joining in the sublime though quaint chorus of, "We're coming, Father Abraham, three hundred thousand more?"

He did talk very earnestly of it with various persons, and, among others, with Doctor Ravenel. The latter approved the young man's warlike inclinations promptly and earnestly.

"It is the noblest duty that you may ever have a chance to perform during your life," said he. "To do something personally towards upholding this Union and striking down slavery is an honor beyond any thing that ever was accorded to Greek or Roman. I wish that I were young enough for the work, or fitted for it by nature or education. I would be willing to have my tombstone set up next year, if it could only bear the inscription, "He died in giving freedom to slaves."

"Oh! do stop," implored Lillie, who entered in time to

D

hear the concluding sentence. "What do you talk about your tombstone for? You will get perfectly addled about abolition, like all the rest. Now, papa, you ought to be more consistent. You didn't use to be so violent against slavery. You have changed since five years ago."

"I know it," says the Doctor. "But that doesn't prove that I am wrong now. I wasn't infallible five years ago. Why, my dear, the progress of our race from barbarism to civilization is through the medium of constant change. If the race is benefited by it, why not the individual? I am a sworn foe to consistency and conservation. To stick obstinately to our old opinions, because they are old, is as foolish as it would be in a soldier-crab to hold on to his shell after he had outgrown it instead of picking up a new one fitted to his increased size. Suppose the snakes persisted in going about in their last year's skins? No, no; there are no such fools in the lower animal kingdom; that stupidity is confined to man."

"The world does move," observed Colburne. "We consider ourselves pretty strict and old-fashioned here in New Boston. But if our Puritan ancestors could get hold of us, they would be likely to have us whipped as heretics and Sabbath-breakers. Very likely we would be equally severe upon our own great-great-grandchildren, if we should get a chance at them."

"Weak spirits are frightened by this change, this growth, this forward impetus," said the Doctor. "I must tell you a story. I was travelling in Georgia three years ago. On the seat next in front of me sat a cracker, who was evidently making his first railroad experience, and in other respects learning to go on his hind legs. Presently the train crossed a bridge. It was narrow, uncovered and without sides, so that a passenger would not be likely to see it unless he sat near the window. Now the cracker sat next the alley of the car, and away from the window. I observed him give a glare at the river and turn away his head suddenly, after which he rolled about in a queer way, and finally went on the floor in a heap. We picked him up; spirits were easily produced, (they always are down there) ; and presently the cracker was brought to his senses. His first words were, 'Has she lit'— He was under the impression that the train had taken the river at a running jump. Now that is very much like the judgment of timid and ill-informed people on the progress of the nation or race at such a time as this. They don't know about the bridge; they think we are flying through the air; and so they go off in general fainting-fits."

Colburne laughed, as many another man has done before him, at this good old story.

" On our train, " said he, " on the train of human progress, we are parts of the engine and not mere passengers. I ought to be revolving somewhere. I ought to be at work. I want to do something—I am most anxious to do something—but I don't know precisely what. I suppose that the inability exists in me, and not in my circumstances. I am like the gentleman who tired himself out with jumping, but never could jump high enough to see over his own standing-collar."

" I know how you feel. I have been in that state myself, often and in various ways. For instance it has occurred to me, especially in my younger days, to feel a strong desire to write, without having anything to say. There was a burning in my brain; there was a sentiment or sensation which led me to seek pens, ink and paper; there was an impatient, uncertain, aimless effort to commence; there was a pause, a revery, and all was over. It was a storm of sheet-lightning. There were glorious gleams, and far off openings of the heavens; but no sound, droppings, no sensible revelation from the upper world.— However, your longings are for action, and I am convinced that you will find your opportunity. There will be work enough in this matter for all."

" I don't know," said Colburne. " The sixth and sev-

enth regiments are full.   I hear that there isn't a lieuten-
antcy left."

" You will have to raise your own company."

" Ah ! But for what regiment ? We shan't raise another,
I am afraid.   Yes, I am actually afraid that the war will
be over in six months."

Miss Ravenel looked up hastily as if she should like to
say " Forty years," but checked herself by a surprising
effort of magnanimity and good nature.

" That's queer patriotism," laughed the Doctor.   But let
me assure you, Mr. Colburne, that your fears are groundless.   There will be more regiments needed."

Miss Ravenel gave a slight approving nod, but still said
nothing, remembering Bull Run and how provokingly she
had shouted over it.

" This southern oligarchy," continued the Doctor, " will
be a tough nut to crack.   It has the consolidated vigor of
a tyranny."

" I wonder where Lieutenant-Colonel Carter is ?" queried
Colburne.   " It is six weeks since he was taken prisoner.
It seems like six years."

Miss Ravenel raised her head with an air of interest,
glanced hastily at her father, and gave herself anew to
her embroidery.   The Doctor made a grimace which was
as much as to say that he thought small beer or sour beer
of Lieutenant-Colonel Carter.

" He is a very fine officer," said Colburne.   " He was
highly spoken of for his conduct at Bull Run."

" I would rather have you for a Colonel," replied the
Doctor.

Colburne laughed contemptuously at the idea of his
fitness for a colonelcy.

" I would rather have any respectable man of tolerable
intellect," insisted the Doctor.   " I tell you that I know
that type perfectly.   I know what he is as well as if I had
been acquainted with him for twenty years.   He is what
we southerners, in our barbarous local vanity, are accus-

tomed to call a southern gentleman. He is on the model
of the sugar-planters of St. Dominic Parish. He needs
somebody to care for him. Let me tell you a story. When
I was on a mineralogical expedition in North Carolina
some years ago, I happened to be out late at night looking
for lodgings. I was approaching one of those cross-road
groggeries which they call a tavern down there, when I
met a most curious couple. It was a man and a goose.
The man was drunk, and the goose was sober. The man
was staggering, and the goose was waddling perfectly
straight. Every few steps it halted, looked back and
quacked, as if to say, Come along. The moon was shining,
and I could see the whole thing plainly. I was obliged to
put up for the night in the groggery, and there I got an
explanation of the comedy. It seems that this goose was
a pet, and had taken an unaccountable affection to its
owner, who was a wretched drunkard of a cracker. The
man came nearly every night to the groggery, got drunk
as regularly as he came, and generally went to sleep on
one of the benches. About midnight the goose would appear and cackle for him. The bar-keeper would shake up
the drunkard and say, 'Here! your goose has come for
you.' As soon as the brute could get his legs he would
start homeward, guided by his more intelligent companion. If the man fell down and couldn't get up, the goose
would remain by him and squawk vociferously for assistance.—Now, sir, there was hardly a sugar-planter, hardly
a southern gentleman, in St. Dominic Parish, who didn't
need some such guardian. Often and often, as I have
seen them swilling wine and brandy at each other's tables,
I have charitably wished that I could say to this one and
that one, Sir, your goose has come for you."

"But you never have seen the Lieutenant-Colonel so
badly off," answered Colburne, after a short meditation.

"Why no—not precisely," admitted the Doctor. "But
I know his type," he presently added with an obstinacy
which Miss Ravenel secretly thought very unjust. She

thought it best to direct her spirit of censure in another direction.

"Papa," said she, " what a countryfied habit you have of telling stories !"

" Don't criticise, my dear," answers papa. "I am a high toned southern gentleman, ·and always knock people on the head who criticise me."

The question still returns upon us, why Mr. Colburne did not join the army. It is time, therefore, to state the hitherto unimportant fact that he was the only son of a widow, and that his life was a necessity to her, not only as a consolation to her loneliness, but as a support to her declining fortunes. Doctor Colburne had left his wife and child an estate of about twenty-five thousand dollars, which at the time of his death was a respectable fortune in New Boston. But the influx of gold from California, and the consequent rise of prices, seriously diminished the value of the family income just about the time that Edward, by growing into manhood and entering college, necessitated an increase of expenses. Therefore Mrs. Colburne was led to put one half of the joint fortune into certain newly-organized manufacturing companies, which promised to increase her annual six per cent to twenty-four —nor was she therein exceedingly to blame, being led away by the example and advice of some of the sharpest New Boston capitalists, many of whom had their experienced pinions badly lamed in these joint-stock adventurings.

" What you want, Mr. Colburne," said a director, " is an investment which is both safe and permanent. Now this is just the thing."

I can not say much for the safety of the investment, but it certainly was a permanent one. During the first year the promised twenty-four per cent was paid, and the widow could have sold out for one hundred and twenty. Then came a free-trade, Democratic improvement on the tariff; the manufacturing interest of the country was paralyzed. and the Braggville stock fell to ninety. Mrs. Colburne might still have sold out at a profit, counting in her first year's dividend; but as it was not in her inexperience to see that this was wisdom, she held on for a—decline. By the opening of the war her certificates of manufacturing stock were waste paper, and her annual income was reduced to eight hundred dollars. Indeed, for a year or two previous to the commencement of this story, she had been forced to make inroads upon her capital.

Of this crisis in the family affairs Edward was fully aware, and like a true-born, industrious Yankee, did his best to meet it. From every lowermost branch and twig of his profession he plucked some fruit by dint of constant watchfulness, so that during the past year he had been very nearly able to cover his own conscientiously economical expenditures. He was gaining a foothold in the law, although he as yet had no cases to plead. If he held on a year or two longer at this rate he might confidently expect to restore the family income and stave off the threatened sale of the homestead.

But this was not all which prevented him from going forth to battle. The cry of his mother's heart was, " My son, how can I let thee go ?" She was an abolitionist, as was almost every body of her set in New Boston; she was an enthusiastic patriot, as was almost every one in the north during that sublime summer of popular enthusiasm; but this war—oh, this strange, ferocious war ! was horrible. Her sensitively affectionate nature, blinded by veils of womanly tenderness, folded in habits of life-long peace, could not see the hard, inevitable necessity of the contest. Earnestly as she sympathised with its loyal and humane objects, she was not logical enough or not firm enough to sympathise with the iron thing itself. Lapped in sweet influences of peace all her loving life, why must she be called to death amid the clamor of murderous contests ? For her health was failing ; a painful and fatal disease had fastened its clutches on her ; another year's course she did not hope to run. And if the hateful strug-

gle must go on, if it must torment her last few days with
its agitations and horrors, so much the more did she need
her only child.   Other women's sons—yes, if there was no
help for it—but not hers—might put on the panoply of
strife, and disappear from anxiously following eyes into
the smoke and flame of battle.   Edward told her every day
the warlike news of the journals, the grand and stern putting on of the harness, the gigantic plans for crushing the
nation's foes.   She could take no interest in such tidings
but that of aversion.   He read to her in a voice which
thrilled like swellings of martial music, Tennyson's Charge
of the Six Hundred.   She listened to the clarion-toned
words with distaste and almost with horror.

Well, the summer wore away, that summer of sombre
preparation and preluding skirmishes, whose scattering
musketry and thin cannonade faintly prophecied the or-
chestral thunders of Gettysburgh and the Wilderness,
and whose few dead preceded like skirmishers the massive
columns which for years should firmly follow them into
the dark valley.   Its forereaching shadows fell upon many
homes far away from the battlefield, and chilled to death
many sensitive natures.   Old persons and invalids sank
into the grave that season under the oppression of its
straining suspense and preliminary horror; and among
these victims, whom no man has counted and whom few
have thought of collectively, was the mother of Colburne.

One September afternoon she sent for Edward.   The
Doctor had gone; his labors were over.   The clergyman
had gone; neither was he longer needed.   There was no
one in the room but the nurse, the dying mother and the
only child.   The change had been expected for days, and
Edward had thought that he was prepared for it; had indeed marvelled and been shocked at himself because he
could look forward to it with such seeming composure;
for, reason with his heart and his conscience as he might,
he could not feel a fitting dread and anguish.   In the
common phrase of humanity, when numbed by unusual

sorrow, he could not realize it. But now, as, leaning over the footboard and looking steadfastly upon his mother's face, he saw that the final hour had come, a sickness of heart fell upon him, and a trembling as if his soul were being torn asunder. Yet neither wept; the Puritans and the children of the Puritans do not weep easily; they are taught, not to utter, but to hide their emotions. The nurse perceived no signs of unusual feeling, except that the face of the strong man became suddenly as pale as that of the dying woman, and that to him this was an hour of anguish, while to her it was one of unspeakable joy. The mother knew her son too well not to see, even with those failing eyes, into the depths of his sorrow.

"Don't be grieved for me, Edward," she said. "I am sustained by the faith of the promises. I am about to return from the place whence I came. I am re-entering with peace and with confidence into a blessed eternity."

He came to the side of the bed, sat down on it and took her hand without speaking.

"You will follow me some day," she went on. "You will follow me to the place where I shall be, at the right hand of the Lord. I have prayed for it often;—I was praying for it a moment ago; and, my child, my prayer will be granted. Oh, I have been so fearful for you; But I am fearful no longer."

He made no answer except to press her hand while she paused to draw a few short and wearisome breaths.

"I can bear to part with you now," she resumed. "I could not bear it till the Lord granted me this full assurance that we shall meet again. I leave you in his hands. I make no conditions with him. I have been sweetly brought to give you altogether up to one who loves you better than I know how to love you. He gave me my love, and he has kept more than he gave. Perhaps I have been selfish, Edward, to hold on to you as I have. You have felt it your duty to go into the army, and perhaps I have been selfish to prevent you. Now you are free; to-morrow I shall not be here. If you still see that to be your duty, go; and the Lord go with you, darling, and give you strength and courage. I do not ask him to spare you, but only to guide you here below, and restore you to me above.———And he will do it, Edward, for his own sake. I am full of confidence; the promises are sure. For you and for myself, I rejoice with a joy unspeakable and full of glory."

While thus speaking, or rather whispering, she had put one arm around his neck. As he kissed her wasted cheek and let fall his first tears on it, she drew her hand across his face with a caressing tenderness, and smiling, fell back softly on her pillow, closing her eyes as calmly as if to sleep. A few broken words, a murmuring of unutterable, unearthly, infinite happiness, echoes as it were of greetings far away with welcoming angels, were her last utterances. To the young man, who still held her hand and now and then kissed her cheek, she seemed to slumber, although her breathing gradually sank so low that he could not perceive it. But after a long time the nurse came to the bedside, bent over it, looked, listened, and said, "She is gone!"

He was free; she was not there.

He went to his room with a horrible feeling that for him there was no more love; that there was nothing to do and nothing to expect; that his life was a blank. He could fix his mind on nothing past or future; not even upon the unparalleled sorrow of the present. Taking up the Bible which she had given him, he read a page before he noticed that he had not understood and did not remember a single passage. In that vacancy, that almost idiocy, which beclouds afflicted souls, he could not recall a distinct impression of the scene through which he had just passed, and seemed to have forgotten forever his mother's dying words, her confidence that they should meet again, her heavenly joy. With the same perverseness, and in spite of repeated efforts to close his ears to the sound,

some inner, wayward self repeated to him over and over
again these verses of the unhappy Poe—

> " Thank Heaven! the crisis,
> The danger is past,
> And the lingering illness
> Is over at last,
> And the fever called Living
> Is conquered at last."

The sad words sounded wofully true to him. For the
time, for some days, it seemed to him as if life were but a
wearisome illness, for which the grave was but a cure. His
mind, fevered by night watching, anxiety, and an unaccustomed grappling with sorrow, was not in a healthy
state. He thought that he was willing to die; he only desired to fall usefully, honorably, and in consonance with
the spirit of his generation; he would set his face henceforward towards the awful beacons of the battle-field. His
resolution was taken with the seriousness of one, who,
though cheerful and even jovial by nature, had been per-
meated to some extent by the solemn passion of Puritanism. He painted to himself in strong colors the risk of
death and the nature of it; then deliberately chose the
part of facing this tremendous mystery in support of the
right. All this while, be it remembered, his mind was
somewhat exalted by the fever of bodily weariness and of
spiritual sorrow.

CHAPTER VII.

CAPTAIN COLBURNE RAISES A COMPANY, AND COLONEL CARTER A REGIMENT.

THE settlement of his mother's estate and of his own pecuniary affairs occupied Colburne's time until the early part of October. By then he had invested his property as well as might be, rented the much-loved old homestead, taken a room in the New Boston House, and was fully prepared to bid good-bye to native soil, and, if need be, to life. Miss Ravenel was a strong though silent temptation to remain and to exist, but he resisted her with the heroism which he subsequently exhibited in combating male rebels.

One morning, as he left the hotel rather later than usual to go to his office, his eyes fell upon a high-colored face and gigantic brown mustache, which he could not have failed to recognize, no matter where nor when encountered. There was the wounded captive of Bull Run, as big chested and rich complexioned, as audacious in eye and haughty in air, as if no hurt nor hardship nor calamity had ever befallen him. He checked Colburne's eager advance with a cold stare, and passed him without speaking. But the young fellow hardly had time to color at this rebuff, when, just as he was opening the outer door, a baritone voice arrested him with a ringing, " Look here !"

" Beg pardon," continued the Lieutenant-Colonel, coming up hastily. " Didn't recognize you. It's quite a time since our pic-nic, you know."

Here he showed a broad grin, and presently burst out laughing, as much amused at the past as if it did not contain Bull Run.

" What a jolly old pic-nic that was !" he went on. " I

have shouted a hundred times to think of myself passing the wine and segars to those prim old virgins. Just as though I had bowsed into the House Beautiful, among Bunyan's damsels, and offered to treat the crowd!"

Again the Lieutenant-Colonel laughed noisily, his insolent black eyes twinkling with merriment. Colburne looked at him and listened to him with amazement. Here was a man who had lately been in what was to him the terrible mystery of battle; who had fallen down wounded and been carried away captive while fighting heroically for the noblest of causes; who had witnessed the greatest and most humiliating overthrow which ever befel the armies of the republic; who yet did not allude to any of these things, nor apparently think of them, but could chat and laugh about a pic-nic. Was is treasonable indifference, or levity, or the sublimity of modesty? Colburne thought that if *he* had been at Bull Run, he never could have talked of any thing else.

"Well, how are you?" demanded Carter. "You are looking a little pale and thin, it seems to me."

"Oh, I am well enough," answered Colburne, passing over that subject with modest contempt, as not worthy of mention. "But how are *you?* Have you recovered from your wound?"

"Wound? Oh! yes; mere bagatelle; healed up some time ago. I shouldn't have been caught if I hadn't been stunned by my horse falling. The wound was nothing."

"But you must have suffered in your confinement," said Colburne, determined to appreciate and pity.

"Suffered! My dear fellow, I suffered with eating and drinking and making merry. I had the deuce's own time in Richmond. I met loads of my old comrades, and they nearly killed me with kindness. They are a nice set of old boys, if they are on the wrong side of the fence. You didn't suppose they would maltreat a brother West Pointer, did you?"

And the Lieutenant-Colonel laughed heartily at the civilian blunder.

"I didn't know, really," answered the puzzled Colburne. "I must say I thought so. But I am as poor a judge of soldiers as a sheep is of catamounts."

"Why, look here. When I left they gave me a supper, and not only made me drunk, but got drunk themselves in my honor. Opened their purses, too, and forced their money on me."

All this, it will be noted, was long previous to the time when Libby Prison and Andersonville were deliberately converted into pest-houses and starvation pens.

"I am afraid they wanted to bring you over," observed Colburne. He looked not only suspicious, but even a little anxious, for in those days every patriot feared for the faith of his neighbor.

"I suppose they did," replied Carter carelessly, as if he saw nothing extraordinary in the idea. "Of course they did. They need all the help that they can get. In fact the rebel Secretary of War paid me the compliment of making me an offer of a regiment, with an assurance that promotion might be relied on. It was done so delicately that I couldn't be offended In fact it was quite natural, and he probably thought it would be bad taste to omit it. I am a Virginian, you know ; and then I was once engaged in some southern schemes and diplomacies—before this war broke out, you understand—oh, no connection with this war. However, I declined his offer. There's a patriot for you."

"I honor you, sir," said Colburne with a fervor which made the Lieutenant-Colonel grin. "You ought at be rewarded."

"Quite so," answered the other in his careless, half-joking style. "Well, I am rewarded. I received a letter yesterday afternoon from your Governor offering me a regiment. I had just finished an elegant dinner with some good fellows, and was going in for a roaring evening. But business before pleasure. I took a cold plunge bath and the next train for New Boston, getting here at midnight. I am off at ten to see his Excellency."

"I am sincerely delighted," exclaimed the young man. "I am delighted to hear that the Governor has had such good sense."

After a moment's hesitation he added anxiously, ".Do you remember your invitation to me ?"

"Certainly. What do you say to it now ? Will you go with me ?"

"I will," said Colburne emphatically. "I will try. I only fear that I can neither raise nor command a company."

"Never fear," answered Carter in a tone which pooh-poohed at doubt. "You are just the man. Come round to the bar with me, and let's drink success to our regiment. Oh, I recollect ; you don't imbibe. Smoke a segar, then, while we talk it over. I tell you that you are just the man. *Noblesse oblige.* Any gentleman can make a good enough company officer in three months' practice. As to raising your men, I'll give you my best countenance, whatever that may amount to. And if you actually don't succeed in getting your quota, after all, why, we'll take somebody else's men. Examinations of officers and consolidations of companies bring all these things right, you know."

"I should be sorry to profit by any other man's influence and energy to his harm," answered the fastidious Colburne.

"Pshaw ! it's all for the good of the service and of the country. Because a low fellow who keeps a saloon can treat and wheedle sixty or eighty stout fellows into the ranks, do you suppose that he ought to be commissioned an officer and a gentleman ? I don't. It can't be in my regiment. Leave those things to me, and go to work without fear. Write to the Adjutant-General of the State to-day for a recruiting commission, and as soon as you get it, open an office.   I guarantee that you shall be one of the Captains of the Tenth Barataria."

" Who are the other field officers ?" asked Colburne.

"Not appointed yet.   I am alone in my glory.   I am the regiment.   But the Lieutenant-Colonel and Major shall be of the right stamp.   I mean to have a word to say as to the choice.   I tell you that we'll have the bulliest regiment that ever sprang from the soil of New England."

" Well, I'll try.   But I really fear that I shall just get my company recruited in time for the next war."

" Never fear," laughed Carter, as though war were a huge practical joke.   " We are in for a four or five years' job of fighting."

" You don't mean it !" said the young man in amazement.   " Why, we citizens are all so full of confidence. McClellan, every body says, is organizing a splendid army.   Did Bull Run give you such an opinion of the superior fighting qualities of the southerners ?"

"Not at all.   Both sides fought timidly, as a rule, just as greenhorns naturally would do.   The best description of the battle that I have heard was given in a single sentence by my old captain, Lamar, now in command of a Georgia regiment.   Said he, ' There never was a more frightened set than our fellows—except your fellows.—Why, we out-fought them in the morning ; we had them fairly whipped until Johnston came up on our right.   The retreat was a mathematical necessity ; it was like saying, Two and two make four.   When our line was turned, of course it had to retreat."

" Retreat !" groaned Colburne in bitterness over the recollection of that calamitous afternoon.   " But you didn't see it.   They ran shamefully, and never stopped short of Washington.   One man reached New Boston inside of twenty-four hours.   It was a panic unparalleled in history."

" Nonsense! Beg your pardon.   Did you never read of Austerlitz and Jena and Waterloo?   Our men did pretty

well for militia. I didn't see the panic, to be sure;—I
was picked up before that happened. But I have talked
with some of our officers who did see it, and they told me
that the papers exaggerated it absurdly. Newspaper
correspondents ought not to be allowed in the army.
They exaggerate every thing. If we had gained a victory,
they would have made it out something greater than
Waterloo. You must consider how easily inexperience is
deceived. Just get the story of an upset from an old stage-
driver, and then from a lady passenger; the first will tell
it as quite an ordinary affair, and the second will make it
out a tragedy. Now when some old grannies of congress-
men and some young ladies of newspaper reporters, none
of whom had ever seen either a victory or a defeat before,
got entangled among half a dozen disordered regiments
they naturally concluded that nothing like it had happened in history. I tell you that it wasn't unparalleled, and
that it ought not to have been considered surprising.
Whichever of those two green armies got repulsed was
pretty sure to be routed. That was a very pretty
manœuvre, though, that coming up of Johnston on
our right. Patterson ought to be court-martialed for his
stupidity."

"Stupidity! He is a traitor," exclaimed Colburne.

"Oh! oh!" expostulated the Colonel with a cough.
"If we are to try all our dull old gentlemen as traitors,
we shall have our hands full. That's something like
hanging homely old women for witches.—By the way,
how are the Allstons? I mean the—the Ravenels. Well,
are they? Young lady as blooming and blushing as ever?
Glad to hear it. Can't stop to call on them; my train
goes in ten minutes.—I am delighted that you are going
to fall in with me. Good bye for to-day."

Away he went, leaving Colburne in wonder over his
contrasts of slanginess and gentility, his mingled audacity
and *insouciance* of character, and all the picturesque ins
and outs of his moral architecture, so different from the

severe plainness of the spiritual temples common in New
Boston. The young man would have preferred that his
future Colonel should not drink and swear; but he would
not puritanically decide that a man who drank and swore
could not be a good officer. He did not know army men
well enough to dare judge them with positiveness; and
he certainly would not try them by the moral standards
according to which he tried civilians. The facts that
Carter was a professional soldier, and that he had shed
his blood in the cause of the country, were sufficient to
make Colburne regard with charity all his frank vices.

I must not allow the reader to suppose that I present
Carter as a type of all regular officers. There were men
in the old army who never tasted liquors, who never
blasphemed, who did not waste their substance in riotous
living, who could be accused of no evil practices, who
were models of Christian gentlemen. The American service, as well as the English, had its Havelocks, its Headly
Vicars, its Colonel Newcomes. Nevertheless I do venture to say that it had also a great many men whose moral
habits were cut more or less on the Carter pattern, who
swore after the fashion of the British army in Flanders,
whose heads could carry drink like Dugald Dalgetty's,
and who had even other vices concerning which my discreet pen is silent.

Within a week after the conversation above reported
Colburne opened a recruiting office, advertised the "Putnam Rangers" largely, and adorned his doorway with a
transparency representing Old Put in a bran-new uniform
riding sword in hand down the stone steps of Horse-
neck. His company, as yet in embryo, was one of the ten
accepted out of the nineteen offered for Carter's regiment.
It was supposed that the name of a West Point colonel
would render the organization a favorite one with the enlisting classes; and accordingly all the chiefs of incomplete
companies throughout the State of Barataria wanted to
sieze the chance for easy recruiting. But Colburne

soon found that the dullness of a young lawyer's office was none too prosy an exordium for the dullness of a recruiting office at this particular period. Passed was that springtide of popular enthusiasm when companies were raised in a day, when undersized heroes wept at being rejected by the mustering officer, when well-to-do youths paid a hundred dollars to buy out a chance to be shot at. Bull Run had disenchanted some romantic natures concerning the pleasures of war, and the vast enlistments of the summer had drawn heavily on the nation's fighting material. Moreover, Colburne had to encounter obstacles of a personal nature, such as did not trouble some of his competitors. A student, a member of a small and shy social circle, neither business man nor one of the bone and sinew, not having belonged to a fire company or militia company, nor even kept a bar or billiard-saloon, he had no retainers nor partisans nor shopmates to call upon, no rummy customers whom he could engage in the war-dance on condition of unlimited whiskey. He had absolutely no personal means of influencing the classes of the community which furnish that important element of all military organizations, private soldiers. For a time he remained almost as solitary in his office as Old Put in the perilous glory of his breakneck descent. In short the raising of his company proved a slow, vexatious and expensive business, notwithstanding the countenance and aid of the Colonel.

Miss Ravenel was much spited in secret when she saw his advertisement; but she was too proud to expose her interest in the matter by opposition. What object had she in keeping him at home and out of danger? Moreover, after the fashion of most southern women, she believed in fighting, and respected a man the more for drawing the sword, no matter for which party. After a while, when his activity and cheerfulness of spirit had returned to him, she began to talk with her old freedom of expression, and indulged in playful prophecies about the Bull

Runs he would fight, the masterly retreats he would accomplish, and the captivities he would undergo.

"When you are a prisoner in Richmond," she said, "I'll write to my Louisiana friends in the southern army and tell them what a spiteful abolitionist you are. I'll get them to put a colored friend and brother into the same cell with you. You won't like it. You'll promise to go back to your law office, if they'll send that fellow to his plantation."

The Doctor was all sympathy and interest, and brimmed over with prophecies of Colburne's success. He judged the people of Barataria by the people of Louisiana; the latter preferred gentlemen for officers, and so of course would the former. Notwithstanding his hatred of slavery he was still somewhat under the influence of its aristocratical glamour. He had not yet fully comprehended that the war was a struggle of the plain people against an oligarchy, and that the plain people had, not very understandingly but still very resolutely, determined to lead the fighting as well as to do it. He had not yet full faith that the northern working-man would beat the southern gentleman, without much guidance from the northern scholar.

"Don't be discouraged," he said to Colburne. "I feel the utmost confidence in your prospects. As soon as it is generally understood who you are and what your character is, you will have recruits to give away. It is impossible that these bar-tenders and tinkers should raise good men as easily as a gentleman and a graduate of the university. They may get a run of ruff-scuff, but it won't last. I predict that your company will be completed sooner and composed of better material than any other in the regiment. I would no more give your chance for that of one of these tinkers than I would exchange a meteorite for its weight in old nails."

The Doctor abounded in promising but unfruitful schemes for helping forward the Putnam Rangers. He proposed that Colburne should send a circular to all the clergymen and Sabbath-school superintendents of the county, calling upon each parish to furnish the subscriber with only one good recruit.

"If they do that," said he, "as they unquestionably will when the case is properly presented to them, why the company is filled at once."

He advised the young man to make an oratorical tour, delivering patriotic speeches in the village lyceums, and circulating an enlistment paper at the close of each performance. He told him that it would not be a bad move to apply to his professional brethren far and near for aid in rousing the popular enthusiasm. He himself wrote favorable notices of the captain and his company, and got them printed in the city journals. One day he came home in a hurry, and with great glee produced the evening edition of the New Boston Patriot.

"Our young friend has hit it at last," he said to Lillie. "He has called the muses to his aid. Here is a superb patriotic hymn of his composition. It is the best thing of the kind that the literature of the war has produced." (The Doctor was somewhat given to hyperbole in speaking well of his friends.) "It can't fail to excite popular attention. I venture to predict that those verses alone will bring him in fifty men."

"Let me see," said Lillie, making an impatient snatch at the paper; but the Doctor drew it away, desirous of enjoying the luxury of his own elocution. To read a good thing aloud and to poke the fire are simple but real pleasures, which some people cannot easily deny themselves— and which belong of right, I think, to the head of a family. The Doctor settled himself in an easy chair, adjusted his collar, put up his eyeglass, dropped it, put on his spectacles in spite of Lillie's remonstrances, and read as follows—

A NATIONAL HYMN.

Tune : AMERICA.

Be thou our country's Chief
In this our year of grief,
   Allfather great ;
Go forth with awful tread,
Crush treason's serpent head,
Bring back our sons misled,
   And save our State.

Uphold our stripes and stars
Through war's destroying jars
   With thy right hand ;
Oh God of battles, lead
Where our swift navies speed,
Where our brave armies bleed
   For fatherland.

Break every yoke and chain,
Let truth and justice reign
   From sea to sea ;
Make all our statutes right
In thy most holy sight ;
Light us, O Lord of light,
   To follow Thee.

God bless our fatherland,
God make it strong and grand
   On sea and shore ;
Ages its glory swell,
Peace in its borders dwell,
God stand its sentinel
   For ever more.

" Let me see it," persisted Lillie, making a second and
more successful reach for the paper. She read the verses
to herself with a slight flush of excitement, and then
quietly remarked that they were pretty. It has been sus-

pected that she kept that paper; at all events, when her father sought it next morning to cut out the verses and paste them in his common-place book, he could not find it; and while Lillie pretended to take an interest in his search, she made no distinct answer to his inquiries. I am told by persons wise in the ways of young ladies that they sometimes lay aside trifles of this sort, and are afterwards ashamed, from some inexplicable cause, of having the fact become patent even to their nearest relatives. It must not be understood, by the way, that Miss Ravenel had lost her slight admiration for that full-blown specimen of the male sex, Colonel Carter. He was too much in the style of a Louisiana planter not to be attractive to her homesick eyes. She welcomed his rare visits with her invariable but nevertheless flattering blush, and talked to him with a vivacity which sent flashes of pain into the soul of Colburne. The young man admitted the fact of these spasms, but tried to keep up a deception as to their cause. In his charity towards himself he attributed them to an unselfish anxiety for the happiness of that sweet girl, who, he feared, would find Carter an unsuitable husband, however grandiose as a social ornament and accomplished as an officer.

In spite of these sentimental possibilities of disagreement between the Colonel and the Captain, their friendship daily grew stronger. The former was not in the least influenced by lovelorn jealousy, and set much store by Colburne as being the only officer in his regiment who was precisely to his taste. He had desired, but had not been able to obtain, the young gentlemen of New Boston, the sons of the college professors, and of the city clergymen. The set was limited in number and not martial nor enthusiastic in character. It had held aristocratically aloof from the militia, from the fire companies, from personal interference in local politics, from every social enterprise which could bring it into contact with the laboring masses. It needed two years of tremendous war to break through the shy reserve of this secluded and almost mon-

astic little circle, and let loose its sons upon the battle-
field.   The Colonel was disgusted with his raft of tinkers
and tailors, as he called his officers, although they were
mostly good drill-masters and creditably zealous in learning the graver duties of their new profession.   The regular army, he said, had not been troubled with any such
kind of fellows.   The brahminism of West Point and of
the old service revolted from such vulgar associations.   It
required the fiery breath of many fierce battles, in which
the gallantry of volunteers shone conspicuous, to blow this
feeling into oblivion.

One day the Colonel related in confidence to the Doctor
a circumstance which had given him peculiar disgust.
The Governor having permitted him to nominate his own
Lieutenant-Colonel, he had selected an ex-officer of a three
months' regiment who had shown tactical knowledge, and
gallantry.   The field position of Major he had finally resolved to demand for Colburne.   Hence an interview, and
an unpleasant one, with the chief magistrate of Barataria.

" Governor," said Carter, " I want that majority for a
particular friend of mine, the best officer in the regiment
and the best man for the place that I know in the State."

The Governor was in his little office reclining in a high-
backed oaken chair, and toasting his feet at a fire.   He
was a tall, thin, stooping gentleman, slow in gait because
feeble in health, with a benign dignity of manner and an
unvarying amiability of countenance.   His eyes were a
pale blue, his hair a light chesnut slightly silvered by fifty
years, his complexion had once been freckled and was still
fair, his smile was frequent and conciliatory.   Like President Lincoln he sprang from the plain people, who were to
conquer in this war, and like him he was capable of intellectual and moral growth in proportion to enlargement of
his sphere of action.   A modest, gentle-tempered, oblig-
ing man, patriotic in every impulse, devout in the severe
piety of New England, distinguished for personal honor

and private virtues, he was in the main a credit to the State which had selected him for its loftiest dignity.

He had risen from his chair and saluted the Colonel with marked respect. Although he did not like his moral ways, he valued him highly for his professional ability and courage, and was proud to have him in command of a Baratarian regiment. To his shy spirit this aristocratic and martial personage was in fact a rather imposing phenomenon. Carter had a fearful eye; by turns audaciously haughty and insolently quizzical; and on this occasion the Governor felt himself more than usually discomposed under its wide open, steady, confident stare. He seemed even a little tremulous as he took his seat; he dreaded to disagree with the representative of West Point brahminism; and yet he knew that he must.

"Captain Colburne."

"Oh—Captain Colburne," hesitated the Governor. "I agree with you, Colonel, in all that you say of him. I hope that there will be an opportunity yet of pushing him forward. But just now," he continued with a smile that was apologetical and almost penitent, "I don't see that I can give him the majority. I have promised it to Captain Gazaway."

"To Gazaway!" exclaimed Carter. A long breath of angry astonishment swelled his broad breast, and his cheek would have flushed if any emotion could have deepened the tint of that dark red bronze.

"You don't mean, I hope, Governor, that you are resolved to give the majority of my regiment to that boor."

"I know that he is a plain man," mildly answered the Governor, who had begun life himself as a mechanic.

"Plain man! He is a plain blackguard. He is a toddy-mixer and shoulder-hitter."

The Governor uttered a little troubled laugh; he was clearly discomposed, but he was not angry.

"I am willing to grant all that you say of him," he answered. "I have no personal liking for the man. Indi-

E

vidually I should prefer Captain Colburne. But if you knew the pressure that I am under—"

He hesitated as if reflecting, smiled again with his habitual gentleness, folded and unfolded his hands nervously, and proceeded with his explanation.

"You must not expose our little political secrets, Colonel. I am obliged to permit certain schemes and plots which personally I disapprove of. Captain Gazaway lives in a very close district, and influences a considerable number of votes. He is popular among his class of people, as you can see by the ease with which he filled his company. He and his friends insist upon the majority. If we refuse it we shall probably lose the district and a member of Congress. That is a serious matter at this time when the administration must be supported by a strong house, or the nation may be shipwrecked. Still, if I were left alone I would take the risk, and appoint good officers and no others to all our regiments, satisfied that success in the field is the best means of holding the masses firm in support of the Government. But in the meantime Burleigh, who is our candidate in Gazaway's district, is defeated, we will suppose. Burleigh and Gazaway understand each other. If Gazaway gets the majority, he promises to insure the district to Burleigh. You see the pressure I am under. All the leading managers of our party concur in urging upon me this promotion of Gazaway. I regret extremely that I can do nothing now for your favorite, whom I respect very much. I hope to do something for him in the future."

"When an election is not so near at hand," suggested Carter.

"Here," continued the Governor, without noticing the satire, I have been perfectly frank with you. All I ask in return is that you will have patience."

"'Pon my honor, I can't of course find fault with you personally, Governor," replied the Colonel. "I see how the cursed thing works. You are on a treadmill, and must keep stepping according to the machinery. But by —! sir, I wish this whole matter of appointments was in the hands of the War Department."

"I almost wish it was," sighed the Governor, still without a show of wounded pride or impatience.

It was this conversation which the Colonel repeated to the scandalized ears of Doctor Ravenel, when the latter urged the promotion of Colburne.

"I hope you will inform our young friend of your efforts in his favor," said the Doctor. "He will be exceedingly gratified, notwithstanding the disappointment."

"No," said the Colonel. "I beg your pardon; but don't tell him. It would not be policy, it would not be soldierly, to inform him of any thing likely to disgust him with the service."

CHAPTER VIII.

THE BRAVE BID GOOD-BYE TO THE FAIR.

ANOTHER circumstance disgusted Colonel Carter even more than the affair of the majority. He received a communication from the War Department assigning his regiment to the New England Division, and directing him to report for orders to Major-General Benjamin F. Butler. Over this paper he fired off such a volley of oaths as if Uncle Toby's celebrated army in Flanders had fallen in for practice in battalion swearing.

"A civilian! a lawyer, a political wire-puller! a militia-man!" exclaimed the high-born southern gentleman, West Point graduate and ex-officer of the regular army. "What does such a fellow know about the organization or the command of troops! I don't believe he could make out the property returns of a company, or take a platoon of

skirmishers into action. And I must report to him, instead of he to me!"

Let us suppose that some inconceivably great power
had suddenly created the Colonel a first-class lawyer, and
ordered the celebrated Massachusetts advocate to act under him as junior counsel. We may conjecture that the
latter might have been made somewhat indignant by such
an arrangement.

"I'll make official application to be transferred to some
other command," continued Carter, thinking to himself.
"If that won't answer, I'll go to the Secretary myself
about it, irregular as personal application may be. And
if that won't answer, I'll be so long in getting ready for
the field, that our Major-General Pettifogger will probably
go without me."

If Carter attempted to carry out any of these plans, he
no doubt discovered that the civilian General was greater
than the West Point Colonel in the eyes of the authorities
at Washington. But it is probable that old habits of soldierly obedience prevented him from offering much if any
resistance to the will of the War Department, just as it
prevented him from expressing his dissatisfaction in the
presence of any of his subordinate officers. It is true that
the Tenth was an unconscionable long time in getting ready for the field, but that was owing to the decay of the
enlisting spirit in Barataria, and Carter seemed to be as
much fretted by the lack of men as any body. Meantime
not even Colburne, the officer to whom he unbosomed himself the most freely, overheard a syllable from him in dis-
paragement of General Butler.

During the leisurely organization and drilling of his regiment the Colonel saw Miss Ravenel often enough to fall
desperately in love with her, had he been so minded. He
was not so minded; he liked to talk with pretty young
ladies, to flirt with them and to tease them; but he did
not easily take sentiment *au grand serieux*. Self-conceit
and a certain hard-hearted indifference to the feelings of

others, combined with a love of fun, made him a habitual
quiz. He acknowledged the charm of Lillie's outlines and
manner, but he treated her like a child whom he could
pet and banter at his pleasure. She, on the other hand,
was a little too much afraid of him to quiz in return; she
could not treat this mature and seemingly worldly-wise
man with the playful impertinence which sometimes
marked her manner towards Colburne.

"Miss Ravenel, have you any messages for New Orleans?" said the Colonel. "I begin to think that we
shall go just there. It will be such a rich pocket for General Butler's fingers."

In speaking to civilians Carter was not always so careful of the character of his superiors as in talking to his
subordinate officers.

"Just think of the twelve millions of gold in the
banks," he proceeded, "and the sugar and cotton too, and
the wholesale nigger-stealing that we can do to varnish
over our robberies. It grieves me to death to think that
the Tenth will soon be street-firing up and down New Orleans. We shall make such an awful slaughter among
your crowds of old admirers!"

"I hope you won't kill them all."

"Oh, I shan't kill them all. I am not going to commit
suicide," said the Colonel with a flippant gallantry which
made the young lady color with a suspicion that she was
not profoundly appreciated.

"Do you really think that you are going to New Orleans?" she presently inquired.

"Ah! Don't ask me. You have a right to command
me; but don't, I beg of you, order me to tell state secrets."

"Then why do you introduce the subject?" she replied,
more annoyed by his manner than by what he said.

"Because the subject has irresistible charms; because it
is connected with your past, and perhaps with your future."

Now if Carter had looked in the least as he spoke, I fear that Miss Lillie would have been flattered and gratified. But he did not; he had a quizzing smile on his audacious face; he seemed to be talking to her as he would to a child of fourteen. Being a woman of eighteen, and sensitive, she was not pleased by his confident familiarity, and in her inexperience she showed her annoyance perhaps a little more plainly than was quite dignified. After watching her for a moment or two with his wide-open, unwinking eyes, he suddenly changed his tone, and addressed her with an air of entirely satisfactory respect. The truth is that he could not help being at times semi-impertinent to young ladies; but then he had delicacy of breeding enough to know when he was so; he did not quiz them in mere boorish stupidity.

"I should be truly delighted," he said, "I should consider it one of the greatest honors possible to me—if I could do something towards opening your way back to your own home."

"Oh! I wish you could," she replied with enthusiasm. "I do so want to get back to Louisiana. But I don't want the South whipped. I want peace."

"Do you? That is a bad wish for me," observed Carter, with his characteristic frankness, coolly wondering to himself how he would be able to live without his colonelcy. As to how he could pay the thousand or two which he owed to tailors, shoemakers, restaurateurs and wine merchants, that was never to him a matter of marvel or of anxiety, or even of consideration.

In obedience to a curious instinct which exists in at least some feminine natures, Miss Ravenel liked the Colonel, or at least felt that she could like him, just in proportion as she feared him. A man who can make some women tremble, can, if he chooses, make them love. Pure and modest as this girl of eighteen was, she could, and I fear, would have fallen desperately in love with this toughened worldling, had he, with his despotic temperament, resolutely

willed it.   In justice to her it must be remembered that
she knew little or nothing about his various naughty ways.
In her presence he never swore, nor got the worse for
liquor, nor alluded to scenes of dissipation.   At church he
decorously put down his head while one could count
twenty, and made the responses with a politeness meant
to be complimentary to the parties addressed.   Her
father hinted; but she thought him unreasonably prejudiced; she made what she considered the proper allowance for men who wore uniforms.   She had very little
idea of the stupendous discount which would have to be
admitted before Colonel Carter could figure up as an angel of light, or even as a decently virtuous member of
human society.   She thought she stated the whole subject fairly when she admitted that he might be " fast;"
but she had an innocently inadequate conception of the
meaning which the masculine sex attaches to that epithet.
She applied it to him chiefly because he had the mu-
mental self-possession, the graceful audacity, the free and
easy fluency, the little ways, the general air, of certain
men in New Orleans who had been pointed out to her as
" fast," and concerning whom there were dubious whisper-
ings among elderly dowagers, but of whom she actually
knew little more than that they had good manners and
were favorites with most ladies.   She had learned to consider the type a satisfactory one, without at all appreciating its moral signification.   That Colonel Carter had
been downright wicked and was still capable of being so
under a moderate pressure of temptation, she did not believe with any realizing and saving faith.   Balzac says
that very corrupt people are generally very agreeable;
and it may be that this extraordinary fact is capable of a
simple and sufficient explanation.   They are seared and
do not take thing seriously; they do not contradict you
on this propriety and that belief, because they care nothing about proprieties and beliefs; they love nothing, hate
nothing, and are as easy to wear as old slippers.   The

strict moralist and pietest, on the other hand, is as hard
and unyielding as a boot just from the hands of the
maker; you must conform to his model, or he will conscientiously pinch your moral corns in a most grievous manner; he cannot grant you a hair's-breadth without bursting his uppers and endangering his sole. But pleasant as
our corrupt friends are apt to be, you must not trust your
affections and your happiness to them, or you may find
that you have cast your pearls before the unclean.

These reflections are not perhaps of the newest, but they
are just as true as when they were first promulgated.

Concerning the possible flirtation to which I have alluded Doctor Ravenel was constanly ill at ease. If he found
on returning from a walk that Lillie had received a call
from the Colonel during his absence, he was secretly
worried and sometimes openly peevish for hours afterward.
He would break out upon that sort of people, though always without mentioning names ; and the absent Carter
would receive a severe lashing over the back of some gentleman whom Lillie had known or heard of in New Orleans.

"I don't see how I ever lived among such a disreputable
population," he would say. "I look upon myself sometimes as a man who has just come from a twenty-five
year's residence among the wealthy and genteel pirates of
the Isle of Pines. I actually feel that I have no claims
upon a decent society to be received as a respectable
character. If a New Boston man should refuse to shake
hands with me on the ground that my associations had
not been what they should be, I could not find it in my
heart to disagree with him. Among that people I used to
wonder at the patience of the Almighty. I obtained a
conception of his long-suffering mercies such as I could
not have obtained in a virtuous community. Just look at
that Colonel McAllister, who used to be the brightest
ornament of New Orleans fashion. A mass of corruption!
The immoral odor of him must have been an offense to the
heavens. I can imagine the angels and glorified spirits

looking down at him with disgust, and actually holding their noses, like the king in Orcagna's picture when he comes across the dead body. There never was a subject brought into our dissecting room so abominable to the physical senses as that man was to the moral sense."

"Oh, papa, don't!" implored Miss Lillie. "You talk most horridly when you get started on certain subjects."

"My conversation is'nt half pungent enough to do justice to the perfume of the subject," insisted the Doctor. "When I speak or try to speak of that McAllister, and of similar people to be met there and everywhere, I am obliged to admit the inadequacy of language. Nothing but the last trump can utter a sound appropriate to such personages."

"But Colonel McAllister is a very respectable middle-aged planter now, papa," said Lillie.

"Respectable! Oh, my child! do not persist in talking as if you were still in the nursery. Saint Paul, Pascal, Wilberforce couldn't have remained respectable if they had been slaveholding planters."

To Colonel Carter personally the Doctor was perfectly civil, as he was to every one with whom he was obliged to come in contact, including the reprobated McAllister and his similars. Even had he been of a combative disposition, or been twice as prejudiced against Carter as he was, he could not have brought himself in these days and with his present loyal enthusiasm, to discourteously entreat an officer who wore the United States uniform and who had bled in the cause of country against treason. Moreover he felt a certain degree of good-will towards our military *roue*, as being the patron of his particular friend Colburne. Of this young man he seemed almost as fond as if he were his father, without, however, entertaining the slightest thought of gaining him for a son-in-law. I never knew, nor read of, not even in the most unnatural novels, an American father who was a matchmaker.

So the autumn and half the winter passed away, with-

out any one falling in love, unless it might be Colburne.
It needed all his good sense to keep him from it; or rather
to keep him from paying Miss Ravenel what are called
significant attentions; for as to his being in love, I admit
it, although he did not. To use old-fashioned language,
alarming in its directness and strength of meaning, I suppose he would have courted her if she would have let him.
But there was something in the young lady's manner towards him which kept him at arm's length; which had
the charm of friendship, indeed, but no faintest odor of
even the possibility of love, just as certain flowers have
beauty but no perfume; which said to him very gently
but also very firmly, "Mr. Colburne, you had better not
be in a hurry."

At times he was under sudden and violent temptation.
The trusting Doctor placed Lillie under his charge to go
to one or two concerts and popular lectures, following
therein the simple and virtuous ways of New Boston,
where young ladies have a freedom which in larger and
wickeder cities is only accorded to married women. On
the way to and from these amusements, Lillie's hand resting
lightly on his arm, and the obscurity of the streets veiling
whatever reproof or warning might sparkle in her eyes,
his heart was more urgent and his soul less timid than
usual.

"I have only one subject of regret in going to the war,"
he once said; "and that is that I shall not see you for a
long time, and may never see you again."

There was a magnetic tremulousness in his voice which
thrilled through Miss Ravenel and made it difficult for her
to breathe naturally. For a few seconds she could not
answer, any more than he could continue. She felt as we
do in dreams when we seem to stand on the edge of a
gulf wavering whether we shall fall backward into safety
or forward into the unknown. It was one of the perilous
and decisive moments of the young lady's life; but the
end of it was that she recovered self-possession enough to

speak before he could rally to pursue his advantage. Ten seconds more of silence might have resulted in an engagement ring.

"What a hard heart you have!" she laughed. "No greater cause of regret than that! And here you are, going to lay waste my country, and perhaps burn up my house. You abolitionists are dreadful."

He immediately changed his manner of conversation with a painful consciousness that she had as good as ordered him to do so.

"Oh! I have no sort of compunction about turning the South into a desert," he said, with a poor attempt at making merry. "I mean to take a bag of salt with me, and sow all Louisiana with it."

And the rest of the dialogue, until he left her at the door of the hotel, was conducted in the same style of laborious and painful trifling.

As the day approached for the sailing of the regiment, Colburne looked forward with dread yet with eagerness to the last interview. At times he thought and hoped and almost expected that it would bring about some decisive expression of feeling which should give a desirable direction to the perverse heart of this inexplicable young lady. Then he reflected during certain flashes of pure reason, how foolish, how cruel it would be to win her affection only to quit her on the instant, certainly for months, probably for years, perhaps for ever. Moreover, suppose he should lose a leg or a nose in his first battle, how could he demand that she should keep her vows, and yet how could he give her up? But these last interviews are frequently unsatisfactory; and the one which Colburne excitedly anticipated was eminently so. It took place in the public parlor of the hotel; the Doctor was present, and so were several dowager boarders. The regiment had marched through the city in the afternoon, surrounded and cheered by crowds of enthusiastic citizens, and was already on board of the coasting steamer which would transfer it to the ocean transport at New York. Colburne had obtained permission to remain in New Boston until the evening through train from the east.

"This is a proud day for you," said the warm-hearted Doctor. "But I must say that it is a sad one for me. I am truly grieved to think how long it may be before we shall see you again."

"I hope not very long," answered the young man with a gravity and sadness which did not consort with his words.

He was pale, nervous and feverish, partly from lack of sleep the night before.

"I really think it will not be very long," he repeated after a moment.

Now that peace was apparently his only chance of returning to Miss Ravenel, he longed for it, and like most young people he could muster confidence to believe in what he hoped. Moreover it was at this time a matter of northern faith that the contest could not last a year; that the great army which was being drilled and disciplined on the banks of the Potomac would prove irresistible when it should take the field; that McClellan would find no difficulty in trampling out the life of the rebellion. Colonel Carter, Doctor Ravenel and a few obstinate old hunker democrats were the only persons in the little State of Barataria who did not give way to this popular conviction.

"Where are you going, Mr. Colburne?" asked Lillie eagerly.

"I don't know, really. The Colonel has received sealed orders. He is not to open them until we have been twenty-four hours at sea."

"Oh! I think that is a shame. I do think that is abominable," said the young lady with excitement. She was very inquisitive by nature, and she was particularly anxious to know if the regiment would reach Louisiana.

"I am inclined to believe that we shall go to Virginia,"

resumed Colburne. "I hope so. The great battle of the war is to be fought there, and I want to take part in it."

Poor young man! he felt like saying that he wanted to be killed in it; mistaken young man! he believed that there would be but one great battle.

"Wherever you go you will be doing your duty as a patriot and a friend of the interests of humanity," put in the Doctor, emphatically. I confidently anticipate for you the greatest successes. I anticipate your personal success. Colonel Carter will undoubtedly be made a general, and you will return the commander of your regiment. But even if you never receive a grade of promotion, nor have a chance to strike a blow in battle, you will still have performed one of the highest duties of manhood and be entitled to our lasting respect. I sincerely and fervently envy you the feelings which you will be able to carry through life."

"Thank you, sir," was all the answer that Colburne could think of at the moment.

"If you find yourself near a post-office you will let us know it, won't you?" asked Lillie with a thoughtless frankness for which she immediately blushed painfully. In the desire to know whether Louisiana would be attacked and assaulted by Colonel Carter, she had said more than she meant.

Colburne brightened into a grateful smile at the idea that he might venture to write to her.

"Certainly," added the Doctor. "You must send me a letter at once when you reach your destination."

Colburne promised as he was required, but not with the light heart which had shone in his face an instant before. It was sadly clear, he thought, that he must not on any account write to Miss Ravenel.

"And now I must say good-bye, and God bless you," he sighed, putting out his hand to the young lady, while his face grew perceptibly whiter, if we may believe the reports of the much affected dowager spectators.

As Miss Ravenel gave him her hand, her cheeks also became discolored, not with pallor however, but only with her customary blush when excited.

"I do hope you will not be hurt," she murmured.

She was so simply kind and friendly in her feelings that she did not notice with any thrill of emotion the fervent pressure, the clinging as of despair, with which he held her hand for a few seconds. An hour afterward she remembered it suddenly, blushing as she interpreted to herself its significance, but with no sentiment either of love or anger.

"God bless you! God bless you!" repeated the Doctor, much moved. "Let me know as early and as often as possible of your welfare. Our best wishes go with you."

Colburne had found the interview so painful, so different from what his hopes had pictured it, that, under pretence of bidding farewell to other friends, he left the hotel half an hour before the arrival of his train. As he passed through the outer door he met the Colonel entering.

"Ah! paid you adieux?" said Carter in his rough-and-ready, jaunty way. "I must say good-bye to those nice people. Meet you at the train."

Colburne merely replied, "Very well sir," with a heart as gloomy as the sour February weather, and strolled away, not to take leave of any more friends, but to smoke an anchorite, uncomforting segar in the purlieus of the station.

"Delighted to have found you," said the Colonel intercepting the Ravenels as they were leaving the parlor for their rooms. "Miss Ravenel, I have neglected my duty for the sake of the pleasure—no, the pain, of bidding you good-bye."

The Doctor cringed at this speech, but expressed delight at the visit. Lillie adorned the occasion by a blush as sumptuous as a bouquet of roses, and led the way back to the parlor, defiant of her father's evident intention to shorten the scene by remaining standing in the hall. The Doctor, finding himself thus out-generalled, retorted by taking the lead in the conversation, and talked volubly for ten minutes of the magnificent appearance of the regiment as it marched through the city, of the probable length of the war, and of the differing characteristics of northerners and southerners. Meanwhile Miss Ravenel sat quietly, after the fashion of a French *demoiselle*, saying nothing, but perhaps thinking all the more dangerously. At last the Colonel broke loose from the father and resolutely addressed himself to the daughter.

"Miss Ravenel, I suppose that you have not a friendly wish to send with me."

"I don't know why I should have," she replied, "until I know that you are not going to harm my people. But I have no very bad wishes."

"Thank you for that," he said with a more serious air than usual. "I do sincerely desire that your feelings were such as that I could consider myself to be fighting your cause. Perhaps you will find before we get through that I am fighting it. If we should go to New Orleans—which is among the possibilities—it may be the means of restoring you to your home."

"Oh! I should thank you for that—almost. I should be tempted to feel that the end justified the means."

"Let me hope that I shall meet you there, or somewhere, soon," he added, rising.

His manner was certainly more earnest and impressive than it had ever been before in addressing her. The tremor of her hand was perceptible to the strong steady hand which took it, and her eyes dropped under the firm gaze which met them, and which for the first time, she thought, had an expression deeply significant to her.

"If she turns out to have any prospects"—thought the Colonel as he went down stairs. "If they ever get back their southern property"—

He left the sentence unfinished on the writing tablets of his soul, to light a segar. His impulses and passions were strong when once aroused, but on this subject they had only begun to awaken.

CHAPTER IX.

FROM NEW BOSTON TO NEW ORLEANS, VIA FORT JACKSON.

"By" (this and that)! swore Colonel Carter to himself when, twenty-four hours out from Sandy Hook, he opened his sealed orders in the privacy of his state-room. "Butler has got an expedition to himself. We are in for a round of Big Bethels as sure as" (this and that and the other.)

I wish it to be understood that I do not endorse the above criticism on the celebrated proconsul of Louisiana. I am not sketching the life of General Butler, but of Colonel Carter—I am not trying to show how things really were, but only how the Colonel looked at them.

Carter opened the door and looked into the cabin. There stood a particularly clean soldier of the Tenth, his uniform carefully brushed, his shoes, belts, cartridge-box and cap-pouch blacked, his buttons and brasses shining like morning suns, white cotton gloves on his hands, and his bayonet in its scabbard, but without a musket. Being the neatest man of all those detailed for guard that morning, he had been selected by the Adjutant as the Colonel's orderly. He saluted his commander by carrying his right hand open to his fore-piece, then well out to the right, then dropping it with the little finger against the seam of his trousers, meanwhile standing bolt upright with his heels well together. The Colonel surveyed him from top to toe with a look of approbation.

"Very well, orderly," said he. "Very clean and soldierly. Been in the old army, I see."

Here he gratified himself with another full-length inspection of this statue of neatness and speechless respect.

"Now go to the captain of the vessel," he added, "give him my compliments, and request him to step to my state-room."

The orderly saluted again, faced about as if on a pivot, and walked away.

"Here, come back, sir," called the Colonel. "What did I tell you?"

"You told me, sir, to give your compliments to the captain of the vessel, and request him to step to your state-room," replied the soldier.

"My God! he understood the first time," exclaimed the Colonel. "Been in the old army, I see. Quite right, sir; go on."

In a few minutes the marine functionary was closeted with the military potentiality.

"Sit down, Captain," said the Colonel. "Take a glass of wine."

"No, thank you, Colonel," said the Captain, a small, brown, quiet-mannered, taciturn man of forty-five, his iron-grey locks carefully oiled and brushed, and his dark-blue morning-suit as neat as possible. "I make it a rule at sea," he added, "never to take any thing but a bottle of porter at dinner."

"Very good: never get drunk on duty—good rule," laughed the Colonel. "Well, here are our orders. Look them over, Captain, if you please."

The Captain read, lifted his eyebrows with an air of comprehension, put the paper back in the envelope, returned it to the Colonel, and remarked, "Ship Island."

"It would be best to say nothing about it at present," observed Carter. "Some accident may yet send us back to New York, and then the thing would be known earlier than the War Department wants."

"Very good. I will lay the proper course, and say nothing."

And so, with a little further talk about cleaning quarters and cooking rations, the interview terminated. It was not till the transport was off the beach of Ship Island that the Tenth Barataria became aware of its destination. Meantime, taking advantage of a run of smooth weather, Carter disciplined his green regiment into a state of cleanliness, order and subserviency, which made it a wonder to itself. He had two daily inspections with regard to personal cleanliness, going through the companies himself, praising the neat and remorselessly punishing the dirty. "What do you mean by such hair as that, sir?" he would say, poking up a set of long locks with the hilt of his sabre. "Have it off before night, sir. Have it cut short and neatly combed by to-morrow morning."

For offences which to the freeborn American citizen seemed peccadilloes or even virtues, (such as saying to a second-lieutenant, "I am as good as you are,") men were seized up by the wrists to the rigging with their toes scarcely touching the deck. The soldiers had to obey orders without a word, to touch their caps to officers, to stop chaffing the sentinels, to keep off the quarter-deck, and out of the cabin.

"By (this and that) I'll teach them to be soldiers," swore the Colonel. "They had their skylarking in Barataria. They are on duty now."

The men were not pleased; freeborn Americans could not at first be gratified with such despotism, however salutary; but they were intelligent enough to see that there was a hard, practical sense at the bottom of it: they not only feared and obeyed, but they respected. Every American who is true to his national education regards with consideration a man who knows his own business. Whenever the Colonel walked on the main deck, or in the hold where the men were quartered, there was a silence, a quiet standing out of the way, a rising to the feet, and a touching of fore-pieces. To his officers Carter was distant and authoritative, although formally courteous. It was,

" Lieutenant, have the goodness to order those men down from the rigging, and to keep them down;" and when the officer of the day reported that the job was done, it was, " Very well, Lieutenant, much obliged to you." Even the private soldiers whom he berated and punished were scrupulously addressed by the title of " Sir."

" My God, sir! I ought not to be obliged to speak to the enlisted men at all," he observed apologetically to the captain of the transport. " A colonel in the old army was a little deity, a Grand Lama, who never opened his mouth except on the greatest occasions. But my officers, you see, don't know their business. I am as badly off as you would be if your mates, sailors and firemen were all farmers. I must attend to things myself."

" Captain Colburne," he said on another occasion, " how about your property returns? Have the goodness to let me look at them."

Colburne brought two packets of neatly folded papers, tied up in the famous, the historical, the proverbial red tape, and endorsed ; the one, " Return of Ordnance and Ordnance Stores appertaining to Co. I, 10th Regt. Barataria Vols., for the quarter ending December 31st, 1861 ;" the other, " Return of Clothing and Camp and Garrison Equipage appertaining to Co. I, 10th Regt. Barataria Vols., for the quarter ending Dec. 31st, 1861." Carter glanced over the footings, the receipts and the invoices with the prompt and accurate eye of a bank accountant.

" Correct," said he. " Very much to your credit, Captain. —Orderly! give my compliments to all the commandants of companies, and request them to call on me immediately in the after cabin."

One after another the captains walked in, saluted, and took seats in obedience to a wave of the Colonel's hand.

" Gentlemen," he began, " those of you who have finished your property returns for the last quarter will send them in to the adjutant this afternoon for examination. Those who have not, will proceed to complete them immediately.

If you need any instructions, you will apply to Captain Colburne. His papers are correct. Gentlemen, the United States Army Regulations are as important to you as the United States Army Tactics. Ignorance of one will get you into trouble as surely as ignorance of the other. Such parts of the Regulation as refer to the army account-ability system are of especial consequence to your pockets. Neglect your returns, and you will get your pay stopped. This is not properly my business. You are responsible for yourselves directly to the War Department. But I wish to set you on the right path. You ought to take a pride, gentlemen, in learning the whole of your profession, even if you are sure that the war will not last three months. If a thing is worth learning at all it should be learned well, if only for the good of a man's own soul. Never do a duty by halves. No man of any self-respect will accept an officer's pay without performing the whole of an officer's duty. And this accountability system is worth study. It is the most admirable system of book-keeping that ever was devised. John C. Calhoun perfected it when he was Secretary of War and at the top of his intel-lectual powers. I have no hesitation in saying that a man who can account truthfully and without loss for all the public property in a company, according to this system, is able to master the business of any mercantile house or banking establishment. The system is as minute and in-exorable as a balance-sheet. When I was a boy, just out of West Point and in command of a company on the Indian frontier, I took part in a skirmish. I was as vain over my first fight as a kitten over its first mouse. I thought the fame of it must illuminate Washington and dazzle the clerks in the department offices. In my next return I accounted for three missing ball-screws as lost in the en-gagement of Trapper's Bluff. I supposed the army ac-countability system would bow to a second-lieutenant who had been under fire. But, gentlemen, it did no such thing. I got a letter from the Chief of Ordnance informing me that I must state circumstantially and on honor *how* the three ball-screws were lost. I couldn't do it, couldn't make out a satisfactory certificate, and had them taken out of my pay. I, the hero of an engagement, who had personally shot a Pawnee, was charged thirty-nine cents for three ball-screws."

Emboldened by the Colonel's smiles of grim humor the audience burst into a laugh.

"I knew another case," he proceeded. "A young fellow was appointed quartermaster at Puget Sound. About a year after he had sent in his first return he was notified by the Quartermaster General that it did not properly account for certain cap letters, value five cents. Indignant at what he considered such small-beer fault-finding, he immediately mailed five cents to Washington, with a statement that it was intended to cover the deficiency. Six months later he received a sharp note from the Quartermaster General, returning him his five cents, informing him that the department was not accustomed to settle accounts in that manner, and directing him to forward the proper papers concerning the missing property under penalty of being reported to the Adjutant General. The last I knew of him he was still corresponding on the subject, and hoping that the rebels would take enough of Washington to burn the quartermaster's department. Now, gentlemen, this is not nonsense. It is business and sense, as any bank cashier will tell you. Red-Tape means order, accuracy, honesty, solvency. A defalcation of five cents is as bad in principle as a defalcation of a million. I tell you these stories to give you an idea of what will be exacted of you some time or other, it may be soon, but certainly at last. I wish you to complete your returns as soon as possible. They ought to have gone in long since. That is all, gentlemen."

"I talked to them like a Dutch uncle," said Carter to the captain of the transport, after relating the above inter·view. The fact is that in the regular army we generally left the returns to the first sergeants. When I was in command of a company I gave mine the ten dollars monthly for accountability, and hardly ever saw my papers except when I signed them, all made up and ready to forward. But here the first sergeants, confound them ! don't know so much as the officers. The officers must do every thing personally, and I must set them the example."

So much at present for Carter as chief of a volunteer. regiment which it was his duty and pride to transform into a regiment of regulars. Professionally if not person- ally, as a soldier if not as a man, he had an imperious conscience ; and his aristocratic breeding and tolerably hard heart enabled him to obey it in this matter of disci- pline without hesitation or pity. And now, in the calm leisure of this winter voyage over summer seas, let us go back a little in his history, and see what kind of a life his had been outside of the regulations and devoirs of the army.

" How rapidly times change !" he said to Colburne in a moment of unusual communicativeness. " Three years ago I expected to take a regiment or so across this gulf on a very different errand. I was, by (this and that) a filibuster and pro-slavery champion in those days; at least by intention. I was closeted with the Lamars and the Soules—the Governor of South Carolina and the Governor of Mississippi and the Governor of Louisiana—the gentle- men who proposed to carry the auction-block of freedom into Yucatan, Cuba, the island of Atalantis, and the moon. I expected to be a second Cortez. Not that I cared much about their pro-slavery projects and palaverings. I was a soldier of fortune, only anxious for active service, pay and promotion. I might have been monarch of all I surveyed by this time, if the world had turned as we ex- pected. But this war broke up my prospects. They saw it coming, and decided that they must husband their re- sources for it. It was necessary to take sides for a greater struggle than the one we wanted. They chose their party, and I chose mine."

These confessions were too fragmentary and guarded to satisfy the curiosity of Colburne; but he subsequently obtained information in the South from which he was able to piece out this part of Carter's history; and the facts are perhaps worth repeating as illustrative of the man and his times. Our knowledge is sufficiently complete to enable us to decide that the part which he played in the filibustering conspiracy was not that of a Burr, but of a Walker, which indeed might be inferred from the fact that he was not intellectually capable of making himself head of a cabal which included some of the cleverest of the keen-sighted (though not far-sighted) statemen of the south. It is no special reflection on the Colonel's brains to say that they were not equal to those of Soule and Jefferson Davis. Moreover a soldier is usually a poor intriguer, because his profession rarely leads him to appeal to any other influence than open authority: he is not obliged to learn the politician's essential arts of convincing, wheedling and circumventing; he simply says to his man Go, and he goeth. Carter, then, was to be the commander of the regiment, or brigade, or division, or whatever might be the proposed force of armed filibusters. There appears to have been no doubt in the minds of the ringleaders as to his fidelity. He was a Virginian born, and of a family which sat in the upper seats of the southern oligarchy. Furthermore, he had married a wife and certain appertaining human property in Louisiana; and although he had buried the first, and dissolved the second (as Cleopatra did pearls) in the wine cup, it was reasonable to suppose that they had exercised an establishing influence on his character; for what Yankee even was ever known to remain an abolitionist after having once tasted the pleasure of living by the labor of others? Moreover he had become agent and honorary stockholder of a company which had a new patent rifle to dispose of; and it was an item of the filibustering bargain that the expeditionary force should be armed with ordnance furnished by this Pennsylvania manufactory. Finally, having melted down his own and his wife's patrimony in the crucible of pleasure, and been driven by debts to resign his lieutenancy for something which promised, but did not provide, a better income, he was known to be dreadfully in need of money.

It is impossible to make the whole conspiracy a matter of plain and positive history. Colburne thought he had learned that at least two or three thousand men were sworn in as officers and soldiers, and that the Governors of several Southern States had pledged themselves to support it, even at the risk of being obliged to bully the venerable public functionary who then occupied the White House. It is certain that councils of state and war were held in the Mills House at Charleston and in the St. Charles Hotel at New Orleans. It is even asserted that a distinguished southern divine was present at some of these sessions, and gave his blessing to the plan as one of the most hopeful missionary enterprises of the day; and the story, ironical as it may seem to misguided Yankees, becomes seriously credible when we remember that certain devout southerners advocated the slave-trade itself as a means of christianizing benighted Africans. Where the expedition was to go and when it was to sail are still points of uncertainty. Carter himself never told, and perhaps was not let into the secret. His part was to draw over as many of his old comrades as possible; to organize the enlisted men into companies and regiments, and to command the force when it should once be landed. Concerning the causes of the failure of the enterprise we know nothing more than what he stated to Colburne. The arch conspirators foresaw the election of Lincoln, and resolved to save the material and enthusiasm of the South for war at home. It is pretty certain, however, that they sought to bring Carter's courage and professional ability into the new channel which they had resolved to open for such qualities; and we can only wonder that a man of such desperate fortunes, apparently such a mere Dugald Dalgetty, was not seduced into treason by their no doubt earnest persuasions and flattering promises. He may have resisted their blandishments merely because he knew that the other side was the strongest and richest; but if we are charitable we will concede that it argued in him some still uneradicated roots of military honor and patriotism. At all events, here he was, confident, cheerful and jealous, going forth to fight for his old flag and his whole country. This vague and unsatisfactory story of the conspiracy would not have been worth relating did it not shed some cloudy light on the man's dubious history and contradictory character.

We may take it for granted that Captain Colburne devoted much of his time during this voyage to meditations on Miss Ravenel. But lovers' reveries not being popular reading in these days, I shall omit all the interesting matter thus offered, notwithstanding that the young man has my earnest sympathies and good wishes.

One summer-like March morning the steam transport, black with men, lay bowing to the snow-like sand-drifts of Ship Island; and by sunset the regiment was ashore, the camp marked out, tents pitched, rations cooking, and line formed for dress-parade; an instance of military promptness which elicited the praises of Generals Phelps and Butler.

It is well known that the expedition against New Orleans started from Ship Island as its base. Over the organization of the enterprise, the battalion and brigade drills on the dazzling sands, the gun-boat fights in the offing with rebel cruisers from Mobile, the arrival of Farragut's frigates and Porter's bomb-schooners, and the grand review of the expeditionary force, I must hurry without a word of description, although I might make up a volume on these subjects from the newspapers of the day, and from three or four long and enthusiastic letters

F

which Colburne wrote to Ravenel.   But these matters do
not properly come within the scope of this narrative,
which is biographical and not historical.   Parenthetically
it may be well to remark that neither Carter nor Colburne ever referred to Miss Ravenel in their few and brief
interviews.   The latter was not disposed to talk of her
to that listener ; and the former was too much occupied
with his duties to give much thought to an absent Dul-
cinea.   The Colonel was no longer in that youthfully tender stage when absence increases affection.   To make him
love it was necessary to have a woman in pretty close
personal propinquity.

In a month or two from the arrival of the Tenth Barataria at Ship Island it was again on board a transport, this
time bound for New Orleans *via* Fort Jackson.

"This part of Louisiana looks as the world must have
looked in the marsupial period," says Colburne in a letter
to the Doctor written from the Head of the Passes.
"There are two narrow but seemingly endless antennæ of
land; between them rolls a river and outside of them
spreads an ocean.   Dry land there is none, for the Mississippi being unusually high the soil is submerged, and
the trees and shrubs of these long ribbons of underwood
which enclose us have their boles in the water.   I do not
understand why the ichthyosauri should have died out in
Louisiana.   It certainly is not fitted, so far as I can see,
for human habitation.   May it not have been the chaos
(*vide* Milton) through which Satan floundered ?   Miss
Ravenel will, I trust, forgive me for this hypothesis when
she learns that it is suggested by your theory that Lucifer
was and is and ever will be peculiarly at home in this part
of the world."

In a subsequent passage he gives a long account of the
famous bombardment of the forts, which I feel obliged to
suppress as not strictly biographical, he not being under
fire but only an eye-witness and ear-witness of the cannonade.   One paragraph alone I deem it worth while to copy,

being a curious analysis of the feelings of the individual in the presence of sublime but monotonous circumstance.

"Here we are, in view of what I am told is the greatest bombardment known in marine, or, as I should call it, amphibious warfare. You take it for granted, I suppose, that we are in a state of constant and noble excitement; but the extraordinary truth is that we are in a condition of wearisome *ennui* and deplorable *desaeuvrement.* We are too ignorant of the great scientific problems of war to take an intelligent interest in the fearful equation of fleets =forts. We got tired a week ago of the mere auricular pleasure of the incessant bombing. We got tired a day or two afterward of climbing to the crosstrees to look at the fading globes of smoke left aloft in the air by the bursting shells. We are totally tired of the monotonous flow of the muddy river, and the interminable parallel curves of its natural levees and the glassy stretches of ocean which seem to slope upwards toward the eastern and western horizon. We pass our time in playing cards, smoking, grumbling at our wretched fare, exchanging dull gossip and wishing that we might be allowed to do something. Happy is the man who chances once a day to find a clear space of a dozen feet on the crowded deck where he can take a constitutional. Waiting for a belated train, alone, in a country railroad station, is not half so wearisome."

But in a subsequent page of the same letter he makes record of startling events and vivid emotions.

"The fleet has forced the passage of the forts. We have had a day and a night of almost crazy excitement. A battle, a victory, a glorious feat of arms has been achieved within our hearing, though beyond our sight and range of action. A submerged iron-clad, one of the wrecks of the enemy's fleet, drifted against our cable, shook us over the edge of eternity, and then floated by harmlessly. Blazing fire-ships have passed us, lighting up the midnight river until its ripples seemed of flame."

In another part of the letter he says, "The forts have

surrendered, and we are steaming up the Mississippi in the track of that amazing Farragut. As I look around me with what knowledge of science there is in my eyes, I feel as if I had lived a few millions of years since yesterday; for within twenty-four hours we have sailed out of the marsupial period into the comparatively modern era of fluvial deposits and luxuriant vegetation. Give my compliments to Miss Ravenel, and tell her that I modify my criticisms on the scenery of Louisiana. On either side the land is a living emerald. The plantation houses are embowered in orange groves—in a glossy mass of brilliant, fragrant verdure. I do not know the names of a quarter of the plants and trees which I see; but I pass the livelong day in admiring and almost adoring their tropical beauty. We are no welcome tourists, at least not to the white inhabitants; very few of them show themselves, and they do not answer our cheering, nor hardly look at us; they walk or ride grimly by, with faces set straight forward, as if they could thereby ignore our existence. But to the negroes we evidently appear as friends and redeemers. Such joyous gatherings of dark faces, such deep-chested shouts of welcome and deliverance, such a waving of green boughs and white vestments, and even of pickaninnies—such a bending of knees and visible praising of God for his long-expected and at last realized mercy, salutes our eyes from morn till night, as makes me grateful to Heaven for this hour of holy triumph. How glorious will be that time, now near at hand, when our re-united country will be free of the shame and curse of slavery!"

Miss Ravenel spit in her angry pussy-cat fashion when her father read to her this passage of the letter.

"We are in New Orleans," proceeds Colburne towards the close of this prodigious epistle. "Our regiment was the first to reach the city and to witness the bareness of the once-crowded wharves, the desertion of the streets and the sullen spite of the few remaining inhabitants. I suspect that your aristocratic acquaintances have all fled at

the approach of the Vandal Yankees, for I see only negroes, poor foreigners, and rowdies more savage-looking
than the tribes of the Bowery. The spirit of impotent but
impertinent hate in this population is astonishing. The
ragged news-boys will not sell us a paper—the beggarly
restaurants will not furnish us a dinner. Wherever I walk
I am saluted by mutterings of 'Damned Yankee !'—'Cut
his heart out !' &c. &c. I once more profess allegiance to
your theory that this is where Satan's seat is. But the
evil spirits who inhabit this city of desolation only grimace
and mumble, without attempting any manner of injury.
If Miss Ravenel fears that there will be a popular insur-
rection and a consequent burning of the city, assure her
from me that she may dismiss all such terrors."

And here, from mere lack of space rather than of interesting matter, I must close my extracts from this incompa-
rably elongated letter. I question, by the way, whether
Colburne would have covered so much paper had he not
been reasonably justified in imagining a pretty family picture of the Doctor reading and Miss Ravenel listening.

CHAPTER X.

THE RAVENELS FIND CAPTAIN COLBURNE IN GOOD QUARTERS.

THE spring and summer of 1862 was a time of such
peace and pleasantness to the Tenth Barataria as if there
had been no war. With the Major General commanding
Carter was a favorite, as being a man who had seen service, a most efficient officer, an old regular and a West
Pointer. The Tenth was a pet, as being clean, admirably
accoutred, well-disciplined and thoroughly instructed in
those formal niceties and watchful severities of guard

duty which are harder to teach to new soldiers than the minutiæ of the manual, or the perplexities of field evolutions, or the grim earnestness of fighting. The Colonel was appointed Major of New Orleans, with a suspicion of something handsome in addition to his pay; the regiment was put on provost duty in the city, instead of being sent into the malarious mud of Camp Parapet or the feverish trenches of Vicksburgh. Colburne's letters of those days are full of braggadocio about the splendid condition of the Tenth and the peculiar favor with which it was viewed by the commanding general. Doctor Ravenel, in his admiration for the young captain, unwisely published some of these complacent epistles, thereby eliciting retorts and taunts from the literary champions of rival regiments, the *esprit du corps* having already grown into a strong and touchy sentiment among the volunteer organizations.

In this new Capua, the only lap of luxury that our armies found during the war, Carter, a curious compound of hardihood and sybaritism, forgot that he wanted to be Hannibal, and that he had not yet fought his Cannæ. He gave himself up to lazy pleasures, and even allowed his officers to run to the same, in which they were not much discountenanced by the commanding general, whose grim, practical humor was perhaps gratified by the spectacle of freeborn mudsills dwelling in the palaces and emptying the wine-cellars of a rebellious aristocracy. If, indeed, an undesirable cub over-stepped some vague boundary, he found himself court-martialed and dismissed the service. But the mass of the regimental officers, being jealous in their light duties and not prominently obnoxious in character, were permitted to live in such circumstances of comfort as they chose to gather about them from the property of self-exiled secessionists. Thus the regiment went through the season : no battles, no marches, no privations, no exposures, no anxieties : not even any weakening loss from the perilous climate. That terrible guardian angel of the land, Yellow Jack, would not come to realize the fond predictions of the inhabitants and abolish the alien garrison as a similar seraph destroyed the host of Sennacherib.

"Don't you find it hot?" said a citizen to Captain Colburne. "You'll find it too much for you yet."

"Pshaw!" answered the defiant youth. "I've seen it hotter than this in Barataria with two feet of snow on the ground."

During the spring Colburn wrote several long letters to the Doctor, with his mind, you may believe, fixed more on Miss Ravenel than on his nominal correspondent. It was a case of moral strabismus, which like many a physical squint, was not without its beauty, and was even quite charming to the gaze of sentimental sympathy. It was a sly carom on the father, with the intention of pocketing the daughter, but done with a hand rendered so timorous by anxiety that the blows seemed to be struck at random. The Captain enjoyed this correspondence; at times he felt all by himself as if he were talking with the young lady; his hazel eyes sparkled and his clear cheeks flushed with the excitement of the imaginary interview; he dropped his pen and pushed up his wavy brown hair into careless tangles, as was his wont in gleesome conversation. But this happiness was not without its counterweight of trouble, so that there might be no failure of equilibrium in the moral balance of the universe. After Colburne had received two responses to his epistles, there ensued a silence which caused him many lugubrious misgivings. Were the Ravenels sick or dead? Had they gone to Canada or Europe to escape the jealous and exacting loyalty of New England? Were they offended at something which he had written? Was Lillie to be married to young Whitewood, or some other conveniently propinquitous admirer?

The truth is that the Doctor had obtained a permit from the government to go to New Orleans, and that the letter in which he informed Colburne of his plan had miscarried, as frequently happened to letters in those days of wide-spread confusion.   On a certain scorching day in June he knocked at the door of the neat little brick house which had been assigned to the Captain as his quarters.   It was opened by an officer in the uniform of a second-lieutenant, a man of remarkable presence, very dark and saturnine in visage, tall and broad-shouldered and huge chested, with the limbs of a Heenan and the ringing bass voice of a Susini. He informed the visitor that Captain Colburne was out, but insisted with an amicable boisterousness up-on his entering. He had an elaborate and ostentatious courtesy of manner which puzzled the Doctor, who could not decide whether he was a born and bred gentleman or a professional gambler.

"Nearly dinner time, sir," he said in a rolling deep tone like mellow thunder.   "The Captain will be in soon for that good and sufficient reason. You will dine with us, I hope. Give you some capital wine, sir, out of Mon-sieur Soulé's own *cave*. Take this oaken arm-chair, sir, and allow me to relieve you of your chapeau. What name, may I ask?—Ah! Doctor Ravenel.—My God, sir ! the Captain has a letter for you.   I saw it on his table a moment ago."

He commenced rummaging among papers and writing materials with an exhilaration of haste which caused Rav-enel to suspect that he had taken a bottle or so of the Soulé sherry.

"Here it is," he exclaimed with a smile of triumph and friendliness. "You had better take it while you see it. If you are a lawyer, sir, you are aware that possession is nine tenths of a title.   I beg pardon ; of course you are not a lawyer. Or have I the honor to address an L. L. D. ?"

"Merely an M. D.," observed Ravenel, and took his letter.

"A magnificent profession !" rejoined the sonorous lieu-tenant. "Most ancient and honorable profession. The

profession of Esculapius and Hippocrates.   The physician
is older than the lawyer, and more useful to humanity."

Ravenel looked at his letter and observed that it was
not post-marked nor sealed ; he opened it, and found that
it was from Colburne to himself—intended to go, no
doubt, by the next steamer.

"I hope it gives you good news from home, sir," observed the lieutenant in the most amicable manner.

The Doctor bowed and smiled assent as he put the letter in his pocket, not thinking it worth while to explain
matters to a gentleman who was so evidently muddled by
the Soulé vintages.   As his interlocutor rattled on he
looked about the room and admired the costly furniture
and tasteful ornaments.   There were two choice paintings
on the paneled walls, and a dozen or so of choice engravings.   The damask curtains edged with lace were superb,
and so were the damask coverings of the elaborately
carved oaken chairs and lounges.   The marble mantels
and table, and the extravagant tortoise-shell *tiroir*, were
loaded with Italian cameos, Parisian bronzes, Bohemian
glass-ware, Swiss wood-sculpture, and other varieties of
European gimcracks.   Against the wall in one corner
leaned four huge albums of photographs and engravings.
The Doctor thought that he had never before seen a house
in America decorated with such exquisite taste and lavish
expenditure.   He had not been in it before, and did not
know who was its proprietor.

"Elegant little box, sir," observed the lieutenant.   "It
belongs to a gentleman who is now a captain in the rebel
service.   He built and furnished it for his affinity, an actress whom he brought over from Paris, which disgusted
his wife, I understand.   Some women are devilish exacting, sir."

Here the humor of a satyr gleamed in his black eyes
and grinned under his black mustache.

"You will see her portrait (the affinity's—not the wife's)
all over the house, as she appeared in her various charac-

ters.   And here she is in her morning-gown, in her own
natural part of a plain, straight-forward affinity."

He pointed with another satyr-like grin to a large pho-
tograph representing the bust and face of a woman apparently twenty-eight or thirty years of age, who could not
have been handsome, but, judging by the air of life and
cleverness, might have been quite charming.

"Intelligent old girl, I should say, sir," continued the
cicerone, regardless of the Doctor's look of disgust ; "but
not precisely to my taste.   I like them more youthful and
innocent, with something of the down of girlhood's purity
about them.   What is your opinion, sir ?"

Thus bullied, the Doctor admitted that he entertained
much the same preferences, at the same time wishing
heartily in his soul that Colburne would arrive.

"We have devilish fine times here, sir," pursued the
other in his remorseless garrulity.   "We finished the rebel
captain's wine-cellar long ago, and are now living on old
Soulé's.   Emptied forty-six bottles of madeira and champagne yesterday.   Select party of loyal friends, sir, from
our own regiment, the bullissimo Tenth Barataria."

"Ah! you belong to the Tenth?" inquired the Doctor
with interest.

"Yes, sir.   Proud to own it, sir.   The best regiment in
either service.   Not that I enlisted in Barataria.   I had
the honor of being the first man to join it here.   I was in
the rebel service, sir, an unwilling victim, dragged as an
innocent sheep to the slaughter, and took a part much
against my inclinations in the defence of Fort Jackson. It
seemed to me, sir, that the day of judgment had come,
and the angel was blowing particular hell out of his
trumpet.   Those shells of Porter's killed men and buried
them at one rap.   My eyes stuck out so to watch for
them that they havn't got back into their proper place yet.
After the fleet forced the passage I was the first man to
raise the standard of revolt, and bid defiance to my officers.   I theu made the best time on record to New Or-

leans, and enlisted under the dear old flag of my country in Captain Colburne's company. I took a fancy to the captain at first sight. I saw that he was a born gentleman and a scholar, sir. I was first made sergeant for good conduct, obedience to orders, and knowledge of my business; and when the second-lieutenant of the company died of bilious fever I was promoted to the vacancy. Our colonel, sir, prefers gentlemen for officers. I am of an old Knickerbocker family, one of the aboriginal Peter Stuyvesant Knickerbockers, as you may infer from my name— Van Zandt, at your service, sir—Cornelius Van Zandt, second-lieutenant, Co. I, Tenth Regiment Barataria Volunteers. I am delighted to make your acquaintance. and hope to see much of you."

I hope not, thought the Doctor with a shudder; but he bowed, smiled, and continued to wait for Colburne.

"Hope to have the pleasure of receiving you here often," Van Zandt went on. "Always give you a decent bottle of wine. When the Soulé *cave* gives out, there are others to be had for the asking. By the way—I beg a thousand pardons—allow me to offer you a bumper of madeira. You refuse! Then, sir, permit me the pleasure of drinking your health."

He drank it in a silver goblet, holding as much as a tumbler, to the astonishment if not to the horror of the temperate Doctor.

"I was remarking, I believe, sir," he resumed, "that I am a descendant of the venerable Knickerbockers. If you doubt it, I beg leave to refer you to Colonel Carter, who knew my family in New York. I am sensitive on the subject in all its bearings. I have a sort of feud, an ancestral vendetta, with Washington Irving on account of his Knickerbocker's History of New York. It casts an undeserved ridicule on the respectable race from which I am proud to trace my lineage. My old mother, sir—God bless her!—never could be induced to receive Washington Irving at her house. By the way, I was speaking of Colonel Carter, I think, sir. He's a judge of old blue blood, sir; comes of an ancient, true-blue cavalier strain himself; what you might call old Virginia particular. A splendid man, sir, a born gentleman, an officer to the back-bone, the best colonel in the service, and soon will be the best general. When he comes to show himself in field service, these militia-generals will have to take the back seats. I assume whatever responsibility there may be in predicting it, and I request you to mark my words. I am willing to back them with a fifty or so ; though don't understand me as being so impertinent as to offer you a bet—I am perfectly well aware of the respect due to your clerical profession, sir—I was only supposing that I might fall into conversation on the subject with a betting character. I feel bound to tell you how much I admire Captain Colburne, of whom I think I was speaking. He saw that I was a gentleman and a man of education. (By the way, did I tell you that I am a graduate of Columbia College ?) He saw that I was above my place in the ranks, and he started me on my career of promotion. I would go to the death for him, sir. He is a man, sir, that you can depend on. You know just where to find him. He is a man that you can tie to."

The Doctor looked gratified at this statement, and listened with visible interest.

" He would have died in the cause of total abstinence, but for Colonel Carter," continued Van Zandt. " The Colonel came in when he was at his lowest."

" Sick !" exclaimed the Doctor. " Has he been sick ?"

" Sick, sir ? Yes, sir ! Wofully broken up—slow bilious typhoid fever—and wouldn't drink, sir—conscientious against it. ' You *must* drink, by —— ! sir,' says the Colonel; ' you must drink and wear woollen shirts.' ' But,' says the Captain, ' if I drink and get well, my men will drink and go to hell.' By the way, those were not his exact words, sir. I am apt to put a little swearing into a story. It's like lemon in a punch. Don't you think so,

sir ?—Where was I ?   Oh, I remember.   ' How can I
punish my men,' says the Captain, ' for doing what I do
myself ?'   ' It's none of their dam business what you do,'
says the Colonel.   ' If they get drunk and neglect duty
thereby, it's your business to punish them.   And if you
neglect duty, it's my business to punish you.   But don't
suppose it is any affair of your men.   The idea is contrary
to the Regulations, sir.'   Those are the opinions of Colonel
Carter, sir, an officer, a gentleman and a philosopher.   Nothing but good old Otard brandy and woollen shirts
brought the Captain around—woollen shirts and good old
Otard brandy with the Soule seal on it.   He was dying of
bilious night-sweats, sir.   Horrible climate, this Louisiana.
But perhaps you are acquainted with it.   By the way, I
was speaking of Colonel Carter, I believe.   *He* knows how
to enjoy himself.   He keeps the finest house and most hospitable board in this city.   He has the prettiest little
French—*boudoir*—"

He was about to utter quite another word, but recollected himself in time to substitute the word *boudoir*,
while a saturnine twinkle in his eye showed that he felt
the humor of the misapplication.   Then, tickled with his
own wit, he followed up the idea on a broad grin.

" I am more envious of the Colonel's *boudoir*, sir, than
of his commission.   Nothing like a trim little French
boudoir for a bachelor.   You are a man of the world, sir,
and understand me."

And so on, prattling *ad nauseam*, meanwhile pouring
down the madeira.   The Doctor, who wanted to say, " Sir,
your goose has come for you," had never before listened
to such garrulity nor witnessed such thirst.   When Colburne entered, Van Zandt undertook to introduce the
two, although they met each other with extended hands
and friendly inquiries.   The Captain was somewhat embarrassed, knowing that his surroundings were of a nature
to rouse suspicion as to the perfect virtuousness of his life,
and thinking, perhaps in consequence of this knowledge,

that the Doctor surveyed him with an investigating expression. Presently he turned his eyes on Van Zandt; and, gently as they had been toned by nature, there was now a something in them which visibly sobered the bacchanalian; he rose to his feet, saluted as if he were still a private soldier, and left the room murmuring something about hurrying up dinner. The Doctor noticed with interest the authoritative demeanor which had usurped the place of the old New Boston innocence.

"And where is Miss Ravenel?" was of course one of the first questions.

"She is in the city," was the answer.

"Is it possible? (With a tremendous beating of the heart.)

"Yes. You may suppose that I could not get her to stay behind when it was a question of re-visiting New Orleans. She is as fierce a rebel as ever."

Colburne laughed, with the merest shadow of hysteria in his amusement, and, patriot as he was, felt that he hated Miss Ravenel none the worse for the announcement. There is a state of the affections in which every peculiarity of the loved object, no matter how offensive primarily or in itself, becomes an additional charm. People who really like cats like them all the better for their cattishness. A mother who dotes on a deformed child takes an interest in all lame children because they remind her of her own unfortunate.

"Besides, there was no one to leave her with in New Boston," continued the Doctor.

"Certainly," assented Colburne in a manifestly cheerful humor.

"But I am truly sorry to see you so thin and pale," the Doctor went on. "You are suffering from our horrible climate. You positively must be careful. Let me beg of you to avoid as much as possible going out in the night air."

Colburne could not help laughing outright at the recommendation.

"I dare say it's good advice," said he. "But when I am officer of the day I must make my rounds after midnight. It puts me in mind of the counsel which one of our Union officers who was in the siege of Vicksburg received from his mother. She told him that the air near the ground is always unhealthy, and urged him never to sleep lower than the third story. This to a man who lay on the ground without even a tent to cover him."

"War is a dreadful thing, even in its lesser details," observed the Doctor.

"What can I do for you?" asked Colburne after a moment's silence.

"I really don't know at present. Perhaps much. I have come here, of course, to get together the fragments of my property. I may be glad of some introductions to the military authorities."

"I will do my best for you. Colonel Carter can do more than I can. But, in the first place, you must dine with me."

"Thank you; no. I dine at five with a relation of mine."

"Dine twice, then. Dine with me first, for New Boston's sake. You positively must."

"Well, if you insist, I am delighted of course.—But what a city! I must break out with my amazement. Who could have believed that prosperous, gay, bragging New Orleans would come to such grief and poverty! I seem to have walked through Tyre and witnessed the fulfillment of the predictions of the prophets. I have been haunted all day by Ezekiel. Business gone, money gone, population gone. It is the hand of the Almighty, bringing to shame the counsels of wicked rulers and the predictions of lying seers. I ask no better proof than I have seen to-day that there is a Divine Ruler. I hope that the whole land will not have to pay as heavy a price as New Orleans to be quit of its compact with the devil. We are are all guilty to some extent. The North thought that it could make money out of slavery and yet evade the natural punishments of its naughty connivance. It thought that it could use the South as a catspaw to pull its chesnuts out of the fires of hell. It hoped to cheat the devil by doing its dirty business over the planter's shoulders. But he is a sharp dealer. He will have his bond or his pound of flesh. None of us ought to get off easily, and therefore I conclude that we shall not."

Now who would suppose that the Doctor had in his mind all the while a moral lecture to Colburne? Yet so it was: for this purpose had he gone back to Tyre and Babylon; with this object in view had he descanted on divine providence and the father of evil. It was his manner to reprove and warn persons whom he liked, but not bluntly nor directly. He touched them up gently, around the legs of other people, and over the shoulders of events which lost their personal interest to most human beings thousands of years ago. Please to notice how gradually, delicately, yet surely he descended upon Colburne through epochal spaces of time, and questions which involved the guilt and punishment of continents.

"Just look at this city," he continued, "merely in its character as a temptation to this army. Here is a chance for plunder and low dissipation such as most of your simply educated and innocent country lads of New England never before imagined. I have no doubt that there is spoil enough here to demoralize a corps of veterans. I don't believe that any thing can be more ruinous to a military force than free licence to enrich itself at the expense of a conquered enemy. There is nobody so needed here at this moment as John the Baptist. You remember that when the soldiers came unto him he exhorted them, among other things, to be content with their wages. I suppose the counsel was an echo of the military wisdom of his Roman rulers. The greatest blessing that could be vouchsafed this army would be to have John the Baptist crying night and day in this wilderness of temptation,

Be content with your wages! I have hardly been here forty-eight hours, and I have already heard stories of cotton speculations and sugar speculations, as they are slyly called, yes, and of speculations in plate, pictures, furniture, and even private clothing. It is sure disgrace and probable ruin. Please to understand that I am not pleading the cause of the traitors who have left their goods exposed to these peculations, but the cause of the army which is thus exposed to temptation. I want to see it subjected to the rules of honor and common sense. I want it protected from its opportunities."

The Doctor had not alluded to plundered wine-cellars, but Colburne's mind reverted to the forty-six emptied bottles of yesterday. John the Baptist had not made mention of this elegant little dwelling, but this convicted legionary glanced uneasily over its furniture and gimcracks. He had not hitherto thought that he was doing any thing irregular or immoral. In his opinion he was punishing rebellion by using the property of rebels for the good or the pleasure of loyal citizens. The subject had been presented to him in a new and disagreeable light, but he was too fair-minded and conscientious not to give it his instant and serious consideration. As for the forty-six bottles of wine, he might have stated, had he supposed it to be worth while, that he had drunk only a couple of glasses, and that he had quitted the orgie in disgust during its early stages.

"I dare say this is all wrong," he admitted. "Unquestionably, if any thing is confiscated, it should be for the direct and sole benefit of the government. There ought to be a system about it. If we occupy these houses we ought to receipt for the furniture and be responsible for it. I wonder that something of the sort is not done. But you must remember charitably how green most of us are, from the highest to the lowest, in regard to the laws of war, the rights of conquerors, the discipline of armies, and every

thing that pertains to a state of hostilities.   It is very
much as if the Quakers had taken to fighting."

"Oh, I don't say that I am right," answered the Doctor.
"I don't pretend to assert.   I only suggest."

"I am afraid there is occasion to offer apologies for my
Lieutenant," continued Colburne.

"A very singular man.   I should say eccentric," admitted the Doctor charitably.

"He annoys me a good deal, and yet he is a valuable
officer.   When he is drunk he is the drunkest man since
the discovery of alcohol.   He isn't drunk to-day.   You
have heard of three-bottle men.   Well, Van Zandt is something like a thirty bottle man.   I don't think he has had
above two quarts of sherry this morning.   I let him have
it to keep him from swallowing camphene or corrosive
sublimate.   But with all his drink he is one of the best
officers in the regiment, a good drill-master, a first-rate dis-
ciplinarian, and able to do army business.   He takes a
load of writing off my hands.   I never saw such a fellow
for returns and other official documents.   He turns them
off in a way that reminds you of those jugglers who
pull dozens of yards of paper out of their mouths.   He was
once a bank accountant, and he has seen five years in the
regular army.   That explains his facility with the pen and
the musket.   Then he speaks French and Spanish.   I believe he is a reprobate son of a very respectable New York
family."

This brief biography of Van Zandt furnished Ravenel
the text for a discourse on the dangers of intemperance,
illustrated by reminiscences of New Orleans society, and
culminating in the assertion that three-quarters of the
southern political leaders whom he remembered had died
drunkards.   The Doctor was more disposed than most
Anglo-Saxons towards monologue, and he had a mixture
of enthusiasm and humor which made people in general
listen to him patiently.   His present oration was interrupted by a mulatto lad who announced dinner.

The meal was elegantly cooked and served. Louisiana has inherited from its maternal France a delicate taste in convivial affairs, and the culinary artist of the occasion was he who had formerly ministered to the instructed appetites of the rebel captain and his Parisian affinity. To Colburne's mortification Van Zandt had paraded the rarest treasures of the Soulé wine-cellar; hermitage that could not have been bought then in New York for two dollars a bottle, and madeira that was worth three times as much; not to enlarge upon the champagne for the dessert, and the old Otard brandy for the *pousse-cafe*. He seemed to have got quite sober, as if by some miracle; or as if there was a fresh Van Zandt always ready to come on when one got over the bay; and he now recommenced to get himself drunk again *ab initio*. He governed his tongue, however, and behaved with good breeding. Evidently he was not only grateful to Colburne, but stood in professional awe of him as his superior officer. After dinner, still amazingly sober, although with ten or twenty dollars' worth of wine in him, he sat down to the piano, and thundered out some pretty-well executed arias from popular operas.

"Four o'clock!" exclaimed the Doctor. "I have just time to get home and see my daughter dine. Captain, we shall see you soon, I hope."

"Certainly. What is the earliest time that I can call without inconveniencing you?"

"Any time. This evening."

The Doctor bade Van Zandt a most amicable good afternoon, but did not ask him to accompany Colburne in the projected visit.

No sooner was he gone than the Captain turned upon the Lieutenant.

"Mr. Van Zandt, I must beg you to be extremely prudent in your language and conduct before that gentleman."

"By Jove!" roared Van Zandt, "it came near being

the cursedest mess.   I have had to pour down the juice of
the grape to keep from fainting."

"What is the matter?"

"Why, Parker brought his ——— cousin here this
morning. You've heard of the girl he calls his cousin?
She's in the smoking-room now. I've been so confoundedly
afraid you would show him the smoking-room! I've been
sweating with fright during the whole dinner, and all
the time looking as if every thing was lovely and the
goose hung high. She couldn't get out, you know; the
side entrance has never been unlocked yet—no key, you
know."

"What in Heaven's name did you let her in here for?"
demanded Colburne in a passion.

"Why—Parker, you see—I didn't like to insult Parker
by refusing him a favor. He only wanted to leave her
while he ran around to head-quarters to report something.
He swore by all his gods that he wouldn't be gone an
hour."

"Well, get her out. See that the coast is clear, and
then get her out. Tell her she must go. And hereafter,
if any of my brother officers want to leave their ———
cousins here, remember, sir, to put a veto on it."

The perspiration stood on his brow at the mere thought
of what might have been the Doctor's suspicions if he had
gone into the smoking-room. Van Zandt went about his
delicate errand with a very meek and sheepish grace.
When he had accomplished it, Colburne called him into
the sitting-room and held the following Catonian discourse.

"Mr. Van Zandt, I want you to take an inventory of
the furniture of the house and the contents of the wine-
cellar, so that when I leave here I can satisfy myself that
not a single article is missing. We shall leave soon. I
shall make application to-day to have my company quartered in the custom-house, or in tents in one of the
squares."

"Upon my honor, Captain!" remonstrated the dismayed Van Zandt, "I pledge you my word of honor that nothing of this kind shall happen again."

He cast a desperate glare around the luxurious rooms, and gave a mournful thought to the now forbidden paradise of the wine-cellar.

"And I give you mine to the same effect," answered the Captain. "The debauch of yesterday answers my purpose as a warning; and I mean to get out of temptation for my sake and yours. Besides, this is no way for soldiers to live. It is poor preparation for the field. More than half of our officers are in barracks or tents. I am as able and ought to be as willing to bear it as they. Make your preparations to leave here at the shortest notice, and meantime remember, if you please, the inventory. The company clerk can assist you."

Poor Van Zandt, who was a luxurious brute, able to endure any hardship, but equally able to revel in any sybaritism, set about his unwelcome task with a crest-fallen obedience. I do not wish to be understood, by the way, as insinuating that all or even many of our officers then stationed in New Orleans were given up to plunder and debauchery. I only wish to present an idea of the temptations of the place, and to show how our friend Colburne could resist them, with some aid from the Doctor, and perhaps more from Miss Ravenel.

As the Doctor walked homeward he put his hand into his pocket for a handkerchief to wipe his brow, and discovered a paper. It was Colburne's letter to him, and he read it through as he strolled onward.

"How singular!" he said. "He doesn't even mention that he has been sick. He is a noble fellow."

The Doctor was too fond of the young man to allow his faith in him to be easily shaken.

CHAPTER XI.

NEW ORLEANS LIFE AND NEW ORLEANS LADIES.

FROM these chapters all about men I return with pleasure to my young lady, rebel though she is. Before she had been twenty-four hours in New Orleans she discovered that it was by no means so delightful a place as of old, and she had become quite indignant at the federals, to whom she attributed all this gloom and desolation. Why not? Adam and Eve were well enough until the angel of the Lord drove them out of Paradise. The felon has no unusual troubles, so far as he can see, except those which are raised for him by the malignity of judges and the sheriff. Miss Ravenel was informed by the few citizens whom she met, that New Orleans was doing bravely until the United States Government illegally blocked up the river, and then piratically seized the city, frightening away its inhabitants and paralyzing its business and nullifying its prosperity. One old gentleman assured her that Farragut and Butler had behaved in the most unconstitutional manner. At all events somebody had spoiled the gayety of the place, and she was quite miserable and even pettish about it.

"Isn't it dreadful !" she said, bursting into tears as she threw herself into the arms of her aunt, Mrs. Larue, who, occupying the next house, had rushed in to receive the restored exile.

She had few sympathies with this relation, and never before felt a desire to overflow into her bosom; but any face which had been familiar to her in the happy by-gone times was a passport to her sympathies in this hour of affliction.

"C'est effrayant," replied Mrs. Larue. "But you are

out of fashion to weep. We have given over that feminine weakness, *ma chère.* That fountain is dry. The inhumanities of these Yankee Vandals have driven us into a despair too profound for tears. We do not flatter Beast Butler with a sob."

Although she talked so strongly she did not seem more than half in earnest. A half smile lurked around her lips of deep rose-color, and her bright, almond-shaped black eyes sparkled with interest rather than with passion. By the way, she was not a venerable personage, and not properly Lillie's aunt, but only the widow of the late Mrs. Ravenel's brother, not more than thirty-three years of age and still decidedly pretty. Her complexion was dark, pale and a little too thick, but it was relieved by the jet black of her regular eye-brows and of her masses of wavy hair. Her face was oval, her nose straight, her lips thin but nicely modeled, her chin little and dimpled; her expression was generally gay and coquettish, but amazingly variable and capable of running through a vast gamut of sentiments, including affection, melancholy and piety. Though short she was well built, with a deep, healthy chest, splendid arms and finely turned ankles. She did not strike a careless observer as handsome, but she bore close examination with advantage. The Doctor instinctively suspected her; did not think her a safe woman to have about, although he could allege no overtly wicked act against her; and had brought up Lillie to be shy of her society. Nevertheless it was impossible just now to keep her at a distance, for he would probably be much away from home, and it was necessary to leave his daughter with some one.

In politics, if not in other things, Mrs. Larue was as double-faced as Janus. To undoubted secessionists she talked bitterly, coarsely, scandalously against the northerners. If advisable she could go on about Picayune Butler, Beast Butler, Traitor Farragut, Vandal Yankees, wooden-nutmeg heroes, mudsills, nasty tinkers, nigger-worshippers, amalgamationists, &c. &c. from nine o'clock in the morning when she got up, till midnight when she went to bed. At the same time she could call in a quiet way on the mayor or the commanding General to wheedle protection out of them by playing her fine eyes and smiling and flattering. Knowing the bad social repute of the Ravenels as Unionists, she would not invite them into her own roomy house; but she was pleased to have them in their own dwelling next door, because they might at a pinch serve her as friends at the Butler court. On the principle of justice to Satan, I must say that she was no fair sample of the proud and stiff-necked slaveholding aristocracy of Louisiana. Neither was she one of the patriotic and puritan few who shared the Doctor's sympathies and principles. As she came of an old French Creole family, and her husband had been a lawyer of note and an ultra southern politician, she belonged, like the Ravenels, to the patrician order of New Orleans, only that she was counted among the Soulé set, while her relatives had gone over to the Barker faction. She had not been reduced to beggary by the advent of the Yankees; her estate was not in the now worthless investments of negroes, plantations, steamboats, or railroads, but in bank stock; and the New Orleans banks, though robbed of their specie by the flying Lovell, still made their paper pass and commanded a market for their shares. But Mrs. Larue was disturbed lest she might in some unforeseen manner follow the general rush to ruin; and thus, in respect to the Vandal invaders, she was at once a little timorous and a little savage.

The conversation between niece and youthful aunt was interrupted by a call from Mrs. and Miss Langdon, two stern, thin, pale ladies in black, without hoops, highly aristocratic and inexorably rebellious. They started when they saw the young lady; then recovered themselves and looked on her with unacquainted eyes. Miss Larue made haste, smiling inwardly, to introduce her cousin Miss Ravenel.

Ah, indeed, Miss Ravenel! They remembered having met Miss Ravenel formerly. But really they had not expected to see her in New Orleans. They supposed that she had taken up her residence at the north with her father.

Lillie trembled with mortification and colored with anger. She felt with a shock that sentence of social ostracism had been passed upon her because of her father's fidelity to the Union. Was this the reward that her love for her native city, her defence of Louisiana in the midst of Yankee-land, had deserved? Was she to be ignored, cut, satirized, because she was her father's daughter? She rebelled in spirit against such injustice and cruelty, and remained silent, simply expressing her feelings by a haughty bow. She disdained to enter upon any self-defence; she perceived that she could not, without passing judgment upon her much adored papa; and finally she knew that she was too tremulous to speak with good effect. The Langdons and Mrs. Larue proceeded to discuss affairs political; metaphorically tying Beast Butler to a flaming stake and performing a scalp dance around it, making a drinking cup of his skull, quaffing from it refreshing draughts of Yankee blood. Lillie remembered that, disagreeably loyal as the New Boston ladies were, she had not heard from their lips any such conversational atrocities. She did not sympathize much when Mrs. Langdon entered on a lyrical recital of her own wrongs and sorrows. She was sorry, indeed, to hear that young Fred Langdon had been killed at Fort Jackson; but then the mother expressed such a squaw-like fury for revenge as quite shocked and rather disgusted our heroine; and moreover she could not forget how coolly she had been treated merely because she was her dear father's daughter. She actually felt inclined to laugh satirically when the two visitors proceeded to relate jointly and with a species of solemn ferocity how they had that morning snubbed a Yankee officer.

G

"The brute got up and offered us his seat in the cars. I didn't look at him. Neither of us looked at him. I said —we both said—'We accept nothing from Yankees.' I remained—we both remained—standing."

Such was the mild substance of the narrative, but it was horrible in the telling, with fierce little hisses and glares, sticking out from it like quills of the fretful porcupine. Miss Ravenel did not sympathize with the conduct of the fair snubbers, and I fear also that she desired to make them feel uncomfortable.

"Really," she observed, "I think it was right civil in him to give up his seat. I didn't know that they were so polite. I thought they treated the citizens with all sorts of indignities."

To this the Langdons vouchsafed no reply except by rising and taking their departure.

"Good-day, Miss Ravenel," they said. "So surprised ever to have seen you in New Orleans again!"

Nor did they ask her to visit them, as they very urgently did Mrs. Larue. It seemed likely to Lillie that she would not find life in New Orleans so pleasant as she had expected. Half her old friends had disappeared, and the other half had turned to enemies. She was to be cut in the street, to be glared at in church, to be sneered at in the parlor, to be put on the defensive, to be obliged to fight for herself and her father. Her temper rose at the thought of such undeserved hardness, and she felt that if it continued long she should turn loyal for very spite.

Doctor Ravenel, returning from his interview with Colburne, met the Langdon ladies in the hall, and, although they hardly nodded, waited on them to the outer door with his habitual politeness. Lillie caught a glimpse of this from the parlor, and was infuriated by their incivility and his lack of resentment.

"Didn't they speak to you, papa?" she cried, running to him. "Then I would have let them find their own way out. What are you so patient for?"

"My dear, I am merely following the Christian example set me by these low Yankees whom we all hate so," said papa, smiling. "I have seen a couple of officers shamefully insulted to-day by a woman who calls herself a lady. They returned not a word, not even a look of retaliation."

"Yes, but—" replied Lillie, and after a moment's hesitation, concluded, "I wouldn't stand it."

"We must have some consideration, too, for people who have lost relatives, lost property, lost all, however their folly may have deserved punishment."

"Havn't *we* lost property?" snapped the young lady.

"Do you ask for the sake of argument, or for information?"

"Well—I should really like to know—yes, for information," said Lillie, deciding to give up the argument, which was likely to be perplexing to a person who had feelings on both sides.

"Our railroad property," stated the Doctor, "won't be worth much until it is recovered from the hands of the rebels."

"But that is nearly all our property."

"Except this house."

"Yes, except the house. But how are we to live in the house without money?"

"My dear, let us trust God to provide. I hope to be so guided as to discover something to do. I have found a friend to-day. Captain Colburne will be here this evening."

"Oh! will he?" said the young lady, blushing with pleasure.

It would be delightful to see any amicable visage in this city of enemies; and moreover she had never disputed that Captain Colburne, though a Yankee, was gentlemanly and agreeable; she had even admitted that he was handsome, though not so handsome as Colonel Carter. Mrs. Larue was also gratified at the prospect of a male visitor. As Sam Weller might have phrased it, had he known the lady, a man was Mrs. Larue's "particular wanity." The kitchen department of the Ravenels not being yet organized, they dined that day with their relative. The meal over, they went to their own house, Lillie to attend to housekeeping duties, and the Doctor to forget all trouble in a box of minerals. Lillie's last words to Mrs. Larue had been, "You must spend the evening with us. This Captain Colburne is right pleasant."

"Is he? We will bring him over to the right side. When he gives up the blue uniform for the grey I shall adore him."

"I don't think he will change his coat easily."

In her own house she continued to think of the Captain's coat, and then of another coat, the same in color, but with two rows of buttons.

"Who did you see out, papa?" she asked presently.

"Who did I see out? Mr. Colburne, as I told you."

"Nobody else, papa?"

"I don't recollect," he said absent-mindedly, as he settled himself to a microscopic contemplation of a bit of ore.

"Don't wrinkle up your forehead so. I wish you wouldn't. It makes you look old enough to have come over with Christopher Columbus."

It was a part of her adoration of her father that she could not bear to see in him the least symptoms of increasing age.

"I don't think that I saw a single old acquaintance," said the Doctor, rubbing his head thoughtfully. "It is astonishing how the high and mighty ones have disappeared from this city, where they used to suppose that they defied the civilized world. The barbarians didn't know what the civilized world could do to them. The conceited braggadocia of New Orleans a year ago is a most comical reminiscence now, in the midst of its speechless terror and submission. One can't help thinking of frogs sitting around their own puddle and trying to fill the universe with their roarings. Some urchin throws a stone into the puddle. You see fifty pairs of legs twinkle in the air, and the uproar is followed by silence. It was just so here. The United States pitched Farragut and Butler into the puddle of secession, and all our political roarers dived out of sight. Many of them are still here, but they keep their noses under water. By the way, I did see two of my old students, Bradley and John Akers. Bradley told me that the rebel authorities maintained a pretence of victory until the last moment, probably in order to keep the populace quiet while they got themselves and their property out of the city. He was actually reading an official bulletin stating that the Yankee fleet had been sunk in passing the forts when he heard the bang, bang, bang of Farragut's cannonade at Chalmette. Akers was himself at Chalmette. He says that the Hartford came slowly around the bend below the fort with a most provoking composure. They immediately opened on her with all their artillery. She made no reply and began to turn. They thought she was about to run away, and hurrahed lustily. Suddenly, whang! crash! she sent her whole broadside into them. Akers says that not a man of them waited for a second salute; they started for the woods in a body at full speed; he never saw such running. Their heels twinkled like the heels of the frog that I spoke of."

"But they made a good fight at the forts, papa."

"My dear, the devil makes a good fight against his Maker. But it is small credit to him—it only proves his amazing stupidity."

"Papa," said Lillie after a few minutes of silence, "I think you might let those stones alone and take me out to walk."

"To-morrow, my child. It is nearly sunset now, and Mr. Colburne may come early."

A quarter of an hour later he laid aside his minerals and picked up his hat.

"Where are you going?" demanded Lillie eagerly and almost pettishly. It was a question that she never failed

to put to him in that same semi-aggrieved tone every time
that he essayed to leave her.   She did not want him to go
out unless she went in his company.   If he would go, it
was, " When will you come back ?" and when he returned
it was, " Where have you been?" and " Who did you
see ?" and " What did he say ?" &c. &c.   Never was a
child so haunted by a pet sheep, or a handsome husband by
a plain wife, as was this charming papa by his doating
daughter.

" I am going to Dr. Elderkin's," said Ravenel.   " I hear
that he has been kind enough to store my electrical machine during our absence.   He was out when I called on
him this morning, but he was to be at home by six this
evening.   I am anxious to see the machine."

" Oh, papa, don't !   How can you be so addled about
your sciences !   You are just like a little boy come home
from a visit, and pulling over his playthings.   Do let the
machine go till to-morrow."

" My dear, consider how costly a plaything it is.   I
couldn't replace it for five hundred dollars."

" When will you come back ?" demanded Lillie.

" By half-past seven at the latest.   Bring in Mrs. Larue
to help entertain Captain Colburne ; and be sure to ask
him to wait for me."

When he quitted the house Lillie went to the window
and watched him until he was out of sight.   She always
had a childish aversion to being left alone, and solitude
was now particularly objectionable to her, so forsaken did
she feel in this city where she had once been so happy.
After a time she remembered Captain Colburne and the
social duties of a state of young ladyhood.   She hurried
to her room, lighted both gas-burners, turned their full
luminosity on the mirror, loosened up the flossy waves of
her blonde hair, tied on a pink ribbon-knot, and then a
blue one, considered gravely as to which was the most
becoming and finally took a profile view of the effect by
means of a hand-glass, prinking and turning and adjusting

her plumage like a canary. She was conscientiously aware, you perceive, of her obligation to put herself in suitable condition to please the eye of a visitor. She was not a learned woman, nor an unpleasantly strong-minded one, but an average young lady of good breeding—just such as most men fall in love with, who wanted social success, and depended for it upon pretty looks and pleasant ways. By the time that these private devoirs were accomplished Mrs. Larue entered, bearing marks of having given her person a similar amount of fastidious attention. Each of these ladies saw what the other had been about, but neither thought of being surprised or amused at it. To their minds such preparation was perfectly natural and womanly, and they would have deemed the absence of it a gross piece of untidiness and boorishness. Mrs. Larue put Lillie's blue ribbon-knot a little more off her forehead, and Lillie smoothed out an almost imperceptible wrinkle in Mrs. Larue's waist-belt. I am not positively sure, indeed, that waist-belts were then worn, but I am willing to take my oath that some small office of the kind was rendered.

Of course it would be agreeable to have a scene here between Colburne and Miss Ravenel; some burning words to tell, some thrilling looks to describe, such as might show how they stood with regard to each other—something which would visibly advance both these young persons' heart-histories. But they behaved in a disappointingly well-bred manner, and entirely refrained from turning their feelings wrong side outwards. With the exception of Miss Ravenel's inveterate blush and of a slightly unnatural rapidity of utterance in Captain Colburne, they met like a young lady and gentleman who were on excellent terms, and had not seen each other for a month or two. This is not the way that heroes and heroines meet on the boards or in some romances; but in actual human society they frequently balk our expectations in just this

manner. Melo-dramatically considered real life is frequent
ly a failure.

"You don't know how pleasant it is to me to meet you
and your father," said Colburne. "It seems like New Boston over again."

The time during which he had known the Ravenels at
New Boston was now a pasture of very delightful things
to his memory.

"It is pleasant to me because it seems like New Orleans," laughed Miss Lillie. "No, not much like New Orleans, either," she added. "It used to be so gay and
amusing ! You have made an awfully sad place of it
with your patriotic invasion."

"It is bad to take medicine," he replied. "But it is
better to take it than to stay sick. If you will have the
self-denial to live ten years longer, you will see New Orleans more prosperous and lively than ever."

" I shan't like it so well. We shall be nobodies. Our
old friends will be driven out, and there will be a new set
who won't know us."

"That depends on yourselves. They will be glad to
know you, if you will let them. I understand that the
Napoleonic aristocracy courts the old out-of-place oligarchy of the Faubourg St. Germain. It will be like that
here, I presume."

Mrs. Larue had at first remained silent, playing off a
pretty little game of shyness ; but seeing that the young
people had nothing special to say to each other, she gave
way to her sociable instincts and joined in the conversation.

"Captain Colburne, I will promise to live the ten years,"
she said. "I want to see New Orleans a metropolis. We
have failed. You shall succeed ; and I will admire your
success."

The patriotic young soldier looked frankly gratified. He.
concluded that the lady was one of the far-famed Unionists
of the South, a race then really about as extinct as the

dedo, but devoutly believed in by the sanguine masses of the North, and of which our officers at New Orleans were consequently much in search. He began to talk gaily, pushing his hair up as usual when in good spirits, and laughing heartily at the slightest approach to wit, whether made by himself or another. Some people thought that Mr. Colburne laughed too much for thorough good breeding.

"I feel quite weighted by what you expect," he said. "I want to go to work immediately and build a brick and plaster State-house like ours in New Boston. I suppose every metropolis must have a State-house. But you mustn't expect too much of me ; you mustn't watch me too close. I shall want to sleep occasionally in the ten years."

"We shall look to see you here from time to time," rejoined Mrs. Larue.

"You may be sure that I shan't forget that. There are other reasons for it besides my admiration for your loyal sentiments," said Colburne, attempting a double-shotted compliment, one projectile for each lady.

At that imputation of loyal sentiments Lillie could hardly restrain a laugh; but Mrs. Larue, not in the least disconcerted, bowed and smiled graciously.

"I am sorry to say," he continued, "that most of the ladies of New Orleans seem to regard us with a perfect hatred. When I pass them in the street they draw themselves aside in such a way that I look in the first attainable mirror to see if I have the small-pox. They are dreadfully sensitive to the presence of Yankees. They remind me of the catarrhal gentleman who sneezed every time an ice-cart drove by his house. Seriously they abuse us. I was dreadfully set down by a couple of women in black this morning. They entered a street car in which I was. There were several citizens present, but not one of them offered to give up his place. I rose and offered them mine. They no more took it than if they knew that I had scalped all their relatives. They surveyed me from head to foot with a lofty scorn which made them seem fifty feet high and fifty years old to my terrified optics. They hissed out, 'We accept nothing from Yankees,' and remained standing. The hiss would have done honor to Rachel or to the geese who saved Rome."

The two listeners laughed and exchanged a glance of comprehension.

" Offer them your hand and heart, and see if they won't accept something from a Yankee," said Mrs. Larue.

Colburne looked a trifle disconcerted, and because he did so Miss Ravenel blushed. In both these young persons there was a susceptibility, a promptness to take alarm with regard to hymenial subjects which indicated at least that they considered themselves old enough to marry each other or somebody, whether the event would ever happen or not.

" I suppose Miss Ravenel thinks I was served perfectly right," observed Colburne. " If I see her standing in a street car and offer her my seat, I suppose she will say something crushing."

He preferred, you see, to talk apropos of Miss Ravenel, rather than of Mrs. Larue or the Langdons.

" Please don't fail to try me," observed Lillie. " I hate to stand up unless it is to dance."

As Colburne had not been permitted to learn dancing in his younger days, and had felt ashamed to undertake it in what seemed to him his present fullness of years, he had nothing to say on the new idea suggested. The speech even made him feel a little uneasy : it sounded like an implication that Miss Ravenel preferred men who danced to men who did not: so fastidiously jealous and sensitive are people who are ever so slightly in love.

In this wandering and superficial way the conversation rippled along for nearly an hour. Colburne had been nonplussed from the beginning by not finding his young lady alone, and not being able therefore to say to her at least a few of the affecting things which were in the bottom of his heart. He had arrived at the house full of pleasant emotion, believing that he should certainly overflow with warm expressions of friendship if he did not absolutely pour forth a torrent of passionate affection. Mrs. Larue had dropped among his agreeable bubbles of expectation like a piece of ice into a goblet of champagne, taking the life and effervescence out of the generous fluid. He was occupied, not so much in talking or listening, as in cogitating how he could bring the conversation into congeniality with his own feelings. By the way, if he had found Miss Ravenel alone, I doubt whether he would have dared say any thing to her of a startling nature. He over-estimated her and was afraid of her; he under-estimated himself and was too modest.

Lillie had repeatedly wondered to herself why her father did not come. At last she looked at her watch and exclaimed with anxious astonishment, "Half past eight! Why, Victorine, where can papa be?"

"At Doctor Elderkin's without doubt. Once that two men commence on the politics they know not how to finish."

"I don't believe it," said the girl with the unreasonableness common to affectionate people when they are anxious about the person they like. "I don't believe he is staying there so long. I am afraid something has happened to him. He said he would certainly be back by half past seven. He relied on seeing Captain Colburne. I really am very anxious. The city is in such a dreadful state!"

"I will go and inquire for him," offered Colburne. "Where is Doctor Elderkin's?"

"Oh, my dear Captain! don't think of it," objected Mrs. Larue. "You, a federal officer, you would really be in danger in the streets at night, in this unguarded part of the city. You would certainly catch harm from our *canaille*. Re-assure yourself, cousin Lillie. Your father, a citizen, is in no peril."

Mrs. Larue really believed that the Doctor ran little

risk, but her main object in talking was to start an interest between herself and the young officer. He smiled at the idea of his being attacked, and, disregarding the aunt, looked to the niece for orders. Miss Ravenel thought that he hesitated through fear of the *canaille*, and gave him a glance of impatience bordering disagreeably close on anger. Smarting under the injustice of this look he said quietly, "I will bring you some news before long," inquired the way to the Elderkin house, and went out. At the first turning he came upon a man sitting on a flight of front-door steps, and wiping from his face with his handkerchief something which showed like blood in the gaslight.

"Is that you, Doctor?" he said. "Are you hurt? What has happened?"

"I have been struck.—Some blackguard struck me.—With a bludgeon, I think."

Colburne picked up his hat, aided in bandaging a cut on the forehead, and offered his arm.

"It does'nt look very bad, does it?" said Ravenel. "I thought not. My hat broke the force of the blow. But still it prostrated me. I am really very much obliged to you."

"Have you any idea who it was?"

"Not the least. Oh, it's only an ordinary New Orleans salutation. I knew I was in New Orleans when I was hit, just as the shipwrecked man knew he was in a Christian country when he saw a gallows."

"You take it very coolly, sir. You would make a good soldier."

"I belong in the city. It is one of our pretty ways to brain people by surprise. I never had it happen to me before, but I have always contemplated the possibility of it. I wasn't in the least astonished. How lucky I had on that deformity of civilization, a stiff beaver! I will wear nothing but beavers henceforward. I swear allegiance to them, as Baillie Jarvie did to guid braidcloth. A brass helmet would be still better. Somebody ought to get up a dress hat of aluminum for the New Orleans market."

" Oh, papa!" screamed Lillie, when she saw him enter on Colburne's arm, his hat smashed, his face pale, and a streak of half-wiped blood down the bridge of his nose. She was the whitest of the two, and needed the most attention for a minute. Mrs. Larue excited Colburne's admiration by the cool efficiency with which she exerted herself—bringing water, sponges and bandages, washing the cut, binding it up artistically, and finishing the treatment with a glass of sherry. Her late husband used to be brought home occasionally in similar condition, except that he took his sherry, and a great deal of it too, in advance.

" It was one of those detestable soldiers," exclaimed Lillie.

" No, my dear," said the Doctor. " It was one of our own excellent people. They are so ardent and impulsive, you know. They have the southern heart, always fired up. It was some old acquaintance, you may depend, although I did not recognize him. As he struck me he said, ' Take that, you Federal spy.' He added an epithet that I don't care to repeat, not believing that it applies to me. I think he would have renewed the attack but for the approach of some one, probably Captain Colburne. You owe him a word of thanks, Lillie, particularly after what you have said about soldiers."

The young lady held out her hand to the Captain with an impulse of gratitude and compunction. He took it, and could not resist the temptation of stooping and kissing it, whereupon her white face flushed instantaneously to a crimson. Mrs. Larue smiled knowingly and said, " That is *very* French, Captain; you will do admirably for New Orleans."

" He doesn't know all the pretty manners and customs of the place," remarked the Doctor, who was not evidently displeased at the kiss. " He hasn't yet learned to knock down elderly gentlemen because they disagree with him in politics. They are awfully behind-hand at the North, Mrs. Larue, in those social graces. The mudsill Sumner was too unpolished to think of clubbing the brains out of the gentleman Brooks. He boorishly undertook to settle a question of right and justice by argument."

"You must'nt talk so much, papa," urged Lillie. "You ought to go to bed."

Colburne bade them good evening, but on reaching the door stopped and said, "Do you feel safe here?"

Lillie looked grateful and wishful, as though she would have liked a guard; but the Doctor answered, "Oh, perfectly safe, as far as concerns that fellow. He ran off too much frightened to attempt any thing more at present. So much obliged to you!"

Nevertheless, a patrol of the Tenth Barataria did arrive in the vicinity of the Ravenel mansion during the night, and scoured the streets till daybreak, arresting every man who carried a cane and could not give a good account of himself. In a general way, New Orleans was a safer place in these times than it had been before since it was a village. I may as well say here that the perpetrator of this assault was not discovered, and that the adventure had no results except a day or two of headache to the Doctor, and a considerable progress in the conversion of Miss Ravenel from the doctrine of state sovereignty. Women, especially warm-hearted women offended in the persons of those whom they love, are so terribly illogical! If Mr. Secretary Seward, with all his constitutional lore and persuasive eloquence, had argued with her for three weeks, he could not have converted her; but the moment a southern ruffian knocked her father on the head, she began to see that secession was indefensible, and that the American Union ought to be preserved.

"It was a mere sporadic outbreak of our local light-heartedness," observed Ravenel, speaking of the outrage. "The man had no designs—no permanent malice. He merely took advantage of a charming opportunity. He saw a loyal head within reach of his bludgeon, and he instinctively made a clutch at it. The finest gentlemen of the city would have done as much under the same temptation."

CHAPTER XII.

COLONEL CARTER BEFRIENDS THE RAVENELS.

CAPTAIN COLBURNE indulged in a natural expectation that the kiss which he had laid on Miss Ravenel's hand would draw him nearer to her and render their relations more sentimentally sympathetic. He did not base his hopes, however, on the impression produced by the mere physical contact of the salute; he had such an exalted opinion of the young lady's spiritual purity that he never thought of believing that she could be influenced by any simply carnal impulses, however innocent; and furthermore he was himself in a too exalted and seraphic state of feeling to attach much importance to the mere motion of the blood and thrillings of the spinal marrow. But he did think, in an unreasoning, blindly longing way, that the fact of his having kissed her once was good reason for hoping that he might some day kiss her again, and be permitted to love her without exciting her anger, and possibly even gain the wondrous boon of being loved by her. Notwithstanding his practical New England education, and his individual sensitiveness at the idea of doing or so much as meditating any thing ridiculous, he drifted into certain reveries of conceivable interviews with the young lady, wherein she and he gradually and sweetly approximated until matrimony seemed to be the only natural conclusion. But the next time he called at the Ravenel house, he found Mrs. Larue there, and, what was worse, Colonel

Carter. Lillie remembered the kiss, to be sure, and
blushed at the sight of the giver; but she preserved her
self-possession in all other respects, and was evidently not
a charmed victim.   I think I am able to assure the reader
that in her head the osculation had given birth to no reveries.   It is true that for a moment it had startled her
greatly, and seemed to awaken in her some mighty and
mysterious influence.   But it is also true that she was half
angry at him for troubling her spiritual nature so po-
tently, and that on the whole he had not advanced himself a single step in her affections by his audacity.   If any
thing, she treated him with more reserve and kept him at
a greater distance than before.

Mrs. Larue did her best to make up for the indifference
of Lillie, and to reward Colburne, not so much for his
friendly offices of the evening previous, as for his other
and in her eyes much greater merits of being young and
handsome.   The best that the widow could offer, however,
was little to the Captain; indeed had she laid her heart,
hand and fortune at his feet he would only have been embarrassed by the unacceptable benificence; and he was
even somewhat alarmed at the dangerous glitter of her
eyes and freedom of her conversation.   It must be understood here that Madame's devotion to him, fervent as it
seemed, was not whole-hearted. She would have preferred
to harness the Colonel into her triumphal chariot, and had
only given up that idea after a series of ineffectual efforts.
Some men can be driven by a cunning hand through flirt-
ations which they do not enjoy, just as a spiritless horse
can be held down and touched up, to a creditable trot;
but Carter was not a nag to be managed in this way,
being too experienced and selfish, too willful by nature
and too much accustomed to domineer, to allow himself
to be guided by a jockey whom he did not fancy.   Could
she have got at him alone and often enough she might
perhaps have broken him in; for she knew of certain
secret methods of rareyizing gentlemen which hardly evei

fail upon persons of Carter's physical and moral nature;
but thus far she had found neither the time nor the juxtaposition necessary to a trial of her system. Accordingly
she had been obliged to admit, and make the best of, the
fact that he was resolved to do the most of his talking
with Miss Ravenel. Leave the two alone she could not,
according to New Orleans ideas of propriety, and so was
compelled for a time to play what might be called a foot-
man's part in conversation, standing behind and listening.
It was a pleasant relief from this experience to take the
ribbons in her own hands and drive the tractable though
reluctant Colburne. While the Colonel and Lillie talked
in the parlor, the Captain and Mrs. Larue held long dia-
logues in the balcony. He let her have the major part of
these conversations because she liked it, because he felt
no particular spirit for it, and because as a listener he could
glance oftener at Miss Ravenel. Although a younger
man than Carter and a handsomer one, he never thought
to outshine him, or, in common parlance, to cut him out;
holding him in too high respect as a superior officer, and
looking up to him also with that deference which most
homebred, unvitiated youth accord to mature worldlings.
The innocent country lad bows to the courtly roué because
he perceives his polish and does not suspect his corruption.
Captain Colburne and Miss Ravenel were similarly innocent and juvenile in their worshipful appreciation of
Colonel Carter. The only difference was that the former,
being a man, made no secret of his admiration, while the
latter, being a marriageable young lady, covered hers under a mask of playful raillery.

" Are you not ashamed," she said, " to let me catch you
tyrannizing over my native city ?"

" Don't mention it. Havn't the heart to go on much
longer. I'll resign the mayoralty to-day if you will accept it."

" Offer it to my father, and see if I don't accept for him."

This was a more audacious thrust than the young lady

was aware of. The idea of a civilian mayor was one that High Authority considered feasible, provided a citizen could be found who was loyal enough to deserve the post, and influential enough to pay for it by building up that so much-desired Union party.

"A good suggestion," said the Colonel. "I shall respectfully refer it to the distinguished consideration of the commanding general."

He entertained no such intention, the extras of his mayoralty being exceedingly important to him in view of the extent and costly nature of his present domestic establishment.

"Oh, don't !" answered Miss Ravenel.

"Why not? if you please."

"Because that would be bribing me to turn Yankee outright."

This brief passage in a long conversation suggested to Carter that it might be well for himself to procure some position or profitable employment for the out-of-work Doctor. If a man seems likely to appropriate your peaches, one of the best things that you can do is to offer him somebody else's apples. Moreover he actually felt a sincere and even strong interest in the worldly welfare of the Ravenels. By a little dexterous questioning he found that, not only was the Doctor's college bare of students, but that his railroad stock paid nothing, and that, in short, he had lost all his property except his house and some small bank deposits. Ravenel smilingly admitted that he had been justly punished for investing in any thing which bore even a geographical relation to the crime of slavery. He received with bewildered though courteously calm astonishment a proposition that he should try his hand at a sugar speculation.

"I beg pardon. I really don't understand," said he. "I am so unaccustomed to business transactions."

"Why, you buy the sugar for six cents a pound and sell it for twenty."

"Bless me, what a profit! Why don't business men take advantage of the opportunity?"

"Because they havn't the opportunity. Because it requires a permit from the powers that be to get the sugar."

"Oh! confiscated sugar. I comprehend. But I supposed that the Government—"

"You don't comprehend at all, my dear Doctor. Not confiscated sugar, but sugar that we can't confiscate—sugar beyond our reach—beyond the lines. You must understand that the rebels want quinine, salt, shoes, gold and lots of things. We want sugar and cotton. A barter is effected, and each party is benefited. I should call it a stupid arrangement and contrary to the laws of war, only that it is permitted by—by very high authority. At all events, it is very profitable and perfectly safe."

"You really astonish me," confessed the Doctor, whose looks expressed even more amazement than his language. "I should have considered such a trade nothing less than treasonable."

"I don't mean to say that it isn't. But I am willing to make allowances for the parties who engage in it, considering whose auspices they act under. As I was saying, the trade is contrary to the articles of war. It is giving aid and comfort to the enemy. But the powers that be, for unknown reasons which I am of course bound to respect, grant permits to certain persons to bring about these exchanges. I don't doubt that such a permit could be obtained for you. Will you accept it?"

"Would you accept it for yourself?" asked the Doctor.

"I am a United States officer," replied the Colonel, squaring his shoulders. "And a born Virginian gentleman," he was about to add, but checked himself.

By the way, it is remarkable how rarely this man spoke of his native State. It is likely enough that he had some remorse of conscience, or rather some qualms of sentiment, as to the choice which he had made in fighting against, instead of for, the Old Dominion. If he ever mentioned her name, it was simply to express his pleasure that he was not warring within her borders.   In other respects it would have been difficult to infer from his conversation that he was a southerner, or that he was conscious of being any thing but a graduate of West Point and an officer of the United States army.   But it was only in political matters that he was false to his birth-place.   In his strong passions, his capacity for domestic sympathies, his strange conscience (as sensitive on some points as callous on others), his spendthrift habits, his inclination to swearing and drinking, his mixture in short of gentility and barbarism, he was a true child of his class and State.   He was a Virginian in his vacillation previous to a decision, and in the vigor which he could exhibit after having once decided.   A Virginian gentleman is popularly supposed to be a combination of laziness and dignity.   But this is an error; the type would be considered a marvel of energy in some countries; and, as we have seen in this war, it is capable of amazing activity, audacity and perseverance. Of all the States which have fought against the Union Virginia has displayed the most formidable military qualities.

"And I am a United States citizen," said the Doctor, as firmly as the Colonel, though without squaring his shoulders or making any other physical assertion of lofty character.

"Very well.—You mean it, I suppose.—Of course you do.—You are quite right.   It isn't the correct thing, this trade, as a matter of course.   Still, knowing that it was allowed, and not knowing how you might feel about it, I thought I would offer you the chance.   It pays like piracy.   I have known a single smuggle to net forty thousand dollars, after paying hush money and every thing."

"Shocking !" said the Doctor.   "But you mustn't think that I am not obliged to you.   I really am grateful for your interest in my well-being.   Only I can't accept. Some men have virtue strong enough to survive such things ; but I fear that my character is of too low and feeble a standard."

"You are not offended, I hope," observed the Colonel after a thoughtful pause, during which he debated whether he should offer the Doctor the mayoralty, and decided in the negative.

"Not at all. I beg you to believe, not at all. But how is it possible that such transactions are not checked !" he exclaimed, recurring to his amazement. "The government ought to be informed of them."

"Who is to inform ? Not the barterers nor their abettors, I suppose. You don't expect that of these business fellows. You think perhaps that I ought to expose the thing. But in the army we obey orders without criticising our superiors publicly. Suppose I should inform, and find myself unable to prove any thing, and be dismissed the service."

The Doctor hung his head in virtuous discouragement, admitting to himself that this world is indeed an unsatisfactory planet.

"You may rely upon my secrecy concerning all this, Colonel," he said.

"I do so ; at least so far as regards your authority. As for the trade itself, I don't care how soon it is blown upon."

If the Colonel had been a quoter of poetry, which he was not, he would probably have repeated as he walked homeward "An honest man's the noblest work of God." What he did say to himself was, "By Jove ! I must get the Doctor a good thing of some sort."

Ten days later he called at the house with a second proposition which astonished Ravenel almost as much as the first.

"Miss Ravenel," he said, "you are a very influential person. Every body who knows you admits it. Mr. Colburne admits it. I admit it."

Lillie blushed with unusual heartiness and tried in vain

to think of some saucy answer. The Colonel's quizzical
smile, his free and easy compliments and confident address, sometimes touched the pride of the young lady, and
made her desire to rebel against him.

"I want you," he continued, "to persuade Doctor Ravenel to be a colonel."

"A colonel!" exclaimed father and daughter.

"Yes, and a better colonel than half those in the service."

"On which side, Colonel Carter?" asked Miss Ravenel,
who saw a small chance for vengeance.

"Good heavens! Do you suppose I am recruiting for
rebel regiments?"

"I didn't know but Mrs. Larue might have brought you
over."

The Colonel laughed obstreperously at the insinuation,
not in the least dashed by its pertness.

"No, it's a loyal regiment; black in the face with loyalty. General Butler has decided on organizing a force
out of the free colored population of the city."

"It isn't possible. Oh, what a shame!" exclaimed
Lillie.

The Doctor said nothing, but leaned forward with
marked interest.

"There is no secret about it," continued Carter. "The
thing is decided on, and will be made public immediately.
But it is a disagreeable affair to handle. It will make an
awful outcry, here and every where. It wouldn't be wise
to identify the Government too closely with it until it is
sure to be a success. Consequently the darkies will be enrolled as militia—State troops, you see—just as your rebel
friend Lovell, Miss Ravenel, enrolled them. Moreover, to
give the arrangement a further local character it is thought
best to have at least one of the regiments commanded by
some well known citizen of New Orleans. I proposed
this idea to the General, and he doesn't think badly of it.
Now who will sacrifice himself for his country? Who

will make the niggers in uniform respectable? Doctor,
will you do it?"

"Papa, you shall do no such thing," cried Lillie, thoroughly provoked. Then, reproachfully, "Oh, Colonel Carter!" The Colonel laughed with immovable good humor,
and surveyed her pretty wrath with calm admiration.

"Be quiet, my child," pronounced the Doctor with an
unusual tone of authority. "Colonel, I am interested,
exceedingly interested in what you tell me. The idea is
admirable. It will be a lasting honor to the man who conceived it."

"Oh, papa!" protested Lillie. She was slightly union-
ized, but not in the least abolitionized.

"I am delighted that General Butler has resolved to
take the responsibility of it," continued the Doctor. "Our
free negroes are really a respectable class. Many of them
are wealthy and well educated. In the whole south General Butler could not have found another so favorable a
place to try this experiment as New Orleans."

"I am glad you think so," answered the Colonel; but
he said it with an air of no great enthusiasm. In fact how
could an old army officer, a West Point military Brahmin
and a Virginian gentleman look with favor at first sight
on the plan of raising nigger regiments?

"But as for the colonelcy," continued the Doctor.
"Are you positively serious in making me that proposition?"

"Positively."

"Why, I am no more fit to be a Colonel than I am to
be a professor of Sanscrit and Chinese literature."

"That need'nt stand in the way at all. That is of no
consequence."

Ravenel laughed outright, and waited for an explanation.

"Your Lieutenant-Colonel and Major will be experienced
officers—that is, for volunteers," said Carter. "They will
know the drill, at any rate. Your part will be simply to

give the thing a local coloring, as if the New Orleans
people had got it up among themselves."

Here he burst into a horse-laugh at the idea of saddling
Louisianians with the imputation of desiring and raising
nigger soldiers for putting down the rebellion and slavery.

"You will have nothing to do with the regiment," he
went on. As soon as it is organized, or under way, you
will be detached. You will be superintendent of negro education, or superintendent of negro labor, or something of
that sort. You will have the rank and pay of Colonel,
you see; but your work will be civil instead of military;
it will be for the benefit of the niggers."

"Oh, indeed!" answered the Doctor, his face for the
first time showing that the proposition had for him a pole
of attraction. "So officers can be detached for such purposes? It is perfectly honorable, is it?"

"Quite so. Army custom. About the same thing as
making an officer a provost-marshal, or military governor,
or mayor."

"Really, I am vastly tempted. I am vastly flattered
and very grateful. I must think of it. I will consider it
seriously."

In his philanthropic excitement he rose and walked the
room for some minutes. The windows were open and admitted what little noise of population there was in the
street, so that Miss Ravenel and the Colonel, sitting near
each other, could exchange a few words without being
overheard by the abstracted Doctor. I suspect that the
young lady was more angry at this moment than on any
previous occasion recorded in the present history. Colburne would have quailed before her evident excitement,
but Colonel Carter, the widower, faced her with a smile of
good-natured amusement. Seeing that there was no prospect of striking a panic into the foe, she made a flanking
movement instead of a direct attack.

"What do you suppose the old army will think of the
negro regiment plan?"

" *Vin ordinaire*, I suppose."

" Then how can you advise my father to go into a thing which you call *vin ordinaire?*" she demanded, her lips trembling with an agitation which was partly anger, and partly alarm at her own audacity.

As this was a question which Carter could not answer satisfactorily without telling her that he knew how poor her father was, and also knew what a bad thing poverty was, he made no reply, but rose and sauntered about the room with his thumbs in his vest pockets. And Lillie was so curiously in awe of this mature man, who said what he pleased and was silent when he pleased, that she made no further assault on him.

" I must confess," said the Doctor, resuming his seat, " that this is a most attractive and flattering proposition. I am vain enough to believe that I could be of use to this poor, ignorant, brutish, down-trodden, insulted, plundered race of pariahs and helots. If I could organize negro labor in Louisiana on a basis just and profitable to all parties, I should consider myself more honored than by being made President of the United States in ordinary times. If I could be the means of educating their darkened minds and consciences to a decent degree of Christian intelligence and virtue, I would not exchange my good name for that of a Paul or an Apollos. My only objection to this present plan is the colonelcy. I should be in a false position. I should feel myself to be ridiculous. Not that it is ridiculous to be a colonel," he explained, smiling, " but to wear the uniform and receive the pay of a colonel without being one—there is the satire. Now could not that point be evaded? Could I not be made superintendent of negro labor without being burdened with the military dignity ? I really feel some conscientious scruples on the matter, quite aside from my desire not to appear absurd. I should be willing to do the work for less pay, provided I could escape the livery. I am sorry to give you any trouble when I am already under such obliga

H

tions. But would you have the kindness to inquire whether this superintendency could not be established without attaching to it the military position ?"

" Certainly. But I foresee a difficulty. Will the General dare to found such an office, and set aside public money for its salary ? I suppose he has no legal right to do it. Detach an officer for the purpose—that is all very simple and allowable ; it's army fashion. But when it comes to founding new civil offices, you trench upon State or Federal authority. Besides, this superintendency of negro labor is going to be a heavy thing, and the General may want to keep it directly under his own thumb, as he can do if the superintendent is an army officer. However, I will ask your question. And, if the civil office can be founded, you will accept it ; is it not so ?"

" I do accept. Most gratefully, most proudly."

" But how if the superintendency can't be had without the colonelcy ?"

" Why, then I—I fear I shall be forced to decline. I really don't feel that I can place myself in a false position. Only don't suppose that I am unconscious of my profound obligations to you."

" What an old trump of a Don Quixote !" mused the Colonel as he lit his segar in the street for the walk homeward. " It's devilish handsome conduct in him ; but, by Jove ! I don't believe the old fellow can afford it. I'm afraid it will be up-hill work for him to get a decent living in this wicked world, however he may succeed in the next."

A few minutes later a cold chill of worldly wisdom struck through his enthusiasm.

" He hasn't starved long enough to bring him to his milk," he thought. " When he gets down to his last dollar, and a thousand or two below it, he won't be so particular as to how he lines his pockets."

The Colonel almost felt that a civilian had no right to such a delicate and costly sense of honor. He would have

been rather glad to have the Doctor enter into some of
these schemes for getting money, inasmuch as this same
filthy lucre was all that Miss Ravenel needed to make her
a very-attractive *partie*. The next day he repaired at the
earliest office hours to head-quarters, and plead earnestly
to have the proposed superintendency founded on the basis of a civil office, the salary to be furnished by the State,
or by the city, or by a per-centage levied on the wages of
the negroes. But the Proconsul did not like to assume
such a responsibility, and moreover would not sympathise
with the Doctor's fastidiousness on the subject of the uniform. The Colonel hurried back to Ravenel and urged
him to accept the military appointment. He repeated to
him, " Remember, this is a matter of twenty-six hundred a
year," with a pertinacity which was the same as to say,
" You know that you cannot afford to refuse such a salary." The Doctor did not dispute the correctness of the
insinuation, but persisted with smiling obstinacy in declining the eagles. I am inclined to think that he was
somewhat unreasonable on the subject, and that the Colonel was not far from right in being secretly a little angry
with him. The latter did not care a straw for the niggers,
but he desired very earnestly to put the Ravenels on the
road to fortune, and he foresaw that a superintendent of
colored labor would infallibly be tempted by very considerable side earnings and perquisites. Even Miss Lillie
was rather disappointed at the failure of the project. To
arm negroes, to command a colored regiment, was aboli-
tionistic and abominable ; but to set the same negroes to
work on a hundred plantations, would be playing the
southerner, the planter, the sugar aristocrat, on a magnificent scale ; and she thought also that in this business her
father might do ever so much good, and make for himself
a noble name in Louisiana, by restoring thousands of run-
away field-hands to their lawful owners. Let us not be
too severe upon the barbarian beliefs of this civilized young
lady. She had not the same geographical reasons for lov-

ing human liberty in the abstract that we have who were
nurtured in the truly free and democratic North. Moreover, for some reason which I shall not trouble myself to
discover, all women love aristocracies.

The Ravenel funds were getting low, and the Doctor,
despairing of finding profitable occupation in depopulated
New Orleans, was thinking seriously of returning to New
Boston, when High Authority sent him an appointment as
superintendent of a city hospital, with a salary of fifteen
hundred dollars.

"I can do that," he said jubilantly as he showed the appointment to Carter, unaware that the latter had been the
means of obtaining it. "My medical education will come
in play there, and I shall feel that I am acting in my own
character. It will not be so grand a field of usefulness as
that which you so kindly offered me, but it will perhaps
approximate more nearly to my abilities."

"It is a captain's pay instead of a colonel's," laughed
Carter. "I don't know any body who would make such
a choice except you and young Colburne, who supposes
that he isn't fit to be a field officer. Some day head-quarters will perhaps be able to do better by you. When the
Western Railroad is recovered—the railroad in which you
hold property—there will be the superintendency of that,
probably a matter of some three or four thousand dollars
a year."

"But I couldn't do it," objected the Doctor, thereby
drawing another laugh from his interlocutor.

He was perfectly satisfied with his fifteen hundred,
although it was so miserably inferior to the annual six
thousand which he used to draw from his scientific labors
in and out of the defunct college. As long as he could
live and retain his self-respect, he was not much disposed
to grumble at Providence. Things in general were going
well; the rebellion would be put down; slavery would
perish in the struggle; truth and justice would prevail.
The certainty of these results formed in his estimation a

part of his personal estate—a wealth which was invisible, it is true, but none the less real, inexhaustible and consolatory—a wealth which was sufficient to enrich and ennoble every true-hearted American citizen.

When it was known throughout the city that he had accepted a position from the Federal authorities, the name of Ravenel became entirely hateful to those who only a few years before accorded it their friendship and respect. The hostile gulf between Lillie and her old friends yawned into such a vast abyss, that few words were ever exchanged across it; and even those that did occasionally reach her anxious ears had a tone of anger which excited, sometimes her grief, and sometimes her resentment. The young lady's character was such that the resentment steadily gained on the grief, and she became from day to day less of a Secessionist and more of a Unionist. Her father laughed in his good-natured way to see how spited she was by this social ostracism.

"You should never quarrel with a pig because he is a pig," said he. "The only wise way is not to suppose that you can make a lap-dog of him, and not to invite him into your parlor. These poor people have been brought up to hate and maltreat every body who does not agree with their opinions. If the Apostle Paul should come here, they would knock him on the head for making a brother of Onesimus."

"But I can't bear to be treated so," answered the vexed young lady. "I don't want to be knocked on the head, nor to have you knocked on the head. I don't even want them to think what they do about me. I wish I had the supreme power for a day or two."

"What progress!" observed the Doctor. "She wants to be General Butler."

"No I don't," snapped Lillie, whose nerves were indeed much worried by her internal struggles and outward trials. "But I would like to be emperor. I would actu-

ally enjoy forcing some of these horrid people to change
their style of talking."

" I don't think you would enjoy it, my dear. I did once
entertain the design of making myself autocrat, and deciding what should be believed by my fellow citizens, and
bringing to deserved punishment such as differed from
me.   It would be such a fine thing, I thought, to manage
in my own way, and manage right, all the religion, politics, business, education, and conscience of the country.
But I dropped the plan, after mature consideration, because I foresaw that it would give me more to do than I
could attend to."

Lillie, working at her embroidery, made no reply, not
apparently appreciating her father's wit.   Presently she
gave token that the current of her thoughts had changed,
by breaking out with her usual routine of questions.
" Who did you see in the streets ?   Didn't you see any
body ?   Didn't you hear any thing ?" etc. etc.

By what has been related in this chapter it will be perceived that Colonel Carter has established a claim to be
received with at least courtesy in the house of the Ravenels.   The Doctor could not decently turn a cold shoulder
to a man who had been so zealous a friend, although he
still admired him very little, and never willingly permitted
him a moment's unwatched intercourse with Lillie.   He
occasionally thought with disgust of Van Zandt's leering
insinuations concerning the little French boudoir ; but he
charitably concluded that he ought not to attach much
importance to the prattle of a man so clearly under the
influence of liquor as was that person at Colburne's quarters ; and finally he reflected with a sigh that the boudoir
business was awfully common in the world as then constituted, and that men who were engaged in it could not
well be ostracised from society.   So outwardly he was
civil to the Colonel, and inwardly sought to control his
almost instinctive repugnance.   As for Lillie, she positively
liked the widower, and thought him the finest gentleman

of the very few who now called on her.   Captain Colburne was very pleasant, lively and good ; but—and here
she ceased to reason—she felt that he was not magnetic.

———

CHAPTER XIII.

THE COURSE OF TRUE LOVE BEGINS TO RUN ROUGH.

In some Arabian Nights or other, there is a story of
voyagers in a becalmed ship who were drifted by irresistible currents towards an unknown island.   As they gazed
at it their eyes were deceived by an enchantment in the
atmosphere, so that they seemed to see upon the shore a
number of beautiful women waiting to welcome them,
whereas these expectant figures were really nothing but
hideous apes with carniverous appetites, whose desire it
was to devour the approaching strangers.

As Miss Ravenel drifted towards Colonel Carter she beheld him in the guise of a pure and noble creature, while
in truth he was a more than commonly demoralized man,
with potent capacities for injuring others.   Mrs. Larue, on
the other hand, perceived him much as he was, and liked
him none the less for it.   Had she lived in the days before
the flood she would not have cared specially for the angels
who came down to enjoy themselves with the daughters
of men, except just so far as they satisfied her vanity and
curiosity.   Seeing clearly that the Colonel was not a seraph, but a creature of far lower grade, very coarse and
carnal in some at least of his dispositions, she would still
have been pleased to have him fall in love with her, and
would perhaps have accepted him as a husband.   It is probable that she did not have a suspicion of the glamour
which humbugged the innocent eyes of her youthful cousin.   But she did presently perceive that it would be Lillie, and not herself, who would receive Carter's offer of

marriage, if it was ever made to either. How should she
behave under these trying circumstances? Painful as the
discovery may have been to her vanity, it had little effect
on a temper so callously amiable, and none on the lucid
wisdom of a spirit so clarified by selfishness. She showed
that she was a person of good worldly sense, and of little
heart. She soon brought herself to encourage the Carter
flirtation, partly because she had a woman's passion for
seeing such things move on, and partly for reasons of
state. If the Colonel married Lillie he would be a valuable friend at court; moreover the match could not hurt
the social position of her relatives, who were ostracised as
Yankees already; it would be all gain and no loss. She
soon discovered, as she thought, that there was no need
of blowing the Colonel's trumpet in the ears of Miss Lillie, and that the young lady could be easily brought to
greet him with a betrothal hymn of, " Hail to the chief who
in triumph advances." But the Doctor, who evidently did
not like the Colonel, might exercise a deleterious influence
on these fine chances. Madame Larue must try to lead
the silly old gentleman to take a reasonable look at his
own interests. What a paroxysm of vexation and contempt she would have gone into, had she known of his
refusal to make forty or fifty thousand dollars on sugar,
merely because the transaction might furnish the Confederate army with salt and quinine! Not being aware of this
act of cretinism, she went at him on the marriage business
with a hopeful spirit.

" What an admirable *parti* for some of our New Orleans
young ladies would be the Colonel Carter!"

The Doctor smiled and bowed his assent, because such
was his habit concerning all matters which were indifferent to him. The fact that he had lived twenty-five years
in New Orleans without ever being driven to fight a duel,
although disagreeing with its fiery population on various
touchy subjects, shows what an exquisite courtesy he must
have maintained in his manners and conversation.

"I must positively introduce him to Mees Langdon or Mees Dumas, and see what will come of it," pursued Madame.

Ravenel professed and looked his delight at the proposition, without caring a straw for the subject, being engaged in a charming mineralogical revery. Mrs. Larue perceived his indifference and was annoyed by it, but continued to smile with the Indian-like fortitude of a veteran worldling.

"He is of an excellent family—one of the best families of Virginia. He would be a suitable *parti* for any young lady of my acquaintance. There is no doubt that he has splendid prospects. He is almost the only regular officer in the department. Of course he will win promotion. I should not be surprised to see him supersede Picayune Butler. I beg your pardon—I mean Major-General Butler. I hear him so constantly called Picayune that I feel as if that was his name of baptism. Mark my prophecy now. In a year that man will be superseded by Colonel Carter."

"It might be a change for the better," admitted the Doctor with the composure of a Gallio.

"The Colonel has a large salary," continued Madame. "The mayoralty gives him three thousand, and his pay as colonel is two thousand six hundred. Five thousand six hundred dollars seems a monstrous salary in these days of poverty."

"It does, indeed," coincided the Doctor, remembering his own fifteen hundred, with a momentary dread that it would hardly keep him out of debt.

Mrs. Larue paused and considered whether she should venture further. She had already got as far as this two or three times without eliciting from her brother-in-law a word good or bad as to the matter which she had at heart. She had been like a boy who walks two miles to a pond, puts on his skates, looks at the thinly frozen surface, shakes his doubtful head, unbuckles his skates and trudges home

H2

again. She resolved to try the ice this time, at no matter what risk of breaking it.

"I have been thinking that he would not be a bad *parti* for my little cousin."

The Doctor laid aside his Robinsonites in some quiet corner of his mind, and devoted himself to the subject of the conversation, leaning forward and surveying Madame earnestly through his spectacles.

"I would almost rather bury her," he said in his excitement.

"You amaze me. There is a difference in age, I grant. But how little! He is still what we call a young man. And then marriages are so difficult to make up in these horrible times. Who else is there in all New Orleans?"

"I don't see why she should marry at all," said the Doctor very warmly. "Why can't she continue to live with me?"

"Positively you are not serious."

"I certainly am. I beg pardon for disagreeing with you, but I don't see why I shouldn't entertain the idea I mention."

"Oh! when it comes to that, there is no arguing. You step out of the bounds of reason into pure feeling and *egoïsme*. I also beg your pardon, but I must tell you that you are *egoïste*. To forbid a girl to marry is like forbidding a young man to engage in business, to work, to open his own *carrière*. A woman who must not love is defrauded of her best rights."

"Why can't she be satisfied with loving me?" demanded the Doctor. He knew that he was talking irrationally on this subject; but what he meant to say was, "I don't like Colonel Carter."

"Because that would leave her an unhappy, sickly old maid," retorted Madame. "Because that would leave you without grandchildren."

Ravenel rose and walked the room with a melancholy step and a countenance full of trouble. Suddenly he stopped short and turned upon Mrs. Larue a look of anxious inquiry.

"I hope you have not observed in Lillie any inclination towards this—this idea."

"Not the slightest," replied Madame, lying frankly, and without the slightest hesitation or confusion.

"And you have not broached it to her?"

"Never!" affirmed the lady solemnly, which was another whopper.

"I sincerely hope that you will not. Oblige me, I beg you, by promising that you will not."

"If such is your pleasure," sighed Madame. "Well—I promise."

"I am so much obliged to you," said the Doctor.

"I know that there is a difference in age," Mrs. Larue recommenced, thereby insinuating that that was the only objection to the match that she could imagine: but her brother-in-law solemnly shook his head, as if to say that he had other reasons for opposition compared with which this was a trifle: and so, after taking a sharp look at him, she judged it wise to drop the subject.

"I hope," concluded the Doctor, "that hereafter, when I am away, you will allow Lillie to receive calls in your house. There is a back passage. It is neither quite decorous to receive gentlemen alone here, nor to send them away."

Mrs. Larue made no objection to this plan, seeing that she could be just as strict or just as careless a duenna as she chose.

"I wonder why he has such an aversion to the match," she thought. Accustomed to see men matured in vice lead innocent young girls to the altar, habituated to look upon the notoriously pure-minded Doctor as a social curiosity rather than a social standard, she scarcely guessed, and could not realize, the repugnance with which such a father would resign a daughter to the doubtful protection of a husband chosen from the class known as men about town.

"Aurait il découvert," she continued to meditate; "ce petit liaison de monsieur le colonel? Il est vraiment curieux mon beau-frere; c'est plutôt une vierge qu'un homme."

I beg the reader not to do this clever lady the injustice to suppose that she kept or ever intended to keep her promise to the Doctor. To him, indeed, she did not for a long time speak of the proposed marriage, intending thereby to lull his suspicions to sleep, and thus prevent him from offering any timely opposition to that natural course of human events which might alone suffice to bring about the desired end. But into Lillie's ears she perpetually whispered pleasant things concerning Carter, besides leaving the two alone together for ten, fifteen, twenty minutes at a time, until Lillie would get alarmed at her unusual position, and become either nervously silent or nervously talkative. For these services the Colonel was not as grateful as he should have been. He was just the man to believe that he could make his own way in a love affair, and need not burden himself with a sense of obligation for any one's assistance. Moreover, valuing himself on his knowledge of life, he thought that he understood Mrs. Larue's character perfectly, and declared that he was not the man to be managed by such an intriguante, however knowing. He did in fact perceive that she was corrupt, and by the way he liked her none the worse for it, although he would not have married her. To Colburne he spoke of her gaily and conceitedly as "the Larue," or sometimes as "La rouée," for he knew French well enough to make an occasional bad pun in it. The Captain, on the other hand, never mentioned her except respectfully, feeling himself bound to treat any relative of Miss Ravenel with perfect courtesy.

But while Carter supposed that he comprehended the Larue, he walked in the path which she had traced out

for him.   From week to week he found it more agreeable
to be with Miss Ravenel.   Those random tête-a-têtes
which to her were so alarming, were to him so pleasant
that he caught himself anticipating them with anxiety.
The Colonel might have known from his past experience,
he might have known by only looking at his high-colored
face and powerful frame in a mirror, that it was not a safe
amusement for him to be so much with one charming lady.   Self-possessed in his demeanor, and, like most roués,
tolerably cool for a little distance below the surface of his
feelings, he was at bottom and by the decree of imperious
nature, very volcanic.   As we say of some fiery wines,
there was a great deal of body to him.   At this time he
was determined not to fall in love.   He remembered how
he had been infatuated in other days, and dreaded the return of the passionate dominion.   To use his own expression, " he made such a blasted fool of himself when he once
got after a woman !"

Nevertheless, he began to be, not jealous; he could not
admit that very soft impeachment ; but he began to want
to monopolize Miss Ravenel.   When he found Colburne in
her company he sometimes talked French to her, thereby
embarrassing and humiliating the Captain, who understood
nothing of the language except when he saw it in print,
and could trace out the meaning of some words by their
resemblance to Latin.   The young lady, either becaase she
felt for Colburne's awkward position, or because she did
not wish to be suspected of saying things which she
might not have dared utter in English, usually restored
the conversation to her mother tongue after a few sentences.   Once her manner in doing this was so pointed that
the Colonel apologized.

" I beg pardon, Captain," he said, to which he added a
white lie.   " I really supposed that you spoke French."

No ; Colburne did not speak French, nor any other modern language ; he did not draw, nor sing, nor play, and
was in short as destitute of accomplishments as are most

Americans.   He blushed at the Colonel's apology, which
mortified him more than the offence for which it was intended to atone.   He would have given all his Greek for
a smattering of Gallic, and he took a French teacher the
next morning.

Another annoyance to Colburne was Mrs. Larue.   He
was still so young in heart matters, or rather in coquetry,
that he was troubled by being made the object of airs of
affection which he could not reciprocate.   I do not mean
to say that the lady was in love with him ; she never had
been in love in her life, and was not going to begin at
thirty-three.   The plain, placid truth was, that she was
willing to flirt with him to please herself, and determined
to keep him away from Lillie in order to give every possible chance to Carter.   Only when Mrs. Larue said "flirt,"
she meant indescribable things, such as ladies may talk of
without reproach among themselves, but which, if introduced into print, are considered very improper reading.
Meantime neither Carter nor Colburne understood her, although the former would have hooted at the idea that he
did not comprehend the lady perfectly.

" By Jove !" soliloquized the knowing Colonel, " she is
sweeter on him than a pailful of syrup.   She puts one in
mind of a boa-constrictor.   She is licking him all over, preparatory to swallowing him.   Not a bad sort of serpent
to have around one, either," pursued the Colonel, almost
winking to himself, so knowing did he feel.   "Not a bad
sort of serpent.   Only I shouldn't care about marrying
her."

Indeed the Colonel reminds one a little of " devilish sly
old Joey Bagstock."

The innocent Colburne acknowledged to himself that he
did not comprehend Mrs. Larue nor her purposes.   He
would have inferred from her ways that she wanted him
for a husband, only that she spoke in a very cool way of
the matrimonial state.

" Marriage will not content me, nor will single life," she

said to him one day. "I have tried both, and I cannot recommend either. It is a choice between two evils, and one does not know to say which is the least."

Widows in search of second husbands do not talk publicly in this style, and Colburne intelligently concluded that he was not to be invited to the altar. At the same time Mrs. Larue went on in this way, she treated him to certain appetizing little movements, glances and words, which led him to suspect with some vague alarm that she did not mean to let him off as a mere acquaintance. Finally, as is supposed, an explanation ensued which was not to his liking. There was an interview of half an hour in a back parlor, brought about by the graceful manœuvres of the lady, of which Colburne steadily refused to reveal the secrets, although straitly questioned by the fun-loving Colonel.

"By Jove! he's been bluffing her," soliloquized Carter, who thought he perceived that from this private confabulation the parties came forth on terms of estrangement. "What a queer fellow he is! Suppose he didn't want to marry her—he might amuse himself. It would be pleasant to him, and wouldn't hurt her. Hanged if he isn't a curiosity!"

The next time that Colburne called on Miss Ravenel the Larue took her revenge for that mysterious defeat, the particulars of which I am unable to relate. To comprehend the nature and efficiency of this vengeance, it is necessary to take a dive into the recesses of New Orleans society. There is a geographical fable of civilized white negroes in the centre of Africa, somewhere near the Mountains of the Moon. This fable is realized in the Crescent City and in some of the richest planting districts of Louisiana, where you will find a class of colored people, who are not black people at all, having only the merest fraction of negro blood in their veins, and who are respectable in character, numbers of them wealthy, and some of them accomplished. These Creoles, as they call themselves, have been free for generations, and until Anglo-Saxon law invaded Louisiana, enjoyed the same rights as other citizens. They are good Catholics; they marry and are given in marriage; their sons are educated in Paris on a perfect level with young Frenchmen; their daughters receive the strict surveillance which is allotted to girls in most southern countries. In the street many of them are scarcely distinguishable from the unmixed descendants of the old French planters. But there is a social line of demarkation drawn about them, like the sanitary cordon about an infected district. The Anglo-Saxon race, the proudest race of modern times, does not marry nor consort with them, nor of late years does the pure French Creole, driven to join in this ostracism by the brute force of Henghist and Horsa prejudice. The New Orleanois who before the war should have treated these white colored people on terms of equality, would have shared in their opprobrium, and perhaps have been ridden on a rail by his outraged fellow-citizens of northern descent.

Now these white negroes from the Mountains of the Moon constituted the sole loyal class, except the slaves, which Butler found in Louisiana. They and their black cousins of the sixteenth degree were the only people who, as a body, came forward with joy to welcome the drums and tramplings of the New England Division; and when the commanding General called for regiments of free blacks to uphold the Stars and Stripes, he met a patriotic response as enthusiastic as that of Connecticut or Massachusetts. Foremost in this military uprising were two brothers of the name of Meurice, who poured out their wealth freely to meet those incidental expenses, never acknowledged by Government, which attend the recruiting of volunteer regiments. They gave dinners and presented flags; they advanced uniforms, sabres and pistols for officers; they trusted the families of private soldiers. The youngest Meurice became Major of one of the regiments, which I take to be the nearest approach to a miracle

ever yet enacted in the United States of America.
Their entertainments became so famous that invitations to
them were gratefully accepted by officers of Anglo-Saxon
organizations.   At their profuse yet elegant table, where
Brillât-Savarin would not have been annoyed by a badly
cooked dish or an inferior wine, and where he might have
listened to the accents of his own Parisian, Colburne had
met New Englanders, New Yorkers, and even stray Ma-
rylanders and Kentuckians.   There he became acquainted
(ignorant Baratarian that he was!) with the *tasse de cafe
noir* and the *petit verre de cognac* which close a French
dinner.   There he smoked cigars which gave him new
ideas concerning the value of Cuba.   For these pleasures
he was now to suffer at the Caucasian hands of Madame
Larue.

"I am afraid that we are doomed to lose you, Captain
Colburne," she said with a smile which expressed some-
thing worse than good-natured raillery.   "I hear that you
have made some fascinating acquaintances in New Orleans.
I never myself had the pleasure of knowing the Meurices.
They are very charming, are they not?"

Colburne's nerves quivered under this speech, not because he was conscious of having done any thing unbecoming a gentleman, but because he divined the clever
malice of the attack.   To gentle spirits the consciousness
that they are the objects of spite, is a dolorous sensation.

"It is a very pleasant and intelligent family," he replied
bravely.

"Who are they?" smilingly asked Miss Ravenel, who
inferred from her aunt's manner that Colburne was to be
charged with a flirtation.

"Ce sont des métis, ma chère," laughed Mrs. Larue.
"Il y a diné plusieurs fois.   Ces abolitionistes oût leur
gonts a eux."

Lillie colored crimson with amazement, with horror,
with downright anger.   To this New Orleans born Anglo-

Saxon girl, full of the pride of lineage and the prejudices of
the slaveholding society in which she had been nurtured,
it seemed a downright insult that a gentleman who called
on her, should also call on a *metis*, and admit it and defend
it. She glanced at Colburne to see if he had a word to
offer of apology or explanation. It might be that he had
visited these mixed bloods in the performance of some
disagreeable but unavoidable duty as an officer of the
Federal army. She hoped so, for she liked him too well to
be willing to despise him.

"Intelligent? But without doubt," assented Madame,
"if they had been stupid, you would not have dined with
them four or five times."

"Three times, to be exact, Mrs. Larue," said Colburne.
He had formed his line of battle, and could be not merely
defiant but ironically aggressive. But the lady was master
of the southern tactics; she had taken the initiative, and
she attacked audaciously; although, I must explain, without the slightest sign of irritation.

"Which do you find the most agreeable," she asked,
"the white people of New Orleans, or the brown?"

Colburne was tempted to reply that he did not see much
difference, but refrained on account of Miss Ravenel; and,
dropping satire, he entered on a calm defence, less of himself than of the mixed race in question. He affirmed their
intelligence, education, good breeding, respectability of
character, and exceptional patriotism in a community of
rebels.

"You, Mrs. Larue, think something of the elegancies of
society as an element of civilization," he said. "Now
then, I am obliged to confess that these people can give a
finer dinner, better selected, better cooked, better served,
than I ever saw in my own city of New Boston, notwithstanding that we are as white as they are and—can't speak
French. These Meurices, for example, have actually given
me new ideas of hospitality, as something which may be
plenteous without being coarse, and cordial without being

boreous. I don't hesitate to call them nice people. As for the African blood in their veins (if that is a reproach) I can't detect a trace of it. I shouldn't have believed it if they hadn't assured me of it. There is a little child there, a cousin, with blue eyes and straight flaxen hair. She has the honor, if it is one, of being whiter than I am."

It will be remembered here that any one who was whiter than Colburne was necessarily much whiter than Mrs. Larue.

"When I first saw the eldest Meurice," he proceeded, "I supposed from his looks that he was a German. The Major bears a striking resemblance to the first Napoleon, and is certainly one of the handsomest men that I have seen in New Orleans. His manners are charming, as I suppose they ought to be, seeing that he has lived in Paris since he was a child."

Mrs. Larue had never transgressed the borders of Louisiana.

"When this war broke out he came home to see if he might be permitted to fight for his race, and for his and my country. He now wears the same uniform that I do, and he is my superior officer."

"It is shameful," broke out Lillie.

"It is the will of authority," answered Colburne,—" of authority that I have sworn to respect."

"A southern gentleman would resign," said Mrs. Larue.

"A northern gentleman keeps his oath and stands by his flag," retorted Colburne.

Mrs. Larue paused, suppressed her rising excitement, and with an exterior air of meekness considered the situation. She had gained her battle; she had wounded and punished him; she had probably detached Lillie from him; now she would stop the conflict.

"I beg pardon," she said, looking him full in the eyes with a charming little expression of penitence. "I am sorry if I have annoyed you. I thought, I hoped, you might perhaps be obliged to me for hinting to you

that these people are not received here in society. You
are a stranger, and do not know our prejudices. I pray
you to excuse me if I have been officious."

Colburne was astonished, disarmed, ashamed, notwithstanding that he had been in the right and was the injured party.

"Mrs. Larue, I beg your pardon," he answered. "I
have been unnecessarily excited. I sincerely ask you pardon."

She accorded it in pleasant words and with the most
amiable of smiles. She was a good-natured, graceful little
grimalkin, she could be pretty and festive over a mouse
while torturing it; so purring and velvet-pawed, indeed,
that the mouse himself could not believe her to be in earnest, and prayed to be excused for turning upon her. It
is probable that, not being susceptible to keen emotions,
she did not know what deep pain she had given the young
man by her attack. The advantage which blasé people
have over innocents in a fight is awful. They know how
to hit, and they don't mind the punishing. It is said that
Deaf Burke's physiognomy was so calloused by frequent
poundings that he would permit any man to give him a
facer for a shilling a crack.

Lillie said almost nothing during the conversation, being quite overcome with amazement and anger at Colburne's degradation and at the wrongheadedness, the indelicacy, the fanaticism with which he defended it. When
the erring young man left the house she did not give him
her hand, after her usual friendly southern fashion. The
pride of race, the prejudices of her education, would not
permit her to be cordial, at least not in the first moments
of offence, with one who felt himself at liberty to go from
her parlor to that of an octoroon. How could a Miss
Ravenel put herself on a level with a Miss Meurice.

"Oh, these abolitionists! these negar worshippers!"
laughed Mrs. Larue, when the social heretic had taken
himself away. "Are they not horrible, these New Eng-

land isms ? He will be joining the vondoos next. I foresee
that you will have rivals, Mees Lillie. I fear that Made-
moiselle Meurice will carry the day. You are under the
disadvantage of being white. Et puis tu n'est pas
descendue d'une race bâtarde. Quel malheur ! Je ne dirais
rien s'il entretenait son octaronne à lui. Voilà qui est
permis, bien que ce n'est pas joli."

"Mrs. Larue, I wish you wouldn't talk to me in that
way ;—I don't like to hear it," said Lillie, in high anger.

"Mais c'est mieux au moins que de les épouser, les octa-
ronnes," persisted Madame.

Miss Ravenel rose and went to her own house and
room without answering. Since her father fled from New
Orleans, openly espousing the cause of the North against
the South, she had not been so vexed, so hurt, as she was
by this vulgar conduct of her friend, Captain Colburne.
Although it cannot be said that she had even begun to
love him, she certainly did like him better than any other
man that she ever knew, excepting her father and Colonel
Carter. She had thought, also, that he liked her too well
to do anything which would be sure to meet her disapprobation ; and her womanly pride was exceedingly hurt
in that her friendship had been risked for the sake of communion with a race of pariahs. There is little doubt that
Colburne now had small chance with Miss Ravenel. He
guessed as much, and the thought cut him even more
deeply that he could have imagined ; but he was too chivalrous to be false to his education, to his principles, to himself, though it were to gain the heart of the only woman
whom he had ever loved. In fact, so fastidious was his
sense of honor that he had disdained to fortify himself
against Mrs. Larue's attack by stating, as he might have
done truthfully, that at one of these Meurice dinners he
had sat by the side of Colonel Carter.

I consider it worth while to mention here that Colburne
committed a great mistake about this time in declining a
regiment which the eldest Meurice offered to raise for him,

providing he would apply for the colonelcy. But it was not for fear of Mrs. Larue nor yet of Miss Ravenel that he declined the proffer. He took the proposition into serious consideration and referred it to Carter, who advised him against it. Public opinion on this subject had not yet become so overpoweringly luminous that the old regular, the West Point Brahmin, could see the negro in a military light.

"I may be all wrong," he admitted with a considerable effusion of swearing. "If the war spins out it may prove me all wrong. A downright slaughtering match of three or four years will force one party or other to call in the nigger. But I can't come to it yet. I despise the low brute. I hate to see him in uniform. And then he never will be used for the higher military operations. If you take a command of niggers, you will find yourself put into Fort Pike or some such place, among the mosquitoes and fever and ague, where white men can't live. Or your regiment will be made road-builders, and scavengers, and baggage guards, to do the dirty work of white regiments. You never will form a line of battle, nor head a storming column, nor get any credit if you do. And finally, just look at the military position of these Louisiana black regiments. They are not acknowledged by the government yet; they are not a part of the army. They are only Louisiana militia, called out by General Butler on his own responsibility. Suppose the War Department shouldn't approve his policy;—then down goes your house. You have resigned your captaincy to get a sham colonelcy; and there you are, out of the service, with a bran-new uniform. Stay in the regiment. You shall have, by" (this and that!) "the first vacancy in the field positions."

In fact it was an *esprit du corps* which more than anything else induced Colburne to cling to the Tenth Barataria. A volunteer, a citizen soldier, new to the ways of armies, he longed to do his fighting under his own State flag, and at the head of the men whom he had himself raised and drilled for the battle-field.

About these times Colonel Carter broke up that more than questionable domestic establishment which Lieutenant Van Zandt had alluded to under the humorous misnomer of " a little French *boudoir.*" Whether this step was taken by the advice of Mrs. Larue, or solely because the Colonel had found some source of truer enjoyment, I am unable to say; but it is certain, and it is also a very natural human circumstance, that from this day his admiration for Miss Ravenel burgeoned rapidly into the condition of a passion.

CHAPTER XIV.

LILLIE CHOOSES FOR HERSELF.

LATE in that eventful summer of 1862, so bloody in Virginia and Kentucky, so comparatively peaceful in the malarious heats of Louisiana, the Colonel of the Tenth Barataria held a swearing soliloquy. In general when he swore it was at somebody or to somebody; but on the present occasion the performance was confined to the solitude of his own room and the gratification of his own ears; unless, indeed, we may venture to suppose that he had a guardian angel whose painful duty it was to attend him constantly. I suspect that I have not yet enabled the reader to realize how remarkable were the Colonel's gifts in the way of profanity; and I fear that I could not do it without penning three or four such astonishing pages as never were printed, unless it might be in the infernal regions. In the appropriate words of Lieutenant Van Zandt, who, by the way, honestly admired his superior officer for this and for his every other characteristic, " it was a nasty old swear."

Carter's quarters were a large brick house belonging to
a lately wealthy but now impoverished and exiled Secessionist. He had his office, his parlor, his private sitting-
room, his dining-room, his billiard-room, and five upper
bedrooms, besides the basement. His life corresponded
with his surroundings; his dinners were elegant, his wines
and segars superior. As it was now evening and his business hours long since over, he was in his sitting-room,
lounging in an easy chair, his feet on a table, a half-
smoked segar in one hand and an open letter in the other.
Only the Colonel or Lieutenant Van Zandt, or men equally
gifted in ardent expressions. could suitably describe the
heat of the weather. Although he wore nothing but his
shirt and pantaloons, his cheeks were deeply flushed, and
his forehead beaded with perspiration. The Louisiana
mosquitoes, a numerous and venomous people, were buzz-
ing in his ears, raising blotches on his face and perforat-
ing his linen. But it was not about them, it was about
the letter, that he was blaspheming. When the paroxysm
was over he restored the segar to his lips, discovered that
it was out, and relighted it; for he was old smoker enough
and healthy enough to prefer the pungency of a stump to
the milder flavor of a virgin weed. While he re-reads his
letter, we will venture to look over his shoulder.

" My dear Colonel," it ran, " I am sorry that I can give
you no better news. Waldo and I have worked like Tro-
jans, but without bringing anything to pass. You will
see by enclosed copy of application to the Secretary, that
we got a respectable crowd of Senators and Representatives
to join in demanding a step for you. The Secretary is all
right; he fully acknowledges your claims. But those
infernal bigots, the Sumner and Wilson crowd, got ahead
of us. They went to headquarters, civil and military. We
couldn't even secure your nomination, much less a senatorial majority for confirmation. These cursed fools mean
to purify the army, they say. They put McClellan's defeat
down to his pro-slavery sentiments, and Pope's defeat to

McClellan. They intend to turn out every moderate man, and shove in their own sort. They talk of making Banks head of the Army of the Potomac, in place of McClellan, who has just saved the capital and the nation. There never was such fanaticism since the Scotch ministers at Dunbar undertook to pray and preach down Cromwell's army. You are one of the men whom they have black-balled. They have got hold of the tail-end of some old plans of yours in the filibustering days, and are making the most of it to show that you are unfit to command a brig-ade in 'the army of the Lord.' They say you are not the man to march on with old John Brown's soul and hang Jeff. Davis on a sour apple-tree. I think you had better take measures to get rid of that filibustering ghost. I have another piece of advice to offer. Mere administrative ability in an office these fellows can't appreciate; but they can be dazzled by successful service in the field, because that is beyond their own cowardly possibilities; also be-cause it takes with their constituents, of whom they are the most respectful and obedient servants. So why not give up your mayoralty and go in for the autumn campaign? If you will send home your name with a victory attached to it, I think we can manufacture a a public opinion to compel your nomination and confirmation. Mind, I am not finding fault. I know that nothing can be done in Louisiana during the summer. But blockheads don't know this, and in politics we are forced to appeal to blockheads; our supreme court of decisions is, after all, the twenty millions of ignorami who do the voting. Accordingly, I advise you to please these twenty millions by putting your-self into the fall campaign.

" Very truly yours, &c."

" D———n it ! of course I mean to fight," muttered the Colonel, when he had finished his second reading. " I'll resign the mayoralty, and ask for active service and a brigade. Then I must write something to explain that filibustering business.—No, I won't. The less that is explained, the better. I'll deny it outright.—Now there's Weitzel. He, by " (this and that) " can have a star, and I can't. My junior, by " (that and the other) " in the service, by " (this and that) " by at least six years. What if he should get the active brigade ? It would be just him, by " (this and that) " to want it, and just like Butler, by " (that and the other) " to give it to him."

The Colonel sat for a long time in vexatious thought, slapping his mosquito bites, relighting his stump and smoking it down to its bitterest dregs. Finally, without having written a word, he gave up the battle with the stinging multitudes, drank a glass of brandy and water, turned off the gas, stepped into the adjoining bedroom, kicked off his trousers (long since unbuttoned), drew the mosquito-curtain, and went to bed as quickly and quietly as an infant. Soldiering habits had enabled him to court slumber with success under all circumstances.

During the month of September was formed that famous organization, composed of five regiments of infantry, with four squadrons and two batteries attached, known officially as the Reserve Brigade, but popularly as Weitzel's. It was intended from the first for active service, and the title Reserve was applied to it simply to mislead the enemy. The regiments were encamped for purposes of drill and preparation on the flats near Carrollton, a village four or five miles above New Orleans. Carter applied for the brigade, but was unable to obtain it. Weitzel was not only his superior in rank, but was Butler's favorite officer and most trusted military adviser. Then Carter threw up his mayoralty and reported for duty to his regiment, in great bitterness of spirit at finding himself obliged to serve under a man who had once been his junior and inferior. His only consolation was that this was not the worst; both he and Weitzel were under the orders of an attorney.

But he went to work vigorously at drilling, disciplining

and fitting out his regiment. His Sunday morning inspections were awful ordeals which lasted the whole forenoon. If a company showed three or four dirty men the Colonel sent for the Captain and gave him such a lecture as made him think seriously of tendering his resignation. When not on drill or guard duty the soldiers were busy nearly all day in brushing their uniforms, polishing their brasses and buttons, blacking their shoes and accoutrements, and washing their shirts, drawers, stockings, and even their canteen strings. The battalion drills of the Tenth were truly laborious gymnastic exercises, performed in great part on the double-quick. The sentinels did their whole duty, or were relieved and sent to the guardhouse. Corporals who failed to make their rounds properly were reduced to the ranks. Privates who forgot to salute an officer, or who did not do it in handsome style, were put in confinement on bread and water. The company cooking utensils were scoured every day, and the camp was as clean as bare, turfless earth could be. Carter was a hard-hearted, intelligent, conscientious, beneficent tyrant. The Tenth Barataria was the show regiment of the Reserve Brigade. I have not time to analyze the interesting feelings of freeborn Yankees under this searching despotism. I can only say that the soldiers hated their colonel because they feared him; that, like true Americans they profoundly respected him because, as they said, "he knew his biz;" that they were excessively proud of the superior drill and neatness to which he had brought them against their wills; and that, on the whole, they would not have exchanged him for any other regimental commander in the brigade. They firmly believed that under "Old Carter" they could whip the best regiment in the rebel service. It is true that there were exceptional ruffians who could not forget that they had been bucked and put in the stocks, and who muttered vindictive prophecies as to something desperate which they would do on the first field of battle.

"Bedad an' I'll not forget to pay me reshpecs to 'im,"

growled a Hibernian pugilist. "Let 'im get in front of the line, an I'll show 'im that I know how to fire to the right and left oblike."

Carter laughed contemptuously when informed of the bruiser's threat.

"It's not worth taking notice of," he said. "I know what he'll do when he comes under the enemy's fire. He'll blaze away straight before him as fast as he can load and pull trigger, he'll be in such a cursed hurry to kill the men who are trying to kill him. I couldn't probably make him fire right oblique, if I wanted to. You never have seen men in battle, Captain Colburne. It's really amusing to notice how eager and savage new troops are. The moment a man has discharged his piece he falls to loading as if his salvation depended on it. The moment he has loaded he fires just where he did the first time, whether he sees anything or not. And he'll keep doing this till you stop him. I am speaking of raw troops, you understand. The old cocks save their powder,—that is unless they get bedeviled with a panic. You must remember this when we ome to fight. Don't let your men get to blazing away at nothing and scaring themselves with their own noise, under the delusion that they are fiercely engaged."

During the month or more which the brigade passed at Carrollton Ravenel frequently visited Colburne, and did not forget to make an incidental call or two of civility on Colonel Carter. On two or three gala occasions he brought out Mrs. Larue and Miss Ravenel. They always came and went by the railroad, their present means not justifying a carriage. When the ladies appeared in camp the Colonel usually discovered the fact, and hastened to make himself master of the situation. He invited them under the marquee of his double tent, brought out store of confiscated Madeira, ordered the regimental band to play, sent word to the Lieutenant-Colonel to take charge of dress-parade, and escorted his visitors in front of the line to show them the exercises. In these high official hospitalities neither

Colburne nor any other company officer was invited to share. Even the lieutenant-colonel, the major, the first surgeon and the chaplain, though ranking as field and staff officers, kept at a respectful distance from the favored visitors and their awful host. For discipline's sake Carter lived in loftier state among these volunteers than he would have done in a regular regiment. Miss Ravenel was amused, but she was also considerably impressed, by the awe with which he was regarded by all who surrounded him. I believe that all women admire men who can make other men afraid.

"Are you as much scared at the general as your officers are at you?" she laughingly asked. "I wish I could see the general."

"I will bring him to your house," said Carter; but this was one of the promises that he did not keep. That gay speech of the young lady must have been a bitter dose to him, as we know who are aware of his professional disappointment.

The ladies were delighted to walk down the open ranks on inspection, and survey the neat packing of the double lines of unslung knapsacks.

"It is like going through a milliner's shop," said Lillie. "How nicely the things are folded! They really have a great deal of taste in arranging the colors. See, here is blue and red and grey, and then blue again, with a black cravat here and a white handkerchief there. It is like the backs of a row of books."

"Yes, this box knapsack is a good one for show," the Colonel admitted. "It is too large, however. When the men come to march they will find themselves overloaded. I shall have to make a final inspection and throw away a few tons of these extra-military gewgaws. What does a soldier want of black cravats and daguerreotypes and diaries and Testaments?"

"How cruelly practical you are!" said Lillie.

"Not in every thing," responded the Colonel with a sigh;

and for some reason the young lady blushed profoundly at the answer.

Of course these visits, the regiment, the Reserve Brigade, and its destination were matters of frequent conversation at the Ravenel dwelling. Through some leak of indiscretion or treachery it transpired that Weitzel was to oust Mouton from the country between the Mississippi and the Atchafalaya, where he was a constant menace to New Orleans. The whole city, rebel and loyal, argued and quarreled about the chances of success. The Secessionists were rampant ; they said that Mouton had fifteen thousand men ; they offered to bet their piles that he would have New Orleans back in a month. At every notable corner and in front of every popular drinking saloon were groups of tall, dark, fierce-looking men, carrying heavy canes, who glared at Union officers and muttered about coming Union defeats. Pale brunette ladies flouted their skirts scornfully at sight of Federal uniforms, and flounced out of omnibusses and street cars defiled by their presence. These feminine politicians never visited Miss Ravenel, however intimately they might have known her before the war ; and if they met her in the street they complimented her with the same look of hate which they vouchsafed to the flag of their country. With Madame Larue they were still on good terms, although they rarely called at her house for fear of encountering the Ravenels. This suited Madame's purposes precisely ; she could thereby be Federal at home and Secessionist abroad.

" You know, my dears," she would say to the female Langdons and Soulés, " that one cannot undo one's self of one's own relatives. That would be unreasonable. So I am obliged to receive the Doctor and his poor daughter at my house. But I understand perfectly that their society must be to you disagreeable. Therefore I absolve you, though with pain, from returning my visits. But, my dears, I shall only call on you the more often. Do not be surprised," she would sometimes add, " if you see a Fed-

eral uniform enter my door from time to time. I have my
objects. I flatter myself that I shall yet be of benefit to
the good cause."

And in fact she did occasionally send to a certain secret
junto scraps of information which she professed to have ex-
tracted from Union officers. This information was of no
value; it is even probable that much of it was a deliberate
figment of her imagination; but in this way she kept her
political odor sweet in the nostrils of the city Secessionists.

In secret she cared for little more than to be on the safe
side and keep her property. She laughed with delighted
malice at the Doctor's sarcasms upon the absurdities of
New Orleans politics, and the rottenness of New Orleans
morals. She sympathized with Lillie's youthful indignation at her own social proscription. She flattered Carter's
professional pride by predicting his success in the field.
She satirized Colburne behind his back, and praised him to
his face, for his Catonian principles. She was all things to
all men, and made herself generally agreeable.

Meantime Lillie had become what she called a Federalist;
for she was not yet so established in the faith as to style
it Loyalist or Patriot. What girl would not have been
thus converted, driven as she was from the mansion of
secession by its bitter inmates, and drawn towards the opposing house by her father and her two admirers? Colonel
Carter's visits were frequent and his influence strong and
increasing, notwithstanding the Doctor's warning tirades.
It made her uneasy, fretful and unhappy, to disagree with
her father; but on the subject of this preference she positively could not hold his opinions. He seemed to her to
be *so* unjust; she could not understand why he should be
so bitterly and groundlessly prejudiced; the reasons
which he hinted at glided off her like rain off a bird's
feathers. She granted no faith to the insinuation that the
Colonel was a bad man, nor, had she credited it, would she
have inferred therefrom that he would make a bad husband.
Let us not be astonished at the delusion of this intelligent

and pure-minded young lady.   I have witnessed more extraordinary assortments and choices than this.   I have
more than once seen an elegant, brilliant, highly-cultured
girl make an inexplicable and hungry snap at a man who
was stupidly, boorishly, viciously her inferior.   The subtle
and potent sense which draws the two sexes together is
an inexorable despot.

The Colonel was one of its victims, although not quite
bereft of reason.   Still, if he did not offer himself to Miss
Ravenel before going on this Lafourche expedition, it was
simply from considerations of worldly prudence, or, as he
phrased it to himself, out of regard to her happiness.   He
thought that his pay was insufficient to support her in the
style to which she had been accustomed, and in which he
wished his wife to live.   That he would be rejected he did
not much expect, being a veteran in love affairs, accustomed to conquer, and gifted by birthright with an audacious confidence.   Nor did he so much as suspect that he
was not good enough for her.   His moral perceptions, not
very keen perhaps by nature, had been still further calloused by thirty-five years of wandering in the wilderness
of sin.   Strange as it may seem to people of staid lives the
Colonel did not even consider himself a fast man.   He allowed that he drank; yes, that he sometimes drank more
than was good for him; but, as he laughingly said, he
never took more than his regulation quart a day; by
which he meant that, according to the army standard, he
was a temperate drinker.   As to gambling, that was a
gentleman's amusement, and moreover he had done very
little of it in the last year or two.   It was true that he
had had various ——; but then all men did that sort of
thing at times and under temptation; they did it more or
less openly, according as they were men of the world or
hypocrites; if they said they didn't, they lied.   The Colonel
did not grant the least faith to the story of Joseph, or, allowing it to be true, for the sake of argument, he considered Joseph no gentleman.   In short, after inspecting him-

self fairly and fully according to his lights, he concluded
that he was rather honorable even in his vices. Had he
not, for instance, entangled himself in that affair of the
French *boudoir* chiefly to get Miss Ravenel out of his head,
and so keep from leading her and himself into a poverty-
stricken marriage? Thus, though he was very frank with
himself, he still concluded that he was a tolerably good
fellow. Yes; and there were many other persons who
thought him good enough; men who knew his ways perfectly but could not see much matter of reproach in them.

In this state of opinion, and temper of feeling, the Colonel
approached his last interveiw with Miss Ravenel. He
meant to avoid the temptation of seeing her alone on this
occasion; but when Mrs. Larue told him that he should
have a private interview of half an hour he could not refuse the offer. It must not be supposed that Lillie was a
party to the conspiracy. Madame alone originated, planned,
and executed. She saw to it beforehand that the Doctor
should be invited out; she stopped Colburne on the door-
step with a message that the ladies were not at home;
lastly she slipped out of the parlor, dodged through the
back passage into the Ravenel house, and remained there
thirty minutes by the watch. It vexed this amiable creature a trifle that the Colonel should prefer Lillie; but
since he would be so foolish, she was determined that he
should make a marriage of it. Leaving her to these reflections as she walks the Doctor's studio, kicking his
minerals about the carpet with her little feet, or watching
at the window lest he should return unexpectedly, let us
go back to Miss Ravenel and her still undecided lover. It
was understood that the expedition was to sail the next
day, although Carter had not said so, not being a man to
tattle official secrets. When, therefore, he entered the
house that evening, she felt a vague dread of him, as if
half comprehending that the occasion might lead him to
say something decisive of her future. Carter on his part
knew that he would not be interrupted for a reasonable

12

number of minutes; and as Mrs. Larue left the room the sense of opportunity rushed upon him like a flood of temptation. He forgot in an instant that she was poor, that he was poor and extravagant, and that a marriage would be the maddest of follies, compared with which all his bygone extravagancies were acts of sedate wisdom. He was now what he always had been, and what people of strong passions very frequently are, the victim of chance and juxtaposition. He rose from the sofa where he had been sitting and worrying his cap, walked straight across the room with a firm step, like the resolute, irresistible advance of a veteran regiment, and took a chair beside her.

"Miss Ravenel," he said, and stopped. There was more profound feeling in his voice and face than we have yet seen him exhibit in this history; there was so much, and it was so electrical in its nature, at least as regarded her, that she trembled in body and spirit. "Miss Ravenel," he resumed, "I did intend to go to this battle without saying one word of love to you. But I cannot do it. You see I cannot do it."

Such a moment as this is one of the supreme moments of a woman's life. There is a fulfillment of hope which is thrillingly delicious; there is a demand, amounting to a decree, which involves her whole being, her whole future; there is a surprise,—it is always a surprise,—which is so sudden and great that it falls like a terror. A pure and loving girl who receives a first declaration of love from the man whom she has secretly chosen out of all men as the keeper of her heart is in a condition of soul which makes her womanhood all ecstacy. There is not a nerve in her brain, not a drop of blood in her body, which does not go delirious with the enthusiasm of the moment. She does not seem really to see, nor to hear, nor to speak, but only to feel that presence and those words, and her own reply; to feel them all by some new, miraculous sense, such as we are conscious of in dreams, when things are communicated to us and by us without touch or voice. It is a mere palpitation of feeling, yet full of utterances; a throbbing of happiness so acute and startling as to be almost pain. That man has no just comprehension of this moment, or is very unworthy of the power vested in his manhood, who can awaken such emotions merely for a passing pleasure, or blight them afterward by unfaithfulness and neglect. In one sense Carter was as noble as his triumph; he was not a good man, but he could love fervently. At the same time he was not timorous, but understood her although she did not answer. Precisely because she did not speak, because he saw that she could not speak, because he felt that no more speech was necessary, he took her hand and pressed it to his lips. The color which had left her skin came back to it and burned like a flame in her face and neck.

"May I write to you when I am away?" he asked.

She raised her eyes to his with an expression of loving gratitude which no words could utter. She tried to speak, but she could only whisper—

"Oh! I should be so happy."

"Then, my dear, my dearest one, remember that I am yours, and try to feel that you are mine."

I shall go no farther in the description of this interview.

CHAPTER XV.

LILLIE BIDS GOOD-BYE TO THE LOVER WHOM SHE HAS CHOSEN, AND TO THE LOVER WHOM SHE WOULD NOT CHOOSE.

Lillie left Mrs. Larue early, without a word as to the great event which had just changed the world for her, and retired to her own house and her own room. She was in a state of being, half stunned, half ecstatic; every faculty seemed to be suspended, except so far as it was

electrified to action by one idea; she sat by the window
with folded hands, motionless, seeing and hearing only
through her memory; she sought to recollect him as he
was when he took her hand and kissed it; she called to
mind all that he had said and looked and done. She
could not tell whether she had been thus occupied five
minutes or half an hour, when she heard the tinkle of the
door-bell, followed by her father's entrance. Then suddenly a great terror and sense of guilt fell upon her spirit.
From the moment when that confession of love had been
uttered down to this moment her mind had been occupied
by but one human being, and that was her lover. Now,
for the first time during the evening, she recollected that
the man of her choice was not the man of her father's
choice, but, more than almost any other person, the object
of his suspicion, if not of his aversion. Yet she loved
them both; she could not take sides with one against the
other; it would kill her to give up the affection of
either. All impulse, all passion, blood and brain as tremulous as quicksilver, she ran down stairs, opened the door
into the study where the doctor stood among his boxes,
wavered backward under a momentary throb of fear, then
sprang forward, threw her arms around his neck and
sobbed upon his shoulder,

"Oh, papa!—I am so happy!—so miserable!"

The doctor stared in astonishment and in some vague
alarm. Hardly aware of how much energy he used, he
detached her from him and held her out at arm's length,
looking anxiously at her for an explanation.

"Oh, don't push me away," begged Lillie, and struggled back to him, trying to hide her face against his
breast.

A suspicion of the truth fell across the Doctor, but he
strove to fling it from him as one dashes off a disagreeable
reptile. Still, he looked quite nervous and apprehensive
as he said, "What is it, my child?"

"Mr. Carter will tell you," she whispered; then, before he could speak, "Do love him for my sake."

He pushed her sobbing into a chair, and turned his back on her with a groan.

"Oh!—*That* man!—I can't—I won't."

He walked several times rapidly up and down the room, and then broke out again.

"I can *not* consent. I will *not* consent. It is *not* my duty. Oh, Lillie! how could you choose the very man of all that —! I tell you this must not be. It must stop here. I have *no* confidence in him. He will *not* make you happy. He will make you miserable. I tell you that you will regret the day that you marry him to the last moment of your life. My child," (persuasively) "you *must* believe me. You *must* trust my judgment. Will you not be persuaded? Will you not stop where you are?"

He ceased his walk and gazed eagerly at her, hoping for some affirmative sign. As may be supposed Lillie could not give it; she could make no very distinct signs just then, either one way or the other; she did not speak, nor look at him, nor shake her head, nor nod it; she only covered her face with her hands, and sobbed. Then the Doctor, feeling himself to be forsaken, and acknowledging it by outward dumb show, after the manner of men who are greatly moved, went to the other end of the room, sat down by himself and dropped his head into his hands, as if accepting utter loneliness in the world. Lillie gave him one glance in his acknowledged extremity of desertion, and, running to him, knelt at his feet and laid her head against his. She was certainly the most unhappy of the two, but her eagerness was even stronger than her misery.

"Oh papa! *why* do you hate him so?"

"I don't hate him. I dread him. I suspect him. I know he will not make you happy. I know he will make you miserable."

"But why?—*why?* Perhaps he can explain it. Tell

him what you think, papa.   I am sure he can explain every
thing."

But the Doctor only groaned, rose up, disentangled
himself from his daughter, and leaving her there on the
floor, continued his doleful walk.

Never having really feared what had come to pass, but
only given occasional thought to it as a possible though
improbable calamity, he had not inquired strictly into
Carter's manner of life, and so had nothing definite to allege against him.   At the same time he knew perfectly
well from trifling circumstances, incidental remarks, general air and bearing, that he was one of the class known in
the world as " men about town :" a class not only obnoxious to the Doctor's moral sentiments as the antipodes of
his own purity, but also as being a natural product of that
slaveholding system which he regarded as a compendium
of injustice and wickedness ; a class the members of which
were constantly coming to grief and bringing sorrow upon
those who held them in affection.   He knew them ; he had
watched and disliked them since his childhood ; he was
familiar by unpleasant observation with their language,
feelings, and doings ; he knew where they began, how they
went on, and in what sort they ended.   The calamities
which they wrought for themselves and all who were connected with them he had witnessed in a hundred similar,
and, so to speak, reflected instances.   He remembered
young Hammersley, who had sunk down in drunken paralysis and burned his feet to a crisp at his father's fire.
Young Ellicot had dashed out his brains by leaping from
a fourth story window in a fit of delirium tremens.   Tom
Akers was shot dead while drunk by a negro whom he had
horribly tortured.   Fred Sanderson beat his wife until she
left him, spent his property at bars and gaming-tables
and died in Cuba with Walker.   Others he recollected, by
the dozen, it seemed to him, who had fallen, wild with
whiskey, in grog-shop broils or savage street rencontres.
Those who lived to grow old had slave-born children, whom

they either shamelessly acknowledged, or more shamelessly
ignored, and perhaps sold at the auction-block. They were
drunkards, gamblers, adulterers, murderers.   Of such was
the kingdom of Hell.   And this man, to whom his only
child, his Lillie, had entrusted her heart, was, he feared,
he almost knew, one of that same class, although not, it
was to be hoped, so deeply stained with the brutish forms
of vice which flow directly from slavery.   He could not
entrust her to him; he could not accept him as a son.
At the same time he could not in this interview make any
distinct charges against his life and character. Accordingly
his talk was vague, incoherent, and sounded to Lillie like
the frettings of groundless prejudice.   The painful interview lasted above an hour, and, so far as concerned a decision, ended precisely where it began.

"Go to your bed, my child," the Doctor said at last.
"And go to sleep if you can.   You will cry yourself sick."

She gave him a silent kiss, wet with tears, and went
away with an aching heart and a wearied frame.

For two hours or more the Doctor continued his miserable walk up and down the study, from the door to the
window, from corner to corner, occasionally stopping to
rest a tired body which yet had no longing for slumber.
He went back over his daughter's life, beginning with the
infantile days when he used to send the servant away from
the cradle in which she lay, and rock it himself for the
pure pleasure of watching her.   He remembered how she
had expanded into the whole of his heart when her mother
died.   He thought how solely he had loved her since that
bereavement, and how her love for him had grown with
her growth and strengthened with every maturing power
of her spirit.   In the enthusiasm, the confidence of this
recollection, he did not doubt at moments but that he could
win her back to himself from this misplaced affection. She
was so young yet, her heart must be so pliable yet, that
he could surely influence her.   As this comforting hope
stole through him he felt a desire to look at her.   Yes, he

must see her again before he could get to sleep ; he would
go gently to her room and gaze at her without waking
her.   Putting on his slippers, he crept softly up stairs and
opened her door without noise.   By the light of a dying
candle he saw Lillie in her night dress, sitting up in bed
and wiping the tears from her cheeks with her hands.

"Papa !" she said in an eager gasp, tremulous with
affection, grief and hope.

"Oh, my child ! I thought you would be asleep," he
answered, advancing to the bedside.

"You are not very angry with me ?" she asked, making
him sit down by her.

"No ; not angry.   But so grieved !"

"Then may he not write to me ?"

She looked so loving, so eager, so sorrowful that he
could not say No.

"Yes ; he may write."

She drew his head towards her with her wet hands, and
gave him a kiss the very gratitude of which pained him.

"But not you," he added, trying to be stern.   "You
must not write.   You must not entangle yourself farther.
I want to make inquiries.   I must have time in this matter.   I will not be hurried.   You must not consider yourself engaged, Lillie.   I cannot allow it."

"Oh, you *will* inquire, papa ?" implored the girl, confident that Carter's character would come unharmed out
of the furnace of investigation.

"Yes, yes.   But give me time.   This is too important,
too solemn a matter to be hurried over.   I will see.   I will
decide hereafter.   There.   Now you must go to sleep.
Good night, my darling."

"Good night, dear papa," she murmured, with the sigh
of a tired child.   "Forgive me."

It was near morning before either of them slept ; and
both came to the breakfast table with pale, wearied faces.
There were dark circles around Lillie's eyes, and her
head ached so that she could hardly hold it up, but still

she put on a piteous, propitiating smile. She hoped and feared unreasonable things every time that her father spoke or seemed to her to be about to speak. She thought he might say that he had given up all his opposition ; and in the same breath she dreaded lest he might declare that it must be all over forever. But the conversation of the evening was not resumed, and the meal passed in absorbed, anxious, embarrassing silence, neither being able to talk on any subject but the one which filled their thoughts. An hour later Lillie suddenly fled from the parlor to her own room. She had seen Carter approaching the house ; she felt certain that he came to demand her of her father ; and at such an interview she could not have been present, she thought, without dying. The mere thought of it as she sat by her window, looking out without seeing anything, made her breath come so painfully that she wondered whether her lungs were not affected, and whether she were not destined to die early. Her fatigue, and still more her troubles, made her babyish, like an invalid. After half an hour had passed she heard the outer door close upon the visitor, and could not resist the temptation of peeping out to see him, if it were only his back. He was looking, with those handsome and audacious eyes of his straight at her window. With a sudden throb of alarm, or shame, or some other womanish emotion, she hid herself behind the curtain, only to look out again when he had disappeared, and to grieve lest she had given him offence. After a while her father called her, and she went down trembling to the parlor.

"I have seen him," said the Doctor. "I told him what I told you. I told him that I must wait,—that I wanted time for reflection. I gave him to understand that it must not be considered an engagement. At the same time I allowed him to write to you. God forgive me if I have done wrong. God pity us both."

Lillie did not think of asking if he had been civil to the Colonel ; she knew that he would not and could not be

discourteous to any human being. She made no answer
to what he said except by going gently to him and kissing
him.

"Come, you must dress yourself," he added. The regiment goes on board the transport at twelve o'clock. I
promised the Colonel that we would be there to bid him—
and Captain Colburne good-bye."

Dressing for the street was usually a long operation
with Lillie, but not this morning. Although she reached
the station of the Carrollton railroad in a breathless condition, it seemed to her that her father had never walked
so slowly; and on board the cars she really fatigued herself with the nervous tension of an involuntary mental
effort to push forward the wheezy engine.

Carrollton is one the suburban offshoots of New Orleans,
and contains some two thousand inhabitants, mostly of
the poorer classes, and of Germanic lineage. Around it
stretches the tame, rich, dead level which constitutes
southern Louisiana. The only raised ground is the levee;
the only grand feature of the landscape is the Mississippi;
all the rest is greenery, cypress groves, orange thickets,
flowers, or bare flatness. As Lillie emerged from the
brick and plaster railroad-station she saw the Tenth and
its companion regiments along the levee, the men sitting
down in their ranks and waiting patiently, after the manner of soldiers. The narrow open place between the river
and the dusty little suburb was thronged with citizens;—
German shopkeepers, silversmiths, &c., who were out of
custom, and Irish laborers who were out of work;—poor
women, (whose husbands were in the rebel army) selling
miserable cakes and beer to the enlisted men; all, white as
well as black, ragged, dirty, lounging, listless hopeless;
none of them hostile, at least not in manner; a discouraged, subduced, stricken population. Against the
bank were moored six steamboats, their smoke-stacks, and
even their upper decks, overlooking the low landscape.
They were not the famous floating palaces of the Mis-

ssisippi, those had all been carried away by Lovell, or burnt at the wharves, or sunk in battle near the forts; these were smaller craft, such as formerly brought cotton down the Red River, or threaded the shallows between Lake Pontchartrain and Mobile. They looked more fragile even than northern steamboats; their boilers and machinery were unenclosed, visible, neglected, ugly; the superstructure was a card-house of stanchions and clap-boards.

The Doctor led Lillie through the crowd to a pile of lumber which promised a view of the scene. As she mounted the humble lookout she caught sight of a manly equestrian figure, and heard a powerful bass voice thunder out a sentence of command. It was so guttural as to be incomprehensible to her; but in obedience to it the loung-ing soldiers sprang to their feet and resumed their ranks; the shining muskets rose straight from the shoulder, and then took a uniform slope; there was a bustle, a mo-mentary mingling, and she saw knapsacks instead of faces.

"Battalion!" the Colonel had commanded. "Shoul-der arms. Right shoulder shift arms. Right face."

He now spoke a few words to the adjutant, who re-peated the orders to the captains, and then signalled to the drum-major. To the sound of drum and fife the right com-pany, followed successively by the others from right to left, filed down the little slope with a regular, resounding tramp, and rapidly crowded one of the transports with blue uniforms and shining rifles. How superb in Lillie's eyes was the Colonel, though his face was grim and his voice harsh with arbitrary power. She liked him for his bronzed color, his monstrous mustache, his air of matured manhood; yes, how much better she liked him for being thirty-five years old than if he had been only twenty-five! How much prouder of him was she because she was a little afraid of him, than if he had seemed one whom she might govern! Presently a brilliant blush rose like a sunrise upon her countenance. Carter had caught sight of them, and was approaching.   A wave of his hand and a stare of his imperious eyes drove away the flock of negroes who had crowded their lookout.   The interview was short, and to a listener would have been uninteresting, unless he had known the sentimental relations of the parties.   The Doctor did nearly all of that part of the talking which was done in words; and his observations, if they were noted at all, probably seemed to the other two mere flatness and irrelevancy.   He prophecied success to the expedition; he wished the Colonel success for the sake of the good cause; finally he warmed so far as to wish him personal success and safety.   But what was even this to that other question of union or separation for life?

Presently the Adjutant approached with a salute, and reported that the transport would not accommodate the whole regiment.

" It must," said the Colonel.   " The men are not properly stowed.   I suppose they won't stow.   They hav'n't learned yet that they can't have a state-room apiece.   I well attend to it, Adjutant."

Turning to the Ravenels, he added, " I suppose I must bid you good-bye.   I shall have little more time to myself. I am so much obliged to you for coming to see us off. God bless you!   God bless you!"

When a man of the Colonel's nature utters this benediction seriously he is unquestionably much more moved than ordinarily.   Lillie felt this: not that she considered Carter wicked, but simply more masculine than most men: and she was so much shaken by his unusual emotion that she could hardly forbear bursting into tears in public. When he was gone she would have been glad to fly immediately, if only she could have found a place where she might be alone.   Then she had to compose herself to meet Colburne.

" The Colonel sent me to take care of you," he said, as he joined them.

" How good of him !" thought Lillie, meaning thereby Carter, and not the Captain.

" Will they all get on board this boat ?" she inquired.

" Yes. They are moving on now. The men of course hate to stow close, and it needed the Colonel to make then do it."

" It looks awfully crowded," she answered, searching the whole craft over for a glimpse of Carter.

The Doctor had little to say, and seemed quite sad; he was actually thinking how much easier he could have loved this one than the other. Colburne knew nothing of the great event of the previous evening, and so was not miserable about it. He hoped to send back to this girl such a good report of himself from the field of impending battle as should exact her admiration, and perhaps force her heart to salute him Imperator. He was elated and confident; boasted of the soldierly, determined look of the men; pointed out his own company with pride ; prophesied brilliant success. When at last he bade them good-bye he did it in a light, kindly brave way which was meant to cheer up Miss Ravenel under any possible cloud of foreboding.

" I won't say anything about being brought back on my shield. I won't ever promise that there shall be enough left to fill a table-spoon."

Yet the heart felt a pang of something like remorse for this counterfeit gayety of the lips.

The gangway plank was hauled in ; a few stragglers leaped aboard at the risk of a ducking; the regimental band on the upper deck struck up a national air; the negroes on shore danced and cackled and screamed with childish delight ; the noisy high-pressure engine began to sob and groan like a demon in pain,—the boat veered slowly into the stream and followed its consorts. Two gunboats and six transports steamed up the yellow river, trailing columns of black smoke athwart the blue sky, and away over the green levels of Louisiana.

Now came nearly a week of anxiety to Lillie and trouble to her father. She was with him as much as possible, partly because that was her old and loving habit, and partly because she wanted him continually at hand to comfort her. She was not satisfied with seeing him morning and evening; she must visit him at the hospitals, and go back and forth with him on the street cars; she must hear from him every half hour that there was no danger of evil tidings, as if he were a newspaper issued by extras; she must keep at him with questions that no man could answer.

"Papa, do you believe that Mouton has fifteen thousand men? Do you believe that there will be a great battle? Do you believe that our side" (she could call it *our* side now) "will be beaten? Do you believe that our loss will be very heavy? What is the usual proportion of killed in a battle? You don't know? Well, but what are the probabilities?"

If he took up a book or opened his cases of minerals, it was, "Oh, please don't read," or, "Please let those stones alone. I want you to talk to me. When do you suppose the battle will happen? When shall we get the first news? When shall we get the particulars?"

And so she kept questioning; she was enough to worry the life out of papa: but then he was accustomed to be thus worried. He was a most patient man, even in the bosom of his own family, which is not so common a trait as many persons suppose. One afternoon those sallow, black-eyed Hectors at the corners of the streets, who looked so much like gamblers and talked so much like traitors, had an air of elation which scared Miss Ravenel; and she accordinglp hurried home to receive a confirmation of her fears from Mrs. Larue, who had heard that there had been a great battle near Thibodeaux, that Weitzel had been defeated and that Mouton would certainly be in the city by next day afternoon. For an hour she was in an agony of unalleviated terror, for her comforter had not returned from the hospital. When he came she flew upon him and ravenously demanded consolation.

"My dear, you must not be so childish," remonstrated the Doctor. "You must have more nerve, or you won't last the year out."

"But what will become of you? If Mouton comes here you will be sacrificed—you and all the Union men. I wish you would take refuge on board some of the ships of war. Do go and see if they will take you. I shan't be hurt. I can get along."

Ravenel laughed.

"My dear, *have* you gone back to your babyhood? I don't believe this story at all. When the time comes I will look out for the safety of both of us."

"But do please go somewhere and see if you can't hear something."

And when the Doctor was thus driven to pick up his hat, she took hers also and accompanied him, not being able to wait for the news until his return. They could learn nothing; the journals had no bulletins out; the Union banker, Mr. Barker, had nothing to communicate; they looked wistfully at headquarters, but did not dare to intrude upon General Butler. As they went homeward the knots of well-dressed Catilines at the corners carried their treasonable heads as high and stared at Federal uniforms as insolently as ever. Ravenel thought sadly how much they resembled in air the well-descended gentleman to whom he feared that he should have to trust the happiness of his only child. Those of them who knew him did not speak nor bow, but glared at him as a Pawnee might glare at the captive hunter around whose stake he expected to dance on the morrow. Evidently his life would be in peril if Mouton should enter the city; but he was a sanguine, man and did not believe in the calamity.

Next morning, as the father set off for the hospital, the daughter said, "If you hear any thing, do come right straight and tell me."

Twenty minutes afterward Ravenel was back at the house, breathless and radiant. Weitzel had gained a victory; had taken cannon and hundreds of prisoners; was in full march on the rebel capital, Thibodeaux.

" Oh ! I am so happy !" cried the heretofore Secessionist. " But is there no list of killed and wounded? Has our loss been heavy? What do you think? What do you think are the probabilities? How strange that there should be no list of killed and wounded! Was that positively all that you heard? So little? Oh, papa, don't, please, go to the hospital to-day. I can't bear to stay alone.—Well, if you must go, I will go with you."

And go she did, but left him in half an hour after she got there, crazy to be near the bulletin boards. During the day she bought all the extras, and read four descriptions of the battle, all precisely alike, because copied from the same official bulletin, and all unsatisfactory because they did not contain lists of killed and wounded. But at the post-office, just before it closed, she was rewarded for that long day of wearying inquiries. There was a letter from Carter to herself, and another from Colburne to her father.

" My dear Lillie," began the first ; and here she paused to kiss the words, and wipe away the tears. " We have had a smart little fight, and whipped the enemy handsomely. Weitzel managed matters in a way that really does him great credit, and the results are one cannon, three hundred prisoners, possession of the killed and wounded, and of the field of battle. Our loss was trifling, and includes no one whom you know. Life and limb being now doubly valuable to me for your sake, I am happy to inform you that I did not get hurt. I am tired and have a great deal to do, so that I can only scratch you a line. But you must believe me, and I know that you will believe me, when I tell you that I have the heart to write you a dozen sheets instead of only a dozen sentences. Good bye, my dear one.

" Ever and altogether yours."

It was Lillie's first love letter; it was from a lover who had just come unharmed out of the perils of battle; it was a blinding, thrilling page to read. She would not let her father take it; no, that was not in the agreement at all; it was too sacred even for his eyes. But she read it to him, all but those words of endearment; all but those very words that to her were the most precious of all. In return he handed her Colburne's epistle, which was also brief.

"My dear Doctor,—I have had the greatest pleasure of my whole life; I have fought under the flag of my country, and seen it victorious. I have not time to write particulars, but you will of course get them in the papers. Our regiment behaved most nobly, our Colonel proved himself a hero, and our General a genius. We are encamped for the night on the field of battle, cold and hungry, but brimming over with pride and happiness. There may be another battle to-morrow, but be sure that we shall conquer. Our men were greenhorns yesterday, but they are veterans to-day, and will face any thing. Ask Miss Ravenel if she will not turn loyal for the sake of our gallant little army. It deserves even that compliment.

"Truly yours."

"He doesn't say that he is unhurt," observed the Doctor.

"Of course he is," answered Lillie, not willing to suppose for him the honor of a wound when her paragon had none. "Colonel Carter says that the loss includes no one whom we know."

"He is a noble fellow," pursued the Doctor, still dwelling on the young man's magnanimity in not thinking to speak of himself. "He is the most truly heroic, chivalrous gentleman that I know. He is one of nature's noblemen."

Lillie was piqued at these praises of Colburne, not considering him half so fine a character as Carter, in eulogy

K

of whom her father said nothing. She thought of asking him if he had noticed how the Captain spoke of the Colonel as a hero—but concluded not to do it, for fear he might reply that the latter ought to have paid the former the same compliment. She felt that for the present, until her father's prejudices should wear away, she must be contented with deifying her Achilles alone. Notwithstanding this pettish annoyance, grievous as it was to a most loving spirit strongly desirous of sympathy, the rest of the day passed delightfully, the time being divided between frequent readings of Carter's letter, and intervals of meditation thereon. The epistle which her father wrote to the Colonel was also thoroughly read, and was in fact so emendated and enlarged by her suggestions that it might be considered her composition.

CHAPTER XVI.

COLONEL CARTER GAINS ONE VICTORY, AND MISS RAVENEL ANOTHER.

AFTER the victory of Georgia Landing, the brigade was stationed for the winter in the vicinity of the little half-Creole, half-American city of Thibodeaux. I have not time to tell of the sacking of this land of rich plantations; how the inhabitants, by flying before the northern Vandals, induced the spoliation of their own property; how the negroes defiled and plundered the forsaken houses, and how the soldiers thereby justified themselves in plundering the negroes; how the furniture, plate and libraries of the Lafourche planters were thus scattered upon the winds of destruction. These things are matters of public and not of private history. If I were writing the life and times of Colonel Carter, or of Captain Colburne, I should relate them with conscientious tediousness, adding a description in the best style of modern word-painting of the winding and muddy Bayou Lafourche, the interminable parallel levees, the flat border of rich bottom land, the fields of moving cane, and the enclosing stretches of swampy forest. But I am simply writing a biography of Miss Ravenel, illustrated by skretches of her three or four relatives and intimates.

To reward Colonel Carter for his gallantry at Georgia Landing, and to compensate him for his disappointment in not obtaining the star of a brigadier, the commanding general appointed him military governor of Louisiana, and stationed him at New Orleans.

In his present temper and with his present intentions he was sincerely delighted to obtain the generous loot of the governorship. In order to save up money for his approaching married life, he tried to be economical, and actually thought that he was so, although he regularly spent the monthly two hundred and twenty-two dollars of his colonelcy. But the position of governor would give him several thousands a year, and these thousands he could and would put aside to comfort and adorn his future wife. Now-a-days there was no private and unwarrantable attachment to his housekeeping establishment; the pure love that was in his heart overthrew and drove out all the unclean spirits who were its enemies. Moreover, he rapidly cut down his drinking habits, first pruning off his cocktails before breakfast, then his absinthe before dinner, then his afternoon whiskeys straight, then his convivial evening punches, and in short everything but the hot night-cap with which he prepared himself for slumber.

"That may have to go, too," he said to himself, "when I am married."

He spent every spare moment with Lillie and her father. He was quite happy in his love-born sanctification of spirit, and showed it in his air, countenance and conversation. Man of the world as he was, or thought he was, *roué* as he had been, it never occurred to him to wonder at the

change which had come over him, nor to laugh at himself because of it. To a nature so simply passionate as
his, the present hour of passion was the only hour that he
could realize. He shortly came to feel as if he had never
lived any other life than this which he was living now.

The Doctor soon lost his keen distrust of Carter; he began to respect him, and consequently to like him. Indeed
he could not help being pleased with any tolerable person
who pleased his daughter; although he sometimes exhibited a petulant jealousy of such persons which was droll
enough, considering that he was only her father.

"Papa, I believe you would be severe on St. Cecilia, or
St. Ursula, if I should get intimate with them," Lillie had
once said. "I never had a particular friend since I was
a baby, but what you picked her to pieces."

And the Doctor had in reply looked a little indignant,
not perceiving the justice of the criticism. By the way,
Lillie had a similar jealousy of him, and was ready to
slander any single woman who ogled him too fondly.
There were moments of great anguish when she feared
that he might be inveigled into admiring, perhaps loving,
perhaps (horrid thought!) marrying, Mrs. Larue. If it
ever occurred to her that this would be a poetically just
retribution for her own sin of giving away her heart without asking his approval, she drew no resignation from the
thought. I may as well state here that the widow did occasionally make eyes at the Doctor. He was oldish, but
he was very charming, and any man is better than no man,
She had given up Carter; our friend Colburne was with
his regiment at Thibodeaux; and the male angels of New
Orleans were so few that their visits were far between.
So those half-shut, almond eyes of dewy blackness and
brightness were frequently turned sidelong upon Ravenel,
with a coquettish significance which made Lillie uneasy in
the innermost chambers of her filial affection. Mrs. Larue
had very remarkable eyes. They were the only features
of her face that were not under her control; they were so

expressive that she never could fully veil their meaning.
They were beautiful spiders, weaving quite visibly webs
of entanglement, the threads of which were rays of dazzling light and subtle sentiment.

" Devilish handsome eyes ! Dangerous, by Jove !" remarked the Colonel, judging in his usual confident, broad-
cast fashion, right rather more than half the time.   " I've
seen the day, by Jove ! when they would have finished
me."

For the present the Doctor was saved from their perilous
witchery by the advent of Colburne, who, having obtained
a leave of absence for ten days, came of course to spend
it with the Ravenels.   Immediately the Larue orbs kin-
dled for him, as if they were pyres whereon his passions, if
he chose, might consume themselves to ashes, She exhibited and felt no animosity on account of bygones.   She
was a most forgiving, cold-hearted, good-natured, selfish,
well-bred little creature.   She never had standing quarrels,
least of all with the other sex ; and she could practice a
marvellous perseverance, without any acrimony in case of
disappointment.   Colburne was favored with private interviews which he did not seek, and visions of conquest
which did not excite his ambition.   He was taken by gentle force up the intricate paths of a mountain of talk, and
shown the unsubstantial and turbulent kingdoms of coquetry, with a hint that all might be his if he would but fall
down and worship.   It became a question in his mind whether Milton should not have represented Satan as a female
of French extraction and New Orleans education.

" Captain Colburne, you do not like women," she once
said.

"I beg your pardon—I repel the horrible accusation."

" Oh, I admit that you like a woman—this one, perhaps,
or that one.   But it is the individual which interests you,
and not the sex.   For woman as woman—for woman because she is woman—you care little."

" Mrs. Larue, it is a very singular charge.   Now that

you have brought it to my notice, I don't know but I must
plead guilty, to some extent. You mean to say, I suppose,
that I can't or won't fall in love with the first woman I
come to, merely because she is handy."

"That is precisely it, only you have phrased it rather
grossly."

"And do you charge it as a fault in my character?"

"I avow that I do not regard it as so manly, so truly
masculine, you comprehend, as the opposite trait."

"Upon my honor!" exclaimed Colburne in amazement.
"Then you must consider,—I beg your pardon—but it
follows that Don Juan was a model man."

"In my opinion he was. Excuse my frankness. I am
older than you. I have seen much life. I have a right to
philosophise. Just see here. It is intended for wise reasons that man should not leave woman alone; that he
should seek after her constantly, and force himself upon
her; that, losing one, he should find another. Therefore
the man, who, losing one, chooses another, best represents
his sex."

She waited for a reply to her argument, but Colburne
was too much crushed to offer one. He shirked his honest
duty as an interlocutor by saying, "Mrs. Larue, this is a
novel idea to me, and I must have time for consideration
before I accept it."

She laughed without a sign of embarrassment, and
changed the subject.

But Mrs. Larue was not the only cause which prevented
Colburne's visit from being a monotony of happiness. He
soon discovered that there was an understanding between
Colonel Carter and Miss Ravenel; not an engagement,
perhaps, but certainly an inner circle of confidences and
sentiments into which he was not allowed to enter. In
this matter Lillie was more open and legible than her lover.
She so adored her hero because of the deadly perils which
he had affronted, and the honor which he had borne from
among their flame and smoke, that she could not always con-

ceal, and sometimes did not care to conceal, her admiration. Not that she ever expressed it by endearments or fondling words: no, that would have been a coarse audacity of which her maidenly nature was incapable: but there were rare glances ot irrepressible meaning, surprised out of her very soul, which came like revelations. When she asked Colburne to tell her the whole story of Georgia Landing, he guessed easily what she most wanted to hear. To please her, he made Carter the hero of the epic, related how impetuous he was during the charge, how superbly cool as soon as it was over, how he sat his horse and waved his sabre and gave his orders. To be sure, the enthusiastic youth took a soldierly pleasure in the history; he was honestly proud of his commander, and he loved to tell the tale of his own only battle. But notwithstanding this slight pleasure, notwithstanding that the Doctor treated him with even tender consideration, and that Mrs. Larue was often amusing as well as embarrassing, he did not enjoy his visit. This mysterious cloud which encompassed the Colonel and Miss Ravenel, separating them from all others, cast upon him a shadow of melancholy. In the first place, of course, it was painful to suspect that he had lost this charming girl; in the second, he grieved on her account, not believing it possible that with that man for a husband she could be permanently happy. Carter was a brave soldier, an able officer, a person of warm and naturally kind impulses; but gentlemen of such habits as his were not considered good matches where Colburne had formed his opinions. No man, whatever his talents, could win a professorship in Winslow University, or occupy a respectable niche in New Boston society, who rarely went to church, who drank freely and openly, who had been seen to gamble, who swore like a trooper, and who did other things which the Colonel had been known to do. All this time he was so over-modest by nature, and so oppressed by an acquired sense of soldierly subordination, that he never seriously thought of setting himself up as a rival against the Colonel. Perhaps I am tedious in my analysis of the Captain's opinions, motives and sentiments. The truth is that I take a sympathetic interest in him, believing him to be a representative young man of my native New England, and that I consider him a better match for Miss Ravenel than this southern "high-toned" gentleman whom she insists upon having.

While Colburne was feeling so strongly with regard to Lillie, could she not devote a sentiment to him? Not many; she had not time; she was otherwise occupied. So selfishly wrapped up in her own affections was she, that, until Mrs. Larue laughingly suggested it, she never thought of his being jealous or miserable on account of her. Then she hoped that he did not care much for her, and was really sorry for him if he did. What a horrible fate it seemed to her to be disappointed in love! She remembered that she had once liked him very much indeed; but so she did even yet, she added, with a comfortable closing of her eyes to all change in the nature of the sentiment; and perhaps he only fancied her in a similar Platonic fashion. Once she had cut out of a paper, and put away in so safe a place that now she could not find it, a little poem which he had written, and which was only interesting because he was the author. She blushed as she called her folly to mind, and resolved that it should never be known to any one. It is curious that she was a little vexed with Colburne because of this reminiscence, and felt that it more than repaid him for all the secret devotion which he might have lavished on her.

"My leave of absence has not been as pleasant as I hoped it would be," he once had the courage to remark.

"Why not?" she asked absent-mindedly; for she was thinking of her own heart affairs.

"I fear that I have lost some sympathies which I once——"

Here he checked himself, not daring to confess how much he had once hoped. With a sudden comprehension of his meaning Lillie colored intensely, after her usual fashion on startling occasions, and glanced about the room in search of some other subject of conversation.

"I have a sense of being a stranger in the family," he explained after a moment of painful silence.

She might surely have said something kind here, but she was too conscientious or too much embarrassed to do it. She made one of those efforts which women are capable of, and sailed out of the difficulty on the wings of a laugh.

"I am sure Mrs. Larue takes a deep interest in you."

Colburne colored in his turn under a sense of mortification mingled with something like anger. Both were relieved when Doctor Ravenel entered, and thereby broke up the fretting dialogue. Now why was not the young man informed of the real state of affairs in the family? Simply because the Doctor, fearful for his child's happiness, and loth to lose dominion over her future, could not yet bring himself to consider the engagement as a finality.

There were no scenes during the leave of absence. Neither Colburne nor Madame Larue made a declaration or received a refusal. Two days before the leave of absence terminated he sadly and wisely and resolutely took his departure for Thibodeaux. Nothing of interest happened to him during the winter, except that he accompanied his regiment in Weitzel's advance up the Teche, which resulted in the retreat of Mouton from Camp Beasland, and the destruction of the rebel iron-clad "Cotton." A narrative of the expedition, written with his usual martial enthusiasm, but which unfortunately I have not space to publish, was received by Doctor Ravenel, and declared by him to be equal in precision, brevity, elegance, and every other classical quality of style, to the Commentaries of Julius Cæsar. The Colonel remarked, in his practical way, that the thing seemed to have been well planned, and that the Captain's account was a good model for a despatch, only a little too long-winded and poetical.

K2

Colburne being absent, Mrs. Larue turned her guns once more upon the Doctor. As the motto of an Irishman at a Donnybrook fair is, "Wherever you see a head, hit it," so the rule which guided her in the Vanity Fair of this life was, "Wherever you see a man, set your cap at him." It must not be supposed, however, that she made the same eyes at the Doctor that she made at Colburne. Her manner would vary amazingly, and frequently did vary to suit her company, just as a chameleon's jacket is said to change color according to the tree which he inhabits ; and this was not because she was simple and easily influenced, but precisely because she was artful and anxious to govern, and knew that soft looks and words are woman's best means of empire. It was interesting to see what a nun-like and saintly *pose* she could take in the presence of a clergyman. To the Colonel she acted the part of Lady Gay Spanker ; to the Doctor she was *femme raisonnable*, and, so far as she could be, *femme savante ;* to Colburne she of late generally played the female Platonic philosopher. It really annoys me to reflect how little space I must allow myself for painting the character of this remarkable woman. "She was nobody's fool but her own," remarked the Colonel, who understood her in a coarse, incomplete way ; nor did she deceive either Lillie or the Doctor in regard to the main features of her character, although they had no suspicion how far she could carry some of her secret caprices. It is hard to blind completely the eyes of one's own family and daily intimates.

As a hen is in trouble when her ducklings take to the water, so was Lillie's soul disturbed when her father was out on the flattering sea of Madame's conversation. Carter was amused at the wiles of the widow and the terrors of the daughter. He comprehended the affair as well as Lillie, at the same time that he did not see so very much harm in it, for the lady was pretty, clever, young enough, and had money. But nothing came of the flirtation—at least not for the present. Although the Doctor was an

eminently sociable being and indefatigably courteous to all
of Eve's daughters, he was not at bottom what you call a
ladies' man. He was too much wrapped up in his daughter and in his scientific studies to be easily pervious to the
shafts of Cupid; besides which he was pretty solidly cuir-
assed by fifty-five years of worldly experience. Madame
even felt that she was kept at a distance, or, to use a more
corporeal and specially correct expression, at arm's length,
by his very politeness.

"Doctor, have you not thought it odd sometimes that
I never consult you professionally?" she asked one day,
changing suddenly from *femme raisonnable* to Lady Gay
Spanker.

"Really, it never occurred to me. I don't expect to
prescribe for my own family. It would be unfair to my
brother doctors. I believe, too, that you are never sick."

"Thanks to Heaven, never! But that is not the only
cause. The truth is—perhaps you have not noticed the
fact—but you are not married. If you want me for a patient, there must first be a Mrs. Ravenel."

"Ah! Yes. Somebody to whom I could confide what is
the matter with you."

"That would not matter. We women always tell our own
maladies. No; that would not matter; it is merely the
look of the thing that troubles me."

The Doctor had the air of being cornered, and remained
smiling at Mrs. Larue, awaiting her pleasure.

"I do not propose to consult you," she continued. "I
am so constantly well that I am almost unhappy about it.
But I do think seriously of studying medicine. What is
your opinion of female doctors?"

"A capital idea!" exclaimed Ravenel, jumping at the
change of subject. "Why not follow it up? You could
master the science of medicine in two or three years, and
you have ability enough to practice it to great advantage.
You might be extremely useful by making a specialty of
your own sex."

" You are a professor of theory and practice, Doctor. Will you instruct me ?"

" Oh! as to that—Elderkin would be better. He is precisely in what ought to be your line. I think that out of kindness to you I ought to say No."

" Not even if I would promise to study mineralogy also ?"

Ravenel pondered an instant, and then eluded her with a story.

" That reminds me of a chaffering which I overheard in a country tavern in Georgia between a Yankee peddler and an indigenous specimen. The Cracker wanted to sell the stranger a horse. 'I don't care particularly for a trade,' says the Yankee, 'but I'll buy the shoes if you'll throw in the creetur.' Medicine is a great science; but mineralogy is a far vaster one."

In short, the Doctor was to Madame like a cold cake to a lump of butter; he calmly endured her, but gave her no encouragement to melt upon his bosom. Just at this time he was more than usually safe from love entanglements because he was so anxious about Lillie's position and prospects. He made what inquiries he could concerning Carter's way of life, and watched his demeanor and conversation closely while talking to him with the politest of smiles. He was unexpectedly gratified by discovering that his proposed son-in-law led—at least for the present—a sober and decent life. With his devotion as a lover no fault could be found by the most exacting of fathers. He called on Lillie every evening and sent her flowers every morning; in short, he bloomed with fair promise of being an affectionate and even uxorious husband. Gradually the Doctor weaned himself from his selfish or loving suspicions, and became accustomed to the idea that from this man his daughter might draw a life-long happiness. Thus when it happened, late in January, nearly four months after the declaration, that Carter requested to be informed definitely as to his prospects, he obtained permission to consider the affair an engagement.

" You know I can't promise wealth to Miss Ravenel," he said frankly. " She may have to put up with a very simple style of life."

" If she can't be contented, I shall not pity her," answered the Doctor. " I don't believe that the love of money is the root of all evil. But I do say that it is one of the most degrading passions conceivable in woman. I sympathise with no woman whose only trouble is that she cannot have and spend a great deal of money. By the way, you know how unable I am to endow her."

" Don't mention it. You have already endowed her. The character that you have transmitted to her, sir—"

The Doctor bowed so promptly and appreciatively that the Colonel did not feel it necessary to round off the compliment.

As men do not talk copiously with each other on these subjects, the interview did not last ten minutes.

I hope that I shall not impress the reader unfavorably concerning Lillie's character when I state that she was frankly happy over the result of her lover's probation. Her delight did not arise merely from the prospect of a smooth course of love and marriage. It sprang in part from the greatly comforting fact that now there was no difference of opinion, no bar to perfect sympathy, between her and that loved, respected, almost adored papa. I have given a very imperfect idea of her if I have not already made it clear that with her the sentiment of filial affection was almost a passion. From very early childhood she had been remarkable for papa-worship, or whatever may be the learned name for the canonization of one's progenitors. At the age of seven she had propounded the question, " Mamma, why don't they make papa President of the United States ?" Some light may be shed on the character of this departed mother and wife by stating that her answer was, " My dear, your father never chose to meddle in politics." Whether Mrs. Ravenel actually deified the Doctor with all the simple faith of the child, or whether the reply was merely

meant to confirm the latter in her filial piety, is a matter of
doubt even to persons who were well acquainted with the
deceased lady.

At last Lillie could prattle to her father about Carter as
much as she liked ; and she used the privilege freely, being
habituated to need, demand and obtain his sympathies.
Not that she filled his ears with confessions of love, or said
that Colonel Carter was " *so* handsome !" or anything of
that sickish nature.   But when her father came in from a
walk, it was, " Papa, did you see Mr. Carter anywhere ?
And what did he say ?"   At another time it was, " Papa,
did Mr. Carter ever tell you about his first campaign
against the Indians ?"   And then would follow the story,
related with glee and a humorous appreciation of the
grandiloquent ideas of a juvenile West Pointer about to
draw his maiden sword. A frequent subject of her conversation was Carter's chance of promotion, not considered with
regard to the pecuniary advantages thereof, but in respect
to the simple justice of advancing such an able and gallant officer.   It was, " Papa, how can the Government be
so stupid as to neglect men who know their duties ?   Mrs.
Larue says that the abolitionists are opposed to Mr. Carter
because he doesn't hold their ultra opinions.   I suppose
they would rather favor a man who talks as they do, even
if he got whipped every time, and never freed a nigger.
If Mr. Carter were on the southern side, he would find
promotion fast enough.   It is enough to make any one
turn rebel."

" My dear," says the Doctor with emphasis, " I would
rather be a private soldier under the flag of my
country, than be a major-general in the army of those
villainous conspirators against country, liberty and humanity.   I respect Colonel Carter for holding fast to his
patriotic sentiments, in spite of unjust neglect, far more
than I would if he were loyal merely because he was sure
of being commander-in-chief.

Lillie could not fail to be gratified by such a compliment

to the moral worth of her hero. After a few moments of agreeable meditation on the various perfections of that great being, she resumed the old subject.

"I think that there is a chance yet of his getting a star when the official report of the battle of Georgia Landing once reaches the minds of those slow creatures at Washington. What do you think, papa? What are the probabilities?"

"Really, my dear, you perplex me. Prophecy never formed a part of my education. There are even a few events in the past that I am not intimately acquainted with."

"Then you shouldn't look so awfully old, papa. If you *will* wrinkle up your forehead in that venerable way, as if you were the Wandering Jew, you must expect to have people ask you all sorts of questions. Why will you do it? I hate to see you making yourself so aggravatingly ancient when nature does her best to keep you young."

About these times the Doctor wrote, with a pitying if not a sad heart, to inform Colburne of the engagement. The young man had looked for some such news, but it nevertheless pained him beyond his anticipations. No mental preparation, no melancholy certainty of forecast, ever quite fits us to meet the avalanche of a great calamity. No matter, for instance, how long we have watched the sure invasion of disease upon the life of a dear friend or relative, we are always astonished with a mighty shock when the last feeble breath leaves the wasted body. Colburne had long sat gloomily by the bedside of his dying hope, but when it expired outright he was seemingly none the less full of anguished amazement.

"Who would have thought it!" he repeated to himself. "How could she choose such a husband, so old, so worldly, so immoral? God help her and watch over her. The love of such a man is a calamity. The tender mercies of the wicked are unintentional cruelties."

As for himself, the present seemed a barren waste without a blossom of happiness, and the future another waste without an oasis of hope. For a time he even lost all desire for promotion, or for any other worldly honor or success ; and he would not have considered it hard, so undesirable did life appear, if he had known that it was his fate to die in the next battle. If he wanted to live it was only to see the war terminate gloriously, and the stars and stripes once more flying over his whole country. The devotional sentiments which his mother had sown throughout his youth, and which had been warmed for a while into some strength of feeling and purpose by the saintly glory of her death, struggled anew into temporary bloom under the clouds of this second bereavement.

" Not my will but Thine be done," he thought. And then, " How unworthy I am to repeat those words !"

There were certain verses of the Bible which whispered to him a comforting sympathy. Many times a day such a phrase as, " A man of sorrows and acquainted with grief," repeated to him as if by some other self or guardian angel, would thrill his mind with the plaintive consolation of requiems.

CHAPTER XVII.

COLONEL CARTER IS ENTIRELY VICTORIOUS BEFORE HE BEGINS HIS CAMPAIGN.

TOWARDS the close of this winter of 1862–3 Banks superseded Butler, and the New England Division expanded into the Nineteenth Army Corps. Every one who was in New Orleans during that season will remember the amazement with which he and all other persons saw transport after transport steam up the river, increasing the loyal forces in and around the city by at least ten thousand men, which rumor magnified into twenty-five thousand. Where did they come from, and where were they going, and what would be the result? Since the opening of the war no expedition of magnitude had been conducted with similar secrecy; and every one argued that a general who could plan with such reticence would execute with corresponding vigor and ability. While the Secessionists shrank within themselves, seeing no more hope of freeing Louisiana from Northern Vandals, our Doctor and his fellow Loyalists exulted in a belief that the war would soon be brought to a triumphant close.

"Three mere transports!" exclaimed Ravenel, coming in from a walk on the levee. "It is a most glorious spectacle, this exhibition of the power of the Republic. It equals the greatest military efforts of the greatest military nations. One is absolutely reminded of consular Rome, carrying on the war with Hannibal in Italy, and at the same time sending one great army to Spain and another to Africa. I pin my faith to the tail of General Scott's anaconda. In the end it will crush Secessia, break every bone in its body, and swallow it. I think, Colonel, that we have every reason to congratulate ourselves on the prospects."

"I really can't see it," answered Carter, with a lugubrious laugh.

"How so? You astonish me."

"Don't you perceive that I lose my Governorship?"

"Oh, but—I don't anticipate an immediate close of the struggle. It may last a year yet; and during that time—"

"That is not the point. King Stork has succeeded King Log. King Stork's men must have the nice places and King Log's men must get out of them."

"Oh, but they won't turn you out," exclaimed Lillie, and then blushed as she thought how her eagerness might be interpreted.

"We shall see," answered the Colonel gravely, and almost sadly. He was so much in love with this girl that a

life in Capua with her seemed more desirable than the
winning of Cannæ's away from her.

"Here is my fate," he said when he called on the following evening, and handed her two official documents,
the one relieving him from his position as Military Governor, the other assigning him to the command of a brigade.

"Now you must go into the battle again," she said,
making a struggle to preserve her self-possession.

"I am sorry,—on your account."

At this answer her effort at stoicism and maidenly
dignity failed; she dropped her head and hid her face in
the sewing work on which she had been engaged. This
was too much for Carter, to whom love had been a reju-
venation and almost a regeneration, so that he was as gentle, virginal, and sensitive as if he had never known the
hardening experiences of a soldier and a man about town.
Sitting down beside his betrothed, he pressed her temples
with both his hands and kissed the light, flossy, amber-
colored ripples of her hair. He could feel the half-sup-
pressed sobs which trembled through her frame, breaking
softly and noiselessly, like summer waves dying on a reedy
shore. How he longed to soothe her by grasping all her
being into his and making her altogether his own! He
was on the point of falling before the temptation which he
had that morning resolved to resist. He knew that he
ought not to marry, with only his colonelcy as a support;
yet he was about to urge an immediate marriage, and
would have done so had he spoken. Lillie would not
have refused him: it would not have been in the nature
of woman: what girl would put off a lover who was going
to the battle-field? Nothing prevented the consummation
of this imprudence but a ring at the door-bell. Miss Ravenel sprang up and fled from the parlor, fearful of being
caught with tears on her cheeks and her hair disordered.
Mrs. Larue entered, gave the Colonel a saucy courtesy,
cast a keen sidelong glance at his serious countenance,

repressed apparently some flippant remark which was on her lips, begged him to excuse her for a few moments, and slid out of the room.

"Confound her!" muttered the Colonel, indignant at Madame without cause, merely because he had been interrupted.

By the time that Lillie had dried her eyes, washed her face and composed herself so far as to dare return to the parlor, Mrs. Larue, ignorant of the good or mischief that she was accomplishing, was there also. Consequently, although Carter stayed late into the evening, there was no second opportunity for the perilous trial of a tête-a-tête farewell.

Next day he went by the first train to Thibodeaux. As commanding officer of a brigade he exhibited his usual energy, practical ability, and beneficent despotism. The colonels were ordered to make immediate inspections of their regiments, and to send in reports of articles necessary to complete the equipment of their men, with requisitions for the same on the brigade quartermaster. During several consecutive days he personally went the rounds of his grand guards and outlying videttes, choosing for this purpose midnight, or a wet storm, or any other time when he suspected that men or officers might relax their vigilance. In such a pelting rain, as if the Father of Waters had been taken up to heaven and poured back into Louisiana, he came upon a picket of five men who had sought refuge in some empty sugar-hogsheads. The closed-up heads were toward the road, because from that direction came the wind; and such was the pattering and howling of the tempest, that the men did not hear the tramp of the approaching horse. Reining up, the Colonel shouted, "Surrender! The first man that stirs, dies!"

Not a soul moved or answered. For a minute or two Carter sat motionless, smiling grimly, with the water streaming down his face and uniform. Then he ordered:

"Come out here, one of you. I want to see what this picket is made of."

A corporal crawled out, leaving his gun behind him in the recumbent hogshead. His face was pale at his first appearance, but it turned paler still when he recognized his brigade commander.

"I—I thought it was a secesh," he stammered.

"And so you surrendered, sir !" thundered the Colonel. "You allowed yourself to be surprised, and then you surrendered! Give me your name, sir, and the names of your men."

Twenty minutes afterward a detachment from the reserve relieved the culprits, and marched them into camp as prisoners. Next day the corporal and the soldier whose turn it had been to stand as sentry, went before a court-martial, and in a week thereafter were on their way to Ship Island, to work out a sentence of hard labor with ball and chain.

On the midnight following this adventure Carter ordered the outlying videttes to fire three rounds of musketry, and then rode from camp to camp to see which regiment got into line the quickest.

The members of his staff, especially his Adjutant-General and Aid, found their positions no sinecures. Every night one or other of these young gentlemen made the rounds of the pickets some time between midnight and daybreak, and immediately on his return to head-quarters reported to the Colonel the condition of the line as regarded practical efficiency and knowledge of the formalities. If the troops fell in at three in the morning to go through the drill of taking position to repel an imaginary enemy, they had at least the consolation of knowing that some poor staff-officer had been roused out of bed half an hour before to disseminate the order. A staff-officer inspected every guard-mounting and every battalion-drill, and made a report as to how the same was conducted. A staff-officer rode through every regimental camp every morning, and made a report of its condition as to cleanliness. If the explosion of a rifle was heard any where about the post, a staff-officer was on the spot in five minutes to learn the circumstances of the irregularity, to order the offender to the guard-house, and to make his report to the all-pervading brigade commander. A false or incomplete statement he did not dare to render, so severe was the cross-questioning which he was liable to undergo.

"Did you see it yourself, Lieutenant?" the Colonel would ask.

"I saw the man cleaning his piece, sir; and he confessed that he had discharged it to get the ball out."

"Who was the man?"

"Private Henry Brown, Company I, Ninth Barataria."

"Very well, Mr. Brayton." (In the regular army a lieutenant is Mr.)   "Now have the kindness to take my compliments to the Colonel of the Ninth Barataria and the field-officer of the day, and request them to step here."

First comes the commanding officer of the regiment in which the offence has been committed.

"Walk in, Colonel," says the brigade commander. "Take a seat, sir. Colonel, a rifle has been fired by one of your men this morning. How is that?"

"It was against my orders, sir. The man is in the guard-house."

"This is not the first offence of the kind—it is the third or fourth within a week."

"The fact is, sir, that the men have no ball-screws. Their rifles get wet on picket duty, and they have no means of drawing the loads. Consequently they are tempted to discharge them, notwithstanding the orders."

"Ah! You must give them the devil until they learn to resist temptation. But no ball-screws! How is that?"

"I was not aware, sir, of the deficiency."

"Not aware of it? My God, Colonel! Not aware of such a deficiency of equipment in your own regiment?"

"I am extremely sorry, sir," apologizes the humiliated

Colonel, who does not know what might be done to him for such neglect, and who, although only three months in the service, is a conscientious officer, anxious to do his whole duty.

"Send up a requisition for ball-screws and for every other lacking article of ordnance," says the brigade commander. "I will forward it to head-quarters and see that you are supplied. But, by the way, how did this fellow get outside your camp-guard with his gun? That is all wrong. Have the goodness to haul your officer of the guard over the coals about it. Make him understand that he is responsible for such irregularities, and that he may get dismissed the service if he doesn't attend to his duties. That is all, Colonel. Will you take a glass of brandy? *Good* morning, sir."

Then, turning to the Adjutant-General: "Captain, make out a circular directing commandants of regiments to see that targets are set up in proper places where the relieved guards may discharge their rifles. The best marksman to be reported to regimental head-quarters, and to be relieved from all ordinary duty for twenty-four hours."

The field-officer of the day is now announced by the orderly.

"Come in, Captain; take a seat, sir. Are you aware, Captain, that a rifle has been fired this morning, outside the camps, in violation of general orders?"

"I—I think I heard it," stammers the Captain, taking it for granted that he is guilty of something, but not knowing what.

"Do you know who the offender is?" demands the Colonel, his brow beginning to blacken like a stormy heaven over the ignoramus.

"I do not, sir. I will inquire, if you wish, Colonel."

"If I wish! My God, sir! of course I wish it. Haven't you already inquired? My God, sir! what do you suppose your duties are?"

"I didn't know that this was one of them," pleads the now miserable Captain.

"Don't you know, sir, that you are responsible for every irregularity that happens within the grand guards and outside the camps, while you are field-officer of the day? Don't you know that you are responsible for the firing of this rifle?"

"Responsible," feebly echoes the Captain, not seeing the fact as yet, but nevertheless very much troubled.

"Yes, sir. It is your business, if any thing goes wrong, to know it, and discover the perpetrators, and report them for punishment. It was your business, as soon as that gun was fired, to find out who fired it, to have him put under guard, and to see that he was reported for punishment. You haven't attended to your duty, sir. And because the officers of the day don't know and don't do their duty, I have to make my staff-officers ride day and night, and knock up their horses. Here is my Aid, who has been doing your business. Mr. Brayton, give the Captain this man's name, &c. Do you know, Captain, *why* muskets should not be fired about the camps at the will and pleasure of the enlisted men?"

"I suppose, sir, to prevent a waste of ammunition."

"Good God! Why, yes, sir; but that isn't all—that isn't half, sir. The great reason, the all-important reason, is that firing is a signal of danger, of an enemy, of battle. If the men are to go shooting about the woods in this fashion, we shall never know when we are and when we are not to be attacked. Without orders from these head-quarters no firing is permissible except by the pickets, and that only when they are attacked. This matter involves the safety of the command, and must be subjected to the strictest discipline. That is all, Captain. *Good* morning, sir."

As the poor officer of the day goes out, the heavens seem to be peopled with threatening brigade commanders, and

the earth to be a wilderness of unexlored and thorny responsibilities.

"Well, Mr. Brayton, what was the cause of the firing?"
inquired Carter one midnight, when the Aid returned from
an expedition of inquiry.

"A sentinel of the Ninth shot a man dead, sir, for neglecting to halt when challenged."

"Good, by" (this and that), exclaimed the Colonel.
"Those fellows are redeeming themselves. It used to be
the meanest regiment for guard duty in the brigade. But
this is the second man the Ninth fellows have shot within
a week. By" (that and the other) "they are learning
their business. What is the sentinel's name, Mr. Brayton?"

"Private Henry Brown, Company I. The same man,
sir, that was punished the other day for firing off his rifle
without orders."

"Ah, by Jove! he has learned something—learned to
do as he is told. Mr. Brayton, I wish you would go to
the Colonel of the Ninth in the morning, and request him
from me to make Brown a corporal at the first opportunity. Ask him also to give the man a good word in an order, to be read before the regiment at dress parade to-
morrow. By the way, who was the fellow who was shot?"

"Private Murphy of the Ninth, who had been to Thibodeaux and over-stayed his pass. He was probably drunk,
sir—he had a half-empty bottle of whiskey in his pocket."

"Bully for him—he died happy," laughed the Colonel.
"You can go to bed now, Mr. Brayton. Much obliged to
you."

A few days later the brigade commander looked over
the proceedings of the court-martial which he had con-
vened, and threw down the manuscript with an oath.

"What a stupid—what a cursedly stupid record! Orderly, give my compliments to Major Jackson, and request
him" (here he rises to a roar) "to report here immediately."

Picking up the manuscript, he annotated it in pencil until Major Jackson was announced.

"My God, sir!" he then broke out. "Is that your style of conducting a court-martial? This record is a disgrace to you as President, and to me for selecting you for such duty. Look here, sir. Here is a private convicted of beating the officer of the guard—one of the greatest offences, sir, which a soldier could commit—an offence which strikes at the very root of discipline. Now what is the punishment that you have allotted to him? To be confined in the guard-house for three months, and to carry a log of wood for three hours a day. Do you call that a suitable punishment? He ought to have three years of hard labor with ball and chain—that is the least he ought to have. You might have sentenced him to be shot. Why, sir, do you fully realize what it is to strike an officer, and especially an officer on duty? It is to defy the very soul of discipline. Without respect for officers, there is no army. It is a mob. Major Jackson, it appears to me that you have no conception of the dignity of your own position. You don't know what it is to be an officer. That is all, sir. Good morning."

"Captain," continues the Colonel, turning to his Adjutant-General, "make out an order disapproving of all the proceedings of this court, and directing that Major Jackson shall not again be detailed on court-martial while he remains under my command."

Carter was a terror to his whole brigade—to the stupidest private, to every lieutenant of the guard, to every commandant of company, to the members of his staff, and even to his equals in grade, the colonels. He knew his business so well, he was so invariably right in his fault-findings, he was so familiar with the labyrinth of regulations and general orders, through which almost all others groped with many stumblings, and he was so conscientiously and gravely outraged by offences against discipline, that he was necessarily a dreadful personage. To use the compo-

L

site expression, half Hibernian and half Hebraic, of Lieutenant Van Zandt, he was a regular West Point Bull of Bashan in the volunteer China-shop. But while he was thus feared, he was also greatly respected; and a word of praise from him was cherished by officer or soldier as a medal of honor. And, stranger still, while he was exercising what must seem to the civilian reader a hard-hearted despotism, he was writing every other day letters full of ardent affection to a young lady in New Orleans.

In a general way one is tempted to speak jestingly of the circumstance of a well-matured man falling in love with a girl in her teens. By the time a man gets to be near forty, his moral physiognomy is supposed to be so pock-marked with bygone amours as to be in a measure ludicrous, or at least devoid of dignity in its tenderness. But Carter's emotional nature was so emphatic and volcanic, so capable of bringing a drama of the affections to a tragic issue, that I feel no disposition to laugh over his affair with Miss Ravenel, although it was by no means his first, nor perhaps his twentieth. Considering the passions as forces, we are obliged to respect them in proportion to their power rather than their direction. And in this case the direction was not bad, nor foolish, but good, and highly creditable to Carter; for Miss Ravenel, though as yet barely adolescent, was a finer woman in brain and heart than he had ever loved before; also he loved her better than he had ever before loved any woman.

He could not stay away from her. As soon as he had got his brigade into such order as partially satisfied his stern professional conscience, he obtained a leave of absence for seven days, and went to New Orleans. From this visit resulted one of the most important events that will be recorded in the present history. I shall hurry over the particulars, because to me the circumstance is not an agreeable one. Having from my first acquaintance with Miss Ravenel entertained a fondness for her, I never could fancy this match of hers with such a dubious person as

Colonel Carter, who is quite capable of making her very unhappy. I always agreed with her father in preferring Colburne, whose character, although only half developed in consequence of youth, modesty, and Puritan education, is nevertheless one of those germs which promise much beauty and usefulness. But Miss Ravenel, more emotional than reflective, was fated to love Carter rather than Colburne. To her, and probably to most women, there was something powerfully magnetic in the ardent nature which found its physical expression in that robust frame, that florid brunette complexion, those mighty mustachios, and darkly burning eyes.

The consequence of this visit to New Orleans was a sudden marriage. The tropical blood in the Colonel's veins drove him to demand it, and the electric potency of his presence forced Miss Ravenel to concede it. When he held both her hands in his, and, looking with passionate importunity into her eyes, begged her not to let him go again into the flame of battle without the consolation of feeling that she was altogether and for ever his, she could only lay her head on his shoulder, gently sobbing in speechless acquiescence. How many such marriages took place during the war, sweet flowers of affection springing out of the mighty carnage! How many fond girls forgot their womanly preference for long engagements, slow preparations of much shopping and needle-work, coy hesitations, and gentle maidenly tyrannies, to fling themselves into the arms of lovers who longed to be husbands before they went forth to die! How many young men in uniform left behind them weeping brides to whom they were doomed never to return!

> " Brave boys are all, gone at their country's call,
>   And yet, and yet,
>   We cannot forget
> That many brave boys must fall."

This sad little snatch from the chorus of a commonplace song Lillie often repeated to herself, with tears in her eyes, when Carter was at the front, without minding a bit the fact that her "brave boy" was thirty-six years old.

The marriage cost the Doctor a violent pang; but he consented to it, overborne by the passion of the period. There was no time to be lost on bridal dresses, any more than in bridal tours. The ceremony was performed in church by a regimental chaplain, in presence of the father, Mrs. Larue, and half a dozen chance spectators, only two days before the Colonel's leave of absence expired. Neither then nor afterward could Lillie realize this day and hour, through which she walked and spoke as if in a state of somnambulism, so stupefied or benumbed was she by the strength of her emotions. The lookers-on observed no sign of feeling about her, except that her face was as pale and apparently as cold as alabaster. She behaved with an appearance of perfect self-possession; she spoke the ordained words at the right moment and in a clear voice— and yet all the while she was not sure that she was in her right mind. It was a frozen delirium of feeling, ice without and fire within, like a volcano of the realms of the pole.

Once in the hackney-coach which conveyed them home, alone with this man who was now her husband, her master, the ice melted a little, and she could weep silently upon his shoulder. She was not wretched; neither could she distinctly feel that she was happy; if this was happiness, then there could be a joy which was no release from pain. She had no doubts about her future, such as even yet troubled her father, and set him pacing by the half-hour together up and down his study. This man by her side, this strong and loving husband, would always make her happy. She did not doubt his goodness so much as she doubted her own; she trusted him almost as firmly as if he were a deity. Yes, he would always love her—and she would always, always, always love him; and what more was there to desire? All that day she was afraid of him, and yet could not bear to be away from him a moment.

He had such an authority over her—his look and voice and touch so tyrannized her emotions, that he was an object of something like terror; and yet the sense of his domination was so sweet that she could not wish it to be less, but desired with her whole beating brain and heart that it might evermore increase. I give no record of her conversation at this time. She said so little! Usually a talker, almost a prattler, she was now silent; a look from her husband, a thought of her husband, would choke her at any moment. He seemed to have entered into her whole being, so that she was not fully herself. The words which she whispered when alone with him were so sacred with woman's profoundest and purest emotions that they must not be written. The words which she uttered in the presence of others were not felt by her, and were not worth writing.

After two days, there was a parting; perhaps, she wretchedly thought, a final one.

"Oh! how can I let you go?" she said. "I cannot. I cannot bear it. Will you come back? Will you ever come back? Will you be careful of yourself? You won't get killed, will you? Promise me."

She was womanish about it, and not heroic, like her Amazonian sisters on the Rebel side. Nevertheless she did not feel the separation so bitterly as she would have done, had they been married a few months or years, instead of only a few hours. Intimate relations with her husband had not yet become a habit, and consequently a necessity of her existence; the mere fact that they had exchanged the nuptial vows was to her a realization of all that she had ever anticipated in marriage; when they left the altar, and his ring was upon her finger, their wedded life was as complete as it ever would be. And thus, in her ignorance of what love might become, she was spared something of the anguish of separation.

She was thinking of her absent husband when Mrs. Larue addressed her for the first time as Mrs. Carter; and yet in her dreaminess she did not at the moment recognize the name as her own : not until Madame laughed and said, " Lillie, I am talking to you." Then she colored crimson and throbbed at the heart as if her husband himself had laid his hand upon her shoulder.

Very shortly she began to demand the patient encouragements of her father. All day, when she could get at him, she pursued him with questions which no man in these unprophetic days could answer. It was, " Papa, do you think there will be an active campaign this summer ? Papa, don't you suppose that Mr. Carter will be allowed to keep his brigade at Thibodeaux ?"

She rarely spoke of her husband except as Mr. Carter. She did not like his name John—it sounded too commonplace for such a superb creature ; and the title of Colonel was too official to satisfy her affection. But " Mr. Carter " seemed to express her respect for this man, her husband, her master, who was so much older, and, as she thought, morally greater than herself.

Sometimes the Doctor, out of sheer pity and paternal sympathy, answered her questions just as she wished them to be answered, telling her that he saw no prospect of an active campaign, that the brigade could not possibly be spared from the important post of Thibodeaux, etc. etc. But then the exactingness of anxious love made her want to know why he thought so ; and her persevering inquiries generally ended by forcing him from all his hastily constructed works of consolation. In mere self-defence, therefore, he occasionally urged upon her the unpleasant but ennobling duties of patience and self-control.

" My dear," he would say, " we cannot increase our means of happiness without increasing our possibilities of misery. A woman who marries is like a man who goes into business. The end may be greatly increased wealth, or it may be bankruptcy. It is cowardly to groan over the fact. You must learn to accept the sorrows of your present life as well as the joys ; you must try to strike a rational balance between the two, and be contented if you can say, 'On the whole, I am happier than I was.' I beg you, for your own sake, to overcome this habit of looking at only the darker chances of life. If you go on fretting, you will not last the war out. No constitution—no woman's constitution, at any rate—can stand it. You positively must cease to be a child, and become a woman."

Lillie tried to obey, but could only succeed by spasms.

CHAPTER XVIII.

DOCTOR RAVENEL COMMENCES THE ORGANIZALION OF SOUTHERN LABOR.

FOR some time previous to the marriage Doctor Ravenel had been plotting the benefit of the human race. He was one of those philanthropic conspirators, those humanitarian Catilines, who, for the last thirty years have been rotten-egged and vilified at the North, tarred and feathered and murdered at the South, under the name of abolitionists. It is true that until lately he has been a silent one, as you may infer from the fact that he was still in the land of the living. If the hundred-headed hydra had preached abolition in New Orleans previous to the advent of Farragut and Butler, he would have had every one of his skulls fractured within twenty-four hours after he had commenced his ministry. Nobody could have met the demands of such a mission except that gentleman of miraculous vitality mentioned by Ariosto, who, as fast as he was cut in pieces, picked himself up and grew together as good as new.

The Doctor was chiefly intent at present upon inducing the negroes to work as freemen, now that they were no longer obliged to work as slaves. He talked a great deal

about his plan to various influential personages, and even
pressed it at department headquarters in a lengthy private
interview.

"You are right, sir," said Authority, with suave dignity.
"It is a matter of great instant importance. It may become a military necessity. Suppose we should have a
war with France, (I don't say, sir, that there is any danger
of it,) we might be cut off from the rest of the Union. Louisiana would then have to live on her own resources, and feed
her own army. These negroes *must* be induced to work.
They must be put at it immediately; they must have their
hoes in the soil before six weeks are over; otherwise we
are in danger of a famine. I have arranged a plan, Doctor. The provost-marshals are to pick up every unem-
ployed negro, give him his choice as to what plantation he
will work on, but see that he works somewhere. There is
to be a fixed rate of wages,—so much in clothes and so
much in rations. Select your plantation, my dear sir, and
I will see that it is assigned to you. You will then obtain
your laborers by making written application to the Superintendent of Negro Labor."

The Doctor was honestly and intelligently delighted.
He expressed his admiration of the commanding general's
motives and wisdom in such terms that the latter, high as
he was in position and mighty in authority, felt flattered.
You could not possibly talk with Ravenel for ten minutes
without thinking better of yourself than before; for, perceiving that you had to do with a superior man, and that
he treated you with deference, you instinctively inferred
that you were not only a person but a personage. But
the compliments and air of respect which he accorded the
commanding general were not mere empty civilities, nor
well-bred courtesies, nor expressions of consideration for
place and authority. Ravenel's enthusiasm led him to believe that, in finding a man who sympathised with him in
his pet project, he had found one of the greatest minds of
the age.

"At last," he said to his daughter when he reached home, "at last we are likely to see wise justice meted out to these poor blacks."

"Is the Major-General pleasant?" asked Lillie, with an inconsequence which was somewhat characteristic of her. She was more interested in learning how a great dignitary looked and behaved than in hearing what were his opinions on the subject of freemen's labor.

"I don't know that a major general is obliged to be pleasant, at least not in war time," answered the Doctor, a little annoyed at the interruption to the train of his ideas. "Yes, he is pleasant enough; in fact something too much of deportment. He put me in mind of one of my adventures among the Georgia Crackers. I had to put up for the night in one of those miserable up-country log shanties where you can study astronomy all night through the chinks in the roof, and where the man and wife sleep one side of you and the children and dogs on the other. The family, it seems, had had a quarrel with a neighboring family of superior pretensions, which had not yet culminated in gouging or shooting. The eldest daughter, a ragged girl of seventeen, described to me with great gusto an encounter which had taken place between her mother and the female chieftain of the hostile tribe. Said she, "Miss Jones, she tried to come the dignerfied over mar. But thar she found her beater. My mar is hell on dignerty."—Well, the Major-General runs rather too luxuriantly to dignity. But his ideas on the subject of reorganizing labor are excellent, and have my earnest respect and approbation. I believe that under his administration the negroes will be allowed and encouraged to take their first certain step toward civilization. They are to receive some remuneration,—not for the bygone centuries of forced labor and oppression,—but for what they will do hereafter."

"I don't see, papa, that they have been treated much worse than they might expect," responds Lillie, who, although now a firm loyalist, has by no means become an abolitionist.

"Perhaps not, my dear, perhaps not. They have no doubt been better off in the Dahomey of America than they would have been in the Dahomey of Africa; and certainly they couldn't expect much from a Christianity whose chief corner-stone was a hogshead of slave-grown sugar. The negroes were not foolish enough to look for much good in such a moral atrocity as that. They have put their trust in the enemies of it; in Frémont a while ago, and in Lincoln now. At present they do expect something. They believe that 'the year of jubilo am come.' And so it is. Before this year closes, many of these poor creatures will receive what they never did before—wages for their labor. For the first time in their lives they will be led to realize the idea of justice. Justice, honesty, mercy, and nearly the whole list of Christian virtues, have hitherto been empty names to them, having no practical signification, and in fact utterly unknown to their minds except as words that for some unexplained purpose had been inserted in the Bible. How could they believe in the things themselves? They never saw them practiced; at least they never felt their influence. Of course they were liars and hypocrites and thieves. All constituted society lied to them by calling them men and treating them as beasts; it played the hypocrite to them by preaching to them the Christian virtues, and never itself practising them; it played the thief by taking all the earnings of their labor, except just enough to keep soul and body together, so that they might labor more. Our consciences, the conscience of the nation, will not be cleared when we have merely freed the negroes. We must civilize and Christianize them. And we must begin this by teaching them the great elementary duty of man in life—that of working for his own subsistence. I am so interested in the problem that I have resolved to devote myself personally to its solution."

"What! And give up your hospital?"

"Yes, my dear. I have already given it up, and got my plantation assigned to me."

"Oh, papa! Where?"

Of course Lillie feared that in her new home she might not be able to see her husband; and of course the Doctor divined this charming anxiety, and hastened to relieve her from it.

"It is at Taylorsville, my dear. Taylorsville forms a part of Colonel Carter's military jurisdiction, and the fort there is garrisoned by a detachment from his brigade. He can come to see us without neglecting his duties."

Lillie colored, and said nothing for a few minutes. She was so unused as yet to her husband, that the thought of being visited by him thrilled her nerves, and took temporary possession of all her mind.

"But, papa," she presently inquired, "will this support you as well as the hospital?"

"I don't know, child. It is an experiment. It may be a failure, and it may be a pecuniary success. We shall certainly be obliged to economize until our autumn crops are gathered. But I am willing to do that, if I meet with no other reward than my own consciousness that I enter upon the task for the sake of a long oppressed race. I believe that by means of kindness and justice I can give them such ideas of industry and other social virtues as they could not obtain, and have not obtained, from centuries of robbery and cruelty."

Lillie was lost in meditation, not concerning the good of the blacks, but concerning the probable visits of Colonel Carter at Taylorsville. Affectionately selfish woman as she was, she would not have given up the alarming joy of one of those anticipated interviews for the chance of civilizing a capering wilderness of negroes.

Taylorsville, a flourishing village before the war, is situated on the Mississippi just where it is tapped by Bayou Rouge, which is one of the dozen channels through which

the Father of Waters finds the Gulf of Mexico. It is on
the western bank of the river, and for the most part on the
southern bank of the bayou; and is protected from both
by that continuous system of levees which alone saves
southern Louisiana from yearly inundations. At the time
of which I speak, a large portion of the town consisted of
charred and smoke-blackened ruins. Its citizens had been
mad enough to fire on our fleet, and Farragut had swept
it with his iron besoms of destruction. On the same bank
of the Mississippi, but on the northern bank of the bayou,
at the apex of the angle formed by the diverging currents,
is Fort Winthrop, a small star-shaped earth-work, faced
in part with bricks, surrounded by a ditch except on the
river side, and provided with neither casemate nor bomb-
proof. Ordered by Butler and designed by Weitzel, it
had been thrown up shortly after the little victory of
Georgia Landing. It was to be within reach of this fort
in case of an attack from raiding rebels, that Ravenel had
selected a plantation for his philanthropic experiment in
the neighborhood of Taylorsville. Haste was necessary to
success, for the planting season was slipping away.
Within a week or so after the marriage he had bought a
stock of tools and provisions, obtained a ragged corps of
negroes from the Superintendent of Colored Labor, shipped
every thing on board a Government transport, and was on
the spot where he proposed to initiate the re-organization
of southern industry.

The plantation house was a large, plain wooden mansion, very much like those which the country gentility of
New England built about the beginning of this century,
except that the necessities of a southern climate had dic-
tated a spacious veranda covering the whole front, two
stories in height, and supported by tall square wooden
pillars. In the rear was a one-storied wing, containing
the kitchen, and rooms for servants. Farther back, at the
extremity of a deep and slovenly yard, where pigs had
been wont to wander without much opposition, was a hol-

low square of cabins for the field-hands, each consisting of two rooms, and all alike built of rough boards coarsely whitewashed. Neither the cabins nor the family mansion had a cellar, nor even a foundation wall; they stood on props of brick-work, leaving room underneath for the free circulation of air, dogs, pigs and pickaninnies. On either side of the house the cleared lands ran a considerable distance up and down the bayou, closing in the rear, at a depth of three or four hundred yards, in a stretch of forest. An eighth of a mile away, not far from the winding road which skirted the sinuous base of the levee, was the most expensive building of the plantation, the great brick sugar-house, with vast expanses of black roof and a gigantic chimney. No smoke of industry arose from it; the sound of the grinding of the costly steam machinery had departed; the vats were empty and dry, or had been carried away for bunks and fire-wood by foraging soldiers and negroes.

There was not a soul in any of the buildings or about the grounds when the Ravenels arrived. The Secessionist family of Robertson had fled before Weitzel's advance into the Lafourche country, and its chief, a man of fifty, had fallen at the head of a company of militia at the fight at Georgia Landing. Then the field-hands, who had hid in the swamps to avoid being carried to Texas, came upon the house like locusts of destruction, broke down its doors, shattered its windows, plundered it from parlor to garret, drank themselves drunk on the venerable treasures of the wine closet, and diverted themselves with soiling the carpets, breaking the chairs, ripping up the sofas, and defacing the family portraits. Some gentle sentiment, perhaps a feeble love for the departed young "missus," perhaps the passion of their race for music, had deterred them from injuring the piano, which was almost the only unharmed piece of furniture in the once handsome parlor. The single living creature about the place was a half-starved grimalkin, who caterwauled dolefully at the visit-

ors from a distance, and could not be enticed to approach
by the blandishments of Lillie, an enthusiastic cat-fancier.
To the merely sentimental observer it was sad to think
that this house of desolation had not long since been the
abode of the generous family life and prodigal hospitality
of a southern planter.

"Oh, how doleful it looks!" sighed Lillie, as she wandered about the deserted rooms.

"It *is* doleful," said the Doctor.   "As doleful as the
ruins of Babylon—of cities accursed of God, and smitten
for their wickedness.   My old friend Elderkin used to say
(before he went addled about southern rights) that he
wondered God didn't strike all the sugar planters of Louisiana dead.   Well He *has* stricken them with stark madness ; and under the influence of it they are getting themselves killed off as fast as possible.   It was time.   The
world had got to be too intelligent for them.   They could
not live without retarding the progress of civilization.
They wanted to keep up the social systems of the middle
ages amidst railroads, steamboats, telegraphs, patent reap-
ers, and under the noses of Humboldt, Leverrier, Lyell,
and Agassiz.   Of course they must go to the wall.   They
will be pinned up to it *in terrorem*, like exterminated
crows and chicken-hawks.   The grand jury of future centuries will bring in the verdict, ' Served them right !'   At
the same time one cannot help feeling a little human sympathy, or at any rate a little poetic melancholy, on stepping thus into the ruins of a family."

Lillie, however, was not very sentimental about the departed happiness of the Robertsons; she was planning how
to get the house ready for the expected visit of Colonel
Carter; in that channel for the present ran her poesy.

"But really, papa, we must go to work," she said.
"The nineteenth century has turned out the Robertsons,
and put us in—but it has left these rooms awfully dirty,
and the furniture in a dreadful condition."

In a few minutes she had her hat off, her dress **pinned**

up to keep it out of the dust, her sleeves rolled back to her elbows, and was flying about with remarkable emphasis, dragging broken chairs, etc., to the garret, and brooming up such whirlwinds of dust, that the Doctor flew abroad for refuge. What she could not do herself she set half a dozen negroes, male and female, to doing. She was wild with excitement and gayety, running about, ordering and laughing like a threefold creature. It was delightful to remember, in a sweet under-current of thought which flowed gently beneath her external glee, that she was working to welcome her husband, slaving for him, tiring herself out for his dear sake. In a couple of hours she was so weary that she had to fling herself on a settee in the veranda, and rest, while the negroes continued the labor. Women in general, I believe, love to work by spasms and deliriums, doing, or making believe do, a vast deal while they are at it, but dropping off presently into languor and headache.

"Papa, we shall have five whole chairs," she called. "You can sit in one, I in another, and that will leave three for Mr. Carter. Why don't you come and do something? I have fagged myself half to death, and you haven't done a thing but mope about with your hands behind your back. Come in now, and go to work."

"My dear, there are so many negroes in there that I can't get in."

"Then come up and talk to me," commanded the young lady, who had meant that all the while. "You needn't think you can find any Smithites or Robinsonites. There isn't a mineral in Louisiana, unless it is a brickbat. Do come up here and talk to me. I can't scream to you all the afternoon."

"I am so glad you can't," grinned papa, and strolled obstinately away in the direction of the sugar-house. He was studying the nature of the soil, and proposing to subject it to a chemical analysis, in order to see if it could not be made to produce as much corn to the acre as the bottom lands of Ohio. Indian corn and sweet potatoes, with a little seasoning of onions, beets, squashes, and other kitchen garden vegetables, should be his only crop that season. Also he would raise pigs and chickens by the hundred, and perhaps three or four cows, if promising calves could be obtained in the country. What New Orleans wanted, and what the whole department would stand in desperate need of, should a war break out with France, was, not sugar, but corn and pork. All that summer the possibility of a war with France was a prominent topic of conversation in Louisiana, so that even the soldiers talked in their rough way of " revelling in the halls of the Montezumas, and filling their pockets with little gold Jesuses." As for making sugar, unless it might be a hogshead or so for family consumption, it was out of the question. It would cost twenty thousand dollars merely to put the sugar-house and its machinery to rights—and the Doctor had no such riches, nor any thing approaching to it, this side of heaven. Nevertheless he was perfectly happy in strolling about his unplanted estate, and revolving his unfulfilled plans, agricultural and humanitarian. He proposed to produce, not only a crop of corn and potatoes, but a race of intelligent, industrious and virtuous laborers. He would make himself analytically acquainted, not only with the elements and possibilities of the soil, but with those of the negro soul. By the way, I ought to mention that he was not proprietor of the plantation, but only a tenant of it to the United States, paying a rent which for the first year was merely nominal, so anxious was Authority to initiate successfully the grand experiment of freedmen's labor.

When he returned to the house from a stroll of two hours Lillie favored him with a good imitation of a sound scolding. What did he mean by leaving her alone so, without anybody to speak a word to ? If he was going to be always out in this way, they might as well live in New Orleans where he would be fussing around his hospital from morning till night. She was tired with over-seeing those stupid negroes and trying to make them set the chairs and tables right side up.

"My dear, don't reproach them for being stupid," said Ravenel. "For nearly a century the whole power of our great Republic, north and south, has been devoted to keep-ing them stupid. Your own State has taken a demoniac interest in this infernal labor. We mustn't quarrel with our own deliberate productions. We wanted stupidity, we have got it, and we must be contented with it. At least for a while. It is your duty and mine to work patiently, courteously and faithfully to undo the horrid results of a century of selfishness. I shall expect you to teach all these poor people to read."

"Teach them to read! what, set up a nigger school!"

"Yes, you born barbarian,—and daughter of a born barbarian,—for I felt that way myself once. I want you in the first place to teach them, and yourself too, how to spell negro with only one *g*. You must not add your efforts to keep this abused race under a stigma of social contempt. You must do what you can to elevate them in sentiment and in knowledge."

"But oh, what a labor! I would rather clean house every day."

"Not so very much of a labor—not so very much of a labor," insisted the Doctor. "Negro children are just as intelligent as white children until they find out that they are black. Now we will never tell them that they are black; we will never hint to them that they are born our inferiors. You will find them bright enough if you won't knock them on the head. Why, you couldn't read your-self till you were seven years old."

"Because you didn't care to have me. I learned quick enough when I set about it."

"Just so. And that proves that it is not too late for our people here to commence their education. Adults can beat children at the alphabet."

"But it is against the law, teaching them to read."

The Doctor burst into a hearty laugh.

"The laws of Dahomey are abrogated," said he. "What a fossil you are! You remind me of my poor doting old friend, Elderkin, who persists in declaring that the invasion of Louisiana was a violation of the Constitution."

By this time the dozen or so of negroes had brought the neglected mansion to a habitable degree of cleanliness, and decked out two or three rooms with what tags and amputated fragments remained of the once fine furniture. A chamber had been prepared for Lillie, and another for the Doctor. A tea-table was set in a picnic sort of style, and crowned with corn cake, fried pork, and roasted sweet potatoes.

"Are you not going to ask in our colored friends?" inquired Lillie, mischievously.

"Why no. I don't see the logical necessity of it. I always have claimed the right of selecting my own intimates. I admit, however, that I have sat at table with less respectable people in some of the most aristocratic houses of New Orleans. Please to drop the satire and put some sugar in my tea."

"Mercy! there is no sugar on the table. The stupid creatures! How can you wonder, papa, that I allow myself to look down on them a little?"

"I don't believe it is possible to get all the virtues and all the talents for nothing a year, or even for ten dollars a month. I will try to induce the Major-General commanding to come and wait on table for us. But I am really afraid I sha'n't succeed. He is very busy. Meantime suppose you should hint to one of the handmaidens, as politely as you can, that I am accustomed to take sugar in my tea."

"Julia!" called Lillie to a mulatto girl of eighteen, who just then entered from the kitchen. "You have given us no sugar. How could you be so silly?"

"Don't!" expostulated the Doctor. "I never knew a woman but scolded her servants, and I never knew a servant but waited the worse for it. All that the good-natured creature desired was to know what you wanted. It didn't clear her head nor soften her heart a bit to call her silly; nor would it have helped matters at all if you had gone on to pelt her with all the hard names in the English language. Be courteous, my dear, to everything that is human. We owe that much of respect to the fact that man is made in the image of his Maker. Politeness is a part of piety."

"When would Mr. Carter be able to visit them?" was Lillie's next spoken idea. Papa really could not say, but hoped very soon—whereupon he was immediately questioned as to the reasons of his hope. Having no special reason to allege, and being driven to admit that, after all, the visit could not positively be counted upon, he was sharply catechised as to *why* he thought Mr. Carter would not come, to which he could only reply by denying he had entertained such a thought. Then followed in rapid succession, "Suppose the brigade leaves Thibodeaux, where will it go to? Suppose General Banks attacks Port Hudson, won't he be obliged to leave Colonel Carter to defend the Lafourche Interior? Suppose the brigade is ordered into the field, will it not, being the best brigade, be always kept in reserve, out of the range of fire?"

"My dear child," deprecated the hunted Doctor, "what happy people those early Greeks must have been who were descended from the immortal gods! They could ask their papas all sorts of questions about the future, and get reliable answers."

"But I am *so* anxious!" said Lillie, dropping back in her chair with a sob, and wiping away her tears with her napkin.

"My poor dear little girl, you must try to keep up a better courage," urged papa in a compassionate tone which only made the drops fall faster, so affecting is pity.

" Nothing has happened to him yet, and we have a right
to hope and pray that nothing will."

" But something *may*," was the persevering answer of
anxiety.

As soon as supper was over she hurried to her room,
locked the door, knelt on the bit of carpet by the bedside,
buried her face in the bed-clothes, and prayed a long time
with tears and sobs, that her husband, her own and dear
husband, might be kept from danger.   She did not even
ask that he might be brought to her; it was enough if he
might only be delivered from the awful perils of battle;
in the humility of her earnestness and terror she had not
the face to require more.   After a while she went down
stairs again with an expression of placid exhaustion, rendered sweeter by a soft glory of religious trust, as the sunset mellowness of our earthly atmosphere is rayed by
beams from a mightier world.   Sitting on a stool at her
father's feet, and laying her head on his knee, she talked
in more cheerful tones of Carter, of their own prospects,
and then again of Carter—for ever of Carter.

" I *will* teach the negroes to read," she said.   " I will
try to do good—and to be good."

She was thinking how she could best win the favor and
protection of Heaven for her husband.   She would teach
the negroes for Carter's sake; she had not yet learned to
do it for Jesus Christ's sake.   She was not a heathen; she
had received the same evangelical instruction that most
young Americans receive; she was perfectly well aware
of the doctrine of salvation by faith and not by works.
But no profound sorrow, no awful sense of helplessness
under the threatening of dangers to those whom she dearly loved, had ever made these things matters of personal
experience and realizing belief.

When the Doctor called in the negroes at nine o'clock,
and read to them a chapter from the Bible, and a prayer,
Lillie joined in the devotions with an unusual sense of humility and earnestness.   In her own room, before going to

bed, she prayed again for Carter, and not for him only, but for herself. Then she quickly fell asleep, for she was young and very tired. How some elderly people, who have learned to toss and count the hours till near morning, envy these infants, whether of twenty months or twenty years, who can so readily cast their sorrows into the profound and tranquil ocean of slumber!

CHAPTER XIX.

THE REORGANIZATION OF SOUTHERN LABOR IS CONTINUED WITH VIGOR.

By six o'clock in the morning the Doctor was out visiting the quarters of his sable dependants. Having on the previous evening told Major Scott, the head man or overseer of the gang, that he should expect the people to rise by daybreak and get their breakfasts immediately, so as to be ready for early work, he was a little astonished to find half of them still asleep, and two or three absent. The Major himself was just leaving the water-butt in rear of the plantation house, where he had evidently been performing his morning ablutions.

"Scott," said the Doctor, " you shouldn't use tnat water. The butt holds hardly enough for the family."

" Yes sah," answered with a reverential bow the Major. " But the butt that we has is mighty dry."

" But there is the bayou, close by."

" Yes sah, so 'tis," assented the Major, with another bow. " I guess I'll think of that nex' time."

"But what are you all about?" asked the Doctor. " I understood that you were all to be up and ready for work by this time."

" I tole the boys so," said the Major in a tone of indignant virtue. " I tole 'em every one to be up an' about right

smart this mornin'. I tole 'em this was the fust mornin' an'
they orter be up right smart, cos everythin' 'pended on
how we took a start. 'Pears like they didn't mine much
about it some of 'em."

"I'm afraid you didn't set them an example, Scott.
Have you had your breakfast?"

"No sah. 'Pears like the ole woman couldn't fetch no-
thin' to pass this mornin'."

"Well, Scott, you must set them an example, if you
want to influence them. Never enjoin any duty upon a
man without setting him an example."

"Yes sah ; that's the true way," coincided the unabashed
Major. "That's the way Abraham an' Isaac an' Jacob
went at it," he added, turning his large eyes upward with
a sanctimoniousness of effect which most men could not
have equalled without the aid of lifted hands, tonsures
and priestly gowns. "An' they was God's 'ticlar child'n,
an 'lightened by his holy sperrit."

The Doctor studied him for a moment with the interest
of a philosopher in a moral curiosity, and said to himself,
rather sadly, that a monkey or a parrot might be educated
to very nearly the same show of piety.

"Are all the people here?" he inquired, reverting from
a consideration of the spiritual harvest to matters connected with temporal agriculture.

"No sah. I'se feared not. Tom an' Jim is gone fo'
suah. Tom he went off las' night down to the fote.
'Pears like he's foun' a gal down thar that he's a co'ting.
Then Jim ;—don' know whar Jim is nohow. Mighty
poor mean nigger he is, I specs. Sort o' no 'count nigger."

"Is he?" said the Doctor, eyeing Scott with a suspicious
air, as if considering the possibility that he too might be a
negro of no account. "I must have a talk with these
people. Get them all together, every man, woman and
pickaninny."

The Major's face was radiant at the prospect of a speech,
a scene, a spectacle, an excitement. He went at his sub-

ordinates with a will, dragging them out of their slumbers by the heels, jerking the little ones along by the shoulder, and shouting in a grand bass voice, " Come, start 'long! Pile out! Git away frum hyer. Mars Ravenel gwine to make a speech."

In a few minutes he had them drawn up in two ranks, men in front, women in the rear, tallest on the right, younglings on the left.

" I knows how to form 'em," he said with a broad smile of satisfied vanity. " I used to c'mand a comp'ny under Gineral Phelps. I was head boss of his cullud 'campment. He fus' give me the title of Major."

He took his post on the right of the line, honored the Doctor with a military salute, and commanded in a hollow roar, " 'Tention!"

" My friends," said the Doctor, " we are all here to earn our living."

" That's so. Bress the Lawd! The good time am a comin'," from the not unintelligent audience.

" Hear me patiently and don't interrupt," continued the Doctor. " I see that you understand and appreciate your good fortune in being able at last to work for the wages of freedom."

" Yes, Mars'r," in a subdued hoarse whisper from Major Scott, who immediately apologized for his liberty by a particularly grand military salute.

" I want to impress upon you," said Ravenel, " that the true dignity of freedom does not consist in laziness. A lazy man is sure to be a poor man, and a poor man is never quite a free man. He is not free to buy what he would like, because he has no money. He is not free to respect himself, for a lazy man is not worthy even of his own respect. We must all work to get any thing or deserve any thing. In old times you used to work because you were afraid of the overseer." " Whip," he was about to say, but skipped the degrading word.

" Now you are to work from hope, and not from fear.

The good time has come when our nation has resolved to declare that the laborer is worthy of his hire."

"Oh, the blessed Scripter!" shouted Madam Scott in a piercing pipe, whereupon her husband gave her a white-eyed glare of reproof for daring to speak when he was silent.

"Your future depends upon yourselves," the Doctor went on. "You can become useful and even influential citizens, if you will. But you must be industrious and honest, and faithful to your engagements. I want you to understand this perfectly. I will talk more to you about it some other time. Just now I wish chiefly to impress upon you your immediate duties while you are on this plantation. I shall expect you all to sleep in your quarters. I shall expect you to be up at daybreak, get your breakfasts as soon as possible, and be ready to go to work at once. You must not leave the plantation during the day without my permission. You will work ten hours a day during the working season. You will be orderly, honest, virtuous and respectable. In return I am to give you rations, clothing, quarters, fuel, medical attendance, and instruction for children. I am also to pay you as wages eight dollars a month for first-class hands, and six for second-class. Each of you will have his little plot of land. Finally, I will endeavor to see that you are all, old and young, taught to read."

Here there was an unanimous shout of delight, followed by articulate blessings and utterances of gratitude.

"Whenever any one gets dissatisfied," concluded the Doctor, "I will apply to find him another place. You know that, if you go off alone and without authority, you are exposed to be picked up by the provost-marshal, and put in the army. Now then, get your breakfasts. Major Scott, you will report to me when they are ready to go to work."

While the Major offered up a ponderous salute, the line dispersed in gleesome confusion, which was a sore disappointment to him, as he wanted to make it right face, clap hands, and break ranks in military fashion. The Doctor went to breakfast with the most cheerful confidence in his retainers, notwithstanding the idle opening of this morning. As soon as the poor fellows knew what he expected of them, they would be sure to do it, if it was anything in reason, he said to Lillie. The negroes were ignorant of their duty, and often thoughtless of it, but they were at bottom zealous to do right, and honestly disposed toward people who paid them for their labor. And here the author ventures to introduce the historical doubt as to whether any other half-barbarous race was ever blessed and beautified with such a lovingly grateful spirit as descended, like the flames of the day of Pentecost, upon the bondsmen of America when their chains were broken by the just hands of the great Republic. Impure in life by reason of their immemorial degradation, first as savages, and then as slaves, they were pure in heart by reason of their fervent joy and love.

Under no urgency but that of their own thankfulness the Doctor's negroes did more work that summer than the Robertsons had ever got from double their number by the agency of a white overseer, drivers, whips and paddles. On the second morning they were all present and up at daybreak, including even Tom the lovelorn, and Jim the "no 'count nigger." In a couple of weeks they had split out many wagon-loads of rails from the forest in rear of the plantation, put the broken-down fences in order, and prepared a sufficient tract of ground for planting. Not a pig nor a chicken disappeared from the Doctor's flocks and herds, if I may be allowed to apply such magnificent terms to bristly and feathered creatures. On the contrary, his small store of live-stock increased with a rapidity which seemed miraculous, and which was inadequately explained by the non-committal commentary of Major Scott, "Specs it mebbe in anser to prayer." Ravenel finally learned, to his intense mortification, that his over-zealous henchmen

M

were in the habit of depredating nightly on the property of adjacent planters of the old Secession stock, and adding such of their spoils as they did not need, to his limited zoological collection. Under the pangs of this discovery he made a tour of apology and restitution through the neighborhood, and on returning from it, called his hands together and delivered them a lecture on the universal application of the law of honesty. They heard him with suppressed titters and hastily eclipsed grins, nudging each other in the side, and exhibiting a keen perception of the practical humor and poetical justice of their roguery.

" 'Pears like you don' wan' to spile the 'Gyptians, Mars Ravenel," observed a smirking, shining darkey known as Mr. Mo. " You's one o' God's chosen people, an' you's been in slavery somethin' like we has, an' you has a right to dese yere rebel chickins."

" My good people," replied the Doctor, " I don't say but that *you* have a right to all the rebel chickens in Louisiana. I deny that I have. I have always been well paid for my labor. And even to you I would say, be forgiving,—be magnanimous,—avoid even the appearance of evil. It is your great business, your great duty toward yourselves, to establish a character for perfect honesty and harmlessness. If you haven't enough to eat, I don't mind adding something to your rations."

" We *has* 'nuff to eat," thundered Major Scott. " Let the man as says we hasn't step out *yere*."

Nobody stepped out ; everybody was full of nourishment and content ; and the interview terminated in a buzz of satisfaction and suppressed laughter. Thenceforward the Doctor had the virtuous pleasure of observing that his legitimate pigs and chickens were left to their natural means of increase.

Lillie's reading schools, held every evening in one of the unfurnished rooms of the second story, were attended regularly by both sexes, and all ages of this black population. The rapidity of their progress at first astonished and eventually delighted her, in proportion as she gradually took her ignorant but zealous scholars to her heart. The eagerness, the joy, the gratitude even to tears, with which they accepted her tuition was touching. They pronounced the words " Miss Lillie " with a tone and manner which seemed to lay soul and body at her feet; and when the Doctor entered the schoolroom on one of his visits of inspection they gave him a dazzling welcome of grins and rolling eyes; the spectacle reminded him vaguely of such spiritual expressions crowns of glory and stars in the firmament. If the gratitude of the humble is a benediction, few people have ever been more blessed than were the Ravenels at this period.

As a truthful historian I must admit that there were some rotten specks in the social fruit which the Doctor was trying to raise from this barbarous stock. Lillie was annoyed, was even put out of all patience temporarily, by occasional scandals which came to light among her sable pupils and were referred to her or to her father for settlement. That eminent dignitary and supposed exemplar of purity, Major Scott, was the very first to be detected in capital sin, the scandal being all the more grievous because he was not only the appointed industrial manager, but the self-elected spiritual overseer of the colored community. He preached to them every Sunday afternoon, and secretly plumed himself on being more fluent by many degrees than Mars Ravenel, who conducted the morning exercises chiefly through the agency of Bible and prayer-book. His copiousness of language, and abundance of Scriptural quotation was quite wonderful. In volume of sound his praying was as if a bull of Bashan had had a gift in prayer; and if Heaven could have been taken, like Jericho, by mere noise, Major Scott was able to take it alone. Had he been born white and decently educated, he would probably have made a popular orator either of the pulpit or forum. He had the lungs for, it, the volubility and the imagination. In pious conversation, venerable air, grand physique, superb bass voice, musical ear, perfection of teeth, and shining white of the eyes, he was a counterpart of Mrs. Stowe's immortal idealism, Uncle Tom. But, like some white Christians, this tolerably exemplary black had not yet arrived at the ability to keep the whole decalogue. He sometimes got a fall in his wrestlings with the sin of lying, and in regard to the seventh commandment he was even more liable to overthrow than King David. Ravenel had much ado to heal some social heart-burnings caused by the Major's want of illumination concerning the binding nature of the marriage contract. He got him married over again by the chaplain of the garrison at Fort Winthrop, and then informed him that, in case of any more scandals, he should report him to the provost-marshal as a proper character to enter the army.

"I'se very sorry for what's come to pass, Mars Ravenel," said the alarmed and repentant culprit. "But now I 'specs to go right forrad in the path of duty. I s'pose now Mars Chaplain has done it strong. Ye see, afore it wasn't done strong. I wasn't rightly married, like 'spectable folks is, nohow. Ef I'd been married right strong, like 'spectable white folks is, I wouldn't got into this muss an fotched down shame on 'ligion, for which I'se mighty sorry an' been about repentin in secret places with many tears. That's so, Mars Ravenel, as true as I hopes to be forgiven."

Here the Major's manhood, what he had of it, broke down, or, perhaps I ought to say, showed itself honorably, and he wept copious tears of what I must charitably accept as true compunction.

"I am a little disappointed, but not much astonished," said the Doctor, discussing this matter with the Chaplain. "I was inclined to hope at one time that I had found an actual Uncle Tom. I was anxious and even ready to believe that the mere gift of freedom had exalted and purified the negro character notwithstanding uncounted centuries of barbarism or of oppression. But in hoping a moral miracle I was hoping too much. I ought not to have expected that a St. Vincent de Paul could be raised under the injustice and dissoluteness of the sugar-planting system. After all, the Major is no worse than David. That is pretty well for a man whom the American Republic, thirty millions strong, has repressed and kept brutish with its whole power from his birth down to about a year ago."

" It seems to me," answered the Chaplain,—" I beg your pardon,—but it seems to me that you don't sufficiently consider the enlightening power of divine grace. If this man had ever been truly regenerated (which I fear is not the case), I doubt whether he would have fallen into this sin."

" My dear sir," said the Doctor warmly, " renewing a man's heart is only a partial reformation, unless you illuminate his mind. He wants to do right, but how is he to know what is right ? Suppose he can't read. Suppose half of the Bible is not told him. Suppose he is misled by half the teaching, and all the example of those whom he looks up to as in every respect his superiors. I am disposed to regard Scott as a very fair attempt at a Christian, considering his chances. I am grieved over his error, but I do not think it a case for righteous indignation, except against men who brought this poor fellow up so badly."

" But Uncle Tom," instanced the Chaplain, who had not been long in the South.

" My dear sir, Uncle Tom is a pure fiction. There never was such a slave, and there never will be. A man educated under the degrading influences of bondage must always have some taint of uncommon grossness and lowness. I don't believe that Onesimus was a pattern of piety. But St. Paul had the moral sense, the Christianity, to make allowance for his disadvantages, and he recommended him to Philemon, no doubt as a weak brother who required special charity and instruction."

Injured husbands of the slave-grown breed are rarely

implacable in their anger; and before a fortnight had passed, Major Scott was preaching and praying among his colored brethren with as much confidence and acceptance as ever.

The season opened delightfully with the Ravenels. Lillie was occasionally doleful at not getting letters from her husband, and sometimes depressed by the solitude and monotony of plantation life. Her father, being more steadily occupied, and having no affectionate worry on his mind, was constantly and almost boyishly cheerful. It was one of his characteristics to be contented under nearly any circumstances. Wherever he happened to be he thought it was a very nice place; and if he afterwards found a spot with superior advantages, he simply liked it better still. I can easily believe that, but for the stigma of forced confinement, he would have been quite happy in a prison, and that, on regaining his liberty, he would simply have remarked, " Why, it is even pleasanter outside than in."

But I am running ahead of some important events in my story. Lillie received a letter from her husband saying that he should visit the family soon, and then another informing her that in consequence of an unforeseen press of business, he should be obliged to postpone the visit for a few days. His two next letters were written from Brashear City on the Atchafalaya river, but contained no explanation of his presence there. Then came a silence of three days, which caused her to torture herself with all sorts of gloomy doubts and fears, and made her fly for forgetfulness or comfort to her housekeeping, her school, and her now frequent private devotions. The riddle was explained when the Doctor procured a New Orleans paper at the fort, with the news that Banks had crossed the Atchafalaya and beaten the enemy at Camp Beasland.

"It's all right," he said, as he entered the house. He waved the paper triumphantly, and smiled with a counterfeit delight, anxious to forestall her alarm.

" Oh ! what is it ?" asked Lillie with a choking sensation, fearful that it might not be quite as right as she wanted.

" Banks has defeated the enemy in a great battle. Colonel Carter is unhurt, and honorably mentioned for bravery and ability."

" Oh, papa !"

She had turned very white at the thought of the peril through which her husband had passed, and the possibility, instantaneously foreseen, that he might be called to encounter yet other dangers.

" We ought to be very grateful, my darling."

" Oh ! why has he gone ? Why didn't he tell me that he was going ? Why did he leave me so in the dark?" was all that Lillie could say in the way of thankfulness.

" My child, don't be unreasonable. He wished of course to save you from unnecessary anxiety. It was very kind and wise in him."

Lillie snatched the paper, ran to her own room and read the official bulletin over and over, dropping her tears upon it and kissing the place where her husband was praised and recommended for promotion. Then she thought how generous and grand he was to go forth to battle in silence, without uttering a word to alarm her, without making an appeal for her sympathy. The greatest men of history have not seemed so great to the world as did this almost unknown colonel of volunteers to his wife. She was in a passion, an almost unearthly ecstasy of grief, terror, admiration and love. It is well that we cannot always feel thus strongly ; if we did, we should not average twenty years of life ; if we did, the human race would perish.

Next day came two letters from Carter, one written before and one after the battle. In his description of the fighting he was as professional, brief and unenthusiastic as usual, merely mentioning the fact of success, narrating in two sentences the part which his brigade had taken in the action, and saying nothing of his own dangers or performances. But there was another subject on which he was more copious, and this part of the letter Lillie prized most of all. "I am afraid I sicken you with such fondness," he concluded. "It seems to me that you must get tired of reading over and over again the same endearing phrases and pet names."

"Oh, never imagine that I can sicken of hearing or reading that you love me," she answered. "You must not cheat me of a single pet name; you must call me by such names over and over in every letter. I always skim through your letters to read those dear words first. I should be utterly and forever miserable if I did not believe that you love me, and did not hear so from you constantly."

At this time Lillie knew by heart all her husband's letters. Let her eye rest on the envelope of one which she had received a week or a fortnight previous, and she could repeat its contents almost verbatim, certainly not missing one of the loving phrases aforesaid. Through the New Orleans papers and these same wonderful epistles she followed the victorious army in its onward march, now at Franklin, now at Opelousas, and now at Alexandria. It was all good news, except that her husband was forever going farther away; the Rebels were always flying, the triumphant Unionists were always pursuing, and there were no more battles. She flattered herself that the summer campaign was over, and that Carter would soon get a leave of absence and come to his own home to be petted and worshipped.

From Alexandria arrived a letter of Colburne's to the Doctor. The young man had needed all this time and these events to fortify him for the task of writing to the Ravenels. For a while after that marriage it seemed to him as if he never could have the courage to meet them, nor even call to their attention the fact of his continued existence. His congratulations were written with labored care, and the rest of the letter in a style of affected gayety. I shall copy from it a single extract, because it bears some relation to the grand reconstruction experiment of the Doctor.

" I hear that you are doing your part towards organizing free labor in Louisiana. I fear that you will find it an up-hill business, not only from the nature of your surroundings but from that of your material. I am as much of an abolitionist as ever, but not so much of a 'nigger-worshipper.' I don't know but that I shall yet become an advocate of slavery. I frequently think that my boy Henry will fetch me to it. He is an awful boy. He dances and gambles all night, and then wants to sleep all day. If the nights and days were a thousand years long apiece, he would keep it up in the same fashion. In order that he may not be disturbed in his rest by my voice, he goes away from camp and curls up in some refuge which I have not yet discovered. I pass hours every day in shouting for Henry. Of course his labors are small and far between. He brushes my boots in the morning because he doesn't go to bed till after I get up ; but if I want them polished during the day,—at dress-parade, for instance,— it is not Henry who polishes them. When I scold him for his worthlessness, he laughs most obstropolously (I value myself on this word, because to my ear it describes Henry's laughter exactly). For his services, or rather for what he ought to do and doesn't, I pay him ten dollars a month, with rations and clothing. He might earn two or three times as much on the levee at New Orleans ; but the lazy creature would rather not earn anything ; he likes to get his living gratis, as he does with me. This is the way he came to join me. When I was last in New Orleans, Henry, whom I had previously known as the body servant of one of my sergeants, paid me a visit. Said I, ' What are you doing ?' "

" ' Workin 'on 'ee levee.'

" ' How much do you get ?'

"'It's 'cordin' to what I doos. Ef I totes a big stent, I gits two dollars; an' ef I totes 'nuff to kill a hoss, I gits two dollars 'n 'aff a day.'

"'Why, that is grand pay. That is a great deal better than hanging around camp for nothing but your board and clothes. I am glad you have gone at some profitable and manly labor. Stick to it, and make a man of yourself. Get some money in the bank, and then give yourself a little schooling. You can make yourself as truly respectable as any white man, Henry.'

"'Ya–as,' he said hesitatingly, as if he thought the result hardly worth the trouble; for which opinion I hardly blame him, considering the nature of a great many white men of this country. 'But it am right hard work, Cap'm.'—Here he chuckled causelessly and absurdly.—'Sometimes I thinks I'd like to come and do chores for you, Cap'm.'

"'Oh no,' I remonstrated. 'Don't think of giving up your respectable and profitable industry. I couldn't afford to pay you more than ten dollars a month."

Here he laughed in his obstropolous and irrational fashion, signifying thereby, I think, that he was embarrassed by my arguments.

"Well, I kinder likes dem terms," he said. "'Pears like I wants to have a good time better'n to have a heap o' money."

And so here he is with me, having a good time, and getting more money than he deserves. Now when you have freed with your own right hand as many of these lazy bumpkins as I have, you will feel at liberty to speak of them with the same disrespectful levity. Wendell Phillips says that the negro is the only man in America who can afford to fold his arms and quietly await his future. That is just what the critter is doing, and just what puts me out of patience with him. Moreover, he can't afford it; if he doesn't fall to work pretty soon, we shall cease to be negrophilists; we shall kick him out of doors and get in somebody who is not satisfied with folding his arms and waiting his future."

"He is too impatient," said the Doctor, after he had finished reading the letter to Lillie. "Just like all young people—and some old ones. God has chosen to allow himself a hundred years to free the negro. We must not grumble if He chooses to use up a hundred more in civilizing him. I can answer that letter, to my own satisfaction. What right has Captain Colburne to demand roses or potatoes of land which has been sown for centuries with nothing but thistles? We ought to be thankful if it merely lies barren for a while."

CHAPTER XX.

CAPTAIN COLBURNE MARCHES AND FIGHTS WITH CREDIT.

THE consideration of Mr. Colburne's letter induces me to take up once more the thread of that young warrior's history. In the early part of this month of May, 1863, we find him with his company, regiment and brigade, encamped on the bank of the Red River, just outside of the once flourishing little city of Alexandria, Louisiana. Under the protection of a clapboard shanty, five feet broad and ten feet high, which three or four of his men have voluntarily built for him, he is lying at full length, smoking his short wooden pipe with a sense of luxury; for since he left his tent at Brashear City, four weeks previous, this is the first shelter which he has had to protect him from the rain, except one or two ticklish mansions of rails, piled up by Henry of the "obstropolous" laughter. The brigade encampment, a mushroom city which has sprung up in a day, presenting every imaginable variety of temporary cabin, reaches half a mile up and down the river, under the shade of a long stretch of ashes and beeches. Hundreds of soldiers are bathing in the reddish-ochre current, regardless of the possibility that the thick woods of the opposite bank may conceal Rebel marksmen.

Colburne has eaten his dinner of fried pork and hard-tack, has washed off the grime of a three days' march, has finished his pipe, and is now dropping gently into a soldier's child-like yet light slumber. He does not mind the babble of voices about him, but if you should say " Fall in !" he would be on his feet in an instant. He is a handsome model of a warrior as he lies there, though rougher and plainer in dress than a painter would be apt to make him. He is dark-red with sunburn; gaunt with bad food, irregular food, fasting and severe marching; gaunt and wiry, but all the hardier and stronger for it, like a wolf. His coarse fatigue uniform is dirty with sleeping on the ground, and with marching through mud and clouds of dust. It has been soaked over and over again with rain or perspiration, and then powdered thickly with the fine-grained, unctuous soil of Louisiana, until it is almost stiff enough to stand alone. He cannot wash it, because it is the only suit he has brought with him, and because moreover he never knows but that he may be ordered to fall in and march at five minutes' notice.

Yet his body and even his mind are in the soundest and most enviable health. His constant labors and hardships, and his occasional perils have preserved him from that enfeebling melancholy which often infects sensitive spirits upon whom has beaten a storm of trouble. Always in the open air, never poisoned by the neighborhood of four walls and a roof, he never catches cold, and rarely fails to have more appetite than food. He has borne as well as the hardiest mason or farmer those terrific forced marches which have brought the army from Camp Beasland to Alexandria on a hot scent after the flying and scattering rebels. His feet have been as sore as any man's ; they have been blistered from toe to heel, and swollen beyond their natural size ; but he has never yet laid down by the roadside nor crawled into an army wagon, saying that he could march no further. He is loyal and manly in his endurance, and is justly proud of it. In one of his letters he says, "I was fully repaid for yesterday's stretch of thirty-five miles by overhearing one of my Irishmen say, while washing his bloody feet, 'Be —— ! but he's a hardy man, the Captin !'—To which another responded, 'An' he had his hands full to kape the byes' courage up; along in the afthernoon, he was a jokin' an' scoldin' an' encouragin' for ten miles together. Be —— ! an' when *he* gives out, it 'ull be for good rayson.'"

From Alexandria, Banks suddenly shifted his army to the junction of the Red River with the Mississippi, and from thence by transport to a point north of Port Hudson, thus cutting it off from communication with the Confederacy. In this movement Weitzel took command of the Reserve Brigade and covered the rear of the column. By night it made prodigious marches, and by day lay in threatening line of battle. The Rebel Cavalry, timid and puzzled, followed at a safe distance without attacking. Now came the delicious sail from Simmsport to Bayou Sara, during which Colburne could lounge at ease on the deck with a sense of luxury in the mere consciousness that he was not marching, and repose his mind, his eyes, his very muscles, by gazing on the fresh green bluffs which faced each other across the river. To a native of hilly New England, who had passed above a year on the flats of Louisiana, it was delightful to look once more upon a rolling country.

It was through an atmosphere of scalding heat and stifling dust that the brigade marched up the bluffs of Bayou Sara and over the rounded eminences which stretched on to Port Hudson. The perspiration which drenched the ragged uniforms and the pulverous soil which powdered them rapidly mixed into a muddy plaster; and the same plaster grimed the men's faces out of almost all semblance to humanity, except where the dust clung dry and gray to hair, beard, eyebrows and eyelashes. So dense was the distressing cloud that it was impossible at times to see the length of a company. It seemed as if the men would go rabid with thirst, and drive the officers mad with their pleadings to leave the ranks for water, a privilege not allowable to any great extent in an enemy's country. A lovely crystal streamlet, running knee-deep over clean yellow sand, a charming contrast to black or brown bayous with muddy and treacherous banks, was forded by the feverish ranks with shouts and laughter of child-like enjoyment. But it was through volumes of burning yet lazy dust, soiling and darkening the glory of sunset, that the brigade reached its appointed bivouac in a large clearing, only two miles from the rebel stronghold, though hidden from it by a dense forest of oaks, beeches and magnolias.

It is too early to tell, it is even too early to know, the whole truth concerning the siege of Port Hudson. To an honest man, anxious that the world shall not be humbugged, it is a mournful reflection that perhaps the whole truth never will be known to any one who will dare or care to tell it. We gained a victory there; we took an important step towards the end of the Rebellion; but at what cost, through what means, and by whose merit? It was a capital idea, whosesoever it was, to clean out Taylor's Texans and Louisianians from the Teche country before we undertook the siege of Gardner's Arkansians, Alabamians, and Mississippians at Port Hudson. But for somebody's blunder at that well-named locality, Irish Bend, the plan would have succeeded better than it did, and Taylor would not have been able to reorganize, take Brashear City, threaten New Orleans, and come near driving Banks from his main enterprise. As it was we opened the siege with fair prospects of success, and no disturbing force in the rear. The garrison, lately fifteen or twenty thousand strong, had been reduced to six thousand, in order to reinforce Vicksburg; and Joe Johnston had already directed Gardner to destroy his fortifications and transfer all his

men to the great scene of contest on the central Mississippi.
Banks arrived from Simmsport just in time to prevent
the execution of this order. A smart skirmish was fought,
in which we lost more men than the enemy, but forced
Gardner to retire within his works, and accept the eventu-
alities of an investment.

At five o'clock on the morning of the 27th of May, Colburne was awakened by an order to fall in. Whether it
signified an advance on our part, or a sally by the enemy,
he did not know nor ask, but with a soldier's indifference
proceeded to form his company, and, that done, ate his
breakfast of raw pork and hard biscuit. He would have
been glad to have Henry boil him a cup of coffee ; but that
idle freedman was " having a good time," probably sleeping, in some unknown refuge. For two hours the ranks
sat on the ground, musket in hand; then Colburne saw
the foremost line, a quarter of a mile in front, advance
into the forest. One of Weitzel's aids now dashed up to
Carter, and immediately his staff-officers galloped away to
the different commanders of regiments. An admonishing
murmur of " Fall in, men !"—" Attention, men !" from the
captains ran along the line of the Tenth, and the soldiers
rose in their places to meet the grand, the awful possibility of battle. It was a long row of stern faces, bronzed
with sunburn, sallow in many cases with malaria, grave
with the serious emotions of the hour, but hardened by the
habit of danger, and set as firm as flints toward the enemy. The old innocence of the peaceable New England
farmer and mechanic had disappeared from these war-
seared visages, and had been succeeded by an expression
of hardened combativeness, not a little brutal, much like
the look of a lazy bull-dog. Colburne smiled with pleasure and pride as he glanced along the line of his company,
and noted this change in its physiognomy. For the purpose for which they were drawn up there they were better men than when he first knew them, and as good men
as the sun ever shone upon.

At last the Lieutenant-Colonel's voice rang out, "Battalion, forward. Guide right. March!"

To keep the ranks closed and aligned in any tolerable fighting shape while struggling through that mile of tangled forest and broken ground, was a task of terrible difficulty. Plunging through thickets, leaping over fallen trees, a continuous foliage overhead, and the fallen leaves of many seasons under foot, the air full of the damp, mouldering smell of virgin forest, the brigade moved forward with no sound but that of its own tramplings. It is peculiar of the American attack that it is almost always made in line, and always without music. The men expected to meet the enemy at every hillock, but they advanced rapidly, and laughed at each other's slippings and tumbles. Every body was breathless with climbing over obstacles or running around them. The officers were beginning to swear at the broken ranks and unsteady pace. The Lieutenant-Colonel, perceiving that the regiment was diverging from its comrades, and fearing the consequences of a gap in case the enemy should suddenly open fire, rode repeatedly up and down the line, yelling, "Guide right! Close up to the right!" Suddenly, to the amazement of every one, the brigade came upon bivouacs of Union regiments quietly engaged in distributing rations and preparing breakfast.

"What are you doing up here?" asked a Major of Colburne.

"We are going to attack. Don't you take part in it?"

"I suppose so. I don't know. We have received no orders."

Through this scene of tardiness, the result perhaps of one of those blunders which are known in military as well as in all other human operations, Weitzel's division steadily advanced, much wondering if it was to storm Port Hudson alone. The ground soon proved so difficult that the Tenth, unable to move in line of battle, filed into a faintly marked forest road and pushed forward by the flank in the ordinary column of march. The battle had already commenced, although Colburne could see nothing of it, and could hear nothing but a dull *pum-pum-pum* of cannon. He passed rude rifle-pits made of earth and large branches, which had been carried only a few minutes previous by the confused rush of the leading brigade. Away to the right, but not near enough to be heard above the roar of artillery, there was a wild, scattering musketry of broken lines, fighting and scrambling along as they best could over thicketed knolls, and through rugged gullies, on the track of the retiring Alabamians and Arkansans. It was the blindest and most perplexing forest labyrinth conceivable ; it was impossible to tell whither you were going, or whether you would stumble on friends or enemies ; the regiments were split into little squads from which all order had disappeared, but which nevertheless advanced.

The Tenth was still marching through the woods by the flank, unable to see either fortifications or enemy, when it came under the fire of artillery, and encountered the retiring stream of wounded. At this moment, and for two hours afterward, the uproar of heavy guns, bursting shells, falling trees and flying splinters was astonishing, stunning, horrible, doubled as it was by the sonorous echoes of the forest. Magnolias, oaks and beeches eighteen inches or two feet in diameter, were cut asunder with a deafening scream of shot and of splitting fibres, the tops falling after a pause of majestic deliberation, not sidewise, but stem downwards, like a descending parachute, and striking the earth with a dull shuddering thunder. They seemed to give up their life with a roar of animate anguish, as if they were savage beasts, or as if they were inhabited by Afreets and Demons.

The unusually horrible clamor and the many-sided nature of the danger had an evident effect on the soldiers, hardened as they were to scenes of ordinary battle. Grim faces turned in every direction with hasty stares of alarm, looking aloft and on every side, as well as to the front, for

destruction. Pallid stragglers who had dropped out of
the leading brigade drifted by the Tenth, dodging from
trunk to trunk in an instinctive search for cover, although
it was visible that the forest was no protection, but rather an additional peril. Every regiment has its two or
three cowards, or perhaps its half-dozen, weakly-nerved
creatures, whom nothing can make fight, and who never
do fight. One abject hound, a corporal with his disgraced stripes upon his arm, came by with a ghastly
backward glare of horror, his face colorless, his eyes projecting, and his chin shaking. Colburne cursed him for
a poltroon, struck him with the flat of his sabre, and
dragged him into the ranks of his own regiment; but
the miserable creature was too thoroughly unmanned by
the great horror of death to be moved to any show of
resentment or even of courage by the indignity; he only gave an idiotic stare with outstretched neck toward
the front, then turned with a nervous jerk, like that of a
scared beast, and rushed rearward. Further on, six men
were standing in single file behind a large beech, holding
each other by the shoulders, when with a stunning crash
the entire top of the tree flew off and came down among
them butt foremost, sending out a cloud of dust and splinters. Colburne smiled grimly to see the paralyzed terror
of their upward stare, and the frantic flight which barely
saved them from being crushed jelly. A man who keeps
the ranks hates a skulker, and wishes that he may be
killed, the same as any other enemy.

"But in truth," says the Captain, in one of his letters,
"the sights and sounds of this battle-reaped forest were
enough to shake the firmest nerves. Never before had I
been so tried as I was during that hour in this wilderness
of death. It was not the slaughter which unmanned me,
for our regiment did not lose very heavily; it was the stupendous clamor of the cannonade and of the crashing trees
which seemed to overwhelm me by its mere physical
power; and it made me unable to bear spectacles which I

had witnessed in other engagements with perfect composure.   When one of our men was borne by me with half
his foot torn off by a round shot, the splintered bones projecting clean and white from the ragged raw flesh, I grew
so sick that perhaps I might have fainted if a brother officer had not given me a sip of whiskey from his canteen.
It was the only occasion in my fighting experience when
I have had to resort to that support.   I had scarcely recovered myself when I saw a broad flow of blood stream
down the face of a color-corporal who stood within arm's-
length of me.   I thought he was surely a dead man; but it
was only one of the wonderful escapes of battle.   The bullet had skirted his cap where the fore-piece joins the cloth,
forcing the edge of the leather through the skin, and making a clean cut to the bone from temple to temple.   He
went to the rear blinded and with a smart headache, but
not seriously injured.   That we were not slaughtered by
the wholesale is wonderful, for we were closed up in a
compact mass, and the shot came with stunning rapidity.
A shell burst in the centre of my company, tearing one
man's heel to the bone, but doing no other damage.   The
wounded man, a good soldier though as quiet and gentle
as a bashful girl, touched his hat to me, showed his bleeding foot, and asked leave to go to the rear, which I of
course granted.   While he was speaking, another shell
burst about six feet from the first, doing no harm at all,
although so near to Van Zandt as to dazzle and deafen
him."

Presently a section of Bainbridge's regular battery came
up, winding slowly through the forest, the guns thump-
ing over roots and fallen limbs, the men sitting superbly
erect on their horses, and the color-sergeant holding his
battle-flag as proudly as a knight-errant ever bore his pen-
non.   In a minute the two brass Napoleons opened with a
sonorous *spang*, which drew a spontaneous cheer from
the delighted infantry.   The edge of the wood was now
reached, and Colburne could see the enemy's position.   In

front of him lay a broad and curving valley, irregular in
surface, and seamed in some places by rugged gorges, the
whole made more difficult of passage by a multitude of
felled trees, the leafless trunks and branches of which
were tangled into an inextricable *chevaux de frise*. On the
other side of this valley rose a bluff or table-land, partially
covered with forest, but showing on its cleared spaces the
tents and cabins of the Rebel encampments. Along the
edge of the bluff, following its sinuosities, and at this distance looking like mere natural banks of yellow earth, ran
the fortifications of Port Hudson. Colburne could see
Paine's brigade of Weitzel's division descending into the
valley, forcing its bloody way through a roaring cannonade and a continuous screech of musketry.

An order came to the commander of the Tenth to deploy
two companies as skirmishers in the hollow in front of
Bainbridge, and push to the left with the remainder of
the regiment, throwing out other skirmishers and silencing
the Rebel artillery. One of the two detached companies
was Colburne's, and he took command of both as senior
officer. At the moment that he filed his men out of the
line a murmur ran through the regiment that the Lieutenant-Colonel was killed or badly wounded. Then came an
inquiry as to the whereabouts of the Major.

"By Jove! it wouldn't be a dangerous job to hunt for
him," chuckled Van Zandt.

"Why? Where is he?" asked Colburne.

"I don't believe, by Jove! that I could say within a
mile or two. I only know, by Jove! that he is *non est
inventus*. I saw him a quarter of an hour ago charging
for the rear with his usual impetuosity. I'll bet my everlasting salvation that he's in the safest spot within ten
miles of this d——d unhealthy neighborhood."

The senior captain took command of the regiment, and
led it to the left on a line parallel with the fortifications.
Colburne descended with his little detachment, numbering
about eighty muskets, into that Valley of the Shadow of

Death, climbing over or creeping under the fallen trunks of the tangled labyrinth, and making straight for the bluff on which thundered and smoked the rebel stronghold. As his men advanced they deployed, spreading outwards like the diverging blades of a fan until they covered a front of nearly a quarter of a mile. Every stump, every prostrate trunk, every knoll and gulley was a temporary breastwork, from behind which they poured a slow but fatal fire upon the rebel gunners, who could be plainly seen upon the hostile parapet working their pieces. The officers and sergeants moved up and down the line, each behind his own platoon or section, steadily urging it forward.

"Move on, men. Move on, men," Colburne repeated. "Don't expose yourselves. Use the covers; use the stumps. But keep moving on. Don't take root. Don't stop till we reach the ditch."

In spite of their intelligent prudence the men were falling under the incessant flight of bullets. A loud scream from a thicket a little to Colburne's right attracted his attention.

"Who is that?" he called.

"It is Allen!" replied a sergeant. "He is shot through the body. Shall I send him to the rear?"

"Not now, wait till we are relieved. Prop him up and leave him in the shade."

He had in his mind this passage of the Army Regulations: "Soldiers must not be permitted to leave the ranks to strip or rob the dead, nor even to assist the wounded, unless by express permission, which is only to be given after the action is decided. The highest interest and most pressing duty is to win the victory, by which only can a proper care of the wounded be ensured."

Turning to a soldier who had mounted a log and stood up at the full height of his six feet to survey the fortifications, Colburne shouted, "Jump down, you fool. You will get yourself hit for nothing."

"Captain, I can't see a chance for a shot," replied the fellow deliberately.

"Get down!" reiterated Colburne; but the man had waited too long already. Throwing up both hands he fell backward with an incoherent gurgle, pierced through the lungs by a rifle-ball. Then a little Irish soldier burst out swearing, and hastily pulled his trousers to glare at a bullet-hole through the calf of his leg, with a comical expression of mingled surprise, alarm and wrath. And so it went on: every few minutes there was an oath of rage or a shriek of pain; and each outcry marked the loss of a man. But all the while the line of skirmishers advanced.

The sickishness which troubled Colburne in the cannon-smitten forest had gone, and was succeeded by the fierce excitement of close battle, where the combatants grow angry and savage at sight of each other's faces. He was throbbing with elation and confidence, for he had cleaned off the gunners from the two pieces in his front. He felt as if he could take Port Hudson with his detachment alone. The contest was raging in a clamorous rattle of musketry on the right, where Paine's brigade, and four regiments of the Reserve Brigade, all broken into detachments by gullies, hillocks, thickets and fallen trees, were struggling to turn and force the fortifications. On his left other companies of the Tenth were slowly moving forward, deployed and firing as skirmishers. In his front the Rebel musketry gradually slackened, and only now and then could he see a broad-brimmed hat show above the earthworks and hear the hoarse whistle of a Minie-ball as it passed him. The garrison on this side was clearly both few in number and disheartened. It seemed to him likely, yes even certain, that Port Hudson would be carried by storm that morning. At the same time, half mad as he was with the glorious intoxication of successful battle, he knew that it would be utter folly to push his unsupported detachment into the works, and that such a movement would probably end in slaughter or capture. Fifteen or twenty, he did not know precisely how many, of his soldiers had been hit, and the survivors were getting short of cartridges.

"Steady, men!" he shouted. "Halt! Take cover and hold your position. Don't waste your powder. Fire slow and aim sure."

The orders were echoed from man to man along the extended, straggling line, and each one disappeared behind the nearest thicket, stump or fallen tree. Colburne had already sent three corporals to the regiment to recount his success and beg for more men; but neither had the messengers reappeared nor reinforcements arrived to support his proposed assault.

"Those fellows must have got themselves shot," he said to Van Zandt. "I'll go myself. Keep the line where it is, and save the cartridges."

Taking a single soldier with him, he hurried rearward by the clearest course that he could find through the prostrate forest, without minding the few bullets that whizzed by him. Suddenly he halted, powerless, as if struck by paralysis, conscious of a general nervous shock, and a sharp pain in his left arm. His first impulse,—a very hurried impulse,—was to take the arm with his right hand and twist it to see if the bone was broken. Next he looked about him for some shelter from the scorching and crazing sunshine. He espied a green bush, and almost immediately lost sight of it, for the shock made him faint although the pain was but momentary.

"Are you hurt, Captain?" asked the soldier.

"Take me to that bush," said Colburne, pointing—for he knew where the cover was, although he could not see it.

The soldier put an arm round his waist, led him to the bush, and laid him down.

"Shall I go for help, Captain?"

"No. Don't weaken the company. All right. No bones broken. Go on in a minute."

The man tied his handkerchief about the ragged and

bloody hole in the coat-sleeve; then sat down and reloaded his musket, occasionally casting a glance at the pale face of the Captain. In two or three minutes Colburne's color came back, and he felt as well as ever. He rose carefully to his feet, looked about him as if to see where he was, and again set off for the regiment, followed by his silent companion. The bullets still whizzed about them, but did no harm. After a slow walk of ten minutes, during which Colburne once stopped to sling his arm in a handkerchief, he emerged from a winding gully to find himself within a few yards of Bainbridge's battery. Behind the guns was a colonel calmly sitting his horse and watching the battle.

"What is the matter?" asked the Colonel.

"A flesh wound," said Colburne. "Colonel, there is a noble chance ahead of you. Do you see that angle? My men are at the base of it, and some of them in the ditch. They have driven the artillerymen from the guns, and forced the infantry to lie low. For God's sake send in your regiment. We can certainly carry the place."

"The entire brigade that I command is engaged," replied the Colonel. "Don't you see them on the right of your position?"

"Is there no other force about here?" asked Colburne, sitting down as he felt the dizziness coming over him again.

"None that I know of. This is such an infernal country for movements that we are all dislocated. Nobody knows where anything is.—But you had better go to the rear, Captain. You look used up."

Colburne was so tired, so weak with the loss of blood, so worn out by the heat of the sun, and the excitement of fighting that he could not help feeling discouraged at the thought of struggling back to the position of his company. He stretched himself under a tree to rest, and in ten minutes was fast asleep. When he awoke—he never knew how long afterwards—he could not at first tell what he remembered from what he had dreamed, and only satisfied himself that he had been hit by looking at his bloody and

bandaged arm. An artilleryman brought him to his full
consciousness by shouting excitedly, "There, by God!
they are trying a charge. The infantry are trying a
charge."

Colburne rose up, saw a regiment struggling across the
valley, and heard its long-drawn charging yell.

"I must go back," he exclaimed. "My men ought to
go in and support those fellows." Turning to the soldier
who attended him he added, "Run! Tell Van Zandt to
forward."

The soldier ran, and Colburne after him. But he had
not gone twenty paces before he fell straight forward on
his face, without a word, and lay perfectly still.

CHAPTER XXI.

CAPTAIN COLBURNE HAS OCCASION TO SEE LIFE IN A HOSPITAL.

W HEN Colburne came to himself he was lying on the
ground in rear of the pieces. Beside him, in the shadow
of the same tuft of withering bushes, lay a wounded lieutenant of the battery and four wounded artillerists. A
dozen steps away, rapidly blackening in the scorching sun
and sweltering air, were two more artillerists, stark dead,
one with his brains bulging from a bullet-hole in his forehead, while a dark claret-colored streak crossed his face,
the other's light-blue trousers soaked with a dirty carna-
tion stain of life-blood drawn from the femoral artery.
None of the wounded men writhed, or groaned, or pleaded
for succor, although a sweat of suffering stood in great
drops on their faces. Each had cried out when he was hit,
uttering either an oath, or the simple exclamation " Oh !"
in a tone of dolorous surprise; one had shrieked spasmodically, physically crazed by the shock administered to
some important nervous centre; but all, sooner or later,

N

had settled into the calm, sublime patience of the wounded
of the battle-field.

The brass Napoleons were still spanging sonorously, and
there was a ceaseless spitting of irregular musketry in the
distance.

"Didn't the assault succeed?" asked Colburne as soon
as he had got his wits about him.

"No sir—it was beat off," said one of the wounded artillerists.

"You've had a faint, sir," he added with a smile.
"That was a smart tumble you got. We saw you go over,
and brought you back here."

"I am very much obliged," replied Colburne. His arm
pained him now, his head ached frightfully, his whole
frame was feverish, and he thought of New England
brooks of cool water. In a few minutes Lieutenant Van
Zandt appeared, his dark face a little paler than usual, and
the right shoulder of his blouse pierced with a ragged and
bloody bullet-hole.

"Well, Captain," said he, "we have got, by Jove! our
allowance of to-day's rations. Hadn't we better look up
a doctor's shop? I feel, by the everlasting Jove!—excuse
me—that I stand in need of a sup of whiskey. Lieutenant
—I beg your pardon—I see you are wounded—I hope
you're not much hurt, sir—but have you a drop of the
article about the battery? No! By Jupiter! You go
into action mighty short of ammunition. I beg your pardon for troubling you. This is, by Jove! the dryest
fighting that I ever saw. I wish I was in Mexico, and
had a gourd of aguaardiente."

By the way, I wish the reader to understand that, when
I introduce a "By Jove!" into Van Zandt's conversation,
it is to be understood that that very remarkably profane
officer and gentleman used the great Name of the True
Divinity.

"Where is the company, Lieutenant?" asked Colburne.

"Relieved, sir. Both companies were relieved and or-

dered back to the regiment fifteen or twenty minutes ago.
I got this welt in the shoulder just as I was coming out of
that damned hollow.   We may as well go along, sir.   Our
day's fight is over."

"So the attack failed," said Colburne, as they took up
their slow march to the rear in search of a field hospital.

"Broken up by the ground, sir; beaten off by the musketry.   Couldn't put more than a man or two on the ramparts.   Played out before it got any where, just like a
wave coming up a sandy beach.   It was only a regiment.
It ought to have been a brigade.   But a regiment might
have done·it, if it had been shoved in earlier.   That was
the time, sir, when you went off for reinforcements.   If
we had had the bully old Tenth there then, we could have
taken Port Hudson alone.   Just after you left, the Rebs
raised the white flag, and a whole battalion of them came
out on our right and stacked arms.   Some of our men
spoke to them, and asked what they were after.   They
said—by Jove! it's so, sir!—they said they had surrendered.   Then down came some Rebel General or other, in
a tearing rage, and marched them back behind the works.
The charge came too late.   They beat it off easy.   They
took the starch out of that Twelfth Maine, sir.   I have
seen to-day, by Jove! the value of minutes."

Before they had got out of range of the Rebel musketry
they came upon a surgeon attending some wounded men
in a little sheltered hollow.   He offered to examine their
hurts, and proposed to give them chloroform.

"No, thank you," said Colburne.   "You have your
hands full, and we can walk farther."

"Doctor, I don't mind taking a little stimulant," observed Van Zandt, picking up a small flask and draining
it nearly to the bottom.   "Your good health, sir; my best
respects."

A quarter of a mile further on they found a second surgeon similarly occupied, from whom Van Zandt obtained
another deep draught of his favorite medicament, reject-

ing chloroform with profane politeness. Colburne refused
both, and asked for water, but could obtain none. Deep
in the profound and solemn woods, a full mile and a half
from the fighting line, they came to the field hospital of
the division. It was simply an immense collection of
wounded men in every imaginable condition of mutilation,
every one stained more or less with his own blood, every
one of a ghastly yellowish pallor, all lying in the open air
on the bare ground, or on their own blankets, with no
shelter except the friendly foliage of the oaks and beeches.
In the centre of this mass of suffering stood several oper-
ating tables, each burdened by a grievously wounded man
and surrounded by surgeons and their assistants. Underneath were great pools of clotted blood, amidst which lay
amputated fingers, hands, arms, feet and legs, only a little
more ghastly in color than the faces of those who waited
their turn on the table. The surgeons, who never ceased
their awful labor, were daubed with blood to the elbows;
and a smell of blood drenched the stifling air, overpower-
ing even the pungent odor of chloroform. The place resounded with groans, notwithstanding that most of the injured men who retained their senses exhibited the heroic
endurance so common on the battle-field. One man, whose
leg was amputated close to his body, uttered an inarticulate jabber of broken screams, and rolled, or rather
bounced from side to side of a pile of loose cotton, with
such violence that two hospital attendants were fully occupied in holding him. Another, shot through the body,
lay speechless and dying, but quivering from head to foot
with a prolonged though probably unconscious agony. He
continued to shudder thus for half an hour, when he gave
one superhuman throe, and then lay quiet for ever. An
Irishman, a gunner of a regular battery, showed astonishing vitality, and a fortitude bordering on callousness.
His right leg had been knocked off above the knee by a
round shot, the stump being so deadened and seared by
the shock that the mere bleeding was too slight to be mor-

tal. He lay on his left side, and was trying to get his left hand into his trousers-pocket. With great difficulty and grinning with pain, he brought forth a short clay pipe, blackened by previous smoking, and a pinch of chopped plug tobacco. Having filled the pipe carefully and deliberately, he beckoned a negro to bring him a coal of fire, lighted, and commenced puffing with an air of tranquillity which resembled comfort. Yet he was probably mortally wounded; human nature could hardly survive such a hurt in such a season; nearly all the leg amputations at Port Hudson proved fatal. The men whose business it is to pick up the wounded—the musicians and quartermaster's people—were constantly bringing in fresh sufferers, laying them on the ground, putting a blanket-roll or havresack under their heads, and then hurrying away for other burdens of misery. They, as well as the surgeons and hospital attendants, already looked worn out with the fatigue of their terrible industry.

"Come up and see them butcher, Captain," said the iron-nerved Van Zandt, striding over prostrate and shrinking forms to the side of one of the tables, and glaring at the process of an amputation with an eager smile of interest much like the grin of a bull-dog who watches the cutting up of a piece of beef. Presently he espied the assistant surgeon of the Tenth, and made an immediate rush at him for whiskey. Bringing the flask which he obtained to Colburne, he gave him a sip, and then swallowed the rest himself. By this time he began to show signs of intoxication; he laughed, told stories, and bellowed humorous comments on the horrid scene. Colburne left him, moved out of the circle of anguish, seated himself on the ground with his back against a tree, filled his pipe, and tried to while away the time in smoking. He was weak with want of food as well as loss of blood, but he could not eat a bit of cracker which a wounded soldier gave him. Once he tried to soothe the agony of his Lieutenant-Colonel, whom he discovered lying on a pile of loose cotton, with a bullet-wound in his thigh which the surgeon whispered was mortal, the missile having glanced up into his body.

"It's a lie!" exclaimed the sufferer. "It's all nonsense, Doctor. You don't know your business. I won't die. I sha'n't die. It's all nonsense to say that a little hole in the leg like that can kill a great strong man like me. I tell you I sha'n't and won't die."

Under the influence of the shock or of chloroform his mind soon began to wander.

"I have fought well," he muttered. "I am not a coward. I am not a Gazaway. I have never disgraced myself. I call all my regiment to witness that I have fought like a man. Summon the Tenth here, officers and men; summon them here to say what they like. I will leave it to any officer—any soldier—in my regiment."

In an hour more he was a corpse, and before night he was black with putrefaction, so rapid was that shocking change under the heat of a Louisiana May.

Amid these horrible scenes Van Zandt grew momentarily more intoxicated. The surgeons could hardly keep him quiet long enough to dress his wound, so anxious was he to stroll about and search for more whiskey. He talked, laughed and swore without intermission, every now and then bellowing like a bull for strong liquors. From table to table, from sufferer to sufferer he followed the surgeon of the Tenth, slapping him on the back violently and shouting, "Doctor, give me some whiskey. I'll give you a rise, Doctor. I'll give you a rise higher than a balloon. Hand over your whiskey, damn you!"

If he had not been so horrible he would have been ludicrous. His Herculean form was in incessant stumbling motion, and his dark face was beaded with perspiration. A perpetual silly leer played about his wide mouth, and his eyes stood out so with eagerness that the white showed a clear circle around the black iris. He offered his assistance to the surgeons; boasted of his education as a graduate

of Columbia College ; declared that he was a better Doctor
than any other infernal fool present ; made himself a torment to the helplessly wounded. Upon a Major of a Louisiana regiment who had been disabled by a severe contu-
sion he poured contempt and imprecations.

"What are you lying whimpering there for ?" he shouted.
"It's nothing but a little bruise. A child, by Jove!
wouldn't stop playing for it. You ought to be ashamed
of yourself. Get up and join your regiment."

The Major simply laughed, being a hard drinker himself, and having a brotherly patience with drunkards.

"That's the style of Majors," pursued Van Zandt. "*We*
are blessed, by Jove! with a Major. He is, by Jove! a
dam incur—dam—able darn coward." (When Van Zandt
was informed the next day of this feat of profanity he
seemed quite gratified, and remarked, "That, by Jove! is
giving a word a full battery,—bow-chaser, stern-chaser
and long-tom amidships.") "Where's Gazaway? (in a
roar). Where's the heroic Major of the Tenth? I am going, by Jove! to look him up. I am going, by Jove! to
find the safest place in the whole country. Where Gazaway
is, there is peace !"

Colburne refused one or two offers to dress his wound,
saying that others needed more instant care than himself.
When at last he submitted to an examination, it was found
that the ball had passed between the bones of the fore-arm,
not breaking them indeed, but scaling off some exterior
splinters and making an ugly rent in the muscles.

"I don't think you'll lose your arm," said the Surgeon.
"But you'll have a nasty sore for a month or two. I'll
dress it now that I'm about it. You'd better take the
chloroform ; it will make it easier for both of us."

Under the combined influence of weakness, whiskey and
chloroform, Colburne fell asleep after the operation. About
sundown he awoke, his throat so parched that he could
hardly speak, his skin fiery with fever, and his whole body
sore. Nevertheless he joined a procession of slightly

wounded men, and marched a mile to a general hospital
which had been set up in and around a planter's house in
rear of the forest. The proprietor and his son were in the
garrison of Port Hudson. But the wife and two grown-
up daughters were there, full of scorn and hatred; so un-
womanly, so unimaginably savage in conversation and
soul that no novelist would dare to invent such characters;
nothing but real life could justify him in painting them.
They seemed to be actually intoxicated with the malignant
strength of a malice, passionate enough to dethrone the
reason of any being not aboriginally brutal. They laughed
like demons to see the wounds and hear the groans of the
sufferers. They jeered them because the assault had failed.
The Yankees never could take Port Hudson; they were
the meanest, the most dastardly people on earth. Joe
Johnson would soon kill the rest of them, and have Banks
a prisoner, and shut him up in a cage.

"I hope to see you all dead," laughed one of these female hyenas. "I will dance with joy on your graves. My
brother makes beautiful rings out of Yankee bones."

No harm was done to them, nor any stress of silence
laid upon them. When their own food gave out they
were fed from the public stores; and at the end of the siege
they were left unmolested, to gloat in their jackal fashion
over patriot graves.

There was a lack of hospital accommodation near Port
Hudson, so bare is the land of dwellings; there was a lack
of surgeons, nurses, stores, and especially of ice, that absolute necessity of surgery in our southern climate; and
therefore the wounded were sent as rapidly as possible to
New Orleans. Ambulances were few at that time in the
Department of the Gulf, and Colburne found the heavy,
springless army-wagon which conveyed him to Springfield
Landing a chariot of torture. His arm was swollen to
twice its natural size from the knuckles to the elbow.
Nature had set to work with her tormenting remedies of
inflammation and suppuration to extract the sharp slivers

of bone which still hid in the wound notwithstanding the searching finger and probe of the Surgeon. During the night previous to this journey neither whiskey nor opium could enable him to sleep, and he could only escape from his painful self-consciousness by drenching himself with chloroform. But this morning he almost forget his own sensations in pity and awe of the multitudinous agony which bore him company. So nearly supernatural in its horror was the burden of anguish which filled that long train of jolting wagons that it seemed at times to his fevered imagination as if he were out of the world, and journeying in the realms of eternal torment. The sluggish current of suffering groaned and wailed its way on board the steam transport, spreading out there into a great surface of torture which could be taken in by a single sweep of the eye. Wounded men and dying men filled the state-rooms and covered the cabin floor and even the open deck There was a perpetual murmur of moans, athwart which passed frequent shrieks from sufferers racked to madness, like lightnings darting across a gloomy sky. More than one poor fellow drew his last breath in the wagons and on board the transport. All these men, thought Colburne, are dying and agonizing for their country and for human freedom. He prayed, and, without arguing the matter, he wearily yet calmly trusted, that God would grant them His infinite mercy in this world and the other.

It was a tiresome voyage from Springfield Landing to New Orleans. Colburne had no place to lie down, and if he had had one he could not have slept. During most of the trip he sat on a pile of baggage, holding in his right hand a tin quart cup filled with ice and punctured with a small hole, through which the chilled water dripped upon his wounded arm. Great was the excitement in the city when the ghastly travellers landed. It was already known there that an assault had been delivered, and that Port Hudson had not been taken; but no particulars had been published which might indicate that the Union army had suffered a

N2

severe repulse. Now, when several steamboats discharged
a gigantic freight of mutilated men, the facts of defeat and
slaughter were sanguinarily apparent. Secessionists of
both sexes and all ages swarmed in the streets, and filled
them with a buzz of inhuman delight. Creatures in the
guise of womanhood laughed and told their little children
to laugh at the pallid faces which showed from the ambulances as they went and returned in frequent journeys
between the levee and the hospitals. The officers and
men of the garrison were sad, stern and threatening in as-
pect. The few citizens who had declared for the Union
cowered by themselves and exchanged whispers of gloomy
foreboding.

In St. Stephen's Hospital Colburne found something of
that comfort which a wounded man needs. His arm was
dressed for the second time; his ragged uniform, stiff with
blood and dirt, was removed; he was sponged from head
to foot and laid in the first sheets which he had seen for
months. There were three other wounded officers in the
room, each on his own cot, each stripped stark naked and
covered only by a sheet. A Major of a Connecticut regiment, who had received a grapeshot through the lungs,
smiled at Colburne's arm and whispered, "Flea-bite."
Then he pointed to the horrible orifice in his own breast,
through which the blood and breath could be seen to bub-
ble whenever the dressings were removed, and nodded
with another feeble but heroic smile which seemed to say,
"This is no flea-bite." Iced water appeared to be the only
exterior medicament in use, and the hospital nurses were
constantly drenching the dressings with this simple
panacea of wise old Mother Nature. But in this early
stage of the great agony, before the citizens had found it
in their hearts to act the part of the Good Samaritan, there
was a lack of attendance. Happy were those officers who
had their servants with them, like the Connecticut Major,
or .who, like Colburne, had strength and members left to
take care of their own hurts. He soon hit upon a device

to lessen his self-healing labors.   He got a nurse to drive
a hook into the ceiling and suspend his quart cup of ice
to it by a triangle of strings, so that it might hang about
six inches above his wounded arm, and shed its dew of
consolation and health without trouble to himself.   In his
fever he was childishly anxious about his quart cup ; he
was afraid that the surgeon, the nurse, the visitors, would
hit it and make it swing.   That arm was a little world of
pain ; it radiated pain as the sun radiates light.

For the first time in his life he drank freely of strong
liquors.   Whiskey was the internal panacea of the hospital,
as iced water was the outward one.   Every time that the
Surgeon visited the four officers he sent a nurse for four
milk punches ; and if they wanted other stimulants, such
as claret or porter, they could have them for the asking.
The generosity of the Government, and the sublime beneficence of the Sanitary Commission supplied every necessary
and many luxuries.   Colburne was on his feet in forty-
eight hours after his arrival, ashamed to lie in bed under
the eyes of that mangled and heroic Major.   He was promoted to the milk-toast table, and then to the apple-sauce
table.   Holding his tin cup over his arm, he made frequent
rounds of the hospital, cheering up the wounded, and finding not a little pleasure in watching the progress of individual cases.   He never acquired a taste, as many did,
for frequenting the operating-room, and (as Van Zandt
phrased it) seeing them butcher.   This *chevalier sans
peur*, who on the battle-field could face death and look upon
ranks of slain unblenchingly, was at heart as soft as a
woman, and never saw a surgeon's knife touch living flesh
without a sensation of faintness.

He often accompanied the Chief Surgeon in his tours of
inspection.   A wonder of practical philanthropy was this
queer, cheerful, indefatigable Doctor Jackson, as brisk and
inspiriting as a mountain breeze, tireless in body, fervent
in spirit, a benediction with the rank of Major.   Iced water,
whiskey, nourishment and encouragement were his cure-

alls. There were surgeons who themselves drank the claret and brandy of the Sanitary Commission, and gave the remnant to their friends; who poured the consolidated milk of the Sanitary Commission on the canned peaches of the Sanitary Commission and put the grateful mess into their personal stomachs; and who, having thus comforted themselves, went out with a pleasant smile to see their patients eat bread without peaches and drink coffee without milk. But Dr. Jackson was not one of these self-centred individuals; he had fibres of sympathy which reached into the lives of others, especially of the wretched. As he passed through the crowded wards all those sick eyes turned to him as to a sun of strength and hope. He never left a wounded man, however near to death, but the poor fellow brightened up with a confidence of speedy recovery.

"Must cheer 'em—must cheer 'em," he muttered to Colburne. "Courage is a great medicine—best in the world. Works miracles—yes, miracles."

"Why! how *are* you, my old boy?" he said aloud, stopping before a patient with a ball in the breast. "You look as hearty as a buck this morning. Getting on wonderfully."

He gave him an easy slap on the shoulder, as if he considered him a well man already. He knew just where to administer these slaps, and just how to graduate them to the invalid's weakness. After counting the man's pulse he smiled in his face with an air of astonishment and admiration, and proceeded, "Beautiful! Couldn't do it better if you had never got hit. Nurse, bring this man a milk-punch. That's all the medicine *he* wants."

When they had got a few yards from the bed he sighed, jerked his thumb backward significantly, and whispered to Colburne, "No use. Can't save him. No vitality. Boneyard to-morrow."

They stopped to examine another man who had been shot through the head from temple to temple, but without

unseating life from its throne. His head, especially about
the face, was swollen to an amazing magnitude; his eyes
were as red as blood, and projected from their sockets, two
awful lumps of inflammation. He was blind and deaf, but
able to drink milk-punches, and still full of vital force.

"Fetch him round, I *guess*," whispered the Doctor with
a smile of gratification. "Holds out beautiful."

"But he will always be blind, and probably idiotic."

"No. Not idiotic. Brain as sound as a nut. As for
blindness, can't say. Shouldn't wonder if he could use his
peepers yet. Great doctor, old Nature—if you won't get
in her way. Works miracles—miracles! Why, in the
Peninsular campaign I sent off one man well, with a rifle-
ball in his heart. *Must* have been in his heart. There's
your room-mate, the Major. Put a walking cane through
him, and *he* won't die. Could, but won't. Too good pluck
to let go. Reg'lar bull terrier."

"How is my boy Jerry? The little Irish fellow with a
shot in the groin."

"Ah, I remember. Empty bed to-morrow."

"You don't mean that there's no hope for him?"

"No, no. All right. I mean he'll get his legs and be
about. No fear for that sort. Pluck enough to pull half
a dozen men through. Those devil-may-care boys make
capital soldiers, they get well so quick. This fellow will
be stealing chickens in three weeks. I wouldn't bet that I
could kill him."

Thus in the very tolerable comfort of St. Stephen's Colburne escaped the six weeks of trying siege duty which
his regiment had to perform before Port Hudson. The
Tenth occupied a little hollow about one hundred and
fifty yards from the rebel fortifications, protected in front
by a high knoll, but exposed on the left to a fire which hit
one or more every day. The men cut a terrace on their
own side of the knoll, and then topped the crest with a
double line of logs pierced for musketry, thus forming a
solid and convenient breastwork. On both sides the sharp-

shooting began at daybreak and lasted till nightfall. On both sides the marksmanship grew to be fatally accurate. Men were shot dead through the loopholes as they took aim. If the crown of a hat or cap showed above the breast-work, it was pierced by a bullet. After the siege was over, a rebel officer, who had been stationed on this front, stated that most of his killed and wounded men had been hit just above the line of the forehead. Every morning at dawn, Carter, who had his quarters in the midst of the Tenth, was awakened by a spattering of musketry and the singing of Minie-balls through the branches above his head, and even through the dry foliage of his own sylvan shanty. Now and then a shriek or oath indicated that a bullet had done its brutal work on some human frame. No crowd collected ; the men were hardened to such tragedies ; four or five bore the victim away ; the rest asked, " Who is it ?" One death which Carter witnessed was of so remarkable a character that he wrote an account of it to his wife, al-though not given to noting with much interest the minor and personal incidents of war.

" I had just finished breakfast, and was lying on my back smoking. A bullet whistled so unusually low as to attract my attention and struck with a loud smash in a tree about twenty feet from me. Between me and the tree a soldier, with his great coat rolled under his head for a pillow, lay on his back reading a newspaper which he held in both hands. I remember smiling to myself to see this man start as the bullet passed. Some of his comrades left off playing cards and looked for it. The man who was reading re-mained perfectly still, his eyes fixed on the paper with a steadiness which I thought curious, considering the bustle around him. Presently I noticed that there were a few drops of blood on his neck, and that his face was paling. Calling to the card-players, who had resumed their game, I said, ' See to that man with the paper.' They went to him, spoke to him, touched him, and found him perfectly dead. The ball had struck him under the chin, traversed the neck, and cut the spinal column where it joins the brain, making a fearful hole through which the blood had already soaked his great-coat. It was this man's head, and not the tree, which had been struck with such a report. There he lay, still holding the New York Independent, with his eyes fixed on a sermon by Henry Ward Beecher. It was really quite a remarkable circumstance.

"By the way, you must not suppose, my dear little girl, that bullets often come so near me. I am as careful of myself as you exhort me to be."

Not quite true, this soothing story ; and the Colonel knew it to be false as he wrote it. He knew that he was in danger of death at any moment, but he had not the heart to tell his wife so, and make her unhappy.

CHAPTER XXII.

CAPTAIN COLBURNE REINFORCES THE RAVENELS IN TIME TO AID THEM IN RUNNING AWAY.

COLBURNE had been two or three weeks in the hospital when he was startled by seeing Doctor Ravenel advancing eagerly upon him with a face full of trouble. The Doctor had heard of the young man's hurt, and as his sensitive sympathy invariably exaggerated danger and suffering, especially if they concerned any one whom he loved, he had imagined the worst, and taken the first boat for New Orleans. On the other hand, Colburne surmised from that concerned countenance that the Doctor brought evil tidings of his daughter. Was she unhappy in her marriage, or widowed, or dead ? He laughed outright, with a sense of relief equivalent to positive pleasure, when he learned that he alone was the cause of Ravenel's worry.

"I am getting along famously," said he. "Ask Doctor Jackson here. I am not sick at all above my left elbow.

Below the elbow the arm seems to belong to some other man."

The Doctor shook his head with the resolute incredulity of a man who is too anxious not to expect the worst.

"But you can't continue to do well here. This air is infected. This great mass of inflammation, suppuration, mortification and death, has poisoned the atmosphere of the hospital. I scented it the moment I entered the door. Am I not right, Dr. Jackson?"

"Just so. Can't help it. Horrid weather for cases," replied the chief surgeon, wiping the perspiration from his forehead. Air *is* poisoned. Wish to God I could get a fresh building. My patients would do better in shanties than they will here."

"I knew it," said Ravenel. "Now then, I am a country doctor. I can take this young man to a plantation, and give him pure air."

"That's what you want," observed Jackson, turning to Colburne. "Your arm don't need ice now. Water will do. Better go, I think. I'll see that you have a month's leave of absence. Come, you can go to Taylorsville, and still not miss a chance for fighting. Tried to send him north," he added, addressing Ravenel. "But he's foolish about it. Wants to see Port Hudson out—what you call a knight-errant."

Colburne was in a tremble, body and soul, at the thought of meeting Mrs. Carter; he had never been so profoundly shaken by even the actuality of encountering Miss Ravenel. Most of us have been in love enough to understand all about it without explanation, and to feel no wonder at him because, after reeling mentally this way and that, he finally said, "I will go." Now and then there is a woman who cannot bear to look upon the man whom she has loved and lost, and who will turn quick corners and run down side streets to escape him, haunting him spiritually perhaps, but bodily keeping afar from him all her life. But stronger natures, who can endure the trial, frequently go to meet it, and seem to find some dolorous comfort in it. As regards Colburne, it may be that he would not have gone to Taylorsville had he not been weak and feverish, and felt a craving for that petting kindness which seems to be a necessity of invalids.

I doubt whether the life in Ravenel's house contributed much to advance his convalescence. His emotions were played upon too constantly and powerfully for the highest good of the temporarily shattered instrument. He had supposed that he would undergo one great shock on meeting Mrs. Carter, and that then his trouble would be over. The first thrill was not so potent as he expected; but it was succeeded by a constant unrest, like the burning of a slow fever; he was uneasy all day and slept badly at night. In the house he could not talk freely and gaily, because of Lillie's presence; and out of it he could not feel with calmness, because he was perpetually thinking of her. After all, it may have been the splinters of bone in the arm, quite as much as the arrow in the heart, which worried him. Of Mrs. Carter I must admit that she was not merciful; she made the doubly-wounded Captain talk a great deal of his Colonel. He might recite Carter's martial deeds and qualities as lengthily as he pleased, and recommence *da capo* to recite them over again, not only without fatiguing her, but without exciting in her mind a thought that he was doing any thing remarkable. She was very much pleased, but she was not a bit grateful. Why should she be! It was perfectly natural to her mind that people should admire the Colonel, and talk much of his glory. Colburne performed this ill-paid task with infinite patience, sympathy, and self-sacrificing love; and no warrior was ever better sung in conversational epics than was Carter the successful by Colburne the disappointed. Under the rude oppression of this subject the bruised shrub a exhaled daily sweetness. It is almost painful to contemplate these two loving hearts: the one sending its anxious sympathies a hundred miles away into the deadly trenches of Port Hudson; the other pouring out its sympathies for a present object, but covertly and without a thought of reward. If the passionate affection of the woman is charming, the unrequited, unhoping love of the man is sublime.

The Doctor perhaps saw what Lillie could not or would not see.

"My dear," he observed, "you must remember that Colonel Carter is not the husband of Captain Colburne."

"Oh papa!" she answered. "Do you suppose that he doesn't like to talk about Colonel Carter? Of course he does. He admires him, and likes him immensely."

"I dare say—I dare say. But nevertheless you give him very large doses of your husband."

"No, papa; not too large. He is such a good friend that I am sure he doesn't object. Just think how unkind it would be not to want to talk about my husband. You don't understand him if you think he is so shabby."

Nevertheless the Doctor was partially right, and shabby as it may have been, Colburne was no better for the conversation which so much gratified Mrs. Carter. His arm discharged its slivers of bone and healed steadily, but he was thin and pale, slept badly, and had a slow fever. It must not be supposed that he wilfully brooded over his disappointment; much less that he was angry about it or felt any desire to avenge it. He was too sensible not to struggle against useless pinings; too gentle-hearted and honorable to be even tempted of base or cruel spirits. Not that he was a moral miracle; not that he was even a marvellously bright exception to the general run of humanity; on the contrary he was like many of us, especially when we are under the influence of elevating emotion. Some by me forgotten author has remarked that no earthly being is purer, more like the souls in paradise, than a young man during his first earnest love.

At one time Colburne entirely forgot himself in his sympathy for Mrs. Carter. When the news came of the

unsuccessful and murderous assault of the fourteenth of
June, she was nearly crazy for three days because of her
uncertainty concerning the fate of her husband. She must
hear constantly from her comforters the assurance that all
was undoubtedly well; that, if the Colonel had been engaged in the fighting, he would certainly have been named
in the official report; that, if he had received any harm, he
would have been all the more sure of being mentioned,
etc., etc. Clinging as if for life to these two men, she demanded all their strength to keep her out of the depths of
despair. Every day they went two or three times to the
fort, one or other of them, to gather information from passing boats concerning the new tragedy. Very honestly
and earnestly gratified was Colburne when he was able to
bring to Mrs. Carter a letter from her husband, written
the day after the struggle, and saying that no harm had
befallen him. How that letter was wept over, prayed
over, held to a beating heart, and then to loving lips! The
house was solemn all day with that immense and unspeakable joy.

Circumstances soon occurred which caused this lonely
and anxious family to be troubled about its own safety.
To carry on the siege of Port Hudson, Banks had been
obliged to reduce the garrison of New Orleans and of its
vast exterior line of defences (a hundred miles from the
city on every side) to the lowest point consistent with
safety. Meantime Taylor reorganized the remnant of his
beaten army, raised new levies by conscription, procured
reinforcements from Texas, and resumed the offensive.
Brashear City on the Atchafalaya, with its immense mass
of commissary stores, and garrison of raw Nine Months'
men, was captured by surprise. A smart little battle was
fought at Lafourche Crossing, near Thibodeaux, in which
Greene's Texans charged with their usual brilliant impetuosity, but were repulsed by our men with fearful slaughter
after a hand-to-hand struggle over the contested cannon.
Nevertheless the Union troops soon retired before superior

numbers, and Greene's wild mounted rangers were at liberty to patrol the Lafourche Interior.

"We can't stay here long," said Colburne, in the council of war in which the family talked these matters over. "Greene will come this way sooner or later. If he can take Fort Winthrop, he will thereby blockade the Mississippi, cut off Banks' supplies, and force him to raise the siege of Port Hudson. He is sure to try it sooner or later."

"Must we leave our plantation, then?" asked Ravenel in real anguish. To lose his home, his invested capital, pigs, chickens, prospective crop of vegetables, and, worse yet, of enlightened and ennobled negroes, was indeed a torturing calamity. Had he known on the afternoon of that day, that before morning the shaggy ponies and long, lank, dirty mosstroopers of Greene's brigade would be upon him, he would not have paused to examine the situation from so many different points of view. Colburne knew by experience the celerity of Texan rangers; he had chased them in forced marches from Brashear City to Alexandria without ever seeing a tail of their horses; and yet even he indulged in a false security.

"I think we have twelve hours before us," he observed. "To-morrow morning we shall have to get up and get, as the natives say. Still it's my opinion—I don't believe Mrs. Carter had better stay here; she ought to go to the fort to-night."

"Are gou going, papa?" asked Mrs. Carter, who somehow was not much alarmed.

"My dear, I must stay here till the last moment. We have so much property here! You will have to go without me."

"Then I won't go," she answered; and so that was settled.

"*You* ought to be off," said the Doctor to Colburne. "As a United States officer you are sure to be kept a prisoner, if taken. I certainly think that you ought to go."

Colburne thought so too, but would not desert his friends;

he shrugged his shoulders in spirit and resolved to endure what might come. The negroes were in a state of exquisite alarm. The entire black population of the Lafourche Interior was making for the swamps or other places of shelter ; and only the love of the Ravenel gang for their good massa and beautiful missus kept them from being swept away by the contagious current. The horror with which they regarded the possibility of being returned into slavery delighted the Doctor, who, even in those circumstances, dilated enthusiastically upon it as a proof that the race was capable of high aspirations.

"They have already acquired the love of individual liberty," said this amiable optimist. "The cognate love of liberty in the abstract, the liberty of all men, is not far ahead of them. How superior they already are to the white wretches who are fighting to send them back to slavery!—Shedding blood, their own and their brothers', for slavery ! Is it not utterly amazing ? Risking life and taking life to restore slavery ! It is the foolishest, wickedest, most demoniacal infatuation that ever possessed humanity. The Inquisition, the Massacre of St. Bartholomew, were common sense and evangelical mercy compared to this pro-slavery rebellion. And yet these imps of atrocity pretend to be Christians. They are the most orthodox creatures that ever served the devil. They rant and roar in the Methodist camp-meetings ; they dogmatize on the doctrines in the Presbyterian church ; they make the responses in the Episcopal liturgy. There is only one pinnacle of hypocrisy that they never have had the audacity to mount. They have not yet brought themselves to make the continuance and spread of slavery an object of prayer. It would be logical, you know ; it would be just like their impudence. I have expected that they would come to it. I have looked forward to the time when their hypocritical priesthood would put up bloody hands in the face of an indignant Heaven, and say, ' O God of Justice ! O Jesus, lover of the oppressed ! bless, extend and perpet-

uate slavery; prosper us in selling the wife away from
the husband, and the child away from the parent; enable
us to convert the blood and tears of our fellow creatures
into filthy lucre; help us to degrade man, who was made
in Thine image; and to Father, Son and Spirit be all the
Glory!'—Can you imagine anything more astoundingly
wicked than such a petition? And yet I am positively astonished that they have not got up monthly concerts of
prayer, and fabricated a liturgy, all pregnant with just
such or similar blasphemies. But God would not wait for
them to reach this acme of iniquity. His patience is ex-
hausted, and He is even now bringing them to punishment."

"They have some power left yet, as we feel to-night,"
said Colburne.

"Yes. I have seen an adder's head flatten and snap
ten minutes after the creature was cut in two. I dare say
it might have inflicted a poisonous wound."

"I think you had better send the hands to the fort."

"Do you anticipate such immediate danger?" inquired
the Doctor, his very spectacles expressing surprise.

"I feel uneasy every time I think of those Texans. They
are fast boys. They outmarch their own shadows sometimes, and have to wait for them to come in after nightfall."

"I really ought to send the hands off," admitted the
Doctor after a minute of reflection. "I never could forgive myself if through my means they should be returned
to bondage."

"It would be a poor result of a freedman's labor experiment."

The Doctor went to the back door and shouted for Major
Scott.

"Major," said he, "you must take all the people down
to the fort as soon as they can get ready."

"They's all ready, Marsr. They's only a waitin' for the
word."

"Very well, Bring them along. I'll write a note to the commandant, asking him to take you in for the night. You can come back in the morning if all is quiet."

"What's a gwine to come of you an' Miss Lillie?"

"Never mind that now. I will see to that presently. Bring the people along."

In five minutes fifteen men, six women and four pickaninnies, the whole laboring force of the plantation, were in the road before the house, each loaded with a portion of his or her property, such as blankets, food, and cooking utensils. The men looked anxious; the women cried loudly with fright and grief; the pickaninnies cried because their mothers did.

"Oh, Mars Ravenel! you'll be cotched suah," sobbed the old mamma who did the family cooking. "Miss Lillie, do come 'long with us."

"We'se gwine to tote some o' your fixin's 'long," observed Major Scott.

"Better let him do it," said Colburne. "It may be your only chance to save necessaries."

So the negroes added to their loads whatever seemed most valuable and essential of the Ravenel baggage. Then Scott received the note to the commandant of the fort, handed it to Julius, the second boss, and remarked with dignity, "I stays with Marsr." The Major was undisguisedly alarmed, but he had a character to sustain, and a military title to justify. He was immediately joined in his forlorn hope by Jim the "no 'count nigger," who, being a sly and limber darkey, fleet of foot, and familiar with swamp life, had a faith that he could wriggle out of any danger or captivity.

"Keep them," said Colburne to Ravenel. "We shall want them as look-outs during the night."

There was an evident hesitation in the whole gang as to whether they should go or stay; but Colburne settled the question by pronouncing in a tone of military command, "Forward, march!"

" Ah! they knows how to mind that sort o' talk," said
Major Scott, highly gratified with the spectacular nature
of the scene.   "I'se a been eddycatin' 'em to millingtary
ways.   They knows a heap a'ready, they doos."

He smiled with a simple and transitory joy, although he
could hear the voice of his wife (commonly called Mamma
Major) rising in loud lament amid the chorus of sorrow
with which the women and children moved away.   The
poor creature kept no grudge against her husband for his
infidelity of a month previous.

In the lonely and imperilled little household Colburne
now took command.

" Since you will fight," he said smiling, " you must fight
under my orders.   I am the military power, and I proclaim
martial law."

He forbade the Ravenels to undress; they must be prepared to run at a moment's notice.   He laughed at the
Doctor's proposition to barricade the doors and windows,
and, instead thereof, opened two or three trunks and scattered articles of little value about the rooms.   The property would be a bait, he said, which might amuse the
raiders while the family escaped.   To gratify Major Scott's
tremulous enthusiasm he loaded his own revolver and the
Doctor's doubled-barreled fowling-piece, smiling sadly to
himself to think how absurd was the idea of fighting off a
band of Texans with such a feeble artillery.   He posted
the two negroes as a vidette a quarter of a mile down the
road, with strict orders not to build a fire, not to sleep,
not to make a noise, but in case of the approach of a party
to hasten to the house and give information.   The Major
begged hard for the fowling-piece, but Colburne would not
let him have it.

" He would be worse than a Nine Months' man," he said
to the Doctor.   " He would be banging away at stumps
and shadows all night.   There wouldn't be a living field
mouse on the plantation by morning."

The Doctor's imagination was seriously affected by these

business-like preparations, and he silently regretted that he had not gone to the fort, or at least sent his daughter thither. Lillie, though quiet, was very pale, and wished herself in the trenches of Port Hudson, safe under the protection of her invincible husband. Colburne urged and finally ordered them to lie down and try to sleep. Two mules were standing in the yard, saddled and ready to do their part in the hegira when it should be necessary. He examined their harness, then returned into the house, buckled on his sword and revolver, extinguished every light, took his seat at an open window looking towards the danger, waited and listened. The youthful veteran was perfectly calm, notwithstanding that he had taken more precautions than a greenhorn, however timorous, would have thought of. Once in each hour he visited the negroes to see if they were awake; then mounted the levee to listen for tramp of men or horses across the bayou; then went to the sugar-house and listened towards the woods which backed the plantation; then resumed his silent watch at the open window. At two o'clock the moon still poured a pale light over the flat landscape. Colburne, feverish with fatigue, want of sleep, and the small remainder of irritation in his wound, was just saying to himself, "We *must* go to-morrow," when he saw two dark forms glide rapidly towards the house under cover of a fence, and rush crouching across the door-yard. Without waiting to hear what the negroes had to say, he stepped into the parlor and awoke the two sleepers on the sofas.

"What is the matter?" gasped the Doctor, with the wild air common to people startled out of an anxious slumber.

"Perhaps nothing," answered Colburne. "Only be ready."

By this time the two videttes were in the house, breathless with running and alarm.

"Oh, Cap'm! they's a comin'," whispered Scott. "They's a comin' right smart. We heerd the hosses. They's a

O

quarter mile off, mebbe; but they's a comin' right smart.
Oh Cap'm, please give me the double-barril gun. I wants
to fight for my liberty an' for Mars Ravenel an' for Miss
Lillie."

"Take it," said Colburne. "Now then, Doctor, you and
Jim will hurry Mrs. Carter directly down the road to the
fort. Jim can keep up on foot. The Major and I will go
to the woods, fire from there, and draw the enemy in that
direction."

Every one obeyed him without a word. The approaching tramp of horses was distinctly audible at the house
when the Ravenels mounted the mules and set off at a lum-
bering trot, the animals being urged forward by resounding whacks from Jim's bludgeon. Colburne scowled and
grated his teeth with impatience and vexation.

"I ought to have sent them away last evening," he
muttered with a throb of self-reproach.

"Scott, you and I will have to fight," he said aloud.
"They never can escape unless we keep the rascals here.
We must fire once from the house; then run to the woods
and fire again there. We must show ourselves men now."

"Yes, Mars Cap'm," replied the Major. His voice was
tremulous, and his whole frame shook, but he was nevertheless ready to die, if need be, for his liberty and his
benefactors. Of physical courage the poor fellow had
little; but in moral courage he was at this moment sublime.

Colburne posted himself and his comrade at a back
corner of the house, where they could obtain a view of the
road which led toward Thibodeaux.

"Now, Scott," he said, "you must not fire until I have
fired. You must not fire until you have taken aim at
somebody. You must fire only one barrel. Then you
must make for the woods along the line of this fence. If
they follow us on horseback we can bother them by dodging over the fence now and then. If they catch us, we
must fight as long as we can. Cheer up, old fellow. It's

all right. It's not bad business as soon as you're used to it."

"Cap'm, I'se ready," answered Scott solemnly. "I'se not gwine for ter be cotched alive."

Then he prayed for some minutes in a low whisper, while Colburne stood at the corner and watched. "Watch and pray," the latter repeated to himself, smiling inwardly at the odd compliance with the double injunction, so strangely does the mind work on such occasions. It was not a deliberate process of intellection with him; it was an instinctive flash of ideas, not traceable to any feeling which was in him at the time; on the contrary, his prevailing emotion was one of extreme anxiety. The tramp which fled toward the fort gently diminished in the distance, while the tramp which approached from the opposite side grew nearer and louder. When the advancing horsemen got within a hundred yards of the house, they slackened their pace to a walk, and finally halted, probably to listen. Some of them must have dismounted at this time, for Colburne suddenly beheld four footmen at the front gate. He scowled at this sign of experienced caution, and gave a hasty glance toward the garden in his rear, to see if others were not cutting off his retreat. He could not discover the features of any of the four, but he could see that they were of the tall and lank Texan type, dressed in brownish clothing, and provided with short guns, no doubt double-barreled fowling-pieces. Inside of the gate they halted and seemed to hearken, while one of them pointed up the road toward the fort, and whispered to his comrades. Colburne had hoped that they would get into the house, and fall to plundering; but they had evidently overheard the fugitives, for there was a simultaneous backward movement in the group—they were going to remount and pursue. Now was his time, if ever, to effect the proposed diversion. Aiming his six-inch revolver at the tallest, he fired a single barrel. The man yelled a curse, staggered, dropped his gun, and leaned against the

fence. Two of his comrades sprang across the road, and
threw themselves behind the levee as a breast-work, while
the fourth, all grit, turned short and brought his fowling-
piece to a level as Colburne drew behind his cover. In
that same moment, Major Scott, wild with a sudden madness of conflict, shouted like a lion, bounded beyond the
angle of the house, planting himself on two feet set wide
apart, his mad black face set toward the enemy, and his
gun aimed. Both fired at the same instant, and both fell
together, probably alike lifeless. The last prayer of the
negro was, "My God!" and the last curse of the rebel
was "Damnation!"

By the light of the moon Colburne looked at his comrade, and saw the brains following the blood from a hole
in the centre of his forehead. He cast a glance at the
levee, fired one more barrel at a broad-brimmed hat which
rose above it, listened for a second to an advancing rush
of hoofs in order to decide whether it came by the road
or by the fields, turned, crossed the garden on a noiseless
run, placed himself on the further side of a high and
close plantation-fence, and followed its cover rapidly toward the forest. The distance was less than a quarter
of a mile, but he was quite breathless and faint before he
had traversed it, so weak was he still, and so little accustomed to exercise. In the edge of the wood he sat
down on a fallen and mouldering trunk to listen. If the
cavalry were pursuing their course up the road, they
were doing it very prudently and slowly, for he could
hear no more trampling of horses. Tolerably satisfied as
to the safety of the Ravenels, he reloaded his two empty
barrels, settled his course in his mind, and pushed as
straight as he could for Taylorsville without quitting
the cover of the forest. Although the fort was not four
miles away in a direct line, it was daybreak when he
came in sight of a low flattened outline, as of a trun-
cated mound, which showed dimly through the yellowish morning mist. He had still to cross a dead level of

four or five hundred yards, with no points of shelter but three small wooden houses. At this moment, when safety seemed so near and sure, he saw on the bayou road, two hundred yards to his right, half a dozen black and indistinct bunches moving in a direction parallel to his own. They were unquestionably horsemen going toward the fort, and nearer to it than he. Changing his direction, he made straight for the river, struck it above the fortification, and got behind the levee, thus securing both a covered way to hide his course, and an earthwork from behind which he could fight. He lost no time in peeping over the top of the mound, but pushed ahead at his best speed, supposing that no cavalry scouts would dare approach very near to a garrison supplied with artillery. He could see a sentry pacing the ramparts, the dark uniform showing clear against the grey sky beyond. He even thought that the man perceived him, and supposed that his dangers were over for the present. He was full of exhilaration, and glanced back at the events of the night with a sense of satisfaction, taking it all for granted with a resolute faith of satisfaction, that the Ravenels had escaped. Major Scott was dead; he was really quite sorry for that; but then two Texans had been killed, or at least disabled; the war was so much nearer its close. In a small way he felt much as a general does who has effected a masterly retreat, and inflicted severe loss upon the pursuing enemy.

Presently a break in the bank forced him to mount the levee. As he reached the top he stared in astonishment and some dismay at a man in butternut-colored clothing, mounted on a rough pony, with the double-barreled gun of Greene's mosstroopers across his saddle-bow, who was posted on the road not forty feet distant. The Butternut immediately said, in the pleasant way current in armies, " Halt, you son of a bitch !"

He fired, but missed, as Colburne skirted the break on a run, and sprang again behind the levee. The Captain then fired in return, with no other effect than to make the Butternut gallop beyond revolver range. From this distance he called out, ironically, "I say, Yank, have you heard from Brashear City?"

Colburne made no reply, but continued his retreat unmolested. When the sentinel challenged, "Halt! who comes there?" he thought he had never heard a pleasanter welcome.

"Friend," he answered.

"Halt, friend! Corporal of the guard, number five," shouted the sentry.

The corporal appeared, recognized Colburne, and let him in through the gate in a palisade which connected one angle of the fort with the river. The garrison was already under arms, and the men were lying down behind the low works, with their equipments on and their muskets by their sides. The first person from the plantation whom Colburne saw was Mauma Major.

"Where is Mrs. Carter, aunty?" he asked.

"They's all here, bress the Lord! And now you's come!" shouted the good fat creature, clapping her hands with delight. "Whar my ole man?"

"In heaven," said Colburne, with a solemn tenderness which carried instant conviction. The woman screamed, and went down upon her knees with an air and face of such anguish as might cast shame upon those philosophers as have asserted that the negro is not a man.

"Oh! the Lord gave! The Lord gave!" she repeated, wildly.

Perhaps she had forgotten, perhaps she never knew, the remainder of the text; but its piteous sense of bereavement, and of more than human consolation, was evidently clear in some manner to her soul.

CHAPTER XXIII.

CAPTAIN COLBURNE COVERS THE RETREAT OF THE SOUTHERN LABOR ORGANIZATION.

COLBURNE soon discovered the Ravenels and their retainers bivouacked in an angle of the fortification. The
Doctor actually embraced him in delight at his escape;
and Mrs. Carter seized both his hands in hers, exclaiming,
"Oh, I am so happy!"

She was full of gayety. She had had a splendid nap;
had actually slept out of doors. Did he see that tent made
out of a blanket? She had slept in that. She could bivouac
as well as you, Captain Colburne; she was as good a soldier as you, Captain Colburne. She liked it, of all things
in the world. She never would sleep in the house again
till she was fif— sixty.

It was curious to note how she checked herself upon the
point of mentioning fifty as the era of first decrepitude.
Her father was over fifty, and therefore fifty could not be
old age, notwithstanding her preconceived opinions on the
subject.

"But oh, how obliged we are to you!" she added, changing suddenly to a serious view. "How kind and noble
and brave you are! We owe you so much!—Isn't it
strange that I should be saying such things to you? I
never thought that I should ever say anything of the kind to
any man but my father and my husband. I am indeed grateful to you, and thankful that you have escaped."

As she spoke, her eyes filled with tears. There was a
singular changeableness about her of late; she shifted
rapidly and without warning, almost without cause, from
one emotion to another; she felt and expressed all emotions
with more than usual fervor. She was sadder at times
and gayer at times than circumstances seemed to justify.
An ordinary observer, a man especially, would have been

apt to consider some of her conduct odd, if not irrational. The truth is that she had been living a new life for the past two months, and that her being, physical and moral, had not yet been able to settle into a tranquil unity of function and feeling. Many women and a few men will understand me here. Colburne was too merely a young man to comprehend anything; but he could stand a little way off and worship. He thought, as she faced him with her cheeks flushed and her eyes the brighter for tears, that she was very near in guise and nature to an angel. It may be a paradox; it may be a dangerous fact to make public; but he certainly was loving another man's wife with perfect innocence.

"What is the matter with Mauma Major?" asked the Doctor.

Colburne briefly related the martyrdom of Scott; and father and daughter hurried to console the weeping black woman.

Then the young soldier bethought himself that he ought to report his knowledge of the rebels to the commandant of the garrison. "You'll find the cuss in there," said a devil-may-care lieutenant, pointing to a brick structure in the centre of the fort. Colburne entered, saw an officer sleeping on a pile of blankets, and to his astonishment recognized him as Major Gazaway. In slumber this remarkable poltroon looked respectably formidable. He was six feet in height and nearly two hundred pounds in weight, large-limbed, deep-chested, broad-shouldered, dark in complexion, aquiline in feature, masculine and even stern in expression. He had begun life as a prize fighter, but had failed in that career, not because he lacked strength or skill, but from want of pluck to stand the hammering. Nevertheless he was a tolerable hand at a rough-and-tumble fight, and still more efficient in election-day bullying and browbeating. For the last ten years he had kept a billiard saloon, had held various small public offices, and had been the Isaiah Rynders of his little city. On the stump he had a low kind of popular eloquence made up of coarse denunciation, slanderous lying, bar-room slang, smutty stories, and profanity. The Rebellion broke out; the Rebel cannon aimed at Fort Sumter knocked the breath out of the Democratic party; and Gazaway turned Republican, bringing over two hundred fighting voters, and changing the political complexion of his district. Consequently he easily got a commision as captain in the three months' campaign, and subsequently as major in the Tenth, much to the disgust of its commandant. He had expected and demanded a colonelcy; he thought that the Governor, in not granting it, had treated him with ingratitude and black injustice; he honestly believed this, and was naively sore and angry on the subject. It needed this trait of born impudence to render his character altogether contemptible; for had he been a conscious, humble coward, he would have merited a pity not altogether disunited from respect. From the day of receiving his commission Gazaway had not ceased to intrigue and bully for promotion in a long series of blotted and ill-spelled letters. How could a mere Major ever hope to go before the people successfully as a candidate for Congress? That distinction was the aim of Gazaway, as of many another more or less successful blackguard. It is true that these horrid battles occasionally shook his ambition and his confidence in his own merits. Under fire he was a meek man, much given to lying low, to praying fervently, to thinking that a whole skin was better than laurels. But in a few hours after the danger was past, his elastic vanity and selfishness rose to the occasion, and he was as pompous in air, as dogmatical in speech, as impudently greedy in his demands for advancement as ever. Such was one of Colburne's superior officers; such was the dastard to whom the wounded hero reported for duty. Colburne, by the way, had never asked for promotion, believing, with the faith of chivalrous youth, that merit would be sure of undemanded recognition.

After several calls of " Major !" the slumberer came to

his consciousness; he used it by rolling over on his side, and endeavoring to resume his dozings. He had not been able to sleep till late the night before on account of his terrors, and now he was reposing like an animal, anxious chiefly to be let alone.

"Major—excuse me—I have something of importance to report," insisted the Captain.

"Well; what is it?" snarled Gazaway. Then, catching sight of Colburne, "Oh! that you, Cap? Where *you* from?"

"From a plantation five miles below, on the bayou. I was followed in closely by the rebel cavalry. Their pickets are less than half a mile from the fort."

"My God!" exclaimed Gazaway, sitting up and throwing off his musquito-net. "What do you think? They ain't going to attack the fort, be they?" Then calling his homespun pomposity to his aid, he added, with a show of bravado, "I can't see it. They know better. We can knock spots out of 'em."

"Of course we can," coincided the Captain. "I don't believe they have any siege artillery; and if we can't beat off an assault we ought to be cat-o'-nine-tailed."

"Cap, I vow I wish I had your health," said the Major, gazing shamelessly at Colburne's thin and pale face. "You can stand anything. I used to think I could, but this cussed climate fetches *me*. I swear I hain't been myself since I come to Louisianny."

It is true that the Major had not been in field service what he once honestly thought he was. He had supposed himself to be a brave man; he was never disenchanted of this belief except while on the battle-field; and after he had run away he always said and tried to believe that it was because he was sick.

"I was took sick with my old trouble, he continued; "same as I had at New Orleans, you know—the very day that we attacked Port Hudson."

By the way, he had not had it at New Orleans; he had

had it at Georgia Landing and Camp Beasland; but Colburne did not correct him.

"By George! what a day that was!" he exclaimed, referring to the assault of the 27th of May. "I'll bet more'n a hundred shots come within five feet of me. If I could a kep' up with the regiment, I'd a done it. But I couldn't. I had to go straight to the hospital. I tell you I suffered there. I couldn't get no kind of attention, there was so many wounded there. After a few days I set out for the regiment, and found it in a holler where the rebel bullets was skipping about like parched peas in a skillet. But I was too sick to stand it. I had to put back to the hospital. Finally the Doctor he sent me to New Orleans. Well, I was just gettin' a little flesh on my bones when General Emory ordered every man that could walk to be put to duty. Nothing would do but I must take command of this fort. I got here yesterday morning, and the boat went back in the afternoon, and here we be in a hell of a muss. I brought twenty such invalids along—men no more fit for duty than I be. I swear it's a shame."

Colburne did not utter the disgust and contempt which he felt; he turned away in silence, intending to look up dressings for his arm, which had become dry and feverish. The Major called him back.

"I say, Cap, if the enemy are in force, what are we to do?"

"Why, we shall fight, of course."

"But we ha'n't got men enough to stand an assault."

"How many?"

"One little comp'ny Louisianny men, two comp'nies nine months' men, and a few invalids."

"That's enough. Have you any spare arms?"

"I d'no. I reckon so," said the Major, in a peevish tone. "I reckon you'd better hunt up the Quartermaster, if there is one. I s'pose he has 'em."

"A friend of mine has brought fifteen able-bodied negroes into the fort. I want guns for them."

"Niggers!" sneered the Major. "What good be they?"

Losing all patience, Colburne disrespectfully turned his back without answering, and left the room.

"I say, Cap, if we let them niggers fight we'll be all massacred," were the last words that he heard from Gazaway.

Having got his arm bound anew with wet dressings, he sought out the Quartermaster, and proceeded to accouter the Ravenel negroes, meanwhile chewing a breakfast of hard crackers. Then, meeting the Lieutenant who had directed him to Gazaway's quarters, and who proved to be the commandant of the Louisiana company, they made a tour of the ramparts together, doing their volunteer best to take in the military features of the flat surrounding landscape, and to decide upon the line of approach which the rebels would probably select in case of an assault. There was no cover except two or three wooden houses of such slight texture that they would afford no protection against shell or grape. The levee on the opposite side of the bayou might shelter sharpshooters, but not a column. They trained a twenty-four-pounder iron gun in that direction, and pointed the rest of the artillery so as to sweep the plain between the fort and a wood half a mile distant. The ditch was deep and wide, and well filled with water, but there was no abattis or other obstruction outside of it. The weakest front was toward the Mississippi, on which side the rampart was a mere bank not five feet in hight, scarcely dominating the slope of twenty-five or thirty yards which stretched between it and the water.

"I wish the river was higher—smack up to the fortifications," said the Louisiana lieutenant. "They can wade around them fences," he added, pointing to the palisades which connected the work with the river.

This officer was not a Louisianian by birth, any more than the men whom he commanded. They were a medley of all nations, principally Irish and Germans, and he had begun his martial career as a volunteer in an Indiana regiment. He was chock full of fight and confidence; this was the only fort he had ever garrisoned, and he considered it almost impregnable; his single doubt was lest the assailants "might wade in around them fences." Colburne, remembering how Banks had been repulsed twice from inferior works at Port Hudson, also thought the chances good for a defence. Indeed, he looked forward to the combat with something like a vindictive satisfaction. Heretofore he had always attacked; and he wanted to fight the rebels once from behind a rampart; he wanted to teach them what it was to storm fortifications. If he had been better educated in his profession he would have found the fort alarmingly small and open, destitute as it was of bomb-proofs, casemates and traverses. The river showed no promise of succor; not a gunboat or transport appeared on its broad, slow, yellow current; not a friendly smoke could be seen across the flat distances. The little garrison, it seemed, must rely upon its own strength and courage. But, after taking a deliberate view of all the circumstances, Colburne felt justified in reporting to Major Gazaway that the fort could beat off as many Texans as could stand between it and the woods, which was the same as to say a matter of one or two hundred thousand. Leaving his superior officer in a state of spasmodic and short-lived courage, he spread his rubber blanket in a shady corner, rolled up his coat for a pillow, laid himself down, and slept till nearly noon. When he awoke, the Doctor was holding an umbrella over him.

"I am ever so much obliged to you," said Colburne, sitting up.

"Not at all. I was afraid you might get the fever. Our Louisiana sun, you know, doesn't dispense beneficence alone. I saw that it had found you out, and I rushed to the rescue."

"Is Mrs. Carter sheltered?" asked the Captain.

"She is very comfortably off, considering the circumstances."

He was twiddling and twirling his umbrella as though he had something on his mind.

"I want you to do me a favor," he said, after a moment. "I should really like a gun, if it is not too much trouble."

The idea of the Doctor, with his fifty-five years, his peaceful habits, and his spectacles, rushing to battle made Colburne smile. Another imaginary picture, the image of Lillie weeping over her father's body, restored his seriousness.

"What would Mrs. Carter say to it?" he asked.

"I should be obliged if you would not mention it to her," answered the Doctor. "I think the matter can be managed without her knowledge."

Accordingly Colburne fitted out this unexpected recruit with a rifle-musket, and showed him how to load it, and how to put on his accoutrements. This done, he reverted to the subject which most interested his mind just at present.

"Mrs. Carter must be better sheltered than she is," he said. "In case of an assault, she would be in the way where she is, and, moreover, she might get hit by a chance bullet. I will tell the Major that his Colonel's wife is here, and that he must turn out for her."

"Do you think it best?" questioned the Doctor. "Really, I hate to disturb the commandant of the fort."

But Colburne did think it best, and Gazaway was not hard to convince. He hated to lose his shelter, poor as it was, but he had a salutary dread of his absent Colonel, and remembering how dubious had been his own record in field service, he thought it wise to secure the favor of Mrs. Carter. Accordingly Lillie, accompanied by Black Julia, moved into the brick building, notwithstanding her late declarations that she liked nothing so well as sleeping in the open air.

"Premature old age," laughed Colburne. "Sixty already."

"It is the African Dahomey, and not the American, which produces the Amazons," observed the Doctor.

"If you don't stop I shall be severe," threatened Lillie. "I have a door now to turn people out of."

"Just as though that was a punishment," said Colburne. "I thought out-of-doors was the place to live."

As is usual with people in circumstances of romance which are not instantly and overpoweringly alarming, there was an exhilaration in their spirits which tended towards gayety. While Mrs. Carter and Colburne were thus jesting, the Doctor shyly introduced his martial equipments into the house, and concealed them under a blanket in one corner. Presently the two men adjourned to the ramparts, to learn the cause of a commotion which was visible among the garrison. Far up the bayou road thin yellow-clouds of dust could be seen rising above the trees, no doubt indicating a movement of troops in considerable force. From that quarter no advance of friends, but only of Texan cavalry and Louisianian infantry, could be expected. Nearly all the soldiers had left their shelters of boards and rubber blankets, and were watching the threatening phenomenon with a grave fixedness of expression which showed that they fully appreciated its deadly significance. Sand-columns of the desert, water-spouts of the ocean, are a less impressive spectacle than the approaching dust of a hostile army. The old and tried soldier knows all that it means; he knows how tremendous will be the screech of the shells and the ghastliness of the wounds; he faces it with an inward shrinking, although with a calm determination to do his duty; his time for elation will not come until his blood is heated by fighting, and he joins in the yell of the charge. The recruit, deeply moved by the novelty of the sight, and the unknown grandeur of horror or of glory which it presages, is either vaguely terrified or full of excitement. Calm as is the exterior of most men in view of approaching battle, not one of them looks upon it with entire indifference. But let the eyes on the fortifications strain as they might, no lines of troops could be distinguished, and there was little, if any, increase in the number of the rebel pickets who sat sentinel in their saddles under the shade of scattered trees and houses. Presently the murmur " A flag of truce !" ran along the line of spectators. Down the road which skirted the northern bank of the bayou rode slowly, amidst a little cloud of dust, a party of four horsemen, one of whom carried a white flag.

" What does that mean," asked Gazaway. " Do you think peace is proclaimed ?"

" It means that they want this fort," said Colburne. " They are going to commit the impertinence of asking us to surrender."

The Major's aquiline visage was very pale, and his outstretched hand shook visibly ; he was evidently seized by the complaint which had so troubled him at Port Hudson.

" Cap, what shall I do ?" he inquired in a confidential whisper, twisting one of his tremulous fingers into Colburne's buttonhole, and drawing him aside.

" Tell them to go to ——, and then send them there," said the Captain, angrily, perceiving that Gazaway's feelings inclined toward a capitulation. " Send out an officer and escort to meet the fellows and bring in their message. They mustn't be allowed to come inside."

" No, no ; of course not. We couldn't git very good terms if they should see how few we be," returned the Major, unable to see the matter in any other light than that of his own terrors. " Well, Cap, you go and meet the feller. No, you stay here ; I want to talk to you. Here, where's that Louisianny Lieutenant? Oh, Lieutenant, you go out to that feller with jest as many men 's he's got ; stop him 's soon 's you git to him, and send in his business. Send it in by one of your men, you know ; and take a white flag, or han'kerch'f, or suthin'."

When Gazaway was in a perturbed state of mind, his conversation had an unusual twang of the provincialisms of tone and grammar amidst which he had been educated, or rather had grown up without an education.

At sight of the Union flag of truce, the rebel one, now only a quarter of a mile from the fort, halted under the shadow of an evergreen oak by the roadside. After a parley of a few minutes, the Louisiana Lieutenant returned, beaded with perspiration, and delivered to Gazaway a sealed envelope. The latter opened it with fingers which worked as awkwardly as a worn-out pair of tongs, read the enclosed note with evident difficulty, cast a troubled eye up and down the river, as if looking in vain for help, beckoned Colburne to follow him, and led the way to a deserted angle of the fort.

"I say, Cap," he whispered, "we've got to surrender."

Colburne looked him sternly in the face, but could not catch his cowardly eye.

"Take care, Major," he said.

Gazaway started as if he had been threatened with personal violence.

"You are a ruined man if you surrender this fort," pursued Colburne.

The Major writhed his Herculean form, and looked all the anguish which so mean a nature was capable of feeling; for it suddenly occurred to him that if he capitulated he might never be promoted, and never go to Congress.

"What in God's name shall I do?" he implored. "They've got six thous'n' men."

"Call the officers together, and put it to vote."

"Well, you fetch 'em, Cap, I swear I'm too sick to stan' up."

Down he sat in the dust, resting his elbows on his knees, and his head between his hands. Colburne sought out the officers, seven in number, besides himself, and all, as it chanced, Lieutenants.

"Gentlemen," he said, "we are dishonored cowards if we surrender this fort without fighting."

"Dam'd if we don't have the biggest kind of a scrimmage first," returned the Louisianian.

The afflicted Gazaway rose to receive them, opened the communication of the rebel general, dropped it, picked it up, and handed it to Colburne, saying, "Cap, you read it."

It was a polite summons to surrender, stating the investing force at six thousand men, declaring that the success of an assault was certain, offering to send the garrison on parole to New Orleans, and closing with the hope that the commandant of the fort would avoid a useless effusion of blood.

"Now them's what I call han'some terms," broke in Gazaway eagerly. "We can't git no better if we fight a week. And we can't fight a day. We hain't got the men to whip six thous'n' Texans. I go for takin' terms while we can git 'em."

"Gentlemen, I go for fighting," said Colburne.

"That's me," responded the Louisiana lieutenant; and there was an approving murmur from the other officers.

"This fort," continued our Captain, "is an absolute necessity to the prosecution of the siege of Port Hudson. If it is lost, the navigation of the river is interrupted, and our army is cut off from its supplies. If we surrender, we make the whole campaign a failure. We must not do it. We never shall be able to face our comrades after it; we never shall be able to look loyal man or rebel in the eye. We *can* defend ourselves. General Banks has been repulsed twice from inferior works. It is an easy chance to do a great deed—to deserve the thanks of the army and the whole country. Just consider, too, that if we don't hold the fort, we may be called on some day to storm it. Which is the easiest? Gentlemen, I say, No surrender!"

Every officer but Gazaway answered, "That's my vote." The Louisiana Lieutenant fingered his revolver threateningly, and swore by all that was holy or infernal that he would shoot the first man who talked of capitulating.

Gazaway's mouth had opened to gurgle a remonstrance, but at this threat he remained silent and gasping like a stranded fish.

"Well, Cap, you write an answer to the cuss, and the Major 'll sign it," said the Louisianian to Colburne, with a grin of humorous malignity. Our friend ran to the office of the Quartermaster, and returned in a minute with the following epistle:

"Sir: It is my duty to defend Fort Winthrop to the last extremity, and I shall do it."

The signature which the Major appended to this heroic document was so tremulous and illegible that the rebel general must have thought that the commandant was either very illiterate or else a very old gentleman afflicted with the palsy.

Thus did the unhappy Gazaway have greatness thrust upon him. He would have been indignant had he not been so terrified ; he thought of court-martialing Colburne some day for insubordination, but said nothing of it at present ; he was fully occupied with searching the fort for a place which promised shelter from shell and bullet. The rest of the day he spent chiefly on the river front, looking up and down the stream in vain for the friendly smoke of gunboats, and careful all the while to keep his head below the level of the ramparts. His trepidation was so apparent that the common soldiers discovered it, and amused themselves by slyly jerking bullets at him, in order to see him jump, fall down and clap his hand to the part hit by the harmless missile. He must have suspected the trick ; but he did not threaten vengeance nor even try to discover the jokers : every feeble source of manliness in him had been dried up by his terrors, He gave no orders, exacted no obedience, and would have received none had he demanded it. Late in the afternoon, half a dozen veritable rebel balls whistling over the fort sent him cowering into the room occupied by Mrs. Carter, where he appropriated a blanket and stretched himself at full length on the floor,

fairly grovelling and flattening in search of safety. It was
a case of cowardice which bordered upon mania or physical
disease. He had just manliness enough to feel a little
ashamed of himself, and mutter to Mrs. Carter that he was
" too sick to stan' up." Even she, novel as she was to the
situation, understood him, after a little study; and the
sight of his degrading alarm, instead of striking her with
a panic, roused her pride and her courage. With what an
admiring contrast of feeling she looked at the brave Colburne and thought of her brave husband!

The last rays of the setting sun showed no sign of an
enemy except the wide thin semicircle of rebel pickets,
quiet but watchful, which stretched across the bayou from
the river above to the river below. As night deepened,
the vigilance of the garrison increased, and not only the
sentinels but every soldier was behind the ramparts, each
officer remaining in rear of his own company or platoon,
ready to direct it and lead it at the first alarm. Colburne,
who was tacitly recognized as commander-in-chief, made
the rounds every hour. About midnight a murmur of
joy ran from bastion to bastion as the news spread that
two steamers were close at hand, coming up the river.
Presently every one could see their engine-fires glowing
like fireflies in the distant, and hear through the breathless
night the sighing of the steam, the moaning of the ma
chinery, and at last the swash of water against the bows.
The low, black hulks, and short, delicate masts, distinctly
visible on the gleaming groundwork of the river, and
against the faintly lighted horizon, showed that they were
gunboats; and the metallic rattle of their cables, as they
came to anchor opposite the fort, proved that they had arrived to take part in the approaching struggle. Even
Gazaway crawled out of his asylum to look at the cheering
reinforcement, and assumed something of his native pomposity as he observed to Colburne, " Cap, they won't dare
to pitch into us, with them fellers alongside."

A bullet or two from the rebel sharpshooters posted on

the southern side of the bayou sent him back to his house of refuge. He thought the assault was about to commence, and was entirely absorbed in hearkening for its opening clamor. When Mrs. Carter asked him what was going on, he made her no answer. He was listening with all his pores; his very hair stood on end to listen. Presently he stretched himself upon the floor in an instinctive effort to escape a spattering of musketry which broke through the sultry stillness of the night. A black speck had slid around the stern of one of the gunboats, and was making for the bank, saluted by quick spittings of fire from the levee above and below the junction of the bayou with the river. In reply, similar fiery spittings scintillated from the dark mass of the fort, and there was a rapid *whit-whit* of invisible missiles. A cutter was coming ashore; the rebel pickets were firing upon it; the garrison was firing upon the pickets; the pickets upon the garrison. The red flashes and irregular rattle lasted until the cutter had completed its return voyage. There was an understanding now between the little navy and the little army; the gunboats knew where to direct their cannonade so as best to support the garrison; and the soldiers were full of confidence, although they did not relax their vigilance. Doctor Ravenel and Mrs. Carter supposed in their civilian inexperience that all danger was over, and by two o'clock in the morning were fast asleep.

CHAPTER XXIV.

A DESPERATE ATTACK AND A SUCCESSFUL DEFENCE.

WHILE it was still darkness Lillie was awakened from her sleep by an all-pervading, startling, savage uproar. Through the hot night came tramplings and yellings of a rebel brigade; roaring of twenty-four-pounders and whirring of grape from the bastions of the fort; roaring of hundred-pounders and flight of shrieking, cracking,

flashing shells from the gunboats; incessant spattering
and fiery spitting of musketry, with whistling and hum-
ming of bullets; and, constant through all, the demoniac
yell advancing like the howl of an infernal tide.   Bedlam,
pandemonium, all the maniacs of earth and all the fiends
of hell, seemed to have combined in riot amidst the crash-
ings of storm and volcano.   The clamor came with the
suddenness and continued with more than the rage of a
tornado.   Lillie had never imagined anything so unearthly
and horrible.   She called loudly for her father, and was
positively astonished to hear his voice close at her side, so
strangely did the familiar tones sound in that brutal uproar.

"What is it?" she asked.

"It must be the assault," he replied, astonished into
telling the alarming truth.   "I will step out and take a
look."

"You shall not," she exclaimed, clutching him.   "What
if you should be hit!"

"My dear, don't be childish," remonstrated the Doctor.
"It is my duty to attend to the wounded.   I am the only
surgeon in the fort.   Just consider the ingratitude of
neglecting these brave fellows who are fighting for our
safety."

"Will you promise not to get hurt?"

"Certainly, my dear."

"Will you come back every five minutes and let me
see you?"

"Yes, my dear.   I'll keep you informed of everything
that happens."

She thought a few moments, and gradually loosened her
hold on him.   Her curiosity, her anxiety to know how
this terrible drama went on, helped her to be brave and
to spare him.   As soon as her fingers had unclosed from
his sleeve he crept to where his rifle stood and softly,
siezed it; and in so doing he stepped on the recumbent
Gazaway, who groaned, whereupon the Doctor politely

apologized. As he stepped out of the building he distinguished Colburne's voice on the river front, shouting, "This way, men !" In that direction ran the Doctor, holding his rifle in both hands, at something like the position of a charge bayonet, with his thumb on the trigger so as to be ready for immediate conflict. Suddenly bang ! went the piece at an angle of forty-five degrees, sending its ball clean across the Mississippi, and causing a veteran sergeant near him to inquire " what the hell he was about."

" Really, that explosion was quite extraordinary," said the surprised Doctor. "I had not the least intention of firing. Would you, sir, have the goodness to load it for me ?"

But the sergeant was in a hurry, and ran on without answering. The Doctor began to finger his cartridge-box in a wild way, intending to get out a cartridge if he could, when a faint voice near him said, " I'll load your gun for you, sir."

" *Would* you be so kind ?" replied the Doctor, delighted. "I am so dreadfully inexperienced in these operations! I am quite sorry to trouble you."

The sick man—one of the invalids whom Gazaway had brought from New Orleans—loaded the piece, capped it, and added some brief instructions in the mysteries of half-cock and full-cock.

" Really you are very good. I am quite obliged," said the Doctor, and hurried on to the river front, guided by the voice of Colburne. At the rampart he tried to shoot one of our men who was coming up wounded from the palisade, and would probably have succeeded, but that the lock of his gun would not work. Colburne stopped him in this well-intentioned but mistaken labor, saying, " Those are our people." Then, " Your gun is at half-cock. —There.—Now keep your finger off the trigger until you see a rebel."

Then shouting, "Forward, men !" he ran down to the

palisade followed by twenty or thirty, of whom one was the Doctor.

The assailing brigade, debouching from the woods half a mile away from the front, had advanced in a wide front across the flat, losing scarcely any men by the fire of the artillery, although many, shaken by the horrible screeching of the hundred-pound shells, threw themselves on the ground in the darkness or sought the frail shelter of the scattered dwellings. Thus diminished in numbers and broken up by night and obstacles and the differing speed of running men, the brigade reached the fort, not an organization, but a confused swarm, flowing along the edge of the ditch to right and left in search of an entrance. There was a constant spattering of flushes, as individuals returned the steady fire of the garrision; and the sharp clean whistle of round bullets and buckshot mingled in the thick warm air with the hoarse whiz of Minies. Now and then an angry shout or wailing scream indicated that some one had been hit and mangled. The exhortations and oaths of the rebel officers could be distinctly heard, as they endeavored to restore order, to drive up stragglers, and to urge the mass forward. A few jumped or fell into the ditch and floundered there, unable to climb up the smooth facings of brickwork. Two or three hundred collected around the palisade which connected the northern front with the river, some lying down and waiting, and others firing at the woodwork or the neighboring ramparts, while a few determined ones tried to burst open the gate by main strength.

The Doctor put the whole length of his barrel through one of the narrow port holes of the palisade and immediately became aware that some on the outside had seized it and was pulling downwards. "Let go of my gun!" he shouted instinctively, without considering the unreasonable nature of the request. "Let go yourself, you son of a bitch!" returned the outsider, not a whit more rational. The Doctor pulled trigger with a sense of just indignation, and

drew in his gun, the barrel bent at a right angle and
bursted. Whether he had injured the rebel or only startled him into letting go his hold, he never knew and did
not then pause to consider. He felt his ruined weapon
all over with his hands, tried in vain to draw the ramrod,
and, after bringing all his philosophical acumen to bear on
the subject, gave up the idea of reloading. Casting about
for a new armament, he observed behind him a man lying
in one of the many little gullies which seemed to slope between the fort and the river, his eyes wide open and fixed
upon the palisade, and his right hand loosely holding a rifle.
The Doctor concluded that he was sick, or tired, or seeking shelter from the bullets.

"Would you be good enough to lend me your gun for
a few moments ?" he inquired.

The man made no reply; he was perfectly dead. The
Doctor being short-sighted and without his spectacles, and
not accustomed, as yet, to appreciating the effects of musketry, did not suspect this until he bent over him, and saw
that his woolen shirt was soaked with blood. He picked
up the rifle, guessed that it was loaded, stumbled back to
the palisade, insinuated the mere muzzle into a port-hole,
and fired, with splintering effect on the woodwork. The
explosion was followed by a howl of anguish from the exterior, which gave him a mighty throb, partly of horror
and partly of loyal satisfaction. "After all, it is only a
species of surgical operation," he thought, and proceeded
to reload, according to the best of his speed and knowledge. Suddenly he staggered under a violent impulse,
precisely as if a strong man had jerked him by the coat-
collar, and putting his hand to the spot, he found that a
bullet (nearly spent in penetrating the palisades) had
punched its way through the cloth. This was the nearest
approach to a wound that he received during the engagement.

Meantime things were going badly with the assailants.
Disorganized by the night, cut up by the musketry, de-

P

moralized by the incessant screaming and bursting of the
one-hundred-pound shells, unable to force the palisade or
cross the ditch, they rapidly lost heart, threw themselves
on the earth, took refuge behind the levees, dropped away
in squads through the covering gloom, and were, in short,
repulsed.   In the course of thirty minutes, all that yelling
swarm had disappeared, except the thickly scattered dead
and wounded, and a few well-covered stragglers, who continued to fire as sharpshooters.

"We have whipped them!" shouted Colburne. "Hurrah
for the old flag!"

The garrison caught the impulse of enthusiasm, and
raised yell on yell of triumph.   Even the wounded ceased
to feel their anguish for a moment, and uttered a feeble
shout or exclamation of gladness.   The Doctor bethought
himself of his daughter, and hurried back to the brick
building to inform her of the victory.   She threw herself
into his arms with a shriek of delight, and almost in the
same breath reproached him sharply for leaving her so long.

"My dear, it can't be more than five minutes," said the
Doctor, fully believing what he said, so rapidly does time
pass in the excitement of successful battle.

"Is it really over?" she asked.

"Quite so.   They are rushing for the woods like pelted
frogs for a puddle.   They are going in all directions, as
though they were bound for Cowes and a market.   I don't
believe they will ever get together again.   We have
gained a magnificent victory.   It is the grandest moment
of my life."

"Is Captain Colburne unhurt?" was Lillie's next question.

"Perfectly.   We haven't lost a man—except one," he
added, bethinking himself of the poor fellow whose gun he
had borrowed.

"Oh!" she sighed, with a long inspiration of relief, for
the life of her brave defender had become precious in her
eyes.

The Doctor had absent-mindedly brought his rifle into the room, and was much troubled with it, not caring to shock Lillie with the fact that he had been personally engaged. He held it behind his back with one hand, after the manner of a naughty boy who has been nearly detected in breaking windows, and who still has a brickbat in his fist which he dares not show, and cannot find a chance to hide. He was slyly setting it against the wall when she discovered it.

"What!" she exclaimed. "Have you been fighting, too? You dear, darling, wicked papa!"

She kissed him violently, and then laughed hysterically.

"I thought you were up to some mischief all the while," she added. "You were gone a dreadful time, and I screaming and looking out for you. Papa, you ought to be ashamed of yourself."

"I have reason to be. I am the most disgraceful ignoramus. I don't know how to load my gun. I think I must have put the bullet in wrong end first. The ramrod won't go down."

"Well, put it away now. You don't want it any more. You must take care of the wounded."

"Wounded!" exclaimed the Doctor. "Are there any wounded?"

"Oh dear! several of them. I forgot to tell you. They are to bring them in here. I am going to our trunks to get some linen."

The Doctor was quite astonished to find that there were a number of wounded; for having escaped unhurt himself, he concluded that every one else had been equally lucky, excepting, of course, the man who lay dead in the gulley. As he laid down his gun he heard a groaning in one corner, and went softly towards it, expecting to find one of the victims of the conflict. Lifting up one end of a blanket, and lighting a match to dispel the dimness, he beheld the prostrate Gazaway, his face beaded with the perspiration of heat and terror.

"Oh!" said the Doctor, with perhaps the merest twang of contempt in the exclamation.

"My God, Doctor!" groaned the Major. "I tell you I'm a sick man. I've got the most awful bilious colic that ever a feller had. If you can give me something, do, for God's sake!"

"Presently," answered Ravenel, and paid no more attention to him.

"If I could have discharged my gun," he afterwards said, in relating the circumstance, "I should have been tempted to rid him of his bilious colic by a surgical operation."

The floor of the little building was soon cumbered with half a dozen injured men, and dampened with their blood. The Doctor had no instruments, but he could probe with his finger and dress with wet bandages. Lillie aided him, pale at the sight of blood and suffering, but resolute to do what she could. When Colburne looked in for a moment, she nodded to him with a sweet smile, which was meant to thank him for having defended her.

"I am glad to see you at this work," he said. "There will be more of it."

"What! More fighting!" exclaimed the Doctor, looking up from a shattered finger.

"Oh yes. We mustn't hope that they will be satisfied with one assault. There is a supporting column, of course; and it will come on soon. But do you stay here, whatever happens. You will be of most use here."

He had scarcely disappeared when the whole air became horribly vocal, as, with a long-drawn, screaming battle-yell, the second brigade of Texans moved to the assault, and the "thunders of fort and fleet" replied. Taking the same direction as before, but pushing forward with superior solidity and energy, the living wave swept up to the fortifications, howled along the course of the ditch, and surged clamorously against the palisade. Colburne was there with half the other officers and half the strength of the garrison, silent for the most part, but fighting desperately. Suddenly there was a shout of, "Back! back! They are coming round the palisade."

There was a stumbling rush for the cover of the fortification proper; and there the last possible line of defence was established instinctively and in a moment. Officers and men dropped on their knees behind the low bank of earth, and continued an irregular, deliberate fire, each discharging his piece as fast as he could load and aim. The garrison was not sufficient to form a continuous rank along even this single front, and on such portions of the works as were protected by the ditch, the soldiers were scattered almost as sparsely as sentinels. Nothing saved the place from being carried by assault except the fact that the assailants were unprovided with scaling ladders. The adventurous fellows who had flanked the palisade, rushed to the gate, and gave entrance to a torrent of tall, lank men in butternut or dirty grey clothing, their bronzed faces flushed with the excitement of supposed victory, and their yells of exultation drowning for a minute the sharp outcries of the wounded, and the rattle of the musketry. But the human billow was met by such a fatal discharge that it could not come over the rampart. The foremost dead fell across it, and the mass reeled backward. Unfortunately for the attack, the exterior slope was full of small knolls and gullies, beside being cumbered with rude shanties, of four or five feet in height made of bits of board, and shelter tents, which had served as the quarters of the garrison. Behind these covers scores if not hundreds sought refuge, and could not be induced to leave them for a second charge. They commenced with musketry, and from that moment the great peril was over. The men behind the rampart had only to lie quiet, to shoot every one who approached or rose at full length, and to wait till daylight should enable the gunboats to open with grape. In vain the rebel officers, foreseeing this danger, strove with voice and example to raise a yell and a rush. The impetuosity of the attack had died out, and could not be brought to life.

"They don't like the way it works," laughed the Louis-iana lieutenant in high glee. "They ain't on it so much as they was."

For an hour the exchange of close musketry continued, the strength of the assailants steadily decreasing, as some fell wounded or dead, and others stole out of the fatal enclosure. Daylight showed more than a hundred fallen and nearly two hundred unharmed men; all lying or crouching among the irregularities of that bloody and bullet-torn glacis. Several voices cried out, "Stop firing. We surrender."

An officer in a lieutenant-colonel's uniform repeated these words, waving a white handkerchief. Then rising from his refuge he walked up to the rampart, leaped upon it, and stared in amazement at the thin line of defenders, soldiers and negroes intermingled.

"By ——! I won't surrender to such a handful," he exclaimed. "Come on, boys!"

A sergeant immediately shot him through the breast, and his body fell inside of the works. Not a man of those whom he had appealed to followed him; and only a few rose from their covers, to crouch again as soon as they witnessed his fate. The fire of the garrison reopened with violence, and soon there were new cries of, "We surrender," with a waving of hats and handkerchiefs.

"What shall we do?" asked the Louisiana lieutenant. "They are three to our one. If we let the d—n scoundrels in, they will knock us down and take our guns away from us."

Colburne rose and called out, "Do you surrender?"

"Yes, yes," from many voices, and a frantic agitation of broadbrims.

"Then throw your arms into the river."

First one, then another, then several together obeyed this order, until there was a general rush to the bank, and a prodigious splashing of double-barreled guns and bowie-knives in the yellow water.

"Now sit down and keep quiet," was Colburne's next command.

They obeyed with the utmost composure. Some filled their pipes and fell to smoking; others produced corn-cake from their havresacks and breakfasted; others busied themselves with propping the wounded and bringing them water. Quite a number crawled into the deserted shanties and went to sleep, apparently worn out with the night's work and watching. A low murmur of conversation, chiefly concerning the events of the assault, and not specially gloomy in its tenor, gradually mingled with the groans of the wounded. When the gate of the palisade was closed upon them and refastened, they laughed a little at the idea of being shut up in a pen like so many chickens.

"Trapped, by Jiminy!" said one. "You must excuse me if I don't know how to behave myself. I never was cotched before. I'm a wild man of the pararies, I am."

On all sides the attack had failed, with heavy loss to the assailants. The heroic little garrison, scarcely one hundred and fifty strong, including officers, camp-followers and negroes (all of whom had fought), had captured more than its own numbers, and killed and wounded twice its own numbers. The fragments of the repulsed brigades had fallen back beyond the range of fire, and even the semicircle of pickets had almost disappeared in the woods. The prisoners and wounded were taken on board the gunboats, and forwarded to New Orleans by the first transport down the river. As the last of the unfortunates left the shore Colburne remarked. "I wonder if those poor fellows will ever get tired of fighting for an institution which only prolongs their own inferiority."

"I am afraid not—I am afraid not," said the Doctor. "Not, at least, until they are whipped into reason. They have been educated under an awful tyranny of prejudice, conceit, and ignorance. They are more incapable of perceiving their own true interests than so many brutes. I have had the honor to be acquainted with dogs who were their superiors in that respect. In Tennessee, on one of my excursions, I stopped over night in the log-cabin of a farmer. It was rather chilly, and I wanted to poke the fire. There was no poker. 'Ah,' said the farmer, 'Bose has run off with the poker again.' He went out for a moment, and came in with the article. I asked him if his dog had a fancy for pokers. '·No,' said he; 'but one of my boys once burnt the critter's nose with a hot poker; and ever since then he hides it every time that he comes across it. We know whar to find it. He allays puts it under the house and kivers it up with leaves. It's curous,' said he, ' to watch him go at it, snuffing to see if it is hot, and picking it up and sidling off as sly as a horse-thief. He has an awful bad conscience about it. Perhaps you noticed that when you asked for the poker, Bose he got up and travelled.'—Now, you see, the dog knew what had burned him. But these poor besotted creatures don't know that it is slavery which has scorched their stupid noses. They have no idea of getting rid of their hot poker. They are fighting to keep it."

When it had become certain that the fighting was quite over, Major Gazaway reappeared in public, complaining much of internal pains, but able to dictate and sigh a pompous official report of his victory, in which he forgot to mention the colic or the name of Captain Colburne. During the following night the flare of widespread fires against the sky showed that the enemy were still in the neighborhood; and negroes who stole in from the swamps reported that the country was "cram full o' rebs, way up beyon' Mars Ravenel's plantashum."

" You won't be able to reoccupy your house for a long time, I fear," said Colburne.

" No," sighed the Doctor. " My experiment is over. I must get back to New Orleans."

" And I must go to Port Hudson. I shall be forgiven, I presume, for not reporting back to the hospital."

Such was the defence of Fort Winthrop, one of the most gallant feats of the war. Those days are gone by, and there will be no more like them forever, at least, not in our forever. Not very long ago, not more than two hours before this ink dried upon the paper, the author of the present history was sitting on the edge of a basaltic cliff which overlooked a wide expanse of fertile earth, flourishing villages, the spires of a city, and, beyond, a shining sea flecked with the full-blown sails of peace and prosperity. From the face of another basaltic cliff two miles distant, he saw a white globule of smoke dart a little way upward, and a minute afterwards heard a dull, deep *pum!* of exploding gunpowder. Quarrymen there were blasting out rocks from which to build hives of industry and happy family homes. But the sound reminded him of the roar of artillery; of the thunder of those signal guns which used to presage battle; of the alarums which only a few months previous were a command to him to mount and ride into the combat. Then he thought, almost with a feeling of sadness, so strange is the human heart, that he had probably heard those clamors, uttered in mortal earnest, for the last time. Never again, perhaps, even should he live to the age of threescore and ten, would the shriek of grapeshot, and the crash of shell, and the multitudinous whiz of musketry be a part of his life. Nevermore would he hearken to that charging yell which once had stirred his blood more fiercely than the sound of trumpets : the Southern battle-yell, full of howls and yelpings as of brute beasts rushing hilariously to the fray : the long-sustained Northern yell, all human, but none the less relentless and stern ; nevermore the one nor the other. No more charges of cavalry, rushing through the dust of the distance ; no more answering smoke of musketry, veiling unshaken lines and squares ; no more columns of smoke, piling high above deafening batteries. No more groans of wounded, nor shouts of victors over positions carried and banners captured, nor reports of triumphs which saved a nation from disappearing off the face of the earth. After thinking of these things for an hour together, almost sadly, as I have said, he walked back to his home; and read with interest a paper which prattled of town elections, and advertised corner-lots for sale ; and decided to make a kid-gloved call in the evening, and to go to church on the morrow.

CHAPTER XXV.

DOMESTIC HAPPINESS, IN SPITE OF ADVERSE CIRCUMSTANCES.

WHEN Colburne reached Port Hudson, it had capitulated ; the stars and stripes were flying in place of the stars and bars. With a smile of triumph he climbed the steep path which zig-zagged up the almost precipitous breast— earth changing into stone—of the gigantic bluff which formed the river front of the fortress. At the summit was a plateau of nearly three-quarters of a mile in diameter, verdant with turf and groves, and pleasantly rolling in surface. He had never been here before ; he and twelve thousand others had tried to come here on the 27th of May, but had failed ; and he paused to take a long look at the spot and its surroundings. Not a sign of fortification was visible, except five or six small semi-lunes of earth at different points along the edge of the bluff, behind which were mounted as many monstrous guns, some smooth-bore, some rifled. Solid shot from these giants had sunk the Mississippi, and crippled all of Farragut's fleet but two in his audacious rush up the river. Shells from them had flown clean over the bluff, and sought out the farthest camps of Banks's army, bursting with a sonorous, hollow thunder which seemed to shake earth and atmosphere. On the land side the long lines of earthworks which had so steadily and bloodily repulsed our columns were all below the line of sight, hidden by the undulations of the ground, or by the forest. The turf was torn and pitted by the bombardments; two-hundred-pound shells, thrown by the long rifles of the fleet, lay here and there, some in fragments, some unexploded; the church, the store, and half a dozen houses, which constituted the village, were more or less shattered. The bullets of the Union sharpshooters had reached as far as here, and had even gone quite over and fallen into the Mississippi. A gaunt, dirty woman told Colburne that on the spot where he stood a soldier of the garrison had been killed by a chance rifle-ball while drinking a glass of beer. Leaving his cicerone, he joined a party of officers who were lounging in the shade of a tree, and inquired for the residence of Colonel Carter.

"Here you are," answered a lieutenant, pointing to the nearest house. "Can I do any thing for you, Captain? I am his aid. I wouldn't advise you to call on him unless you have something very particular to say. Every body has been celebrating the surrender, and the Colonel isn't exactly in a state for business."

Colburne hesitated; but he had letters from Carter's wife and father-in-law, and of course he must see him, drunk or sober. At that moment he heard a voice that he recognized; a voice that had demanded and obtained what he had not dared to ask for—a voice that, as he well knew, *she* longed for as the sweetest of earth's music.

"Hi! hi!" said the Colonel, making his appearance upon the unpainted, warped, paralytic verandah of his dwelling. Through the low-cut window from which he issued could be seen a sloppy table, with bottles and glasses, and the laughing faces of two bold-browed, slatternly girls, the one seventeen, the other twenty. He had on an old dressing-gown, fastened around his waist with a sword-belt, and his trousers hung loose about the heels of a pair of dirty slippers. His face was flushed and his eyes blood-shot; he was winking, leering, and slightly unsteady.

Colburne slunk behind a tree, humiliated for his sake, and ready to rave or weep as he thought of the young wife to whom this man's mere name was a comfort.

"Hi! hi!" repeated Carter. "Where are all these fellows?"

The aid advanced and saluted. "Do you want any one, Colonel?"

"No, no. Don't want any one. What for? Celebrate it alone. Man enough for it."

Presently catching the eye of another officer, he again chuckled, "Hi! hi!"

The person thus addressed approached and saluted.

"I say," observed the Colonel, "I got letters last night addressed General Carter—Brigadier-General John T. Carter. What do you think of that?"

"I hope it means promotion," said the officer. "Colonel, do you think we shall go into quarters?"

"No, no; no go into quarters; no go into quarters for us. Played out—quarters. In ole, ole times, after fought a big battle, used to stop—look out good quarters, and stop. But now nix cum rouse the stop."

Back he reeled through the window, to sit down to his whiskey and water, amidst the laughter and rather scornful blandishments of the Secession lasses.

Nevertheless I must see him, decided Colburne. "Ask Colonel Carter," he said to an orderly, "if he can receive Captain Colburne, who brings letters and messages from Mrs. Carter."

In a minute the man returned, saluted and said, "The Colonel sends his compliments and asks you to walk in, sir."

When Colburne entered Carter's presence he found him somewhat sobered in manner; and although the bottles and glasses were still on the table, the bold-faced girls had disappeared.

"Captain, sit down. Take glass plain whiskey," were

the Colonel's first words. "Good for your arm—good for every thing. Glad you got off without a—cut-off."

He would have used the word amputation, only he knew that his tongue could not manage it.

"Thank you, Colonel. Here are two letters, sir, from Mrs. Carter and the Doctor. Just as I was leaving, when it was too late to write, Mrs. Carter charged me to say to you that her father had decided to go at once to New Orleans, so that your letters must be directed to her there."

"I understand," answered Carter slowly and with the solemnity of enforced sobriety. "Thank you."

He broke open his wife's letter and glanced hurriedly through it.

"Captain, I'm 'bliged to you," he said. "You've saved my wife from im-prisn—ment. She's 'bliged to you. You're noble fellah. I charge myself with your pro—mosh'n."

It was so painful to see him struggle in that humiliating manner to appear sober, that Colburne cut short the interview by pretexting a necessity of reporting immediately to his regiment.

"Come to-morrow," said Carter. "All right to-morrow. Business to-morrow. To-day—celebrash'n."

The Colonel, although not aware of the fact, was far advanced in the way of the drunkard. He had long since passed the period when it was necessary to stimulate his appetite for spirituous liquors by sugar, lemon-peel, bitters and other condiments. He had lived through the era of fancy drinks, and entered the cycle of confirmed plain whiskey. At the New Orleans bars he did not call for the fascinating mixtures for which those establishments are famous; he ran his mind's eye wearily over the milk-punches, claret-punches, sherry-cobblers, apple-toddies, tom-and-jerries, brandy-slings, and gin-cocktails; then said in a slightly hoarse *basso profondo*, "Give me some plain whiskey." He had swallowed a great deal of strong

drink during the siege, and since the surrender he had not
known a sober waking moment. His appetite was poor,
especially at breakfast. His face was constantly flushed,
his body had an appearance of being bloated, and his hands
were tremulous. Nevertheless, obedient to a delusion
common to men of his habits, he did not consider himself
a hard drinker. He acknowledged that he got intoxicated
at times and thoroughly, but he thought not more frequently or thoroughly than the average of good fellows.
He was kept in countenance by a great host of comrade
inebriates in the old service and in the new, in the navy
as well as in the army, in high civilian position and at the
front, in short throughout almost every grade and class of
American society. He could point to men whose talents
and public virtues the nation honors, and say, "They get
as drunk as I do, and as often." He could point to such
cases on this side of the water and on the other. Does
anybody remember the orgies of the *viri clari et venera-*
bili, who gathered at Boston to celebrate the obsequies
of John Quincy Adams, and at Charleston to lament over
the remains of John C. Calhoun ? Does anybody remember the dinner speeches on board of Sir Charles Napier's
flagship, just before the Baltic fleet set out for Cronstadt ?
Latterly this vice has increased upon us in America, thanks
to the reaction against the Maine liquor law, thanks to the
war. Perhaps it is for the best ; perhaps it is a good thing
that hundreds of leading Americans and hundreds of thousands of led Americans should be drunkards ; it may be,
in some incomprehensible manner, for the interest of humanity. To my unenlightened mind the contrary seems
probable ; but I am liable to error, and sober at this moment of writing : a pint of whiskey might illuminate me to
see behind the veil. It is wonderful to me, a member of
the guzzling Anglo-Saxon race, that the abstemious Latin
nations have not yet got the better of us. Nothing can
account for it, unless it is that spiritual, and intellectual,
and political tyranny more than counterbalance the advant-

ages of temperance. Boozing John Bull and Jonathan
have kept an upper hand because their geographical conditions have enabled them to remain free ; and on their
impregnable islands and separated quarters of the globe
they have besotted themselves for centuries with political
impunity.

Next day, as Carter had promised, he was able to attend to business. His first act was to issue an order assigning Captain Colburne to his staff as " Acting Assistant
Adjutant-General, to be obeyed and respected accordingly." When the young officer reported for duty he
found the Colonel sober, but stern and gloomy with the
woful struggle against his maniacal appetite, and shaky
in body with the result of the bygone debauch.

" Captain," said he, " I wish you would do me the favor
to join my mess. I want a temperance man. No more
whiskey for one while ! — By the way, I owe you so
much I never can repay you for saving my wife from those
savages. If admiration is any reward, you have it. My
wife and her father both overflow with your praises."

Colburne bowed and replied that he had done no more
than his duty as an officer and a gentleman.

" I am glad it was you who did it," replied the Colonel.
" I don't know any other person to whom I would so willingly be under such an obligation."

It was certainly rather handsome in Carter that he should
cheerfully permit his wife to feel admiration and gratitude
towards so handsome a young man as Colburne.

" That infernal poltroon of a Gazaway !" he broke out
presently. " I ought to have cashiered him long ago. I'll
have him court-martialed and shot. By the way, he was
perfectly well when you saw him, wasn't he ?"

" I should think so. He looked like a champion of the
heavy weights. The mere reflection of his biceps was
enough to break a looking-glass."

" I thought he had run away from the service altogether.
He came up to the regiment once during the siege. The

officers kicked him out, and he disappeared. Got in at some hospital, it seems—By (this and that) three quarters of the hospitals are a disgrace to the service. They are asylums for shirks and cowards. I wish you would make it your first business to inform yourself of all Gazaway's sneakings—misbehavior in presence of the enemy, you understand—violation of the fifty-second article of war—and draw up charges against him. I want charges that will shoot him."

Here I may as well anticipate the history of the Major. When the charges against him were forwarded, he got wind of them, and, making a personal appeal to high authority, pleaded hard for leave to resign on a surgeon's certificate of physical disability. The request was granted for some mysterious reason, probably of political origin ; and this vulgar poltroon left the army, and the department with no official stigma on his character. On reaching Barataria he appealed to his faithful old herd of followers and assailed Colonel Carter and Captain Colburne as a couple of aristocrats who would not let a working man hold a commission.

Two days subsequent to Colburne's arrival at Port Hudson the brigade sailed to Fort Winthrop and from thence followed the trail of the retreating Texans as far as Thibodeaux, where Carter established his head-quarters. A week later, when the rebels were all across the Atchafalaya and quiet once more prevailed in the Lafourche Interieur, he sent to New Orleans for his wife, and established her in a pretty cottage, with orange trees and a garden, in the outskirts of the little French American city. The Doctor's plantation house had been burned, his agricultural implements destroyed, and his cattle eaten or driven away by the rebels, who put a devout zeal into the task of laying waste every spot which had been desecrated by the labor of manumitted bondsmen. His grand experiment of reorganizing southern industry being thus knocked on the head, he had applied for and obtained his old position in the hospital. Lillie wept at parting from him, but nevertheless flew to live with her husband.

The months which she passed at Thibodeaux were the happiest that she had ever known. The Colonel did not drink; was with her every moment that he could spare from his duties; was strongly loving and noisily cheerful, like a doting dragoon as he was; abounded with attentions and presents, bouquets from the garden, and dresses from New Orleans; was uneasy to make her comfortable, and exhibit his affection. The whole brigade knew her, and delighted to look at her, drilling badly in consequence of inattention when she cantered by on horseback. The sentinels, when not watched by the lieutenant of the guard, gratified themselves and amused her with the courteous pleasantry of presenting arms as she passed. Such officers as were aristocratic enough or otherwise fortunate enough to obtain a bowing acquaintance, still more to be invited to her receptions and dinner parties, flattered her by their evident admiration and devotion. A second lieutenant who once had a chance to shorten her stirrup leather, alluded to it vain-gloriously for weeks afterward, and received the nickname from his envious comrades of "Acting Assistant Flunkey General, Second Brigade, First Division, Nineteenth Army Corps." It made no difference with the happy youth; he had shortened the stirrup of the being who was every body's admiration; and from his pedestal of good fortune he smiled serenely at detraction. Lillie was the queen, the goddess, the only queen and goddess, of the Lafourche Interieur. In the whole district there was no other lady, except the wives of two captains, who occupied a much lower heaven, and some bitter Secessionists, who kept aloof from the army, and were besides wofully scant in their graces and wardrobe. The adulation which she received did not come from the highest human source, but it was unmixed, unshared, whole-souled, constant. She thought it was the most delightful thing conceivable to keep house, to be married, to be the wife of Colonel Carter. If she had been twenty-five or thirty years old, a veteran of society, I should be inclined to laugh at her for the child-like pleasure she took in her conditions and surroundings; but only twenty, hardly ever at a party, married without a wedding, married less than six months, I sympathise with her, rejoice with her, in her unaccustomed intoxication of happiness. It was curious to see how slowly she got accustomed to her husband. For some time it seemed to her amazing and almost incredible that any man should call himself by such a title, and claim the familiarity and the rights which it implied. She frequently blushed at encountering him, as if he were still a lover. If she met the bold gaze of his wide-open brown eyes, she trembled with an inward thrill, and wanted to say, " Please don't look at me so !" He could tyrannize over her with his eyes ; he could make her come to him and try to hide from them by nestling her head on his shoulder ; he used to wonder at his power, and gratify his vanity as well as his affection by using it.

An officer of the staff, who believed in the marvels of the so-called psychologists, observed the emotion awakened in the wife by the husband's gaze, and mentioned it to Colburne as a proof of the actuality of magnetico-spiritualistic influence. The Captain was not convinced, and felt a strong desire to box the officer's ears. What right had the fellow to make the movements and inclinations of that woman's soul an object of curiosity and a topic of conversation? He offered no reply to the remark, and glared in a way which astonished the other, who had the want of delicacy common to men of one idea. Colburne divined Mrs. Carter too well to adopt the magnetic theory. Judging her nature out of the depths of his own, he believed that love was the true and all-sufficient explanation of her nervousness under the gaze of her husband. It was a painful belief: firstly, for the very natural reason that he was not himself the cause of the emotion; secondly, because he feared that the Colonel might be a blight to the delicate affection which clasped him with its tendrils.

His relations with both were the most familiar, the frankest, the kindest. When Carter could not ride out with his wife, he detailed Colburne for the agreeable duty. When Mrs. Carter made a visit to headquarters, and did not find the Colonel there, she asked for the adjutant-general. The friend sent the lady bouquets by the hands of the husband. Carter knew to some extent how Colburne adored Lillie, but he had a fine confidence in the purity and humility of the adoration, and he trusted her to him as he would have trusted her to her father. The Captain was not a member of the family: the cottage was too far from his official duties to allow of that; but he dined there every Sunday, and called there every other evening. Ravonel's letters to one or the other, were the common property of both. If Lillie did not hear from her father twice a week, and therefore became anxious about him, because it was the yellow fever season, or because of the broad fact that man is mortal, she applied to Colburne as well as to her husband for comforting suggestions and assurances. In company with some chance fourth, these three had the gayest evenings of whist and euchre. Lillie never looked at her cards without exciting the laughter of the two men, by declaring that she hadn't a thing in her hand—positively not a single thing—couldn't take a trick—not one. She talked perpetually, told what honors she held, stole glances at her opponent's hand, screamed with delight when she won, and in short violated all the venerable rules of whist. She forgot the run of the cards, trumped her partner's trick, led diamonds when he had trashed on hearts, led the queen when she held ace and king. To her trumps she held on firmly, never showing them till the last moment, and scolding her partner if he called them out. She invariably claimed the deal at the close of each hand, thereby getting it oftener than she had a right to it. But she might do what she pleased, sure that those who played

with her would not complain.   Was she not queen and
goddess, Semiramis and Juno ?   Who would rebel, even
in the slightest particular, against the dominion of a happiness which overflowed in such gayety, such confidence
in all around, such unchangeable amiability ?

She was in superb health of body, and spirit without a
pain, or a sickly moment, or a cloud of foreboding, or a
thrill of pettishness.   A physical calmness so deliciously
placid as to remind one of that spiritual peace which passeth
understanding, bore her gently through the summer,
smiling on all beholders.   Do you remember the serene
angel in the first picture of Cole's Voyage of Life, who
stands at the helm of the newly launched bark, guiding it
down the gentle river ?   It is the mother voyaging with
her child, whether before its birth or after.   Just now she
looked much like this angel, only more frolicsomely happy.
Her blue eyes sparkled with the lustre of health so perfect
that the mere consciousness of a life was a pleasure.   Her
cheeks, usually showing more of the lily than of the rose,
were so radiant with color that it seemed as if every throb
of emotion might force the blood through the delicate skin.
Her arms, neck and shoulders were no longer Dianesque,
but rounded, columnal, Junonian.   It was this novel, this
almost superwomanly health which gave her such an
efflorescence of happiness, amiability and beauty.

She had repeatedly hinted to her husband that she had
a secret to tell him.   When he asked what it was she
blushed, laughed at him for the question, and declared
that he should never know it, that she had no secret at all,
that she had been joking.   Then she wondered that he should
not guess it ; thought it the strangest thing in the world
that he should not know it.   At last she made her confession : made it to him alone, with closed doors and in darkness ; she could no more have told it in the light of day
than in the presence of a circle.   Then for many minutes
she nestled close to him with wet cheeks and clinging
arms, listening eagerly to his assurances of love and devo-

tion, hungering unappeaseably for them, growing to him, one with him.

After this Carter treated his wife with increased tenderness. Nothing that she desired was too good for her, or too difficult to get. He sought to check the constant exercise which she delighted in, and especially her long rides on horseback; and when with a sweet, laughing wilfulness she defied his authority, he watched her with evident anxiety. He wrote about it all to her father, and the consequence was a visit from the Doctor. This combination of natural potentates was victorious, and equestrianism was given up for walking and tending flowers. At this time she had so much affection to spare that she lavished treasures of it, not only on plants, but on birds, cats, dogs, and ponies. Here Colburne drifted into the circle of her sympathies. He was fond of pets, especially of weak ones, for instance liking cats better than dogs, and liking them all the more because most people abused and, as he contended, misunderstood them. He had stories to tell of feline creatures who had loved him with a love like that of Jonathan for David, passing the love of woman. There was the abnormally sensitive Tabby who pined away with grief when his mother died, and the uncomformably intelligent Tom who persisted in getting into his trunk when he was packing it to go to the wars.

"I am confident," he asserted, "that Puss knew I was about to leave, and wanted to be taken along."

Lillie did not question it; all love, even that of animals, seemed natural to her; she felt (not thought) that love was the teacher of the soul.

By the way, Colburne's passion for pets had deep roots in his character. It sprang from his pitying fondness for the weak, and was closely related to his sympathies with humanity. It extended to the feebler members of his own race, such as children and old ladies, whom he befriended and petted whenever he could, and who in return granted him their easily-won affection. For flowers, and in general for inanimate nature, he cared little; never could be induced to study botany, nor to understand why other people should study it; could not see any human interest in it. Geology he liked, because it promised, he thought, some knowledge of the early history of man, or at least of the grand cosmical preparation for his advent. Astronomy was also interesting to him, inasmuch as we may at some future time traverse sidereal spaces. The most interesting star in the heavens, to his mind, was that one in the Pleiades which is supposed to be the central sun of our solar and planetary system. Around this all that he knew and all whom he loved revolved, even including Mrs. Carter.

I presume that this summer was the happiest period in the life of the Colonel. He was in fine health, thanks to his present temperate ways, although they reduced his weight so rapidly that his wife thought he was sick, and became alarmed about him. He frequently recommended marriage to Colburne, and they had long conversations on the subject; not, however, before Mrs. Carter, whose entrance always caused the Captain to drop the subject. The Telemachus was as fully persuaded of the benefits, happiness and duty of wedded life as the Mentor, and was much the best theorizer.

"I believe," he said, "that neither man nor woman is a complete nature by himself or herself, and that you must unite the two in one before humanity is perfected, and, to use an Emersonianism, comes full circle. The union is affection, and the consecration of it is marriage. You remember Baron Munchausen's horse; how he was cut in two, and the halves got on very poorly without each other; and how they were reunited with mutual benefit. Now this is the history of every bachelor and single woman, who having miserably tried for a while to go it alone, finally coalesce happily in one flesh."

"By Jove, Captain, you talk like a philosopher," said the Colonel. "You ought to write something. You ought to practice, too, according to your preaching. There is Mrs. Larue, now. No," he added seriously. " Don't take her. She isn't worthy of you. You deserve the best."

Colburne was a better conversationalist than Carter, except in the way of small talk with comparative strangers, wherein the latter's confidence in himself, strengthened by habits of authority, gave him an easy freedom. Indeed, when Carter was actually brilliant in society, you might be sure he had taken five or six plain whiskeys, and that five or six more (what a head he sported!) would make him moderately drunk. If my readers will go back to the dinner at Professor Whitewood's, and the evening which followed it, and the next day's pic-nic when he was under the influence of a whiskey fever, they will see the best that he could do as a talker. With regard to subjects which implied ever so little scholarship, the Colonel accorded the Captain a facile admiration which at first astonished the latter. Talking one day of the earth-works of Port Hudson, Colburne observed that the Romans threw up field fortifications at the close of every day's march, one legion standing under arms to protect the workmen, while another marched out and formed line of battle to cover the foragers. If the brigade commander had ever known these things, he had evidently forgotten them. He looked at Colburne with undisguised astonishment, and set him down from that moment as a fellow of infinite erudition. This was far from being the only occasion on which the volunteer captain was led to notice the narrow professional basis from which most of the officers of the old service talked and thought. Now and then he met a philosopher like Phelps, or a chemist like Franklin; but in general he found them as little versed in the ways and ideas of the world as so many old sea-captains; and even with regard to their own profession they were narrowly practical and technical.

Amidst all these pleasant sentiments and conversings, Carter had his perplexities and anxieties. He was spending more than his income, and neither knew how to increase it, nor how to curtail his outlay. Besides his colonel's pay he had no resources, unless indeed dunning letters could be made into negotiable paper. He was not very sensitive on the subject of these missives; and in fact he was what most people would consider disgracefully callous to their influence; but he looked forward with alarm to a time when his credit might fail altogether, and his wife might suffer for luxuries.

CHAPTER XXVI.

CAPTAIN COLBURNE DESCRIBES CAMP AND FIELD LIFE.

A PERUSAL of the letters of Colburne has decided me to sketch some of the smaller incidents of his experience in field service. The masculine hardness of the subject will perhaps be an agreeable relief to the reader after the scenes of domestic felicity, not very comprehensible or interesting to bachelors, which are depicted in the preceding chapter.

The many minor hardships of a soldier are, I presume, hardly suspected by a civilian. As an instance of what an officer may be called on to endure, even under favorable circumstances, when for instance he is not in Libby Prison, nor in the starvation camp at Andersonville, I cite the following passage from the Captain's correspondence:

"I think that the severest trial I ever had was on a transport. The soldiers were on half rations; and officers, you know, must feed themselves. We had not been paid for four months, and I commenced the voyage, which was to last three days, with seventy-five cents in my pocket. The boat charged a quarter of a dollar a meal. Such were the prospects, and I considered them solemnly. I said to myself, 'Dinner will furnish the greatest amount of nourishment, and I will eat only dinner.' The first day I went without breakfast and supper. On the morning of the second day I awoke fearfully hungry, and could not resist the folly of breakfast. I had character enough to refuse dinner, but by night I was starving again. Possibly you do not know what it is to be ravening after food. I ate supper. That was my last possible meal on board the steamer. I had no chance of borrowing, for every one was about as poor as myself; and to add to my sufferings, the weather was superb and I had a seafaring appetite. I was truly miserable with the degrading misery of hunger, thinking like a dog of nothing but food, when a brother officer produced a watermelon which he had saved for this supreme moment of destitution. He was charitable enough to divide it among four fellow paupers; and on that quarter of a watermelon I lived twenty-six hours, very wretchedly. When we landed I was in command of the regiment, but could hardly give an order loud enough to be heard by the shrunken battalion. Two hours afterwards Henry brought me a small plate of stewed onions, without meat or bread, not enough to feed a Wethersfield baby. I ate them all, too starved to ask Henry whether he had anything for himself or not. Shameful, but natural. Ridiculous as it may seem, I think I can point to this day as the only thoroughtly unhappy one in two years of service. It was not severe suffering; but it was so contemptible, so animal; there was no heroic relief to it. I felt like a starved cur, and growled at the Government, and thought I wanted to resign. Hunger, like sickness, has a depressing effect on the morale, and changes a young man into his grandmother."

It appears that these little starvation episodes were of frequent recurrence. In one letter he speaks of having marched all day on a single biscuit, and in another, written during his Virginia campaign, of having lived for eighteen hours on green apples. He often alluded with pride to the hardihood of soul which privations and dangers had given to the soldiers.

"Our men are not heroes in battle alone," he writes.

Q

"Three months without shelter, drenched by rain or scorched by the sun, tormented by mosquitoes, tainted with fever, shaking with the ague, they appear stoically indifferent to all hardships but their lack of tobacco. Out of the four hundred men whom we brought to this poisonous hole [Brashear City], forty are dead and one hundred and sixty are in hospital. We can hear their screams a mile away as they go into the other world in their chariots of delirium. The remainder, half sick themselves, thin and yellow ghosts in ragged uniforms, crawl out of their diminutive shanties and go calmly to their duties without murmuring, without a desertion. What a scattering there would be in a New England village, in which one tenth of the inhabitants should die in six weeks of some local disease! Yet these men are New Englanders, only tempered to steel by hardships, by discipline, by a profound sense of duty. How I have seen them march with blistered and bleeding feet! march all night after having fought all day! march when every step was a crucifixion! Oh, these noblemen of nature, our American common soldiers! In the face of suffering and of death they are my equals; and while I exact their obedience, I accord them my respect."

The mud of Louisiana appears to have been as troublesome a footing, as the famous sacred soil of Virginia.

"It is the most abominable, sticky, doughy stuff that ever was used in any country for earth," he says. "It 'balls up' on your feet like damp snow on a horse's hoofs. I have repeatedly seen a man stop and look behind him, under the belief that he had lost off his shoe, when it was merely the dropping of the immense mud-pie which had formed around his foot. It is like travelling over a land of suet saturated with pudding sauce.

"Just now the rain is coming down as in the days of Noah. I am under a tent, for an unusual mercy; but the drops are driven through the rotten canvass by the wind. The ditch outside my dwelling is not deep enough to carry off all the water which runs into it, and a small stream is stealing under my bedding and forming a puddle in the centre of my floor. But I don't care for this;—I know that my rubber-blanket is a good one : the main nuisance is that my interior will be muddy. By night I expect to be in a new tent, enlarged and elevated by a siding of planks, so that I shall have a promenade of eight feet in length sheltered from the weather. I only fear that the odor will not be agreeable; for the planks were plundered from the molasses-vats of a sugar-mill and are saturated with treacle; not sticky, you understand, but quite too saccharinely fragrant."

It appears that the army, even in field service, is not altogether barren of convivialities. In the letter following the one, quoted above he says, " My new dwelling has been warmed. I had scarcely taken possession of it when a brother officer, half seas over, and with an inscrutable smile on his lips, stalks in and insists upon treating the occasion. I cannot prevent it without offending him, and there is no strong reason why I should prevent it. He sends to the sutler for two bottles of claret, and then for two more, and finishes them, or sees that they are finished. It is soon evident that he is crowded full and can't carry any more for love or politeness. At dress parade I do not see him out, and learn that he is in his tent, with a prospect of remaining there for the next twelve hours. Yet he is a brave, faithful officer, this now groggiest of sleepers, and generally a very temperate one, so that everybody is wondering, and, I am sorry to say, giggling, over his unusual obfuscation."

In another letter he describes a "jollification by division" on the anniversary of the little victory of Georgia Landing.

" All the officers, not only of the old brigade but of the entire division, were invited to headquarters. Being a long way from our base, the eatables were limited to dried beef, pickles and hard-tack, and the only refreshments to be had in profusion were commissary whiskey and martial music. Such a roaring time as there was by midnight in and around the hollow square formed by the headquarter tents. By dint of vociferations the General was driven to make the first speech of a life-time. He confined himself chiefly to reminiscences of our battles, and made a very pleasant, rambling kind of talk, most of it, however, inaudible to me, who stood on the outside of the circle. When he closed, Tom Perkins, our brave and bossy banddrummer, roared out, 'General, I couldn't hear much of what you said, but I believe what you said was right'."

"This soldierly profession of faith was followed by three-times-three for our commander, everybody joining in without regard to grade of commission. Then Captain Jones of our regiment shouted, 'Tenth Barataria ! three cheers for our old comrades at Georgia Landing and everywhere else, the Seventy-Fifth New York !' and the cheers were given. Then Captain Brown of the Seventy Fifth replied, 'There are not many of us Seventy-Fifth left ; but what there are, we can meet the occasion ; three cheers for the Tenth Barataria !' Then one excited officer roared for Colonel Smith, and another howled for Colonel Robinson, and another screamed for Colonel Jackson, in consequence of which those gentlemen responded with speeches. Nobody seemed to care for what they said, but all hands yelled as if it was a bayonet charge. As the fun got fast and furious public attention settled on a gigantic, dark-complexioned officer, stupendously drunk and volcanically uproarious ; and twenty voices united in shouting, 'Van Zandt ! Van Zandt !'—The great Van Zandt, smiling like an intoxicated hyæna, plunged uncertainly at the crowd, and was assisted to the centre of it. There, as if he were about to make an oration of an hour or so, he dragged off his overcoat, after a struggle worthy of Weller Senior in his pursiest days ; then, held up by two friends, in a manner which reminded me obscurely of Aaron, and Hur sustaining Moses, he stretched out both hands, and delivered himself as follows. 'G'way from th' front thar! G'way from the front thar! An' when say g'way from th' front —thar——'

"He probably intended to disperse some musicians and contrabands who were grinning at him; but before he could explain himself another drunken gentleman reeled against him, vociferating for Colonel Robinson. Van Zandt gave way with a gigantic lurch, like that of an over-balanced iceberg, which carried him clean out of the circle. Somebody brought him his overcoat and held him up while he surged into it. Then he fell over a tent rope and lay across it for five minutes, struggling to regain his feet and smiling in a manner incomprehensible to the beholder. He made no effort to resume his speech, and evidently thought that he had finished it to public satisfaction; but he subsequently addressed the General in his tent, request-ing, so far as could be understood, that the Tenth might be mounted as cavalry. Tom Perkins also staggered into the presence of our commander, and made him a pathetic address, weeping plentifully over his own maudlin, and shaking hands repeatedly, with the remark, 'General, allow me to take you by the hand.'

"It was an All Fools' evening. For once distinctions of rank were abolished. This morning we are subordinates again, and the General is our dignified superior officer."

One of the few amusements of field service seems to con-sist in listening to the facetiæ of the common soldiers, more particularly the irrepressible Hibernians.

"These Irishmen," he says, "are certainly a droll race when you get used to their way of looking at things. My twenty-five Paddies have jabbered and joked more since they entered the service than my seventy Americans backed up by my ten Germans. To give you an idea of how they prattle I will try to set down a conversation which I over-heard while we were bivouacking on the field of our first battle. The dead are buried; the wounded have been car-ried to a temporary hospital; the pickets are out, watchful, we may be sure, because half-frozen in the keen October wind; the men who remain with the colors are sitting up around camp fires, their knapsacks, blankets and overcoats three miles to the rear. This seems hard measure for fellows who have made a twenty-mile march, and gained a victory since morning. But my Irishmen are as jolly as ever, blathering and chaffing each other after their usual fashion. The butt of the company is Sweeney, a withered little animal who walks as if he had not yet thoroughly learned to go on his hind legs, a most curious mixture of simplicity and humor, an actual Handy Andy.

'Sweeney,' says one, ' you ought to do the biggest part of the fightin'. You ate more'n your share of the rashins.'

' I don't ate no more rashins than I get,' retorts Sweeney. indignant at this stale calumny. ' I'd like to see the man as did.'

' Oh, you didn't blather so much whin thim shells was a-flying about your head.'

Here Sweeney falls back upon his old and sometimes successful dodge of trying to turn the current of ridicule upon some one else:

' Wasn't Mickey Emmett perlite a-comin' across the lot ?' he demands. ' I see him bowin' like a monkey on horseback. He was makin' faces as 'ud charrm the head off a whalebarry. Mickey, you dodged beautiful.'

Mickey. Thim shells 'ud make a wooden man dodge. Sweeney's the bye for dodgin'. He was a runnin' about like a dry pea in a hot shovel.

Sweeney. That's what me legs was made for.

Sullivan. Are ye dead, Sweeney ? (An old joke which I do not understand.)

Sweeney. An I wud be if I was yer father, for thinkin' of the drrunken son I had.

Sullivan. Did ye see that dead rebel with his oye out ?

Sweeney. The leftenant ate up all his corn cake while he wasn't noticin'.

Sullivan. It was lookin' at Sweeney put his oye out.

Sweeney. It's lucky for him he didn't see the pair av us.

Jonathan. Stop your yawping, you Paddies, and let a fellow sleep if he can. You're worse than an acre of tom-cats.

Sullivan. To the divil wid ye! It's a pity this isn't all an Oirish company, for the credit of the Captin.

Touhey. Byes, it's mighty cowld slapin' with niver a blanket, nor a wife to one's back.

Sweeney. I wish a man 'ud ask me to lisht for three years more. Wouldn't I knock his head off?

Sullivan. Ye couldn't raich the head av a man, Sweeney. Ye hav'n't got the hoight for it.

Sweeney. I'd throw him down. Thin I'd be tall enough.

" And so they go on till one or two in the morning, when I fall asleep, leaving them still talking."

Even the characteristics of a brute afford matter of comment amid the Sahara-like flatness of ordinary camp life.

" I have nothing more of importance to communicate," he says in one letter, " except that I have been adopted by a tailless dog, who, probably for the lack of other following, persists in laying claim to my fealty. If I leave my tent door open when I go out, I find him under my bunk when I come in. As he has nothing to wag, he is put to it to express his approval of my ways and character. When I speak to him he lies down on his back with a meekness of expression which I am sure has not been rivalled since Moses. He is the most abnormally bobbed dog that ever excited my amazement. I think I do not exaggerate when I declare that his tail appears to have been amputated in the small of his back. How he can draw his breath is a wonder. In fact, he seems to have lost his voice by the operation, as though the docking had injured his bronchial tubes, for he never barks, nor growls, nor whines. I often lose myself in speculation over his absent appendage, questioning whether it was shot away in battle, or left behind in a rapid march, or bitten off, or pulled out. Perhaps it is on detached service as a waggin-

master, or has got a promotion and become a brevet lion's
tail.   Perhaps it has gone to the dog heaven, and is wag-
ging somewhere in glory.   Venturing again on a pun I
observed that it is very proper that an army dog should
be detailed.   I wish I could find his master;—I have just
one observation to make to that gentleman;—I would say
to him, 'There is your dog.—I don't want the beast, and I
don't see why he wants me; but I can't get rid of him,
any more than I can of Henry, who is equally useless.'   I
sometimes try to estimate the infinitessimal loss which the
world would experience if the two should disappear together, but always give up the problem in despair, not
having any knowledge of fractions small enough to figure
it."

"In a general way," says Colburne, "we are sadly off for
amusements.   Fowling is not allowed because the noise of
the guns alarms the pickets.   Even alligators I have only
shot at once, when I garrisoned a little post four miles
from camp, and, being left without rations, was obliged to
subsist my company for a day on boiled Saurian.   The
meat was eatable, but not recommendable to persons of
delicate appetite, being of an ancient and musky flavor,
as though it had been put up in its horny case a thousand
years ago.   By the way, a minie ball knocks a hole in these
fellows' celebrated jackets without the slightest difficulty.
As for riding after hounds or on steeple chases, or boxing,
or making up running or rowing matches, after the gymnastic fashion of English officers, we never think of it.
Now and then there is a horse-race, but for the most part
we play euchre.   Drill is no longer an amusement as at
first, but an inexpressibly wearisome monotony.   Conversation is profitless and dull, except when it is professional
or larkish.   With the citizens we have no dealings at all,
and I have not spoken to a lady since I left New Orleans.
Books are few because we cannot carry them about, being
limited in our baggage to a carpet-sack; and moreover
I have lost my taste for reading, and even for all kinds of

thinking except on military matters. My brother officers, you know, are brave, sensible and useful men, but would not answer to fill the professorial chairs of Winslow University. They represent the plain people whose cause is being fought out in this war against an aristocracy. When I first went into camp with the regiment they humorously recognized my very slight fashionable elevation by styling my company, which then numbered eighteen men, 'The Upper Ten Thousand.' Now all such distinctions are rubbed out; it is, who can fight best, march best, com mand best; each one stands on the base of his individual manhood. In the army a man cannot remain long on a social pedestal which will enable him to overlook the top of his own head. He can obtain no respect which is not accorded to rank or merit; and very little merit is acknowledged except what is of a professional character."

With true *esprit du corps* he frequently expatiates on the excellencies of his regiment.

" The discipline in the Tenth is good," he declares, " and consequently there are no mutinies, no desertions and not much growling. Ask the soldiers if they are satisfied with the service, and they might answer, 'No;' but you cannot always judge of a man by what he says, even in his impulsive moments; you must also consider what he does. Look at an old man-of-war's man : he growls on the forecastle, but is as meek as Moses on the quarter-deck; and, notwithstanding all his mutterings, he is always at his post and does his duty with a will. Just so our soldiers frequently say that they only want to get out of the service, but never run away and rarely manœuvre for a discharge."

This, it will be observed, was before the days of substitutes and bounty-jumpers, and while the regiments were still composed of the noble fellows who enlisted during the first and second years of the war.

From all that I can learn of Captain Colburne I judge that he was a model officer, at least so far as a volunteer

Q2

knew how to be one.   While his men feared him on account of his reserve and his severe discipline, they loved him for the gallantry and cheerful fortitude with which he shared their dangers and hardships.   The same respect which he exacted of them he accorded, at least outwardly, to all superior officers, even including the contemptible Gazaway.   He did this from principle, for the good of the service, believing that authority ought not to be questioned lightly in an army.   By the way, the Major did not like him : he would have preferred to have the Captain jolly and familiar and vulgar ; then he would have felt at ease in his presence.   This gentlemanly bearing, this dignified respect, kept him, the superior, at a distance.   The truth is that, although Gazaway was, in the emphatic language of Lieutenant Van Zandt, " an inferior cuss," he nevertheless had intelligence enough to suspect the profound contempt which lay behind Colburne's salute.   Only in the Captain's letters to his intimate friend, Ravenel, does he speak unbecomingly of the Major.

" He is," says one of these epistles, " a low-bred, conceited, unreasonable, domineering ass, who by instinct detests a gentleman and a man of education.   He will issue an order contrary to the Regulations, and fly into a rage if a captain represents its illegality.   I have got his illwill in this way, I presume, as well perhaps as by knowing how to spell correctly.   His orders, circulars, etc., are perfect curiosities of literature until they are corrected by his clerk, who is a private soldier.   Sometimes I am almost tired of obeying and respecting my inferiors ; and I certainly shall not continue to serve a day after the war is over."

However, these matters are now by-gones, Gazaway being out of the regiment.   I mention them chiefly to show the manliness of character which this intelligent and educated young officer exhibited in remaining in the service notwithstanding moral annoyances more painful to bear than marches and battles.   He is still enthusiastic ; has not by any means had fighting enough; wants to go to Virginia in order to be in the thickest of it. He is disappointed at not receiving promotion; but bears it bravely and uncomplainingly, for the sake of the nation; bears it as he does sickness, starvation, blistered feet and wounds.

CHAPTER XXVII.

COLONEL CARTER MAKES AN ASTRONOMICAL EXPEDITION WITH A DANGEROUS FELLOW TRAVELLER.

A PROSPECT of flat peace and boundless prosperity is tiresome to the human eye. Although it is morally agreeable to think about the domestic happiness and innocence of the Carters, as sketched in a late chapter, there is danger that the subject might easily prove tiresome to the reader, and moreover it is difficult to write upon it. I announce therefore with intellectual satisfaction that our Colonel is summoned to the trial of bidding good-bye to his wife, and undertaking a journey to Washington.

It was his own work and for his own interests. He felt the necessity of adding to his income, and desired the honor and claimed the justice of promotion. High Authority in the department admitted that the star of a brigadier was not too high a reward for this brave man, thoroughly instructed officer, model colonel. High Authority was tired of gerrymandering seniorities so as to give a superb brigade of three thousand men to the West Point veteran, Carter, and a skeleton division of nine hundred men to the ex-major-general of militia, ex-mayor of Pompoosuc, Brigadier-General John Snooks. Accordingly when the Colonel applied for a month's leave of absence, with the understood purpose of sueing for an acknowledgment of his services, High Authority made him bearer of dispatches to Washington, so that, being on duty, he might pay his travelling expenses out of the Government pocket. The same mail which brought him his order informed him that a steamer would sail for the north on the next day but one. Acting with the rapidity which always marked his movements when he had once decided on his course, he took the next morning's train for New Orleans, first pressing his wife for many times to his breast and kissing away such of her tears as he could stay to witness. To good angels, and other people capable of appreciating such things, it would have been a pretty though pathetic spectacle to see this slender, blonde-haired girl clinging to the strong, bronzed, richly colored man with the burning black eyes.

"Oh, what shall I do without you?" she moaned. "What shall I do with myself?"

"My dear little child," he said, "you will do just what you like. If you choose to stay here and keep house, Captain Colburne will see that you are cared for. Perhaps it may be best, however, to join your father. Here are two hundred dollars, all the money that I have except what is necessary to take me to New Orleans. I shall get a month's pay there. Don't settle any bills. Tell people that I will attend to them when I come back.—There. Don't keep me, my dear one. Don't make me lose the train."

So he went, driving to the railroad in an ambulance, while Lillie looked after him with tearful eyes, and waved her handkerchief and kissed her hand till he was out of sight. At first she decided that she would remain at Thibodeaux and think of her husband in every room of the house, and every walk of the garden; but after two days she found herself so miserably lonesome that she shut up the cottage, went to New Orleans and threw herself upon her father for consolation. Having told so much in anticipation we will go back to the Colonel. The two hundred dollars which he left with his wife had been borrowed from the willing Colburne. Carter had no pay due him as he had hinted, but he hoped to obtain a month's ad-

vance from a paymaster, or, failing in that, to borrow from
some one, say the commanding general. In fact, one hundred and fifty dollars, abstracted from Government funds.
I fear, were furnished him by a neglected quartermaster,
who likewise wanted promotion and was willing to run
this risk for the sake of securing the benign influences of
Carter's future star. With this friend in need the Colonel
took the first glass of plain whiskey which he had swallowed
in three months. To this followed other glasses, proffered
by other friends, whose importunity he could not now resist, although yesterday he had repulsed them with ease.
Every brother colonel, every appreciating brigadier,
seemed possessed of Satan to lead him to a bar or to his
own quarters and there to toast his health, or his luck, or
his star. It was "Here's how!" and "Here's towards
you!" from ten o'clock in the morning when he got his
money, until four in the afternoon when he sprang on
board the Creole just as she loosed her moorings from the
shaky posts of the tattered wooden wharf. Being in that
state of exhilaration which enabled Tam O'Shanter to gaze
on the witches of Alloway kirk-yard without flinching, the
Colonel was neither astonished nor alarmed at encountering on the quarter-deck the calm, beautiful, dangerous eyes
of Madame Larue. The day before he would have been almost willing to lose the steamer rather than travel with her.
Now, in the fearlessness of plain whiskey, he shook both her
hands with impetuous warmth and said, " 'Pon honor, Mrs.
Larue, perfectly delighted to see you."

"And so am I delighted," she answered with a flash of
unfeigned pleasure in her eyes, which might have alarmed
the Carter of yesterday but which gratified the Carter of
to-day.

"Now I shall have a cavalier," she continued, allowing
him to pull her down on a seat by his side. " Now I shall
have a protector and adviser. I have had such need of
one. Did you know that I was going on this boat ? I am
so flattered if you meant to accompany me ! I am going

north to invest my little property. I still fear that it is
not safe here. No one knows what may happen here. As
soon as I could sell for a convenable sum, I resolved to
go north. I shall expect you to be my counsellor how to
invest."

Carter laughed boisterously.

"My dear, I never invested a picayune in my life," he
said.

She noticed the term of endearment and the fact of
semi-intoxication, but she was not vexed nor alarmed by
either. She was tolerably well accustomed to drunken
gentlemen, and she was not easily hurt by love-making,
no matter how vigorous.

"You have always invested in the Bank of Love," she
remarked with one of those amatory glances which black
eyes, it seems to me, can make more effective than blue
ones.

"And in monte and faro, and bluff and euchre," he
added, laughing loudly again. "In wine bills, and hotel
bills, and tailors' bills, and all sorts of negatives."

The debts which weighed somewhat heavily yesterday
were mere comicalities and piquancies of life to-day.

"Oh! you are a terrible personage. I fear you are not
the protector I ought to choose."

He made no reply, feeling vaguely that the conversation was growing dangerous, and sending back a thought
to his wife like a cry for help. Mrs. Larue divined his
alarm and changed the subject.

"What makes you voyage north?" she asked with a
knowing smile. "Are you in search of a new planet?"

Through his plain whiskey the Colonel could not see her
joke on the star which he was seeking, but he was still
clever enough to shun the confession that he was on an expedition in search of promotion.

"I am bearer of dispatches," he said. "Nothing to do
now in Louisiana. I shall be back before any more fighting comes off."

"Shall you? I am enchanted of it. I shall return soon, and hope to make the voyage with you. I am not going to forsake New Orleans. I love the city well enough—and more, I cannot sell my house. Remember, you must let me know when you return, and arrange yourself to come on my steamer."

Next morning, in possession of his sober senses, Carter endeavored to detach himself a little from Mrs. Larue, impelled to this seeming lack of chivalry by remembrance of his wife, and mistrust of his own power of self-government. But this prudent course soon appeared to be impossible for a variety of reasons. In the first place it happened, whether by chance or through her forethought he did not know, that their state-rooms opened on the same narrow passage. In the second place, he was the only acquaintance that Mrs. Larue had on board, and there was not another lady to take her up, the Creole being a Government transport, and civilian travel being in those times rare between New York and New Orleans. Moreover, the other passengers were in his estimation low, or at least plain people, such as sutlers, speculators, and rough volunteer officers—so that, if he left her, she was alone, and could not even venture on deck for a breath of fresh air. At any rate, that was the way that she chose to put it, although there was not the least danger that she would be insulted, and although, had Carter been absent, she would not have failed to strike up a flirtation with some other representative of my noble sex. Finally, he was obliged to consider that she was a relative of his wife. Thus before the second day was over, he found himself under bonds of courtesy to be the constant attendant of Mrs. Larue. They sat together next the head of the table, the lady being protected from the ignoble crowd of volunteers by the Colonel on one side, and the captain of the Creole on the other. Opposite them were a major and a chaplain, highly respectable persons so far as one could judge from their conversation, but who never got a word, rarely a look, from Mrs. Larue or Carter. The captain talked, first with one party, then with the other, but never with both at once. He was a polite and considerate man, accustomed to his delicate official position as a host, and he saw that he would not be thanked for making the conversation general. Except to him, to Carter, and to the servants, Mrs. Larue did not speak one word during the first seven days of the passage. All the volunteer officers admired her nun-like demeanor. Kept afar off, and with no other woman in sight, they began to worship her, much as the brigade at Thibodeaux adored that solitary planet of loveliness, Mrs. Carter. The fact that she was a widow, which crept out in some inexplicable manner, only heightened the enthusiasm.

"By Heavens!" declared one flustered Captain, "if I only had Colonel before my name, and a hundred thousand dollars after it, I would rush to her and say, 'Madame, are you inconsolable? *Could* I persuade you to forget the dear departed?'"

While these gentlemen worshipped her, Carter hoped she would get sea-sick. This great, brawny, boisterous, domineering, heroic fighter had just enough moral vitality to know when he was in danger of falling, and to wish for safety. Those were perilous hours at evening, when the ship swept steadily through a lulling whisper of waters, when a trail of foamy phosphorescense, like a transitory Milky Way, followed in pursuit, when a broad bar of rippling light ran straight out to the setting moon, when the decks were deserted except by slumberers, and Mrs. Larue persisted in dallying. The temptation of darkness, the temptation of solitude, the fever which begins to turn sleepless brains at midnight, made this her possible hour of coquettish conquest. She varied from delicately phrased sentimentalities to hoydenish physical impertinences. He was not permitted for five minutes together to forget that she was a bodily, as well as a spiritual presence. He was not checked in any transitory license of speech or gesture.

Meantime she quoted fine rhapsodies from Balzac, and repeated telling situations from Dumas le Jeune, and commented on both in the interest of the *sainte passion de l'amour*. Once, after a few moments of silence and revery, she said with an air of earnest feeling, " Is it not a horrible fate for a woman—solitude ? Do you not pity me ? Thirty years old, a widow, and childless ! No one to love ; no right to love any one."

She changed into French now, as she frequently did when she was animated and wished to express herself freely. Such talk as this sounds unnatural in the language of the Anglo-Saxon, but is not so unbecoming to the tongue of the Gauls.

" A woman to whom the affections are forbidden, is deprived of the use of more than half her being. Whatever her possibilities, she is denied all expansion beyond a certain limit. She may not explore, much less use, her own heart. It contains chambers of joy which she can only guess of, and into which she must not enter. There is a nursery of affections there, but she can only stand with her ear to the door, trying to hear the sweet prattle within. There is an innermost chapel, with an altar all set for the communion of love, but no priest to invite her to the holy banquet. She is capable of a mother's everlasting devotion, but she scarcely dares suspect it. She is fitted to enter upon the tender mysteries of wifehood, and yet she is constantly fearing that she shall never meet a man whom she can love. That is the old maid, horrible name ! The widow is less ashamed, but she is more unhappy. She has been taught her possibilities, and then suddenly forbidden the use of them."

Had the Colonel been acquainted with Michelet and his fellow rhapsodists on women, he might have suspected Madame of a certain amount of plagiarism. But he only thought her amazingly clever, at the same time that he was unable to answer her in her own style.

" Why don't you marry ?" he asked, striking with Anglo-Saxon practicality at the root of the matter.

" Satirical question !" responded Madame, putting her face close to his, doubtless in order to make her smile visible by moonlight.   " It is not so easy to marry in these frightful times. Besides,—shall I avow it ?—what if I cannot marry the man of my choice ?"

" That's bad."

" What if he *would* marry some one else ?—Is it not a humilating confession ?—Do you know what is left to a woman then ?   Either hidden love, or spiritual self-murder.   Which is the greater of the two crimes ?   *Is* the former a crime ?   Society says so.   But are there not exceptions to all rules, even moral ones ?   Love always has this great defence—that nature prompts it, commands it.   As for self-repression, asphyxia of the heart, Nature never prompts that."

The logical conclusion of all this sentimental sophistry was clear enough to Carter's intellect, although it did not deceive his Anglo-Saxon conscience. He understood, briefly and in a matter of fact way that Madame was quite willing to be his wife's rival. He was not yet prepared to accept the offer ; he only feared and anticipated that he should be brought to accept it.

Mrs. Larue was a curious study.   Her vices and virtues (for she had both) were all instinctive, without a taint of education or effort. She did just what she liked to do, unchecked by conscience or by anything but prudence. She was as corrupt as possible without self-reproach, and as amiable as possible without self-restraint. Her serenity was at all times as unrippled as was that of Lillie in her happiest conditions. Her temper was so sunny, her smile so ready, and her manner so flattering, that few persons of the male sex could resist liking her. But she was the detestation of most of her lady acquaintance—who were venomously jealous of her attractions—or rather seductions—and abhorred her for the unscrupulous manner in which she put them to use, abusing her in a way which was enough to make a man rally to her rescue. She really cared little for that *divin sens du genesiaque* concerning which she prattled so freely to her intimates; and therefore she was cool and sure in her coquetries, at the same time that vanity gave her motive force which some naughty flirts derive from passion. She took a pride in making conquests of men, at no matter what personal sacrifice.

Carter saw where he was drifting to, and groaned over it in spirit, and made resolutions which he broke in half an hour, and rowed desperately against the tide, and then drifted again.

"A woman in the same house has so many devilish chances at a fellow," he repeated to himself with a bitter laugh; and indeed he coarsely said as much to Mrs. Larue, with a desperate hope of angering and alienating her. She put on a meekly aggrieved air, drew away from him, and answered, "That is unmanly in you. I did not think you could be so dishonorable."

He was deeply humiliated, begged her pardon, swore that he was merely jesting, and troubled himself much to obtain forgiveness. During the whole of that day she was distant, dignified and silently reproachful. Yet all the while she was not a bit angry with him; she was as malicious as Mephistopheles, but she was also as even-tempered; moreover she was flattered and elated by the evident desperation which drove him to the impertinence. In his efforts to obtain a reconciliation Carter succeeded so thoroughly that the scene took place late at night, his arm around her waist and his lips touching her cheek. You must remember—charitably or indignantly, as you please—that she was his wife's relative. From this time forward he pretty much stopped his futile rowing against the tide. He let Mrs. Larue take the helm and guide him down the current of his own emotions, singing meawhile her syren lyrics about *la sainte passion*, etc. etc. There were hours, indeed, when he grated over reefs of remorse.

At the thought of his innocent, loving, trusting wife he
shut his eyes as if to keep out the gaze of a reproachful
spectre, clenched his hands as if trying to grasp some rope
of escape, and cursed himself for a fool and a villain.   But
it was a penitence without fruit, a self-reproach without
self-control.

Mrs. Larue treated him now with a familiar and confid-
ing fondness which he sometimes liked and sometimes not,
according as the present or the past had the strongest hold
on his feelings.

" I am afraid that you do not always realize that we are
one for life," she said in one of her earnest, French speaking moods. " You are my sworn friend forever. You
must never hate me ; you cannot. You must never change
towards me ; it would be a perjury of the heart. But I
do not doubt you, my dear friend. I have all confidence
in you. Oh, I am so happy in feeling that we are united
in such an indissoluble concord of sympathy."

Carter could only reply by taking her hand and pressing it in silence. He was absolutely ashamed of himself
that he was able to feel so little and to say nothing.

" I never shall desire a husband," she proceeded. " I can
now use all my heart. What does a woman need more ? How
strangely Heaven has made us ! A woman is only happy
when she is the slave, body and soul, of some man. She
is happy, just in proportion to her obedience and self-
sacrifice. Then only she is aware of her full nature. She
is relieved from prison and permitted the joy of expansion.
It is a seeming paradox, but it is solemnly true."

Carter made no answer, not even by a look. He was
thinking that his wife never philosophised concerning her
love, never analyzed her sentiments, and a shock of self-
reproach, as startling as the throb of a heart-complaint,
struck him as he called to mind her purity, trust and affection. It is curious, by the way, that he suffered no remorse on account of Mrs. Larue. In his opinion she fared
no worse than she deserved, and in fact fared precisely as

she desired, only he had not the nerve to tell her so.
When, late one night, on the darkened and deserted
quarter-deck, she cried on his shoulder and whispered, " I
am afraid you don't love me—I have a right to claim
your love," he felt no affection, no gratitude, not even any
profound pity. It annoyed him that she should weep, and
thus as it were reproach him, and thus trouble still further
his wretched happiness. He was not hypocrite enough to
say, " I *do* love you;" he could only kiss her repeatedly,
penitently and in silence. He still had a remnant of a conscience, and a mangled, sore sense of honor. Nor should
it be understood that Mrs. Larue's tears were entirely hypocritical, although they arose from emotions which were
so trivial as to be somewhat difficult to handle, and so
mixed that I scarcely know how to assort them. In the
first place she was not very well that evening, and was
oppressed by the despondency which all human beings, especially women, suffer from when vitality throbs less vigorously than usual. Moreover a little emotion of this sort
was desirable, firstly to complete the conquest of Carter by
reminding him how much she had sacrificed for him, and
secondly to rehabilitate herself in her own esteem by proving that she possessed a species of conscience. No woman likes to believe herself hopelessly corrupt: when
she reaches that point she is subject to moral spasms which
make existance seem a horror; and we perhaps find her
floating in the river, or asphyxiated with charcoal. Therefore let no one be surprised at the temporary tenderness,
similar to compunction, which overcame Mrs. Larue.

Now that these two had that conscience which makes
cowards of us all, they dropped a portion of the reserve
with which they had hitherto kept their fellow-passen-
gers at a distance. The captain was encouraged to introduce his two neighbors, the major and chaplain; and
Mrs. Larue cast a few telling glances at the former and
discussed theological subjects with the latter. To one
who knew her, and was not shocked by her masquerades,

nothing could be more diverting than the nun-like airs
which she put on *pour achalander le prêtre.* Carter and
she laughed heartily over them in their evening asides.
She would have made a capital actress in the natural comedy school known on the boards of the Gymnase and at
Wallack's, for it was an easy amusement to her to play a
variety of social characters. She had no strong emotions
nor profound principles of action, it is true, but she was
sympathetic enough to divine them, and clever enough to
imitate their expression. Her manner to the chaplain was
so religiously respectful as to pull all the strings of his
unconscious vanity, personal and professional, so that he
fell an easy prey to her humbugging, declared that he considered her state of mind deeply interesting, prayed for
her in secret, and hoped to convert her from the errors of
papacy. Indeed her profession of faith was promising if
not finally satisfactory.

"I believe in the holy catholic church," she said. "But
I am not *dogmatique.* I think that others also may have
the truth. Our faith, yours and mine, is at bottom one,
indivisible, uncontradictory. It is only our human weakness which leads us to dispute with each other. We dispute, not as to the faith, but as to who holds it. This is
uncharitable. It is like quarrelsome children."

The chaplain was charmed to agree with her. He thought
her the most hopefully religious catholic that he had ever
met ; he also thought her the wittiest, the most graceful,
and on the whole the handsomest. Her eyes alone were
enough to deceive him : they were inexhaustible green-
rooms of sparkling masks and disguises ; and he was
especially taken with the Madonnesque gaze which issued
from their recesses. He was bamboozled also by the prim,
broad, white collar, like a surplice, which she put on ex-
pressly to attract him ; by the demure air of childlike piety
which clothed her like a mantle ; by her deference to his
opinion ; by her teachable spirit. Perhaps he may also
have been pleased with her plump shoulders and round

arms, and he certainly did glance at them occasionally as
their outlines showed through the transparent muslin; but
he said nothing of them in his talks concerning Mrs. Larue
with his room-mate the Major.

" *J'ai apprivoisé le prêtre*," she observed laughingly to
Carter. " I have assured myself a firm friend in his reverence. He will defend me the character always. He has
asked me to visit his family, and promised to call to see
me at New York. Madame La Prêtresse is to call also.
He is quite capable of praying me to stand godmother to
his next child. If he were not married, I should have an
offer. I believe I could bring him to elope with me in a
fortnight."

" Why don't you?" asked Carter. " It would make a
scandal that would amuse you," he added somewhat bitterly, for he was at times disgusted by her heartlessness.

" No, my dear," she replied gently, pressing his arm.
" I am quite satisfied with my one conquest. It is all I
desire in the world."

They were leaning against the taffrail, listening to the
gurgling of the waters in the luminous wake and watching
the black lines of the masts waving against the starlit sky.

" You are silent," she observed. " Why are you so sad?"

" I am thinking of my wife," he replied, almost sullenly.

" Poor Lillie! I wish she were here," said Mrs. Larue.

" My God! what a woman you are!" exclaimed the
Colonel. " Don't you know that I should be ashamed to
look her in the face?"

" My dear, why do you distress yourself so? You can
love her still. I am not exacting. I only want a corner
in your heart. If I might, I would demand the whole;
but I know I could not have it. You ought not to be unhappy; that is my part in the drama. I have sacrificed
much. What have you sacrificed? A man risks nothing,
loses nothing, in these affairs *du cœur*. He has a bonne fortune, *voilà tout*."

Carter was heavy laden in secret with his bonne fortune.

He was glad when the voyage ended, and he could leave Mrs. Larue at New York, with a pleasing chance that he might never meet her again, and a hope that he had heard the last of her *sainte passion de l'amour*. Of course he was obliged, before he quitted her, to see that she was established in a good boarding house, and to introduce her to one or two respectable families among his old acquaintance in the city. Of course also he said nothing to these families about her propensities towards the *divin sens* and the *sainte passion*. She quickly made herself a character as a southern loyalist, and as such became quite a pet in society. Before she had been a week in the city she was an inmate of the household of the Rev. Dr. Whitehead, a noted theologian and leading abolitionist, who worked untiringly at the seemingly easy task of converting her from the errors of slavery and papacy. It somewhat scandalized his graver parishioners, especially those of Copperhead tendencies, that he should patronize so gay a lady. But the Reverend Doctor did not see her pranks, and did not believe the tale when others related them. How could he when she looked the picture of a saint, dressed entirely in black and white, wore her hair plain *a la Madonne*, and talked theology with those earnest eyes, and that childlike smile? To the last he honestly regarded her as very nigh unto the kingdom of heaven. It was to shield her from envious slanders, to cover her with the ægis of his great and venerable name, that the warmhearted, unsuspicious old gentleman dedicated to her his little work on moral reform, entitled " St. Mary Magdalen." How ecstatically Mrs. Larue laughed over this book when she got to her own room with it, after the presentation ! She had not had such a paroxysm of merriment before, since she was a child ; for during all her adult life she had been too *blasee* to laugh often with profound heartiness and honesty : her gayety had been superficial, like most of her other expressions of feeling. I can imagine that she looked very attractive in her spasm of jollity, with her black eyes sparkling, her brunette cheeks flushed, her jetty streams of hair waving and her darkly roseate arms and shoulders bare in the process of undressing. Before she went to bed she put the book in an envelope addressed to Carter, and wrote a playful letter to accompany it, signed "Your best and most loving friend, St. Marie Madeleine."

CHAPTER XXVIII.

THE COLONEL CONTINUES TO BE LED INTO TEMPTATION.

ON the cars between New York and Washington Carter encountered the Governor of Barataria. After the customary compliments had been exchanged, after the Governor had acknowledged the services of the famous Tenth, and the Colonel had eulogized the good old State, the latter spoke of the vacant lieutenant-colonelcy in the regiment, and asked that it might be given to Colburne.

"But I have promised that to Mr. Gazaway," said the Governor, looking slightly troubled.

"To Gazaway!" roared Carter in wrathful astonishment. "What! to the same Gazaway? Why—Governor—are you aware—are you perfectly aware why he left the regiment?"

The Governor's countenance became still more troubled, but did not lose its habitual expression of mild obstinacy.

"I know—I know," he said softly. "It is a very miserable affair."

"Miserable! It is to the last degree scandalous. I never heard of anything so utterly contemptible as this fellow's behavior. You certainly cannot know—— If you did, you wouldn't think of letting this infernal poltroon back into the regiment. He ought to have been court-martialed. It is a cursed shame that he was not shot for misbehavior in presence of the enemy. Let me tell you his story."

R

The Governor had an air which seemed to say that it would be of no use to tell him anything; but he folded his hands, bowed his head, crossed his legs, put a pastille in his mouth, and meekly composed himself to listen.

"This Gazaway is the greatest coward that I ever saw," pursued the Colonel. "I positively think he must be the greatest coward that ever lived. At Georgia Landing he left his horse, and dodged, and ducked, and squatted behind the line in such a contemptible way that I came near rapping him over the head with the flat of my sabre. At Camp Beasland he shammed sick, and skulked about the hospitals, whimpering for medicine. I sent in charges against him then; but they got lost, I believe, on the march; at any rate, they never turned up. At Port Hudson I released him from arrest, and ordered him into the fight, hoping he would get shot. I privately told the surgeon not to excuse him, and I told the blackguard himself that he must face the music. But he ran away the moment the brigade came under fire. He was picked up at the hospital by the provost-guard, and sent to the regiment in its advanced position. The officers refused to obey his orders unless he proved his courage first by taking a rifle and fighting in the trenches. They equipped him, but he wouldn't fight. He trembled from head to foot, said he didn't know how to load his gun, said he was sick, cried. Then they kicked him out of camp—actually and literally booted him out—put the leather to him, sir. That is the last time that he was seen with the regiment. He was next picked up in the hospitals of New Orleans, and sent to the front by Emory, who would have shot him if he had known what he was. He was in command of Fort Winthrop, and wanted to surrender at the first summons. Nothing but the high spirit of his officers, and the gallantry of the whole garrison, saved the fort from its own commander. I tell you, sir, that he is a redemptionless sneak. He is a disgrace to the regiment, and to the State, and to the country. He is a disgrace to every man in both services—to evey man who calls himself an American. And you propose to restoré him to the regiment!"

The Governor sighed, and looked very sad, but at the same time as meékly determined as Moses.

"My dear Colonel, I knew it all," he said. "But I think I am right. I think I am acting out our American principle—the greatest good of the greatest number. I must beg your patient hearing and your secrecy. In the first place, Gazaway is not to keep the commission. It is merely given to whitewash him. He will accept it, and then resign it. That is all understood."

"But what the —— do you want to whitewash him for? He ought to be gibbeted."

"I know. Very true. But see here. We *must* carry the elections. We *must* have the government supported by the people. We *must* give the administration a clear majority in both houses of Congress. Otherwise, you see, Copperheadism and Secession, false peace and rebellion will triumph."

But the way to carry the elections is to whip the rebels, my God!—to have the best officers and the best army, and win all the victories, my God!"

The Governor smiled as if from habit, but pursued his own course of reasoning resolutely, without noticing the new argument. His spunk was rising a little, and he had no small amount of domination in him, notwithstanding his amiability.

"Now Gazaway's Congressional district is a close one," he continued, "and we fear that his assistance is necessary to enable us to carry it. I grieve to think that it is so. It is not our fault. It is the fault of those men who will vote a disloyal ticket. Well, he demands that we shall whitewash him by giving him a step up from his old commission. On that condition he agrees to insure us the district. Then he is to resign."

"My God! what a disgraceful muddle!" was Carter's indignant comment.

The Governor looked almost provoked at seeing that the Colonel would not appreciate his difficulties and necessities.

"I sacrifice my own feelings in this matter," he insisted. "I assure you that it is a most painful step for me to take."

He forgot that he was also sacrificing the feelings of Captain Colburne and of other deserving officers in the gallant Tenth.

I wouldn't take the step," returned the Colonel. "I'd let the election go to hell before I'd take it. If that is the way elections are carried, let us have done with them, and pray for a depotism."

After this speech there was a silence of some minutes. Each of these men was a wonder to the other; each of them ought to have been a wonder to himself. The Governor knew that Carter was a roué, a hard drinker, something of a Dugald Dalgetty; and he could not understand his professional chivalry, his passion for the honor of the service, his bitter hatred of cowards. The Colonel knew the Governor's upright moral character as an individual, and was amazed that such a man could condescend to what he considered dirty trickery. In one respect, Carter had the highest moral standpoints. He did wrong to please himself, but it was under the pressure of overwhelming impulse, and he paid for it in frank remorse. The other did wrong after calm deliberation, sadly regretting the alleged necessity, but chloroforming his conscience with the plea of that necessity. He was at bottom a well-intentioned and honorable man, but blinded by long confinement in the dark labyrinths of political intrigue, as the fishes of the Mammoth Cave are eyeless through the lack of light. He would have shrunk with horror from Carter had he known of that affair with Madame Larue. At the same time he could commission a known coward above the heads of heroes, to carry a Congressional district. And, in order that we may not be too hard upon him, let us consider his difficulties; let us suppose that he had elevated the Bayard and thrown the Bardolph overboard. In the first place all the wire-pullers of his following would have been down upon him with arguments and appeals, begging him in the name of the party, of the country, of liberty, not to lose the election. His own candidate in the doubtful district, an old and intimate friend, would have said, " You have ruined my chances." All the capitalists and manufacturers who depended on this candidate to get this or that axe sharpened on the Congressional grindstone, would have added their outcries to the lamentation. Thinking of all this, and thinking too of the Copperheads, and what they would be sure to do if they triumphed, he felt that what he had decided on was for the best, and that he must do it. Gazaway must have the lieutenant-colonelcy until the spring election was over ; and then, and not before, he must make way for some honorable man and brave officer.

" But how can this fellow have such a political influence ?" queried the Colonel. " It ought to be easy enough to expose him in the newspapers, and smash him."

" The two hundred men or so who vote as he says never read the newspapers, and wouldn't believe the exposure."

" There is the majority left," observed Carter, after another pause. " Captain Colburne might have that—if he would take promotion under Gazaway."

" I have given that to my nephew, Captain Rathbun," said the Governor, blushing.

He was not ashamed of his political log-rolling with a vulgar coward, but he was a little discomposed at confessing his very pardonable and perhaps justifiable nepotism.

" Captain Rathbun," he pursued hastily, " has been strongly recommended by all the superior officers of his corps. There is no chance of promotion in the cavalry, as our State has only furnished three companies. I have therefore transferred him to the infantry, and I placed him in your regiment because there were two vacancies."

" Then my recommendation goes for nothing," said Carter, in gloomy discontent.

"Really, Colonel, I must have some authority in these matters. I am called commander-in-chief of the forces of the State. I am sorry if it annoys you. But there will be—I assure you there will soon be—a vacancy for Captain Colburne."

"But he will have to come in under your nephew, I suppose."

"I suppose so. I don't see how it can be otherwise. But it will be no disgrace to him, I assure you. He will find Major Rathbun an admirable officer and a comrade perfectly to his taste. He graduated from the University only a year after Captain Colburne."

"Excuse me if I leave you for half an hour," observed Carter, without attempting to conceal his disgust. "I want to step into the smoking-car and take a segar."

"Certainly," bowed the Governor, and resumed his newspaper. He was used to such unpleasant interviews as this; and after drawing a tired sigh over it, he was all tranquillity again. The Colonel was too profoundly infuriated to return to his companion during the rest of the journey, much as he wanted his influence to back up his own application for promotion.

"Horrible shame, by Jove!" he muttered, while chewing rather than smoking his segar. "I wish the whole thing was in the hands of the War Department. Damn the States and their rights! I wish, by (this and that) that we were centralized."

Thus illogically ruminated the West Pointer; not seeing that the good is not bad merely because it may be abused; not seeing that Centralism is sure to be more corrupt than Federalism. The reader knows that such cases as that of Gazaway were not common. They existed, but they were exceptional; they were sporadic, and not symptomatic. In general the military nominations of the Governor did honor to his heart and his head. It was Colburne's accidental misfortune that his State contained one or two doubtful districts, and that one of them was in the

hands, or was supposed to be in the hands, of his contemptible superior officer.   In almost any other Baratarian regiment the intelligent, educated, brave and honorable young
captain would have been sure of promotion.

Carter was troubled with a foreboding that his own
claims would meet with as little recognition as those of
Colburne.   He took plain whiskeys at nearly every stop-
ping-place, and reached Washington more than half drunk,
but still in low spirits.   Sobered and rested by a night's
sleep, he delivered his dispatches, was bowed out by General Halleck, and then sought out a resident Congressional
friend, and held a frank colloquy with him concerning the
attainment of the desired star.

" You see, Colonel, that you are a marked man," said
the M. C.   " You have been known to say that the war
will last five years."

" Well, it will.   It has lasted nearly three, and it will
kick for two more.   I ought to be promoted, by (this and
that) for my sagacity."

" Just so," laughed the M. C.   " But you won't be.   The
trouble is that you say just what the Copperheads say;
and you get credit for the same motives.   It is urged,
moreover, that men like you discourage the nation and
cheer the rebels."

" By Jove!   I'd like to see the rebel who would be
cheered by the news that the war will last two years
longer."

The honorable member laughed again, in recognition of
the hit, and proceeded :

" Then there is that old filibustering affair.   When you
went into that you were not so good a prophet as you are
now ; and in fact it is a very unfortunate affair at present;
it stands in your way confoundedly.   In fact, you are not
a favorite with our left wing—our radicals.   The President
is all right.   The War Department is all right.   They admit your faithfulness, ability and services.   It is the Senate that knocks you.   I am afraid you will have to wait

for something to turn up. In fact, I don't see my way to a
confirmation yet."

Carter swore, groaned, and chewed his cigar to a pulp.

" But don't be discouraged," pursued the M. C.   " We
have brought over two or three of the radicals to your
side.   Three or four more will do the job.   Then we can
get a nomination with assurance of a confirmation.   I
promise you it shall be attended to at the first chance.   But
you must come out strong against slavery.   Abolition is
your card.   New converts must be zealous, you know."

" By Jove, I *am* strong.   I didn't believe in arming the
negro once ; but I do now.   It was a good movement.
I'll take a black brigade."

" Will you ?"   Then you can have a white one, I guess.
By the way, perhaps you can do something for yourself.
A good many of the Members are in town already.   I'll
take you around—show you to friends and enemies.   In
fact you can do something for yourself."

Carter did something in the way of treating, giving
game-suppers, flattering and talking anti-slavery, smiling
outwardly the while, but within full of bitterness.   It
seemed to him a gross injustice that the destiny of a man
who had fought should be ruled by people who slept in
good beds every night and had never heard a bullet whistle.   He thought that he was demeaning himself by bowing down to members of Congress and State wire-pullers ;
but he was driven to it by his professional rage for promotion, and still more urgently by the necessity of increasing
his income.   When he left Washington after the two
weeks' stay which was permitted to him, his nomination to
a brigadiership was promised, and he had strong hopes of
obtaining the Senatorial confirmation.   At New York he
called on Mrs. Larue.   He had not meant to do it when
he quitted the virtuous capital of the nation, but as he approached her he felt drawn towards her by something
stronger than the engine.   Moreover, he thought to himself that she might do something for his promotion if she

could be induced to go to Washington and try the ponderosity of the United States Senate with that powerful social lever of hers, *la sainte passion*, etc.

"Why didn't you tell me this before?" she exclaimed. "Why were you not frank with me, *mon ami?* I would have gone. I would have worked day and night for you. I would have had such fun! It would have been delicious to humbug those abolitionist Senators. I would have been the ruin of Mr. Sumnaire and Mr. Weelsone. There would have been yet more books dedicated to Sainte Marie Madeleine."

She burst into a laugh at these jolly ideas, and waltzed about the room with a mimicry of love-making in her eyes and gestures.

"But I can not go alone, you perceive; do you not?" she resumed, sitting down by his side and laying one hand caressingly on his shoulder. "I should have no position alone, and there is not the time for me to create one. Moreover, I have paid for my passage to New Orleans in the Mississippi."

"Well, we shall be together," said Carter. "That is my boat. But what a cursed fool I was in not taking you to Washington!"

"Certainly you were, *mon ami*. It is most regrettable. It is *désespérant*."

As far as these two were concerned, the voyage south was much like the latter part of the voyage north, except that Carter suffered less from self-reproach, and was generally in higher spirits. He had not money enough left to pay for his meals and wine, but he did not hesitate to borrow a hundred dollars from the widow, and she lent it with her usual amiability.

"You shall have all I can spare," she said. "I only wish to live and dress *comme il faut*. You are always welcome to what remains."

What could the unfortunate man do but be grateful? Mrs. Larue began to govern him with a mild and insinuat-

ing domination ; and, strange to say, her empire was not
altogether injurious. She corrected him of a number of
the bearish ways which he had insensibly acquired by life
in the army, and which his wife had not dared to call his
attention to, worshipping him too sincerely. She laughed
him out of his swearing, and scolded him out of most of his
drinking. She mended his stockings, trimmed the frayed
ends of his necktie, saw to it that his clothes were brushed ;
in short, she greatly improved his personal appearance,
which had grown somewhat shabby under the influences
of travelling and carousing ; for the Colenel was one of
those innumerable male creatures who always go to seedi-
ness as soon as womankind ceases to care for them. With
him she had no more need of coquetries and sentimental
prattle ; and she treated him very much as a wife of five
years' standing treats her husband. She was amiable,
pains-taking, petting, slightly exacting, slightly critical,
moderately chatty, moderately loving. They led a peaceable, domestic sort of life, without much regard to
secrecy, without much terror at the continual danger of
discovery. They were old sinners enough to feel and behave much like innocent people. Carter's remorse, it must
be observed, had arisen entirely from his affection for his
wife, and his shame at having proved unworthy of her
affectionate confidence, and not at all from any sense of
doing an injury to Mrs. Larue, nor from a tenderness of
conscience concerning the abstract question of right and
wrong. Consequently, after the first humiliation of his fall
was a little numbed by time, he could be quite comfortable in spirit.

But his uneasiness awakened at the sight of Lillie, and
the pressure of her joyful embrace. The meeting, affectionate as it seemed on both sides, gave him a very miserable
kind of happiness. He did not turn his eyes to Mrs.
Larue, who stood by with a calm, pleased smile. He was
led away in triumph ; he was laid on the best sofa and
worshipped ; he was a king, and a god in the eyes of that

pure wife ; but he was a very unhappy, and shamefaced deity.

"Oh, what charming letters you wrote !" whispered Lillie. "How good you were to write so often, and to write such sweet things ! They were such a comfort to me !"

Carter was a little consoled. He *had* written often and affectionately; he had tried in that way to make amends for a concealed wrong ; and he was heartily glad to find that he had made her happy.

"Oh, my dear child !" he said. "I am so delighted if I have given you any pleasure !"

He spoke this with such a sigh, almost a groan, that she looked at him in wonder and anxiety.

"What is the matter, my darling?" she asked. "What makes you sad ? Have you failed in getting your promotion ? Never mind. I will love you to make up for it. I know, and you know, that you deserve it. We will be just as happy."

"Perhaps I have not altogether failed," he replied, glad to change the subject. "I have some hopes yet of getting good news."

"Oh, that will be so delightful ! Won't it be nice to be prosperous as well as happy ! I shall be so overjoyed on your account ! I shall be too proud to live."

In his lonely meditations Carter frequently tried himself at the bar of his strange conscience, and struggled hard to gain a verdict of not guilty. What could a fellow do, he asked, when a woman would persist in flinging herself at his head ? He honestly thought that most men would have done as he did; that no one but a religious fanatic could have resisted so much temptation ; and that such resistance would have been altogether ungentlemanly. To atone for his wrong he was most tender to his wife; he followed her with attentions, and loaded her with presents. As the same time that he had a guilt upon his soul which might have killed her had she discovered it, he would not

stint her wardrobe, nor forget to kiss her every time he
went out, nor fail to bring her bouquets every evening.
He has been known to leave his bed at midnight and
walk the street for hours, driving away dogs whose howling prevented her from sleeping. Deeds like this were
his penance, his expiation, his consolation.

He was now on duty in the city. High Authority, determined to make amends for the neglect with which this
excellent officer was treated, offered him the best thing
which it had now to give, the chief-quartermastership of
the Department of the Gulf. His pay would thereby be
largely increased in consequence of his legal commutations
for rooms and fuel, besides which there was a chance of
securing large extra-official gleanings from such a broad
field of labor and responsibility. But Carter realized little
out of his position. He could keep his accounts of Government property correctly; but except in his knowledge
of returns, and vouchers, and his clerk-like accuracy, he
was not properly speaking a man of business; that is to
say, he had no faculty for making money. He was too
professionally honorable to lend Government funds to
speculators for the sake of a share of the profits. He would
not descend to the well-known trickery of getting public
property condemned to auction, and then buying it in for
a song to sell it at an advance. In the case of a single
wagon he might do something of the sort in order to rec-
tify his balances in the item of wagons; or he might make
a certificate of theft in a small affair of trousers or havresacks which had been lost through negligence, or issued
without a receipt. But to such straits officers were frequently driven by the responsibility system; he sheltered
himself under the plea of necessity; and did nothing worse.
In fact, his position was a temptation without being
a benefit.

It was a serious temptation. A great deal of money
passed through his hands. He paid out, and received on
account of the Government, thousands of dollars daily;

and the mere handling of such considerable sums made him feel as if he were a great capitalist. Money was an every day, vulgar commodity, and he spent it with profusion. Before he had been in his place two months he was worm-eaten, leaky, sinking with debts. No one hesitated to trust a man who had charge over such an abounding source of wealth as the chief-quartermastership of the Department of the Gulf. He lived sumptuously, drank good wines, smoked the best segars, and marketed for the Ravenel table in his own name, blaspheming the expense whether of cost or credit. Remembering that his wife needed gentle exercise, and had a right to every comfort which he could furnish, he gave her a carriage, and pair of ponies, and of course set up a coachman.

"Can you afford it, my dear?" asked Lillie, a little anxious, for she was aware of his tendency to extravagance.

"I can afford anything, my little one, rather than the loss of you," replied the Colonel after a moment's hesitation.

She wanted to believe that all was well, and therefore the task of convincing her was easy. Her trust was constant, and her adoration fervent; they were symptomatic of her physical condition; they were for the present laws of her nature. It was more than usually painful to her now to be separated long from her deity. When he went out it was, " Where are you going? When will you come back?"—When he returned it was, " How long you have been gone! Oh, I though you would come an hour ago?" It was childish, but she did not perceive it, and if she had, she could not have helped it. She clung to him, and longed after him because she must; there was a bond of unity between them which clasped her inmost life.

Meanwhile how about Mrs. Larue? No one could have been more discreet, more corruptly sagacious, more sunnily amiable, than this singular woman. She petted Lillie like a child, helped her in her abundant sewing labors,

brought her as many bouquets as the Colonel himself,
scolded her for imprudencies, forbade this dish and recommended that, laughed at her occasional despondencies, and
cheered her as women know how to cheer each other. She
seemed like the truest friend of the young woman whom
she would not have hesitated much to rob of her husband,
provided she could have wished to do it. This kindness
was not hypocrisy, but simple, unforced good nature. It
was natural, and therefore, agreeable to her to be amiable ;
and as she always did what she liked to do, she was a
pattern of amiability. To have quarreled seriously with
Lillie would have been a downright annoyance to her, and
consequently she avoided every chance of a disagreement,
so far at least as was consistent with her private pleasures.
She had not the slightest notion of eloping with the Colonel ;
she did not take passions sufficiently *au grand sérieux* for
that ; she would not have isolated herself from society for
any man.

Notwithstanding Mrs. Larue's sugar mask Lillie was at
times disposed to fight her ; not, however, in the slightest
degree on account of her husband ; only on account of her
father. The sly Creole, partly for her own amusement indeed, but chiefly to divert suspicion from her familiarity
with Carter, commenced a coquettish attack upon the
Doctor. Lillie was sometimes in a desperate fright lest
she should entrap him into a marriage. She thought that
she understood Mrs. Larue perfectly, and she felt quite
certain that she was by no means good enough for her
father. In her estimation there never was a man, unless
it might be her husband, who was so good, so noble, so
charming as this parent of hers ; and if she had been called
on to select a wife for him, I doubt whether any woman
could have passed the examination to which she would
have subjected the candidates.

"I perfectly spoil you, papa," she said, laughing. "I
pet you and admire you till I suppose I shall end by ruin-
ing you. If ever you go out into the world alone,

what will become of you? You will miss my care dreadfully. You mustn't leave me; it's for your own good—hear? You mustn't trust yourself to anybody else—hear?"

"I hear, my child," answers the Doctor. "What a charming little Gold Coast accent you have!"

"Pshaw! It isn't negro at all. Everybody talks so. But I wonder if you are trying to change the subject."

"Really I wasn't aware of a subject being presented for my consideration."

"Oh, you don't understand, or you won't understand. I do believe you have a guilty conscience."

"A guilty conscience about what, my child? Have the kindness to speak plainly. My mind is getting feeble."

"Ain't you ashamed to ask me to speak plainly? I don't want to speak plainly. Do you actually want to have me?"

"If it wouldn't overpower your reason, I should like it. It would be such a convenience to me."

"Well, I mean, papa," said Lillie, coloring at her audacity, "that I don't like Mrs. Larue!"

"Don't like Mrs. Larue! Why, she is as kind to you as she can possibly be. I thought you were on the best of terms."

"I mean that I don't like her well enough to call her Mamma."

"Call her Mamma!" repeated the Doctor, staring over his spectacles in amazement. "You don't mean?—upon my honor, you are too nonsensical, Lillie."

"Am I? Oh, I am so delighted!" exclaimed Lillie eagerly. "But I *was* so afraid."

"Do you think I am in my dotage?" inquired the Doctor, almost indignant.

"No no, papa. Don't be vexed with me. I dare say it was very absurd in me. But I do think she is so artful and designing."

"She is a curious woman, we know," observed Ravenel. "She certainly has some—peculiarities."

Lillie laughed outright, and said, "Oh yes," with a gay little air of satire.

"But she is too young to think of me," pursued the Doctor. "She can't be more than twenty-five."

"Papa!!" protested Lillie. "She is thir—ty! Have you lost your memory?"

"Thirty! Is it possible? Really, I am growing old. I am constantly understating other people's ages. I have caught myself at it repeatedly. I don't know whether it is forgetfulness, or inability to realize the flight of time, or an instinctive effort to make myself out a modern by showing that my intimates are youthful. But I am constantly doing it. Do you recollect how I have laughed about Elderkin for this same trick? He is always relating anecdotes of his youth in a way which would lead you to suppose that the events happened some fifteen or twenty years ago. And yet he is seventy. I mustn't laugh at Elderkin any more."

"Nonsense!" said Lillie. "You are not a bit like him. He blacks his hair to correspond with his dates. He means to humbug people. And then you are not old."

"But, to return to Mrs. Larue," observed the Doctor. "She has a clear head; she is pretty sensible. She is not a woman to put herself in a false or ridiculous position. I really have not observed anything of what you hint."

"Oh no. Of course not. Men never do; they are *so* stupid! Of course you wouldn't observe anything until she went on her knees and made you a formal declaration. I was afraid you might say, 'Yes,' in your surprise."

"My dear, don't talk in that way of a lady. You degrade your own sex by such jesting."

However, the Doctor did in a quiet way put himself on his guard against Mrs. Larue; and Lillie, observing this, did also in a quiet way feel quite elated over the condition of things in the family. She was as happy as she had ever been, or could desire to be. It was a shocking state of deception; corruption lilied over with decorum and smiling amiability ; whited sepulchres, apples of Sodom, blooming Upas.   Carter saw Mrs. Larue as often as he wanted, and even much oftener, in a private room, which even his wife did not know of, in rear of his offices.   Closely veiled she slipped in by a back entrance, and reappeared at the end of ten minutes, or an hour, or perhaps two hours.   It was after such interviews had taken place that his wife welcomed him with those touching words. "Oh, where have you been? I thought you never would come."

He would have been glad to break the evil charm, but he was too far gone to be capable of virtuous effort.

CHAPTER XXIX.

LILLIE REACHES THE APOTHEOSIS OF WOMANHOOD.

WOMAN is more intimately and irresponsibly a child of Nature than man.   She comes oftener, more completely, and more evidently under the power of influences which she can neither direct nor resist, and which make use of her without consulting her inclination.   Her part then is passive obedience and uncomplaining suffering, while through her the ends of life are accomplished.   She has no choice but to accept her beneficent martyrdom.   Like Jesus of Nazareth she agonzies that others may live ; but, unlike Him, she is impelled to it by a will higher than her own.   At the same time, a loving spirit is given to her, so that she is consoled in her own anguish, and does not seriously desire that the cup may pass from her before she has drunk it to the dregs.   She has the patience of the lower animals and of inanimate nature, ennobled by a heavenly joy of self-sacrifice, a divine pleasure in suffering for those whom she loves.   She is both lower and higher than man, by instinct rather than by reason, from necessity rather than from choice.

There came a day to Lillie during which she lay between

two worlds, not caring which she entered, submissive to
whatever might be, patient though weeping with pain.
Her father did not dare trust her to his own care, but
called in his old friend and colleague, Doctor Elderkin.
These two, with Carter, Mrs. Larue, and a hired nurse, did
not quit the house for twenty-four hours, and all but the
husband and father were almost constantly in the room of
the invalid. The struggle was so long and severe that
they thought it would end in death. Neither Mrs. Larue
nor the nurse slept during the whole night, but relieved
each other at the bedside, holding by turns the quivering,
clutching hand of Lillie, and fanning the crimson cheeks
and the brow covered with a cold sweat as of a death agony.
The latent womanliness of Mrs. Larue, the tenderness which
did actually exist in some small measure beneath her
smooth surface of amiability and coquetry, was profoundly
stirred by her instinctive sympathy for a suffering which
was all feminine. She remembered that same anguish in
her own life, and lived it over again. Every throe of the
sick girl seemed to penetrate her own body. She thought
of the child which had been given and taken years ago,
and then she wiped away a tear, lest Lillie might see it
and fear for herself. When she was not by the bedside
she stood at the window, now looking for a glimpse of
dawn as if that could bring any hope, and then turning to
gaze at the tossing invalid.

The Doctor only once allowed Carter to enter the room.
The very expansion of Lillie at sight of him, the eagerness
with which her soul reached out to him for help, pity, love,
was perilous. There was danger that she might say, "My
dear, good-bye;" and in the exaltation of such an impulse
she might have departed. As for him, he had never before witnessed a scene like this, and he never forgot it.
His wife held both his hands, clasping them spasmodically,
a broad spot of fever in either cheek, the veins of her forehead swollen, and her neck suffused, her eyes preternatur-
ally open and never removed from his, her whole express-

ion radiant with agony. The mortal pain, the supernatural expectation, the light of that other world which was so near, spiritualized her face, and made it unhumanly beautiful. He seemed to himself to be standing on earth and joining hands with her in heaven. He had never before reached so far; never so communed with another life. His own face was all of this world, stern with anxiety and perhaps remorse; for the moment was so agitating and imperious that he could not direct his emotions nor veil his expression. Happy for her that she had no suspicion of one thing which was in his heart. She believed that he was solely tortured by fear that she would die; and if she could have thought to speak, she would have comforted him. On her own account she did not desire to live; only for his sake, and for her father's, and perhaps a little for her child's. The old Doctor watched her, shook his head, signed to the husband to leave the room, and took his wife's hands in his place. As Carter went out Mrs. Larue followed him a few steps into the passage.

"What is between you and me must end," she whispered.

"Yes," he replied in the same tone, and went to his room somewhat comforted.

At seven in the morning he was awakened by a tremulous knocking at his door. Springing from the sofa, on which he had dozed for an hour or two without undressing, he opened, and encountered Mrs. Larue, pale with sleeplessness but smiling gaily.

"*Venez*," she said, speaking her mother tongue in her haste, and hastened noiselessly, like a swift sprite, back to the sick room. Carter followed, entered with a sense of awe, passed softly around the screen which half encircled the bed, and saw his wife and child lying side by side. Lillie was very pale; her face was still spiritualized by the Gethsemane of the night; but her eyes were still radiant with a purely human happiness. She was in eager haste to have him drink at the newly-opened fountain of joy.

Even as he stooped to kiss her she could not wait, but turned her head towards the infant with a smile of exultation and said, " Look at him."

" But how are *you* ?" he asked, anxiously ; for a man does not at once forget his wife in his offspring ; and Carter had a stain of remorse on his soul which he needed to wash away with rivers of tenderness.

" Oh, I am perfectly well," she answered. " Isn't he pretty ?"

At that moment the child sneezed ; the air of this world was too pungent.

" Oh, take him !" she exclaimed, looking for the nurse. " He is going to die."

The black woman lifted the boy and handed him to the father.

" Don't drop him," said Lillie. " Are you sure you can hold him ? I wouldn't dare to take him."

As if she could have taken him ! In her eagerness she forgot that she was sick, and talked as if she were in her full strength. Her eyes followed the infant so uneasily about the room that Elderkin motioned Carter to replace him on the bed.

" Now he won't fall," she said, cheerfully.—" It was only a sneeze," she added presently, with a little laugh which was like a gurgle, a purr of happiness. " I thought something was the matter with him."—Shortly afterward she asked, " How soon will he talk ?"

" I am afraid not for two or three weeks, unless the weather is favorable," replied Elderkin, with a chuckle which under the circumstances was almost blasphemous.

" How strange that he can't talk !" she replied, without noticing the old gentleman's joke. " He looks so intelligent !"

" She wouldn't be a bit surprised to hear him sing an Italian opera," said Ravenel. " She has seen a miracle to-day. Nothing could astonish her."

Lillie did not laugh nor answer ; nothing interested her

which did not say, Baby! Baby was for the time the whole thought, the whole life, of this girl, who a little previous existed through her husband, and before that through her father. Each passion had been stronger than its predecessor; but now she had reached the culminating point of her womanhood : higher than Baby it was impossible for her to go. Even her father distressed and alarmed her a little by an affection for the newly-arrived divinity which lacked what she felt to be the proper reverence. Not content with worshiping afar off, he picked up the tiny god and carried him to the partial day of a curtained window, desiring, as he said, the honor of being the first to give him an idea.

"The first to give him an idea!" laughed the father. "Why, he looks as if he had been thinking for centuries. He looks five thousand years old."

Seeing that Lillie began to weary, the old Doctor replaced the deity on the pillow which served him for an altar, and turned the male worshipers out of the room.

"How delighted they are with him!" she said when the door had closed behind them. "Doctor, isn't he an uncommonly handsome child?" she added with the adorable simplicity of perfect love. "I thought babies were not pretty at first."

The room was now kept still. The mother and child lay side by side, reposing from their night-long struggle for life. The mother looked steadily at the infant; the infant looked with equal fixity at the window : each gazed and wondered at an unaccustomed glory. In a few minutes both dropped to sleep, overcome by fatigue, and by novel emotions, or sensations. For three days a succession of long slumbers, and of waking intervals similar to tranquilly delightful dreams, composed their existence. When they were thus reposed they tasted life with a more complete and delicious zest. Lillie entertained her husband and father for hours at a time with discoursing on the attributes of the baby, pointing out the different elements of his glory, and showing how he grew in graces. She was quite indifferent to their affectionate raillery; nothing could shake her faith in the illimitability of the new deity. They two, dear as they were, were nevertheless human, and were not so necessary as they had been to her faith in goodness, and her happiness in loving. So long as she had the baby to look at, she could pass the whole day without them, hardly wondering at their absence.

"We are dethroned," said the Doctor to the Colonel. "We are a couple of Saturns who have made way for the new-born Jupiter."

"Nonsense!" smiled Lillie. "You think that you are going to spend all your time with your minerals now. You are perfectly happy in the idea. I sha'n't allow it."

"No. We must remain and be converts to the new revelation. Well, I suppose we sha'n't resist. We are ready to make our profession of faith at all times and in all places."

"This is the place," said Lillie. "Isn't he sweet?"

The grandfather knew a great deal better than either the father or mother how to handle the diminutive Jupiter. He took him from the pillow, carried him to the window, drew the curtain slowly, and laughed to see the solemn little eyes, after winking slowly, turn upward and fix themselves steadily on the broad, mild effulgence of the sky.

"He looks for the light, as plants and trees lean towards it," said he. "He is trying to see the heavenly mansions which he may some day inhabit. Nobody knows how soon. They get up their chariots very suddenly sometimes, these little Elijahs."

"Oh, don't talk so," implored Lillie. "He sha'n't die."

The Doctor was thinking of his own only boy, who had flown from the cradle to Heaven more than twenty years ago.

Aside from tenderness for his wife, Carter's principal

emotion all this while was that of astonishment at his position. It cost him considerable mental effort, and stretch
of imagination, to conceive himself a relative of the new-
comer. He did not, like Lillie, love the child by passionate
instinct; and he had not yet learned to love him as he had
learned to love her. He was tender of the infant, as a
creature whose weakness pleaded for his protection; but
when it came to the question of affection, he had to confess that he loved him chiefly through his mother. He
was a poor hand at fondling the boy, being always afraid
of doing him some harm. He was better pleased to see
him in Lillie's arms than to feel him in his own; the little
burden was curiously warm and soft, but so evidently susceptible to injury as to be a terror.

"I would rather lead a storming party," he said. "I
have been beaten in that sort of thing, and lived through
it. But if I should drop this fellow—"

And here the warrior absolutely flinched at the thought
of how he would feel in such a horrible case.

Now commenced a beautiful reciprocal education of
mother and child. Each discovered every day new mysteries, new causes of admiration and love, in the other.
Long before a childless man or even woman would have
imagined signs of intelligence in the infant, the mother had
not merely imagined but had actually discovered them.
You would have been wrong if you had laughed incredu-
lously when she said, "He begins to take notice." Of
course her fondness led her into errors: she mistook symptoms of mere sensation for utterances of ideas; she perceived prophetically rather than by actual observation:
but some things, some opening buds of intellect, she saw
truly. She deceived herself when she thought that at the
age of three weeks he knew his father; but at the same
time she was quite correct in believing that he recognized
and cried for his mother. This delighted her; she would
let him cry for a moment, merely for the pleasure of being
so desired; then she would fold him to her breast and be

his comforter, his life. They were teachers, consolers, deities, the one to the other.

Her love gave a fresh inspiration to her religious feeling. Here was a new object of thanksgiving and prayer: an object so nearly divine that only Heaven could have sent it: an object so delicate that only Heaven could preserve it. For her baby she prayed with an intelligence, a feeling, a faith, such as she had never known before, not even when praying for her husband during his times of battle. It seemed certain to her that the merciful All-Father and the Son who gave himself for the world would sympathize compassionately with the innocence, and helplessness of her little child. These sentiments were not violent: she would have withered under the breath of any passionate emotion: they were as gentle and comforting as summer breezes from orange groves. Once only, during a slight accession of fever, there came something like a physical revelation; a room full of mysterious, dazzling light; a communication of some surprising, unutterable joy; an impression as of a divine voice, saying, "Thy sins are forgiven thee."

Forgiven of God, she wished also to be forgiven of man. The next morning, moved by the remembrance of the vision, although its exaltation had nearly vanished with the fall of the fever, she beckoned her husband to her, and with tears begged his pardon for some long since forgotten petulance. This was the hardest trial that Carter had yet undergone. To have her plead for his forgiveness was a reproach that he could hardly bear with self-possession. He must not confess—no such relief was there for his burdened spirit—but he sank on his knees in miserable penitence.

"Oh! forgive me," he said. "I am not half good enough for you. I am not worthy of your love. You must pray for me, my darling."

For the time she was his religion: his loving, chastening,

though not all-seing deity : uplifting and purifying him, even as she was exalted and sanctified by her child.

Her sick-bed happiness was checkered by some troubles. It was hard not to stir; not to be able to help herself; not to tend the baby. When her face was washed for her by the nurse, there would be places where it was not thoroughly dried, and which she sought to wipe by rubbing against the pillow. After a few trials of this sort she forbade the nurse to touch her, and installed her husband in the duty. It was actually a comfort to him to seek to humiliate himself by these dressing-maid services; and it seemed to him that he was thereby earning forgiveness for the crime which he dared not confess. He washed her face, took her meals in, and put them out, fed her with his own hands, fanned her by the hour, and all, she thought, as no one else could.

"How gentle you are!" she said, her eyes suddenly moistening with gratitude. "How nicely you wait on me! And to think that you have led a storming party! And I have seen men afraid of you! My dear, what did you ever mean by saying that you are not good enough for me? You are a hundred times better than I deserve."

Carter laid his forehead in her gently clasping hands without speaking.

"What are you going to call him?" he asked presently.

"Why, Ravenel;—didn't you know?" she answered with a smile.

She had been calling him Ravenel to herself for several days, without telling any one of it. It was a pleasure to think that she alone knew his name; that she had so much in him of an unshared, secret possession.

"Ravenel Carter," she repeated. "We can make that into Ravvie. Don't you like it?"

"I do," he answered. "It is the best name possible. It contains the name of at least one good man."

"Of two good men," she insisted. "A good husband and a good father."

S

Her first drive in the pony carriage was an ecstacy. By her side sat the nurse holding Ravvie, and opposite sat her husband and father. Presently she made the Colonel and the nurse change places.

"I want my child where I can see him, and my husband where I can lean against him," she said.

"I don't come in," observed the Doctor. "I am Monsieur De Trop—Mr. No Account."

"No you are not. I want you to look at Ravvie and me."

Soon she was anxious lest the child should catch cold by riding backwards.

"No more danger one way than the other," said the Doctor. "The back of his head goes all around."

"I dare say his hair will protect him; won't it?" she asked.

"His hair is about as heavy as his whiskers," laughed the Doctor. "He is in no danger of Absalom's fate."

The nurse having pulled up a shawl in rear of the little bobbing head, Lillie was satisfied, and could turn her attention to other things. She laid her slender hand on her husband's knee, nestled against his strong shoulder and said, "Isn't it lovely—isn't the whole world beautiful!"

They had taken the nearest cut out of the city, and were passing a surburban mansion, the front yard of which was full of orange trees and flowers. A few weeks before she would have wanted to steal the flowers; now she eagerly asked her husband to get out and beg for some. When he returned with a gorgeous bouquet she was full of gratitude, exclaiming, "Oh, how lovely! Did you thank the people? I am so obliged to them. Did they see the child in the carriage?"

"Yes," said the Colonel, smiling with pleasure at her naïve delight. "The lady saw the child, and said this rose was for him."

Accordingly the rose, carefully stripped of all thorns,

was put into the dimpled fist of Ravvie, who of course proceeded to suck it.

"He is smelling of it," cried Lillie, with a charming faith in the little god's precocity.

"He is trying it by his universal test—his all-sufficient crucible," said the Doctor. "Everything must go into that mouth. It is his only medium for acquiring knowledge at present. If it was large enough and he could reach far enough, he would investigate the nature of the solar system by means of it. It is lucky for the world that he is not sufficiently big to put the sun in his mouth. We should certainly find ourselves in darkness—not to mention that he might burn himself. My dear, I am afraid he will swallow some of the leaves," he added. "We must interfere. This is one of the emergencies when a grandfather has a right to exercise authority."

The rose was gently detached from Ravvie's fat grasp, and stuck in his little silk bonnet, his eyes following it till it disappeared.

"You see he is an eating animal," continued the Doctor. "That is pretty much all at present, and that is enough. He has no need of any more wisdom than what will enable him to demand nourishment and dispose of it; and God, in his great kindness towar ls infants, has not troubled him with any further revelations so far. God has provided us to do all the necessary thinking in his case. The infant is a mere swallower, digestor, and assimilator. He knows how to convert other substances into himself. He does it with energy, singleness of purpose, perseverance, and wonderful success. Nothing more is requisite. In eating he is performing the whole duty of man at his age. So far as he goes he is a masterpiece."

"But you are making a machine of him—an oyster," protested Lillie.

"Very like," said the Doctor. "Very like an oyster. His existence has a simplicity and unity very similar to that of the lower orders of creation. Of course I am not speaking of his possibilities. They are spiritual, grand, perhaps gigantic. If you could see the inferior face of his brain, you would be able to perceive even now the magnificent capacities of the as yet untuned instrument."

" Oh don't, papa !" implored Lillie. " You trouble me. Do they ever dissect babies ?"

" Not such lively ones as this," said the Doctor, and proceeded to change the subject. " I never saw a healthier creature. I shouldn't wonder if he survived this war, which you used to say would last forty years. Perhaps he will be the man to finish it."

" I don't say so now. I didn't think my husband would be on the Union side when I said that. I think we shall beat them now."

" Since the miracle all other things seem possible," philosophised the Doctor.

I do not repeat the Colonel's talk. It was not so appropriate as that of the others to the occasion ; for he knew little as yet of the profounder depths of womanly and infantile nature ; his first marriage had been brief and childless. In fact, Carter was rather a silent man in family conclaves, unless the conversation turned on some branch of his profession, or the matters of ordinary existence. He occupied himself with watching alternately his wife and child ; with wrapping up the former, and occasionally fondling the latter.

" How very warm he feels !—how amazingly he pulls hair !—I believe he wants to get my head in his mouth," are samples of his observations on the infant wonder. He felt that the baby was either below him or above him, he really could not tell which. Of his wife's position he was certain : she was far higher than his plane of existence : when she took his hand it was from the heavens.

From Mrs. Larue he was thoroughly detached, and with a joyful sense of relief, freedom, betterment. They talked very little with each other, and only on indifferent subjects and in the presence of others. It is possible that this separation would not have lasted if they had been thrown together unguarded, as had been the case on board the Creole; but here, caring for his infant and for the wife who had suffered so much and so sweetly for his sake, the Colonel felt no puissance of passionate temptation.

Mrs. Larue had no conscience, no sense of honor; but like many cold blooded people, she valued herself on her firmness. In an unwonted burst of enthusiasm she had told him that all must be over between them, and she meant to make her words good, no matter what he might desire. She was a little mortified to see how easily he had cut loose from her; but she knew how to explain it so as not to wound her vanity, nor tempt her to break her resolution.

" If he did not love his wife now, he would be a brute," she reflected. " And if he had had the possibilities of a brute in him, I never should have had a caprice for him. After all, I do not care much for the merely physical human being. *C'est par le côte morale qu 'on s'empare de moi. Apres tout je suis presque aussi pure dans les sentiments que ma petite cousine.*"

Meanwhile her self-restraint was something of a trial to her. At times she thought seriously of marrying again, with the idea of putting an end to these risky intrigues and harassing struggles. Perhaps it was under this impression that she wrote a letter to Colburne, informing him of the birth of Ravvie, and sketching some few items of the scene with a picturesqueness and sympathy that quite touched the young gentleman, astonished as he was at the frankness of the language.

" After all," she concluded, " married life has exquisite pleasures, as well as terrific possibilities of sorrow. I do not really know whether to advise a young man like you to take a wife or not. Whether you marry or remain single you will be sorry. I think that in either state the pains outweigh the pleasures. It follows that we are not to consider our own happiness, but to do what we think is for the happiness of others. Is not this the true secret of life?"

"Is it possible that I have been unjust?" queried Colburne. "Those are not the teachings of a corrupted nature."

He did not know and could not have conceived the unnatural conscience, the abnormal ideas of purity and duty, which this woman had created for her own use and comfort, out of elements that are beyond the ken of most New Englanders. He was the child of Puritanism, and she of Balzac's moral philosophy.

CHAPTER XXX.

COLONEL CARTER COMMITS HIS FIRST UNGENTLEMANLY ACTION.

WE come now to the times of the famous and unfortunate Red River expedition. During the winter of 1863–4 New Orleans society, civil as well as military, was wild with excitement over the great enterprise which was not only to crush the rebel power in the southwest, but to open to commerce the immense stores of cotton belonging to the princely planters of the Red River bottoms. Cotton was gold, foreign exchange, individual wealth, national solvency. Thousands of men went half mad in their desire for cotton. Cotton was a contagion, an influenza, a delirium.

In the height of this excitement a corpulent, baldish, smiling gentleman of fifty was closeted, not for the first time, with the chief quartermaster. His thick feet were planted wide apart, his chubby hands rested on his chubby knees, his broad base completely filled the large office chair in which he sat, his paunchy torso and fat head leaned forward in an attitude of eagerness, and his twinkling grey eyes, encircled by yellowish folds, were fixed earnestly upon the face of Carter.

" Colonel, you make a great mistake in letting this chance slip," he said, and then paused to wheeze.

The Colonel said nothing, smoked his twenty cent Havana slowly, and gazed thoughtfully at the toes of his twenty dollar boots. With his aristocratic face, his lazy pride of expression, his bran-new citizen's suit, his boots and his Havana, he looked immensely rich and superbly indifferent to all pecuniary chances.

" You see, here is a sure thing," continued the oleaginous personage. " Banks' column will be twenty thousand strong. Steele's will be ten thousand. There are thirty thousand, without counting Porter's fleet. The Confederates can't raise twenty thousand to cover the Red River country, if they go to hell. Besides, there is an understanding. Tit for tat, you know. Cotton for cash. You see I am as well posted on the matter as you are, Colonel."

Here he paused, wheezed, nodded, smiled and bored his corkscrew eyes into Carter. The latter uttered not a word and gave no sign of either acquiescence or denial.

" You see the cotton is sure to come," continued the stout man, withdrawing his ocular corkscrew for a moment. " Now what I propose is, that you put in the capital, or the greater part of it, and that I do the work and give you the lion's share of the profits. I can't furnish the capital, and you can. You can't do the work, and I can. Or suppose I guarantee you a certain sum on each bale, Colonel, for a hundred thousand dollars, I promise you a square profit of two hundred thousand."

" Mr. Walker, if it is sure to pay so well, why don't you go in alone ?" asked Carter.

Mr. Walker pointed at his coarse grey trousers and then took hold of the frayed edge of his coarse grey coat.

" See here, Colonel," said he. " The man who wears this cloth hasn't a hundred thousand dollars handy. When I knew you in old times I used to go in my broadcloth. I hope to do it again—not that I care for it. That's one

reason I don't go in alone—a short bank balance. Another
is that I haven't the influence at headquarters that you have.
I need your name as well as your money to put the business through quick and sure. That's why I offer you four
fifths of the profits. Colonel, it's a certain thing and a good
thing. I am positively astonished at finding any hesitation
in a man in your pecuniary condition."

"What do you know about my condition?" demanded
Carter imperiously.

"Well, it's my interest to know," replied Walker, whose
cunning fat smile did not quail before the Colonel's leonine
roar and toss of mane. "I have bought up a lot of your
debts and notes. I got them for an average of sixty, Colonel."

"You paid devilish dear, and made a bad investment,"
said Carter, "I wouldn't have given thirty."

A bitter smile twisted his lips as he thought how poor
he was, how bad his credit was, and how mean it was to
be poor and discredited.

"Perhaps I have. I believe I have, unless you go into
this cotton. I bought them to induce you to go into it.
I thought you would oblige a man who relieved you from
forty or fifty duns. I took a four thousand dollar risk on
you, Colonel."

Carter scowled and stopped smoking. He did not know
what Walker could do with him; he did not much believe that he legally could do anything; his creditors never
had done more than dun him. But High Authority might
perhaps be led to do unpleasant things: for instance, in the
way of relieving him from his position, if the fact should
be forced upon its notice, that so responsible an officer as
the chief quartermaster of the Gulf Department was burdened by private indebtedness. At all events it was unpleasant to have a grasping, intriguing, audacious fellow
like Walker for a creditor to so large an amount. It
would be a fine thing to get out of debt once for all; to
astonish his duns (impertinent fellows, some of them) by

settling every solitary bill with interest ; to be rich once
for all, without danger of recurring poverty ; to be rich
enough to force promotion. Other officials—quartermas-
ters, paymasters, etc.—were going in for cotton on the
strength of Government deposits. The influenza had
caught the Colonel ; indeed it was enough to corrupt any
man's honesty to breathe the moral atmosphere of New Orleans at that time ; it could taint the honor derived from
blue ancestral blood and West Point professional pride.

Carter did not, however, give way to his oily Mephistopheles during this interview. Walker's victory was
not so sudden as Mrs. Larue's ; his temptation was not so
well suited as hers to the character of the victim ; the love
of lucre could not compare as a force with *le divin sens du
genesiaque*. It was not until Walker had boldly threatened
to bring his claims before the General Commanding, not
until the army had well nigh reached the Red River, not
until the chance of investment had almost passed, that the
Colonel became a speculator. Once resolved, he acted
with audacity, according to his temperament. But here,
unfortunately for the curious reader, we enter upon cavern-
ous darkness, where it is impossible to trace out a story
except by hazardous inference, our only guides being common rumor, a fragment of a letter, a conversation half-
overheard, and other circumstances of a like unsatisfactory
nature. Before giving my narrative publicity I feel bound
to state that the entire series of alleged events may be a
fiction of the excited popular imagination, founded on
facts which might be explained in accordance with an as-
sumption of Carter's innocence, and official honor.

I am inclined to believe, or at least to admit, that he
drew a large sum (not less than one hundred thousand
dollars) of the Government money in his charge, and
placed it in the hands of his agent for the purchase of cotton from the planters of the Red River. It is probable
that Walker expected to complete the transaction within
a month, and to place the cotton, or the proceeds of it, in

the hands of his principal early enough to enable the latter to show a square balance on his official return at the close of the current quarter. Such claims as might come in during this period could be put off by the plea of " no funds," or the safer devices of, " disallowed,"—" papers returned for correction," etc., etc. That the cotton could be sold at a monstrous profit was unquestionable. At New Orleans there were greedy capitalists, who had not been lucky enough to get into the Ring, and so accompany the expedition, who were anxious to pay cash down for the precious commodity immediately on its arrival at the levee, or even before it quitted the Red River. No body entertained a doubt of the military and commercial success of the great expedition, with its fleet, its veteran infantry, its abundant cavalry, all splendidly equipped, and its strategic combination of concentric columns. Even rabid secessionists were infected by the mania, and sought to invest their gold in cotton. It is probable that Carter's hopes at this time were far higher than his fears, and that he pretty confidently expected to see himself a rich man inside of sixty days. I am telling my story, the reader perceives, on the presumption that rumor has correctly stated these mysterious events.

If the materials for the tale were only attainable it would be a delightful thing to follow the corpulent Walker through the peaceful advance and sanguinary retreat of the great expedition. It is certain that from some quarter he obtained command of a vast capital, and that, in spite of his avoirdupois, he was alert and indefatigable in seeking opportunities for investment. Had Mars been half as adroit and watchful in his strategy as this fat old Mercury was in his speculations, Shreveport would have been taken, and Carter would have made a quarter of a million. But the God of Lucre had great reason to grumble at the God of War. It was in vain that Mercury lost fifty pounds of flesh in sleepless lookout for chances, in audacious rides to plantations haunted by guerrillas, shot at from swamps, and thickets, half starved or living on raw pork and hard-tack, bargaining nearly all night after riding all day, un-tiring as a savage, zealous as an abolitionist, sublime in his passion for gain.   Mars incautiously stretched his splendid army over thirty miles of road, and saw it beaten in de-tachments by a force one quarter smaller, and vastly in-ferior in discipline and equipment.   There was such a panic at Sabine Cross Roads as had not been seen since Bull Run.   Cavalry, artillery, and infantry, mingled to-gether in hopeless confusion, rushed in wild flight across the open fields, or forced their way down a narrow road encumbered with miles of abandoned baggage wagons. Through this chaos of terror advanced the saviours of the day, the heroic First Division of the Nineteenth Corps, marching calmly by the flank, hooting and jeering the runaways, filing into line within grape range of the enemy, and opening a withering fire of musketry which checked until nightfall the victorious, elated, impetuous Rebel masses.   Then came an extraordinary midnight retreat of twenty miles, and in the afternoon of the next day a hardly-won, unimproved victory.   The first division of the Nine-teenth Corps, and seven thousand men of the Sixteenth Corps, the one forming the right and the other the left, resisted for hours the violent charges of the rebels, and then advanced two miles, occupying the field of battle. The soldiers were victorious, but the General was beaten. A new retreat was ordered, and Mercury went totally to grief.

The obese Walker was last seen by loyal eyes on the night which followed the barren triumph of Pleasant Hill. He had had his horse shot under him in the beginning of the fighting at Sabine Cross Roads, while in advance of the column ; had effected a masterly retreat, partly on foot and partly on a Government mule which he took from a negro driver, who had cut it loose from an entangled wagon ; had fed himself abundantly from the havresacks of defunct rebels on the field of victory ; and then had he-

roically set to work to make the best of circumstances.
Believing with the confidence of his sanguine nature that
the army would advance in the morning, he started on his
mule, accompanied by two comrades of the Ring, for the
house of a neighboring planter, to whom it is supposed
that he had advanced cash for cotton. No one knows to
this day what became of him, or of his funds, or investments, or fellow adventurers. All alike disappeared utterly
and forever from the knowledge of the Union army when
the three rode into that night of blood and groans beyond
the flickering circle of light, thrown out by the camp fires.

The news of the calamity, we may suppose, nearly paralyzed Carter. Defalcation, trial by court-martial, disgraceful dismissal from the service, hard labor at Tortugas,
ball and chain, a beggared family, a crazed wife, must
have made up a terrific spectre, advancing, close at hand,
unavoidable, pitiless. It would be a laborious task to analyze and fully conceive the feelings of such a man in such
a position. Naturally and with inexorable logic followed
the second act of the moral tragedy. A deed which some
men would call merely a blunder led straight to another
deed which all men would call a crime. He could not,
as men have sometimes done, hope to annul his indebtedness
by the simple commission of murder. Irresistible necessity
drove him (if our hypothetical tale is correct) into a species
of wickedness which was probably more repugnant to his
peculiarly educated conscience than the taking of human
life.

Carter wanted, we will say, one hundred and ten thousand dollars to make himself square with the United States
and his private creditors. Looking over the Government
property for which he had receipted and was responsible,
he found fifteen steamboats, formerly freight or passenger
boats on the Mississippi and its branches, but now regular
transports, part of them lying idly at the levee, the others
engaged in carrying reinforcements to the army at Grande
Ecore or in bringing back the sick and wounded. If ten

of these boats were sold at an average of ten thousand dollars apiece and re-bought at an average of twenty-five thousand dollars apiece, the transaction would furnish a profit of one hundred and fifty thousand dollars, which would settle all his debts, besides furnishing collusion-money. First, he wanted a nominal purchaser, who had that sort of honor which is necessary among thieves, fortune enough to render the story of the purchase plausible, and character enough to impose on the public. Carter went straight to a man of known fortune, born in New Orleans, high in social position, a secessionist who had taken the oath of allegiance. Mr. Hollister was a small and thin gentleman, with sallow and hollow cheeks, black eyes, iron gray hair, mellow voice, composed and elegant manners. His air, notwithstanding his small size, was remarkably dignified, and his expression was so calm that it would have seemed benignant but for a most unhappy eye. It was startlingly black, with an agitated flicker in it, like the flame of a candle blowing in the wind; it did not seem to be pursuing any object without, but rather flying from some horrible thought within. What intrigue or crime or suffering it was the record of it is not worth while to inquire. There had been many dark things done or planned in Louisiana during the lifetime of Mr. Hollister. His age must have been sixty-five, although the freshness of his brown morning suit, the fineness and fit of his linen, the neat brush to his hair, the clean shave on his face, took ten years off his shoulders. As he dabbled in stocks and speculations, he had his office. He advanced to meet the chief quartermaster, shook hands with respectful cordiality, and conducted him to a chair with as much politeness as if he were a lady.

"You look pale, Colonel," he said. "Allow me to offer you a glass of brandy. Trying season, this last summer. There was a time when I never thought of facing our climate all the year round."

Taking out of a cupboard one of the many bottles of

choice old cognac with which he had enriched his wine-cellar, before the million of former days had dwindled to the hundred thousand of to-day, he set it beside a pitcher of ice-water and some glasses which stood on a table. The Colonel swallowed half a tumbler of pure brandy, and dashed some water after it. The broker mixed a weak sling, and sipped it to keep his visitor in countenance.

"Mr. Hollister," said Carter, "I hope I shall not offend you if I say that I know you have suffered heavily by the war."

"I shall certainly not be offended. I am obliged to you for showing the slightest interest in my affairs."

"You have taken the oath of allegiance—haven't you?"

Mr. Hollister said "Yes," and bowed respectfully, as if saluting the United States Government.

"It is only fair that you should obtain remuneration for your losses."

The black eyes flashed a little under the iron-gray, bushy eyebrows, but the sallow face showed no other sign of interest and none of impatience.

"I know of a transaction—an investment—" pursued Carter, "which will probably enable you to pocket—to re-alize—perhaps twenty thousand dollars."

"I should be indebted to you for life. Whatever service I can render in return will be given with all my heart."

"It requires secrecy. May I ask you to pledge your word?"

"I pledge it, Colonel—my word of honor—as a Louisi-ana gentleman."

Carter drew a long breath, poured out another dose of brandy, partially raised it and then set it, down without drinking.

"There are ten river steamboats here," he went on—"ten transports which are not wanted. I have received a message from headquarters to the effect that we no longer need our present large force of transports. The army will

not retreat from Grande Ecore.   It is sufficiently reinforced
to go to Shreveport.   I am empowered to select eight of
these transports for sale—you understand."

"Precisely," bowed Hollister.   "If the army advances,
of course it does not need transports."

As to the military information he neither believed nor
disbelieved, knowing well that the Colonel would not
honestly tell him anything of consequence on that score.

"Well, they will be sold," added Carter, after a pause,
during which he vainly tried to imagine some other method
of covering his enormous defalcation.   "They will be sold
at auction.   They will probably bring next to nothing.   I
propose that you be present to buy them."

The broker closed his eyes for a moment or two, and
when he had opened them he had made his calculations.
He inferred that the United States Government was not to
profit much by the transaction; that, in plain words, it
was to be cheated out of an amount of property more or
less considerable; and, being a Confederate at heart, he
had no objection.

"Why not have a private sale?" he asked.

"It is contrary to the Regulations."

"Ah!   Then it might be well not to have the auction
made too public."

"I suppose so.   Perhaps that can be arranged."

"I can arrange it, Colonel.   If I may select the parties
to be present, men of straw, you understand—the auction
will wear a sufficient air of publicity, and will yet be sub-
stantially a private sale.   All that is easily enough managed, provided we first understand each other thoroughly.
Listen, if you please.   The ten steamboats are worth, we
will say, an average of twenty-five thousand dollars, or
two hundred and fifty thousand for the lot.   If I buy them
for an average of ten thousand, which is respectable——"

Here he looked gravely at Carter, and, seeing assent in
his eyes, continued.

"If I buy them at an average of ten thousand, there

will remain a profit—in case of sale—of one hundred and
fifty thousand. That is very well—exceedingly well. Of
course I should only demand a moderate proportion of so
large a sum. But there are several other things to be considered. If I am to pay cash down, it will oblige me to
borrow immensely, and perhaps to realize at a loss by
forcing sales of my stocks. In that case I should want—
say a third—of the profit in order to cover my risk and
my losses, as well as my expenses in the way of—to be
plain—hush-money. If I can pay by giving my notes,
and moreover can be made sure of a purchaser before the
notes mature, I can afford to undertake the job for one
sixth of the profits, which I estimate to be twenty-five
thousand dollars."

There was a flash of pleasure in Carter's eyes at discovering that the broker was so moderate in his expectations.
There was a similar glitter in the dark orbs of Hollister at
seeing that the Colonel tacitly accepted his offer, from
which he would have been willing to abate a few thousands
rather than lose the job.

"The boats will have to go before an Inspector before
they can be sold," said the Colonel, after a few moments
of reverie, during which he drank off his brandy.

"I hope he will be amenable to reason," said Hollister.
"Perhaps he will need a couple of thousands or so before
he will be able to discover his line of duty. It may answer if he is merely ignorant of steamboats."

"Of course he is. What can an army officer know about
steam engines or hulls?"

"I will see that he is posted. I will see that he has entirely satisfactory evidence concerning the worthless
nature of the property from the captains, and engineers,
and carpenters. That will require—say three thousand—
possibly twice that. I will advance the money for these
incidental expenses, and you will reimburse me one half
when the transaction is complete."

The Colonel looked up uneasily, and made no reply.

He did not want to make money out of the swindle: curiously enough he still had too much conscience, too much honor, for that; but he must be sure of enough to clear off his defalcation.

"Well, we will see about that afterward," compromised Hollister. "I will pay these expenses and leave the question of reimbursement to you. By the way, what are the names of the boats? I know some of them."

"Queen of the South, Queen of the West, Pelican, Crescent City, Palmetto, Union, Father of Waters, Red River, Gulf State, and Massachusetts," repeated Carter, with a pause of recollection before each title.

The broker laughed.

"I used to own three of them. I know them all, except the Massachusetts, which is a northern boat. All in running order?"

"Yes. Dirty, of course."

"Very well. Now permit me to make out a complete programme of the transaction. The boats are recommended for the action of an Inspector. I see to it that he receives sufficient evidence to prove their unserviceable condition. It is ordered that they be sold at public auction. I provide the persons who are to be present at the auction. These men—my agents—will purchase the boats at a net cost of one hundred thousand dollars, for which they will give my notes payable a month from date. Within the month I am supposed to refit the boats and make them serviceable, while the Government is certain to need them back again. I then sell them to you—the purchasing agent of the Government—for a net sum of at least two hundred and fifty thousand dollars. I receive my notes back, and also a cash balance of one hundred and thirty thousand dollars, of which I only take thirty thousand, leaving the rest in your hands under a mutual pledge of confidence. I desire to make one final suggestion, which I consider of great importance. It would be well if the boats, when re-bought, should accidentally take fire and be destroyed, as it would prevent inspection as to the amount which I might have expended in repairs. Colonel, is that perfectly to your satisfaction?"

The unfortunate, unhappy, degraded officer and gentleman could only reply, "Yes."

Such is the supposed secret history of this scandalous stroke of business. It is only certain that the boats were inspected and condemned; that at an auction, attended by a limited number of respectably dressed persons, they were sold for sums varying from seven to fifteen thousand dollars; that the amounts were all paid in the notes of L. M. Hollister, a well-known broker, and capitalist of supposed secession proclivities; that within a month the transports were repurchased by the Government at sums varying from fifteen to thirty thousand dollars; that thus a net profit of one hundred and fifty thousand dollars accrued to the said Hollister; and that three days after the sale the boats caught fire and burned to the water's edge. Of course there was talk, perhaps unjustifiable; suspicions, which perhaps had no foundation in fact. But there was no investigation, possibly no serious cause for it, probably no chance for it.

Colonel Carter sent a square balance-sheet to the Quartermaster's Department at Washington, and paid all his private debts in New Orleans. But he grew thin, looked anxious, or ostentatiously gay, and resumed to some extent his habits of drinking. Once he terrified his wife by remaining out all night, explaining when he came home in the morning that he had been up the river on pressing business. The truth is that the Colonel had got himself stone-blind drunk, and had slept himself sober in a hotel.

CHAPTER XXXI.

A TORTURE WHICH MIGHT HAVE BEEN SPARED.

A WEEK after the conflagration Carter received his commission as Brigadier-General. His first impression was one of exultation : his enemies and his adverse fate had been beaten; he was on the road to distinction: he could wear the silver star. Then came a feeling of despondency and fear, while he remembered the crime into which he had been driven, as he thought or tried to think, by the lack of this just recognition of his services. Oh the bitterness of good fortune, long desired, which comes too late !

"A month ago this might have saved me," he muttered, and then burst into curses upon his political opponents, his creditors, himself, all those who had brought about his ruin.

"My only crime! The only ungentlemanly act of my life !" was another phrase which dropped from his lips. Doubtless he thought so: many people of high social position hold a similarly mixed moral creed; they allow that a gentleman may be given to expensive immoralities, but not to money-getting ones; that he may indulge in wine, women, and play, but not in swindling. All over Europe this curious ethical distinction prevails, and very naturally, for it springs out of the conditions of a hereditary aristocracy, and makes allowance for the vices to which wealthy nobles are tempted, but not for vices to which they are not tempted. A feeble echo of it has traversed the ocean, and influenced some characters in America both for good and for evil.

Carter was almost astonished at the child-like joy, so contradictory to his own angry remorse, with which Lillie received the news of his promotion.

"Oh !—My General !" she said, coloring to her forehead

with delight, after a single glance at the commission which he dropped into her lap. She rose up and gave him a mock military salute; then sprang at him and covered his bronzed face and long mustache with kisses.

"I am so happy! They have done you justice at last—a little justice. Oh, I am so glad and proud! I am going with you to buy the star. You shall let me choose it."

Then, her mind taking a forward leap of fifteen years, she added, "We will send Ravvie to West Point, and he shall be a general, too, He is going to be very intelligent. And brave, also. He isn't in the least timid."

Carter laughed for the first time since he had received the commission.

"My dear," said he, "Ravvie will probably become a general long after I have ceased to be one. I am a volunteer. I am only a general while the war lasts."

"But the war will last a long time," hopefully replied the monster in woman's guise, who loved her husband a hundred times as much as she did her country.

"There is one unpleasant result of this promotion," observed Carter.

"What! You are not going to the field?" asked Lillie, clutching him by the sleeve. "Oh, don't do that!"

"My little girl, I cannot hold my present position. A Brigadier-General can't remain quartermaster, not even of a department. I must resign it and report for duty. Headquarters may order me to the field, and I certainly ought to go."

"Oh no! It can't be necessary. To think that this should come just when we were so happy. I wish you hadn't been promoted."

"My darling, you want to make a woman of me," he said, holding her close to his side. "I must show myself a man, now that my manhood has been recognized. My honor demands it."

He talked of his honor from long habit; conscious, however, that the word stung him.

"But don't ask to be sent to the field," pleaded Lillie. "Resign your place and report for duty, if you must. But please don't ask to be sent to the field. Promise me that; won't you?"

Looking into his wife's tearful eyes, with his strong and plump hands on her sloping shoulders, the Colonel promised as she asked him. But that evening, writing from his office, he sent a communication to the headquarters of the Department of the Gulf, requesting that he might be relieved from his quartermastership and assigned to duty with the army in the field. What else should he do? He had proved himself unfit for family life, unfit for business; but, by (this and that and the other) he could command a brigade and he could fight. He would do what he had done, and could do again, with credit. Besides, if he should win distinction at Grande Ecore, it might prevent an investigation into that infernal muddle of cotton and steamboats. A great deal is pardoned by the public, and even by the War Department, to courage, capacity, and success.

In a few days he received orders from the General commanding, directing him to report to the headquarters of the army in the field. He signed his last quartermaster papers gaily, kissed his wife and child sadly, shook hands with Ravenel and Mrs. Larue, and took the first boat up the river.

Lillie was amazed and shocked at discovering how little she missed him. She accused herself of being wicked and heartless; she would not accept the explanation that she was a mother. It was all the more hateful in her to forget him, she said, now that he was the father of her child. Still, she could not be miserable; she was almost always happy with her baby. Such a lovely baby he was; charming because he was heavy, because he ate, because he slept, because he cried! His wailing troubled her because it denoted that he was ill at ease, and not because the sound was in itself disagreeable to her ear. If she heard it at a little distance from the house, for instance when re-

T

returning from a walk, she quickened her step and smiled gaily, saying, "He is alive. You will see how he will stop when I take him."

People who feel so strongly are rarely interesting except to those who share their feelings, or who have learned to love them under any circumstances, and though all the metamorphoses of which a single character is capable. She would have been perfectly tedious at this period to any ordinary acquaintance who had not been initiated into the sweet mystery of love for children. Her character and conversation seemed to be all solved in the great alembic of maternity. She was a mother as passionately as she had been a betrothed and a wife; and indeed it appeared as if this culminating condition of her womanhood was the most absorbing of all. This exquisite life, delicious in spite of her occasional anxieties and self-reproaches concerning her husband, flowed on without much mixture of trouble until one day she picked up a letter on the floor of her father's study which opened to her a hitherto inconceivable fountain of bitterness. Let us see how this unfortunate manuscript found its way into the house.

Doctor Ravenel, deprived for the last two years of his accustomed summer trip to Europe, or the north, or other countries blessed with a mineralogy, sought health and amusement in long walks about New Orleans and its flat, ugly vicinity. Lillie, who used to be his comrade in these exercises, now took constitutionals in the pony carriage or in company with the wicker wagon of Master Ravvie. These strolls of the Doctor were therefore somewhat dull business. A country destitute of stones was to him much like a language destitute of a literature. He fell into a way of walking without paying much attention to his surroundings, revolving the while new systems of mineralogy, crystallizing his knowledge into novel classifications, recalling to memory the characteristics of his specimens, as Lillie recollected the giggles and cunning ways of her baby. In one of these absent-minded moods he was surprised by a heavy shower, three or four miles from home.   The only shelter was a deserted shanty, once probably the dwelling of a free negro.   A minute or two after the Doctor found himself in its single room, and before he had discovered the soundest part of its leaky roof, a man in the undress uniform of a United States officer, dripping wet, reeled into the doorway, with the observation, "By Jove! this is watering my rum."

The Doctor immediately recognized in the herculean form, bronzed face, black eyes and twisted nose, the personality of Lieutenant Van Zandt.   He had not seen him for nearly two years, but the man's appearance and voice were unforgettable.   The Doctor was charitable in philosophising concerning coarse and vicious people, but he abominated their society and always avoided it if possible.   He looked about him for a means of escape and found none ; the man filled up the only door-way, and the rain was descending in torrents.   Accordingly the Doctor turned his back on the Lieutenant and ruminated mineralogy.

"I prefer plain whisky," continued Van Zandt, staring at the rain with a contemptuous grin.   "I don't want, by Jove! so much water in my grog.   None of your mixed drinks, by Jove!   Plain whisky!"

After a minute more of glaring and smiling, he remarked, "Dam slow business, by Jove!   Van Zandt, my bully boy, we won't wait to see this thing out.   We'll turn in."

Facing about with a lurch he beheld the other inmate of the shanty.

"Hullo!" he exclaimed.   Then recollecting the breeding of his youth, he added, "I beg pardon, sir.   Am I intruding?"

"Not at all; of course not," replied Ravenel.   "Our rights here are the same."

"I am glad to hear it. And, by the way, have the kindness to understand me, sir.   I didn't mean to insinuate that I supposed this to be your residence.   I only thought that you might be the proprietor of the estate."

"Not so unfortunate," said the Doctor.

The Lieutenant laughed like a twelve-pound brass howitzer, the noisiest gun, I believe, in existence.

"Very good, sir. The more a man owns here in Louisiana, the poorer he is. That's just my opinion, sir. I feel honored in agreeing with you, sir. By Jove, I own nothing. I couldn't afford it—on my pay."

A stream of water from a hole in the roof was pattering on his broad back, but he took no notice of it, and probably was not conscious of it. He stared at the Doctor with unblinking, bulging eyes, not in the least recollecting him, but perfectly conscious that he was in the presence of a gentleman. Drunk or sober, Van Zandt never forgot that he came of old Knickerbocker stock, and never failed to accord respect to aristocratic demeanor wherever he found it.

"I beg your pardon, sir," he resumed. "You must excuse me for addressing you in this free and easy way. I only saw you indistinctly at first, sir, and couldn't judge as to your social position and individual character. I perceive that you are a gentleman, sir. You will excuse me for mentioning that I come of an old Knickerbocker family which dates in American history from the good old jolly Dutch times of Peter Stuyvesant—God bless his jolly old Dutch memory! You will understand, sir, that a man who feels such blood as that in his veins is glad to meet a gentleman anywhere, even in such a cursed old hovel as this, as leaky and rickety, by Jove! as the Southern Confederacy. And, sir, in that connection allow me to say, hoping no offence if you hold a contrary opinion, that the Confederacy is played out. We licked them on the Red River, sir. The bully old First Division—God bless its ragged old flags! I can't speak of them without feeling my eyes water—much as I hate the fluid—the jolly, fighting old First Division fairly murdered them at Sabine Cross Roads. At Pleasant Hill the old First, and Andrew Jackson Smith's western boys laid them out over two miles square of prairie. If we had had a cracker in our havresacks we would have gone bang up to Shreveport—if we had had a cracker apiece, and the firm of W. C. Do you know what I mean, sir, by W. C? Weitzel and Carter! Those are the boys for an advance. That's the firm that our brigade and division banks on. Weitzel and Carter would have taken us to Shreveport, with or without crackers, by Jove! We wanted nothing but energy. If we had had half the go, the vim, the forward march, to lead us, that the rebels had, we would have finished the war in the southwest. We must take a leaf out of Johnny Reb's book. *Fas est ab hostes doceri.* I believe I quote correctly. If not, please correct me. By the way, did I mention to you that I am a graduate of Columbia College in New York City? Allow me to repeat the statement. I have reason to be proud of the fact, inasmuch as I took the Greek salutatory, the second highest honor, sir, of the graduation. You are a college man yourself, sir, I perceive, and can make allowance for my vanity in the circumstance. But I am wandering fron my subject. I was speaking, I believe, of Colonel Carter—I beg his pardon— General Carter. At last, sir, the Administration has done justice to one of the most gallant and capable officers in the service. So much the better for the Administration. Colonel Carter—I beg pardon—General Carter is not only an officer but a gentleman; not one of those plebeian humbugs whom our ridiculous Democracy delights to call nature's gentlemen; but a gentleman born and bred— *un echantillon de bonne race*—a jet of pure old sangre azul. I, who am an old Knickerbocker—as I believe I had the honor to inform you—I delight to see such men put forward. Don't you, sir?"

The Doctor admitted with a polite smile that the promotion of General Carter gave him pleasure.

"I knew it would, sir. You came of good blood yourself. I can see it in your manners and conversation, sir. Well, as I was saying, the promotion of Carter is one of

T

the most intelligent moves of the Administration. Carter—
I beg pardon—I don't mean to insinuate that I am on
familiar terms with him—I acknowledge him as my superior officer and keep my distance—General Carter is born
for command and for victory. Wherever he goes he conquers. He is triumphant in the field and in the boudoir.
He is victorious over man and women. By Jove, sir,"
(here he gave a saturnine chuckle, and leer.) "I came
across the most amusing proof of his capacity for bringing
the fair sex to a surrender."

The Doctor grew uneasy, and looked out anxiously at
the pouring rain, but saw no chance of effecting an escape.

"You see, sir, I am wounded," continued Van Zandt.
"They gave me a welt at Port Hudson, and they gave me
another at Pleasant Hill."

"My dear sir, you will catch your death, standing under the dripping in that way," said the Doctor.

"Thank you, sir," replied Van Zandt, changing his position. "No great harm, however. Water, sir, doesn't
hurt me, unless it gets into my whiskey. Exteriorly it is
simply disagreeable; interiorly the same, as well as injurious. Not that I am opposed to bathing. On the contrary, it is my practice to take a sponge bath every morning—that is, when I don't sleep within musket range of
the enemy. Well, as I was saying, they gave me a welt
at Pleasant Hill—a mere flesh wound through the thigh—
nothing worth blathering about—and I was sent to St.
James Hospital. I can't stand the hospital. I don't fancy
the fare at the milk-toast table, sir. (This with a grimace of
unutterable disgust.) I took out a two-legged leave of
absence to-day, and went over to the Lake House; lost my
horse there, and had to foot it back to the city. That is
how I came to have the pleasure of listening to your conversation here, sir. But I believe I was speaking of General Carter. Some miserable light wine which I had the
folly to drink at the Lake has muddled my head, I fancy.
Plain whisky is the only safe thing. Allow me to recom-

mend you to stick to it. I wish we had a canteen of honest commissary now; we could pass the night very comfortably, sir. But I was speaking of General Carter, and his qualities as an officer. Ah! I remember. I mentioned a letter. And, by Jove! here it is in my breast-pocket, soaked with this cursed water. If you will have the goodness to peruse it, you will see that I am not exaggerating when I boast of the conquests of my superior officer. The lady frankly owns up to the fact that she has surrendered to him; no capitulation, no terms, no honors of war; unconditional surrender, by Jove! a U. S. G. surrender. It is an unreserved coming down of the coon."

"It is one of Lillie's letters," thought Ravenel. "This drunkard does not know that the General is married, and mistakes the frank affection of a wife for the illicit passion of an *intriguante*. It is best that I should expose the mistake and prevent further misrepresentation."

He took the moist, blurred sheet, unfolded it, and found the envelope carefully doubled up inside. It was addressed to "Colonel J. T. Carter," with the addition in one corner of the word "personal." The handwriting was not Lillie's, but a large, round hand, foreign in style, and, as he judged, feigned. Glancing at the chirography of the note itself, he immediately recognized, as he thought, the small, close, neat penmanship of Mrs. Larue. Van Zandt was too drunk to notice how pale the Doctor turned, and how his hand trembled.

"By Jove! I am tired," said the Bacchanal. "I shall, with your permission, take the d—st nap that ever was heard of since the days of the seven sleepers. Don't be alarmed, sir, at my snoring. I go off like a steamboat bursting its boiler."

Tearing a couple of boards from the wall of the shanty, he laid them side by side in one corner, selected a blackened stone from the fire-place for a pillow, put his cap on it, stretched himself out with an inebriated smile, and was fast asleep before the Doctor had decided whether he would or would not read the letter. He was most anxious to establish innocence; if there was any guilt, he did not want to know it. He ran over all of Mrs. Larue's conduct since the marriage, and could not call to mind a single circumstance which had excited in him a suspicion of evil. She was coquettish, and, he feared, unprincipled; but he could not believe that she was desperately wicked. Nevertheless, as he did not understand the woman, as he erroneously supposed her to be of an ardent, impulsive nature, he thought it possible that she had been fascinated by the presence of such a masculine being as Carter. Of him as yet he had no suspicion: no, he could not have been false, even in thought, to his young wife; or, as Ravenel phrased it to himself, " to my daughter." He would read the letter and probe the ugly mystery and discover the falsity of its terrors. As he unfolded the paper he was checked by the thought that to peruse unbidden a lady's correspondence was hardly honorable. But there was a reply to that: the mischief of publicity had already commenced; the sleeping drunkard there had read the letter. After all, it might be a mere joke, a burlesque, an April-Fool affair; and if so, it was properly his business to discover it and to make the explanation to Van Zandt. And if, on the other hand, it should be really a confession of criminal feeling, it was his duty to be informed of that also, in order that he might be able to protect the domestic peace of his daughter.

He read the letter through, and then sat down on the door-sill, regardless of the driving rain. There was no charitable doubt possible in the matter; the writer was a guilty woman, and she addressed a guilty man. The letter alluded clearly and even grossly to past assignations, and fixed the day and hour for a future one. Carter's name did not appear except on the envelope; but his avocations and business hours were alluded to; the fact of their voyage together to New York was mentioned; there was no doubt that he was the man. The Doctor was more miserable than he remembered to have been before since the death of his wife. After half an hour of wretched meditation, walking meanwhile up and down the puddles which had collected on the earthen floor of the shanty, he became aware that the rain had ceased, and set out on his miserable walk homeward.

Should he destroy the letter ? Should he give it to Mrs. Larue and crush her ? Should he send it to Carter ? Should he show it to Lillie ? How could he answer any one of these horrible questions ? What right had Fate to put such questions to him ? It was not his crime.

On reaching home he changed his wet clothes, put the billet in his pocket-book, sat down to the dinner-table and tried to seem cheerful. But Lillie soon asked him, " What is the matter with you, papa ?"

" I got wet, my dear. It was a very hard walk back through the mud. I am quite worn out. I believe I shall go to bed early."

She repeated her question two or three times : not that she suspected the truth, or suspected anything more than just what he told her : but because she was anxious about his health, and because she had a habit of putting many questions. Even in the absorption of his inexplicable trouble she worried him, so that he grew fretful at her importunity, and answered her crisply, that he was well enough, and needed nothing but quiet. Then suddenly he repented himself with invisible tears, wondering at his irrational and seemingly cruel peevishness, and seeming to excuse himself to himself by calling to mind that he was tormented on her account. He almost had a return of his vexation when Lillie commenced upon him about her husband, asking, " Isn't it time to hear, papa ? And how soon do you think I will get a letter ?"

" Very soon, my dear," he replied gloomily, remembering the wicked letter in his pocket, and clenching his hands under the table to resist a sudden impulse to give it to her.

"I hope there will be no more battles.   Don't you think that the fighting is over?"

"Perhaps it may be best for him to have a battle."

"Oh no, papa! He has his promotion. I am perfectly satisfied. I don't want him to fight any more."

The father made no answer, for he could not tell her what he thought, which was that perhaps her husband had better die. It must be remembered that he did not know that the intrigue had terminated.

"Here comes the little Brigadier," said Lillie, when the baby made his usual after-dinner irruption into the parlor.

"Isn't he sweet?" she asked for the ten thousandth time, as she took him from the hands of the nurse and put him in her father's lap. The cooing, jumping, clinging infant clawing at watch-chain, neck-tie and spectacles, soft, helpless and harmless, gave the Doctor the first emotion similar to happiness which he had felt for the last three hours. How we fly for consolation to the dependent innocence of childhood when we have been grievously and lastingly wounded by the perfidy or cruelty of the adult creatures in whom we had put our trust! Stricken ones who have no children sometimes take up with dogs and cats, knowing that, if they are feeble, they are also faithful. But with the baby in his arms, Ravenel could not decide what to do with the baby's father; and so he handed the boy back to his mother, saying with more significance of manner than he intended, "There, my dear, there is your comfort."

"Papa, you are sick," replied Lillie, looking at him auxiously. "Do lie down on the sofa."

"I will go to my room and go to bed," said he. "It is eight o'clock; and it will do me no harm if I sleep twelve hours to-night. Now don't follow me, my child; don't tease me. I only want rest."

After kissing her and the child he hurried away, for he heard Mrs. Larue coming through the back hall toward the parlor, and as frequently happens, the innocent had not the audacity to face the guilty. In the passage he paused, glanced back through the crack of the door, and was amazed, almost infuriated, to see that woman kneel at Lillie's feet and fondle the baby with her usual air of girlish gayety.

"What infernal hypocrisy !" he muttered as he turned away, a little indignant at the giggling delight with which Ravvie welcomed the well-known visitor.   His charitable philosophy had all evaporated for the time, and he could not believe that this wicked creature had a spark of good in her, not even enough to smile upon a child honestly. To his mind the caresses which she lavished on Ravvie were part of a deep-laid plan of devilish deceit.

Four wretched hours passed over him, and at midnight he was still undecided what to do.   There were fathers in Louisiana who did not mind this sort of thing ; but he could not understand those fathers ; he minded it.   There were fathers who would simply say to an erring son-in-law over a glass of wine, "Now look here, my dear sir, you must be cautious about publicity ;" or who would quietly send Mrs. Larue her letter, with a note politely requesting that she would make arrangements which would not interfere with the quiet of, "Yours very respectfully," etc.   But such fathers could not love their daughters as he loved his, and could not have such a daughter as he had. To be false to Lillie was an almost unparalleled crime— a crime which demanded not only reproach but punishment ; a crime which, if passed over, would derange the moral balance of the universe.   It seemed to him that he must show Lillie the letter, and take her away from this unworthy husband, and carry her north or somewhither where she should never see him more.   This was what ought to be ; but then it might kill her. Late in the night, when he fell asleep on the outside of his bed, still dressed, his light still burning, the letter in his hand, he had not yet decided what to do.

About dawn, awakened early as usual by the creeping

of Ravvie, Lillie thought of her father, and slipping on a
dressing-gown, stole to his room to see if he were well or
ill. She was alarmed to find him dressed, and looking
pale and sunken. Before she had decided whether to let
him sleep on, or to awaken him and tell him to go to bed
as a sick man should, her eye fell upon the letter. It must
be that which had made him so gloomy and strange. What
could it be about? Had he lost his place at the hospital?
That need not trouble him, for her husband had left her
two thousand dollars in bank, and he would not object to
have her share it with her father. Her husband was so
generous and loving, that she could trust his affection for
any thing! She was accustomed to open and read her father's letters without asking his permission. She took up
this one, and glanced through it with delirious haste. The
Doctor was awakened by a shriek of agony, and found
Lillie senseless on the floor, with the open letter under her
hand.

Now he knew what to do; she must go far away at once
—she must never again see her husband.

CHAPTER XXXII.

A MOST LOGICAL CONCLUSION.

WHEN Lillie came to her senses she was lying on her
father's bed. For some minutes he had been bending over
her, watching her pulse, bathing her forehead, kissing her,
and calling her by name in a hoarse, frightened whisper.
He was aware that insensibility was her best friend; but
he must know at once whether she would live or die. At
first she lay quiet, silent, recollecting, trying not to believe; then she suddenly plunged her face into the pillow
with a groan of unspeakable anguish. It was not for five
or ten minutes longer, not until he had called her by every
imaginable epithet of pity and tenderness, that she turned

toward him with another spasmodic throe, clasped his head to her bosom, and burst into an impetuous sobbing and low crying. Still she did not speak an intelligible word; her teeth were set firm, as if in bodily pain, and her sobs came through her parted lips; she would not look at him either, and kept her eyes closed, or turned upward distractedly. It seemed as if, even in the midst of her anguish, she was stung by shame at the nature of the calamity, so insulting to her pride as a woman and wife. After a while this paroxysm ceased, and she lay silent again, while another icy wave of despair flowed over her, her consciousness being expressed solely in a trembling of her cheeks, her lips, and her fingers. When he whispered, "We will go north, we will never come back here," she made no sign of assent or objection. She did not answer him in any manner until he asked her if she wanted Ravvie; but then she leaped at the proffered consolation, the gift of Heaven's pity, with a passionate "Yes!" For an anxious half hour the Doctor left her alone with her child, knowing that it was the best he could do for her.

One thing he must attend to at once. Steps must be taken to prevent Mrs. Larue from crossing his daughter's sight even for a moment. See the woman himself he could not; not, at least, until she were dead. He enclosed her billet to her in a sealed envelope, adding the following note, which cost him many minutes to write—

"Madame: The accompanying letter has fallen into the hands of my daughter. She is dangerously ill. I hope that you will have the humanity not to meet her again."

When the housemaid returned from delivering the package he said to her, "Julia, did you give it to Mrs. Larue?"

"Yes sah."

"Did you give it into her own hands?"

"Yes sah. She was in bed, an' I gin it to herself."

"What—how did she look?" asked the Doctor after a moment's hesitation.

T 2

"She did'n look nohow. She jess lit a match an' burned the letter up."

The Doctor was aghast at the horrible, hard-hearted corruptness implied by such coolness and forethought. But in point of fact, Mrs. Larue had been startled far beyond her common wont, and was now more profoundly grieved than she had ever been before in her life.

"What a pity!" she said several times to herself. "I have made them very miserable. I have done mischief when I meant none. Why didn't the stupid creature burn the letter! I burned all his. What a pity! Well, at any rate it will go no farther."

She had her trunks packed and drove immediately after breakfast to Carrollton, where she remained secluded in the hotel until she found a private boarding house in the unfrequented outskirts of the village. If the Ravenels moved away, her man servant was to inform her, so that she might return to her house. She realized perfectly the inhumanity of encountering Lillie, and was resolved that no such meeting should take place, no matter what might be the expense of keeping up two establishments. In her pity and regret she was almost willing to sell her house at a loss, or shut it up without rent, and pinch herself in some northern city, supposing that the Ravenels concluded to stay in New Orleans. "I owe them that much," she thought, with a consciousness of being generous, and not bad-hearted. Then she sighed, and said aloud, "Poor Lillie! I am so sorry for her! But she has a baby, and for his sake she will forgive her husband."

And then a feeling came over her that she would like to see the baby, and that it would have been a pleasure to at least kiss it good-bye.

The family with which she lived consisted of a man of sixty and his wife, with two unmarried daughters of twenty-eight and thirty, the parents New Englanders, the children born in Louisiana, but all alike orthodox, devout, silent, after the old fashion of New England. The father was a cotton broker, nearly bankrupted by the Rebellion, and was glad for pecuniary reasons to receive a respectable boarder. Such a household Mrs. Larue had chosen as an asylum, believing that she would be benefited just now by an odor of sanctity, if it were only derived from propinquity. Something might get out; Lillie might go delirious and make disclosures; and it was well to build up a character for staidness. The idea of entering a convent she rejected the moment that it occurred to her. "This is monastic enough," she thought with a repressed smile as she looked at the serious faces of her Presbyterian hosts male and female.

The Allens became as much infatuated with her as did the Chaplain on board the Creole, or the venerable D. D. in New York city. Her modest and retiring manner, her amiability, cheerfulness, and sprightly conversation, made her the most charming person in their eyes that they had ever met. The daughters regained something of their blighted youthfulness under the sunny influences of her presence, aided by the wisdom of her counsel, and the cunning of her fingers in matters of the toilet. Mrs. Allen kissed her with motherly affection every time that she bade the family good-night. The old trick of showing a mind ripe for conversion from Popery was played with the usual success. After she had left the house, and when she was once more receiving and flirting in New Orleans, Mr. Allen used to excite her laughter by presenting her with tracts against Romanism, or lending her volumes of sermons by eminent Protestant divines. Not that she ever laughed at him to his face: she would as soon have thought of striking him with her fist; she was too good-natured and well-bred to commit either impertinence.

For the sake of appearances she remained in the country a week or more after the Ravenels had left the city. Restored to her own house, she found herself somewhat lonely for lack of her relatives, and somewhat gloomy, or at least annoyed, when she thought of the cause of the

separation. But there was no need of continuing solitude ; any quantity of army society could be had by such
New Orleans ladies as wished it ; and Mrs. Larue finally
resolved to break with treason, and flirt with loyalty in
gilt buttons. In a short time her parlor was frequented
by gentlemen who wore silver leaves and eagles and stars
on their shoulders, and the loss of Colonel Carter was more
than made up to her by the devotion of persons who were
mightier in counsel and in war than he. The very latest
news from her is of a highly satisfactory character. It is
reported that she was fortunate enough to gain the special
favor of an official personage very high in authority in
some unmentionable department of the South, who, as a
mark of his gratitude, gave her a permit to trade for several thousand bales of cotton. This curious billet-doux she
sold to a New York speculator for fifteen thousand dollars, thereby re-establishing her somewhat dilapidated fortunes.

Just as a person whose dwelling falls about his head is
sometimes preserved from death by some fragment of the
wreck which prostrates him, but preserves him from the
mass, so Lillie was shielded from the full pressure of her
misery by a short fever, bringing with it a few days of
delirium, and a long prostration, during which she had not
strength to feel acutely. When we must bend or break,
Nature often takes us in her own pitying hands, and lays
us gently upon beds of insensibility or semi-consciousness.
Thanks be to Heaven for the merciful opiate of sickness !

During the fever two letters arrived from Carter, but
Ravenel put them away without showing them to the invalid. For some time she did not inquire about her husband ; when she thought of him too keenly she asked with
a start for her baby. Nature continually led her to that
tender, helpless, speechless, potent consoler. The moment
it was safe for her to travel, Ravenel put her on board a
vessel bound to New York, choosing a sailing craft, not
only for economy's sake, but to secure the benefit of a

lengthy voyage, and to keep longer away from all news of earth and men. She made no objection to going; her father wished it to be so; it was right enough. The voyage lasted three weeks, during which she slowly regained strength, and as a consequence something of her old cheerfulness and hopefulness. The Doctor had a strong faith that she would not be broken down by her calamity. Not only was her temper gay and remarkable for its elasticity, but her physical constitution seemed to partake of the same characteristics, and she had always recovered from sickness with rapidity. Not a bit disposed to brooding, taking a lively interest in whatever went on around her, she would not fall an easy prey to confirmed melancholy. The Doctor never alluded to her husband, and when Lillie at last mentioned his name, it was merely to say, " I hope he will not be killed."

" I hope not," replied Ravenel gently, and stopped there. He could not, however, repress a brief glance of surprise and investigation. Could it be that she would come to forgive that man? Had he been too hasty in dragging her away from New Orleans, and giving up the moderate salary which was so necessary to them both? But no : it would kill her to meet Mrs. Larue : they must never go back to that Sodom of a city.

The question of income was a serious one. He was nearly at the end of his own resources, and he had not suffered Lillie to draw any of her perfidious husband's money. But he did not dwell much on these pecuniary questions now, being chiefly occupied with the moral future of his child, wondering much whether she would indeed forgive her husband, and whether she would ever again be happy. Of course it was not until they reached New York that they learned the events which I must now relate.

Carter joined the army at Grande Ecore just before it resumed field operations. Bailey's famous dam had let Porter out of his trap; the monitors, the gunboats, the Ad-

miral, were on their way down the river; it was too late
to go to Shreveport, or to gather cotton; and so the column
set out rearward. That it was strong enough to take care
of itself against any force which the rebels could bring to
cut off the retreat was well known; and Carter assumed
command of his new brigade with a sense of elation at the
prospect of fighting, which he had little reason to doubt
would be successful. By the last gunboat of the depart-
ing fleet he sent his wife a letter, full of gay anticipations,
and expressions of affection, which she was destined never
to answer. By the last transport which came to Grande
Ecore arrived a letter from Ravenel, which, owing to the
hastiness of the march, did not reach him until the evening
before the battle of Cane River. In the glare of a camp-
fire he read of the destruction which he had wrought in
the peace of his own family. Ravenel spoke briefly and
without reproaches of the discovery; stated that he believed it to be his duty to remove his child from the scene
of such a domestic calamity; that he should therefore take
her to the north as soon as she was able to travel.

"I beg that you will not force yourself upon her," he
concluded. " Hitherto she has not mentioned your name
to me, and I do not know what may be her feelings with
regard to you. Some time she may pardon you, if it is
your desire to be pardoned. I cannot say. At present I
know of nothing better than to take her away, and to ask
your forbearance, in the name of her sickness and suffering."

This letter was a cruel blow to Carter. If the staff
officers who sat with him around the camp-fire could have
known how deeply and for what a purely domestic reason
the seemingly stern and hard General was suffering, they
would have been very much amazed. He was popularly
supposed to be a man of the world, with bad morals and
a calloused heart, which could neither feel much anguish
of its own nor sympathise keenly with the anguish of other
hearts. But the General was indeed so wretched that he
could not talk with them, and could not even sit among

them in silence. He went on one side and walked for an hour up and down in the darkness. He tried to clear up the whole thing in his mind, and decide distinctly what was the worst that had happened, and what was the best that could be done But his perceptions were very tumultuous and incoherent, as is usually the case with a man when first overtaken by a great calamity. It was a horrible affair; it was a cursed, infernal affair; and that was about all that he could say to himself. He was intolerably ashamed, as well as grieved and angry. He thought very little about Mrs. Larue, good or bad; he was not mean enough to curse her, although she had been more to blame than he; only he did wish that he never had seen her, and did curse the day which brought them together on the Creole. The main thing, after all, was that he had ill-treated his wife, and it did not matter who had been his accomplice in the wicked business. He set his teeth into his lips, and felt his eyes grow moist, as he thought of her, sick and suffering because she loved him, and he had not been worthy of her love. Would she ever forgive him, and take him back to her heart? He did not know. He would try to win her back; he would fight desperately, and distinguish himself; he would offer her the best impulses and bravest deeds of manhood. Perhaps if he should earn a Major-General's star and high fame in the nation, and then should go to her feet, she would receive him. A transitory thrill of pleasure shot through him as he thought of reconciliation and renewed love.

At last the General was recalled to the fire to read orders which concerned the movements of the morrow, and to transmit them to the regiments of his own command. Then he had to receive two old friends, regular officers of the artillery, who called to congratulate him on his promotion. Whiskey was produced for the visitors, and Carter himself drank freely to drown trouble. When they went away, about midnight, he found himself wearied out, and very soon dropped asleep, for he was a soldier and could slumber under all circumstances.

At Grande Ecore the Red River throws off a bayou which rejoins it below, the two currents enclosing an island some forty miles in length. This bayou, now called the Cane River, was once the original stream, and in memory of its ancient grandeur flows between high banks altogether out of proportion to its modest current. Over the dead level of the island the army had moved without being opposed, or harassed, for the rebels had reserved their strength to crush it when it should be entangled in the crossing of the Cane River. Taylor with his Arkansas and Louisiana infantry had followed the march closely but warily, always within striking distance but avoiding actual conflict, and now lay in line of battle only a few miles in rear of Andrew Jackson Smith's western boys. Polignac with his wild Texan cavalry had made a great circuit, and already held the bluffs on the southern side of the Cane River confronting Emory's two divisions of the Nineteenth Corps. The main plan of the battle was simple and inevitable. Andrew Jackson Smith must beat off the attack of Taylor, and Emory must abolish the obstacle of Polignac.

The veteran and wary commander of the Nineteenth Corps had already decided how he would go over his ground, should he find it occupied by the enemy. He had before him a wood of considerable extent, then an open plain eight hundred yards across, and then a valley in the nature of a ravine, at the bottom of which flowed a river, not fordable here, and with no crossing but a ferry. A single narrow road led down through a deep cut to the edge of the rapid, muddy stream, and, starting again from the other edge, rose through a similar gorge until it disappeared from sight behind the brows of high bluffs crowned with pines. Under the pines and along the rim of the bluffs lay the line of Polignac. There had been no time to reconnoitre his dispositions; indeed, his presence in strong force was not yet positively known to the leaders of the Union army; but if there, his horses had no doubt been sent to the rear, and his men formed to fight as infantry. And if this were so, if an army of several thousand Texan riflemen occupied this strong position, how should it be carried? Emory had already decided that it would never do to butt at it in front, and that it could only be taken by a turning movement. Thus this part of the battle had a plan of its own.

Such was the military situation upon which our new Brigadier opened his heavy eyes at half-past three o'clock on the morning after getting that woeful letter about his wife. The army was to commence its march at half-past four, and Carter was aroused by the bustle of preparation from the vast bivouac. Thousands of men were engaged in rolling their blankets, putting on their equipments, wiping the dew from their rifles, and eating their hasty and unsavory breakfasts of hard-tack. Companies were falling in; the voices of the first-sergeants were heard calling the rolls; long-drawn orders resounded, indicating the formation of regimental lines; the whinnies of horses, the braying of mules, and the barking of dogs joined in the clamor; but as yet there was no trampling of the march, no rolling of the wheels of artillery. Nothing could be seen of this populous commotion except here and there where a forbidden cooking-fire cast its red flicker over little knots of crouching soldiers engaged in preparing coffee.

In the moment of coming to his senses, and before memory had fully resumed its action, the General was vaguely conscious that something horrible was about to happen, or had already happened. But an old soldier is not long in waking up, especially when he has gone to sleep in the expectation of a battle, and Carter knew almost instantaneously what was the nature of the burden that weighed upon his soul. He lay full dressed at the foot of a tree, with no shelter but its branches. He was quite still for a minute or more, staring at the dark sky with steady, gloomy eyes. His first act was to put his hand to the breast pocket of his blouse and draw out that cruel letter, as if to read it anew by the flicker of a fire which reached his resting place. But there was no need of that : he knew all that was in it as soon as he looked at the envelope ; he remembered at once even the blots and the position of the signature. Next the sight of it angered him, and he thrust it back crumpled into his pocket. There was no need, he felt, of making so much of the affair ; such affairs were altogether too common to be made so much of ; he could not and would not see any sense in the Doctor's conduct. He sprang to his feet in his newly-found indignation, and glared fiercely around the bivouac of his brigade.

"How's this ?" he growled. "I ordered that not a fire should be lighted. Mr. Van Zandt, did you pass the order to every regiment last evening ?"

"I did, sir," answers our old acquaintance, now a staff officer, thanks to his Dutch courage, and his ability with the pen.

"Ride off again. Stop those fires instantly. My God! the fools want to tell the enemy just when we start."

This outburst raised his spirits, and after swallowing a cocktail he sat down to breakfast with some appetite. The toughness of the cold boiled chicken, and the dryness and hardness of the army biscuit served as a further distraction, and enabled him to utter a joke about such delicacies being very suitable for projectiles. But he was still nervous, uneasy, eager, driven by the sin which was past, and dragged by the battle which was before, so that any long reveling at the banquet was impossible. He quitted the empty cracker box which served him for a table, and paced grimly up and down until his orderly came to buckle on his sword, and his servant brought him his horse.

"How are the saddle-pockets, Cato ?" he asked.

"Oh, day's chuck full, Gen'l. Hull cold chicken in dis yere one, an' bottle o' whisky in dis yere."

Carter swung himself slowly and heavily into his saddle. He was weary, languid and feverish with want of sleep, and trouble of mind. In truth he was physically 'and morally a much discomforted Brigadier General. Without waiting for other directions than his example, his five staff officers mounted also and fell into a group behind him. In their rear was the brigade flag-bearer escorted by half-a-dozen cavalry-men. The sombre dawn was turning to red and gold in the east. A monstrous serpent of blue and steel was already creeping toward the ferry, increasing in length as additional regiments streamed into the road from the fields which had served for the bivouac. When Carter had seen his entire brigade file by, he set off at a canter, placed himself at the head of it, and rode on at a walk, silent and gloomy of countenance. Not even the thought that he was now a general, and had a chance to make a reputation for himself as well as for others, could enable him to quite throw off the seriousness and anxiety which beclouds the minds of men during the preliminaries of battle. The remembrance of the misery which he had wrought for his wife was no pleasant distraction. It was like a foreboding ; it overshadowed him even when he was not thinking of it distinctly ; it seemed to have a menacing arm which pointed him to punishment, calamity, perhaps a grave. He was like a haunted man who sees his following phantom if he turns his head ever so little. Nevertheless, when he squarely faced the subject, and dragged it out separately from the general sombreness of the situation, it did not seem such a very hopeless misfortune. It surely was not possible that she had broken with him for life. He would win her back to him ; it must be that she loved him enough to forgive him some day ; he would win her back with repentance and victories. As he thought this he dashed a little way into the fields, gave a glance at the line of his brigade, and dispatched a couple of his staff to close up the rearmost files of his regiments.

Presently there was a halt : something probably going

on in front : perhaps a reconnoisance : perhaps battle. The
men were allowed to stack arms and sit down by the roadside. Then came news : Enemy in force at the crossing : a
direct attack in front out of the question : turning movements to be made somewhere by somebody. It was a full
hour after sunrise when an aid of General Emory's arrived
with orders for General Carter to report for duty to General Birge.

"What is the situation?" asked the General.

"Two brigades are forming in front," replied the aid.
"We have an immense line of skirmishers stretching from
the Cane River on the right all along the edge of the
woods, and out into the fields. But we can't go at them
in front. Their ground is nearly a hundred feet higher
than ours, and the crossing isn't fordable. We have got
to flank them. Closson is going up with some artillery to
establish a position on our left, and from that the cavalry
will turn the right wing of the enemy. Birge is to do the
same thing on this side with three brigades. He will go
up about a mile—three miles from the ferry—ford the
river—it's fordable up there—come round on the fellows,
and give it to them over the left."

"Very good," said Carter. "If I shouldn't come back,
give the General my compliments for his plan. Much
obliged, Lieutenant."

At this moment the flat, dull report of a rifled iron gun
came from the woods far away in front, followed a few
seconds afterward by another report, still flatter in sound
and much more distant, the bursting of a shell.

"There goes Closson," laughed the young officer. "Two
twenty-pound Parrotts and four three-inch rifles ! He'll
wake 'em up when he gets fairly a-talking. Good luck to
you, General."

And away he rode gaily, at a gallop, in the direction of
the ferry.

While Birge's column countermarched, and Carter's
brigade filed into the rear of it, the cannonade became

lively in the front, the crashes of the guns alternating rapidly with the crashes of the shells, as Closson went in with all his six pieces, and a Rebel battery of seven responded. After half an hour of this the enemy found that a range of two thousand yards was too long for them, and became silent. Then Closson ceased firing also, and waited to hear from Birge. And now for five or six hours there was no more sound of fighting along this line, except an occasional shot from the skirmishers aimed at puffs of rifle smoke which showed rarely against the pines of the distant bluffs. The infantry column struggled over its long detour by the right; the cavalry tried in vain to force a way through the jungles on the left; the centre listened to the roar of A. J. Smith's battle in the rear, and lunched and waited. At two o'clock Emory put everything in order to advance whenever Birge's musketry should give notice that he was closely engaged. Closson was to move forward on the left, and fire as fast as he could load. The remainder of the artillery was to gallop down the river road to the ferry, and open with a dozen or fifteen pieces. The two supporting brigades were to push through the woods as rapidly as possible and cover the artillery. The skirmishers were to cross the river wherever they could ford it, and keep up a heavy fire in order to occupy the attention of the enemy. Closson started at once, forced five of his three-inch rifles through the wood, went into battle at a range of a thousand yards, and in ten minutes dislodged the Rebel guns from their position. But all this was mere feinting; the heavy fighting must be done by Birge.

The flanking column had a hard road to travel. After fording the Cane River it entered a country of thickets, swamps and gullies so difficult of passage that five hours were spent in marching barely five miles. Two regiments were deployed in advance as skirmishers; the others followed in columns of division doubled on the centre. At one time the whole force went into line of battle on a false alarm of the near presence of the enemy. Then the nature

of the ground forced it to move for nearly a mile in the
ordinary column of march. It floundered through swampy
undergrowths; it forded a deep and muddy bayou. About
two o'clock in the afternoon it came out upon a clearing
in full view of a bluff, forty or fifty feet in height, flanked
on one side by the river, and on the other by a marshy
jungle connecting with a lake. Along the brow of this
bluff lay Polignac's left wing, an unknown force of Texan
riflemen, all good shots, and impetuous fighters, elated
moreover with pursuit and the expectation of victory.
Here Carter received an order to charge with his brigade.

"Very good," he answered, in a loud, satisfied, confident tone, at the same time throwing away his segar.
"Let me look at things first. I want to see where to go
in."

A single glance told him that the river side was unas-
sailable. He galloped to the right, inspected the boggy
jungle, glared at the lake beyond, and decided that nothing could be done in that quarter. Returning to the brigade he once more surveyed the ground in its front. It
would be necessary to take down a high fence, cross an
open field, take down a second fence, and advance up the
hill under a close fire of musketry. But he was not dis-
pirited by the prospect; he was no longer the silent,
sombre man of the morning. The whizzing of the Texan
bullets, the sight of the butternut uniforms, and ugly
broadbrims which faced him, had cleared his deep breast
of oppression, and called the fighting fire into his eyes.
He swore loudly and gaily; he would flog those dirty
rapscallions; he would knock them high and dry into the
other world; he would teach them not to get in his way.

"Go to the regimental commanders," he shouted to
his staff officers. "Tell them to push straight at the hill.
Tell them, Guide right."

On went the regiments, four in number, keeping even
pace with each other. There was a halt at the first fence
while the men struggled with the obstacle, climbing it in

some places, and pushing it over in others. The General's brow darkened with anxiety lest the temporary confusion should end in a retreat; and spurring close up to the line he rode hither and thither, cheering the soldiers onward.

"Forward, my fine lads," he said. "Down with it. Jump it. Now then. Get into your ranks. Get along, my lads."

On went the regiments, moving at the ordinary quick-step, arms at a right-shoulder-shift, ranks closed, gaps filled, unfaltering, heroic. The dead were falling; the wounded were crawling in numbers to the rear; the leisurely hum of long-range bullets had changed into the sharp, multitudinous *whit-whit* of close firing; the stifled crash of balls hitting bones, and the soft *chuck* of flesh-wounds mingled with the outcries of the sufferers; the bluff in front was smoking, rattling, wailing with the incessant file-fire; but the front of the brigade remained unbroken, and its rear showed no stragglers. The right hand regiment floundered in a swamp, but the other hurried on without waiting for it. As the momentum of the movement increased, as the spirits of the men rose with the charge, a stern shout broke forth, something between a hurrah and a yell, swelling up against the rebel musketry, and defying it. Gradually the pace increased to a double-quick, and the whole mass ran for an eighth of a mile through the whistling bullets. The second fence disappeared like frost-work, and up the slope of the hill struggled the panting regiments. When the foremost ranks had nearly reached the summit, a sudden silence stifled the musketry. Polignac's line wavered, ceased firing, broke and went to the rear in confusion. The clamor of the charging yell redoubled for a moment, and then died in the rear of a tremendous volley. Now the Union line was firing, and now the rebels were falling. Such was the charge which carried the crossing, and gained the battle of Cane River.

But Brigadier-General John Carter had already fallen gloriously in the arms of victory.

At the moment that the fatal shot struck him he had forgotten his guilt and remorse in the wild joy of successful battle. He was on horseback, closely following his advancing brigade, and watching its spirited push, and listening to its mad yell, with such a smile of soldierly delight and pride that it was a pleasure to look upon his bronzed, confident, heroic face. It would have been strange to a civilian to hear the stream of joyful curses with which he expressed his admiration and elation.

"God damn them! see them go in!" he said. "God damn their souls! I can put them anywhere!"

He had just uttered these words when a Minie-ball struck him in the left side, just below the ribs, with a *thud* which was audible ten feet from him in spite of the noise of the battle. He started violently in the saddle, and then bent slowly forward, laying his right hand on the horse's mane. He was observed to carry his left hand twice toward the wound without touching it, as if desirous, yet fearful, of ascertaining the extent of the injury. The blow was mortal, and he must have known it, yet he retained his ruddy bronze color for a minute or two. With the assistance of two staff officers he dismounted and walked eight or ten yards to the shade of a tree, uttering not a groan, and only showing his agony by the manner in which he bent forward, and the spasmodic clutch with which he held to those supporting shoulders. But when he had been laid down, it was visible enough that there was not half an hour's life in him. His breath was short, his forehead was thickly beaded with a cold perspiration, and his face was of an ashy pallor stained with streaks of ghastly yellow.

"Tell Colonel Gilliman," he said, mentioning the senior colonel of the brigade, and then paused to catch his breath before he resumed, "tell him to keep straight forward."

These were the first words that he had spoken since he

was hit. His voice had already sunk from a clear, sonorous bass to a hoarse whisper. Presently, as the smoking and roaring surge of battle rolled farther to the front a chaplain and a surgeon came up, followed by several ambulance men bearing stretchers. The chaplain was attached to Carter's old regiment, and had served under him since its formation. The surgeon, a Creole by birth, a Frenchman by education, philosophical and roué, belonged to a Louisiana loyal regiment, and had known the General in other days, when he was a dissipated, spendthrift lieutenant of the regular army, stationed at Baton Rouge. He gave him a large cup of whiskey, uncovered the wound, probed it with his finger, and said nothing, looked nothing.

"Why don't you do something?" whispered the chaplain eagerly, and almost weeping.

"I have done all that is—essential," he replied, with a slight shrug of the shoulders.

"How do you feel, General?" asked the chaplain, turning to his dying commander.

"Going," was the whispered answer.

"Going!—Oh, going where?" implored the other, sinking on his knees. "General, have you thought of the sacrifice of Jesus Christ?"

For a moment Carter's deep voice returned to him, as, fixing his stern eyes on the chaplain, he answered, "Don't bother!—where is the brigade?"

Perhaps he thought it unworthy of him to seek God in his extremity, when he had neglected Him in all his hours of health. Perhaps he felt that he owed his last thoughts to his country and his professional duties. Perhaps he did not mean all that he said.

It was strange to note the power of military discipline upon the chaplain. Even in this awful hour, when it was his part to fear no man, he evidently quailed before his superior officer. Under the pressure of a three years' habit of obedience and respect, cowed by rank and that audacious will accustomed to domination, he shrank back

U

into silence, covering his face with his hands, and no doubt praying, but uttering no further word.

"General, the brigade has carried the position," said one of the staff-officers..

Carter smiled, tried to raise his head, dropped it slowly, drew a dozen labored breaths, and was dead.

"*Il a maintena jusq' au bout son personnage,*" said the surgeon, letting fall the extinct pulse. "*Sa mort est tout ce qu' il y a de plus logique.*"

So he thought, and very naturally. He had only known him in his evil hours; he judged him as all superficial acquaintances would have judged; he was not aware of the tenderness which existed at the bottom of that passionate nature. With another education Carter might have been a James Brainard or a St. Vincent de Paul. With the training that he had, it was perfectly logical that in his last moments he should not want to be bothered about Jesus Christ.

The body was borne on a stretcher in rear of the victorious columns until they halted for the night, when it was buried in the private cemetery of a planter, in presence of Carter's former regiment. Among the spectators was Colburne, stricken with real grief as he thought of the bereaved wife. Throughout the army the regret was general and earnest over the loss of this brave and able officer, apparently just entering upon a career of long-deserved promotion. In a letter to Ravenel, Colburne related the particulars of Carter's death, and closed with a fervent eulogium on his character as a man and his services as a soldier, forgetting that he had sometimes drunk too deeply, and that there were suspicions against him of other vices. It is thus that young and generous spirits are apt to remember the dead, and it is thus always that a soldier laments for a worthy commander who has fallen on the field of honor.

CHAPTER XXXIII.

LILLIE DEVOTES HERSELF ENTIRELY TO THE RISING GENERATION.

LILLIE wished to return, at least for a while, to her old quarters in the New Boston House. A desire to go back by association to some part of her life which had been happy may have influenced her in this choice; and she was so quietly earnest in it that her father yielded, although he feared that the recollections connected with the place would increase her melancholy. They had been there only three days when he read with a shock the newspaper report of the battle of Cane River, and the death of "the lamented General Carter." He did not dare mention it to her, and sought to keep the journals out of her reach. This was easy enough, for she never went out alone, rarely spoke to any one but her father, and devoted her time mostly to her child and her sewing. But about a week after their arrival, as the Doctor came in to dinner from a morning's reading in the college library, he found her weeping quietly over a letter which lay open in her lap. She handed it to him, merely saying, "Oh, papa!"

He glanced through it hastily; it was Colburne's account of Carter's death.

"I knew this, my dear," he said. "But I did not dare to tell you. I hope you are able to bear it. There is a great deal to bear in this world. But it is for our good."

"Oh, I don't know," she replied with a weary air. She was thinking, not of his general consolations, but of his hope that she could endure her trial; for a trial it was, this sudden death of her husband, though she had thought of him of late only as separated from her forever. After a short silence she sobbed, "I am so sorry I quarreled with him. I wish I had written to him that I was not angry."

She went on crying, but not passionately, nor with a show of unendurable sorrow. From that time, as he watched the patient tranquillity of her grief, the Doctor conceived a firm hope that she would not be permanently crushed by her afflictions. She kept the letter in her own writing desk, and read it many times when alone; sometimes laying it down with a start to take up the unconscious giggling comforter in the cradle; sometimes telling him what it all meant, and what her tears meant, saying, "Poor baby! Baby's papa is dead."

Only once did an expression savoring of anger at any one force its way through her lips.

"I don't see why I should have been made miserable because others are wicked," she said.

"It is one of the necessary consequences of living," answered the Doctor. "Other people's sins are sometimes brought to our doors, just as other people's infants are sometimes left there in baskets. God has ordained that we shall help bear the burdens of our fellow creatures, even down to the consequences of their crimes. It is one way of teaching us not to sin. I have had my small share of this unpleasant labor. I lost my home and my income because a few men wanted to found a slave-driving oligarchy on the ruins of their country."

"We have had nothing but trials," sighed Lillie.

"Oh yes," said the Doctor. "Life in the average is a mass of happiness, only dotted here and there by trials. Our pleasures are so many that they grow monotonous and are overlooked."

I must now include the history of eight months in a few pages. The Doctor, ignorant of the steamboat transaction, allowed his daughter to draw the money which she had left behind on deposit, considering that Carter's child unquestionably had a right to it. Through the good offices of that amiable sinner, Mrs. Larue (of which he was equally unaware), he was enabled to let his house in New Orleans as a Government office. Thus provided with ready money and a small quarterly payment, he resumed his literary and scientific labors, translating from a French Encyclopedia for a New York publisher, and occasionally securing a job of mineralogical discovery. The familiar life of former days, when father and daughter were all and all to each other, slowly revived, saddened by recollections, but made joyful also by the new affection which they shared. As out of the brazen vase of the Arabian Nights arose the malignant Jinn whose head touched the clouds, and whose voice made the earth tremble, so out of the cradle of Ravvie arose an influence, perhaps a veritable angel, whose crown was in the heavens, and whose power brought down consolation. There was no cause of inner estrangement; nothing on which father and child could not feel alike. Ravenel had found some difficulty in liking his daughter's husband, but he had none at all in loving his daughter's baby. So, agreeing on all subjects of much importance to either, and disposed by affection and old habit to take a strong interest in each other's affairs, they easily returned to their former ways of much domestic small-talk. Happily for Lillie she was not taciturn, but a prattler, and by nature a light-hearted one. Now prattlers, like workers of all kinds, physical and moral, unconsciously dodge by their activity a great many shafts of suffering which hit their quieter brothers and sisters. A widow who orders her mourning, and waits for it with folded hand and closed lips, is likely to be more melancholy than a widow who must trim her gowns, and make up her caps with her own fingers, and who is thereby impelled to talk of them to her mother, sisters, and other born sympathisers. It was a symptom of returning health of mind when Lillie could linger before the glass, arrange her hair with the old taste, put on a new cap daintily and say, "Papa, how does that look?"

"Very well, my dear," answers papa, scratching away

at his translation.   Then, remembering what his child had suffered, and transferring his thoughts to the subject which she proffers for consideration, he adds, "It seems to me that it is unnecessarily stiff and parchment like.   It looks as if it was made of stearine."

"Why, that's the material," says Lillie.   "Of course it looks stiff; it ought to."

"But why not have some other material?" queries the Doctor, who is as dull as men usually are in matters of the female toilet.   "Why not use white silk, or something?"

"Silk, papa!" exclaims Lillie, and laughs heartily. "Who ever heard of using silk for mourning?"

Woe to women when they give up making their own dresses and take to female tailors!   Five will then die of broken hearts, of ennui, of emptiness of life, where one dies now.

But her great diverter and comforter was still her child. Like most women she was born for maternity more distinctly and positively even than for love.   She had not given up her dolls until she was fourteen; and then she had put them reverentially and tenderly away in a trunk where she could occasionally go and look at them; and less than seven years later she had a living doll, her own, her soul's doll, to care for and worship.   It was charming to see this slender, Diana-like form, overloaded and leaning, but still bearing, with an affection which was careless of fatigue, the disproportionate weight of that healthy, succulent, ponderous Ravvie.   His pink face, and short flaxen hair bobbed about her shoulders, and his chubby hands played with her nose, lips, hair, and white collars.   When he went out on an airing she almost always went with him, and sometimes took the sole charge of his wicker wagon, proud to drag it because of its illustrious burden. Ravvie had a promenade in the morning with mamma and nurse, and another late in the afternoon with mamma and grandpapa.   Lillie meant to make him healthy by keeping him constantly in the open air, and burning him brown in the sunshine, after the sensible fashion of southern nurseries, and in consonance with the teaching of her father. The old Irish nurse, a veteran and enthusiast in her profession, had more than one contest with this provokingly devoted mother. Not that Rosánn objected to the child being out; she would have been glad to have him in the wicker wagon from breakfast to dinner, and from dinner to sundown; but she wanted to be the sole guide and companion of his wanderings. When, therefore she was ordered to stay at home and do the small washing and ironing, while the mistress went off with the baby, she set up an indignant·ullaloo, and threatened departure without warning. Sometimes Lillie was satirical and said, " Rosann, since you can't nurse the baby, I hope you will allow me to do so."

To which Rosann, with Irish readiness, and with an apologetic titter, would reply, " An' since God allows ye to do it, ma'am, I don't see as I can make an objection."

" I would turn her away if she wasn't so fond of Ravvie," affirmed Lillie in a pet. " She is the most selfish creature that I ever saw. She wants him the whole time. I declare, papa, I only keep her out of pity. I believe it would break her heart to deprive her of the child."

" It's a very odd sort of selfishness," observed the Doctor. " Most people would call it devotion, self-abnegation, or something of that sort."

" But he isn't her child," answered Lillie, half vexed, half smiling. " She thinks he is. I actually believe she thinks that she had him. But she didn't. I did."

She tossed her head with a pretty air of defiance, which was as much as to say that she was not ashamed of the feat.

Long before Master Ravvie could say a word in any language, she had commenced the practice of talking to him only in French. He should be a linguist from his cradle; and she herself would be his teacher. When he got old enough her father should instruct him in the sciences, and, if he chose to be a doctor, in the theory and practice of medicine. They would never send him to school, nor to college: thus they would save money, have him always by them and keep him from evil. Concerning this project she had long arguments with her father, who thought a boy should be with boys, learn to rough it away from home, study human nature as well as languages and sciences, and grow up with a circle of emulators and life comrades.

"You will give up this little plan of yours," he said, "when he gets old enough to make it necessary. When he is fifteen he won't wear the shell that fits him now, and meantime we must let another one grow on his back against he needs it."

But Lillie could not yet see that her child ought even to be separated from her. She was constantly arranging, and re-arranging her imaginary future in such ways as seemed best fitted to make him a permanent feature of it. In every cloud-castle that she built he occupied a central throne, with her father sitting on the right hand and she on the left. Of course, however, she was chiefly occupied with his present, desiring to make it as delightful to him as possible.

"I wonder if Ravvie would like the sea-shore," she said, on one of the first warm days of summer.

"Why so?" asks papa.

"Oh, it would be so pleasant to spend a week or so on the sea-shore. I think I could get a little fatter and stronger if I might have the sea-breeze and sea-bathing. I am tired of being so thin. Besides, it would be such fun to take Ravvie down to the beach and see him stare at the waves rolling in. How round his eyes would be! Do you remember how he used to turn his head up when he was a month old, and stare at the sky with his eyes set like a doll-baby's. I wish I knew what he used to think of it."

"I presume he thought just about as much as the holly-hocks do when they turn their faces toward the sun," says the Doctor.

"For shame, papa! Do you compare him to a vege-table?"

"Not now. But in those days he was only a grade above one. There wasn't much in him but possibilities. Well; he may have perceived that the sky was very fine; but then the hollyhocks perceive as much."

"What! don't you suppose he had a soul?"

"Oh yes. He had a tongue too, but he hadn't learned to talk with it. I doubt whether his soul was of much use to him in that stage of his existence."

"Papa, it seems to me that you talk like an infidel. Now if Ravvie had died when he was a month old, I should have expected to meet him in Heaven—that is, if I am ever fit to go there."

"I have no doubt you would—no doubt of it," affirmed the Doctor with animation. "I never intended to dispute the little man's immortality."

"Then why did you call him a hollyhock?"

"My dear, I take it all back. He isn't a hollyhock and never was."

"If we can hire a house I want it in the suburbs," said Lillie, after a meditation. "I want it outside the city so that Ravvie can have plenty of air. His room must be on the sunny side, papa—hear?"

"Yes," answered papa, who had also had his revery, probably concerning Smithites and Brownites.

"You don't hear at all," said Lillie. "You don't pay any attention."

"Well, my child, there is plenty of time. We sha'n't have a house for the next five minutes."

"I know it. Not for five years perhaps. But I want you to pay attention when I am talking about Ravvie."

Meantime the two were very popular in New Boston. As southern refugees, as martyrs in the cause of loyalty,

as an organizer of free black labor, as the widow of a
distinguished Union officer, both and each were personages whom the fervent Federalists of the little city delighted to honor. As soon as they would receive calls or
accept of new acquaintances they had all that they wanted.
Professor Whitewood had been killed at Chancellorsville,
although bodily more than three hundred miles from
the field of battle; and his son was now worth eighty
thousand dollars, besides seven hundred dollars yearly
from a tutorship, and the prospect of succeeding to his
father's position. This well-to-do, virtuous, amiable, and
intelligent young gentleman was more than suspected of
being in love with the penniless widow. His sister made
the affair a subject of much meditation, and even of prayer,
being anxious above all things on earth, that her brother
should be happy. Whitewood was more than once observed to drop his Hindustani, sidle out upon the green
and beg the privilege of drawing Ravvie's baby-wagon;
and what was particularly suspicious about the matter
was, that he never attempted to join Rosann in this manner, but only Mrs. Carter. Lillie colored at the significance of the shyly-preferred request, and would not consent to it, but nevertheless was not angry. Her bookish
admirer's interest in her increased when he found that she
aided her father in his translations; for from his childhood
he had been taught to like people very much in proportion to their intellectuality and education. Of evenings
he was frequently to be seen in the little parlor of the
Ravenels on the fourth floor of the New Boston House.
Lillie would have been glad to have him bring his sister,
so that they four could make up a game of whist; but since
the dawn of history no Whitewoods had ever handled a
pack of cards, and the capacity of learning to do so was
not in them. Moreover they still retained some of the old
New England scruples of conscience on the subject.
Whitewood talked quite as much with the Doctor as with
Lillie; quite as much about minerals and chemistry as

about subjects with which she was familiar; but it was easy to see that, if he had known how, he would have made his conversation altogether feminine. At precisely ten o'clock he rose with a start and sidled to the door; stuck there a few moments to add a postcript concerning science or classic literature; then with another start opened the door, and said, " Good evening " after he was in the passage.

" How awkward he is !" Lillie would sometimes observe.

" Yes—physically," was the Doctor's answer. " But not morally. I don't see that he tramples on any one's feelings, or breaks any one's heart."

The visitor gone, father and daughter walked in the hall while Rosann opened the windows for ventilation. After that the baby's cradle was dragged into the parlor with much ceremony, the whole family either directing or assisting; a mattress and blankets were produced from a closet and made up on the floor into a bed for the nurse; grandpapa kissed both his children and went to his own room next door; and Lillie proceeded to undress, talking to Rosann about Ravvie.

" An' do ye know, ma'am, what the little crater did to me to-day ?" says the doting Irishwoman. " He jist pulled me spectacles off me nose an' stuck 'em in his own little mouth. He thought, mebbe, he could see with his mouth. An' thin he lucked me full in the face as cunnin as could be, an' give the biggest jump that iver was. I tell ye, ma'am, babies is smarter now than they used to be."

This remarkable anecdote, with the nurse's commentary, being repeated to the Doctor in the morning, he philoso- phised as follows.

" There may be something in Rosann's statement. It is not impossible that the babies of a civilized age are more exquisitely sensitive beings than the babies of antique barbarism. It may be that at my birth I was a little ahead of my Gallic ancestor at his birth. Perhaps I was able to compare two sensations as early in life as he was able to perceive a single sensation. It might be something like this. He at the age of ten days would be capable of thinking, ' Milk is good.' I at the same age could perhaps go so far as to think, 'Milk is better than Dally's Mixture.' Babies now-a-days have need of being cleverer than they used to be. They have more dangers to evade, more medicines to spit out."

"I know what you mean," said Lillie. "You always did rebel against Dally. But what was I to do? He *would* have the colic."

"I know it! He would! But Dally couldn't help it. Don't, for pity's sake, vitiate and torment your poor little angel's stomach, so new to the atrocities of this world, with drugs. These mixers of baby medicines ought to be fed on nothing but their own nostrums. That would soon put a stop to their inventions of the adversary."

"Oh dear," sighed Lillie. "I don't know what to do with him sometimes. I am *so* afraid of not doing enough, or doing too much!"

Then the *argumentem ad hominem* occurred to her: that *argumentem* which proves nothing, and which women love so well.

" But you have given him things, papa. Don't you remember the red fluid ?"

" I never gave it to him," asserted the Doctor.

" But you gave it to me to give to him—when you threw the Dally out of the window."

" And do you know what the red fluid was ?"

" No. It did him good. It was just as powerful as the Dally. Consequently it must have been a drug."

"It was pure water, slightly colored. That was all, upon my honor—as we say down south. It used to amuse me to see you drop it according to prescription—five drops for a dose—very particular not to give him six. He might have drunk the vial full."

"Papa," said Lillie when she had fully realized this

awful deception, "you have a great many sins to repent of."

"Poisoning my own grandchild is not one of them, thank Heaven!"

"But suppose Ravvie had become really sick?" she suggested more seriously.

"Ah! what a clear conscience I should have had! Nobody could have laid it to me."

"How healthy, and strong, and big he is?" was her next observation. "He will be like you. I would bet anything that he will be six feet high."

Ravenel laughed at a bet which would have to wait some sixteen or eighteen years for a decision, and said it reminded him of a South Carolinian who offered to wager that in the year two thousand slavery would prevail the world over.

"This whole subject of infancy's perceptions, and opinions is curious," he observed presently. "What a world it would be, if it were exactly as these little people see it! Yes, and what a world it would be, if it were as we grown people see it in our different moods of depression, exhilaration, vanity, spite, and folly! I suppose that only Deity sees it truly."

In this kind of life the spring grew into summer, the summer sobered into autumn, and the autumn began to grow hoary with winter. Eight months of paternal affection received, and maternal cares bestowed had decided that Lillie should neither die of her troubles nor suffer a lifelong blighting of the soul. In bloom she was what she used to be; in expression alone had she suffered a change. Sometimes sudden flashes of profoundly felt pain troubled her eyes, as she thought of her venture of love and its great shipwreck. She had not the slightest feeling of anger toward her husband; she could not be angry with the buried father of her child. But she felt, and sometimes reproached herself for it, that his crime had made her grieve less over his death, just as his death had led her

to pardon his crime. She often prayed for him, not that
she believed in Purgatory and its deliverance, but rather
because the act soothed painful yearnings which she could
not dispel by reason alone. Her devotional tendencies
had been much increased by her troubles. In fact, she
was far more religious than some of the straiter New
Bostonians were able to believe when they knew that she
played whist, and noted how tastefully she was dressed,
and how charmingly graceful she was in social intercourse.
She never went to sleep without reading a chapter in the
Bible, and praying for her child, her father, and herself.
It is possible that she may have forgotten the heathen, the
Jews, and the negroes. Well, she had not been educated
to think much of far away people, but rather to interest
herself in such as were near to her, and could be made
daily happy or unhappy by her conduct. She almost offended Mrs. Whitewood by admitting that she loved Ravvie a thousand times more than the ten tribes, or, as Mrs.
W. called them, the wandering sheep of the house of
Israel. Nor could this excellent lady enlist her interest
in favor of the doctrine of election, owing perhaps to the
adverse remarks of Doctor Ravenel.

"My dear madame," he said, "let us try to be good,
repent of our short-comings, trust in the atonement,
and leave such niceties to those whose business it is to
discuss them. Doctrines are no more religion than geolo-
gical bird-tracks are animated nature. Doctrines are the
footprints of piety. You can learn by them where devout-
minded men have trod in their searchings after the truth.
But they are not in themselves religion, and will not save
souls."

"But think of the great and good men who have made
these doctrines the study and guide of their lives," said
Mrs. Whitewood. "Think of our Puritan forefathers."

"I do," answered the Doctor. "I think highly of them.
They have my profoundest respect. We are still moving
under the impetus which they gave to humanity. Dead

as they are, they govern this continent. At the same time
they must have been disagreeable to live with. Their
doctrines made them hard in thought and manner. When
I think of their grimness, uncharity, inclemency, I am
tempted to say that the sinners of those days were the salt
of the earth. Of course, Mrs. Whitewood, it is only a
temptation. I don't succumb to it. But now, as to these
doctrines, as to merely dogmatic religion, it reminds me
of a story. This story goes (I don't believe it), that an
ingenious man, having found that a bandage drawn tight
around the waist will abate the pangs of hunger, set up a
boarding-house on the idea. At breakfast the waiters
strapped up each boarder with a stout surcingle. At dinner the waistbelts were drawn up another hole—or two,
if you were hungry. At tea there was another pull on the
buckle. The story proceeds that one dyspeptic old bachelor found himself much better by the evening of the second
day, but that the other guests rebelled and left the house
in a body, denouncing the gentlemanly proprietor as a
humbug. Now some of our ethical purveyors remind me
of this inventor. They put nothing into you; they give
you no sustaining food. They simply bind your soul, and
now and then take up a hole in your moral waistbelt."

It is pretty certain that Lillie even felt more interest in
Captain Colburne than in the vanished Hebrews. It will
be remembered that she has never ceased to like him since
she met him, more than three years ago, in this same New
Boston House, which is now in some faint degree fragrant
to her with his memory. Here commenced that loyal
affection which has followed her through her love for another, her marriage, and her maternity, and which has
risked life to save her from captivity. She would be ungrateful if she did not prefer him in her heart to every
other human being except her father and Ravvie. Next
to her intercourse with this same parent and child, Colburne's letters were her chief social pleasures. They were
invariably directed to the Doctor; but if she got at them

first, she had no hesitation about opening them. It was her business and pleasure also to file them for preservation.

"If he never returns," she said, "I will write his life. But how horrible to hear of him killed!"

"In five months more his three years will be up," observed the Doctor. "I hope that he will be protected through the perils that remain."

"I hope so," echoed Lillie. "I wonder if the war will last long enough to need Ravvie. He shall never go to West Point."

"He is pretty certain not to go for the next fourteen years," said Ravenel, smiling at this long look ahead.

Lillie sighed; she was thinking of her husband; it was West Point which had ruined his noble character; nothing else could account for such a downfall; and her child should not go there.

In July (1864) they heard that the Nineteenth Corps had been transferred to Virginia, and during the autumn Colburne's letters described Sheridan's brilliant victories in the Shenandoah Valley. The Captain was present in the three pitched battles, and got an honorable mention for gallantry, but no promotion. Indeed advancement was impossible without a transfer, for, although his regiment had only two field-officers, it was now too much reduced in numbers to be entitled to a colonel. More than two-thirds of the rank and file, and more than two-thirds of the officers had fallen in those three savage struggles. Nevertheless the young man's letters were unflagging in their tone of elation, bragging of the bravery of his regiment, describing bayonet charges through whistling storms of hostile musketry, telling of captured flags and cannon by the half hundred, affectionate over his veteran corps commander, and enthusiastic over his youthful general in chief.

"Really, that is a most brilliant letter," observed Ravenel, after listening to Colburne's account of the victory of Cedar Creek. "That is the most splendid battle-piece that ever was produced by any author, ancient or modern," he went on to say in his enthusiastic and somewhat hyperbolical style. "Neither Tacitus nor Napier can equal it. Alison is all fudge and claptrap, with his granite squares of infantry and his billows of calvalry. One can understand Colburne. I know just how that battle of Cedar Creek was fought, and I almost think that I could fight such an one myself. There is cause and effect, and their relations to each other, in his narrative. When he comes home I shall insist upon his writing a history of this war."

"I wish he would," said Lillie, with a flash of interest for which she blushed presently.

* * *

CHAPTER XXXIV.

LILLIE'S ATTENTION IS RECALLED TO THE RISING GENERATION.

ON or about the first of January, 1865, Lillie chanced to go out on a shopping excursion, and descended the stairway of the hotel just in time to catch sight of a newly arrived guest, who was about entering his room on the first story. One servant directed the unsteady step and supported the wavering form of the stranger, while another carried a painted wooden box eighteen or twenty inches square, which seemed to be his sole baggage. As Lillie was in the broad light and the invalid was walking from her down a dark passage, she could not see how thin and yellow his face was, nor how weather-stained, threadbare, and even ragged was his fatigue uniform. But she could distinguish the dark blue cloth, and gilt buttons which her eye never encountered now without a sparkle of interest.

She had reached the street before the question occurred to her, Could it be Captain Colburne? She reasoned that it could not be, for he had written to them only a fortnight

ago without mentioning either sickness or wounds, and
the time of his regiment would not be up for ten days yet.
Nevertheless she made her shopping tour a short one for
thinking of that sick officer, and on returning to the hotel
she looked at the arrival-book, regardless of the half-dozen
students who lounged against the office counter. There,
written in the clerk's hand, was "Capt. Colburne, No. 18."
As she went up stairs she could not resist the temptation
of passing No. 18, and was nearly overcome by a sudden
impulse to knock at the door. She wanted to see her best
friend, and to know if he were really sick, and how sick,
and whether she could do anything for him. She determined to send a servant to make instant inquiries; but on
reaching her room she found her father playing with
Ravvie.

"Papa, Captain Colburne is here," were her first words.

"Is it possible!" exclaimed the Doctor, leaping up with
delight. "Have you seen him?"

"Not to speak with him. I am afraid he is sick. He
was leaning on the porter's arm. He is in number eighteen. Do go and ask how he is."

"I will. You are certain that it is our Captain Colburne?"

"It must be," answered Lillie as he went out; and then
thought with a blush, "Will papa laugh at me if I am
mistaken?"

When Ravenel rapped at the door of No. 18, a deep but
rather hoarse voice answered, "Come in."

"My dear friend!" exclaimed the Doctor, rushing into
the room; but the moment that he saw the Captain he
stopped in surprise and dismay.

"Don't get up," he said. "Don't stir. Bless me! how
long have you been in this way?"

"Only a little while—a month or two," answered Colburne with his customary cheerful smile. "Soon be all
right again. Sit down."

He was stretched at full length on his bed, evidently

quite feeble, his eyes underscored with lines of blueish yellow, his face sallow and features sharpened. The eyes
themselves were heavy and dull with the effects of the
opium which he had taken to enable him to undergo the
day's journey. Besides his long brown mustache, which
had become ragged with want of care, he had on a beard
of three weeks' growth; and his face and hands were
stained with the dust and smirch of two days' continuous
railroad travel, which he had not yet had time to wash
away—in fact, as soon as he had reached his room he had
thrown himself on the bed and fallen asleep. His only
clothing was a summer blouse of dark blue flannel, a common soldier's shirt of knit woolen, Government trousers
of coarse light-blue cloth without a welt, and brown Government stockings worn through at toe and heel. On the
floor lay his shoes, rough kip-skin brogans, likewise of Government issue. All of his clothing was ineradically stained
with the famous mud of Virginia; his blouse was threadbare where the sword-belt went, and had a ragged bullet-
hole through the collar. Altogether he presented the
spectacle of a man pretty thoroughly worn out in field
service.

"Is that all you wear in this season?" demanded, or
rather exclaimed the Doctor. "You will kill yourself."

Colburne's answering laugh was so feeble that its cheerfulness sounded like mockery.

"There isn't a chance of killing me," he said. "I am
not cold. On the contrary, I am suffering with the heat
of these fires and close rooms. It's rather odd, considering how run down I am. But actually I have been quar-
reling all the way home to keep my window in the car
open, I was so stifled for want of air. Three years spent
out of doors makes a house seem like a Black Hole of Cal-
cutta."

"But no vest!" urged the Doctor. "It's enough to
guarantee you an inflammation of the lungs."

"I hav'n't seen my vest nor any part of my full uniform

for six months," said Colburne, much amused. "You don't know till you try it how hardy a soldier can be, even when he is sick. My only bed-clothing until about the first of November was a rubber blanket. I will tell you. When we left Louisiana in July we thought we were going to besiege Mobile, and consequently I only took my flannel suit and rubber blanket. It was enough for a southern summer campaign. Henry had all he could do to tote his own affairs, and my rations and frying-pan. You ought to have seen the disgust with which he looked at his bundle. He began to think that he would rather be respectable, and industrious, and learn to read, than carry such a load as that. His only consolation was that he would soon steal a horse. Well, I hav'n't seen my trunk since I left it on store in New Orleans, and I don't know where it is, though I suppose it may be in Washington with the rest of the baggage of our division. I tell you this has been a glorious campaign, this one in the Shenandoah; but it has been a teaser for privations, marching, and guard-duty, as well as fighting. It is the first time that I ever knocked under to hardships. Half-starved by day, and half-frozen by night. I don't think that even this would have laid me out, however, if I hadn't been poisoned by the Louisiana swamps. Malarious fever is what bothers me."

"You will have to be very careful of yourself," said the Doctor. He noticed a febrile agitation in the look and even in the conversation of the wasted young hero which alarmed him.

"Oh no," smiled Colburne. "I will be all right in a week or two. All I want is rest. I will be about in less than a week. I can travel now. You don't realize how a soldier can pick himself up from an ordinary illness. Isn't it curious how the poor fellows will be around on their pins, and in their clothes till they die? I think I am rather effeminate in taking off my shoes. I only did it out of compliment to the white coverlet. Doesn't it look reproachfully clean compared with me? I am positively ashamed of my filthiness, although I didn't suspect it until I got into the confines of peaceful civilization. I assure you I am a tolerably tidy man for our corps in its present condition. I am a very respectable average."

"We are all ready here to worship your very rags."

"Well. After I get rid of them. I must have a citizen's suit as soon as possible."

"Can't you telegraph for your trunk?"

"I have. But that's of no consequence. No more uniform for me. I am home to be mustered out of service. I can't stay any longer, you understand. I am one of the original officers, and have never been promoted, and so go out with the original organization. If we could have re-enlisted eighteen men more, we should have been a full veteran regiment, and I could have staid. I came home before the organization. I was on detached duty as staff-officer, and so got a leave of absence. You see I wanted to be here as early as possible in order to make out my men's account, and muster-out rolls. I have a horrible amount of work to do this week."

"Work!" exclaimed Ravenel. "You are no more fit to work than you are to fly. You can't work, and you sha'n't."

"But I must. I am responsible. If I don't do this job I may be dismissed the service, instead of being mustered out honorably. Do you think I an going to let myself be disgraced? Sooner die in harness!"

"But, my dear friend, you can't do it. Your very talk is feverish; you are on the edge of delirium."

"Oh no! I can't help laughing at you. You don't know how much a sick man can do, if he must. He can march and fight a battle. I have done it, weaker than this. Thank God, I have my company papers. They are in that box—all my baggage—all I want. I can make my first muster-out roll to-morrow, and hire somebody to do the four copies. You see it must be done, for my men's

sake as well as mine. By Jove! we get horrible hard
measure in field service. I have gone almost mad about
that box during the past six months; wanted it every day
and couldn't have it for lack of transportation; the War
Department demanding returns, and hospitals demanding
descriptive lists of wounded men; one threatening to stop
my pay, and another to report me to the Adjutant-General; and I couldn't make out a paper for lack of that box.
If I had only known that we were coming to Virginia, I
could have prepared myself, you see; I could have made
out a memorandum-book of my company accounts to
carry in my pocket; but how did I know?"

He spoke as rapidly and eagerly as if he were pleading
his case before the Adjutant-General, and showing cause
why he should not be dishonorably dismissed the service.
After a moment of gloomy reflection he spoke again, still
harping on this worrying subject.

"I have six months' unfinished business to write up, or
I am a disgraced man. The Commissary of Musters will
report me to the Adjutant-General, and the Adjutant-General will dismiss me from the service. It's pretty justice, isn't it?"

"But if you are a staff-officer and on detached service?"

"That doesn't matter. The moment the muster-out day
comes, I am commandant of company, and responsible for
company papers. I ought to go to work to-day. But I
can't. I am horribly tired. I may try this evening."

"No no, my dear friend," implored the Doctor. "You
mustn't talk in this way. You will make yourself sick.
You *are* sick. Don't you know that you are almost delirious on this subject?"

"Am I? Well, let's drop it. By the way, how are
you? And how is Mrs. Carter? Upon my honor I have
been shamefully selfish in talking so much about my
affairs. How is Mrs. Carter, and the little boy?"

"Very well, both of them. My daughter will be glad
to see you. But you mustn't go out to-day."

"No no. I want some clothes. I can't go out in these filthy rags. I am loaded and disreputable with the sacred southern soil. If you will have the kindness to ring the bell, I will send for a tailor. I must be measured for a citizen's suit immediately."

"My dear fellow, why won't you undress and go to bed? I will order a strait-jacket for you if you don't."

"Oh, you don't know the strength of my constitution," said Colburne, with his haggard, feverish, confident smile.

"Upon my soul, you look like it!" exclaimed the Doctor, out of patience. "Well, what will you have for dinner? Of course you are not going down."

"Not in these tatters—no. Why, I think I should like —let me see—some good—oysters and mince pie."

The Doctor laughed aloud, and then threw up his hands desperately.

"I thought so. Stark mad. I'll order your dinner myself, sir. You shall have some farina."

"Just as you say. I don't care much. I don't want anything. But it's a long while since I have had a piece of mince pie, and it can't be as bad a diet as raw pork and green apples."

"I don't know," answered the Doctor. "Now then, will you promise to take a bath and go regularly to bed as soon as I leave you?"

"I will. How you bully a fellow! I tell you I'm not sick, to speak of. I'm only a little worried."

When Ravenel returned to his own apartment he found Lillie waiting to go down to dinner.

"How is he?" she asked the moment he opened the door.

"Very badly. Very feverish. Hardly in his right mind."

"Oh no, papa," remonstrated Lillie. "You always exaggerate such things. Now he isn't very bad; is he? Is he as sick as he was at Donnelsonville? You know how

fast he got well then.   I don't believe he is in any danger.
Is he?"

She took a strong interest in him; it was her way to
take an interest and to show it.   She had much of what
the French call expansion, and very little of self-repression
whether in feeling or speech.

"I tell you, my dear, that I am exceedingly anxious.
He is almost prostrated by weakness, and there is a febrile
excitement which is weakening him still more.   No immediate danger, you understand; but the case is certainly
a very delicate and uncertain one.   So many of these noble
fellows die after they get home!   I wouldn't be so anxious,
only that he thinks he has a vast quantity of company
business on hand which must be attended to at once."

"Can't we do it, or some of it, for him?"

"Perhaps so.   I dare say.   Yes, I think it likely.   But
now let us hurry down.   I want to order something suitable for his dinner.   I must buy a dose of morphine, too,
that will make him sleep till to-morrow morning.   He
must sleep, or he won't live."

"Oh, papa!   I hope you didn't talk that way to *him.*
you are enough to frighten patients into the other world,
you are always so anxious about them."

"Not much danger of frightening him," groaned the
Doctor.   "I wish he could be scared—just a little—just
enough to keep him quiet."

After dinner the Doctor saw Colburne again.   He had
bathed, had gone to bed, and had an opiated doze, but
was still in his state of fevered nervousness, and showed
it, unconsciously to himself, in his conversation.   Just now
his mind was running on the subject of Gazaway, probably in connection with his own lack of promotion; and
he talked with a bitterness of comment, and an irritation
of feeling which were very unusual with him.

"You know the secret history of his rehabilitation,"
said he.   "Well, there is one consolation in the miserable
affair.   He fooled our sly Governor.   You know it was

agreed, that, after Gazaway had been whitewashed with a lieutenant-colonelcy, he should show his gratitude by carrying his district for our party, and then resign to make way for the Governor's nephew, Major Rathbun. But it seems Gazaway had his own ideas. He knew a trick or two besides saving his bacon on the battle-field. His plan was that he should be the candidate for Congress from the district. When he found that he couldn't make that work, he did the next best thing, and held on to his commission. Wasn't it capital? It pays me for being overlooked, during three years, in spite of the recommendations of my colonel and my generals. There he is still, Lieutenant-Colonel, with the Governor's nephew under him to do his fighting and field duty. I don't know how Gazaway got command of the conscript camp where he has been for the last year. I suppose he lobbied for it. But I know that he has turned it to good account. One of my sergeants was on detached duty at the camp, and was taken behind the scenes. He told me that he made two hundred dollars in less than a month, and that Gazaway must have pocketed ten times as much."

"How is it possible that they have not ferreted out such a scoundrel!" exclaims the horror-stricken Doctor.

"Ah! the War Department has had a great load to carry. The War Department has had its hands too full of Jeff Davis to attend to every smaller rascal."

"But why didn't Major Rathbun have him tried for his old offences? It was the Major's interest to get him out of his own way."

"Those were condoned by the acceptance of his resignation. Gazaway died officially with full absolution; and then was born again in his reappointment. He could go to work with clean hands to let substitutes escape for five hundred dollars a-piece, while the sergeant who allowed the man to dodge him got fifty. Isn't it a beautiful story?"

"Shocking! But this is doing you harm. You don't

X

need talk—you need sleep. I have brought you a dose to make you hold your tongue till to-morrow morning."

" Oh, opium. I have been living on it for the last forty-eight hours—the last week."

" Twelve more hours won't hurt you. You must stop thinking and feeling. I tell you honestly that I never saw you in such a feverish state of excitation when you were wounded. You talk in a manner quite unlike yourself."

" Very well," said Colburne with a long-drawn sigh, as if resigning himself by an effort to the repugnant idea of repose.

Here we may as well turn off Lieutenant-Colonel Gazaway, since he will not be executed by any act of civil or military justice. Removed at last from the conscript camp, and ordered to the front, he at once sent in his resignation, backed up by a surgeon's certificate of physical disability, retired from the service with a capital of ten or fifteen thousand dollars, removed to New York, set up a first-class billiard-saloon, turned democrat once more, obtained a couple of city offices, and now has an income of seven or eight thousand a-year, a circle of admiring henchmen, and a reputation for ability in business and politics. When he speaks in a ward meeting or in a squad of speculators on 'Change, his words have ten times the influence that would be accorded in the same places to the utterances of Colburne or Ravenel. I, however, prefer to write the history of these two gentlemen, who appear so unsuccessful when seen from a worldly point of view.

Fearing to disturb Colburne's slumbers, Ravenel did not visit him again until nine o'clock on the following morning. He found him dressed, and looking over a mass of company records, preparatory to commencing his muster-out roll.

" You ought not to do that," said the Doctor. " You are very feverish and weak. All the strength you have is from opiates, and you tax your brain fearfully by driving it on such fuel."

"But it must be done, Doctor," he said with a scowl, as if trying to see clearly through clouds of fever and morphine. "It is an awful job," he added with a sigh. "Just see what it is. I must have the name of every officer and man that ever belonged to the company—where, when, and by whom enlisted—where, when, and by whom mustered in—when and by whom last paid—what bounty paid and what bounty due—balance of clothing account —stoppages of all sorts—facts and dates of every promotion and reduction, discharge, death and desertion—number and date of every important order. Five copies! Why don't they demand five hundred? Upon my soul, it doesn't seem as if I could do it."

"Why not make some of your men do it?"

"I have none here. I am the only man who will go out on this paper. There is not a man of my original company who has not either re-enlisted as a veteran, or deserted, or died, or been killed, or been discharged because of wounds, or breaking down under hardships."

"Astonishing!"

"Very curious. That Shenandoah campaign cut up our regiment wonderfully. We went there with four hundred men, and we had less than one hundred and fifty when I left."

The civilian stared at the coolness of the soldier, which seemed to him much like hard-heartedness. The latter rubbed his forehead and eyes, not affected by these tremendous recollections, but simply seeking to gain clearness of brain enough to commence his talk.

"You must not work to-day," said the Doctor.

"I have only three days for the job, and I *must* work to-day."

"Well—go on then. Make your original, which is, I suppose, the great difficulty ; and my daughter and I will make the four others."

"Will you? How kind you are!"

At nine o'clock of the following morning Colburne de-

livered to Ravenel the original muster-out roll. During
that day and the next the father and daughter finished
the four copies, while Colburne lay in bed, too sick and
dizzy to raise his head. On the fourth day he went by
railroad to the city of   , the primary rendezvous of
the regiment, and was duly mustered out of existence as
an officer of the United States army. Returning to New
Boston that evening, he fainted at the door of the hotel,
was carried to his room by the porters, and did not leave
his bed for forty-eight hours. At the end of that time he
dressed himself in his citizen's suit, and called on Mrs.
Carter. She was astonished and frightened to see him,
for he was alarmingly thin and ghastly. Nevertheless,
after the first startled exclamation of "Captain Colburne!"
she added with a benevolent hypocrisy, "How much better you look than I thought to see you!"

He held both her hands for a moment, gazing into her
eyes with a profound gratification at their sympathy, and
then said, as he seated himself, "Thank you for your anxiety. I am going to get well now. I am going to give
myself three months of pure, perfect rest."

The wearied man pronounced the word *rest* with a
touching intonation of pleasure.

"Don't call me Captain," he resumed. "The very word
tires me, and I want repose. Besides, I am a citizen, and
have a right to the Mister."

"He is mortified because he was not promoted," thought
Lillie, and called him by the threadbare title no more.

"It always seems to be our business to take care of you
when you are sick," she said. "We nursed you at Taylorsville—that is, till we wanted some fighting done."

"That seems a great while ago," replied Colburne med-
itatively. "How many things have happened since then!"
he was about to say, but checked the utterance for fear of
giving her pain.

"Yes, it seems a long time ago," she repeated soberly,
for she too thought how many things had happened since

then, and thought it with more emotion than he could give to the idea. He continued to gaze at her earnestly and with profound pity in his heart, while his memory flashed over the two great incidents of maternity and widowhood. "She has fought harder battles than I have," he said to himself, wondering meanwhile to find her so little changed, and deciding that what change there was only made her more charming. He longed to say some word of consolation for the loss of her husband, but he would not speak of the subject until she introduced it. Lillie's mind also wondered shudderingly around that bereavement, and then dashed desperately away from it, without uttering a plaint.

"Can I see the baby?" he asked, after these few moments of silence.

She colored deeply, not so much with pleasure and pride, as with a return of the old virginity of soul. He understood it, for he remembered that she had blushed in the same manner when she met him for the first time after her marriage. It was the modesty of her womanhood, confessing, "I am not what I was when you saw me last."

"He is not a baby," she laughed. "He is a great boy, more than a year old. Come and look at him."

She led the way into her room. It was the first time that he had ever been in her room, and the place filled him with delicious awe, as if he were in the presence of some sweet sanctity. Irish Rosann, sitting by the bedside, and reading her prayer-book, raised her old head and took a keen survey of the stranger through her silver-rimmed spectacles. On the bed lay a chubby urchin, well grown for a yearling, his fair face red with health, sunburn, and sleep, arms spread wide apart, and one dimpled leg and foot outside of the coverlet.

"There is the Little Doctor," she said, bending down and kissing a dimple.

It was a long time since she had called him "Little General," or, "Little Brigadier." From the worship of the husband she had gone back in a great measure, perhaps altogether, to the earlier and happier worship of the parent.

" Does he look like his grandfather?" asked Colburne.

" Why! Can't you see it? He is wonderfully like him. He has blue eyes, too. Don't you see the resemblance?"

" I think he has more chins than your father. He has double chins all the way down to his toes," said Colburne, pointing to the collops on the little leg.

" You mustn't laugh at him," she answered. " I suppose you have seen him enough. Men seldom take a longer look than that at a baby."

" Yes. I don't want to wake him up. I don't want the responsibility of it. I wouldn't assume the responsibilities of an ant. I haven't the energy for it."

They returned to the little parlor. The Doctor came in, and immediately forced the invalid to lie on a sofa, propping him up with pillows and proposing to cover him with an Affghan.

" No," said Colburne. " I beg pardon for my obstinacy, but I suffer with heat all the time."

" It is the fever," said the Doctor. " Remittent malarious fever. It is no joke when it dates from Brashear City."

" It it not being used to a house," answered Colburne, stubborn in faith in his own health. " It is wearing a vest and a broadcloth coat. I really am not strong enough to bear the hardships of civilization."

" We shall see," said the Doctor gravely. " The Indians die of civilization. So does many a returned soldier. You will have to be careful of yourself for a long time to come."

" I am," said Colburne. " I sleep with windows open."

" Why didn't you write to us that you were sick?" asked Lillie.

" I didn't wish to worry you. I knew you were kind enough to be worried. What was the use?"

She thought that it was noble, and just like him, but she said nothing. She could not help admiring him, as he lay there, for looking so sick and weak, and yet so cheer ful and courageous, so absolutely indifferent to his state of bodily depression. There was not in his face or manner a single shadow of expression which seemed like an appeal for pity or sympathy. He had the air of one who had become so accustomed to suffering as to consider it a common-place matter not worthy of a moment's despondency, or even consideration. His look was noticeably resolute, and energetic, yet patient.

"You are the most resigned sick man that I ever saw," she said. "You make as good an invalid as a woman."

"A soldier's life cultivates some of the Christian virtues," he answered; "especially resignation and obedience. Just see here. You are roused at midnight, march twenty miles on end, halt three or four hours, perhaps in a pelting rain; then you are faced about, marched back to your old quarters and dismissed, and nobody ever tells you why or wherefore. You take it very hard it first, but at last you get used to it and do just as you are bid, without complaint or comment. You no more pretend to reason concerning your duties than a millstone troubles itself to understand the cause of its revolutions. You are set in motion, and you move. Think of being started out at early dawn and made to stand to arms till daylight, every morning, for six weeks running. You may grumble at it, but you do it all the same. At last you forget to grumble and even to ask the reason why. You obey because you are ordered. Oh! a man learns a vast deal of stoical virtue in field service. He learns courage, too, against sickness as well as against bullets. I believe the war will give a manlier, nobler tone to the character of our nation. The school of suffering teaches grand lessons."

"And how will the war end?" asked Lillie, anxious, as every citizen was, to get the opinion of a soldier on this great question.

" We shall beat them, of course."

" When ?"

" I can't say. Nobody can. I never heard a military man of any merit pretend to fix the time. Now that I am a civilian, perhaps I shall resume the gift of prophecy."

" Mr. Seward keeps saying, in three months."

" Well, if he keeps saying so long enough he will hit it. Mr. Seward hasn't been serious in such talk. His only object was to cheer up the nation."

" So we shall beat them ?" cheerfully repeated the converted secessionist. " And what then ? I hope we shall pitch into England. I hate her for being so underhandedly spiteful toward the North, and false toward the South."

" Oh no ; don't hate her. England, like every body else, doesn't like a great neighbor, and would be pleased to see him break up into small neighbors. But England is a grand old nation, and one of the lights of the world. The only satisfaction which I should find in a war with England would be that I could satisfy my curiosity on a point of professional interest. I would like to see how European troops fight compared with ours. I would cheerfully risk a battle for the spectacle."

" And which do you think would beat ?" asked Lillie.

" I really don't know. That is just the question. Marengo against Cedar Creek, Leipsic against the Wilderness. I should like, of all things in the world, to see the trial."

Thus they talked for a couple of hours, in a quiet way, strolling over many subjects, but discussing nothing of deep personal interest. Colburne was too weak to have much desire to feel or to excite emotions. In studying the young woman before him he was chiefly occupied in detecting and measuring the exact change which the potent incidents of her later life had wrought in her expression. He decided that she looked more serious and more earnest than of old ; but that was the total of his fancied discoveries ; in fact, he was too languid to analyze.

CHAPTER XXXV.

CAPTAIN COLBURNE AS MR. COLBURNE.

DURING three months Colburne rested from marches, battles, fatigues, emotions. He was temporarily so worn out in body and mind that he could not even rally vigor enough to take an interest in any but the greatest of the majestic passing events. It is to be considered that he had been case-hardened by war to all ordinary agitations; that exposure to cannon and musketry had so calloused him as that he could read newspapers with tranquillity. Accordingly he troubled himself very little about the world; and it got along at an amazing rate without his assistance. There were no more Marengos in the Shenandoah Valley, but there was a Waterloo near Petersburg, and an Ulm near Raleigh, and an assassination of a greater than William of Orange at Washington, and over all a grand, re-united, triumphant republic.

As to the battles Colburne only read the editorial summaries and official reports, and did not seem to care much for "our own correspondent's" picturesque particulars. Give him the positions, the dispositions, the leaders, the general results, and he knew how to infer the minutiæ. To some of his civilian friends, the brother abolitionists of former days, this calmness seemed like indifference to the victories of his country; and such was the eagerness and hotness of the times that some of them charged him with want of patriotism, sympathy with the rebels, copperheadism, etc. One day he came into the Ravenel parlor with a smile on his face, but betraying in his manner something of the irritability of weakness and latent fever.

"I have heard a most astonishing thing," he said. "I have been called a Copperhead. I who fought three

years, marched the skin off my feet, have been wounded,
starved, broken down in field service, am a Copperhead.
The man who inferred it ought to know; he has lived
among Copperheads for the last three years. He has never
been in the army—never smelled a pinch of rebel powder.
There were no Copperheads at the front; they were all
here, at the rear, where he was. He ought to know them,
and he says that I am one of them. Isn't it amazing !"

" How did he discover it ?" asked the Doctor.

" We were talking about the war. This man—who has
never heard a bullet whistle, please remember—asserted
that the rebel soldiers were cowards, and asked my opinion. I demurred. He insisted and grew warm. ' But,'
said I, ' don't you see that you spoil my glory ? Here I
have been in the field three years, finding these rebels a
very even match in fighting. If they are cowards, I am a
poltroon. The inference hurts me, and therefore I deny
the premise.' I think that my argument aggravated him.
He repeated positively that the rebels were cowards, and
that whoever asserted the contrary was a southern sympa-
thiser. ' But,' said I, ' the rebel armies differ from ours
chiefly in being more purely American. Is it the greater
proportion of native blood which causes the cowardice ?'
Thereupon I had the Copperhead brand put upon my
forehead, and was excommunicated from the paradise of
loyalty. I consider it rather stunning. I was the only
practical abolitionist in the company—the only man who
had freed a negro, or caused the death of a slaveholder.
Doctor, you too must be a Copperhead. You have suffered a good deal for the cause of freedom and country ;
but I don't believe that you consider the rebel armies
packs of cowards."

The Doctor noted the excitement of his young friend,
and observed to himself, " Remittent malarious fever."

" I get along very easily with these earnest people," he
added aloud. " They say more than they strictly believe,
because their feelings are stronger than can be spoken.

They are pretty tart; but they are mere buttermilk or lemonade compared with the nitric acid which I used to find in Louisiana; they speak hard things, but they don't stick you under the fifth rib with a bowie-knife. Thanks to my social training in the South, I am able to say to a man who abuses me for my opinions, ' Sir, I am profoundly grateful to you for not cutting my throat from ear to ear. I shall never forget your politeness.' "

The nervous fretfulness apparent in Colburne's manner on this occasion passed away as health and strength returned. Another phenomenon of his recovered vigor was that he began to show a stronger passion for the society of Mrs. Carter than he had exhibited when he first returned from the wars. On his well days he made a span with young Whitewood at the baby wagon; only it was observable .that, after a few trials, they came to a tacit understanding to take turns in this duty; so that when one was there, the other kept away, in a magnaminous, man fashion. Colburne found Mrs. Carter, in the main, a much more serious person in temper than when he bade her good-bye in Thibodeaux. The interest which this shadow of sadness gave her in his eyes, or, perhaps I should say, the interest with which she invested the subject of sadness in his mind, may be inferred from the somewhat wordy fervor of the following passage, which he penned about this time in his common-place book.

" *The Dignity of Sorrow.* Grand is the heart which is ennobled, not crushed, by sorrow; by mighty sorrows worn, not as manacles, but as a crown. Try to conceive the dignity of a soul which has suffered deeply and borne its sufferings well, as compared with another soul which has not suffered at all. Remember how we respect a veteran battle-ship—a mere dead mass of timber, ropes, and iron—the Hartford—after her decks have run with blood, and been torn by shot. No spectacle of new frigates just from the stocks, moulded in the latest perfected form, can stir our souls with sympathy like the sight of the battered hulk. Truly there is something of divinity in the man of sorrows, acquainted with grief, even when his body is but human, provided always that his soul has grown purer by its trials."

At one time Colburne was somewhat anxious about Mrs. Carter lest her character should become permanently sombre in consequence of lonely brooding over her troubles. He remembered with pleasure her former girlish gayety, and wished that it might be again her prevailing expression.

" Do you think you see people enough ?" he asked her. " I mean, a sufficient variety of people. Monotony of intellectual diet is as bad for the spirit as monotony of physical nourishment for the body."

" I am sure that papa and Mr. Whitewood constitute a variety," she answered.

Colburne was not badly pleased with this speech, inasmuch as it seemed to convey a slight slur upon Mr. Whitewood. He was so gratified, in fact, that he lost sight of the subject of the conversation until she recalled him to it.

" Do you think I am getting musty ?" she inquired.

" Of course not. But there is danger in a long-continued uniformity of spiritual surroundings: danger of running into a habit of reverie, brooding, melancholy : danger of growing spiritually old."

" I know it. But what can a woman do ? It is one of the inconveniences of womanhood that we can't change our surroundings—not even our hoops—at our own pleasure. We can't run out into the world and say, Amuse us."

" There are two worlds for the two sexes. A man's consists of all the millions of earth and of future time—unless he becomes a captain in the Tenth Barataria—then he stays where he began. A woman's consists of the people whom she meets daily. But she can enlarge it ; she can make it comprehend more than papa and Mr. Whitewood."

" But not more than Ravvie," said Lillie.

As Colburne listened to this declaration he felt something like jealousy of the baby, and something like indignation at Mrs. Carter. What business had she to let herself be circumscribed by the limits of such a diminutive creature? This was not the only time that Lillie shot this single arrow in her quiver at Mr. Colburne. She talked a great deal to him about Ravvie, believing all the while that she kept a strict rein upon her maternal vanity, and did not mention the boy half as often as she would have been justified in doing by his obesity and other remarkable characteristics. I do not mean to intimate that the subject absolutely and acrimoniously annoyed our hero. On the whole her maternal fondness was a pleasant spectacle to him, especially when he drew the inference that so good a mother would be sure to make an admirable wife. Moreover his passion for pets easily flowed into an affection for this infant, and the child increased the feeling by his grateful response to the young bachelor's attentions. Mrs. Carter blushed more than once to see her baby quit her and toddle across the room and greet Colburne's entrance.

"Ravvie, come here," she would say. "You trouble people."

"No, no," protested Colburne, picking up the little man and setting him on his shoulder. "I like to be troubled by people who love me."

Then after a slight pause, he added audaciously, "I never have been much troubled in that way."

Mrs. Carter's blush deepened a shade or two at this observation. It was one of those occasions on which a woman always says something as mal-apropos as possible; and in accordance with this instinct of her sex, she spoke of the Russian Plague, which was then a subject of gossip in the papers.

"I am so afraid Ravvie will take it," she said. "I have heard that there is a case next door, and I am really tempted to run away with him for a week or two."

"I wouldn't," replied Colburne. "You might run into it somewhere else. One case is not alarming. If I had forty children to be responsible for, I wouldn't break up for a single case."

"If you had forty you mightn't be so frightened as if you had only one," remarked Mrs. Carter, seriously.

Then the Doctor came in, to declare in his cheerful way that there was no Russian Plague in the city, and that, even if there were, it was no great affair of a disease among a well-fed and cleanly population.

"We are more in danger of breaking out with national vanity," said he. "They are singing anthems, choruses, pæans of praise to us across the water. All the nations of Europe are welcoming our triumph, as the daughters of Judea went out with cymbals and harps to greet the giant killing David. Just listen to this."

Here he unfolded the Evening Post of the day, took off his eye-glasses, put on his spectacles, and read extracts from European editorials written on the occasion of the fall of Richmond and surrender of Lee.

"They are more flattering than Fourth of July orations," said Colburne. "I feel as though I ought to go straight down to the sea-shore and make a bow across the Atlantic. It is enough to make a spread peacock-tail sprout upon every loyal American. I am not sure but that the next generation will be furnished with the article, as being absolutely necessary to express our consciousness of admiration. On the Darwinian theory, you know; circumstances breed species."

"The Europeans seem to have more enthusiastic views of us than we do of ourselves," observed Lillie. "I never thought of our being such a grand nation as Monsieur Laboulaye paints us. You never did, papa."

"I never had occasion to till now," said the Doctor. "As long as we were bedraggled in slavery there was not much room for honest, intelligent pride of country. It is different now. These Europeans judge us aright; we have

done a stupendous thing.   They are outside of the struggle, and can survey its proportions with the eyes with
which our descendants will see it.   I think I can discover
a little of its grandeur.   It is the fifth act in the grand
drama of human liberty.   First, the Christian revelation.
Second, the Protestant reformation.   Third, the war of
American Independence.   Fourth, the French revolution.
Fifth, the struggle for the freedom of all men, without
distinction of race and color; this Democratic struggle
which confirms the masses in an equality with the few.
We have taught a greater lesson than all of us think or
understand.   Once again we have reminded the world of
Democracy, the futility of oligarchies, the outlawry of
Cæsarism."

"In the long run the right conquers," moralized Colburne.

"Yes, as that pure and wise martyr to the cause of
freedom, President Lincoln, said four years ago, right
makes might.   A just system of labor has produced power,
and an unjust system has produced weakness. The North,
living by free industry, has twenty millions of people, and
wealth inexhaustible.   The South, living by slavery, has
twelve millions, one half of whom are paupers and secret
enemies.   The right always conquers because it always
becomes the strongest.   In that sense ' the hand of God '
is identical with ' the heaviest battalions.'   Another thing
which strikes me is the intensity of character which our
people have developed.   We are no longer a mere collection of thirty millions of bores, as Carlyle called us.
There never was greater vigor or range.   Look at Booth,
the new Judas Iscariot.   Look at Blackburn, who packed
up yellow fever rags with the hope of poisoning a continent.   What a sweep, what a gamut, from these satanic
wretches to Abraham Lincoln ! a purer, wiser and greater
than Socrates, whom he reminds one of by his plain sense
and homely humor.   In these days—the days of Lincoln,
Grant and Sherman—faith in the imagination—faith in

the supernatural origin of humanity—becomes possible. We see men who are demoniacal and men who are divine. I can now go back to my childhood, and read Plutarch as I then read him, believing that wondrous men have lived because I see that they do live. I can now understand the Paradise Lost, for I have beheld Heaven fighting with Hell."

"The national debt will be awful," observes Lillie, after the brief pause which naturally follows the Doctor's Cyricism. "Three thousand millions! What will my share be?"

"We will pay it off," says the Doctor, "in a series of operatic entertainments, at a hundred thousand dollars the dress seats—back seats fifty thousand."

"The southern character will be improved by the struggle," observed Colburne, after another silence. "They will be sweetened by adversity, as their persimmons are by frost. Besides, it is such a calming thing to have one's fight out! It draws off the bad blood. But what are we to do about punishing the masses? I go for punishing only the leaders."

"Yes," coincided the Doctor. "They are the responsible criminals. It is astonishing how imperiously strong characters govern weak ones. You will often meet with a man who absolutely enters into and possesses other men, making them talk, act and feel as if they were himself. He puts them on and wears them, as a soldier crab puts on and wears an empty shell. For instance, you hear a man talking treason; you look at him and say, 'It is that poor fool, Cracker.' But all the while it is Planter, who, being stronger minded than Cracker, dwells in him and blasphemes out of his windows. Planter is the living crab, and Cracker is the dead shell. The question comes up, 'Which shall we hang, and which shall we pardon?' I say, hang Planter, and tell Cracker to get to work. Planter gone, some better man will occupy Cracker and make him speak and live virtuously."

But strange as it may seem, unpatriotic as it may seem, there 'was a subject which interested Colburne more than these great matters. It was a woman, a widow, a mother, who, as he supposed, still mourned her dead husband, and only loved among the living her father and her child. How imperiously, for wise ends, we are governed by the passion of sex for sex, in spite of the superficial pleas of selfish reason and interest! What other quality, physical or moral, have we that could take the place of this beneficently despotic instinct? Do you believe that conscience, sense of duty, philanthropy, would induce men and women to bear with each other—to bring children into the world—to save the race from extinction? Strike out the affection of sex for sex, and earth would be, first a hell, then a desert. God is not very far from every one of us. The nation was not more certainly guided by the hand of Providence in overthrowing slavery, than was this man in loving this woman. I do not suspect that any one of these reflections entered the mind of Colburne, although he was intellectually quite capable of such a small amount of philosophy. We never, or hardly ever think of applying general principles to our own cases; and he believed, as a matter of course, that he liked Mrs. Carter simply because she was individually loveable. On other subjects he could think and talk with perfect rationality; he could even discourse transcendentally to her concerning her own heart history. For instance, one day when she was sadder than usual, nervous, irritable, and in imperious need of a sympathising confidant, she alluded shyly to her sorrows, and, finding him willing to listen, added frankly, "Oh, I have been so unhappy!"

It is rather strange that he did not sieze the opportunity and say, "Let me be your consoler." But he too was in a temporarily morbid state, his mind unpractical with fever and weakness, wandering helplessly around the ideas of trouble and consolation like a moth around the bewilderment of a candle, and not able to perceive that the great comforter of life is action, labor, duty.

"So have multitudes," he answered. "There is some comfort in that."

"How *can* you say so?" she asked, turning upon him in astonishment.

"Look here," he answered. "There are ten thousand blossoms on an apple tree, but not five hundred of them mature into fruit. So it is with us human beings : a few succeed, the rest are failures. It is a part of the method of God. He creates many, in order that some may be sure to reach his proposed end. He abounds in means ; he has more material than he needs ; he minds nothing but his results. You and I, even if we are blighted blooms, must be content with knowing that his purposes are certain to be fulfilled. If we fail, others will succeed, and in that fact we can rejoice, forgetting ourselves."

"Oh! but that is very hard," said Lillie.

"Yes ; it is. But what right have we to demand that we shall be happy ? That is a condition that we have no right and no power to make with the Creator of the Universe. Our desire should be that we might be enabled to make others happy. I wonder that this should seem hard doctrine to you. Women, if I understand them, are full of self-abnegation, and live through multitudes of self-sacrifices."

"And still it sounds hard," persisted Lillie. "I could not bear another sacrifice."

She closed her eyes under an impulse of spiritual agony, as the thought occurred to her that she might yet be called on to give up her child.

"I am sorry you have been unhappy," he said, much moved by the expression of her face at this moment. "I have sympathised with you, oh, so much! without ever saying a word before."

She did not stop him from taking her hand, and for a few moments did not withdraw it from his grasp. Far deeper than the philosophy, which she could understand but not feel, these simple and common-place words, just such as any child might utter stole into her heart, conveying a tearful sense of comfort and eliciting a throb of gratitude.

But their conversation was not often of so melancholy and sentimental a nature. She had more gay hours with this old friend during a few weeks than she had had during six months previous to his arrival. She often laughed when the tears were ready to start; but gradually the spirit of laughter was expelling the spirit of tears. She was hardly sensible, I suspect, how thoroughly he was winding himself into all her emotions, her bygone griefs, her present consolations, her pitying remembrance of her husband, her love for her father and child, her recollections of the last four years, so full for her of life and feeling. His presence recalled by turns all of these things, sweeping gently, like a hand timid because of affection, over every chord of her heart. Man has great power over a woman when he is so gifted or so circumstanced that he can touch that strongest part of her nature, her sentiments.

However, it must not be supposed that Mr. Colburne was at this time playing a very audible tune on Mrs. Carter's heart-strings, or that he even distinctly intended to touch that delicate instrument. He was quite aware that he must better his pecuniary condition before he could honorably meddle in such lofty music.

" I must go to work," he said, after he had been at home nearly three months. " I shall get so decayed with laziness that I sha'n't be able to pick myself up. I shall cease to be respectable if I lounge any longer than is obsolutely necessary to restore my health."

" Yes, work is best," answered the Doctor. " It is our earthly glory and blessing. It is a great comfort to think that the evil spirit of no-work is pretty much exorcised from our nation. The victory of the North is at bottom the triumph of laboring men living by their own industry, over non-laboring men who wanted to live by the industry of others. Europe sees this even more plainly than we do. All over that continent the industrious classes hail the triumph of the North as their own victory. Slavery meant in reality to create an idle nobility. Liberty has established an industrious democracy. In working for our own living we are obeying the teachings of this war, the triumphant spirit of our country and age. The young man who is idle now belongs to bygone and semi-barbarous centuries; he is more of an old fogy than the narrowest minded farm-laborer or ditch-digging emigrant. What a prosperous hive this will be now that it contains no class of drones! There was no hope of good from slavery. It was like that side of the moon which never sees the bright face of the Earth and whose night is always darkness, no matter how the heavens revolve. Yes, we must all go to work. That is, we must be useful and respectable. I am very glad for your sake that you have studied a profession. A young man brought up in literary and scientific circles is subject to the temptation of concluding that it will be a fine thing to have no calling but letters. He is apt to think that he will make his living by his pen. Now that is all wrong; it is wrong because the pen is an uncertain means of existence; for no man should voluntarily place himself in the condition of living from hand to mouth. Every university man, as well as every other man, should learn a profession, or a business, or a trade. Then, when he has something solid to fall back upon, he may if he chooses try what he can do as a scholar or author."

" I shall re-open my law office," said Colburne.

" I wonder if it would be unhandsome or unfair," queried the Doctor, " if I too should open an office and take such patients as might offer."

"I don't see it. I don't see it at all," responded Colburne.

"Nor do I, either—considering my necessities," said Ravenel, meanwhile calculating internally how much longer his small cash capital would last at the present rate of decrease.

Within a week after this conversation two offices were opened, and the professional ranks of New Boston were reinforced by one doctor and one lawyer.

"Papa, now that you have set up a sign," said Lillie, "I will trust you entirely with Ravvie."

"Yes, women always ask after a sign," observed Ravenel. "It is astonishing how much the sex believes in pretense and show. If I should advertise myself—no matter how ignorant I might be—as a specialist in female maladies, I could have all the lady invalids in New Boston for patients. Positively I sometimes get out of patience with the sex for its streaks of silliness. I am occasionally tempted to believe that the greatest difficulty which man has overcome in climbing the heights of civilization is the fact that he has had to tote women on his shoulders."

"I thought you never used negro phrases, papa."

"I pass that one. Tote has a monosyllabic vigor about it which pleads for it."

"You know Mrs. Poyser says that women are fools because they were made to match the men."

"Mrs. Poyser was a very intelligent woman—well worthy of her son, Ike," returned the Doctor, who knew next to nothing of novels.

"Now go to your office," said Lillie, "and if Mrs. Poyser calls on you, don't give her the pills meant for Mrs. Partington. They are different ladies."

Colburne did not regret that he had been a soldier; he would not have missed the battle of Cedar Creek alone for a thousand dollars; but he sometimes reflected that if he had remained at home during the last three years, he might now be in a lucrative practice. From his salary as captain he had been able to lay up next to nothing. Nominally it was fifteen hundred and sixty dollars; but the in-

come tax took out thirty dollars, and he had forfeited the
monthly ten dollars allowed for responsibility of arms,
etc., during the time he was on staff duty; in addition to
which gold had been up to 290, diminishing the cash value
of his actual pay to less than five hundred dollars. Furthermore he had lent largely to brother officers, and in
consequence of the death of the borrowers on heroic fields,
had not always been repaid. Van Zandt owed him two
hundred dollars, and Carter had fallen before he could return him a similar sum. Nevertheless, thanks to the industry and economy of a father long since buried, the
young man had a sufficient income to support him while
he could plant the slowly growing trees of business and
profit. He could live; but could he marry? Gold was
falling, and so were prices; but even before the war one
thousand dollars a year would not support two; and now
it certainly would be insufficient for three. He considered
this question a great deal more than was necessary for a
man who meant to be a bachelor; and occasionally a
recollection of Whitewood's eighty thousand gave him a
pang of envy, or jealousy, or both together.

The lucre which he so earnestly desired, not for its own
stupid sake, but for the gratification of a secretly nursed
purpose, began to flow in upon him in small but constant
driblets. Some enthusiastic people gave him their small
jobs in the way of conveyancing, etc., because he had
fought three years for his country; and at least, somewhat
to his alarm, a considerable case was thrust upon him,
with a retaining fee which he immediately banked as being
too large for his pocket. Conscious that his legal erudition was not great, he went to a former fellow student
who during the past four years had burrowed himself
into a good practice, and proposed that they should take
the case in partnership.

"You shall be counsellor," said he, "and I will be advocate. You shall furnish the law skeleton of the plea,
and I will clothe it with appeals to the gentlemen of the

jury. I used to be famous for spouting, you know; and I think I could ask a few questions."

" I will do it for a third," said the other, who was not himself a pleader.

" Good !"

It was done and the case was gained. The pecuniary profits were divided, but Colburne carried away all the popular fame, for he had spouted in such a manner as quite to dissolve the gentlemen of the jury. The two young men went into partnership on the basis afforded by their first transaction, and were soon in possession of a promising if not an opulent business. It began to seem possible that, at a not very distant day, Colburne might mean something if he should say, " I endow thee with my worldly goods."

CHAPTER XXXVI.

A BRACE OF OFFERS.

At last Colburne gave Mrs. Carter a bouquet. It was a more significant act than the reader who loves flowers will perceive without an explanation. Fond as he was of pets and of most things which are, or stand as emblems of innocence, he cared very little for flowers except as features of a landscape. He was conscious of a gratification in walking along a field path which ran through dandelions, buttercups, etc. ; but he never would have thought of picking one of them for his own pleasure any more than of picking a maple tree. In short, he was deficient in that sense which makes so many people crave their presence, and could probably have lived in a flowerless land without any painful sentiment of barrenness. Therefore it was only a profound and affectionate study into Mrs. Carter's ways and tastes which brought him to the point of buying and bringing to her a bouquet.

He was actually surprised at the flush of pleasure with which she received it: a pleasure evidently caused in great measure by the nature of the gift itself; and only in small part, he thought, by a consciousness of the motives of the giver. He watched her with great interest while she gaily filled a vase with water, put the bouquet in it, placed it on the mantel piece, stepped back to look at it, then set it on her work-table, took in the effect once more, drew a pleased sigh and resumed her seat. Her Diana-like, graceful form showed to advantage in the plain black dress, and her wavy blonde hair seemed to him specially beautiful in its contrast with her plain widow's cap. Youth with its health and hope had brought back the rounded outlines which at one time had been a little wasted by maternity and sorrow. Her white and singularly clear skin had resumed its soft roseate tint and could show as distinctly as ever the motions of the quickly-stirred blood. Her blue eyes, if not as gay as they were four years ago were more eloquent of experience, thought, and feeling. Mr. Colburne must be pardoned for thinking that she was more beautiful than the bouquet, and for wondering how she could prize a loveliness so much inferior in grace and expression to her own.

"Do you know?" she said, and then checked herself. She was about to remind him that these were the first flowers which he ever gave her, and to laugh at him good humoredly for having been so slow in divining one of her passions. But the idea struck her that the gift might be, for the very reason of its novelty, too significant to be a proper subject for her comments.

"Do you know," she continued, after a scarcely perceptible hesitation, "that I am not so fond of flowers as I was once? They remind me of Louisiana, and I—don't love Louisiana."

"But this is thanking you very poorly for your pre-

sent," she added, after another and longer pause. " You
know that I am obliged to you. Don't you ?"

" I do," said Colburne. He had been many times repaid for his offering by seeing the pains which she took to
preserve it and place it to the best advantage.

" It is very odd to me, though, that you never seemed
to love them," she observed, reverting to her first thought.

" It is my misfortune. I have a pleasure the less. It is
like not having an ear for music."

" How can you love poetry without loving flowers ?"

" I knew a sculptor once who couldn't find the slightest
charm or the slightest exhibition of capacity in an opera. I
had a soldier in my company who could see perfectly well
by daylight, but was stone blind by moonlight. That is
the way some of us are made. We are but partially developed or, rather, not developed equally in all directions.
My æsthetic self seems to be lacking in button-holes for
bouquets. If I could carry a landscape about in my hand,
I think I would ; but not a bunch of flowers."

" But you love children ; and they are flowers."

" Ah ! but they are so human ! They make a noise;
they appreciate you comprehensibly ; they go after a
fellow."

So you like people who go after you ? thought Mrs.
Carter, smiling to herself at the confession. Somehow she
was interested in and pleased with the minutest peculiarities of Mr. Colburne.

From that day forward her work table rarely lacked a
bouquet, although her friend's means, after paying his
board bill, were not by any means ample. In fact there
soon came to be two bouquets, representing rival admirers
of the lady. Young Whitewood, who loved flowers, and
had a greenhouse full of them, but had never hitherto
dared present one to the pretty widow, took courage from
Colburne's example, and far exceeded him in the sump-
tuousness of his offerings. By the way, I must not neglect
this shy gentleman's claims to a place in my narrative. He

Y

was a prominent figure of evenings in the Ravenel parlor,
and did a great deal of talking there on learned subjects
with the Doctor, sitting the while on the edge of his
chair, with his thin legs twisted around each other in such
a way as to exhibit with painful distinctness their bony
outlines. Each of these young men was considerably
afraid of the other. Colburne recognized the fact that a
fortune of eighty thousand dollars would be a very suitable adjunct to Mrs. Carter's personal and social graces,
and that it would be perfectly proper in her to accept it if
offered, as it seemed likely to be. Whitewood bowed
modestly to Colburne's superior conversational cleverness,
and humbled himself in the dust before his honorable fame
as a soldier. What was he, a man of peace, a patriot who
had only talked and paid, in comparison with this other
man who had shed his blood and risked his life for their
common country and the cause of human progress? So
when the Captain talked to Mrs. Carter, the tutor contented himself with Doctor Ravenel. He was painfully
conscious of his own stiffness and coldness of style, and
mourned over it, and envied the ease and warmth of these
southerners. To this subject he frequently alluded, driven
thereto by a sort of agony of conviction; for the objective
Whitewood imperfectly expressed the subjective, who
thought earnestly and felt ardently.

"I don't understand," he said mournfully, "why people of the same blood should be so different—in fact, so
opposed—in manner, as are the northerners and southerners."

"The difference springs from a radical difference of purpose in their lives," said the Doctor. "The pro-slavery
South meant oligarchy, and imitated the manners of the
European nobility. The democratic North means equality
—every man standing on his own legs, and not bestriding
other men's shoulders—every man passing for just what
he is, and no more. It means honesty, sincerity, frankness, in word as well as deed. It means general hard

work, too, in consequence of which there is less chance to cultivate the graces. The polish of the South is superficial and semi-barbarous, like that of the Poles and all other slaveholding oligarchies. I confess, however, that I should like to see a little more sympathy and expansion in the northern manners. A native, untravelled New Bostonian is rather too much in the style of an iceberg. He is enough to cause atmospheric condensation and changes of temperature. It is a story that when a new Yankee arrives in the warm air of Louisiana, there is always a shower. But that, you know, is an exaggeration."

Whitewood laughed in a disconcerted, conscience-stricken manner.

"Nevertheless, they do a vast deal of good," continued the Doctor. "They purify as well as disturb the atmosphere. To me, a southerner, it is a humiliating reflection, that, but for these Yankees and their cold moral purity, we should have established a society upon the basis of the most horrible slavery that the world has known since the days of pagan Rome."

Whitewood glanced at Mrs. Carter. She smiled acquiescence and sympathy; her conversion from secession and slavery was complete.

All this while Colburne boarded at the New Boston House, and saw the Doctor and Mrs. Carter and Ravvie every day. When they went down to the sea-shore for a week during the hot weather, he could not leave his business to accompany them, as he wished, but must stay in New Boston, feeling miserably lonesome of evenings, although he knew hundreds of people in the little city. It was an aggravation of his troubles to learn that Mr. Whitewood had followed the Ravenels to the watering-place. When the family returned, still accompanied by the eighty thousand dollar youth, Colburne looked very searchingly into the eyes of Mrs. Carter to discover if possible what she had been doing with herself. She noticed it, and blushed deeply, which puzzled and troubled him through hours of subsequent meditation. If they were engaged, they would certainly tell me, thought he; but nevertheless he was not entirely easy about the matter.

It happened the next evening that he lounged into one of the small parlors of the hotel, intending to pass out upon a little front balcony and look at the moonlit, elm-arched glories of the Common. A murmur of two voices —a male voice and a female—came in from the balcony and checked his advance. As he hesitated young White-wood entered the room through the open window, hastily followed a moment afterward by Mrs. Carter.

"Mr. Whitewood, please say nothing about this," she whispered. "Of course you will not. I never shall."

"Certainly, not," replied the young man. The tone in which he spoke was so low that Colburne could detect no expression in it, whether of despondency or triumph. Entering as they did from the moonlight into a room which had been left unlighted in order to keep out summer insects, neither of them perceived the involuntary listener. Whitewood went out by the door, and Mrs. Carter returned to the balcony. In order that the reader may be spared the trouble of turning over a few pages here, I will state frankly that the young man had proposed and been refused, and that Mrs. Carter had begged him not to let the affair get abroad because—well, because a sudden impulse came over her to do just that, whether it concerned her or not to keep the secret.

Colburne remained alone, in such an agony of anxiety as he had not believed himself capable of feeling. All the stoicism which he had learned by forced marches, starvations, and battles was insufficient, or was not of the proper kind, to sustain him comfortably under the torture inflicted by his supposed discovery. The Rachel whom he had waited for more than four years was again lost to him. But was she lost? asked the hope that never dies in us. It was not positively certain; words and situations may have different meanings; his rival did not seem much elated. He would ask Mrs. Carter what the scene meant, and learn his fate at once. She would not keep the secret from him when he should tell her the motives which induced him to question her. Whether she refused him or not, whether she was or was not engaged to another, he would of course be entirely frank with her, only regretting that he had not been so before. He was whole-souled enough, he had learned at least this much of self-abnegation, not to try to save his vanity in such a matter as loving for life. As the most loveable woman that he had ever known, it was due to her that she should be informed that his heart was at her command, no matter what she might do with it. The feeling of the moment was a grand one, but not beyond the native power of his character, although three years ago he had not been sufficiently developed to be capable of it.

He stepped to the window, pushed apart the long damask curtains and stood by her side.

"Oh! Is it you!" she exclaimed. "You quite startled me." Then, after a moment's hesitation, "When did you come in?"

"I was in the room three minutes ago," he answered, and paused to draw a long breath. "Tell me, Mrs. Carter," he resumed, "what is it that Mr. Whitewood is to keep secret?"

"Mr. Colburne!" she replied, full of astonishment that he should put such a question.

"I did not overhear intentionally," he went on. "I did not hear much, and I wish to know more than I heard."

Mr. Colburne was master of the situation, although he was not aware of it. Surprise was the least of Lillie's emotions; she was quite overwhelmed by her lover's presence, and by the question which he put to her; she could not have declared truly at the moment that her soul was altogether her own.

"Oh, Mr. Colburne! I cannot tell you," was all she could say, and that in a whisper.

She would have told him all, if he had insisted, but he did not. He had manliness enough, he was sufficiently able to affront danger and suffering, to say what was in his own heart, without knowing what had passed between her and his rival. He stood silent a moment, pondering, not over his purpose, but as to what his words should be. Then flashed across him a suspicion of the truth, that Whitewood had made his venture and met with ship-wreck. A wave of strong hope seemed to lift him over reefs of doubt, and shook him so, like a ship trembling on a billow, that for an instant longer he could not speak. Just then Rosann's recognizable Irish voice was heard, calling, " Mrs. Carter ! Mrs. Carter ! Might I spake t' ye ?"

" What is it ?" asked Lillie, stepping by Colburne into the parlor. Ravvie was cutting a double tooth, was feverish and fretful, and she had been anxious about him.

" Ma'am, I'd like t' have ye see the baby. I'm thinkin' he ought t' have somethin' done for 'm. He's mightily worried."

"Please excuse me, Mr. Colburne," said the mother, and ran up stairs. Thus it happened that Lillie unintention-ally evaded the somewhat remarkable and humiliating circumstance of receiving two declarations of love, two offers of marriage, in a single evening. She did not, how-ever, know precisely what it was that she had escaped ; and, moreover, she did not at first think much about it. except in a very fragmentary and unsatisfactory manner ; for Ravvie soon went into convulsions and remained in a precarious condition the whole night, absorbing all her time and attention. Of course he had his gums lanced, and his chubby feet put in hot water, and medicine poured down his patient throat. In the morning he was so com-fortable that his mother went to bed and slept till noon. When she awoke and found Ravvie quite recovered, and had kissed his cheeks, his dimpled neck, and the fat col-lops in his legs a hundred times or so, and called him her

own precious, and her dearest darling, and her sweet little
man at every kiss, she began to dress herself and to think
of Mr. Colburne, and of his unexplained anxieties to say—
what ? She went tremulously to dinner, blushing scarlet
after her sensitive manner as she entered the dining-room,
but quite unnecessarily, inasmuch as he was not at table.
She could not say whether she was most relieved or annoyed by his unexpected absence. It is worthy of record
that before tea-time she had learned through some roundabout medium, (Rosann and the porter, I fear,) that Mr.
Colburne had been summoned to New York by a tele-
gram and was not expected back for a day or two. Her
father was away on a mineralogical hunt, unearthing bur-
rows and warrens of Smithites and Brownites. Thus she
had plenty of opportunity for reflection, and she probably
employed it as well as most young women would under
similar circumstances, but, of course, to no purpose at all
so far as concerned taking any action. In such matters a
woman can do little more than sit still while others trans-
act her history. She was under the spell : it was not she
who would control her own fate : it was Mr. Colburne.
She was ashamed and almost angry to find that she was
so weak ; she declared that it was disgraceful to fall in
love with a man who had not yet told her plainly that he
loved her ; but all her shame, and anger, and declarations
could not alter the stubborn fact. She would never own
it to any one else, but she was obliged to confess it to herself, although the avowal made her cry with vexation.
She had to remember, too, that it was not quite two years
and a half since she was married, and not quite eighteen
months since she had become a widow. She walked
through a valley of humiliation, very meek in spirit, and
yet, it must be confessed, not very unhappy. At times
she defended herself, asking the honest and rational question, How could she help loving this man ? He had been
so faithful and delicate, he was so brave and noble, that
she wondered that every woman who knew him did not

ădore him.   And then, as she thought of his perfections,
she went tremblingly back to the inquiry, Did he love her?
He had not gone so far as to say it, or anything approaching to it; and yet he surely would not have asked her
what had passed between another man and herself unless
he meant to lay bare to her his inmost heart; she knew
that he was too generously delicate to demand such a
confidence except with a most serious and tender purpose.
She did not indeed suppose that he would have gone on
then to say everything that he felt for her; for it did not
seem to her that any one moment which she could fix
upon would be great enough for such a revelation.   But
it would have come in time, if she had answered him suitably; it might come yet, if she had not offended him, and
if he did not meet some one whom he should see to be
more desirable.   *Had* she offended him by her manner, or
by what she had said, or failed to say?   Oh, how easy it
is to suspect that those whom we love are vexed with us!
If it should be so that she had given him cause of anger,
how could she make peace with him without demeaning
herself?   Well, let the worst come to the worst, there
was her boy who would always be faithful and loving.
She kissed him violently and repeatedly, but could not
keep a tear or two from falling on him, although why they
were shed the child could have explained as rationally as
she.

Of all these struggles Colburne knew nothing and
guessed nothing.   He too had his yearnings and anxieties,
although he did not express them by kissing anything or
crying upon anything.   He was sternly fearful lest he was
losing all-important moments, and he attended to his business in New York as energetically as he would have stormed
a battery.   Had he offended Mrs. Carter? Had Whitewood
succeeded, or failed, or not tried?   He could not answer
any of these questions, but he was in a fury to get back
to New Boston.

Lillie trembled when she heard his knock upon the door

at eight o'clock that evening.   She knew it was his by instinct ; she had known it two or three times during the day when it was only a servant's ; but at last she was right in her divination.   She was trying at the moment to write a letter to her father, with the door open into her bed-room, where Ravvie sat under the benign spectacles of Rosann.   In answer to her " Come in," Colburne entered, looking pale with want of sleep, for he had worked nights and travelled days.

" I am so glad you have come back," she said in her frank way.

" And I am so glad to get back," he replied, dropping wearily into an easy chair.   " When does your father return ?"

" I don't know.   He told me to write to him at Springfield until I got word to stop."

Colburne was pleased ; the Doctor would not be at home for a day or two ; that would give him other opportunities in case this one should result in a failure.   The little parlor looked more formidable than the balcony, and the glare of the gas was not so encouraging as the mellow moonlight.   He did not feel sure how he should be able to speak here, where she could see every working of his countenance. He did not know that from the moment he began to speak of the subject which filled his heart she would not be able to look him in the face until after she had promised to be his altogether and forever.

Women always will talk at such times.   They seem to dread to be caught, and to know that silence is a dangerous trap for the feelings; and consequently they prattle about anything, no matter what, provided the prattle will prolong the time during which the hunter is in chase.

" You look quite worn out with your journey," she said. " I should think you had made a forced march to New York and back on foot."

" I have been under the necessity of working nights," he answered, without telling her that it was the desire to return as quickly as possible to her which had constituted the forcing power.

"You shouldn't do it. You will wear yourself down again, as you did in field service."

"No. There are no privations here; no hunger, and no food more unwholesome than hunger; no suffering with cold; no malaria. If I fall sick here, it will only be with living too well, and having too easy a time. Somebody says that death is a disgrace; that man ought to be ashamed of himself for dying. I am inclined to admit it, unless the man is in field service. In field service I have suffered keenly now and then, so as to become babyish about it, and think of you and how glad you would be to give me something to eat."

She made no reply, except to look at him steadily for a moment, admiring what seemed to her the heroism of speaking so lightly of hardships.

"You see I confided strongly in your kindness," he resumed. "I do so still."

The color flooded her face and neck as she divined from his manner that he was about to resume the conversation of the balcony. He rose, walked to the door which led into the bed-room, closed it gently and came back. She could not speak nor raise her eyes to his face as he stood before her. If he had kept silence for a few moments she would probably have recovered herself and said, "Won't you sit down," or some such insanity. But he did not give her time for that; he took one of her hands in both of his and said, "Lillie!"

There was a question in the tone, but she could not answer it except by suddenly raising her other hand to her face, as if to hide the confession which was glowing there.

"You know that I have loved you four years," he went on, bending down to her and whispering.

She never knew how it was that she found herself a moment afterwards on her feet, leaning against his breast, with her head on his shoulder, sobbing, trembling, but full of joy. The man whom she ought always to have loved, the man whom she now did love with the whole strength of her being, whom she could trust perfectly and forever, had claimed her as his, and she had resigned herself to him, not desiring to reserve a drop of her blood or a thought of her soul. Nothing could separate them but death; nothing could make them unhappy but losing each other: for the moment there was nothing in the world but they two and their love. After a time—it might have been five minutes, or half an hour—she remembered—positively recollected with a start—that she had a child.

"Come and see him," she said. "Come and look at our boy."

She caught him by the arm, and dragged him, willing to go, into the room where Ravvie lay asleep. She never thought of her flushed face and disordered hair, although Rosann's spectacles were fixed upon her with an astonishment which seemed to enlarge their silver-bound orbits.

"Isn't he beautiful!" she whispered. "He is yours—mine—ours."

Rosann gave her head a toss of comprehension and satisfaction in which I heartily join her, as does also, I hope, the reader.

Colburne and then Lillie kissed the child—all unconscious of the love which was lavished on him, which filled the room, and was copious enough to fill lives.

It had all come like a great surprise to Lillie. As much as she may have desired it, as much as she may have hoped it in moments for which she reproached herself at the time as absurd and almost immodest, it nevertheless descended upon her, this revelation, with wings of dazzling astonishment. In the night she awoke to disbelieve, and then to remember all with a joyful faith. And while thinking it over, in a delicious reverie which could not justly be called thought, but rather a thrilling succession of recollections and sentiments, there came to her among the multitude of impressions a wonder at her own happiness.

She seemed with amazement to see herself in double: the one figure widowed and weeping, seated amid the tombs of perished hopes: the other also widowed in garb, but about to put on garments of bridal white, and with a face which lit up the darkness.

"How can it be!" she exclaimed aloud, as she remembered the despair of eighteen months ago. Then she added, smiling with a delicious consciousness of justification, " Oh ! I love him better than I ever loved any other. I am right in loving him."

After that she commended the once-loved one, who was dead, to Heaven's pity—and then prayed long and fervently for the newly loved one who was living—but brokenly, too, and stopping now and then to smile at his bright image painted on the night. Last came a prayer for her child, whom she might have forgotten in these passionate emotions, only that she could hear his gentle breathing through the quiet midnight.

" I wonder how you can love me so, when I kept you so long away from me," she said to Colburne at their next meeting.

"You are all the dearer for it," he answered. "Yes, even because another stood for a long time between us, you are all the dearer. Perhaps it ought not to be so; but so it is, my darling."

Her gratitude was uttered in a silent, fervent pressure of her lips against his cheek. These were the only words that passed between them concerning her first marriage.

" Where are we to live ?" he asked. " Do you want to go back to New Orleans?"

" Oh, never !" she replied. " Always at the North ! I like it so much better !"

She was willing at all times now to make confession of her conversion.

CHAPTER XXXVII.

A MARRIAGE.

Doctor Ravenel was delighted when Lillie, blushing monstrously and with one arm around his neck, and her face at first a little behind his shoulder, confided to him the new revelation which had made her life doubly precious.

"I never was more happy since I came into the world, my dear," he said. "I am entirely satisfied. I do most heartily return thanks for this. I believe that now your happiness and well-being are assured, so far as they can be by any human circumstance. He is the noblest young man that I ever knew."

"Shall I send him to you to implore your consent?" she asked roguishly. "Do you want a chance to domineer over him?"

The Doctor laughed outright at the absurdity of the idea.

"I feel," said he, "as though I ought to ask his consent. I ought to apologize to the municipal authorities for taking the finest fellow in the city away from the young ladies of native birth. Seriously, my dear child, you will have to try hard in order to be good enough for him."

"Go away," answered Lillie with a little push. "Papas are the most ungrateful of all human beings. Well, if I am not good enough, there is Ravvie, and you. I throw you both in to make it an even bargain."

It was soon decided that the marriage should take place early in September. Lillie had never had a long engagement, and did not now specially care for one, being therein, I understand, similar to most widows when they are once persuaded to exchange their mourning for bridal attire. Men never like that period of expectation, and

Colburne urged an early day for his inauguration as monarch of a heart and household. His family homestead, just now tenantless, was made fine by the application of much paint and wall-paper, and the introduction of half-a-dozen new articles of furniture. Lillie and he visited it nearly every day during their brief betrothal, usually accompanied by Ravvie in the wicker baby-wagon, and were very happy in dressing up the neglected garden, arranging and re-arranging the chairs, and tables, and planning how the rooms should be distributed among the family. To the Doctor was assigned the best front bedroom, and to the Smithites and Brownites, etc., an adjoining closet of abundant dimensions.

"Ravvie and Rosann shall have the back chamber," said Lillie, " so that Ravvie can look out on the garden and be away from the dust of the street. I am so delighted that the little fellow is at last to have a garden and flowers. You and I will take the other front bedroom, next to papa's."

Here she colored at her own frankness, and hurried on to other dispositions.

" That will leave us two little rooms for servants up stairs ; and down stairs we shall have a parlor, and dining-room, and kitchen ; we shall fairly lose ourselves. How much pleasanter than a hotel !"

Colburne had noticed her blush with a sense of pleasure and triumph ; but he was generous enough and delicate enough to spare her any allusion to it.

" You have left no place for friends," he merely observed.

" Oh, but we mustn't entertain much, for a while. We —you—cannot afford it. I have been catechising Mrs. Whitewood about the cost of meat and things. Prices are dreadful."

After a little pause she broke out, " Oh, won't it be delightful to have a house, and garden, and flowers ! Ravvie will be so happy here ! We shall all be so happy ! I can't think of anything else."

"And you don't want a wedding tour?"

"Oh yes! I *do* want it. But, my darling, you cannot afford it. You must not tempt me. We will have the wedding tour five years hence, when we come to celebrate our wooden wedding. Then you will be rich, perhaps."

The grand ceremony which legalized and ratified all these arrangements took place at five o'clock in the afternoon in the little church of St. Joseph. The city being yet small enough to feel a decided interest in the private affairs of any noted citizen, a crowd of uninvited spectators collected to witness the marriage of the popular young captain with the widow of the lamented Union General. Stories of how the father had given up his all for the sake of the Republic, how Colburne had single-handed saved Mrs. Carter from a brigade of Texans, and how the dying General had bequeathed the care of his family to the Captain on the field of victory, circulated among the lookers on and inflamed them to an enthusiasm which exhibited itself in a violent waving of handkerchief as the little bridal party came out of the church and drove homeward. Since New Boston was founded no other nuptials had been so celebrated, if we may believe the oldest inhabitant.

At last Colburne had his wife, and his wife had her home. For the last four years they have sailed separately over stormy seas, but now they are in a quiet haven, united so long as life shall last.

It grieves me to leave this young woman thus on the threshold of her history. Here she is, at twenty-three, with but one child, and only at her second husband. Two-thirds of her years and heart history are probably before her. Women are most interesting at thirty: then only do they in general enter upon their full bloom, physical, moral and intellectual: then only do they attain their highest charm as members of society. But a sense of artistic fitness, derived from a belief that now she has a sure start in the voyage of happiness, compels me to close the biography of my heroine at her marriage with my

favorite, Mr. Colburne.   Moreover, it will be perceived
that, if I continue her story, I shall have to do it through
the medium of prophecy, which might give it an air of im-
probability to the reader, besides leading me to assume
certain grave responsibilities, such, for instance, as deciding the next presidential election without waiting for the
verdict of the people.

We need have no fears about the prospects of Colburne.
It is true that during his military career luck has been
against him, and he has not received promotion although
he deserved it; but his disappointment in not obtaining
great military glory will finally give strength to his
character and secure to him perfect manliness and success.
It has taken down his false pride, and taught him to use
means for ends; moreover, it will preserve him from being
enfeebled by a dropsy of vanity.   Had he been mustered
out of service as a Brigadier-General of volunteers, he
might possibly have disdained the small beginnings of a
law business, demanded a foreign consulate or home col-
lectorship, and became a State pauper for life.   As it is,
he will stand on his own base, which is a broad and solid
one; and the men around him will have no advantage
over him, except so far as their individual bases are better
than his; for in civilian life there is no rank, nor seniority,
and the close corporation of political cabal has little influence.   The chivalrous sentiment which would not let
him beg for promotion will show forth in a resolute self-
reliance and an incorruptible honor, which in the long run
will be to his outward advantage.   His responsibilities
will take all dreaminess out of him, and make him practical, industrious, able to arrive at results.   His courage
will prolong his health, and his health will be used in
effective labor.   He has the patience of a soldier, and a
soldier's fortitude under discouragement.   He is a better
and stronger man for having fought three years, out-facing
death and suffering.   Like the nation, he has developed,
and learned his powers. Possessing more physical and

intellectual vigor than is merely necessary to exist, he will succeed in the duties of life, and control other men's lives, labors, opinions, successes. It is greatly to his honor, it is a sure promise of his future, that he understands his seeming failure as a soldier, and is not discouraged by it, but takes hold of the next thing to do with confident energy.

He is the soldier citizen: he could face the flame of battle for his country: he can also earn his own living. He could leave his office-chair to march and fight for three years; and he can return to peaceful industry, as ennobling as his fighting.

It is in millions of such men that the strength of the Republic consists.

As for his domestic history, I think that we need have no terrors either for his happiness or that of Mrs. Colburne.

"I don't see but that you get along very well together," said the Doctor, addressing the young couple, a week, or so after the marriage. "I really don't see why I can't hereafter devote myself exclusively to my Brownites and Robinsonites."

"Papa," answered Lillie, "I never felt so near saying that I could spare you."

Colburne listened, happily smiling, conscious of a loved and loving wife, of a growing balance in bank, of surroundings which he would not have exchanged for a field of victory.

THE END.